TIME *and* CHANCE

A MARIAN WOOD BOOK

published by

G.P. PUTNAM'S SONS

a member of Penguin Putnam Inc.

NEW YORK

Sharon Kay Penman

TIME
· and ·
CHANCE

A Marian Wood Book
Published by G. P. Putnam's Sons
Publishers Since 1838
a member of
Penguin Putnam Inc.
375 Hudson Street
New York, NY 10014

Grateful acknowledgment is made for permission
to reproduce from the following:
"A Love Poem," by Hywel ab Owain, translated by Carl Lofmark,
Bards and Heroes (Llanerch Enterprises); "Battle of Tal y Moelfre," by
Hywel ab Owain, translated by Joseph Clancy, *The Penguin Book of
Welsh Verse* (Penguin Books); "The Killing of Hywel," by Peryf ap
Cedifor, translated by Tony Conran, *Welsh Verse* (Poetry Wales Press,
Ltd); "Ceridwen," by Hywel ab Owain, translated by Robert
Gurney, *Bardic Heritage* (Chatto & Windus Ltd).

Library of Congress Cataloging-in-Publication Data

Penman, Sharon Kay.
Time and chance / Sharon Kay Penman.
p.   cm.
"A Marian Wood book."
ISBN 0-399-14785-3
1. Eleanor, of Aquitaine, Queen, consort of Henry II, King of England, 1122?–1204—Fiction.   2. Great Britain—History—Henry II,
1154–1189—Fiction.   3. Henry II, King of England, 1133–1189—
Fiction.   4. Marriages of royalty and nobility—Fiction.
5. Queens—Fiction.   I. Title.

PS3566.E474 T56   2002   2001048255
813'.54—dc21

Printed in the United States of America
1   3   5   7   9   10   8   6   4   2

Book design by Judith Stagnitto Abbate / Abbate Design
Map by John Burgoyne

TO JILL DAVIES

ENGLAND & FRANCE

SCOTLAND

Isle of Man

IRISH SEA

Isle of Mon

York

TRAETH COCH
Pentraeth
Llan-faes
Aberffraw
Aber
Corwen
Trefriw
GWYNEDD
Chester
BERWYN MTS
Shrewsbury
POWYS
WALES
Ludlow
Averton
St. Davids Abbey
Pembroke
Worcester
Northampton
DEHEUBARTH

Woodstock
Oxford
Colchester
London
THAMES
Salisbury (Old Sarum)
Winchester
Clarendon
Southampton
Canterbury
Isle of Wight
Portsmouth
Dover

ENGLISH CHANNEL

Wissant

Barfleur
Bures
Caen
Falaise
Rouen
Morlaix
NORMANDY
Argentan
Domfront
BRITTANY
Paris
Montmirail
LeMans
Pontigny
Fréteval
ANJOU
Angers
Tours
POITOU
Chinon
Poitiers
Lusignan
Périgueux
Bordeaux
AQUITAINE
Cahors
Toulouse

N
W   E
S

Again I saw that under the sun the race is

not to the swift,

nor the battle to the strong, nor bread to the wise,

nor riches to the intelligent, nor favor to men of skill

but time and chance happen to them all.

ECCLESIASTES

CAST *of* CHARACTERS

ROYAL HOUSE OF ENGLAND

Henry Fitz Empress, second of that name to rule since the Conquest, also Duke of Normandy, Count of Anjou; first king of the Plantagenet dynasty

Eleanor, Duchess of Aquitaine in her own right, Henry's queen; former consort of Louis VII, King of France

The Empress Maude, Henry's mother, daughter of English king, Henry I; widow of Holy Roman Emperor and Count of Anjou

Geoffrey, late Count of Anjou, Henry's father

Geoffrey and Will, Henry's younger brothers

Rainald, Earl of Cornwall, illegitimate son of Henry I; Henry's uncle

Ranulf Fitz Roy, illegitimate son of Henry I; Henry's uncle

Rhiannon, Ranulf's first cousin and wife

Maud, widowed Countess of Chester, daughter of Robert Fitz Roy, Earl of Gloucester; Henry's first cousin and Bishop of Worcester's sister

Petronilla, widowed Countess of Vermandois, Eleanor's sister

ROYAL HOUSE OF WALES

Owain Gwynedd, Welsh king
Cristyn, his concubine
Davydd and Rhodri, their sons
Hywel ab Owain, Owain's firstborn son by an Irish noblewoman

HOLY ROMAN CHURCH

Thomas Becket, Henry's chancellor
Theobald, Archbishop of Canterbury
John of Salisbury, Theobald's secretary
William Fitz Stephen and Herbert of Bosham, Becket's chancellery clerks
Gilbert Foliot, Bishop of Hereford and later, London
Roger, Bishop of Worcester, son of Robert Fitz Roy, Earl of Gloucester;
    Henry's cousin
Henry of Blois, Bishop of Winchester, King Stephen's brother
Roger de Pont l'Eveque, Archbishop of York
Hilary, Bishop of Chichester
Jocelin de Bohun, Bishop of Salisbury

PROLOGUE

*I*T BEGAN WITH A SHIPWRECK on a bitter-cold November eve in God's Year 1120. The English king Henry, son of William the Bastard, conqueror of England, lost his only lawfully begotten son in the sinking of the White Ship. In his despair, he named his daughter Maude, widow of the Holy Roman Emperor, as his heir. But his lords balked at being governed by a woman, and when the old king died, Maude's cousin Stephen seized the throne.

Stephen was not feared by his lords, who dismissed him as a mild man, gentle and good, who did no justice. When the Empress Maude and her bastard brother Robert, the Earl of Gloucester, led an army onto English shores, many rallied to her cause. Even more served only themselves or the Devil. Outlaws roamed the roads and barons became bandits, raising up stone castles by forced labor, emerging from these wolf lairs to raid towns and plunder the countryside. Women, pilgrims, priests—none were spared by the lawless and the damned. Because men feared to venture into the fields, the earth was not tilled, crops did not grow, and hunger stalked the land. In this wretched way did nineteen years pass, years of suffering and anarchy, and people said openly that Christ and his saints slept.

The Empress Maude failed in her attempt to reclaim her stolen crown. But by her marriage to Geoffrey, Count of Anjou, she had given birth to a son who vowed to recover his lost birthright. He called himself Henry Fitz Empress and men began to hope that he might deliver them from their misery. It was said that he was Fortune's favorite; when that was reported to him, he said a man makes his own luck and some thought that was blasphemy. He was only nineteen when he stunned Christendom by wedding Eleanor, the beautiful and headstrong Duchess of Aquitaine, less than two months after she'd been freed from her marriage to the King of France. He then turned his gaze upon Stephen's unhappy realm. Within a twelvemonth, he had forced Stephen to recognize him as the rightful heir, and it was agreed that Stephen would rule for the rest of his days and then Henry would be king. In less than a year, it came to pass. He was but one and twenty when he was crowned as the second Henry to rule England since the Conquest, and the people rejoiced, for he promised them justice and peace.

CHAPTER ONE

✦

July 1156
Chinon Castle
Touraine, France

S THE KING OF ENGLAND crossed the inner bailey of Chinon Castle, his brother watched from an upper-story window and wished fervently that God would smite him dead. Geoffrey understood perfectly why Cain had slain Abel, the firstborn, the best-beloved. Harry was the firstborn, too. There were just fifteen months between them, fifteen miserable months, but because of them, Harry had gotten it all—England and Anjou and Normandy—and Geoffrey had naught but regrets and resentments and three wretched castles, castles he was now about to forfeit.

He'd rebelled again, and again he'd failed. He was here at Chinon to submit to his brother, but he was not contrite, nor was he cowed. His heart sore, his spirit still rebellious, he began to stalk the chamber, feeling more wronged with every stride. Why should Harry have the whole loaf and he only crumbs? What had Harry ever been denied? Duke of Normandy at seventeen, Count of Anjou upon their father's sudden death the following year, King of England at one and twenty, and, as if that were not more than enough for any mortal man, he was wed to a celebrated beauty, the Duchess of Aquitaine and former Queen of France.

Had any other woman ever worn the crowns of both England and France? History had never interested Geoffrey much, but he doubted it. Eleanor always seemed to be defying the natural boundaries of woman-hood, a royal rebel who was too clever by half and as willful as any man. But her vast domains and her seductive smile more than made up for any defects of character, and after her divorce from the French king, Geoffrey had attempted to claim this glittering prize, laying an ambush for her as she journeyed back to Aquitaine. It was not uncommon to abduct an heiress, then force her into marriage, and Geoffrey had been confident of success, sure, too, that he'd be able to tame her wild nature and make her into a proper wife, dutiful and submissive.

It was not to be. Eleanor had evaded his ambush, reached safety in her own lands, and soon thereafter, shocked all of Christendom by marrying Geoffrey's brother. Geoffrey had been bitterly disappointed by his failure to capture a queen. But it well nigh drove him crazy to think of her be-longing to his brother, sharing her bed and her wealth with Harry—and of her own free will. Where was the justice or fairness in that?

Geoffrey was more uneasy about facing his brother than he'd ever ad-mit, and he spun around at the sound of the opening door. But it was not Harry. Their younger brother, Will, entered, followed by Thomas Becket, the king's elegant shadow.

Geoffrey frowned at the sight of them. As far back as he could re-member, Will had been Harry's lapdog, always taking his side. As for Becket, Geoffrey saw him as an outright enemy, the king's chancellor and closest confidant. He could expect no support from them, and well he knew it. "I suppose you're here to gloat, Will, as Harry rubs my nose in it."

"No, I'm here to do you a favor—if you've the wits to heed me." The most cursory of glances revealed their kinship; all three brothers had the same high coloring and sturdy, muscular build. Will's hair was redder and he had far more freckles, but otherwise, he and Geoffrey were mirror im-ages of each other. Even their scowls were the same. "Harry's nerves are on the raw these days, and he's in no mood to put up with your bluster-ing. So for your own sake, Geoff, watch your tongue—"

"Poor Harry, my heart bleeds for his 'raw nerves,' in truth, it does! Do you never tire of licking his arse, Little Brother? Or have you acquired a taste for it by now?"

Color seared Will's face. "You're enough to make me believe those tales of babes switched at birth, for how could we ever have come from the same womb?"

"Let him be, lad." Thomas Becket was regarding Geoffrey with chill distaste. "'As a dog returneth to his vomit, so a fool returneth to his folly.'"

"You stay out of this, priest! But then," Geoffrey said with a sneer, "you are not a priest, are you? You hold the chancellorship, yet you balk at taking your holy vows . . . now why is that?"

"I serve both my God and my king," Becket said evenly, "with all my heart. But you, Geoffrey Fitz Empress, serve only Satan, even if you know it not."

Geoffrey had no chance to retort, for the door was opening again. A foreigner unfamiliar with England would not have taken the man in the doorway for the English king, for he scorned the trappings of kingship, the rich silks and gemstones and furred mantles that set men of rank apart from their less fortunate brethren. Henry Fitz Empress preferred comfort to style: simple, unadorned tunics and high cowhide boots and mantles so short that he'd earned himself the nickname "Curtmantle." Equally indifferent to fashion's dictates and the opinions of others, Henry dressed to please himself, and usually looked more like the king's chief huntsman than the king.

To Geoffrey, who spent huge sums on his clothes, this peculiarity of his brother's was just further proof of his unfitness to be king. Henry looked even more rumpled than usual today, his short, copper-colored hair tousled and windblown, his eyes slate-dark, hollowed and bloodshot. Mayhap there was something to Will's blathering about Harry's "raw nerves" after all, Geoffrey conceded. Not that he cared what was weighing Harry down. A pity it was not an anchor.

What did trouble Geoffrey, though, was his brother's silence. The young king was notorious for his scorching temper, but those who knew Henry best knew, too, that these spectacular fits of royal rage were more calculated than most people suspected, deliberately daunting. His anger was far more dangerous when it was iced over, cold and controlled and unforgiving, and Geoffrey was soon squirming under that unblinking, implacable gaze. When he could stand the suspense no longer, he snapped, "What are you waiting for? Let's get it over with, Harry!"

"You have no idea what your rebellion has cost me," Henry said, much too dispassionately, "or you'd be treading with great care."

"Need I remind you that you won, Harry? It seems odd indeed for you to bemoan your losses when I'm the one who is yielding up my castles."

"You think I care about your accursed castles?" Henry moved forward into the chamber so swiftly that Geoffrey took an instinctive backward step. "Had I not been forced to lay siege to them, I'd have been back in England months ago, long ere Eleanor's lying-in was nigh."

Geoffrey knew Eleanor was pregnant again, for Henry had announced it at their Christmas court. Divorced by the French king for her failure to give him a male heir, Eleanor had then borne Henry two sons in their first three years of marriage. To Geoffrey, her latest pregnancy had been another drop of poison in an already noxious drink, and he could muster up no sympathy now for Henry's complaint.

"What of it? You'd not have been allowed in the birthing chamber, for men never are."

"No . . . but I'd have been there to bury my son."

Geoffrey's mouth dropped open. "Your son?"

"He died on Whitsunday," Henry said, softly and precisely, the measured cadence of his tones utterly at variance with what Geoffrey could read in his eyes. "Eleanor kept vigil by his bedside as the doctors and priests tried to save him. She stayed with him until he died, and then she made the funeral arrangements, accompanied his body to Reading for burial. He was not yet three, Geoff, for his birthday was not till August, the seventeenth, it would have been—"

"Harry, I . . . I am sorry about your son. But it was not my fault! Blame God if you must, not me!"

"But I do blame you, Geoff. I blame you for your treachery, your betrayals, your willingness to ally yourself with my enemies . . . again and again. I blame you for my wife's ordeal, which she need not have faced alone. And I blame you for denying me the chance to be at my son's deathbed."

"What do you want me to say? It was not my fault! You cannot blame me because the boy was sickly—" Geoffrey's breath caught in his throat as Henry lunged forward. Twisting his fist in the neck of his brother's tunic, Henry shoved him roughly against the wall.

"The *boy* has a name, damn you—William! I suppose you'd forgotten, for blood-kin means nothing to you, does it? Well, you might remember his name better once you have time and solitude to think upon it!"

Geoffrey blanched. "You . . . you cannot mean to imprison me?"

Henry slowly unclenched his fist, stepped back. "There are men waiting outside the door to escort you to a chamber in the tower."

"Harry, what are you going to do? Tell me!"

Henry turned aside without answering, moved to the door, and jerked it open. Geoffrey stiffened, eyes darting in disbelief from the men-at-arms to this stranger in his brother's skin. Clutching at the shreds of his pride, he stumbled across the chamber, determined not to plead, but betraying himself, nonetheless, by a panicked, involuntary glance of entreaty as the door closed.

Will untangled himself from the settle, ambled over to the door, and slid the bolt into place. "Harry . . . do you truly mean to imprison him? God knows, he deserves it . . ." He trailed off uncertainly, for his was an open, affable nature, uncomfortable with shadings or ambiguities, and it troubled him that his feelings for his brother could not be clear-cut and uncomplicated.

Henry crossed to the settle and took the seat Will had vacated. "If I had my way, I'd cast him into Chinon's deepest dungeon, leave him there till he rotted."

"But you will not," Becket predicted, smiling faintly as he rose to pour them all cups of wine.

"No," Henry admitted, accepting his cup with a wry smile of his own. "There would be two prisoners in that dungeon—Geoff and our mother. She says he deserves whatever punishment I choose to mete out, but that is her head talking, not her heart." After two swallows, he set the cup aside, for he drank as sparingly as he ate; Henry's hungers of the flesh were not for food or wine. "I'm going to try to scare some sense into Geoff. But since he has less sense than God gave a sheep, I do not have high hopes of success."

"Just do not give him his castles back this time," Will chided, in a tactless reminder of Henry's earlier, misplaced leniency. "It would serve him right if he had to beg his bread by the roadside."

"Sorry, lad, but Scriptures forbid it. Thomas can doubtless cite you chapter and verse," Henry gibed, "but I am sure it says somewhere that brothers of kings cannot be beggars."

"I thought it said that brothers of beggars cannot be kings." Becket tasted the wine, then grimaced. "Are your servants trying to poison you with this swill, Harry? Someone ought to tell them that hemlock would be quicker and more merciful."

"This is why men would rather dine with my lord chancellor than with me," Henry told Will. "He'd drink blood ere he quaffed English wine. Whereas for me, it is enough if it is wet!" Becket's riposte was cut off by a sudden knock. Henry, the closest to the door, got to his feet; he was never one to stand on ceremony. But his amusement faded when a weary, travel-stained messenger was ushered into the chamber, for the man's disheveled appearance conveyed a message of its own: that his news was urgent.

Snatching up the proffered letter, Henry stared at the familiar seal, then looked over at Will. "It is from our mother," he said, moving toward the nearest lamp. Will and Becket were both on their feet by now, watching intently as he read. "I have to go to Rouen," he said, "straightaway."

Will paled. "Not Mama . . . ?"

"No, lad, no. She is not ailing. She has written to let me know that Eleanor is in Rouen."

IF THE ENGLISH KING'S WIFE had a remarkable history, so, too, did his mother. Sent to Germany as a child to wed the Holy Roman Emperor, Maude had been summoned back to England by her father, the king, after her husband's death. Forced into a miserable marriage with the Count of Anjou, Maude had sought comfort in their sons and in her hopes of succeeding to the English throne. But her crown was usurped by her cousin Stephen, and she'd fought a long and bloody civil war to reclaim it, fought and failed. She would never be England's queen, and that was a grievance she'd take to her grave. But she'd lived to see her son avenge her loss, and she took consolation in his kingship, a bittersweet satisfaction in his victory, one that had been denied her.

Maude had continued to make use of the regal title of empress even after her marriage to Count Geoffrey of Anjou, and she still did so, although she no longer lived in a regal style. The woman who'd sought a throne with such single-minded intensity had chosen to pass her twilight years in the cloistered quiet of Nôtre-Dame-du-Pré, dwelling in the guest quarters of the priory on the outskirts of Rouen. But upon her grieving daughter-in-law's arrival from England, she'd made haste to join Eleanor in residence at the castle.

A summer storm had drenched the city at dusk, and rain still fell hours later. Maude had ordered a fire built in the great hall's center hearth, and she was stitching an elegant altar cloth by the light of the flickering flames;

needlework was the lot of all women, even queens. She was not surprised when a servant announced that her son had ridden into the bailey, for Henry never let the weather interfere with his plans; he'd sailed in a winter gale to claim England's crown.

Within moments, he'd swept into the hall, and as always, her spirits soared at the sight of him. Flinging off his sodden mantle, he gave her a damp hug and she resisted the impulse to urge him closer to the fire. He'd just laugh and remind her that he was twenty-three, nigh on two years a king, no longer a stripling in need of a mother's coddling.

Maude suppressed a sigh. Henry had reached manhood years ago, but she doubted if Geoffrey would ever cross the border into that adult domain. She very much feared that he'd be as irresponsible and immature at forty as he'd been at sixteen, as he was now at two and twenty. "I do hope you brought an escort," she said, half-seriously, for Henry was known for traveling fast and light.

"Only those who could keep up with me." Henry strode over to greet Minna, the elderly German widow who'd been his mother's companion since her girlhood at the imperial court. Minna beamed and blushed when he kissed her cheek; in her eyes, Henry could do no wrong. Even when he'd hired mercenaries and sailed for England to help his mother in her war against Stephen—at the ripe age of fourteen—Minna had found excuses for his reckless folly. Maude rarely joked, but she sometimes teased Minna that if she saw Henry slit a man's throat, she'd claim it was just a very close shave.

Beckoning Henry away from Minna, Maude touched her hand gently to his face and then said, low-voiced, "What mean you to do with Geoffrey?"

"I would to God I knew. . . ." He found a smile for her, hoping it might give her the reassurance that his words could not. But then Geoffrey was forgotten and he was striding hastily toward the woman just entering the hall. She was a sight to draw most male eyes, a slim, dark-haired daughter of the South, the Lady Petronilla, widowed Countess of Vermandois, his sister by marriage.

"How is she, Petra?"

"How do you think? Hurting." Petronilla's green eyes were coolly appraising. He supposed she blamed him for not being with Eleanor when she'd most needed him and he resented the injustice of that, but not enough to stay and argue with her. Instead, he went to find his wife.

✦

CRESSET LAMPS still burned in the nursery. A young wet-nurse was drowsing by the fire, a swaddled baby suckling hungrily at an ample breast. The infant paid no heed to Henry's entry, but the woman jumped to her feet, flustered and stammering as she sought to cover herself. Henry ordinarily had an appreciative eye for female charms. Now, though, he hardly glanced at the girl's exposed bosom. "Let me see my daughter," he said, and she hastily complied.

The baby wailed in protest as her meal was interrupted, showing she had a healthy set of lungs. Her hair was wispy and soft, as bright as the flames licking at the hearth log, and her tiny face was reddening, puckered up into a fretful pout. Henry stroked her cheek with his forefinger and then handed her back to the nurse.

There were two cradles, but there ought to have been three. That missing bed cut at Henry's heart like the thrust of a sword. His eyes stinging, he halted by one of the cradles, gazing down at his second son and namesake. Hal was sucking on his thumb, the firelight gleaming on his cap of curly fair hair, and even in sleep, his resemblance to his dead brother was wrenching. Henry was tempted to wake him up. He was afraid, though, that the little boy would not remember him. He'd been gone for the past six of the child's sixteen months on earth.

Will would have known him. But he'd been away so often in Will's pitifully brief life, too. He'd meant to be a good father, to forge a bond with his sons that could never be broken. His own childhood had been a turbulent one, he and his brothers held hostage upon the battlefield that his parents had made of their marriage. He'd wanted to do better by his children, and when the duties of kingship relegated them to the outer edges of his life, he told himself that it could not be helped, that there would be time later to make amends for these lost, early years. But for Will, there would be no more time, no more chances. For Will, it was too late—for them both, too late.

ELEANOR HAD NOT yet undressed, but she'd unbound her hair and it cascaded down her back in dark swirls and spirals, flowing toward her hips. Henry's pulse still quickened at the sight of her, even after four years of marriage. She'd obviously been told of his arrival, for she showed no surprise. They'd often been separated for months at a time, had been apart for more than a year when he'd been fighting in England to regain his stolen birthright. Their reunions had always been incendiary; Henry could remember days when they'd never even left their bed. This was the first time that no passion flared between them. Crossing the chamber, he kissed her gently on the corner of her mouth, and they stood for several moments in a wordless embrace.

"I am sorry," he said softly, "that I was not there . . ."

"So was I." Eleanor's hazel eyes had darkened. "It was dreadful, Harry. Once the fever took him, those fool doctors were useless. You know Will, he was never quiet, never still for a moment. And to see him lying in that bed, getting weaker and weaker . . . It was like watching a candle burn out, and there was nothing I could do." Her mouth twisted. "Nothing!"

Henry's throat constricted. His only defense against such pain was to push it away. "Do you want some wine?" She shook her head, but he went over to the table and poured a cupful from the flagon nonetheless. "I saw the baby. She looks like you."

"No, she does not," Eleanor said, so sharply that he swung away from the table, the wine sloshing over the rim of the cup. "I do not want to talk about the baby, Harry, not now. Tell me . . . did you weep for Will?"

"Of course I did!"

"Did anyone see you shed those tears?" When he frowned, she said, "No . . . I thought not."

"What is this about, Eleanor? You blame me for not being there? Petra clearly does, but I expected better of you. Christ Jesus, woman, I was putting down a rebellion in Anjou, not roistering in the bawdy-houses of Paris!"

"I do not blame you for not being with me then, Harry. I blame you for not being with me now!"

"I damned near killed my horse getting here!"

"That is not enough, not nearly enough!"

"What do you want from me?"

"We could not bury our child together. But I thought that at least we could grieve for him together!"

"You dare to say I do not mourn our son?"

She did not flinch from his anger. "No, I know you do. But I need you to mourn with me." She looked at him and then slowly shook her head. "You cannot do that, can you? You trust no one enough to let down your guard, not even me."

"This serves for naught," he said tautly. He was still holding the dripping wine cup and fought back an impulse to fling it against the wall. Setting it down, very deliberately, upon the table, he strode toward the door. He slid the bolt back, but then his fingers clenched on the latch. After a long moment, he turned reluctantly to face his wife.

"Do you truly want to quarrel with me, Eleanor?"

Her shoulders sagged. "No," she said bleakly, "no, I do not . . ."

Coming back into the room, he stopped before her and held out his hand. Her eyes flicked to the jagged scar that tracked across his palm toward his thumb. "How did you do that?"

"I was hearing Mass when they brought me word of Will's death. I put my fist through a stained-glass window."

She ran her fingers lightly over the scar, and when he took her into his arms, she shuddered, then clung fast. "Come on, love," he said, "let's go to bed."

She nodded, letting him lead her toward the bed. Kicking off her shoes, she started to remove her stockings, then gave him an oblique glance through her lashes. "Do you want to help?"

His surprise was obvious. "It is not too soon?"

"Maude was born on the second Wednesday after Whitsun, and today is the twenty-third. That makes six weeks by my count."

"Two days short," Henry said; he'd always been good at math.

Eleanor lay back against the pillows. "Would you rather wait?"

"I've never been one for waiting," he said and kissed her, softly at first, until her arms went up around his neck. When he spoke again, his voice was husky and he sounded out of breath. "You were wrong about my not trusting anyone. I may be wary of the rest of mankind, but I do trust you, my mother, and Thomas Becket."

Eleanor's eyes shone in the firelight, golden and catlike. "Not necessarily in that order," she murmured, and after that, they had no further need of words, finding in their lovemaking a familiar pleasure and even a small measure of solace.

CHAPTER TWO

✦

May 1157
St John's Abbey
Colchester, England

ADAME, WAIT!" The hospitaller hurried along the cloister walkway, hoping to intercept the queen before she reached her destination: the abbey chapter house. He did not have high expectations of success, but he had to try. A woman—even a highborn one—could not be allowed to wander at will in this hallowed sanctum of holy men. He was taken aback when Eleanor stopped abruptly, then swung around to face him.

"You wish to speak with me, Brother Clement?"

"Indeed, Madame, I . . . I wanted to show you our herb gardens."

"That is kind of you, but I've already seen them."

He could think of no other pretext, could only blurt out the truth. "My lady, forgive me for speaking so boldly, but you do not want to enter the chapter house just now. The lord king and our abbot and Archbishop Theobald are discussing a Church matter and . . . and so lovely a lady would be bound to be a distraction."

His patronizing attempt at gallantry had Eleanor's ladies, Barbe and Melisent, avoiding each other's gaze lest they burst out laughing. No monk in Aquitaine would have dared to presume so, but this English monk clearly knew little of his young king's consort. Grateful that they were to be present at his epiphany, they smiled at him with malicious mischief that he, in his innocence, took for coquetry.

His sudden blush made him look so young and vulnerable that Eleanor felt a glimmer of pity and chose not to prolong his ordeal. "Your 'Church matter' is, in actuality, a trial, Brother Clement. When the Bishop of Chichester sought to exercise jurisdiction over the abbey at Battle, the abbot balked, contending that the abbey was exempted from episcopal authority by royal charter. Eventually this dispute came before my lord husband, the king, and we expect the issue to be resolved today."

The hospitaller was staring at her, mouth agape, and she wasted no more time in driving the stiletto home. "Now you may escort me to the chapter house," she said in a tone that he recognized at once, for all that it was sheathed in silk: the voice of authority, absolute and indisputable.

Eleanor's entrance put a temporary halt to the proceedings. The chamber was studded with stars of the Church: the Archbishop of Canterbury, the Archbishop of York, the Bishops of Chichester, Hereford, and Winchester. Eleanor harbored genuine respect only for the venerable Theobald of Canterbury. York and Chichester she considered to be self-seekers, men whose ambitions were thoroughly secular in nature. She did not know Gilbert Foliot, Bishop of Hereford, well enough to assess, and the aged Bishop of Winchester she utterly mistrusted, for he was the brother of the usurping Stephen, damned both by blood and history.

Henry was seated in a high-backed chair, more formally attired than usual for this was Whitsuntide, one of the rare times when he wore his crown. He was flanked by lords of his court: his brother Will; his uncle Rainald, Earl of Cornwall; the Earls of Leicester and Salisbury; his justiciar, Richard de Lucy; and his chancellor, Thomas Becket. Sitting nearby was the other litigant, Walter de Lucy, who was both brother to Henry's justiciar and abbot of St Martin's at Battle, the abbey under episcopal siege. The abbot was looking so complacent that Eleanor assumed the tide must be going his way.

The churchmen were regarding her with poorly disguised disapproval. They were far more worldly than the abbey's hapless hospitaller, though, and none raised any objections to her presence, however unseemly they considered it. As she glanced toward Thomas Becket, Eleanor thought she detected the faintest shadow of disfavor, but if so, it was swiftly gone. Coming toward her with the grave courtliness that was his hallmark, he escorted her to a front-row seat, and she conceded that his manners were impeccable even if he did come from the merchant class. He found a cushion for her bench, which she graciously accepted; she was in her fifth month of another pregnancy and inclined to take what comforts she could get. She looked over then at Henry, curious to see how he was responding to her intrusion. She doubted that he'd be troubled by her trampling upon tradition, and he justified her confidence; as their eyes met, a corner of his mouth curved slightly and he winked.

Abbot Walter had royal charters from the last three kings; if he had one from Stephen, too, he was wise enough not to mention it. Becket was passing them to the king for Henry's inspection. As he did, the justiciar continued the argument Eleanor had interrupted: that the wishes of the abbey's founder, King William of blessed memory, ought to be honored, and his wishes were clearly set forth in the charter.

Eleanor was not surprised to see the bishops frowning at that; even Theobald, a man so good-hearted that some saw him as saintly, was jealous of the Church's prerogatives, ever vigilant for Crown encroachment into clerical domains. Emboldened by the support of his fellow prelates, the Bishop of Chichester launched a counterattack, insisting that to exempt the abbey from episcopal jurisdiction was to violate canon law.

"The 'wishes' of King William, may God assoil him, are therefore not relevant, much less dispositive. I daresay he did want to exempt his abbey, as contended by Abbot Walter's brother, the justiciar." Chichester paused, then, to make sure that none in the room missed his unspoken accusation: that the abbot was trading upon his connections with one of the king's chief officers. "But not even a king's wishes can always prevail. Would a king be able to amend canon law to meet his own needs? No more than he could depose one of his bishops!"

Henry leaned over to murmur something to Thomas Becket, too softly for other ears to hear. Becket grinned, and Henry then turned his gaze upon Chichester. "Very true," he agreed amiably, "a bishop cannot be deposed. But he can be driven out." He demonstrated by pantomiming a shove, and the chamber erupted into the indulgent laughter that a king's humor could inevitably evoke, no matter how lame the sally.

Chichester was not about to be sidetracked by a jest he found dubious at best. "The spiritual power of the Holy Mother Church must not be diminished or debased by temporal authority. No layman, not even a king, can confer ecclesiastical liberties or exemptions without the consent of the Pope. Therefore, since the original act of King William in granting a charter was *ultra vires,* it must stand that the exemption, too, was invalid."

Henry leaned back in his seat, studying the bishop through suddenly narrowed eyes. "This is a strange thing I am hearing, that the charters of past kings, charters confirmed by the full authority of the Crown of England, should be pronounced worthless and arbitrary by you, my lord bishop."

He'd spoken so quietly that Chichester did not at once realize how badly he'd blundered. "I am not saying they are worthless, my liege, merely that they are immaterial in this particular case. St Peter conferred his power solely upon—"

"What you seem to be saying, my lord bishop, is that the Crown must always defer to the Church. Have you forgotten that a king exercises his authority by God's Will?"

Chichester flushed darkly. "It was never my intent to offend your royal honor or dignity, my lord."

"But you did offend, my lord bishop," Becket pointed out coolly. "You knew that the royal charters supported Abbot Walter's claim to exemption. You knew, too, that if the charters were accepted as valid, you would lose your case. And so you sought to circumvent the king's authority by soliciting a papal bull. Instead of trusting to the judgment of the king, whose liegeman you are, you secured from the Holy Father a letter warning Abbot Walter to submit to your authority, upon pain of excommunication."

Hilary of Chichester was a man both clever and learned. But he lacked the fortitude to stand fast in the face of Henry's anger, fearing the loss of his king's favor far more than he did the loss of his claim against Battle Abbey. He realized that Becket had succeeded in putting his papal appeal in the worst possible light, implying that he'd been both underhanded and disloyal, and he panicked. "That is not true! I did nothing of the sort!"

Becket blinked, as if surprised. "You deny that you appealed to Pope Adrian? How, then, do you explain this?" Holding up a parchment roll that seemed to have materialized in his hand as if by magic. "I have here the very letter that His Holiness wrote to Abbot Walter, at your behest!"

It had been so adroitly done that Eleanor, watching with a cynical smile, wondered if it had been rehearsed. She had rather enjoyed seeing

Chichester so thoroughly discomfited. Even his fellow bishops were recoiling, Theobald because he was truly offended by perjury and Winchester because he deplored ineptitude. She did regret, though, that Thomas Becket had been the instrument of Chichester's downfall, for she felt he was already too well entrenched in her husband's favor. Eleanor was astute enough to recognize a potential rival in whatever the guise.

THE TRIAL WAS OVER. There had been no need to declare a verdict. Theobald had passed judgment with his sorrowful observation that the Bishop of Chichester's words had been "ill advised and derogatory to the king's royal dignity." Faced with the need to appease both his archbishop and his sovereign, Chichester renounced any and all claims to authority over Battle Abbey, and he and Abbot Walter solemnly exchanged a ceremonial Kiss of Peace. Henry was usually a gracious winner, an unexpected virtue in a son of the Empress Maude and Count Geoffrey of Anjou, and all had been concluded with civility, at least on the surface.

Afterward, Henry and Eleanor and Becket stole a few moments of privacy in the abbot's lodging, temporarily turned into a royal residence for their stay. Eleanor listened without comment as the two men rehashed the events of the morning, sounding inordinately pleased with themselves. She did not begrudge them their satisfaction, for they had shrewdly anticipated their adversary's weakness, then made the most of it. That was, she knew, a quality of the best battle commanders, and she was glad that Henry had been blessed with such a keen strategic sense. Now that the Bishop of Chichester had been thwarted, her husband had another fight looming on the horizon. From Colchester, he was heading west, for his next foe was Welsh.

RANULF FITZ ROY stood at the cliff's edge, staring down into the abyss. The drop was not that great, for Rhaeadr Ewynnol was not one of the highest waterfalls in North Wales. But he felt at that moment as if a vast chasm was yawning at his feet.

He of all men ought not to have been surprised by how fast life could alter forever, in the blink of an eye or the fading of a heartbeat. Born a king's son on the wrong side of the blanket, he'd come to manhood during those harrowing years when England was convulsed by a savage civil war. Ranulf had been forced to choose between his cousin Stephen and his half-sister Maude. He'd stayed loyal to his sister, but it had cost him the woman he loved.

They'd been plight-trothed, but when Ranulf balked at accepting Stephen's coup, Annora's father had disavowed the betrothal, wedding her to one of Stephen's barons. Eventually the fortunes of war had reunited them, and they'd begun a high-risk adulterous affair. It had ended badly, inadvertently resulting in the death of Ranulf's best friend, a consequence he'd never foreseen and could not bear. Fleeing his grieving and his guilt, he'd blundered into Wales and there he'd found unexpected refuge with his Welsh kin.

Until then, they had been strangers to him, as unknown as the cloud-kissed rough-hewn Eden they called Cymru and their enemies Wales. Ranulf's mother, Angharad, had been Welsh, taken by the English king as spoils of war. She'd died in Ranulf's eighth year, leaving him only a few shadowy memories and a vague curiosity about the land of her birth.

When fate finally brought him together with his mother's Welsh family, he would not have blamed them had they shunned him, the spawn of an alien, conquering king. But they'd welcomed him as one of their own, nursing his ailing body and wounded soul back to health, giving him the courage to face down his ghosts, to learn to live with his regrets. Without realizing it, he'd fallen under the spell of this small, Celtic country his mother had so loved. In time, he took a Welsh bride, and made his home in the deeply wooded hills above the River Conwy.

Overhead, a kestrel stalked the skies in search of prey. Ranulf watched the hawk soar on the wind, higher and higher until it vanished from view. For seven years he had dwelled in his hard-won Welsh haven. His wife had given him a son, now in his sixth year, and a daughter, not yet two. He had been happy and he had been fool enough to think it would last.

Standing on the grassy bluff above the white waters of Rhaeadr Ewynnol, he gazed down into the rain-surged cauldron below and thought of Scriptures, the prophetic dream of Egypt's pharaoh. Seven good years, years of plenty and peace, followed by seven lean years, years of sorrow. With the arrival of the king's letter, Ranulf feared that he was about to pay a high price for those seven years of quiet contentment.

Ranulf DID NOT RETURN to Trefriw until the daylight had begun to fade. He would have delayed even longer if only he could, for he knew what awaited him. They spilled from the hall as he rode in, gathering about him in the twilight dusk: his Welsh family. Rhodri, his uncle, with whom he shared this hillside manor. Rhodri's much younger second wife, the lovely, complacent Enid. Eleri, his lively sister-by-marriage, and Celyn, her husband. And in the doorway, Rhiannon, his cousin and wife.

As Ranulf dismounted, they assailed him with anxious questions, for they knew about the letter, knew what it portended. For months the winds of war had been blowing toward Wales. They'd long raked the borderlands, but they were now about to sweep into the Welsh heartland, into the high mountain domains of the man known as Owain Gwynedd.

"Ranulf, where have you been? Papa says the English king has commanded you to fight against the Welsh!"

"No . . . he has merely summoned me to his encampment at Saltney."

Eleri looked at him blankly. "Is that not what I just said?"

"No, it is not," Ranulf insisted, without much conviction, for even to him, that sounded like a distinction without a difference. "I owe knight service to the Crown for my English manors, but Harry has not demanded that of me. He asks only that I come into Cheshire to talk."

"Talk?" Rhodri echoed incredulously. "What is there to talk about? How much of Wales he means to gobble up?"

Celyn, towering over Eleri like a lofty oak, was as laconic and deliberate as she was impulsive and forthright, usually content to let her do the talking for them both. Now, though, he overcame his innate reticence long enough to offer a practical solution. "If Ranulf were to send word to the English king that he was ailing—"

"Christ's pity, Celyn!" Rhodri glared at his son-in-law. "Why should Ranulf concoct excuses? He ought to refuse outright, letting the English king know that his loyalties are to Wales now!"

"I cannot do that, Uncle." Ranulf's despair was yielding to anger, for he resented being forced to declare himself out here in the bailey, before them all. This was not the way he'd meant to do it. He'd wanted to tell Rhiannon first. She was still standing, motionless, in the doorway, and he started toward her. But he'd taken only a few steps before his uncle exclaimed in horror:

"What are you saying, Ranulf? You cannot mean to obey that summons!"

"I must obey it. Harry is my nephew. But he is also my king."

"So is Owain Gwynedd!"

"I do not need you to remind me of my loyalties, Eleri!"

"I think you do! You've not thought this through, Ranulf. Let's say you go into Cheshire to meet with the English king. What then? Lest you forget, whilst you are visiting and catching up on family news, he is making ready to invade Wales. What will you do as he turns his army loose upon Gwynedd—wish him well?"

"Stay out of this, Eleri. I owe you no explanations, for this is none of your concern."

"And what of me?" Rhodri demanded. "You are my son by marriage and my heir. I would not stand by and watch as you plunged off a cliff, nor will I keep silent now. You cannot do this, lad."

Shifting awkwardly on his crutch, he limped toward Ranulf, dragging the leg broken and imperfectly set last year after he'd been trampled by a panicked, runaway horse. Pointing at his twisted limb, he said bitterly, "This crippled leg will keep me from riding to fight beside our lord king, Owain. But Celyn will answer his summons to arms. So will our neighbors, our friends. Do you want to face Celyn and your countrymen across a battlefield, Ranulf?"

Ranulf's face contorted. "Christ Jesus, Rhodri, you know I do not!"

"Listen to your heart, then, lad," the older man pleaded. "Tell the English king to rot in Hell as he deserves!"

"If you do not," Eleri warned, "you will never be welcome again in my house, and I say that who has loved you like a brother. Tell him, Celyn."

Celyn looked acutely unhappy, for he hated confrontations and was genuinely fond of Ranulf. But he did not hesitate. "If you do this," he confirmed bleakly, "our door will be closed to you."

"You hear them?" Rhodri grabbed for Ranulf's arm. "If you back the English in this, Lord Owain might well cast you out of Gwynedd, and how could I blame him? You must—"

"Stop!" The cry was shrill, filled with such pain that they all fell silent. The color had drained from Rhiannon's face and her dark, sightless eyes were brimming with unshed tears. "Stop," she entreated again, and when Ranulf called out her name, she followed the sound, moving swiftly toward him.

Rhiannon had been blind since childhood and had long ago memorized the boundaries of the only home she'd ever known. It often seemed to Ranulf as if she carried a mental map, so detailed that every stone, every tree root, found its reflection in her memory's mirror. Now, though, she was too distraught to heed her interior landscape, and as Ranulf and the others watched, appalled, she headed straight for the well.

Shouting a warning, Ranulf lunged forward, but it was too late. Rhiannon hit the well's stone wall with bruising impact, the windlass crank striking her on the temple, just above her eye. She reeled backward, blood streaming down her face.

Ranulf reached her first, with Rhodri a step behind. She had yet to utter a sound, but she was trembling visibly. She had a deep fear of falling, for she had more at risk than contusions or scratches. What to a sighted person would be a minor mishap was to Rhiannon a cruel reminder of her vulnerability, painful proof that her defenses were forever flawed.

Knowing that, Ranulf fought back the urge to sweep her up into his arms and carry her to safety. "You're bleeding freely," he said, "but head wounds usually do. Let's go inside and tend to it."

She nodded, fumbling for his arm. But when Rhodri and Eleri started to follow, she said, "No! I want only Ranulf."

Bringing a laver of water to the bed, Ranulf sat beside his wife and sponged the blood from her face. She lay still, her lashes shadowing her cheek, her breathing soft and shallow. Putting the basin aside, he took her hand. "I did not mean for you to find out like this . . ."

"I knew," she said. "As soon as you got the letter, I knew you'd go to him." A tear squeezed through her lashes and she turned her face away so he'd not see. Her father and sister kept talking about Ranulf's loyalty to the English king. She would to God it was that simple.

"He is my nephew, Rhiannon."

She could have reminded him that he had Welsh kin, too. But what good would it do? He was bound to Henry Fitz Empress by more than blood, by more than love. Another tear escaped, trickling slowly down her cheek. Her husband was an honorable man and he'd long ago pledged his honor to the English Crown, first to his sister and now to her son. His heart might belong to Wales, but his soul would forever be England's. She'd always known the time would come when the English king would claim his own.

Ranulf was silent. When he'd refused to forsake his sister, Annora had stormed and wept and threatened, warning that she'd never forgive him. Nor had she. She'd committed a grave sin for him, betraying her husband

and risking the safe, comfortable life she'd thought she wanted, but she'd never understood why he could not accept Stephen's stolen kingship, why he could not put her first. What could he say to make Rhiannon understand?

"If you ask me not to go, Rhiannon . . ."

She did not need to see his face. His voice was hoarse, hurting. He was offering her what he'd not offered Annora. Sitting up, she held out her arms. She could hear his heart thudding against her cheek, and she listened intently until it seemed as if there was no other sound in her world, just the rapid rhythm of her husband's heartbeat.

"RANULF!" THE EBULLIENT BELLOW rang out even above the considerable clamor of an army encampment. "Ranulf, over here!"

Ranulf recognized the voice at once; his brother could out-bay a pack of lymer hounds on the scent of prey. Turning, he saw Rainald Fitz Roy bearing down upon him. He'd put on weight since Ranulf had seen him last, a paunch and jowls testifying to the good living he was enjoying as Earl of Cornwall. Like Ranulf, he was one of Henry I's many by-blows. Ranulf was the youngest but one of that misbegotten crop, and his elder brothers had all taken it upon themselves to look out for him, whether he'd liked it or not. He was thirty-eight now and his boyhood only a memory, but Rainald's vision was clouded by nostalgia and he still saw Ranulf as the little brother, in need of older and wiser guidance, preferably his.

"I'm right glad to see you, lad. Not that I ever doubted you. It was the others who did. I wagered Fitz Alan and Clifford ten marks each that you'd come. Let's go find them so I can collect my winnings and do a bit of gloating!"

Ranulf was not surprised that William Fitz Alan and Walter Clifford would wager against him. They were Marcher lords, men of Norman-French stock whose wealth was rooted in Wales, founded upon conquest. They often intermarried with the Welsh, so neither Ranulf's Welsh wife nor his Welsh blood made him suspect in their eyes. It was that he did not share the cornerstone of Marcher faith—their belief that the Welsh were a primitive people in need of the civilizing influence of their superior culture.

"Who else is here besides the Marcher lords?"

Rainald cursed good-naturedly when a soldier lurched clumsily into their path. "Who else? Becket, of course, for wherever you find Harry these days, you'll find our chancellor; a dog should be so faithful. Harry's brother, the likable one, not Geoff. A few earls: Leicester and Salisbury and Hertford." As an afterthought, he added, "And our nephew Will.

"The Welsh are here, too," Rainald continued, "so that ought to ease your conscience somewhat. Owain Gwynedd's own brother will be fighting against him."

"It is hardly surprising to find Cadwaladr in the English ranks. In the five years since Owain chased him out of Gwynedd, he has done whatever he could to kindle a border war. For the chance to avenge himself upon Owain, he'd have made a pact with the Devil himself, or in this case, the King of England."

Hearing his own words then, Ranulf smiled bleakly, knowing full well that his Welsh kin would say he, too, was making a Devil's deal with the English king.

THE ENGLISH KING was not in his encampment at Saltney, having ridden over to inspect the defenses of Shotwick Castle. As it was only six miles away, it was not long before Ranulf saw in the distance the sun-glazed sheen of the Dee estuary. He found the young king on the castle battlements. Shouting down a cheerful greeting, Henry beckoned him up, and they were soon standing side by side, elbows resting upon the embrasure, looking out across the estuary.

They'd not seen each other since Henry's coronation more than two years ago. They had much to share in consequence, and for a while, they were able to ignore the awkward fact that an English army was encamped just six miles to the south.

Henry had surprising news about his black sheep brother. He'd contrived to have the citizens of Nantes accept Geoffrey as their count. Buying Geoff's cooperation was a gamble, he acknowledged wryly. "But Geoff is too boneheaded to scare and too highborn to hang. If I were Almighty God, I'd have decreed that all kings be only children."

"If I were Almighty God," Ranulf countered, "I'd have adopted the Welsh law code and allowed bastards to inherit." He hesitated, then, not wanting to open an old wound. But would the wound left by a child's death ever truly heal? "I was very sorry about your son," he said, sounding as awkward as he felt.

"I know." Henry's tone was terse, almost curt, but Ranulf understood. They were silent for several moments, listening to the waves surging against the rocks below them. Down on the beach, gulls were shrieking, squabbling over a stolen fish. The sun was warm on their faces and Ranulf lamented that cloudless, summer sky. Welsh weather was usually as wet as it was unpredictable; more than one English army had been defeated by those relentless rains and gusting mountain winds. It was just Harry's luck, he thought, to pick the driest, warmest August within memory for his invasion. Did even the weather do his bidding?

"I suppose you have not heard, then," Henry said at last. "Eleanor is with child, the babe due in September."

"Again?" Ranulf marveled. Four children in five years. Not bad for a "barren" queen. "Congratulations, although you truly are pouring salt into poor Louis's wounds!"

Henry swung away from the battlements with a grin. "As hard as it may be for you to believe, Uncle, when I'm in bed with my wife, I have nary a thought to spare for the French king."

Henry waited until echoes of their laughter had floated away on the wind. "I think it is time," he said, "to talk of less pleasant matters. I know you do not want to be here, Uncle. I knew you would come, though, and it gladdens me greatly."

"I wish I could say the same."

"It is not as bad as you think, Ranulf. I want your counsel, not your sword. What I have in mind is not conquest. I know full well what it would take to subdue the Welsh: more than I'm willing to spend, in lives or money. I mean to remind Owain of the respective realities of our positions, preferably with as little bloodshed as possible. No more than that."

"You truly do not intend to claim Gwynedd for the English Crown?"

Ranulf sounded so dubious that Henry laughed. "You doubt me? You ought to know by now that I do my lusting in the bedchamber, not on the battlefield."

Ranulf did know that. His nephew had never lacked for courage, but his early introduction to war had left him with a jaundiced view of combat. He fought when he had to, and fought well, yet took no pleasure in it. Unlike most men of youth and high birth, Henry saw no glory in war and drank sober from the cup that sent so many into battle drunk on illusions. Remembering that now, Ranulf felt a flicker of hope.

"So why, then, are you leading an army into Gwynedd?"

Henry raised a mocking brow. "Since when are you so disingenuous? You may not want me here, but you know why I am here. Owain

Gwynedd poses a serious threat to the English Crown. He is an able, ambitious man and if I turned a blind eye to his scheming for long, Cheshire
and Shropshire would soon be speaking Welsh."

"You exaggerate, Harry."

"A king's prerogative, Uncle. But I do not exaggerate by much.
Owain has proved himself to be much too adroit at exploiting English
weaknesses. Look what happened during the chaos of Stephen's reign. He
seized control of the entire cantref of Tegeingl. Need I remind you how
close that is to Chester? Or that the present Earl of Chester is a ten-year-
old boy? Moreover, Owain has been casting out bait toward the Marcher
lords, and some of them are greedy enough to snap it up, hook and all. After all, loyalty has never been a conspicuous Marcher virtue."

When Ranulf did not respond, Henry correctly interpreted his silence as reluctant assent. "You know I speak true, Uncle, however little
you want to admit it. But I do not begrudge your affection for the Welsh."
He glanced sideways at the older man, grey eyes glinting in the sun. "I
never said, 'Thou shalt have no other gods before me,' now did I?"

Ranulf smiled. "You're your father's son, for certes, lad. That perverse
humor of yours most surely does not come from my sister, God love her!
So . . . why am I here, then? What do you want from me?"

"I am hoping that a show of force will be enough to tame Owain's rebellious urges. If so, I'll need you to negotiate peace terms. Right now I
want the benefit of your seven years in Wales. You know the man, Ranulf. Tell me about him. What sort of foe—or friend—is he?"

Ranulf leaned back against the wall, shading his eyes from the glare of
sun on water. "I respect him," he said, doling out the words with miserly
precision. "And there are few men I'd say that about."

"Dare I ask if you include me in that small, select group? No . . . better you do not answer," Henry joked. "So you respect him. Why?"

"On your side of the border, the Welsh are viewed as a rash, passionate people. Whether that be true or not, Owain is neither. He is as shrewd
as any fox, farsighted and pragmatic, deliberate in all that he does. He
keeps his temper in check, his enemies close, and his thoughts to himself.
He forgives, but I doubt that he forgets. Above all, he understands what
Stephen never did—that he must put the king's needs above the man's."

"He sounds like a man worthy of your respect," Henry conceded. "A
pity he is not more like his brother. Cadwaladr is a ship without a rudder;
no one ever knows where the winds or his whims will take him. Owain is
much the older of the two, is he not?"

"I think there are about ten years between them, mayhap a few years less. I know Owain's next birthday is his fifty-seventh, for he was born in God's Year 1100. But he is aging like an oak, stunting the sons growing in that vast shadow. He has nigh on a dozen, some by his wife, several by his current concubine, the rest by other bedmates, including the best of the lot, Hywel, whom I count as a friend. I would not want to encounter Hywel on a battlefield, Harry."

Ranulf said it smiling, but Henry caught the undertone. "I hope you will not, Uncle. Truly I do."

"But no promises?"

"No," Henry said slowly. "No promises. Mine would not be worth much on its own. You'd need one, too, from Owain Gwynedd."

"Yes," Ranulf agreed, "I suppose I would." And after that, they stood without talking for a time, gazing toward the west, toward Wales.

CHAPTER THREE

✦

August 1157
Aber, North Wales

S SHE ENTERED THE GREAT HALL, all eyes followed the Welsh king's concubine. By the standards of their age, Cristyn was no longer young at thirty-seven. But she still turned male heads with ease. Dressed richly in a vibrant red gown, she defied Welsh fashion by wearing her hair long, a curly, midnight cloud set off by a veil of gauzy gold, as transparent as summer sunlight. The colors were deliberately dramatic. She'd have been just as compelling, though, in mourning garb, for her vital, passionate nature burned brighter and hotter than any fire. All knew she held their king's heart in the palm of her hand, and few seeing her now wondered why.

One who did watched from the shadows with a sardonic smile. Hywel ab Owain could not deny that Cristyn made his father happy or that he'd have wed her years ago if not for the inconvenient existence of his wife, Gwladys. It even amused Hywel that he might one day have a stepmother younger than he was, although it had taken him years to see the ironic humor in that. In the beginning of their liaison, Hywel had been horrified that his father would bed a girl of seventeen. It had not helped that he'd found her so damnably desirable himself. He still did, but no longer with the shamed, hungry yearning of raw youth. When he looked upon his father's leman now, it was with an oddly impersonal desire, the poet's innate love of beauty continually at war with the prince's deep-rooted dislike of the woman.

"I see the queen bee has set all the drones to buzzing about her again. You think she'll ever grow tired of preening her tail feathers in public?"

The speaker mixing metaphors with such reckless abandon was Hywel's half-brother, Cynan, who'd come up unnoticed behind him. Like Hywel, Cynan was born out of wedlock. But in Wales, it was enough that the father recognized the child as his, and so Cynan and Hywel and their other illegitimate half-brothers were on an equal footing with Iorwerth and Maelgwn, the sons of Owain's lawful wife. Hywel, the result of Owain's youthful love affair with the daughter of an Irish lord, was the firstborn, the oldest at thirty-eight, of Owain's considerable brood. The rest ranged in age through their thirties and twenties down to Cristyn's two sons, nineteen-year-old Davydd and twelve-year-old Rhodri.

Cynan never referred to Cristyn by her given name if he could help it. It was always the "queen bee," although not in his father's hearing; even Cynan was not that rash. Hywel's private name for her was the "lioness," after reading in a bestiary that the female lion was fiercely protective of her cubs. Cristyn's eldest cub was now swaggering across the hall toward her, the younger cub nowhere in sight. Cynan, who detested Davydd fully as much as he did Cristyn, muttered an obscenity. Hywel snagged a cup of mead from a passing servant and waited for Cristyn to come to him.

That she would, he did not doubt; a lioness was always wary when male lions were on the prowl. Hywel had no false pride, for he had won fame at an early age and was renowned throughout Wales as a poet and soldier. He and Cristyn both knew that he was the most formidable of her foes, the son most like Owain.

Cristyn greeted Hywel with a cool smile. "I'd heard that you had ridden in, Hywel. Is my lord Owain expecting you?"

His own smile was wry, acknowledging the deft thrust: a polite welcome for an interloper. "I daresay he is, Cristyn. When has he ever ridden off to war without me at his side?"

Cristyn's smile held steady. Davydd, following in his mother's footsteps, had neither her self-control nor her skill at verbal jousting. Glaring at Hywel, he said belligerently, "My father does not need your help to defeat the English."

Hywel had done enough hell-raising in his own youth to understand Davydd's need to chase after trouble and court confrontations. Usually he overlooked his half-brother's bravado. Tonight, though, he was tired and Davydd's barb rankled. "Tell me, Davydd, have you bloodied your own sword yet?"

Davydd's face flooded with color. "Whoreson!" he snarled, and people nearby gave up any polite pretense that they were not eavesdropping. Others had begun to drift over and they soon had a large, expectant audience. Cristyn put a hand on her son's arm, saying softly, "Do not take his bait, Davydd. Let it lie."

Davydd was no fool, and the part of his brain not inflamed by anger was sending him the same message. But at nineteen, pride had a louder voice than common sense. "Hywel owes me an apology," he insisted. "If he says he is sorry, I'll be satisfied."

He sounded so young that Hywel could not help smiling. It was both his blessing and his curse that he could never stay angry for long; his sense of the absurd was too well developed for that.

"Are you laughing at me?" Davydd balled his fists, shrugging off his mother's restraining hold. "Say you're sorry, damn you, or by God, I'll . . ." He paused, not sure exactly what he would do, and Cynan chose that inopportune moment to join in the fun.

"I'll say it if Hywel won't. I am indeed sorry, lad, sorrier than I can say that you're such a hotheaded half-wit. It reflects badly upon us all, what with your being kin—"

Davydd lunged at Cynan, who pivoted just in time. Before the younger man could launch another attack, Hywel and Cristyn, working in tandem for once, stepped between the combatants. Cynan was willing to cooperate, for he'd merely been amusing himself. Davydd was too furious, though, to heed reason, or even his mother. When Hywel caught his arm, he jerked free with such violence that he stumbled. Only then did he become aware of the sudden silence. All around him, people were backing away, when only moments before, they'd been pressing in eagerly to watch. Davydd froze and then turned slowly to face his father.

When men said that Owain Gwynedd cast a long shadow, they were speaking both literally and figuratively, for he was taller than most Welshmen. He was fairer in coloring, too; in his youth, his hair had been as bright as beaten gold, now silvered like moonlight. He bore his fifty-seven years well, but his cares had chased the laughter from his soul. Inspiring both admiration and awe in his subjects, he was a redoubtable figure even to those who loved him.

Owain said nothing; he'd long ago learned the tactical advantages that waiting could confer. Davydd and Cynan were soon squirming under the piercing power of those flint-grey eyes. "Did something happen here that I ought to know about?" Posed as a question, it was not. He controlled their response as thoroughly as he controlled the moment, and Davydd and Cynan hastily assured him that nothing had happened, nothing at all.

Owain regarded them impassively, just long enough to communicate an unmistakable message: that he knew better. "One of our scouts has ridden in from the east," he said. "The English king's army is breaking camp at Saltney, getting ready to cross into Wales."

A murmur swept the hall, subdued and unsurprised. Cristyn moved unobtrusively to her lover's side. The others, too, had drawn closer to Owain, putting Hywel in mind of the way people huddled before an open hearth on a blustery winter's day. Only this storm would strike in August.

"Papa . . ." Owain's youngest son had followed his father into the hall. Rhodri's eyes were as round as coins and his voice held the hint of a tremor. "What . . . what will you do?"

Owain glanced down at the boy, letting his hand rest on Rhodri's shoulder. "Well, lad, we shall have to teach this young English king how wars are fought in Wales."

THE ENGLISH KING'S command tent was lit by sputtering cresset lamps that gave off more smoke than light, and the men had to crowd in to see the map spread out upon the trestle table. The Marcher lords were dominating the discussion, for they claimed to know Wales better than the Welsh themselves. William Fitz Alan was embellishing his conversation with such sweeping arm gestures that he'd already caused one lamp's flame to gutter out, and Walter Clifford was using his dagger for dramatic effect, stabbing down at the map as if he were thrusting into the heartland of Wales itself.

"Here," he said, "here is where our war begins and ends." The dagger flashed, the knife biting deeply into the table.

Henry looked down at the target pierced by that quivering blade. "I already know Owain awaits us at Basingwerk, Walter," he said coolly, for he had little patience with posturing. "If he fights, it'll be here. Was it really necessary to mutilate the table for that?"

Most men were flustered by royal rebukes. Walter Clifford was oblivious to the sarcasm, as thick-skinned as he was single-minded. "What is more important, my liege?" he asked brashly. "A table or a chance to outflank your enemy?"

"How?" Henry sounded skeptical. "We've agreed that we must march along the coast. What would you have us do, try to take an army over the goat tracks that pass for roads in most of Wales?"

Clifford grinned triumphantly. "No, my lord king. But you could send a smaller force through the Cennadlog Forest."

"I know it sounds rash at first hearing," William Fitz Alan said hurriedly. Furious with Clifford for presenting the Marcher plan as his own, he glared at the other man even as he sought to persuade the king. "The forest trails are indeed narrow and not easily followed. But with trustworthy guides, a body of lightly armed horsemen could penetrate those woods and reach the coast—behind Owain's army."

Henry glanced inquiringly at Owain Gwynedd's brother. "What say you, my lord? Can this be done?"

Cadwaladr nodded vigorously. A tall, robust man in his late forties, with a cocky grin and thick chestnut hair that had not yet begun to grey, he was not one to pass unnoticed in any company. Only in his brother's presence was he somehow diminished, a paler, lesser copy of the original. When seeing the two men together, Ranulf had occasionally felt an involuntary pang of pity for Cadwaladr, no more able to eclipse Owain than a man could outrun his own shadow. He was not surprised now that Cadwaladr should back the Marcher plan, for the Welshman's courage was equaled only by his confidence.

"I can do it," the Welsh prince said, with just enough emphasis on the "I" to hint at doubts about the corresponding capabilities of these alien allies of his. "Give me the command and we'll salt Owain's tail for you, good and proper!" An uproar at once ensued, as the Marcher lords began to object strenuously to the idea of turning over command to Cadwaladr.

Henry heard them all out. Ranulf sensed that he was intrigued by the Marcher suggestion. There was an inherent boldness in the idea that was sure to appeal to him. Ranulf said nothing as the discussion swirled about him, drawing further back into the shadows. He was accustomed to feeling like an outsider, for he'd lived much of his life as one, half Welsh, half Norman-French, a king's bastard, neither fish nor fowl, as he put it in his more whimsical moods. But rarely had he felt as isolated as he did now, or as helpless, watching as war's insidious fever claimed first one victim and then another. Was it burning, too, amongst the Welsh?

His silence did not go unnoticed by Henry, who rarely missed much. "It is getting hotter than Hades in this tent," he complained. "I am going to take a walk around the camp, and will give my decision when I return. Uncle . . . you want to help me walk the wolf?" he asked, gesturing toward the large black alaunt napping under the table.

Rainald half-rose from his seat, then sank back in disappointment as he realized he was the wrong uncle. Ranulf got slowly to his feet, waiting as Henry slipped a lead on the dog's collar, and then followed his nephew out into the night.

Henry's pretext had some basis in truth, for it had been an uncommonly hot August so far. The sky above their heads held not even a wisp of cloud, just stars beyond counting. Soldiers nudged one another as they recognized the king, and one of the inevitable camp-followers, a buxom young woman with fiery red hair, called out cheekily, "Good hunting, my liege!"

"You, too, sweetheart," Henry shot back, stirring laughter in all within hearing range. Glancing over at Ranulf as they paused to let the alaunt sniff a wagon wheel, he said quietly, "You do not like this flank attack. Tell me why, Uncle."

"I do not like this war!" Ranulf said, too loudly, for heads turned in their direction. "I know you say this campaign is meant only to intimidate Owain and the Welsh, and I do not doubt your intent, Harry. Set a fire to contain a fire. But what if it gets away from you? If you and Owain misread each other, all of Wales could go up in flames."

Henry did not deny it. "I never promised you that there would be no fighting, Uncle. I'd not lie, at least not to you. I would much prefer that we come to terms with the Welsh, but if it take some bloodshed to bring that about, so be it. However little you like to admit it, Ranulf, I have the right in this argument."

Ranulf knew that Owain Gwynedd would say the same. But there was no use in pointing that out to his nephew. He had an uneasy sense that events were taking on their own momentum, already beyond the power of either Henry or Owain to control.

"What do you think of this flank attack?" Henry persisted. "Is it worth the risk?"

"I have a bad feeling about it." Even to Ranulf, that sounded lame.

Henry whistled to the dog and they started back toward his tent. Neither spoke for several moments. Ranulf studied his nephew's moonlit profile; it was bright enough to see the freckles scattered across Henry's nose. "You're going to do it, though," he concluded. "So who gets the command? Cadwaladr? Hertford or Salisbury?"

He caught a sudden flash of white as Henry smiled. "The command," he said, "goes to me."

HENRY HAD NEVER seen woods so thick and tangled. Clouds of rustling foliage shut out the sun, and by the time it filtered through that leafy web, the summer heat had lost its oppressive edge. The forest trail was overgrown in spots, but at least it was not mired in mud, and their Welsh guides followed its meandering track as if every hollow and fallen log and brambled barrier were branded into their memories. They'd only ridden a few miles so far, but they'd left the known world behind, all that was familiar and safe. This was the Wales of legend, primal and impenetrable.

"My liege?" Eustace Fitz John urged his mount to catch up with Henry and Ranulf. "Are we sure that Owain is with his army at Dinas Basing?"

He used the Welsh name rather than the Norman-French Basingwerk, and Ranulf liked him for that. It offended him that his father's countrymen were so loath to use the names given by the Welsh to their own castles, towns, and abbeys. He'd had a few dealings with Eustace Fitz John, the Constable of Chester, and had always found him to be a decent sort, not as high-handed as most of the Marcher lords. It seemed such a pity that so many good men, Norman and Welsh, were putting their lives at risk on this hot August afternoon.

Ranulf would have thought that he'd be used to tallying up casualties by now; he had, after all, fought in the very worst of that bloody war for his sister's stolen crown. But a few years of peace had stripped away those hard-won defenses. He was a battle-seasoned soldier with a monk's loathing for bloodshed, and he could expect neither the Welsh nor the Normans to understand. He'd learned the hard way that most people could see no side but their own. Snapping out of his reverie, he saw that Henry and Fitz John were discussing the most lethal weapon in Henry's arsenal: the royal fleet sailing up the Welsh coast from Pembroke. Ranulf had been dismayed to learn of the naval force; the Welsh king had no warships of his own. Nor could Owain match the manpower of the English Crown. The bulk of Henry's army, now making its way along the coast toward Dinas Basing, was sure to outnumber the Welsh. Ranulf's instinctive empathy for the underdog had fused with his love for his adopted homeland, and if it did come to outright war, his deepest sympathies would be with Wales.

The fact that he'd be bleeding for England only underscored the perversity of his plight. With a flicker of forced humor, he wondered how the Almighty would view his muddled prayers for victory. *Let the Welsh win, O Lord, but not by much.* That sounded suspiciously like St Augustine's memorable plea for chastity—eventually.

Henry happened to glance in his direction at that moment, catching a glimpse of Ranulf's self-mocking smile. "What are you laughing at, Uncle?"

"Myself." Ranulf swatted a fly off his stallion's withers, squinting as a bead of sweat trickled into the corner of his eye. While it was cooler in the depths of the woods than out in the full glare of sun, their chain-mail armor was stifling. "I was curious why you decided against letting Cadwaladr accompany us?"

"If I had," Henry explained, "that would have set all those Marcher noses out of joint. Just as Cadwaladr would have been sorely vexed if I'd brought Clifford along. Better to send the lot of them by the coast road with Fitz Alan's archers. I said I had need of you to talk truce terms with Owain, but that glib tongue of yours might be called into service sooner—to make peace midst our own men."

"I'll leave that to your chancellor," Ranulf said and Henry grinned.

"You're right. I daresay Thomas could talk a nun out of her habit. Not that he would. Even after two years in my constant company, he remains remarkably indifferent to the sins of the flesh."

Ranulf laughed. "Well, he is an archdeacon, Harry. And the last I heard, the Church took a rather negative view of sins of the flesh."

"A man can be virtuous without being a zealot about it." Henry laughed, too, reaching up under the nose guard of his helmet to rub his chafed skin. "Thomas claims I do enough sinning for the both of us."

They could see a pool of sunlight up ahead as the trail widened, dappled brightness briefly dispelling some of the deeper shadows. A small woodland creature darted across the path, too swiftly to be identified. As they rode on, there was a sudden flurry and a flock of chittering birds burst from a nearby tree, a shower of feathered arrows aiming at the sky.

Ranulf gazed upward, following their soaring flight with the beginning of a smile. But then he saw Tegid, one of their guides. The young Welshman was staring up at the fleeing birds, too, and on his face was an expression of dawning horror.

"*Rhagod!*" Only Ranulf understood that hoarse cry, a warning of ambush come too late. The urgency in the guide's voice needed no translation, though. Henry checked his stallion, starting to draw his sword from its scabbard. Tegid's second shout was choked off as he was slammed backward, knocked from his saddle by the force of the spear protruding from his chest.

An arrow thudded into a tree trunk above Ranulf's head. Another shaft found a target in flesh, and a knight slumped across his stallion's neck, sliding to the ground as the horse reared up in fright. Then the killing began in earnest. With savage-sounding yells, the Welsh, charging from the woods on both sides of the road, sought to drag the English from their horses. The English in turn slashed and thrust with deadly effect in such close quarters, and blood splattered the combatants, the trampled grass, even the leaves of low-hanging branches.

Ranulf had passed some sleepless hours in recent weeks, envisioning a battle in which he found himself fighting against the Welsh. What if he saw someone he knew amongst them? Celyn, his brother-by-marriage? Hywel? Now that the dreaded moment was here, he had no time to spare for such fears. His only concern was defending himself against men set upon killing him, and when a Welsh soldier grabbed his arm, jerking to pull him from the saddle, he spurred his stallion into rearing up. His attacker lost his balance, falling in front of those flailing hooves.

A few feet away, Eustace Fitz John was not as lucky. His horse had bolted and a tree branch caught him in the throat. He crashed heavily to the ground and before he could regain his feet, a Welshman was astride him, plunging a spear downward. Ranulf tore his gaze away from the constable's body, seeking his nephew. Henry was struggling to control his panicked stallion, while fending off a swarthy Welshman wielding a mace. His sword was already bloody, and as Ranulf watched, an arrow scorched past his face, almost grazing his cheek.

Before Ranulf could go to Henry's assistance, he was again under attack himself. When at last he looked back at Henry, the young king was still holding his own. But then he saw the royal standard dip, disappear into the dust churned up by the thrashing horses.

The impact was immediate and devastating. "The king is dead!" The cry went up from a dozen throats, and Ranulf knew what would happen next. Believing that Henry was slain, his men would lose heart, think only of flight. Ranulf raced his horse across the clearing, leaned recklessly from the saddle and snatched up the fallen standard. Some of the English had already bolted, but the reassuring sight of that red and gold banner steadied the others, forestalling a rout.

"Sound the retreat!" Ranulf thanked God that his nephew had a voice made for shouting. Henry's command rose above the din of battle, followed by the blare of trumpets. Bunching together, the English began an agonizingly slow-paced withdrawal, keeping their horses under tight rein though they yearned to spur into a wild gallop, knowing that such a flight would doom them all.

Ranulf had been in running battles before, but this one was nightmarish, for they were walled in by the dense woods, trapped on a winding trail that made speed impossible, and under unrelenting attack by the pursuing Welsh. They had to abandon their dead, even their wounded. But after several harrowing miles, they succeeded in fighting their way free.

The danger had eased, but not ended. Henry was too tempting a target for Welsh bowmen; they'd be back, and in greater numbers. The English rode on, pushing their horses, relieved but still wary once they left the woods behind. They'd not yet counted their dead. Ranulf knew that the toll would be a high one. But it could have been worse, Christ Jesus, so much worse. Glancing from time to time at his nephew, he wondered if Harry realized just how close he'd come to dying.

Henry did. He could still feel the hot rush of air on his skin as that Welsh arrow whistled past his ear. He was no novice to battle—he'd bloodied his sword for the first time at sixteen—but this had been different. This time his luck had almost run out.

They were heading for the coast road, hoping to catch up with the rest of their army before the Welsh could rally for another attack. But they'd only covered a few miles before they saw dust up ahead. Drawing their swords, they waited, and soon were cheering, for the riders galloping toward them were friends, not foes.

A scout on a lathered horse reached them first, explaining that a few of the English fugitives from the battle had overtaken the rearguard, claiming that the king had been slain, the rest lost. "But your uncle the earl would not believe it, my liege," the scout told Henry. "Nor would the chancellor." His begrimed, sweat-streaked face lit up in a wide grin. "The sight of you is going to gladden their eyes, and that's God's Blessed Truth!"

Rainald began to whoop as soon as he was in recognition range. "I knew those fools were wrong, by God, I did!"

Thomas Becket was more restrained in his greeting, but his jubilation burned no less brightly than Rainald's, just at a lower flame. "Do you realize what you almost put me through, Harry?" He shook his head in mock reproach. "I'd have had to be the one to tell your queen that you got yourself killed in some godforsaken corner of Wales!"

"That was foremost in my mind. Whilst I was fighting for my life, I kept thinking, 'I cannot do this to Thomas!'"

"You think telling Eleanor would have been rough? God pity the man who'd have had to tell my sister Maude!" Rainald's grimace was partly for effect, partly quite genuine. "So . . . tell us. How bad was it, truly?"

"Well, I've passed more pleasant afternoons," Henry allowed, and they all grinned. But as his gaze met Ranulf's, there was no levity, no laughter in either man's eyes, only a haunted awareness of what might have been.

AFTER HENRY'S ESCAPE from the Welsh ambush, Owain withdrew his forces before the advance of the much larger English army, and Henry continued along the coast to Rhuddlan Castle, awaiting the arrival of his fleet. But when word came, it was not good. Acting against orders, the English ships had anchored at Tal Moelfre on the island of Môn and the sailors had gone ashore, plundering and looting and burning the churches of Llanbedr Goch and Llanfair Mathafarn Eithaf. The island residents were so outraged that they staged a counterattack, led by Owain's son Hywel. In the fighting that followed, the English took much the worst of it, suffering many casualties, including a half-brother to Ranulf and Rainald.

IT WAS DUSK when Ranulf and his men reached the encampment of the Welsh king at Bryn y pin. The day's sweltering heat had yet to ebb and the English flag of truce drooped limply in the still, humid air. The Englishmen's spirits were sagging, too, for they were convinced that Ranulf's mission was doomed and they lacked his confidence in the worth of

Owain's word. They were greeted with predictable antagonism, subjected to jeers and catcalls as they were escorted through the camp. But no hands were raised against them, and the only weapons to threaten them were the fabled sharp edges of the Welsh tongue.

Ranulf dismounted from his stallion, then stiffened at the sight of the man striding toward him. Slowly unsheathing his sword, he offered it to Owain's son. Hywel accepted it awkwardly and they walked together across the encampment. The Welshman was finding this meeting as uncomfortable as Ranulf, and after a few moments he said, "So . . . how has your summer been so far, Ranulf? You keeping busy?"

"Nothing out of the ordinary. How about you?"

"You were there, were you not? With the English king in the Cennadlog Forest?"

Not for the first time, Ranulf found himself marveling at the efficiency of Owain Gwynedd's espionage system. "Tell me, Hywel, does a leaf fall in the forest without your father's learning of it within the hour?"

"A stray leaf or two may get past him. But we've tried to keep an eye on you—for your own good, of course."

"Of course." Ranulf decided not to ask why, not sure he wanted to know the answer. "That ambush almost worked. If only they'd waited until we'd gotten deeper into the woods, we'd never have been able to fight our way out. Lucky for us you Welsh are such an impatient, impulsive people."

"Lucky for you I was not in command. That honor went to my brothers, Cynan and Davydd." Hywel's sly smile told Ranulf he was not entirely displeased that his brothers' timing had been off. "I was occupied elsewhere, teaching greedy English sailors that plunder has its price."

They'd reached Owain's tent, but neither man was in a hurry to enter. Hywel's eyes were solemn now, for once devoid of all amusement. "I've always had a way with words; with a Welsh father and an Irish mother, how could I not? But tonight I hope you're the eloquent one. You'll have to be more than persuasive, Ranulf, if you expect to convince my father to make peace. You'll have to be downright spellbinding."

Hywel didn't wait for Ranulf's response. Instead, he handed him back his sword. "It is never wise," he said, "to go unarmed into the lion's den."

RANULF WAS NOT as cynical as Hywel; his expectations were usually much more optimistic. Not this time, though. He agreed wholeheartedly with Hywel's pessimistic assessment of his chances. The tent was poorly lit by a single torch and crowded with as hostile an audience as he'd ever faced. Owain's seneschal was regarding him balefully. So were his lords and four of his sons: Cynan, Davydd, Iorwerth, and Maelgwn.

Owain was not as easy to read as the other men. He never was. They were seated on the ground, for the Welsh scorned the campaign comforts of their English enemies. Signaling for Ranulf to join them, Owain said, "Give the man some mead, Hywel."

Davydd started to object, caught Owain's eye, and reconsidered. Ranulf gratefully accepted a cup from Hywel and took a deep, bracing swallow. "I am here, my lord Owain, at the behest of King Henry. He does not want all-out war with the Welsh. It is his hope that you and he can come to terms."

Owain drank from his cup, keeping his eyes on Ranulf all the while. "His terms, I'd wager."

There was no way to temper the blow, and Ranulf was wise enough not even to try. "King Henry would expect you to do homage to him for your domains, to offer up hostages as a show of good faith, to restore your brother Cadwaladr to his lands in Meirionydd, and to renounce all claims to the cantref of Tegeingl."

He knew what reaction he'd get, but it was even more heated than he'd expected. Owain's sons were the most vocal in expressing their outrage. Cynan vowed passionately that he'd die ere he gave up his share of Meirionydd to Cadwaladr, Maelgwn and Iorwerth fumed at the insufferable arrogance of the English, while Davydd was reduced to sputtering incredulous oaths. Even Hywel dipped his oar in, pointing out acidly that the English fleet had been defeated at Tal Moelfre, just in case that had escaped King Henry's notice.

Ranulf made no attempt to defend himself, letting their indignation run its course. Owain, too, waited for the tumult to subside. "Your king's notion of peace is a curious one. It sounds suspiciously like Welsh surrender to these ears. Suppose you tell me, Lord Ranulf, why I should even consider such one-sided terms. What could I possibly get out of it?"

"You'd get the English army out of North Wales."

Owain smiled skeptically. "For how long?"

Ranulf leaned forward tensely. "That would be up to you."

Owain's eyes narrowed, but his expression did not change as the others began to heap scorn on this "English peace," and when Owain got to his feet, Ranulf reluctantly rose too, taking it as a dismissal. So did Owain's sons, and they were all caught by surprise when the Welsh king beckoned to Ranulf, saying, "Come with me."

Ranulf hastily followed Owain from the tent. Ignoring the stares and speculation of his soldiers, Owain began to walk, and Ranulf fell in step beside him. A turquoise twilight was spilling over the hills, and the few clouds overhead were darkening to a deep purple. Off to the south, Ranulf thought he glimpsed the fading gleam of the River Elwy. They were just a few miles from Rhuddlan and the English army. A few miles and a few days and then Armageddon. Unless he could convince Owain to accept the English terms. Unless the Almighty deigned to work a miracle solely on his behalf.

"What did you mean," Owain asked abruptly, "when you said it would be up to me?"

"King Henry's terms are not easy to swallow. But if you can force them down this once, you'll not have to drink from that cup again. If you keep faith with him, he'll keep out of Wales."

"How can you be so sure of that?"

"Because," Ranulf said, "I know my nephew, about as well as any man can."

Owain had led them into the shadowed circle cast by a sky-scraping oak. "I've spoken to your uncle about you," he said unexpectedly. "Rhodri swears that your soul is Welsh. He says you are that rarity, a man as honorable as he is honest. But can you be loyal to Wales and Henry, too?"

Ranulf summoned up a grimacing smile. "God knows, I am trying."

"The English campaign has hardly been a rousing success so far. Your nephew's attempt to outflank me almost cost him his life, and his fleet was badly mauled in that raid on Môn. Why should I make peace when I am winning?"

"Because we both know that you can win battles, but not the war," Ranulf said bluntly. "Wales can match neither the resources nor the armies of the English Crown. For every Welsh child born, the Lord God has chosen to let twenty be begotten across the border. I am not saying it would be easy to conquer Wales. But I fear it could be done."

"And you think this young lordling is the man to do it?"

"You mock him at your peril, my lord Owain. Yes, Harry is young. He learns fast, though, rarely making the same mistake twice. And he gets what he wants. You need proof of that? Both his crown and his queen were once claimed by other men. But by the time he was one and twenty, he'd won the English throne and taken Eleanor of Aquitaine into his bed."

Ranulf paused, taking a deep, deliberate breath before saying then, with all the conviction at his command, "Trust me in this if nothing else, my lord. Henry Fitz Empress is no 'young lordling,' but the most dangerous foe you've ever faced. His will was forged in the same fire that tempered the blade of his sword. If you provoke him into war to the uttermost, he'll do whatever he must to win that war."

"You say he gets what he wants. How do I know he does not want Wales?"

"Harry is ambitious, not rapacious. For all that gluttony is one of the Seven Deadly Sins, it is not amongst his. He does not bite off more than he can chew, and he well knows that Wales would be a tough mouthful. Moreover, he has shown himself to be a fair and just liege lord to the diverse lands within his domains. He rules Anjou, Normandy, Maine, Touraine, England, and his wife's Aquitaine, without meddling in their customs, laws, or languages. He told me once that was his father's deathbed advice: Always to ride with a light hand on the reins."

"That may be so, but he is heavy-handed in his demands. He asks a lot for a man who has yet to gain a victory on Welsh soil."

"And that is telling, too, my lord. Another man might have forced a battle, just to prove to you—and himself—that he could win. Another man might also have made the terms much harsher, punishing you for his mistakes. But Harry needs to prove his manhood to no one. Nor does he seek out scapegoats. He accepts rebellion, fairly fought. It is betrayal he cannot abide—or forgive."

"I assume that is a warning," Owain said dryly. "You put me in mind, Lord Ranulf, of a man trying to ride two horses at once. At the moment, you seem to have a foot planted firmly in each saddle. But I wonder how long you can keep such a precarious balance."

"I wonder, too," Ranulf said, with a rueful smile. "I've tried to be honest with you, my lord, more honest than men usually are with kings. If I may, I'd do a bit more plain speaking now. I know that Harry's terms leave a sour taste in your mouth. But in truth, they are not that unreasonable or onerous. It would vex you, I daresay, to have Cadwaladr underfoot again. We both know, though, that you can keep him in check. It might even be better to have him back under your control, rather than conniving freely at the English court. As for Tegeingl, you cannot truly blame

Harry for wanting you out of a cantref that borders on Chester. He told me recently that if he turned a blind eye to the border for long, the people of Cheshire and Shropshire would soon be speaking Welsh, and that, my lord Owain, is the highest compliment he could pay you."

He'd taken a gamble with that last remark, saw that he'd won it when the corner of Owain's mouth quirked, a smile almost too quick to catch. He did not dare to ask, though, if he'd been persuasive. There was too much at stake to risk hearing that he'd failed.

"Stay the night," Owain said. "I'll give you my answer in the morning."

"Thank you, my lord." Ranulf watched as Owain strode off into the darkness. Suddenly he felt very tired, body and soul. A tree stump was off to his right, a primitive seat at best, but close at hand. He was still sitting there when Hywel strolled over.

"My father will say only that he has some thinking to do. Naturally, that has alarmed my brothers, few of whom do any thinking at all. They cannot understand why he does not just send you back to the English camp with a blistering refusal scorching your ears. Nor would they stop at that. If it were up to them, you'd be banished from ever setting foot on Welsh soil again, even in your dreams."

That was Ranulf's secret fear, that even if he managed to stave off a war, he could still be the loser. "Am I likely to end up in exile, Hywel? Would your father do that?"

Hywel looked surprised, then amused. "Do not be a dolt. Of course he will not."

Ranulf was heartened by the other man's certainty. "You must have more influence than I realized."

"As much as I'd like to claim the credit, there is a simple reason why my father will let you remain in Wales. You're the English king's uncle. You might well become our window to the English court. Or," Hywel added mischievously, "a useful pawn or hostage. No, rest assured that we'll not be booting you out of Gwynedd, whatever my father decides on the morrow."

"I'm gladdened to hear that," Ranulf admitted, for with Hywel he could let down his guard. "It would break Rhiannon's heart to go off into English exile. Nor would I fancy it much, either."

Getting to his feet, he moved so stiffly that Hywel, who was a year younger, made a joke about aging English bones. By now the moon had risen above the surrounding hills, casting a soft, silvered light upon the

Welsh encampment. Ranulf studied the face of his friend, familiar but not always expressive; Hywel could be as inscrutable as his father when he chose.

"It is going to be a long night, Hywel. You know your father's thinking, better than most. Do you believe he will agree to the English terms?"

Hywel was quiet for a moment. "Well," he said, "if I were a gambling man—and we both know I am—I'd put my money on peace. Or what passes for peace in Wales."

CHAPTER FOUR

✦

August 1157
Rhuddlan Castle
Gwynedd, Wales

HENRY'S CHARM WAS GENUINE, for it sprang from his
love of life and his unquenchable curiosity. But it also con-
tained an element of calculation. He'd learned at an early age
the disarming power of a smile or jest. He'd learned, too, that not all men
could be won over with charm, and he sensed at the outset that Owain
Gwynedd was one of them. The Welsh king was courteous, dignified in
his submission, and beyond reach. When Henry looked into his eyes, grey
unto grey, he got only the most guarded glimpse into the older man's soul.
Gwynedd's defenses might be vulnerable to English attack, but Owain's
defenses were intact, impressive even in defeat.

Across the great hall, Ranulf watched as Henry and Owain talked together, their voices low, their faces unrevealing. Occasionally, they smiled,
seemingly oblivious of all the eyes upon them. The ceremony was over.
Owain had done homage to Henry, yielded hostages and the cantref of
Tegeingl and accepted the submission of his brother, Cadwaladr. Ranulf
doubted if that particular peace would last long. Cadwaladr's smirk did not
bode well for future harmony. But Cadwaladr's prospects held no interest

for Ranulf. If he was foolish enough to provoke Owain again, he deserved whatever he got. The only peace that mattered to Ranulf was the one that now existed between Owain Gwynedd and Henry Fitz Empress.

"Intriguing, is it not?" Hywel materialized without warning at Ranulf's side; for a big man, he could move as quietly as any cat when he chose. "Watching them take each other's measure, like two stallions vying for the same mares. The young challenger versus the seasoned sire. Which would you wager upon, Ranulf? Youth or experience?"

"Does it matter? They've agreed, after all, to share the herd."

Hywel smiled skeptically, for he thought that neither stallions nor kings were ones for sharing. But he refrained from saying so. It was hardly sporting, after all, to kick a man's crutch out from under him. "So what happens next? I trust we get fed now that we've surrendered? Even the doomed Christians got a last meal ere being thrown to the lions."

"Actually, they were the meal and the lions were the ones who got fed. But we'll have a better supper than you'll usually see on the royal table, for Thomas Becket brought his cooks along. Tonight we'll dine on venison stew and stuffed goose and the lord chancellor's finest Gascon wines, and on the morrow, Harry will return to England, Owain to Aber, and you, I expect, will find some absent husband's wife to help you celebrate the Peace of Rhuddlan."

Hywel grinned into his wine cup, not bothering to deny it; he loved to hunt and he loved women, and in pursuit of those twin passions, he felt no conscience pangs about trespassing. "What of you, Ranulf? When you return to Trefriw, will you be welcome?"

"I do not know, Hywel," Ranulf admitted reluctantly. "My uncle and sister-in-law were wroth with me for answering Harry's summons. They may not want me back."

"But you did avert further bloodshed, convincing my lord father to accept the English terms. Surely that must count in your favor?"

Ranulf shrugged. "It is not a popular peace, though. I've heard the talk. Many Welshmen feel that they were winning and do not understand why Owain yielded. My uncle and Eleri may well be amongst them."

"True enough," Hywel conceded, but then he smiled. "Suppose I accompany you? After they hear me laud you as a blessed peacemaker, how can they not forgive you?"

"Just be sure," Ranulf warned, "that you do not lure Eleri off for some private persuasion. Her husband may be a man of few words, but you make a cuckold of him at your peril."

"Of course I will not try to seduce Eleri." Hywel managed to look both innocent and offended, yet his dark eyes were gleaming. "I promise," he said, "to confine my attentions to your wife," and sauntered away with Ranulf's laughing curse ringing in his ears.

"That is Owain's firstborn?" Henry arrived just as Hywel was departing. "The poet?"

Poets were greatly esteemed in Wales, not so revered across the border. Henry had a higher regard for learning, though, than many of his countrymen; both his parents had valued education and had seen to it that he'd received an excellent one. Many lords scorned writing as a lowly clerk's skill, but Henry never traveled without a book in his saddlebags. Knowing that, Ranulf had no qualms about confirmation and he nodded. "Yes, the poet."

Henry looked after Hywel with kindled interest. "Is he any good?"

"Actually, he is. And he wields a sword as deftly as he does a pen. It was Hywel who rallied the citizens of Môn to repel your invasion."

"Can you not even pretend to regret our rout from Môn?" The reproach was playful, Henry's smile sympathetic. "You deserve credit for this peace, Uncle. I'll not be forgetting what you did."

"I hope the Welsh forget," Ranulf said wryly, knowing they would not. Too many of his Welsh brethren would see his actions as proof that he was—and would always be—an *alltud,* a foreigner.

"Let them grumble in the alehouses and taverns; you do have alehouses in Wales? When courting popularity, Ranulf, aim high. You've gained a king's favor by this campaign. No, not mine; you've always had that. I meant Owain. You proved yourself to be honorable and, even better, useful."

Ranulf smiled in spite of himself. "I can see that you and Owain speak the same tongue, one common to kings. A pity poor Stephen never learned it."

"I'm glad he did not," Henry said forthrightly, "for if he had, he might have held on to his stolen crown. You are right, though. I think Owain and I do understand each other." For a moment, his gaze shifted, his eyes resting thoughtfully upon the Welsh king. All in all, Henry was pleased with the results of his campaign. He'd gotten what he wanted, and without paying too high a price for it. He knew, of course, that he had not bought peace with the Welsh, merely rented it for a time. He knew, too, that his uncle believed otherwise, and that would be the one regret he'd take back to England. But he said nothing, for in this, he and Hywel ab Owain were of one mind. *Llawer gwir, gorau ei gelu.* All truths are not for telling.

D INNER WAS SERVED in England between eleven and twelve in the forenoon, in Wales at day's end. Because Eleri had visited Trefriw rarely in the weeks since war began, her stepmother, Enid, had instructed their cook to prepare a more elaborate meal than usual: roast capon, cabbage and almond soup, gingered carp, and apple fritters. But the dinner was not a success. To Enid's annoyance, Eleri and Rhiannon and Rhodri seemed indifferent to the fine fare set before them. Only the children ate with gusto. The adults pushed the food about on their trenchers, taking an occasional absentminded bite, and Enid realized she could have served them straw for all the notice they'd taken. Conversation was equally listless, desultory, and labored. Enid was soon wishing that her stepdaughter had stayed away.

Rhiannon was wishing the same. It was unbearably painful, this estrangement with her sister. She could feel Eleri's eyes upon her. When she misjudged her reach and almost tipped over her cider cup, Eleri had instinctively leaned over to help. As Rhiannon steadied the cup, their fingers touched, briefly, before Eleri pulled back. Rhiannon knew Eleri was hurting, too. But neither one knew how to mend this rift. Whenever they'd tried to talk about it, they ended up arguing again. Even the news of the Rhuddlan pact had not restored peace to their household.

Picking up her spoon, Rhiannon dipped it into her soup. The silence was as oppressive as the heat; this was the hottest, driest summer she could remember. Rhodri was too disheartened by the family discord to keep the conversation afloat, Enid seemed to be sulking, and when shouts echoed across the bailey, Eleri grasped gratefully at an excuse to flee the table.

"Someone is coming," she announced, flinging her napkin aside; she was halfway across the hall before it landed. Swinging the door back, she gave a joyful cry, as sweet and clear as birdsong. "It is Celyn!" Her voice changing, she added flatly, "And Ranulf." But then she gasped. "Jesú, Prince Hywel is with them, too!"

As the men dismounted, Eleri came flying through the doorway and threw herself into Celyn's arms. Rhiannon wisely elected to let Ranulf come to her, and they were soon enveloped in a close embrace. It was left to Hywel to accept Rhodri's flustered greetings. Stammering a bit, for he was not accustomed to entertaining royalty, Rhodri bade the prince welcome, while Enid blessed her luck for having served a dinner fit for a king's son.

With squeals of "Papa!" Ranulf's children bolted out into the bailey. Ranulf swung Gilbert up into his arms and then hastened to catch Mallt as she tripped. As strong-willed as her namesake, the Empress Maude, Mallt took her stumble in stride, picking herself up with admirable aplomb. "Papa! What you bring me?"

Ranulf laughed and then set the little girl upon her feet as his uncle limped toward him. For the span of a lifetime, they looked at each other. "Welcome back, lad," Rhodri said at last. "Welcome home."

THE CELEBRATION LASTED long after darkness had fallen. As word got out, borne on the wind across the hills and down into the river valley, neighbors began to trickle in, for Hywel attracted crowds as surely as nectar enticed bees. He liked nothing better than an audience and soon had the men laughing and the women bedazzled, telling them of the English raid upon Môn, describing his father's meeting with the English king at Rhuddlan, praising Ranulf extravagantly for the part he'd played in the peacemaking, shrewdly mentioning how pleased Lord Owain was with Ranulf's efforts. That baffled some of Ranulf's neighbors, impressed others, and offended a few. But even the most unforgiving of them dared not challenge their king's verdict. Before the evening was done, Hywel would see to it that Ranulf was protected by armor far more effective than chainmail, the redoubtable shield of Owain Gwynedd's favor.

It was almost midnight when Rhiannon slipped from the hall and crossed the bailey toward the chambers she shared with Ranulf. Both her children were in bed, Gilbert tangled up in the sheets and Mallt with her arms wrapped tightly around her cherished rag doll. Rhiannon leaned over their pallets, listening to the soft cadence of their breathing. Reassured that they slept, she backed away.

The chamber was dark, but she navigated with confidence, for she knew the location of every chair, every coffer; it was a grave offense in her household to move furniture at whim. She had been blind for twenty-six of her thirty-four years, and she'd long ago learned how to cope with her disability, relying upon memory and her other senses and courage to compensate for her lack of sight. She invariably amazed people with her prowess, misleading them by how easy she made it appear. That was an illusion, for her victories were all hard won, her battle begun anew with each day's dawning.

Outside, the air was cool on her skin, a welcome relief after so many hours of stifling summer heat. She'd meant to return to the hall, but instead she found herself following the seductive perfume of honeysuckle wafting across the bailey from her garden. Seating herself on a wooden bench, she breathed in the delicate fragrances scenting the night, smiling when one of her cats interrupted its nocturnal prowling to rub against her ankles.

Many people looked askance at cats, and they were not commonly kept as pets. But Rhiannon loved the sensual, plush feel of their fur, the throaty murmur of their purring, the lithe lines of their bodies, and they seemed to sense that, for they invariably sought her out. Now she allowed the young cat to settle in her lap, gently stroking it as she thought about her husband's homecoming.

She'd always liked Hywel. He was one of the few men who'd ever flirted with her, for most males could not see past her blindness. But that fondness seemed such a pallid, tepid emotion when compared with what she felt for Hywel now—a surge of gratitude that ran like a river through her veins, deep and swift-flowing and sure to last until her final breath. Hywel had been her husband's friend. Tonight he had been Ranulf's savior. For she did not doubt that life in Trefriw would have been intolerable for him—for them both—if not for Hywel.

But what mattered far more to Rhiannon than the goodwill of her neighbors was the olive branch offered, rather awkwardly, by her sister. Eleri still did not understand why Ranulf could not refuse the English king's summons. From the first, she'd idolized him, this English cousin come so suddenly and dramatically into their lives, almost as if the Almighty had sent him to replace the brothers He'd claimed, too often and too young. Rhiannon knew that Eleri's anger was fueled by pain. Knowing this, though, had not made it any easier to douse its flames. It had taken Hywel to do that, giving Eleri the excuse she needed to welcome her brother-in-law back into the fold, back into her good graces.

Laughter had been floating from the open windows of the great hall, and the abrupt silence caught Rhiannon's notice. Tilting her head, she listened intently, nervously. But the stillness was not ominous, merely the prelude to a performance.

Summer I love, when the stamping horse is unstilled.
And lord against valiant lord, comes fierce to the field.
And swift upon Flint, the flurrying wave is o'erspilled,
And newly the apple-trees blossom, their beauty fulfilled.
Bright on my shoulder is borne my shield to the fight.
How long to my wooing will my wedded lover not yield?

That was vintage Hywel; when he waxed most lyrical, there was sure
to be a sting in the tail. His next verse was momentarily drowned out by
laughter and cheers, and Rhiannon rose, planning to rejoin the revelries.
But she changed her mind at the sound of a familiar step on the graveled
garden path. Smiling, she turned in the moonlight, waiting for her husband to reach her.

FROM THE UPPER WINDOW of St George's Tower, Henry
looked upon the city of Oxford, spreading out to the east. It was nigh on
fifteen years since his mother had staged an amazing escape from this castle, lowering herself by ropes from this very chamber onto the iced-over
moat below, then somehow slipping through the lines of Stephen's besieging army. It was an incredible feat, for she'd had as much to fear from
the weather as from Stephen's soldiers; a fierce winter snowstorm had
been raging that night.

Henry was very proud of his mother's daring flight. On this particular September day, though, his thoughts were focused upon an ordeal of
another sort. Just north of the city walls, in the palace known as the king's
house, his wife was laboring to give birth to their fourth child.

This was the first time that he'd been present for one of Eleanor's lying-
ins, and with each passing hour, he was regretting it more and more. He'd
always considered waiting to be an earthly foretaste of eternal Hell; even
minor delays could wreak havoc upon his patience. And now he could do
nothing but wait, knowing all the while that so much could go wrong in
a birthing. The babe could be stillborn, strangled by the cord, positioned
wrong in the mother's womb. The woman's life could bleed away then
and there, or she could sicken afterward. Death stalked the birthing chamber as relentlessly as it did the battlefield.

In a far corner of the room, his brother and chancellor watched him
with the wary sympathy of men trapped in close quarters with an injured

lion. "Mayhap we can get him to go hunting," Will murmured. "Harry would likely rise from his deathbed for one last chance to hunt."

"I already suggested it." Becket signaled to a hovering servant to pour more wine. "Not only did he balk, he well nigh bit my head off."

"There is no hope then," Will said, with a melodramatic sigh. "We're doomed."

"Do not despair, lad. To save ourselves, we can always urge Harry to find out for himself how the queen fares."

Will took Becket's jest literally and his eyes widened. "But men are barred from the birthing chamber," he objected. "Harry could not just burst in . . ." After a moment to reflect, he grinned. "What am I saying? Harry would storm Heaven's own gates if he had a mind to!"

"A pity that the queen chose to join Harry here at Oxford. She was already great with child, and I'd not be surprised if the rigors of the journey brought on an early labor. It would have made more sense for her to have remained at Westminster and given birth there."

Will glanced curiously at the chancellor, wondering if all churchmen listened only to their heads, not their hearts. "You can hardly blame Eleanor for wanting to be with Harry as the birth drew nigh," he said mildly. "She came close to losing him in Wales, after all."

Becket's response was lost as Henry swung away from the window with an explosive oath. "By the Blood of Christ, enough of this! For all we know, she gave birth hours ago and the fool midwife has forgotten to send word!"

As he headed for the door, Will scrambled to his feet. "Harry, do nothing rash! You'll just upset the women if you go charging in, and what good will that do Eleanor?"

"The lad is right," Becket observed calmly. "You cannot hasten the birth. The babe will be born in God's Time, no sooner, no later."

Seeing Henry's hesitation, Will hastily groped for further persuasion. "The child might even come faster if you're not there," he insisted. "Everyone knows that hovering over a pot will not make it cook any faster."

Henry gave his brother a look that was incredulous, irked, and amused in equal measure. "That is not an analogy I'd suggest you make in Eleanor's hearing," he said dryly. "What would the two of you have me do, then?"

"You can pray," Becket said and Henry scowled, unwilling to entrust Eleanor's safety to another higher power, even the Almighty's. But it was then that they heard the footsteps out in the stairwell.

When the messenger came catapulting through the doorway, Henry's spirits soared, for no man would be in such a hurry to deliver dire news. Skidding to a halt in the floor rushes, the messenger dropped to his knees before his king. "God has indeed smiled upon you, my liege. He has given you a fine son."

PETRONILLA POURED a cupful of wine, carefully carried it back to her sister's bed. "Here, Eleanor, drink this. God knows, you've earned it."

Eleanor thought so too. "You'd think this would get easier. I'm getting enough practice, for certes."

She heard laughter beyond her range of vision and a low, throaty voice teased, "Well, dearest, what would you tell a farmer who had an overabundant harvest? To plant less, of course!"

Eleanor was amused by that impudent familiarity, for no daughter of Aquitaine could be offended by bawdy humor. Moreover, she was quite fond of the speaker, Henry's cousin Maud, Countess of Chester.

Maud was a handsome widow in her mid-thirties, niece to the Empress Maude, whose namesake she was. She shared more than a name with her royal aunt; they were both women of uncommon courage and sharp intelligence. But laughter had never come readily to the Empress, and the younger Maud laughed as easily as she breathed. To the surprise of many, including Henry, Eleanor and her prickly mother-in-law had gotten along well from their first meeting. With the second Maud, though, a genuine friendship had quickly formed, for in this worldly, irreverent kinswoman of her husband's, Eleanor had recognized a kindred spirit.

"I am not complaining about the frequency of the planting," she said. "I'd just rather not reap a crop every year."

Maud retrieved the wine cup, setting it on the table within Eleanor's reach. "After four crops in five years, I'd think not!"

"It proves," Petronilla chimed in, "that letting a field lie fallow truly does make it more fertile."

Maud's eyes shone wickedly. "Nigh on fifteen years fallow, was it not, Eleanor?"

Sometimes it astonished Eleanor to remember that she'd actually endured fifteen years as France's bored, unhappy queen. "But you may be sure I was the one blamed for those barren harvests," she said, with a twisted smile. "As if I could cultivate soil without seed!"

"Does that truly surprise you? Women have been taking the blame ever since Eve listened to that fork-tongued serpent, who most assuredly was male!" Maud turned then toward the door, smiling. "To judge by the commotion outside, either we are under siege or Harry has just arrived."

Somewhere along the way from the castle, Henry had found a garden to raid, for he was carrying an armful of Michaelmas daisies. These he handed to Petronilla, rather sheepishly, for romantic gestures did not come easily to him. Crossing the chamber in several quick strides, he leaned over the bed to give his wife a kiss that roused a wistful sort of envy in both widows, for Petronilla had been blessed with a happy marriage of her own and Maud had been denied one.

"Are you hurting, love?"

Eleanor's smile was tired, but happy. "Not at all," she lied. "By now the babes just pop right out, like a cork from a bottle."

Henry laughed. "Well . . . where is the little cork?"

A wet-nurse came forward from the shadows, bobbing a shy curtsy before holding out a swaddled form for his inspection. Henry touched the ringlets of reddish-gold hair, the exact shade as his own, and grinned when the baby's hand closed around his finger. "Look at the size of him," he marveled, and as his eyes met Eleanor's, the same thought was in both their minds: heartfelt relief that God had given them such a robust, sturdy son. No parent who'd lost a child could ever take health or survival for granted again.

"We still have not decided what to name him," Henry reminded his wife. "I fancy Geoffrey, after my father."

"The next one," she promised. "I have a name already in mind for this little lad."

He cocked a brow. "Need I mention that it is unseemly to name a child after a former husband?"

Eleanor's lashes were drooping and her smile turned into a sleepy yawn. "I would not name a stray dog after Louis," she declared, holding out her arms for her new baby. She was surprised by the intensity of emotion she felt as she gazed down into that small, flushed face. Why was this son so special? Had God sent him to fill the aching void left by Will's death? "I want," she said, "to name him Richard."

CHAPTER FIVE

✦

May 1158
London, England

THOMAS BECKET WAS CELEBRATED for his hospitality; his great hall was filled at most hours with knights, petitioners, barons, and clerks. He spent such large sums on candles, rushlights, and torches that men joked night was the one unwelcome guest. His servants swept up and changed the floor rushes on a daily basis, sweet-smelling hay in winter and fragrant herbs in summer. His agents ranged far and wide, procuring the finest wines and spices for his buttery and kitchen, and his tables gleamed with gold and silver plate. Men came from foreign courts to meet with England's king, but they hoped to dine with England's chancellor.

Becket's Ascension Day feast for the Archbishop of Canterbury was lavish even by the chancellor's bountiful standards. The tables were draped in linen cloths whiter than milk, the washing lavers were scented with rosemary, and the rich fare included capon, heron, venison, pike, cream of almonds, custard, and angel wafers, all washed down with varied wines and spiced hippocras and sweet malmsey. If any of the guests saw the irony in providing such a banquet for the unassuming, ascetic Theobald, none commented upon it.

Seated at a side table, one of the clerks of the chancellory, William Fitz Stephen, was exchanging discreet gossip with John of Salisbury, Archbishop Theobald's secretary. The dinner was clearly a great success. Yet Fitz Stephen had been hearing an undercurrent of disapproval directed at their host. It was no secret that the archbishop was deeply disappointed in his protégé. Theobald had recommended Becket as chancellor in the belief that he would be a strong advocate of the rights of the Church. Instead, Becket had become the king's man in word and deed. Although the archbishop retained his fondness for his former clerk, some in his inner circle were bitter at what they saw as Becket's defection to the Crown, and they were not loath to criticize the chancellor even while enjoying his hospitality.

Fitz Stephen was disdainful of these disingenuous critics, for he scorned hypocrites and his loyalty to the chancellor was wholehearted. But because John of Salisbury's own friendship with Thomas Becket dated back to their years together in the archbishop's service, Fitz Stephen did not feel he had to be on his guard with John. And so when John made passing mention of the Bishop of Chichester's failed case against Battle Abbey, Fitz Stephen did not become defensive, as he might have done with others in Theobald's household. He contented himself by merely reminding John that even the archbishop had disapproved of Chichester's perjured denials.

"Chichester has less backbone than a conger eel," John said scornfully. "His panic notwithstanding, the underpinnings of his argument remain sound. It sets a poor precedent to exempt an abbey from episcopal jurisdiction, and I'd not be surprised if this comes back to haunt us. Already the king is showing undue interest in the Scarborough case."

Fitz Stephen was familiar with this particular case. When the king had been in York in January, a Scarborough citizen had petitioned him for justice, contending that a local dean had extorted money from him by falsely accusing the man's wife of adultery and then demanding a payment to withdraw the calumny. Henry had wanted the dean charged and had been enraged when the Treasurer of York insisted the king could not punish the dean because he was in holy orders and thus subject only to Church discipline.

Fitz Stephen sighed, for like his master, Thomas Becket, he was both an officer of the Crown owing loyalty to the king and a subdeacon owing loyalty to the Church. He sometimes felt like one of those rope dancers who entertained at fairs, balancing upon a tautly drawn cord high above the ground, knowing that a single misstep could result in a nasty fall.

"I agree that we do not want the Crown intruding into the Church's domains," he said quietly. "But the complaints about lawless clerics are too often justified, as with that Scarborough dean using his position in the Church for extortion. If we took better care to discipline our own, people would not be coming to the king with their woes and he'd have no opportunity to meddle in matters best left to ecclesiastical courts."

John, too, deplored the way unscrupulous men could plead their clergy to elude punishment for crimes against the king's peace. But when he weighed the evils, his fear that the Crown might erode Church liberties was far stronger than his reluctance to see guilty clerics escape a temporal reckoning.

Just then a commotion erupted outside, loud enough to swivel all heads toward the unshuttered windows. Two servants were hurrying to fling open the doors. John looked baffled, but Fitz Stephen was grinning, for this was a familiar occurrence in the chancellor's household. They were about to have a royal visitor.

As the doors swung back, the noise intensified, male voices nearly drowned out by the baying of hounds. Much to John's astonishment, a horse and rider appeared in the doorway, hooves striking sparks against the flagstones. Maneuvering the stallion with ease, Henry guided it over the threshold and into the hall. He was clad in a sweat-stained green tunic, a soft, stalked cap, knee-high cowhide boots, a quiver slung over his shoulder, a bow carried casually in one hand, and his face was streaked with dirt, his eyes unreadable in the blinding, bright sunlight streaming into the hall behind him.

"Another feast, my lord chancellor? My invitation must have gone astray."

John of Salisbury gasped. It was not so long ago that he'd been in severe disfavor with the king, relying upon his friendship with Thomas Becket to appease Henry's anger. He was alarmed now to think that Becket might have drawn that very same anger down upon himself, and he reached out, his hand closing around Fitz Stephen's wrist in an instinctive bid for reassurance.

Fitz Stephen did not share his anxiety. Nor did the target of Henry's pointed query. Thomas Becket was regarding his king with complete composure. "Had I invited you, my liege, you'd have been compelled to pass the afternoon on a cushioned seat, dining on pike in doucette and Galantine pie. As it was, you were able to eat on horseback, washing down strips of dried beef with English ale."

John spun in his seat, staring at Becket's wine cup. He knew the chancellor was sparing in his own habits, yet if he were not drunk, what had possessed him to offend the king like this? His moment of consternation was brief, however, for Henry had already begun to laugh.

"When you put it like that, my lord chancellor, I am in your debt!" he said, and as Becket joined in his laughter, John realized that this was an old game between them, played out for their amusement whenever they had a credulous audience.

Rising, Becket detoured around the table, offering his own wine cup with a flourish. "Will you dine with us, my lord? I'm sure we can squeeze in another place if we try."

Accepting the wine cup, Henry pretended to ponder the invitation. By now the others in his hunting party had followed him into the hall, although they'd made a more conventional entrance, having dismounted first. Gesturing toward his justiciar, his brother Will, and the Earls of Salisbury and Leicester, all of whom were just as bedraggled and disheveled as he, Henry shook his head ruefully. "You'd have to feed that wolf pack, too, if I stay. No, better that we depart whilst you still have some leftovers to distribute to the poor gathering at your gate."

Handing the cup back to Becket, Henry turned to salute the Archbishop of Canterbury, who responded with a paternal smile, and singled out a young priest, Roger Fitz Roy, for some brief badinage. Roger, brother of the Earl of Gloucester and the Countess of Chester, shared with his sister a finely honed wit and he more than held his own with his cousin the king. Henry then exchanged greetings with several of the other guests before bringing his attention again to Theobald.

"We need to talk, my lord archbishop, about that rapacious dean up in Scarborough. My justiciar tells me that the Treasurer of York thinks I'm meddling in matters best left to the Church."

Theobald had won his archbishop's mitre during two of the most turbulent decades in English history, and it was not by chance that he had steered Canterbury and the Church through the worst of the civil war. While he could be sharp-tongued and abrupt in private, he'd long ago learned a valuable lesson, that a soft answer was particularly effective in turning away royal wrath. Showing none of his inner disquiet, he smiled easily.

"I would hope that the treasurer did not express himself in such intemperate terms, my liege. The king's concern for justice in his realm can hardly be considered 'meddling.' But it is true that many in holy orders feel very passionately about the need to safeguard the Church's exclusive right to deal with its own. I would, of course, be pleased to discuss this case with you at greater length, and I will dispatch one of my clerks to your court to arrange a meeting upon this matter."

Henry's smile was no less politic than the archbishop's. "I look forward, my lord archbishop, to these discussions, as I have utter confidence that you will bring your customary prudence and wisdom to bear upon this thorny issue. And now I ask you all to resume your meal, for I've too long kept you from my chancellor's fine fare." With another salute for the archbishop and Becket, he turned his stallion in a semicircle, tossing a nonchalant "Godspeed" over his shoulder as he headed toward the door.

An oppressive silence settled over the hall, for Becket's guests were all men of the cloth, experienced in the shifting nature of boundaries and the predatory practices of kings. Theobald's shoulders slumped, and for a moment, he showed every burdensome one of his more than sixty years. His gaze came to rest upon the tall, courtly figure of Henry's chancellor, and he felt a surge of sadness, a baffled regret that Thomas had not been more outspoken in his defense of the Church.

Becket was standing alone in the middle of the hall. When he called out, "My lord king!" Theobald's hope flared in a sudden spark of faith; he still believed that the heart of his pious, dedicated clerk beat on in the chest of the king's worldly chancellor.

Reining in his stallion, Henry glanced back at Becket, his expression quizzical. "My lord?"

"You did not tell us, my liege, how the hunt went."

Their eyes held steady for a moment, long enough for Theobald's hope to gutter out. And then Henry grinned. "I got," he said, "what I aimed for, Thomas."

THIS WAS RHIANNON'S second visit to the English court, but it was still alien territory. Cities like Winchester were cauldrons always on the boil, alarming places to a woman accustomed to the seclusion and stillness of the Welsh countryside. She'd long ago learned to deal with the calloused curiosity of strangers, but it was easier, somehow, to deflect the hurtful, heedless questions if they were posed in her own language. Even as a welcome guest, aunt by marriage to the King of England, she never felt so vulnerable as she did on English soil.

On this warm August evening in the great hall of Winchester Castle, she was doing her best to play the role expected of her, but so far events seemed to be conspiring to shred her poise. Ranulf had been waylaid by Henry and soon swept away, for trying to resist his nephew was like battling a headwind. Left in the care of Ranulf's brother Rainald, Rhiannon found herself being coddled and cosseted until she yearned to startle Rainald by some outrageous act. She did not, of course, constrained by courtesy and her ironic awareness of the reason for Rainald's clumsy kindness: his own wife was addled in her wits, given to fits of weeping and melancholy and irrational fears.

She'd finally been able to evade Rainald's well-meaning clutches. Listening to the music swirling around her, she slowly began to relax. The shock was all the greater, therefore, when she caught snatches of a nearby conversation, malicious gossip that targeted her as "Ranulf's blind Welsh wench" and marveled how she'd ever ensnared him into marriage, speculating whether it was by drink or the Black Arts.

From the way they were bandying her husband's name about, they appeared to be well acquainted with him. Such careless cruelty would have been easier to tolerate from strangers. Coming from Ranulf's friends, it kindled a spark of rare rage. Turning toward the sound of their voices, she said, "I am blind, not deaf."

There was a sudden silence, and then a mumbled apology. The voices were receding, taking advantage of her disability to escape unscathed. The unfairness of that was more than Rhiannon could accept and she stubbornly sought to hinder their retreat. "Do I know you? Have we met?"

Her challenge went unanswered. She bit her lip, conceding defeat, when another voice alerted her that there was a new player in this unpleasant game. "If you have not met them, Rhiannon, count your blessings."

Those stinging words were accompanied by a whiff of exotic perfume and a soft breath on Rhiannon's cheek. The whispered name was needlessly offered, for she'd recognized the voice at once. But the Countess of Chester was always conscientious about identifying herself, unable to believe that other senses could be as reliable as sight.

Maud gave her no chance to reply. "Rhiannon, as much as it grieves me to admit this, these ill-mannered dolts are kin: my brother Will and his harpy of a wife, Hawise."

There was an outraged sputter from Hawise, and Gloucester said sharply, "This was an unfortunate misunderstanding, Maud. Your meddling will only make it worse."

"Spare me your righteous indignation, Will. I overheard enough to judge your rudeness for myself!"

"For God's Sake, lower your voice!" Gloucester sounded alarmed, for Maud was capable of making an enormously embarrassing scene and well he knew it.

In this concern, he had an unlikely ally in Rhiannon, for her anger was cooling as fast as it had flared now that she knew the identity of her defamers. Family faults were better discussed in private, and she said hastily, "Let it lie, Maud. It does not matter."

"What does not matter?" This was a new voice, low pitched and sultry, infused with the unique confidence that high birth and beauty confer, and Rhiannon quickly dropped a curtsy to the English queen. Eleanor's perfume was more subtle and elusive than Maud's. Breathing it in as Eleanor kissed her cheek in a kinswoman's greeting, Rhiannon was momentarily transported to a far-off garden where mysterious, elegant flowers bloomed by midnight.

The others had the advantage of Rhiannon, though, for they could see the expression on Eleanor's face. As those greenish-gold eyes appraised the Earl of Gloucester and his wife, they thought not of summer gardens, but of cats on the scent of prey.

"You are very pale of a sudden, Hawise. Mayhap you have not fully recovered from your ordeal." Eleanor gently squeezed Rhiannon's arm. "Did you hear about the woeful mishap that befell my husband's cousin and his wife, Rhiannon? They and their son were abducted from the bedchamber of their own castle at Cardiff, dragged off as spoils of war in a daring Welsh raid. Poor Will had to pay a huge ransom for his release, did you not, Will?"

"Yes," Gloucester muttered, acutely aware of the audience that Eleanor was attracting.

"I can only imagine how humiliating that must have been for you." Eleanor's sympathy was as lethal as hemlock. "I daresay they were laughing at how easily they'd breached your defenses, adding insult to injury by making you the butt of their jests and jokes. I do hope that at least they let you both dress ere they carried you off into the night?"

Maud, watching with a grin, thought it a pity that Rhiannon could not savor the peculiar color of her brother's complexion. Hawise was equally flustered, and Maud wondered gleefully which rankled more: the implicit slur upon her husband's manhood or the suggestion that she'd been abducted stark naked.

Satisfied with her victory, Eleanor allowed the discomfited couple to flee the field, trailed by amused titters from some of the spectators. Slipping her arm through Rhiannon's, Eleanor guided the Welshwoman up onto the dais. "I need to sit down," she confessed, not surprisingly, for she was in the eighth month of yet another pregnancy.

"That was a highly enjoyable spectacle," Maud declared, "watching my lout of a brother be minced into sausage. But ought I to warn Cousin Harry how sharp your claws can be, Eleanor?"

"Harry knows," Eleanor said, with a complacent smile that faded as she glanced toward Rhiannon. "Gloucester is a fool, wed to another one. Try not to let their spite spoil your evening."

"It does not matter," Rhiannon repeated. This time she meant it. "It hurt me to think that they were making sport of my blindness," she confided, and then she smiled. "But now that I know they scorn me merely for being Welsh, I can return their hostility in good conscience and full measure." And the last sour aftertaste of the Gloucesters' rancor was washed away by the approving, amused laughter of Chester's countess and England's queen.

THE CHILDREN WERE shrieking again and a nurse hurried over to make peace between three-year-old Mallt and two-year-old Maude, now nicknamed Tilda. Although the floor of the solar was strewn with toys, the cousins invariably set their hearts upon playing with the same puppet. Richard kept trying to claim that puppet, too, but at eleven months, he was too wobbly on his feet to offer a serious challenge. Hal, a handsome, cheerful youngster of three and a half, was more interested in teasing his mother's greyhound, using a wafer to lure the dog within reach. Slouched on a coffer seat, Rhiannon's son, Gilbert, was disconsolately bouncing a ball against the wall over his head. After a time, that irritating, rhythmic thud attracted Eleanor's attention.

Gilbert was feeling very sorry for himself, trapped here with his little sister and cousins when he yearned to be outside, playing games like hoodman blind or hunt the fox. After all, he reasoned, he was nigh on seven, old enough to be having fun on his own. When the queen said his name, he glanced up incuriously, finding these English adults no more interesting than their children. He didn't understand why they were in Winchester, yearned to be back home in Wales with his friends.

Eleanor was beckoning to one of the young women working upon an embroidered cushion. "Beatrix, I'd like you to take Gilbert down to the stables and show him the roan mare's new foal."

Gilbert sprang to his feet, remembering just in time to toss a plaintive "Mama?" in Rhiannon's direction. "Go on," she said reluctantly, hoping that Eleanor had chosen a sharp-eyed caretaker for her spirited young son, whose mischief-making capabilities were truly awesome. The banging door told her that he was now on the prowl and Winchester Castle in God's Keeping. Getting to her feet, she moved cautiously across the solar to join Eleanor at the window.

It was unshuttered, open to the August heat. "Sit beside me," Eleanor invited, "and I'll tell you what I see as I look out upon the city."

Rhiannon did, appreciative of Eleanor's matter-of-fact acceptance of her blindness. Most people were too self-conscious to make such an offer, so fearful of offending her that they denied her the opportunity to envision new surroundings. "I would like that," she said. "Ranulf often talks of Winchester, for he was under siege here during the war between his sister and King Stephen."

"Yes, I've heard those stories, too. To judge by all the men who've boasted to me that they were at the Winchester siege with the Empress Maude, there was nary a soul who supported Stephen. Which makes it very mysterious that he managed to cling to power for nineteen years."

Rhiannon laughed, and Eleanor began to describe the view. "In the distance, I can see the spire of St Swithun's Priory. High Street or the Cheap runs through the center of the town, east to west. It is not visible from here, but off to the southwest lies Wolvesey Palace, where the Bishop of Winchester will be dwelling again now that he's made his peace with Harry. And to the north of the palace is the convent commonly called Nunminster, not far from the East Gate."

Eleanor stopped suddenly, smiling. "And below us, the men have just ridden into the bailey."

Rhiannon sighed with relief, for she'd feared they'd get so caught up in the thrill of the chase that they'd be gone for days. While she didn't understand that particular passion, she knew many men found it as compelling an urge as lust. "I hope," she said politely, "that they had a successful hunt."

"Usually the dirtier and sweatier they are, the more fun they've had. So this hunt must have been truly memorable!"

When the men came trooping into the solar, Rhiannon soon discovered that Eleanor had not been exaggerating. Ranulf was pungent, muddied, soaked with perspiration, and in very high spirits for a man who'd been in the saddle since daybreak. So was Henry, who startled Rhiannon by planting an exuberant kiss on her cheek before grabbing for his wife. "Here you go, love," he declared. "I saved the hunt's prize for you."

Eleanor looked dubiously at the object he'd dropped into her lap. "This had better not ruin my appetite," she warned, gingerly unwrapping the deerskin covering. "What is it?" she asked, puzzled. "It looks like . . . like gristle."

"It is a bone from a hart's heart," Henry explained, grinning at the wordplay. "Well, actually you are right and it is gristle. But legend has it that this so-called bone is what prevents the hart from ever dying of fear. They say that if it is made into an amulet, it protects a woman in childbirth."

"Harry, you spoil me. Other husbands may give their wives gemstones, but how many women ever get gristle from a dead deer?"

"Not just any deer," Henry protested, "a hart of twelve of the less!" And so universal was the love of hunting that even Rhiannon knew enough of its terminology to comprehend that he meant a stag with twelve tines on its antlers.

"Oh, that does make all the difference," Eleanor agreed dryly and gave Henry a kiss that got her face smeared with some of her husband's mud. Sprawling beside her in the window seat, he shouted for wine and launched into an enthusiastic account of the hunt, with his brother Will and his uncles Ranulf and Rainald and the Earl of Leicester all interrupting freely whenever they felt he was claiming too much credit. Servants hastily fetched flagons of wine and Eleanor gave orders for baths to be made ready, warning that not a one of them would be allowed to take supper that night without being scrubbed down first. The mood was ebullient and raucous, and Ranulf realized just how much he'd missed the humor and energy of his nephew's court. He and Rhiannon would have to spend more time in England, he decided.

Having exhausted the dramatic possibilities of the day's events, the talk ranged back to past hunts, each man summoning up his favorite story. Ranulf told them of Loth, his beloved Norwegian dyrehund, who'd once brought a stag down by himself, and Henry boasted of tracking a huge black wolf who'd been slaughtering livestock in the villages around Angers. When it was his turn, Rainald told of a hunt for the most dangerous prey of all, a tusked wild boar that he and Henry and Thomas Becket had brought to bay in the New Forest. The men had retreated into a pond to await the boar's charge, a common practice that enabled the hunters to take advantage of their longer legs. The trick, as Rainald explained it, was to get far enough from shore so that the boar could no longer touch the bottom.

"Becket balked at going into the water, though. He was not fearful of facing the boar's tusks, but he was loath to get his new furred mantle wet—you remember, Harry? So he braced for the charge on the bank. But the boar sped right by him, plunged into the pond, and impaled himself on Harry's spear, as clean a kill as I've ever seen."

"It was a good kill," Henry agreed. "Though when he came churning through the water straight at me, there was a moment when I thought it would take one of God's own thunderbolts to stop him!"

Ranulf was not surprised Rainald's tale had not put Thomas Becket in the best of lights, for Rainald was no friend to the chancellor. He'd always found Becket to be good company, though, and he said curiously, "Just where is Thomas these days? Off on some mysterious mission for the Crown?"

Henry looked amused. "You might say that. I am meeting the French king soon to discuss the future of the Vexin, amongst other matters. So I sent Thomas ahead to blaze a trail for me. I'd wanted to send Eleanor, for she's had some experience at charming Louis—" He pretended to flinch when Eleanor jabbed him in the ribs with her elbow. "But she balked, so I had to settle for Thomas."

"Tell Ranulf and Rhiannon about his entry into Paris," Eleanor prompted her husband. "Better yet, read from his letter, for you'll never remember all the glittering details otherwise." Adding, "And whilst you're up, I need a cushion for my back."

Henry unfolded himself from the window seat. "Imagine how she'd order me around if I were not a king." Tossing Eleanor a cushion, he began to sort through a pile of letters spread out on the table.

"Here it is. Envision this if you will. First came two hundred and fifty footmen, followed by Thomas's hounds and greyhounds and eight wagons, each pulled by five horses and guarded by a chained mastiff. Ah, yes, each of the wagon horses also had a monkey riding on its back."

Henry's mouth twitched. "Then came twenty-eight packhorses laden with gold and silver plate, clothes, money, books, gifts, and such. After that came Thomas's retinue: two hundred squires, knights, falconers with hawks, clerks, stewards, and servants. And finally came Thomas himself, mounted on a stallion whiter than milk, looking more like a king than most, I daresay." With that, his grin broke free. "For certes, more kingly than me!"

"Well," Ranulf acknowledged, "if his aim was to bedazzle the French with English wealth and splendor, he must surely have accomplished that. Mayhap too well! For how can you possibly overshadow him? You plan to bring along elephants and trained bears and Saracen dancing girls?"

Henry laughed, glancing over at Eleanor. "Saracen dancing girls? Alas, as intriguing as that suggestion sounds, I doubt that—" Interrupted by the sound of the opening door, he strode forward to confer briefly with the man who'd just entered, not loudly enough for the others to hear, and then startled them by plunging out into the stairwell. They could hear his boots echoing on the stairs, and then silence. No one spoke after that, waiting uneasily for his return.

He was soon back, a crumpled letter in his hand. "Will," he said, and his brother tensed, for Maude had been ailing again. Henry read his fear and swiftly shook his head. "It is not our mother," he said. "It is Geoff. Will . . . he is dead."

His brother's mouth dropped open. The others shared his astonishment, for Geoffrey was just twenty-four. "What happened, Harry? Was he thrown from his horse?"

"Or caught with another man's wife?" Rainald blurted out, before thinking better of it, relieved when no one paid his tactless suggestion any heed.

Henry was shaking his head again. "He got a chill after going swimming, and a fever followed. It was very quick . . ." His voice trailed off, and as his eyes met Will's, he saw the same thought was in both their minds. This was how their father had died, too, death coming without warning to claim him in his prime.

What puzzled Rhiannon was the lack of sorrow in their voices. They sounded shocked, but not grief-stricken. Tugging at her husband's sleeve, she whispered, "Are there none to mourn him, Ranulf?"

"Yes," he said somberly. "There is one." Crossing the solar, he said, "Will you be going to France straightaway?" When Henry nodded, he said, "I want to come with you."

Henry nodded again, unsurprised. But Rhiannon gasped and Ranulf heard. "I must go, lass. My sister has lost a son."

Rhiannon could not hide her dismay. She did her best, murmuring that she understood. But Eleanor knew better. Leaning over, she touched Rhiannon's hand in silent sympathy, for they would be stranded together in England. Once again, she thought morosely, Harry would be miles away when she gave birth to his child.

THOMAS BECKET WAS STANDING by an open window, watching as monks from the priory went about their daily chores. As soon as word had reached him in Paris of Geoffrey's death, he'd ridden for Rouen to pay his condolences to the empress and to await Henry's arrival. Knowing Henry, he'd known, too, that he would not have long to wait.

Henry was now with Maude on the settle, their voices low, faces intent. When Will offered his mother a wine cup, she thanked him absently, setting it down untasted, and Ranulf felt a twinge of pity for the youth. Maude's rapport with her firstborn was so complete that it inevitably and unintentionally shut others out, even Will. Ranulf had not seen his sister in seven years. His elder by sixteen years, she was fifty-six now, too thin for his liking and too pale. She was dry-eyed, which didn't surprise him; Maude would let only the Almighty see her tears. But her pain was apparent in the rigid stiffness of her posture, in the lines grooved around her mouth, even in the unnatural stillness of the fingers loosely linked in her lap.

Rising, Ranulf crossed the chamber and joined Becket at the window. "How did your talks go with the French king?"

"Quite well."

Ranulf glanced curiously at the other man. He knew his nephew had a specific purpose in seeking a meeting with Louis, and he would have liked to know what it was. But there was no point in asking, for Becket shared none of Henry's secrets.

Feeling Ranulf's gaze upon him, Becket smiled quizzically. He was in his thirty-eighth year, a man of intriguing contrasts, handsome but apparently chaste, educated but no scholar, an articulate and eloquent speaker who'd had to overcome a slight stammer, an archdeacon who'd not taken priestly vows, worldly and prideful and pious, closer to the king than any man alive, and yet with few other friends or intimates. People were invariably impressed by his competence, but he remained a stranger in their midst and they sensed that, however imperfectly.

"Is there some reason why you are staring at me, Ranulf?" Becket asked good-naturedly. "I get the uneasy sense that you are trying to see into the depths of my soul!"

"Actually," Ranulf confessed, "I was speculating about your mission to the French court. It could not have been easy, acting as Harry's emissary to his wife's former husband. Even your powers of persuasion must have been sorely tried under those circumstances."

Becket smiled, not denying that he was a gifted mediator or that this had been a particularly challenging task. "Harry does seem to enjoy sending me into the lion's den."

"And then wagering upon whether you'll come out alive," Ranulf joked. "But he often says that naming you as chancellor was one of the best decisions of his life, although he's not likely ever to say it in your hearing."

"I am gladdened that I've done well as chancellor. But I expected no less." Becket flashed a quick smile to dispel any hint of arrogance. "I learned at an early age that an undertaking must be done wholeheartedly or not at all."

"That may explain why you and Harry see eye to eye so often. God knows, he is half-hearted in nothing that he does!"

They turned then to welcome Will, who'd finally stopped hovering on the fringes of his mother and brother's conversation. When Ranulf asked how he was faring, he shrugged. "I ought to be more grieved," he said, sounding very young, "for we were brothers, after all. But I feel more pity than sorrow. I'm sorry Geoff was cheated of so much. But in truth, he could be such a swine."

Will drew a deep breath then, as if unburdened by his honesty. Almost at once, though, his eyes flicked across the chamber, reassuring himself that his mother had not heard. When he spoke again, he sounded bemused. "Do you know what Harry and Mama are talking about, Uncle Ranulf? She is urging him to lay claim to the county of Nantes as Geoff's heir."

Ranulf and Becket were both amused by Will's naïveté. It would never have occurred to them that Henry would do otherwise than claim Nantes, for if he did not, the Duke of Brittany would swallow the county whole. When Will wandered away to the settle, Becket said softly:

"It was fortunate for all concerned that Harry was the eldest of the Lady Maude's sons."

Ranulf nodded slowly. Geoff would have been a disaster as king, and—in a different way—so would Will, for he was far too good-hearted and easygoing to command other men. "A king needs steel in his soul," he agreed, thinking sadly of Stephen.

"Harry has that, in plenitude. But that raises an interesting point. Which comes first, the kingship or the steel?"

"Ah . . . so you are asking, Thomas, if Harry is ruthless because he is king? Or because he is ruthless, did he become king? I suspect we'd best leave that to the same philosophers who debate how many angels can dance on the head of a pin." Ranulf's smile vanished, though, as he looked across the chamber at his sister. Maude in earnest conversation with Henry, exhorting him to claim Nantes straightaway, doing what she'd always done, submerging her grief in dreams of glory for her first-born, her best beloved son.

CHAPTER SIX

✦

August 1158
Gisors, France

THE GREAT HALL of Gisors Castle was overflowing with men, music, and avid curiosity. Most eyes kept straying toward the dais, where the Kings of France and England presided over an elaborate meal, for the true entertainment of the evening was not the minstrels; it was the sight of these two men sitting side by side in such incongruous harmony.

They were as unlike in appearance as they were in temperament. Louis was tall and slim, with delicate features and fair hair just beginning to thin around the temples. Pledged to God in his cradle, he had been raised by the monks of St-Denis, snatched from the cloistered world he'd come to love by the unexpected death of his elder brother. He was unfailingly courteous and genuinely kindhearted, with an innate dignity that had nothing to do with kingship, so pious that he was rumored to wear a hair shirt under his royal robes. But although he'd been King of France for more than twenty years, he still seemed to be playing a role not of his choosing.

Watching the two kings from his vantage point farther down the table,

Ranulf could not help thinking that Louis was but a candle to Harry's bonfire. As far as he could determine, they had nothing in common but the woman they'd both wed. It made their apparent amity now all the more amazing. Ranulf had long ago learned not to underestimate his nephew. But even he had not been prepared for such dazzling legerdemain as this. How, he marveled, had Harry done it? How had he been able to befriend a man with so many reasons to resent him?

"I find myself thinking of Scriptures." Thomas Becket leaned over so that his voice reached Ranulf's ear alone. "I daresay you know the verse I mean. 'The wolf shall dwell with the lamb, and the leopard shall lie down with the kid.'"

A burst of royal laughter echoed down the table. Ranulf was not close enough to hear what Louis and Henry were saying, but he was struck by the anxious frown of Hugh de Champfleury, the French king's chancellor. It was obvious that de Champfleury was viewing this rapprochement in the same stark biblical terms as Becket; obvious, too, whom he'd cast as the wolf.

Reaching for his wine cup, Ranulf clinked it against Becket's. Still wondering what quarry his nephew was pursuing at the French court, he said, "Let's drink to a successful hunt."

IT WAS LATE when the festivities ended and Henry and Louis bade each other a cordial good night. As the French left, Henry caught Ranulf's eye. They'd always communicated well without words, and Ranulf nodded. Finding his way abovestairs to Henry's bedchamber, he met Thomas Becket at the door and they entered together.

Henry had stripped off his tunic, but was still in his shirtsleeves. No servants were in attendance, for he wanted no other ears pricking up at his news. At the sight of his uncle and his chancellor, Henry grinned. "Well," he said, "Louis has agreed to give me a free hand in Brittany."

Ranulf whistled softly. Duke Conan of Brittany had wasted no time in claiming Nantes after Geoffrey's death. It was only to be expected that Henry would seek to regain Nantes and punish Conan for his rashness. But it was quite surprising that Louis would acquiesce in it, for it was not in the interest of the French Crown to see Henry's influence expand into Brittany. "Now however did you manage that?"

Henry's grin widened. "Louis has decided to make me a seneschal of France, conferring upon me the authority to make peace in Brittany."

"Very clever," Ranulf said admiringly, for that was an adroit, face-saving maneuver, giving Henry the authority to intervene in Brittany without eroding any of the French Crown's purported sovereignty over the duchy. "I'd wager that was your idea and not Louis's."

"Actually," Henry conceded cheerfully, "it was Eleanor's. Women seem to have a natural instinct for subtlety."

Becket was frowning impatiently. "But what of the rest, Harry? Has the deal been struck?"

Henry playfully dragged out the suspense before nodding. "You sowed the seeds well, Thomas. It was only for me to harvest the crop. Louis has agreed to cede me the Vexin."

Becket looked gratified, but Ranulf was dumbfounded. As the high price of recognizing first Geoffrey of Anjou and then his son Henry as successive Dukes of Normandy, the French king had demanded that the Vexin be yielded up. But the castles of the Vexin controlled the River Seine from Paris to Rouen, making it much too strategic for Henry to accept its loss with good grace. Ranulf knew how determined his nephew was to recover the Vexin. He could not imagine what bait he might have used to tempt Louis into giving it up. "Good God Almighty," he said, "what did you do—cast a spell upon the man?"

Henry was obviously enjoying himself. "The Vexin," he said, "cannot compare to a crown, and that is what we are offering Louis: the opportunity to see his daughter as Queen of England one day."

Ranulf was speechless. Louis's Spanish queen, Constance, had given him a daughter early in the year, a bitter disappointment to a man desperate to have sons. It did not surprise Ranulf that Louis would contract a marriage for the little girl at such an early age; that was the way of their world. But as pragmatic as people were about marital unions, it still had not occurred to him that a match could be made between Eleanor's son and Louis's daughter. Could the children truly wade to the altar through so much bad blood?

"Louis agreed to this marriage?" he asked, sounding so incredulous that both Henry and Becket laughed.

"Indeed he did, Uncle. Our eldest lad will wed Louis's little lass when they are of a suitable age, and the Vexin will be her marriage portion. The Knights Templar are to hold the castles of Gisors, Neaufles, and Neufchâtel until the marriage takes place, at which time they will be yielded to me. Louis did prove prickly on one point, though. He refused flat-out to allow his daughter to be raised at our court, in accordance with custom.

Whilst he was too well-mannered to say so, it was plain that he fears Eleanor would exert a sinister influence upon the child! I had to agree that Marguerite would be looked after in Normandy by that pillar of rectitude, Robert de Newburgh."

Becket was glowing with satisfaction. "I had my doubts that we'd ever bring this to fruition," he confessed to Ranulf. "When Harry first proposed the idea to me, the sheer audacity of it well nigh took my breath away. Even after Louis showed an interest, I feared it could all fall apart at any moment. Fortunately for us, Louis retains a monkish distrust of the female sex and blames Eleanor far more than Harry."

"Yet even a crown would not have been enough," Ranulf pointed out, "had Louis not taken to Harry straightaway. That is what baffles me. How in God's Name did you win him over, Harry?"

Henry's mouth quirked. "Must you make it sound as if I've been practicing the Black Arts upon the poor man? The truth is far simpler. There is a bond between us, as kings. And we could each find qualities to respect in the other. It surprised me somewhat, I admit, for I did not expect it. But Louis is an easy man to like." He laughed then, silently. "And if you love me, Uncle, do not ever quote me on that to Eleanor!"

AFTER A HIGHLY successful visit to Paris, Henry headed west to deal with the Duke of Brittany. That proved easier than he'd anticipated, for Conan wanted no war with the King of England. Hastening to meet Henry at Avranches, he made peace by yielding up Nantes. Henry then rode into Poitou, where he taught a sharp lesson to one of Eleanor's more troublesome vassals, the Viscount of Thouars, in just three days capturing a castle that was said to be invincible.

In England, Eleanor gave birth on September 23 to another son, naming the baby Geoffrey in honor of her husband's father.

A COLD NOVEMBER RAIN had been falling since dawn. Rhiannon was seated so close to the hearth that Maud kept an uneasy eye upon her, not totally trusting Rhiannon's insistence that she could judge the fire's distance accurately by its heat. Absently stroking Eleanor's favorite greyhound, Rhiannon was struggling to keep her depression at bay. She'd begun to envision her homesickness as a wolf stalking her relentlessly across the English countryside. Kent, Hampshire, Berkshire, Wiltshire, Devonshire. The shire names meant nothing to Rhiannon, blurred one into the other. She'd known that the English royal court was migratory, but she'd not anticipated that Eleanor would spend so little time in any one place, so much time on the road. She could have elected to remain behind, but she preferred the hardships of travel to the alternative: time to dwell upon her unhappiness.

Eleanor was acting as co-regent with Henry's two justiciars, and Rhiannon was impressed by the sheer volume of work that entailed, especially for a woman just two months risen from childbed. But Eleanor seemed to thrive on it, holding court and issuing writs in her absent husband's name. As November drew to a damp, chilly close, they reached Old Sarum, where Eleanor settled a dispute in favor of Ranulf's niece Maud, Countess of Chester. Rhiannon hoped they would linger here for a while, but she wasn't counting upon it.

Letters from their husbands had been few and far between. Ranulf had written to describe Henry's entry into Paris, as deliberately understated as Becket's had been ostentatious. Modestly declining all ceremonial honors, Henry had impressed the Parisians by traveling with a small escort, visiting the city's shrines, and graciously deferring to his host, the French king, at every opportunity. The letter was circumspect, for Ranulf knew it must be read to Rhiannon, but his unspoken amusement echoed throughout the narrative. It was becoming all too evident to Rhiannon that he was enjoying himself, and so she was not totally surprised when he explained that he felt honor-bound to accompany his nephew on an expedition against the rebellious Viscount of Thouars. Rhiannon had been assuring her mutinous young son that they'd be home for Christmas. But in recent weeks, she'd begun to wonder if their English exile might last far longer.

She'd not seen her children for hours. Gilbert was laboring over his lessons with Maud's youngest son, who'd soon be sent off to serve as a page in some noble household, as his elder brother had. Mallt was in the nursery with Eleanor's children, under a nurse's care; it had shocked Rhiannon to realize how little the queen was involved in their daily routine. She supposed that was why royalty could bear to send their children away to be raised by strangers. Ever since she'd learned that the French queen would be yielding up her infant daughter to Henry, she'd been overwhelmed with pity for Constance. Princesses were bartered away for peace, for gain, for gold, their futures often determined while they were still in the cradle. Constance would have known that, expected that. But

Rhiannon found herself wondering if the mother was as accommodating as the queen.

Across the hall, Eleanor was conversing with her husband's justiciars, Richard de Lucy and Robert Beaumont, Earl of Leicester. Maud and Eleanor's sister, Petronilla, were playing a game of hazard, under the disapproving eye of the Bishop of Salisbury, who felt that gambling was an even greater sin when engaged in by the female sex. Left to her own devices on this rain-soaked afternoon, Rhiannon let her defenses slip. Her sister was with child again, the babe due in January. Eleri's two earlier pregnancies had been difficult ones, her birthings prolonged and painful. She ought to be there for Eleri, not stranded here at the English court, feeling like a flower put down in foreign soil.

"Rhiannon!" The familiar bellowing of her brother-in-law jolted her back to the castle's great hall. By the time Rhiannon had gotten to her feet, Rainald had already reached her. "I've a surprise for you, lass," he said jovially. "Guess who I just met out in the bailey?"

Rhiannon had already recognized the footsteps of Rainald's companion. With a joyful cry, she flung herself into Ranulf's arms, giving him the most enthusiastic greeting of their entire marriage. When they finally ended the embrace, they were surrounded by grinning spectators and Eleanor was moving swiftly toward them.

"Lord Ranulf! Did my husband come back with you?" Eleanor's smile flickered. "No . . . I suppose not."

Ranulf hastened to kiss her hand, murmuring a formal "My lady" for the benefit of their audience. "He has gone on pilgrimage with the French king to the abbey of Mont St Michel."

Eleanor's lips parted, freezing her smile in place. "Did he, indeed? Then he has no plans to return to England in the near future?"

"No, Madame. He wants you to join him at Cherbourg for Christmas, and he gave me a letter to deliver . . ." Ranulf was fumbling within his mantle. "Ah, here it is."

Eleanor took the letter. "Welcome home, my lord Ranulf," she said, and this time the smile was dazzling. Ranulf could not help noticing, though, that she seemed in no hurry to open Henry's letter.

RANULF HAD RACED a winter storm from Southampton to Old Sarum, and it was soon besieging the castle in earnest. The wind was battering at closed shutters and barred doors, its high, keening wail chasing sleep away. Most people tossed restively, yearning for the coming of day. In Ranulf and Rhiannon's bedchamber, though, the mood was one of drowsy contentment, for they were still basking in the afterglow of an especially passionate reunion.

"I must have been stark mad to be gone so long from your bed," Ranulf confided, laughing softly when she agreed that indeed he must have been. "I had intended to return to England after we went to Paris, but then Harry summoned his knights in Normandy to Avranches, planning a campaign in Brittany, and I could not leave. Once Duke Conan submitted to Harry, I made plans again to depart. But then we had to ride south to deal with the Viscount of Thouars. It was never my wish to be gone three months, love."

"Nigh on four," she corrected. "At least you did not go off to tour the religious shrines of Brittany with Harry and the French king."

"Eleanor seemed vexed about that, too."

"Does that truly surprise you, Ranulf?"

"Yes," he admitted, "it does somewhat. She is a queen, after all, and well accustomed to the demands of kingship."

"She is a woman, too, and I doubt that there is a woman alive who'd not expect her husband to come home to see his newborn son. I'm sure she understands his reasons for threatening to make war against Conan, and she'd hardly complain about his success in rousting her rebellious vassal from Thouars Castle. But it is another matter altogether for him then to go off blithely on a pleasure jaunt with her former husband, especially when he has yet to lay eyes upon their babe!"

"But she approved of the marriage betwixt their children, Rhiannon. Harry assured me it was so."

"I know, and I'll own up that I was taken aback by that. Eleanor is far more pragmatic than I am, I fear. But I can assure you that she is not so pragmatic that she wants Harry and Louis to become the best of friends! She loves Louis not, with cause, for he will not allow her to see their daughters. And for all the talk about his saintly nature, he has not scrupled to besmirch her name and their memories of her. Can you blame her for being bitter about that?"

"No, of course not . . ." Ranulf pulled more blankets about them as the wind's howling intensified. "Harry once told me that his father cautioned him against wedding a woman he loved. Geoffrey claimed that the best marriages were based upon goodwill or benign indifference. I thought that was unduly cynical, even for Geoffrey. But I can see that passion might not be the soundest of foundations for a marriage, especially a royal one. The expectations would be different, and marital wounds would cut more deeply, for the weapons would have sharper blades."

He frowned, then was quiet for several moments. "I hope that Harry and Eleanor have the good sense not to let their wounds go untended, lest they fester. It would grieve me greatly to think there was a serpent in their Eden, just biding its time."

Rhiannon realized that he was quite oblivious to their own snake, the woman he'd risked his mortal soul for, the dark-eyed Annora Fitz Clement. Whenever Ranulf crossed the border back into England, Rhiannon's fear rode with him, the fear that this would be the time he'd encounter Annora at the English court. Was it true that a flame was more easily kindled from the embers of an old fire? She didn't know, prayed to God that she never found out. "If you love me, Ranulf," she whispered, "take me home."

Turning, he kissed her mouth and then the hollow of her throat. "I do," he said, "and I will. We leave for Wales on the morrow."

Eleanor's ship landed at Barfleur in mid-December. From there she rode the few miles to Cherbourg, where she was reunited with her husband. Their Christmas court that year was said to be splendid.

CHAPTER SEVEN

April 1159
Trefriw, North Wales

IN JUST TWO DAYS, the churches of Gwynedd would be
pealing out the advent of Palm Sunday, but winter still held fast
in the high mountain passes and heavily wooded hillsides. Patches
of snow glistened above the timberline of Moel Siabod and a raw, wet
wind was making life miserable for men and animals alike. It would not
normally be a day for visiting and so the dusk appearance of a lone rider
caused a stir. A groom was soon hastening into the hall, blurting out that
Lord Owain's son was dismounting in the bailey.

Rhodri and Enid made much of their unexpected royal guest, ushering Hywel toward the hearth, taking his muddied mantle, calling for mead
and cushions. Rhiannon's greeting was equally warm, for Hywel was now
firmly lodged in her good graces. All of them wanted to know what he
was doing out in such wretched weather, expressing astonishment that he
did not have an escort and reminding him that it was both dangerous and
unseemly for a king's son to venture about on his own.

Ranulf thought he had the answer to that particular puzzle. If Hywel
was alone, it meant he'd been paying a discreet, clandestine visit to yet an-

other light o' love, one with either a protective father or a jealous husband. As their eyes met, he had confirmation of his suspicions in Hywel's sudden grin. He wondered idly who this latest conquest was; women came and went with such frequency in Hywel's life that it was hard to keep track of them, even for Hywel.

Hywel's secret liaison had obviously gone well, for he was in high spirits, flirting with Enid and Rhiannon, joking with Rhodri, eating heartily of their plain Lenten fare. Over a dinner of salted herring, onion soup, and dried figs, he regaled them with tales of the recent English expedition into South Wales against the rebellious King of Deheubarth, Rhys ap Gruffydd. Henry had dispatched the Earls of Cornwall, Gloucester, and Salisbury to lift Rhys's siege of Carmarthen Castle. Although Rhys was his sister's son, Owain Gwynedd had been compelled by the English king to contribute a contingent to the royal force, too, led by his brother Cadwaladr and his sons, Hywel and Cynan. Yet this formidable English-Welsh alliance had failed to bring Rhys to heel and they'd had to settle for another truce, a rather inglorious end to such a redoubtable campaign.

Ranulf couldn't resist pointing this out to Hywel, but the Welsh prince took the raillery in good humor. "You do not truly expect me to lose any sleep over the English king's feuding with Rhys? Life is too fleeting to waste time fretting about other men's troubles."

They laughed and urged him to tell them more about the campaign. He did, relating several comical stories that ridiculed both the heroics of war and his English allies, garnering more laughter for his efforts. But Hywel had a poet's keen eye and he was not deceived by the apparent harmony in Ranulf's household. During the course of the dinner, he'd taken note of Rhiannon's reddened, swollen eyes, and he'd noticed the sidelong, surreptitious glances Rhodri cast in his nephew's direction from time to time. Even the complacent Enid was showing signs of distraction, for she had neglected to apologize profusely and needlessly to Hywel for the quality of their meal, as she'd unfailingly done in the past. As for Ranulf, his laugh was too hearty and his humor hollow, at least to one who knew him as well as Hywel.

Putting aside the last of his dried figs, Hywel complimented Enid extravagantly upon the dinner and then insisted that Ranulf accompany him out to the stables to see his new stallion. Ignoring Ranulf's halfhearted protests, he collected their mantles and a lantern, then headed for the door, giving Ranulf no choice but to follow. The rainstorm heralded by the day's damp wind had finally arrived, and they hastened across the bailey, pulling up their hoods.

The horses had been fed and bedded down for the night, their groom over in the hall having his own dinner. Raising the lantern, Ranulf started toward one of the stalls, saying, "Come on, show me this wonder horse so we can get back inside where it is warm." When the flickering light revealed a dappled grey muzzle, he turned to stare at Hywel in surprise. "Either this new stallion of yours is a twin to your Smoke or you had far too much mead tonight. Which is it?"

"You're right, that is Smoke. I needed an excuse to talk to you alone."

Ranulf frowned. "Why? What is wrong?"

"You tell me." Hywel moved closer so that they were both standing within the small pool of light spilling from the lantern. "What has your wife and uncle so distraught? And why do I suspect the King of England's name will soon be creeping into our conversation?"

Ranulf smiled tiredly. "You do not miss much, do you?" Turning aside, he sat down on a workbench and gestured for Hywel to join him. "My nephew is about to go to war against the Count of Toulouse and he has issued a summons to his barons, myself included, to meet at Poitiers on June twenty-fourth."

"And your family does not want you to go."

"They are adamantly opposed, and I cannot seem to make them understand that I have no choice. Rhiannon has turned a deaf ear to my arguments, reminding me that she did not object when I answered Harry's summons two years ago, as if that were a debt she can now collect. I know women can be unreasonable . . ." And for a moment, an unbidden ghost flitted across his memory, strong-willed and stubborn. Startled, he shook his head, banishing Annora Fitz Clement back to the past where she belonged. "But I thought Rhiannon would be more sensible—"

Hywel's laughter cut off the rest of his complaint. "Let me see if I have this right. You will be going off to foreign parts to fight in a war that has nothing whatsoever to do with Wales and you have no idea how long you'll be gone. And you wonder that your wife is balking?"

"Rhiannon does have a legitimate grievance. I know that. But it changes nothing. This is a summons from my king, not a neighbor's invitation to dinner! Refusal is not an option, Hywel."

"I know," Hywel conceded. "You think I was eager to ally myself with that milksop Gloucester? I did it because my lord father wanted it done; why else?"

"Exactly. There are things men must do. Since we are speaking so plainly, I very much doubt that Lord Owain took any pleasure in helping the King of England defeat one of his own. Rhys is a rival and often a thorn in your father's side, but he is still Welsh, and a kinsman in the bargain. Yet your father had done homage to the English king, so he had no choice. No more than I do. I only wish there were some way I could make Rhiannon see that."

"You will not. She will never understand. But she will accept it, because she has no choice, either." Hywel unhooked a flagon from his belt, passed it to Ranulf. "Take a swig and then tell me where Toulouse is and why the English king is willing to fight a war over it. Which motive are we dealing with—greed or revenge?"

"Most likely lust."

Hywel blinked. "What?"

"This war can be explained in three words: Eleanor of Aquitaine. Toulouse is a rich region to the south, with Mediterranean ports and fertile harvests. The Count of Toulouse, Raymond de St Gilles, is not only the French king's vassal, he is also his brother-in-law, for Louis wed his sister Constance to Raymond five years ago. Poor Constance has not had much luck with husbands. Previously she'd been wed to King Stephen's son Eustace, about whom nothing good can be said. And gossip has it that Raymond maltreats her, too, for all that she has borne him three sons in as many years."

"I like gossip as well as the next man, but this woman's marital woes can wait. Where does Eleanor come into this?"

"Eleanor's grandmother Philippa was the only child of Count William of Toulouse. But upon his death, Toulouse passed to his brother, not to Philippa. Philippa was wed to the Duke of Aquitaine, and they always viewed Toulouse as rightfully theirs."

"I see. So you think Eleanor has prodded her husband into asserting her claim to Toulouse?"

Ranulf nodded. "Whilst wed to the French king, she coaxed him into taking that same road. Nigh on twenty years ago, Louis led an armed force into Toulouse, was soundly rebuffed, and withdrew in humiliating haste. But a second husband gives her a second chance, and she's not one to let an opportunity go by unheeded."

"Neither is Henry," Hywel pointed out dryly. "I doubt that he needed much persuasion. But in their eagerness to return the lost sheep to the fold, so to speak, they seem to have forgotten about the sheepdog."

"Would you care to translate that for me?"

"What about their most unlikely alliance with the French king? Surely they do not expect Louis to sit by placidly whilst they make war upon one of his vassals, his own sister's husband?"

"Louis is in an awkward position. How can he refute Harry's claim to Toulouse when it is the very same claim he once made himself on Eleanor's behalf?"

"Somehow I suspect he'll find a way. Men can be very inventive when their own interests are threatened." Hywel took the flagon back, drank, regarded Ranulf thoughtfully, and drank again. "This sounds to me like the wrong war in the wrong place at the wrong time, fought for all the wrong reasons. So . . . when do we leave?"

"You're not serious, Hywel? Why in God's Name would you be willing to risk your life in Toulouse?"

Hywel shrugged. "I do not have any other plans for the summer. I've always wanted to see foreign lands. And what man would not leap at the chance to meet Eleanor of Aquitaine?"

"I would be right glad of your company," Ranulf acknowledged. "But I'll not hold you to it if you change your mind once you sober up."

Hywel grinned. "Some of my best decisions have been made whilst I was in my cups. Now let's go back to the hall ere we both freeze." And as they plunged out into the downpour, he soon had Ranulf laughing, for he'd begun to sing:

Were the lands all mine
From the Elbe to the Rhine,
I'd count them little case
If the Queen of England
Lay in my embrace.

ON TUESDAY, the thirtieth of June in the French town of Périgueux, the English king bestowed the honor of knighthood upon his seventeen-year-old cousin, Malcolm, King of Scotland. The ceremony was an elaborate one and Hywel ap Owain found it fascinating, for he'd never witnessed the ritual before. Malcolm had been bathed to wash away his sins, then clothed in a white tunic, which symbolized his determination to defend God's Law. Within the great cathedral of St Front, Malcolm's sword was blessed, and Henry then gave him his gilded spurs and bright, shining blade, instructing him that he must use his weapon to serve the Almighty and to fight for Christ's poor. A light blow to the shoulder and it was done.

As they milled about outside in the garth after the ceremony, Ranulf told Hywel that Malcolm's grandfather had been the one to knight the sixteen-year-old Henry Fitz Empress. "I can scarcely believe that was ten years ago," he said, "but I suppose I'll be saying that, too, when another ten years have raced by and it is my son whom Harry is knighting."

Hywel was only half-listening, his mind on getting back to the Castle Barière, where an abundance of wine and food and shade awaited them. Gazing up at the bleached-bone expanse of sky, he winced. The abbey was built upon a hill and afforded them a fine view of the cité's brown-red roofs and the moss-green surface of the River Isle, as sluggish and slow-moving as the few townspeople out and about in the noonday sun. His temples were damp with perspiration and Hywel was suddenly very homesick, not for family or friends or even absent bedmates, but for the incessant rains, cooling winds, and early morning mists of Wales.

He glanced toward Henry, but the king was still deep in conversation with Malcolm and his newfound allies, the Count of Barcelona and the Viscount of Beziers and Carcassonne, embittered enemies of the man they would soon face at Toulouse. The turnout of highborn lords to the English king's banners had been impressive. Virtually every baron of England, Normandy, Anjou, and Aquitaine had come in answer to his summons. Henry had allowed his English knights to pay scutage in lieu of military service, and used the money to hire soldiers, mercenaries who would fight as long as he had need of them. He had the most formidable siege engines Hywel had ever seen, trebuchets and mangonels and even Greek fire, the incendiary weapon of the crusaders. Despite the stifling summer heat, the thought of this army being turned loose upon Wales was one that Hywel found chilling.

"There is William de Tancarville," Ranulf said suddenly, nudging Hywel with his elbow.

Hywel had met the Chamberlain of Normandy on several occasions, but he did not understand why Ranulf should be pointing him out now with such enthusiasm. "So?"

"You see de Tancarville's squire? Not the one with freckles, the other. I heard an amazing story about that lad yesterday, told to me by William d'Aubigny, who was a witness and swears it to be gospel truth."

Hywel's interest was piqued. "I am listening."

"The lad is John Marshal's son. Are you familiar with Marshal? He was one of my sister Maude's supporters, but he is presently out of favor with Harry, who recently deprived him of Marlborough Castle. I've always been convinced that Marshal's veins flow with ice water, not blood, for he was once trapped in a burning bell tower and still balked at surrendering, an act of bravado that cost him an eye. But I'd never heard about the incident at Newbury, mayhap because I was dwelling in Wales by then."

"What happened at Newbury?"

"Stephen was still king then, and he'd demanded that Marshal yield up his castle at Newbury. Marshal requested a truce so he could consult with my sister Maude in Normandy, and he offered his youngest son, William, as a hostage. He then took advantage of the truce to refortify Newbury. And when Stephen warned him that the boy's life would be forfeit if he did not surrender the castle, he sent a message back that Stephen could go ahead and hang the boy, for he had the hammer and anvil to forge other and better sons."

"Jesú! Not only does the man have ice water for blood, he has a stone where his heart ought to be. What saved the boy, then? Did Marshal relent at the last moment?"

"No. Luckily for the lad, Stephen did. They'd taken him out to be hanged. He was only about four or five and thought it was a game of some sort. But once the hangman put the noose around the boy's neck, Stephen could not go through with it."

Hywel turned for a better look at young William Marshal, truly one of Fortune's favorites, and then slapped away a buzzing horsefly. "If we do not get into the shade soon, I'm going to be broiled alive. When I calculated all the risks I'd be encountering on this campaign, I was most worried about French arrows or the French pox. Who knew that the French sun would be my greatest foe?"

Ranulf shook his head slowly. "For the life of me, I cannot figure out why you did come along. No more talk about being bored or wanting to see Paris. Tell me the truth, Hywel. Why are you here?"

"To keep you out of trouble, why else? I am much too fond of Rhiannon to see her a widow."

Neither one had heard Henry's approach and they both jumped at the sudden sound of his voice. "What are you two arguing about?" he asked, for they'd been speaking in Welsh, a language that still eluded him.

"I've been trying to get Hywel to reveal the real reason behind his inexplicable desire to see the Toulousin."

"I need another reason besides my wish to serve the king?" Hywel asked, so blandly and blatantly disingenuous that Henry and Ranulf both burst out laughing.

"I think I could hazard a guess as to why Lord Hywel wanted to come," Henry said to Ranulf. "What better way to take the measure of a man than to fight alongside him?" And although Hywel laughed, too, Ranulf saw his eyes narrow slightly, as if from the sun's glare, and knew that his nephew had solved the mystery of the Welsh prince's presence in the army of the English king.

SIMON DE MONTFORT, Count of Evreux, leaned against a wall, arms folded across his chest, listening impassively as the French king was berated by his brothers. Robert, Count of Dreux, and Philippe, Bishop of Beauvais, were both outraged by what they saw as Louis's failure to stand up to the English king and they were not shy about making their feelings known.

Louis did not seem troubled by their effrontery. For a man who was God's Anointed, he was remarkably unassuming, shrugging off familiarities that would have enraged other kings. His chancellor, Hugh de Champfleury, looked much more offended than his royal master, gnawing at his lower lip as if to bite back his protests.

The chancellor held no high opinion of the king's brothers. He thought Robert was a blustering bully and Philippe a fool. He did not doubt that Louis would get to Heaven long before either one of them made it through those celestial gates; Robert was especially sure to spend several centuries in Purgatory. He'd never known a better man than Louis Capet. But the qualities that made him such a good Christian did not necessarily make him a good king, and he feared Louis would fare badly in this test of wills with Henry Fitz Empress, a fear shared by every man in the abbey guest hall.

Louis had moved to a window and he stood gazing out at the sun-dappled cloisters; whenever he had a choice, he preferred the hospitality of monasteries to neighboring castles. Now, as Robert stopped fulminating, he said, "I understand your consternation, and I assure you that I share it."

"How very comforting," his brother said with a sneer. "We can all grieve together for the loss of Toulouse. But mark my words well, Louis, for who's to say what that Angevin whoreson and his slut will set their eyes upon next? You let him gobble up Toulouse and you could end up fending him off at the very gates of Paris!"

As usual, Robert had vastly overstated his case, but there was still enough truth in his complaint to cause the other men to nod and mutter amongst themselves. Literal, as always, Louis patiently explained that Henry Fitz Empress had no claim to the French throne, thus making any assault upon Paris unlikely in the extreme. This was not an argument to win any favor with his barons, still less with his brothers. Nor did he help matters any by adding honestly, "Alas, I cannot say as much for Toulouse. How can I dismiss his claim out of hand when it was one I once made myself?"

"And what of your nephews' claims?" Philippe demanded. "What of Constance's sons? Are you truly going to stand aside whilst they lose their patrimony, Louis?"

Simon de Montfort thought there was a more compelling argument to be made than that. Raymond de St Gilles, Count of Toulouse, was a vassal of the French Crown. Louis had a legal responsibility to come to his aid; their society was predicated upon the mutual obligations of vassal and liege lord. But Louis seemed more distressed by his nephews' plight. When he turned from the window, his misery was laid bare for all to see.

"I do not want to jeopardize my alliance with England," he said plaintively, and Simon de Montfort rolled his eyes, thinking sourly that what Louis did not want to jeopardize was the chance to see his daughter as Queen of England one day.

"Is that what you told the Angevin?" Robert shook his head in disgust. "Little wonder he is now halfway to Toulouse!"

"I told him that I could not countenance the disinheriting of my sister's sons." Even Louis's forbearance was not inexhaustible, and the look he now gave his brother was a mixture of wounded dignity and weary exasperation. "I fear that he did not believe me, though."

"I'd say that was a safe wager." This acerbic observation came from Theobald, Count of Blois, Louis's future son-in-law, plight-trothed to Louis and Eleanor's nine-year-old daughter, Alix. His elder brother, Henry, Count of Champagne, was plight-trothed to Alix's older sister, fourteen-year-old Marie, and both young men were amongst the English king's most implacable foes, for King Stephen was their uncle.

Louis's mouth tightened. "I have no intention of abandoning my sister and her children."

As sincere as that declaration sounded, his audience took little comfort from it, for the French king was the least warlike of monarchs; his attempt to punish Henry and Eleanor for their marriage had been a fiasco, with Henry needing just six weeks to send the French army reeling back across the border.

"So what mean you to do?" Robert scoffed. "Pray for their deliverance?"

"Yes, I shall pray. But I shall do more than that," Louis said, so stoutly that he raised both eyebrows and hopes.

"You have a plan in mind?" Robert sounded skeptical. "Well, tell us!"

Louis did.

The response was not what he'd expected. Instead of congratulations and approval, he gained only blank looks. "Is that it?" Philippe asked at last. "That is your grand plan to thwart the Angevin?"

When Louis nodded, Robert spoke for them all. "God save Toulouse."

"He will," Louis said. "He will."

THE DAY WAS SWELTERING and the dust clouds churned up by the English army were visible for miles. Chestnut trees drooped in the heat, as did the men. They were more than twelve hundred feet above sea level, riding across windswept plateaus brown with bracken and wilted high grass. At dusk, they mounted the crest of a hill and had their first glimpse of Cahors, ensconced in a loop of the River Lot far below them.

Drawing rein, they gazed down upon the city. "Shrewsbury," Hywel said softly, and Ranulf nodded somberly, for like that Marcher town, Cahors lay within a horseshoe curve of wide, swift-flowing water. Surrounded on three sides by a natural moat, the city's only land approach was from the north, and it was well fortified by stone ramparts. Until now, they had advanced almost without challenge, castles and towns yielding to their superior show of force. But Cahors was no ripe pear for the picking. For this prize, there would be a price demanded, one paid in blood.

"WELL?" HENRY ASKED, and his herald slowly shook his head.

"They refused to surrender, my liege."

Henry hadn't truly expected any other answer, even though he'd offered generous terms. But he felt a sharp pang of disappointment, nonetheless. "So be it," he said, gazing toward the city walls. "We attack at dawn."

Thomas Becket was appraising their target, too. "I will tell the others," he said. "I hope you will give me the honor of leading the first assault." His face was deeply tanned, his eyes crinkling at the corners, filled with light. He was immaculately turned out, as always, wearing a finely woven slit surcoat over a chain-mail hauberk that glinted like silver in the last rays of the sun. Ranulf had never seen him as animated as on this campaign. He was showing an unexpected flair for soldiering and an equally unforeseen enthusiasm for his new duties.

Henry had been surprised, too, by his chancellor's zeal, joking that Thomas had turned their campaign to oust Raymond de St Gilles from Toulouse into a holy quest to free Jerusalem from the infidels. But he made no jests now in response to Becket's request. He merely nodded, then turned away from Cahors, heading back toward their encampment.

Ranulf, Hywel, and Rainald stayed where they were, sitting their horses on a rise of ground overlooking the city, which was on a war footing, gates barred, sentries patrolling the battlements. Those who'd wanted to flee were already gone; those remaining were making ready for the suffering of a long siege.

Hywel shifted in the saddle, watching as Henry's stallion broke into a gallop. "Your nephew does not look nearly as eager to spill blood on the morrow as his chancellor."

"Harry finds pleasure in many places, but not on the battlefield. He much prefers to get what he wants by other means, although he'll do what he must if it comes to that. As for Thomas, he does seem keen to make a name for himself on the field; he brought fully seven hundred knights at his own expense, which has to be a staggering cost. Passing strange, for he never seemed to me to be a man ruled by his passions."

"Your chancellor strikes me," Hywel said, "as a man who throws himself totally into any role he undertakes. How else explain why he could have well served two such different masters as the Archbishop of Canterbury and the King of England? I understand the archbishop is a saintly soul, and not even the king's mother would claim that could be said of him. Yet these utterly dissimilar men hold Becket in the highest esteem possible. Interesting, is it not?"

Rainald kneed his mount closer. "Are you saying Becket is a hypocrite?" he asked, and looked let down when Hywel shook his head.

"No . . . a chameleon."

"What in hellfire is that?"

"A small lizard that possesses a truly remarkable talent. It can change its color to reflect its surroundings."

Rainald considered that and then nodded emphatically. "By God, you're right, Hywel," he declared, mangling the Welshman's name so atrociously that Hywel looked away to hide a smile. "Think on it, Ranulf," he insisted, glancing toward his younger brother. "Whenever Harry wants Becket to act as the king's envoy, he boasts a silvered tongue and a statesman's fine manners. Then when Harry needs him to raise money, he counts every coin like an accursed moneylender. And now that he rides with the king to subdue our enemies, he fancies himself another Roland. I daresay he even sleeps with his sword!"

"I believe his weapon of choice is a mace," Ranulf pointed out, "in deference to the Church's stricture against 'smiting with the sword.' But it seems to me, Hywel, that you are indeed accusing the man of hypocrisy, for are you not questioning his sincerity? Unfairly so, I believe."

Hywel looked amused. "Your loyalty to your friends does you credit. I hope you are so quick to defend my sins, too. But for your friend the chancellor, I was not impugning his sincerity. A chameleon cannot be faulted for following his own nature, after all."

He and Rainald both laughed, and after a moment, Ranulf joined in, not because he agreed with them, but because moments of mirth were never to be squandered, not on the eve of battle.

S WIRLING EMBERS LIT the night sky and fires still burned in the city's northern quarter. But the worst was over. The battle had been fierce, but far more brief than either side had anticipated. Pounded mercilessly by the English king's powerful mangonels and trebuchets, the defenders were unable to foil his iron-bound battering rams, which were swung back and forth on rope pulleys until they'd gained enough momentum to smash into the city's gates. After they'd made that first fateful breach, Becket's men charged into the gap, while others flung scaling ladders over the walls and began to scramble up. Once the fighting reached the streets, Cahors was doomed, for its river defenses now made flight impossible. By dusk, Henry's banner was flying over the city and the dying was done, wine now flowing instead of blood.

Ranulf had been in captured towns before. The sights were all too familiar: plundered shops, jubilant soldiers, fearful citizens desperate to placate their conquerors, smoldering ruins that had once been homes or churches, bodies stacked like kindling for swift burial. The streets were crowded with men, many laden with loot, for that was looked upon as a soldier's right. Ranulf had injured his leg in the assault and he was limping, as much from exhaustion as pain. Jostled on all sides, he'd begun to feel as if he were swimming against the tide, but he finally reached the marketplace, where he sank down, winded, upon a mounting block. Somewhere a woman screamed; closer at hand, a dog was whimpering, unseen in the darkness. Ahead Ranulf could distinguish the blurred outlines of the great cathedral of St Etienne, where he hoped to find Henry. But for the moment, he was content to sit and catch his breath.

Men on horses were forcing their way up the narrow, clogged street, shouting vainly for the celebrating soldiers to clear a path for them. As they drew closer, Ranulf recognized Patrick d'Evereaux, the Earl of Salisbury, among them. They were not friends, but they'd been allies, fighting together to gain the English crown for the Empress Maude. Salisbury reined in at the sight of Ranulf. "What an easy victory," he chortled. "We had to work a lot harder at this in the old days, remember?"

"Yes," Ranulf said, "I remember."

"We are seeking the king. The Bishop of Cahors is in a tearing rage, for some of our men sacked his palace," Salisbury said, with a conspicuous lack of regret. "We had to promise we'd take his protests to the king, if only to shut him up. Have you seen him? Or Becket?"

"I heard they were at the cathedral." Declining Salisbury's invitation to accompany them, Ranulf watched as they rode on. Light suddenly spilled into the street as a door opened across the square, raucous laughter resounding on the cooling night air. Ranulf debated going over to the tavern and getting himself a drink, but it was easier just to stay where he was.

"Ranulf?" Hywel was weaving through the crowd, one arm around a remarkably pretty young woman, the other cradled in a jaunty red sling. "Have a drink," he offered, proffering a wine flask that turned out to be empty.

Switching to French, he said, "This is Emma," introducing the girl with a gallant flourish that made her giggle. "A few of our men were pressing their unwanted attentions upon her, but I was able to persuade them to be on their way, and this dear lass then insisted upon giving me her own chemise to bind up my wound."

"He fought for me," Emma said proudly, "against the other English. For me, he did that!"

"I never thought to hear myself called 'English,'" Hywel said with a grimace. "But how can I take offense when it comes from such a honey-sweet mouth?"

Emma giggled again and tilted her face up so he could taste some of that sweetness. Once he'd taken his fill, he scowled at Ranulf with mock indignation. "So why are you sitting out here alone in the dark? Why are you not in one of the taverns, celebrating?"

"Celebrating what? This great victory?"

"No, you fool, that you survived the assault!"

When Ranulf shrugged, Hywel gave him a closer inspection. "What ails you? I see no blood, so why so glum? You're no battle virgin. You spent nigh on twenty years fighting for your sister, and from what I've heard, that war was as savage as any ever fought on English soil. So surely nothing you've seen this day is like to unman you?"

"You're right," Ranulf admitted. "This was child's play compared to the bloody Battle of Lincoln or the Siege of Winchester."

"But?" Hywel prompted, and Ranulf shrugged again.

"That was different, Hywel. We were fighting to recover my sister's stolen crown. Whilst I always regretted the suffering and the deaths, I never doubted the justice of our cause. I truly believed we were in the right and that Maude would rule England better than Stephen. I was willing to die to make her Queen of England. But I see no reason that men should die to see Eleanor as Countess of Toulouse. Christ Jesus, she and Harry already hold England, Normandy, Aquitaine, Anjou, Touraine, and Maine!"

"If you start demanding rational reasons for your wars, Ranulf, you'll never get to fight another one!" The moonlight was bright enough to reveal Hywel's smile. "Have you truly lived through forty winters without learning that just wars are as rare as mermaids and unicorns? One man's just war is another man's unholy slaughter. English, French, Scots, Welsh, even Saracen infidels—we're all convinced we have God on our side."

"What are you saying, that God does not care who wins our wars?"

"Well, I'd not go that far. I surely hope He cares whether I succeed my lord father as King of Gwynedd." With another moonlit gleam, Hywel reached down and hauled Ranulf to his feet. "If we are going to wax philosophical, I demand that we do it over a flagon. Emma claims that Cahors has the best red wine in all of Quercy. I say we put her boast to the test."

Ranulf hesitated, glancing up at the towering silhouette of the cathedral, where his nephew was occupied with the myriad burdens of conquest. "You're right," he said. "Let's find a tavern to liberate." And he followed Hywel and Emma toward the torchlit haven beckoning across the street.

THE LAND SOUTH of Cahors was desolate, dry and sun-seared and barren of life, for the inhabitants of these high plateaus and deep, narrow valleys had fled before the approach of the English army. The town of Montauban offered no resistance, and the road to Toulouse lay open before them.

Toulouse was nestled in a wide curve of the River Garonne, a city of dusky-rose brick under a sky so blue it looked unreal. It seemed deceptively peaceful, and far in the distance was the cloud-crowned splendor of the most magnificent mountains Hywel had ever seen, the soaring peaks of the Pyrenees. They so dwarfed the heights of the Welsh Eryri that he felt a stab of envy; if only God had blessed Wales with such formidable boundaries, they could have kept the English out with ease.

He spotted Ranulf with the English king, and urged his stallion forward to join them. They were all looking intently at the city's high red walls, well manned and fortified, for here Count Raymond would make his stand. The siege of Toulouse would be a long and bloody one.

Hywel reined in at Ranulf's side, and they listened without comment as Henry's lords offered suggestions about how best to begin. Thomas Becket was arguing that they ought to start building belfry towers straightaway when Henry's sharp eyes caught a glimpse of the blue and gold banner flying from the Castle Narbonais. Drawing an audible breath, he stared at the flag in dismayed disbelief, reluctant to admit what he was seeing. Alerted by his silence, the more discerning of the men were turning questioningly in his direction.

"Look," he said, his voice flat and harsh, and they followed his gesture, recognizing with gasps and curses the fleur de lys of the French Crown.

Hywel was not as quick to comprehend, for heraldry had been slow to take root in Wales. As usual, he turned to Ranulf, his interpreter in this alien culture. "What does this mean?"

"It means," Ranulf said, "that the King of France has taken up residence in the city. When we attack Toulouse, we will be attacking, too, the man who is Harry's liege lord."

CHAPTER EIGHT

July 1159
Toulouse, France

I SAID NO." Henry's voice was even, but a muscle twitched
along his jawline and his fists were clenched, incontrovertible evidence that he was fast losing control of his fabled Angevin temper,
evidence that his chancellor brashly ignored. Thomas Becket's disappointment had gotten the better of his customary discretion, and he blurted out:

"How can you, of all men, be taken in by such a foolish superstition?"

"It is not superstition!" Henry's eyes shone with a hard grey glitter. "I
swore homage to the King of France for Normandy. That makes him my
liege lord. I will not lay siege to Toulouse as long as he remains within the
city walls."

"But you've fought him in the past!"

"I was attacked first and defending myself! I had no choice then. I do
now and there will be no assault upon the city. How often do I have to
say it?"

Both men were flushed. Becket shook his head slowly, as if unable to
believe what he was hearing. "And so what now? We've come all this way
for nothing?"

"We will continue the war against the Count of Toulouse," Henry said, through gritted teeth.

"Right up to the walls of Toulouse," Becket retorted, with such lethal sarcasm that Henry slammed his fist down onto the table, causing them all to jump.

"The decision has been made. The discussion is done." His eyes roamed the tent, challenging the other men to protest. None did, for they either shared Henry's qualms about a vassal's attack upon his liege lord or they were daunted by even that brief glimpse of royal rage.

The tent was lit by smoky, reeking torches that seemed to suck out the last of the air. Suddenly Henry could not abide another moment in that stifling, crowded space. Turning on his heel, he shoved his way out into the encampment.

The sun was in full retreat. The day's oppressive heat still lingered, though; even the westerly wind felt hot upon his skin. The soldiers he passed seemed to sense his mood and backed off. Only a slat-thin stray dog dared to trail after him, hopeful for a handout. Lights had begun to flicker in the city, glimmering in the twilight like his lost hopes for victory. Picking up a stone, he squeezed it absently, keeping his gaze upon Toulouse as the sky darkened above his head.

"Harry?"

He glanced over his shoulder, then waited for Ranulf to catch up. "Once I was gone, did the rest of them start singing Thomas's song?"

"A few may have been humming it under their breath, but the Count of Barcelona backed your decision so emphatically that he quelled dissent. The Viscount of Carcassonne shares Becket's indignation. He would, since he is in rebellion against his own liege lord, Count Raymond. As for the others, they either agree or they understand."

"Then why does Thomas not understand?" Henry sounded more baffled now than angry. "Why cannot he see that I have no choice? If I attack the man to whom I've sworn homage, how can I expect my own vassals to keep faith with me?"

Ranulf felt laughter welling up and stifled it with difficulty. He should have known that his nephew's decision would be an utterly pragmatic one, based upon practical considerations of common sense. He was more of an idealist himself, but he could still appreciate Henry's stripped-to-the-bone realism, for he did not think England had been well served by its last chivalrous king, the gallant, sentimental Stephen.

"Moreover," Henry continued with an aggrieved frown, "what would

I have done with Louis if we'd seized the town? Send him off to Eleanor for safekeeping? It would be damnably awkward, to say the least. Kings do not take other kings captive."

"Especially not if they hope to marry off their children." Ranulf's mockery was gentle and coaxed a reluctant half-smile from Henry.

"Well, there is that, too," he acknowledged. After a moment, he returned to his primary concern. "For the life of me, Ranulf, I cannot see why Thomas is being so troublesome about this. He is usually so clearsighted and sensible."

"You mean he is usually in full agreement with you," Ranulf teased. "I'm sure he'll come around once his anger cools down."

"Thomas does have a temper, for certes. Most times he keeps it under tighter rein. I suppose I was so vexed with his bullheadedness because we've always been of the same mind." Henry paused and then conceded with a sardonic smile, "Mine."

When he moved to get a better look at Toulouse's russet-red walls, Ranulf followed. They stood in silence for a time, staring at the French king's safe haven. Opening his fist, Henry glanced down at the forgotten stone, then threw it into the shadows.

"You remember, Uncle, when the Archbishop of Canterbury urged me to invade Ireland and give it over to my brother Will?"

"I remember. I was never sure how serious you were about it, but I thought it was for the best when you abandoned the idea."

"My mother talked me out of it. She felt that I'd be overreaching and that Will would be better off with English estates rather than a precarious hold upon a far-off, foreign isle as prone to rebellion as Ireland."

Ranulf felt a surge of admiration for his sister's shrewd assessment of her youngest son. For all his fine qualities, Will was never meant to carve out an empire, still less to hold on to it afterward. "I'd say Maude gave you sound advice."

Henry nodded, and then startled Ranulf with an abrupt, mirthless laugh. "I am beginning to wish," he said, "that she'd talked me out of this accursed venture, too."

H ENRY'S ATTEMPTS to lure the Count of Toulouse out to do battle were futile. He ravaged the count's lands and soon had all of the province of Quercy under his control. But Raymond refused to stir beyond the city walls, and Louis seemed determined to stay as long as his sister had need of him. By September, Henry's supplies were running low and his men had begun to sicken. Turning command over to Becket, he headed north to deal with the French king's brothers, who'd taken advantage of his absence to raid into Normandy. His war with Toulouse sputtered to an inconsequential end.

"I CANNOT BELIEVE IT!" Eleanor spun around, a letter crumpled in her hand. "Harry has withdrawn his army from Toulouse. He has ridden away, leaving Louis in possession of the city."

Petronilla gasped. "He has given up? It is over?"

"So it would seem." Eleanor glanced again at the letter, then flung it from her with an oath. "How could he, Petra? He knew how much this meant to me, to my family. My grandmother was cheated of her rightful inheritance. My father was born in Toulouse's great castle, walked its streets as a child, and loved it almost as much as Poitiers. The city is mine!"

Petronilla hastened over to commiserate with her sister, but Maud, Countess of Chester, stayed where she was in the window seat. It was unshuttered and the October sun was warm upon her face. She wondered if autumn was always this mild in Poitou. If so, little wonder that Eleanor yearned for her homeland and complained of the harshness of English winters, the suffocating grey dampness of English fogs. Reaching for her cup, Maud sipped one of Aquitaine's robust red wines and listened as Eleanor berated her husband for his failure to take Toulouse.

"When I learned that he would not lay siege to the city, I was dumbfounded. I sought to convince myself that he must have some other strategy in mind, for Harry can be quite cunning. I refused to lose faith in him, even though I did not understand. And this . . . this is my reward. He lets himself be outwitted by Louis, Louis of all men!"

"Do not despair, Eleanor. I daresay you can coax him into making another attempt."

"I am not so sure of that, Petra." Eleanor had begun to pace restlessly. "Harry can be stubborn beyond all belief. He is not easily coaxed into anything, except into bed."

"Well, then, make that your battlefield. Give him your body if you must, but not your passion. Indifference is a most effective weapon, Sister. It always won me victory in my skirmishes with Raoul." Petronilla added a conventional "May God assoil him" for her late husband that was also heartfelt; hers had been that rarest of marriages, one made for love. Turning aside to pour more wine, she frowned upon finding the flagon empty, and frowned again when no servant came in response to her summons. "I will be back straightaway," she promised, "as soon as I put the fear of God into those laggards down in the hall."

Once she had gone, Maud set her wine cup down, rose to her feet, and crossed to the queen. "I know you are very fond of your sister," she said, "but she gives you poor advice. I would hope you not heed her."

Eleanor's eyes glinted, green to gold and then green again. "You are Harry's cousin. Defend him if you must, but not this day, not to me. I am entitled to my anger, will not let you rob me of it."

"I speak as your friend. If you reject what I say, do so because you like not the message. But doubt not the messenger, Eleanor. My loyalty is not given only to blood-kin. It is yours, too, if you want it."

Eleanor searched the other woman's face. "You think I am in the wrong? That I have no right to feel disappointed, even betrayed?"

"I think that your anger has been a long-smoldering fire, feeding on grievances that lie far from the borders of Toulouse. I am not saying you have no cause for it. But let that fire kindle in your marriage bed and your marriage itself could be left in charred ruins. Think long and hard ere you let that happen, Eleanor. You may not have found all you hoped to gain in wedlock with Harry, but surely what you do have is worth holding on to."

"So you'd have me swallow my pride and play the role of submissive, compliant wife? Is that the best you can do, Maud? What very ordinary advice. If I wanted a tiresome lecture about my duty to obey my husband, I could get that from my confessor!"

"You misread me, Madame. I preach no sermons. Heed me or not, as you will. But at least hear me out."

"Why should I?"

"Because," Maud said, "I know more than you of a woman's lot. I know more, too, about compromise and caution and survival. These were lessons I had to learn, and at a very early age."

"I know your marriage was not a happy one, Maud, but—"

"No, you do not know, Eleanor. You could not possibly know." Maud's usual insouciance was utterly gone; her dark eyes held only shadows and secrets she'd never before shared. "You see," she said, "my husband was quite mad."

Eleanor was momentarily startled into silence. "I've heard stories about Randolph," she said, "stories about his ungodly rages and his treachery. Harry said he'd sooner have trusted Judas than Chester. I know he was so hated that when he was poisoned, the only surprise was that it had not happened earlier. But Harry and Ranulf led me to believe that you did not fear him as others did, that you—"

"I learned not to show him my fear. And in time, the fear did lessen, for I found that my boldness was the best shield I could have against Randolph's cruelty. He scented out weakness, the way they say wolves can smell blood for miles. Because I never cowered, because I never let him see my tears, he grudgingly gave me a reluctant respect. So few people ever dared to stand up to him that I suppose the novelty of it disarmed him. And it helped greatly, of course, that he was always so hot to share my bed."

"Did you never think to leave him?"

"I was seventeen when we wed, too young and too proud to be scorned for a failed marriage. For I knew that I'd be blamed, just as my aunt Maude was when her marriage to Geoffrey of Anjou foundered on the rocks of their mutual loathing. Geoffrey was more brutal to her than Randolph was to me, yet that counted for naught. People still saw the failure as hers. So I knew what I could expect. I did not want to disappoint my parents, to bring dishonor upon our family. And so I chose to make the best of it."

"Jesú, Maud, your life must have been hellish!"

"No . . . surprisingly, it was not. I learned to take my pleasures where I could find them, even in Randolph's bed. I also enjoyed the privileges that came to me as Countess of Chester. And in time, I had my sons to love. I suppose ours was not the worst of marriages, given how wretched some of them can be. But when Randolph died," she concluded coolly, "I felt like a prisoner suddenly shoved from the dark up into the light of day."

Eleanor turned abruptly toward the bed, sat down, and beckoned for Maud to join her. "So what would you have me do? Follow in your footsteps?"

"No, there is no need for you to go down that rock-strewn road." Maud grinned suddenly. "You could not even if you wanted to, for it is not in your nature to make 'the best' of things. If it were, you'd still be Queen of France."

"God forbid," Eleanor said, and they both smiled.

"As for Toulouse, I think you must resign yourself to its loss."

Eleanor arched an elegant brow. "Must I, indeed?" she said, but with none of her earlier asperity, and Maud nodded.

"If two men as utterly unlike as Harry and Louis could not win it, does that not tell you something about your chances?" Maud paused, unable to resist adding, "Unless you mean to try again with a third husband?"

"Do not tempt me," Eleanor retorted, but there was a hint of amusement hovering in the corners of her mouth. "A pity I could not ride against Toulouse myself. If only women were not so damnably dependent upon men to get what we want in this life!"

"Amen," Maud said fervently. "But you cannot in fairness blame Harry for that, Eleanor. It is not his fault that men get to soar high and wide whilst we are earthbound, birds with clipped wings."

"Ah, here it comes, the loyal kinswoman rallying to her cousin's defense," Eleanor mocked, and Maud grinned again.

"A defense, yes, but a qualified one. For all that I think the world of Harry, I am not blind to his flaws. He is stubborn and single-minded and surely not the easiest of men to live with. But he is also a man who does love you deeply . . . if reluctantly."

Eleanor stared at her and then burst out laughing. "You do understand Harry," she said, "much better than I realized! Harry was prepared, even eager, to give me his name, his body, his crown, but not his heart. That caught him by surprise, and even now I suspect that he is not entirely easy about it."

"Harry has good reason to be mistrustful of love. His parents' union was not so much a marriage as a war, and he was their hostage, for he was unlucky enough to love them both."

"He rarely talks to me of his childhood, usually shrugging off my questions with one of his jokes. I suspect that you know more than I do, Maud, about his family's bloodletting."

"What I know comes mainly from Ranulf and from my own parents. My father was very protective of Maude and felt strongly that she was ill-used by Geoffrey. Of course there are those to argue that she was equally to blame for their feuding. I do know that the marriage got off to the worst possible start, for Maude had been forced by her father to wed Geoffrey and she was not loath to let him know of her unwillingness to be his wife. Their most bitter quarrels took place in those first years of the marriage, and by all accounts, Maude's sharp tongue was a poor match for Geoffrey's fists. I would wager," she said unexpectedly, "that Harry has never struck you . . . has he?"

Eleanor shook her head. "No."

"Did you never wonder why? Most men feel it is their God-given right to chastise their wives as they would their children, and why not, when Holy Church tells them that woman was born to be ruled by man? But I knew Harry would not, for I remember a talk I once had with him and Ranulf on that subject. Not surprisingly, Ranulf disapproved of wife-beating. God save him, he is the last truly chivalrous soul in all of Christendom. But Harry was no less emphatic, saying a man ought not to take advantage of his superior strength, and Ranulf and I knew he was thinking of his mother."

Eleanor reached for a pillow, positioning herself more comfortably on the bed. "Harry has never lacked for advocates, but you make a particularly effective one. I daresay you could even find excuses for his unfortunate habit of always being half a world away whenever one of my lying-ins begins."

"No, for some sins, no excuses will do and penance is required. I'd suggest you demand it be done in the bedchamber, but then, that is what got you so often into those birthing chambers in the first place."

Eleanor could not help laughing, and Maud joined in. "I guess I did a bit of preaching, after all," she admitted, "even if that was not my intent. Thank you for taking my meddling in good humor. It may be that I envy you, just a little, for I think you and Harry have found happiness in your marriage, and we both know how rare that is. I suppose I have been urging you to give more than Harry, and that may not be fair, but it is realistic. You cannot change a man, Harry least of all. You will always come second with him, for his kingship will come first. But to come second with the most powerful man in the known world is not such a bad thing . . . now is it?"

"I suppose there are worse fates," Eleanor agreed wryly. "So you are saying, then, that I must accept Harry as he is. But what if I cannot?"

Maud shrugged. "Then learn to love him less."

Eleanor had not been expecting such an uncompromising answer. She'd always prided herself upon her pragmatism, but she realized now that she was an outright romantic compared to Maud. "I've never been one to settle for less. But you need not fret on our behalf, Cousin Maud. I think I can content myself with what Harry has to give. Although," she added, half-joking, half-serious, "I'd have been far more contented had he been able to give me Toulouse!"

THE STRONGHOLD OF GERBEROY was in its death throes. Henry's lightning assault had taken its garrison by surprise, for he was thought to be still raiding south of Beauvais. But Henry was already famed and feared for the speed with which he could move his army, and his men had appeared without warning out of the mist of a damp November dawn. The castle had soon fallen, and now Henry's commanders were supervising its destruction.

Rainald's face was streaked with smoke and grime, his eyes puffy with fatigue. His smile, however, was jubilant. "I thought Harry's seizure last year of Thouars Castle was a dazzling feat. But taking Gerberoy was even easier. The Bishop of Beauvais must be quaking under his bed by now!"

"I hope so," Ranulf said, watching as flames consumed the castle stables, began to lick at the roof of the great hall. "I heard that Thomas Becket had ridden into camp. Do you know if that is true?"

Rainald nodded. "He and Harry are back there now and seem to have mended their rift. When I left, Becket was boasting about the havoc he'd wrought in Quercy, taking three castles and putting towns to the torch. Rather bloodthirsty for a man of the Church, wouldn't you say, Little Brother?"

Ranulf smiled, for it had been years since he'd been called that. "I've never known Becket to be much for boasting," he said mildly. "Why do you dislike him so, Rainald?"

His brother shrugged. "I've never seen him drunk."

Ranulf laughed. "You've never seen Harry drunk either, have you?"

"That is different. Harry is good company, drunk or sober. Becket always seems to be standing apart, watching the rest of us sin."

Ranulf suspected that Rainald's animosity was based upon that most common of all motives, jealousy; any man so close to the king was bound to make more enemies than friends. "Well, if he is counting up your sins, he'd better have a tally stick to keep track of them all."

Rainald guffawed, then clouted him on the shoulder. "You're one to talk! You may not stray far from home and hearth nowadays, but I remember when—" He stopped abruptly, awkwardly, not wanting to remind Ranulf of those dark times when his adulterous passion for Annora Fitz Clement had nearly brought him to ruin. Fumbling for another topic, he said hastily, "You've not heard about Stephen's son, have you? We got word this afternoon that he died at Limoges."

"No, I had not heard." Ranulf sketched a cross, feeling a twinge of sadness. William, the Count of Boulogne and Earl of Surrey, had fallen ill on their withdrawal from Toulouse, but he was a young man and Ranulf had expected him to recover. How sad to die in a foreign land, so far from home and family, in the service of the king who'd been his father's implacable foe. "He had no children by his de Warenne wife, did he?"

"No, and that is the trouble. Boulogne is now up for grabs, since the only one left of Stephen's children is William's sister, Mary, and she cannot very well rule it from Romsey's nunnery. Harry was right vexed, says the vultures will soon be circling—"

"Ranulf!" Hywel was coming toward them across the smoke-wreathed bailey. "Padarn has been hurt."

Ranulf felt a jolt of alarm; the young Welshman had once been his squire and had insisted upon being included in the contingent of Welsh he and Hywel were commanding. "How badly?"

"A flaming rafter from the stables came crashing down, killing one of the king's hired Flemings. Padarn was able to dive clear in time, but his arm was burned and I think we ought to get him back to camp straightaway."

As Ranulf turned toward his brother, Rainald waved him on. "Go," he said. "Find the lad a doctor. We've men enough to take care of things here."

Ranulf glanced once more at the wreckage of Gerberoy, then hastened after Hywel. Enough men had already died in a country not their own. He meant to make sure that Padarn was not one of them.

RANULF AND HYWEL left Padarn in the doctor's tent, his burns being treated with goose-grease salve, his pain with spiced red wine. Day was waning and shadows lengthening. Hywel glanced toward the north, where the glowing horizon attested to Gerberoy's fiery demise. "I promised Padarn we'd find him some mead. Are we going to have to ferment it ourselves?"

"Probably." Henry's command tent lay ahead and Ranulf quickened his step. Just then the flap was pulled up and a tall man emerged, dark and saturnine and vaguely familiar. As Ranulf watched, he signaled imperiously to his waiting attendants, then strode over to a tethered bay stallion. Once he and his men were mounted, they galloped out of the encampment at a pace to send soldiers scattering, but he seemed as indifferent to their hurled curses as he'd been to their safety, never once looking back.

Hywel cursed, too, for he'd turned his ankle jumping out of the way. "Who is that arrogant whoreson?"

"I've seen him somewhere," Ranulf said, "but my memory needs prodding. Let's find out from Harry."

Henry and Thomas Becket had spread a map out upon a trestle table and were studying it intently. They looked so pleased with themselves that Ranulf knew something was afoot. And it was then that he remembered where he'd seen the swaggering stranger: last year in Paris, at the court of the French king.

"Good God Almighty, that was Simon de Montfort!"

"You think so?" Henry asked innocently, but his eyes were full of laughter.

"Who," Hywel asked, "is Simon de Montfort?"

"The Count of Évreux, a highborn and high-handed lord who happens to be a vassal of the French king. What was he doing here, Harry?"

"Betraying Louis," Henry said, and gestured for a servant to fetch them wine. "He has agreed to do homage to me . . ." He paused deliberately, savoring the drama. "And to turn over into my keeping the castles of Montfort, Rochefort, and Epernon."

"Which means," Becket chimed in, "that Louis's domains will be cut in half, as this map plainly shows."

"I am impressed," Ranulf said. "Dare I ask how you brought this about?"

Henry merely smiled, leaving it to Becket to answer for him. "De Montfort saw what befell the Bishop of Beauvais's lands and, quite understandably, became alarmed that his own estates might suffer the same fate. It was not difficult to persuade him that he'd fare better as Harry's vassal than he would as Louis's."

Hywel had followed Ranulf over to look at the map. "With his brothers in full retreat and his vassals deserting him, will the French king be able to continue the war?"

Becket shook his head. "We very much doubt it. De Montfort's defection puts him in a perilous position, and even if he does not realize that, there will be plenty to point it out to him."

Henry perched on the edge of the table, running his hand absently through his unruly coppery hair. "Louis has neither the desire nor the stomach to turn Normandy and France into a bloody battlefield. He'll soon seek a truce, which I will agree to, and then we can all go home."

"Now that you mention it," Ranulf said, "Hywel and I are both eager to get back to Wales."

"You and Lord Hywel can have the use of one of my ships," Becket said, and when Ranulf looked inquiringly at his nephew, Henry nodded.

"I see no reason for you to wait upon the truce. Take Thomas up on his offer. He has six ships, you know, whilst the Crown only has the one. I ofttimes have to borrow one of his myself!"

Ranulf's smile was brilliant, radiant with relief. "Is the morrow too soon? It's been more than six months since I've seen my wife, after all."

"It's been nigh on that long since I've seen my wife, too," Henry said, then smiled ruefully, for he suspected that making peace with the French king would be easier than making peace with Eleanor.

The great fortress of William the Bastard was situated on an escarpment high above the Norman town of Falaise. One of the most formidable of Henry's castles, it was here that he had chosen to hold his Christmas court, and it was here that he was to have his long delayed reunion with his wife.

Sleet was lashing the streets of Falaise, and few of the townspeople came out to watch as the king rode up the hill toward the castle. An earlier snowfall had yet to melt and the road was half-hidden, perilously icy in patches. Winter's siege that year had begun early and seemed likely to be a long and brutal one, and Henry's men were shivering from the cold, hunched over their saddles in a futile attempt to escape the wind's buffeting fury. They were all looking forward to the roaring hearths and warm beds awaiting them at the castle; Henry alone felt no sense of relief as they rode into the bailey.

He didn't think he was nervous; how could a man be uneasy at facing his own wife? But he felt an unfamiliar edginess, nonetheless, as he strode into the great hall. Eleanor was standing by the hearth, and as always when they'd been long apart, he was struck anew by the sheer physical impact of her beauty. Her youth was behind her, for she was thirty-seven, and she was not as willow-slim as on their wedding day, not after five pregnancies in seven years. But the body clad in a clinging green gown had a voluptuous, feline grace, and her finely sculpted cheekbones, full, sensual mouth, and slanting hazel eyes gave her a look uniquely her own, at once elegant and provocative. The first time he'd laid eyes upon her, in the Paris palace of the French king, she'd quite literally stolen his breath away. She still did, for she was too passionate and too self-willed and too reckless a woman ever to be taken for granted. As she moved to meet him, he wanted only to sweep her into his arms and off to bed. But it would not be that simple. Life with Eleanor was by turns exciting and unpredictable and occasionally infuriating, but never simple.

His mother had traveled from Rouen for his Christmas court, and she and his brother, Will, hastened forward to welcome him home. Eleanor followed, more slowly. Her greeting was appropriately formal in a hall filled with highborn guests. When he grazed her cheek with a deliberately casual kiss, her smile was unwavering, her eyes unrevealing. They had no chance to speak, for the nurses were ushering his children toward him.

Six months was a significant span in a child's life, and Henry was startled to see how rapidly they'd grown in his absence. Hal was nigh on five, Tilda three, Richard two, and Geoffrey, the baby, tottering unsteadily at fifteen months. They all had Henry's vivid coloring, as did his illegitimate son, another Geoffrey, who would celebrate his sixth birthday in less than a week's time. Beckoning the boy forward when he hung back shyly, Henry glanced over at Eleanor, remembering her reaction when he'd told her about Geoffrey. He hadn't been sure how she'd react to his revelation of a bastard child, one he meant to raise as his own. But she'd taken the news with aplomb, saying she was not likely to get jealous because he'd scratched an itch.

Maude at once began to question him about the truce with the French king, but the mother soon prevailed over the empress. "Harry, your clothes are soaked through," she chided softly. "You'd best change out of them straightaway."

"I'll send servants to prepare a bath for you," Eleanor said, showing a proper wifely concern that gave Henry no comfort, for those luminous hazel eyes remained inscrutable.

As MEN POURED steaming buckets of hot water into the tub, Henry sat on a coffer so his squire could pull off his boots. His fatigue took him by surprise, for he was accustomed to long, hard hours in the saddle in weather even worse than this. Hastily stripping off his sodden clothes, he sank down gratefully in the tub, waving away the youth's offer of further assistance.

"You look half-frozen, too, lad. Go find yourself a flagon of wine or a willing lass, whatever it takes to warm you up."

Miles grinned and disappeared. Henry dismissed the rest of the servants, too; he'd never liked being hovered over. Leaning back, he rested his neck against the padded rim of the tub. The water was caressing his aching muscles, soothing away cramps and stiffness. A tantalizingly familiar scent filled his nostrils; after a moment, he realized that they'd given him

Eleanor's perfumed soap. He poured some into his palms and lathered his chest. He did not usually linger in his bath, but the warm water was lulling, even seductive, and he soon closed his eyes.

He did not even realize when he fell asleep, and when he awoke, it was with a start, unsure how much time had passed. Something cold touched his cheek and he sat up with a splash, staring into the soft brown eyes of Felice, Eleanor's brindle greyhound. Reaching out, he fondled the dog's silky ears, and then turned so hastily that he churned up a wave of water. His wife was seated across from him on the coffer, her feet tucked comfortably under her, regarding him impassively over the rim of a silver gilt wine cup.

The silence spun out between them, a spider's web made of memories and the tangled skeins of miscommunication. It was a contest of wills Henry was bound to lose, and he knew it. "So," he said, falling back upon humor that was somewhat defensive, too, "were you planning to drown me whilst I slept?"

"Have you given me reason to want to drown you?"

"You tell me."

Eleanor lifted her wine cup, drinking slowly. "Are we talking of Toulouse, Harry?"

"What else? I know you had your heart set upon reclaiming it. But it was not to be, Eleanor. Go ahead, blame me if you will. I'll hear you out. It will change nothing, though."

"I know."

Henry's eyes narrowed. "You're taking this much better than I expected."

"Is that why you avoided Poitiers on your withdrawal from Toulouse?"

Henry's first instinct was to justify his absence, to remind her that he'd been occupied in chasing Louis's brothers out of Normandy. But she'd spoken so matter-of-factly that he found himself conceding, "I suppose I may have been somewhat reluctant to face you then." Adding, with just the glimmer of a smile, "After all, I could only fight one war at a time." He waited for her response, but she continued to sip her wine, saying nothing. "Are you going to tell me that I was wrong?" he challenged. "That you were not wroth with me?"

"No, I was indeed wroth with you, Harry. So it was probably for the best that you did stay away as long as you did."

"And now that I'm back?"

She finished the last of her wine, reached for a nearby flagon, and poured another cupful. Coming to her feet, she leaned over the tub. "Now that you're back," she said, "I think we have better things to do than argue."

As she held out the cup, he made no move to take it, letting her tilt it to his lips. The water had begun to cool, but his body was suddenly flooded with heat, centering in his groin and radiating outward. He'd never known another woman able to stir his desire so fast, and he groped hastily for a towel, saying huskily, "I've spent enough time in this bath."

But as he started to rise, she put her hands on his shoulders and pushed him back. "No . . . wait," she said, and as he watched, she unfastened her veil and wimple, began to loosen her long, dark braid. Lifting her skirt, she kicked off her shoes. He expected her to remove her stockings next, but instead she straightened up, and then swung her leg over the rim of the tub. A moment later, she'd slid down into the water, smiling at his startled expression. Running her fingers along the sopping silk that now molded to her body like a second skin, she said, "You owe me a new gown."

Henry began to laugh. "I owe you more than that," he said, and pulled her into his arms. The water was soon spilling over the tub's rim, drenching the floor rushes. But by then, they were too busy to care, even to notice.

ELEANOR STIRRED and sighed. Usually she was an early riser. But this morning she and Henry had slept late, for their lovemaking had been ardent and frequent, and it was almost dawn before they'd finally fallen into an exhausted, satisfied sleep. Her thigh muscles were as sore as if she'd spent a day in the saddle, and she smiled drowsily as the night's memories came surging back.

The ruin of a favored gown had been well worth it, for that calculated plunge into his bath had aroused her husband even more than she'd dared hope. Once a man's imagination was inflamed, his body kept catching fire of its own accord. Not that Harry ever needed much encouragement. His sexual hungers were usually as boundless as his energy. Unlike the monkish Louis, he was delighted when her own passion flared out of control, fondly calling her "hellcat" if she left scratches down his back, teaching her ways to pleasure a man that would have horrified her confessor.

Beside her, Henry slept on, one arm draped across her hip, his face pillowed in her hair. Laying her hand over his heart, she entwined bright golden strands of chest hair around her forefinger, tugging gently. He already had an early morning erection, and she could feel it swelling against her thigh as her fingers trailed across his belly. He kept his eyes shut, pretending still to sleep until her intimate caresses evoked an involuntary gasp. Laughing, she rolled over into his arms, and did her very best to reward him for being so responsive to her overtures.

Eleanor would never have admitted, even to herself, that she was beginning to feel the first stirrings of insecurity. She had a beautiful woman's confidence, which had indeed often bordered on arrogance, for she'd been accustomed to bedazzling men since her fifteenth year. But marriage to a much younger man, one with a roving eye, had made her vulnerable in a way she'd never anticipated and was not yet willing to acknowledge, not consciously. For now, she assuaged these instinctive and unfamiliar pricklings of foreboding with the sweet balm of seduction, finding reassurance as well as pleasure in her husband's eager embrace.

THE FIRE HAD BURNED OUT during the night and servants were attempting to rekindle it. Henry's squire was searching in a coffer, selecting his king's clothes for the day while he flirted with Veronique, the newest and youngest of Eleanor's ladies-in-waiting. Listening to the commotion filling the chamber, Henry and Eleanor realized that they could no longer keep the world at bay. But for now, the bedcurtains remained drawn, giving them a few more moments of precious semiprivacy. Leaning over, Henry smoothed his wife's dark cloud of hair back from her face. "I'd better get out of this bed ere you cripple me."

He didn't move, though, and Eleanor smiled at him lazily. "Well, then you could boast it was a war wound, gotten in the service of your queen."

Henry laughed and tightened his arms around her. "Ah, but I am going to miss you," he said, and then reluctantly reached out to open the bed hangings and start their day.

Eleanor sat up, too, catching his hand. "You're here but one night and already planning your departure?" she asked, not able to hide her dismay. "Where do you mean to go now?"

"Not me, love . . . you. I need you to return to England."

"Why?"

"Because I've been gone from its shores for more than a year and I cannot leave Normandy just yet, not until I've patched up a peace with

Louis and made sure our plans to wed our children have not been jeopardized. I know I have a good man in Leicester. But I'd feel more secure, Eleanor, if you were there to watch over our English interests. Leicester is merely my justiciar; you're my consort."

Eleanor was silent for a moment, sorting out conflicting urges. As Henry's wife, she was troubled by the prospect of another long separation, and even more troubled that he was not. But as his queen, she was pleased that he had such faith in her. She'd been disappointed that he'd not given her a larger role in his decision-making, and she harbored an unwelcome suspicion that he valued his mother's advice more than he did hers. It was heartening, therefore, that he wanted her to be his eyes and ears in England, even if it did mean sleepless nights in a cold, lonely bed.

"When do you want me to go, Harry?"

"Soon, love, mayhap after the Christmas revelries. Is that agreeable to you?"

"No," she said, "but it is acceptable."

THE SEACOAST MANOR OF ABER was the favorite residence of Owain Gwynedd. On this frigid night in late December, not even a well-stoked hearth could dispel the chill that was pervading his bedchamber. Settling back in his chair, Owain studied his son. Hywel was drinking deeply from a brimming cup of mead, putting the cup down with a satisfied smile.

"I got to fancy some of the French wines, but I missed mead and, believe it or not, the wet Welsh climate. I suffered a few minor injuries in the course of Harry's war, but nothing gave me more discomfort than the sunburn I got in Quercy!"

Owain smiled, too. "And did you get to meet the English queen, as you'd hoped?"

"At Poitiers. She is as beautiful as men say, and too clever by half, I suspect." Hywel could not resist glancing toward his father's concubine as he spoke, an insinuation that was not lost upon Cristyn. Taking up her mantle, she slipped unobtrusively from the chamber.

Owain's interest in Eleanor was peripheral. "Tell me," he said, "of the English king. I notice you call him Harry now. You found him likable, then?"

"Yes, I suppose I did. He looks upon life with a humorous eye, and for a man reputed to have the Devil's own temper, I never saw him unleash it upon the truly defenseless. It helped, too, that he laughed at my jokes!"

"What are his failings?" Owain asked, and leaned forward intently to hear his son's answer.

"He thinks he can get whatever he sets his mind upon."

"God help him, then," Owain said dryly. "Is that why he attempted to lay claim to Toulouse?"

"I think it was in part to please his woman, and in part because he thought he could win it without paying too high a price. Becoming a king at one and twenty has made him rather cocky, prone to overvalue his own abilities and undervalue those of his opponents."

"Does he, indeed?" Owain said thoughtfully. "That is most useful to know, Hywel. But I'll confess that I am uneasy about his hunger for lands not his. Your friend Ranulf sought to assure me that he had no desire to swallow Wales whole. Think you that he is right?"

"Well . . . we are a much poorer country than Toulouse and that probably works to our advantage. Harry is a practical man for all his youth, and I cannot see him lusting after a land that has no towns, little sun, and more sheep than people!"

"Ranulf said also that if we provoked him into all-out war, he'd be the most dangerous foe I've ever faced. What say you to that, Hywel?"

Hywel didn't hesitate. "Ranulf spoke true. I have no doubts whatsoever about that."

"I would say, then, that your time in these foreign lands has served us well."

Owain was usually sparing with his praise and Hywel flushed with pleasure. Draining his cup, he pushed his chair away from the table. "It is late," he said, "and I'd best find a bed over in the hall ere they are all taken."

Owain nodded. "I am glad," he said, "to have you home," and Hywel departed with a light step and a lingering smile.

Outside, the sky was clear, stars gleaming in its ebony vastness like celestial fireflies. It was bitterly cold, and Hywel's every breath trailed after him in pale puffs of smoke. The glazed snow crackled underfoot as he started toward the great hall. He'd taken only a few steps when a ghostly, graceful figure glided from the shadows into his path.

Hywel came to a halt. "Were you waiting to bid me good night, Cristyn? How kind."

Cristyn pulled down her hood. The face upturned to his was bleached by the moonlight, her eyes dark and fathomless. "I was hoping," she said, "that you'd not come back."

"I missed you, too," he drawled and heard her draw a breath, sharp as a serpent's hiss.

"I know what you are up to," she warned, "and it will avail you naught. You may be Owain's spy, but you'll never be his heir."

"You might want to check with my father ere you settle the succession for him. I daresay he has an idea or two on that particular subject."

Cristyn gave him a stare colder even than the December night. "You will not cheat Davydd of his birthright."

Hywel laughed softly. "Now if I were facing you across a battlefield, darling, I might be worried. But little brother Davydd? He could not outfight a flock of drunken whores. Ask him to tell you sometime about the night he balked at paying for services rendered and the outraged bawd chased him through the streets of Bangor, walloping him with a broom."

Hywel waited to see if she would respond. When she did not, he walked on, still laughing under his breath. Cristyn stayed where she was, as if rooted to the frozen earth, watching as he sauntered toward the hall. But he never looked back.

CHAPTER NINE

✦

June 1160
Chester, England

FRIDAY, THE TWENTY-FOURTH OF JUNE, was the
Nativity of St John the Baptist, and Chester's annual fair was in
full swing. Booths and stalls had been set up in front of the abbey
of St Werbergh's Great Gate, and merchants were doing a brisk business.
Enticed by the aroma of freshly baked apple wafers, Eleri fumbled in the
purse dangling from her belt. Finding only a few farthings, she scowled,
then tugged at her sister's sleeve.

"I wish to God our kings minted money of their own. I hate having
to use English coins for everything. Speaking of which, do you have any,
Rhiannon? I want to buy the children some wafers."

"Ranulf gave me a full purse. Here, take what you need."

They'd been speaking in Welsh, and Eleri now glanced toward the
young Englishwoman standing a few feet away, one of the Countess of
Chester's ladies-in-waiting. "Your French is much better than mine, Rhiannon. Ask her if she wants a wafer, too."

Isolda did, and Eleri was soon shepherding the children toward the baker's booth. Left alone with Isolda, Rhiannon made polite conversation for a while, but the other woman's responses were so terse that she soon gave up the attempt, unsure whether Isolda's discomfort was a reaction to her blindness, her Welsh blood, or both. Reminding herself that there were plenty of Welsh made uneasy by her blindness, too, she concentrated instead upon the sounds and smells of the fair.

The savory aroma of the baked wafers mingled with the fragrances of perfumes and spices and the more pungent odors associated with summer heat and crowds and animals. Rhiannon had never been to a fair before; they had nothing of this scope in Wales. But Eleri was skilled at acting as her sister's eyes and she'd been providing vivid descriptions of the activities and fairgoers.

The variety of goods for sale was truly amazing, she'd reported: bolts of linen and silk, cowhide boots, felt hats, jars of honey and olive and almond and linseed oil, wines and cider and candles and even a bright green African parrot in a wicker cage. Equally remarkable was the range of entertainment offered. There were acrobats and jugglers and musicians and a rope dancer and archery contests, bouts with the quarter staff, wrestling matches, and cock fighting. There were also cutpurses and thieves and harlots on the prowl, keeping their eyes peeled for the sheriff's men, and an occasional belligerent drunkard. For Rhiannon, it was an experience both exhilarating and overwhelming.

"Lady Isolda, where are they selling cider?" Getting no answer, Rhiannon repeated her question. But again there was no response. With a pang of dismay, she realized that the other woman had gone off, leaving her alone. She had a moment of instinctive panic, which quickly subsided once she remembered that Eleri would soon be back.

Still, it was unnerving to be surrounded by jostling strangers, people she could neither see nor understand, for although Ranulf had taught her French, most of the Chester fairgoers were speaking English, and that only increased her sense of isolation. Damning Isolda under her breath, she stumbled when someone bumped her from behind. Her first fear was that a cutpurse had seen her as an easy target, but she soon realized that something else was amiss. All around her, people were pushing and shoving. They did not seem fearful, though, for they were laughing and shrieking. Confused, she struggled to keep her footing, but she was caught up in the surging crowd like a twig carried along by flood waters. She was soon dizzy and disoriented, her cries for Eleri going unheard. When an elbow slammed into her ribs, she reeled backward, losing her balance.

She did not fall, though. An arm snaked around her waist, keeping her upright, and a familiar voice murmured soothingly in Welsh, "Easy, darling, I've got you."

Rhiannon gasped with relief, but also astonishment. "Hywel? Whatever are you doing here?"

"What I do best, rescuing a damsel in distress. Of course I usually have to fend off dragons, not greased pigs, but—"

"Greased pigs! What are you talking about, Hywel?"

"That was the cause of all the commotion. One of the greased pigs escaped from its pen and made a dash for freedom, with a pack of eager youths in noisy pursuit." Hywel chuckled and gave Rhiannon a hug. "It must have been a Welsh pig, for he ran circles around those English lads, and when last seen, was heading west as fast as those stubby little legs would carry him. Now . . . why are you wandering about Chester's fair by yourself and where is that roving husband of yours?"

"You first," she insisted, as he led her toward the greater security of the closest booth.

"We happened to be passing by and decided to stop in at the fair. Why else did we make peace with the English except for the opportunity to shop in Chester?"

Rhiannon wished he wouldn't joke about the peace, for she still fretted—especially late at night—that it would not last. "My turn," she said. "We are visiting Ranulf's niece. She was waylaid by the abbot, told us to go on into the fair. Eleri is at the baker's booth with the children, hers and mine."

"And Ranulf?"

"He had to ride over to one of his Cheshire manors and meet with his steward. We're staying with Maud until he gets back. Can you wait until she joins us? I would like you to meet her."

"We did meet," Hywel said, smiling at her surprise, "in Poitiers last June. Did Ranulf never tell you?" Hearing his name called then, he gave an answering shout. "Over here!" Turning back to Rhiannon, he said, "You remember my foster brother, Peryf ap Cedifor?"

"Of course," she said, holding out her hand for Peryf to kiss. The sound of his voice was just as she remembered, gruff and so deep that she'd envisioned him as a veritable giant, a vast, sturdy oak of a man. It had come as a shock when Ranulf described Peryf as being only of average height, nowhere near as tall as Hywel.

"And here is my son, Caswallon," Hywel said fondly as they were

joined by a youth of fifteen. "You remember the lovely Lady Rhiannon, lad?"

The boy nodded, ducking his head. He had inherited neither his father's uncommon height nor his coloring, the fair hair and dark eyes that
gave Hywel such a striking appearance. Caswallon had hair the shade of
rust, a multitude of freckles, and greyish-green eyes that looked at life
sidelong, rarely head-on. Unlike Peryf, Caswallon's physical description
tallied well with Rhiannon's mental image of the boy, as one easily overlooked. Each time Rhiannon had met him, he'd been so tongue-tied that
all of her maternal instincts were aroused. The problem, she suspected,
was most likely Hywel; it might well be daunting for a shy youngster,
growing up in the shadow of such a celebrated and flamboyant father.

"Rhiannon, I've been looking all over for you! Why did you not stay
by the— Oh!" Eleri's indignant protest was forgotten at the sight of the
Welsh prince. "Lord Hywel, what a surprise! What brings you to Chester?"

"Lady Eleri, you know I'd follow you to the ends of the earth," Hywel professed gallantly. After dispatching his son to buy more wafers and
cider for them all, he and Peryf ushered the women toward the shade of
a nearby elder tree. "I'm sorry that we'll miss seeing Ranulf. I rely upon
him for gossip about the English king's court."

Eleri giggled; her sister had long ago noted that she laughed immod-
erately at all of Hywel's jokes. "Well, you are in luck," she declared, "for
Rhiannon and I have a truly wicked scandal to relate, one involving a nun
and a count's son!"

Hywel was immediately intrigued. "Do not keep us in suspense,
sweetheart. And spare none of the lurid details!"

Eleri was happy to oblige. "You remember when the Count of
Boulogne died on that ill-fated expedition against Toulouse? Naturally the
English king at once began to think about finding a suitable husband for
the count's sister Mary, the new heiress to Boulogne. Unfortunately, Mary
also happened to be the abbess of Romsey's nunnery. Now that would
have discouraged most men from pursuing any matrimonial schemes."

Eleri stifled another giggle, adding archly, "The Church does not look
kindly upon marriage for its Brides of Christ, after all. But the English
king is not one to balk at trivial obstacles like holy oaths of chastity. So . . .
he either coerced or coaxed our Mother Abbess out of Romsey, somehow obtained a dispensation—to the horror of his own chancellor,
Becket—and married the new countess off to his cousin Matthew,
younger son of the Count of Flanders!"

Rhiannon saw no humor in the tale, for it troubled her that Henry felt so free to play by his own rules; moreover, she could not help sympathizing with the convent-bred Mary, wondering how willing a bride she'd been. But Hywel and Peryf were roaring with laughter.

"Bless you, lass, that is more than choice gossip. It is almost too good to be true, for it has all the classic elements of a truly great scandal; the best ones always involve the Church, the Crown, and clandestine conspiracies. Throw in a virgin nun-bride and it is well nigh perfect!"

Eleri joined in their mirth, delighted with the success of her story. They were laughing too hard to hear the approaching female footsteps, lightly treading upon the summer grass. "What," Maud asked, "is provoking so much merriment?" Her dark eyes widened as they turned toward Hywel. "If it is not the poet-prince!"

Hywel kissed her hand with his usual panache. "I am flattered beyond words that you remember me, my lady."

"You . . . beyond words? Now why do I doubt that?"

Hywel grinned. "Why are the most beautiful of women always the cruelest?" After introducing Maud to Peryf, he collected his son, just returning with a sackful of wafers and several cider flasks. Munching on the wafers, they corralled the children and sauntered back toward the booths, stopping to watch as a daring youth juggled knives and axes and even flaming torches.

It was a dazzling performance, and the audience responded with generous applause and a shower of coins. Leaving the juggler to count his booty, they moved on. Eleri soon dropped back to walk beside her sister. "It is shameless," she hissed, "the way Maud is flirting so blatantly with Hywel! You'd think she'd have more pride, would you not?"

Rhiannon made a noncommittal reply. She would much rather Hywel do his flirting with Maud than with Eleri, for the widowed countess was far more worldly than her little sister and better able to deal with Hywel's formidable charm. While she was convinced that Eleri loved her husband, she knew, too, that Hywel was dangerously adept at seduction, and she wasn't sure his friendship with Ranulf would restrain him if Eleri offered encouragement. No, better that he turn that beguiling smile upon Maud, a more worthy adversary in every sense. Even without sight, she could detect the unmistakable sparks flying between them, and she found herself wondering about that first meeting of theirs in Poitiers.

They were strolling side by side, Maud's arm linked in Hywel's, and their laughter drifted back upon the breeze, bringing a fresh frown to

Eleri's face. Peryf had fallen in behind them, escorting Maud's ladies-in-waiting, Clarice and Isolda, who'd hastily reappeared to attend her mistress. Eleri was keeping watch over the children, and Caswallon trailed after the others, digging in his sack for the last of the wafers.

Up ahead, a crowd had gathered and they were starting in that direction when Maud was intercepted by another woman. What drew Rhiannon's attention was the contrast between their voices. While the stranger seemed delighted by the chance meeting, Maud showed little enthusiasm, sounding polite but wary. The woman was talking with considerable animation, arousing Rhiannon's curiosity, for her demeanor bespoke an intimacy that Maud was not acknowledging. She was almost upon them when her husband's name was unexpectedly thrust into the conversation.

"I am gladdened that you are so well, Lady Maud. Tell me . . . how is Ranulf? How has he been faring?"

Rhiannon came to an abrupt halt. She knew suddenly, with a certainty that owed nothing to logic, that this was Annora Fitz Clement, the woman Ranulf had once loved to distraction. She felt the blood rushing to her face, and for a moment, all she could hear was the thudding of her own heart. And then Maud had slid an arm around her shoulders, saying warmly:

"Ranulf has been faring very well indeed, Annora. And here is the proof, a woman dearer to me than any sister could be, the Lady Rhiannon . . . Ranulf's wife."

The rest of the introductions passed in a blur for Rhiannon. Annora made the proper responses, saying that she'd heard Ranulf had wed a Welsh cousin, and offering her belated congratulations and well-wishes. But the liveliness had drained from her voice and the conversation soon trailed off into an awkward silence. Rhiannon did not doubt that she was being subjected to a critical scrutiny, and she felt a rush of rage, directed against Annora and the Almighty in equal measure, that she could not even look upon her rival's face.

She hoped that she'd regained her poise, although she knew that betraying color still stained her cheeks. As uncomfortable as the encounter was, it would have been far worse if not for Maud. The other woman's silent support was as bracing as the arm around her shoulders, and Maud made a conspicuous point of introducing Rhiannon's children to Annora, while mentioning ever so casually that Ranulf was not expected back in Chester for several days. Annora soon found an excuse to withdraw, but her presence continued to be felt long after she'd vanished into the crowd. Rhiannon felt no surprise at that. She, above all others, needed no one to tell her of Annora's ghostly tenacity, for had she not haunted the shadows of their marriage for fully ten years?

"Is that the one?" Eleri squeezed Rhiannon's arm. "The woman Ranulf was so besotted with? I thought her quite plain. He could surely have done better for himself, dearest!"

"He did," Maud said emphatically, "he did." Lowering her voice for Rhiannon's ear alone, she murmured, "I never cared much for Annora, always found her to be rather forgettable. In fact, she seems to be fading from memory even as we speak."

Rhiannon's smile was forced. "No," she said, "I'll keep nothing from Ranulf. What if he learned from others that we'd met this woman? How would I explain our silence?"

"As you wish, Rhiannon. It matters for naught, though. I'd wager Ranulf has spared nary a thought for Annora in years."

Rhiannon said nothing, wishing she could be as sure of that as Maud. She yearned to ask if Annora was truly plain, or if that was merely a sister's loyalty. But her pride kept her quiet, as did her common sense. What did it matter, after all, if Annora was no great beauty? Ranulf had still loved her, had risked his life and his immortal soul for that love.

They continued on, pausing to watch an acrobatic tumbling act. Judging from the hearty applause of the audience, the performance was a good one. Rhiannon smiled as Gilbert and Mallt cheered and clapped, but not even her children's pleasure could banish Annora from her thoughts.

"Rhiannon?" Hywel's breath was warm on her cheek. "How are you doing, darling?"

"I am well enough," she insisted. "Why should I fear a memory?"

Hywel knew that few temptations were as seductive as memories of lost youth and lost love. He suspected that Rhiannon did, too. "You've nothing to fear from any other woman, sweetheart. And if you ever get tired of that husband of yours, I'll be camping outside your door in the blink of an eye!"

"You're such a liar," Rhiannon laughed. "I do not doubt that you are a good lover, but you are an even better friend."

"You have it backward," he said. "I am a good friend, an even better lover." And his eyes shifted from Rhiannon to Maud, who spoke little Welsh, but who seemed to understand exactly what he was saying.

✦

W<small>INCHESTER</small> <small>WAS</small> <small>IN</small> the grip of an oppressive August heat wave, and Petronilla was not surprised to find the castle gardens deserted. She was turning to go back into the great hall when she spied a recumbent figure sprawled on one of the turf benches. He had a cap pulled down over his face to shut out the sun's glare, but she still recognized her half-brother. Moving swiftly along the graveled path, she bent over and shook his shoulder. "Jos!"

Joscelin opened his eyes, blinking up at her drowsily. "Petra? What is it?"

"I've been searching everywhere for Eleanor. Have you seen her?"

"Not since dinner this morning." Yawning, he slid over to make room for her on the bench, an invitation she ignored. "Why are you seeking Eleanor? Is something amiss?"

"That is what I am trying to find out. I heard that an urgent letter arrived for her from Normandy."

"So?" Joscelin yawned again. "Mayhap it is just a love letter from her husband, telling her how much he misses their bedsport."

"Harry is not a man for writing love letters," Petronilla said impatiently, and Joscelin gave her a quizzical look.

"Not to you, no. But since I see no reason why Eleanor would share hers with you, how do you know what he writes? Why are you always so ready to find fault with the man, Petra?"

"Why do you think? Because he neglects our sister shamefully!"

"For the Lord's pity, woman, he gave her a crown!"

"And you truly think that is enough?"

"Mayhap not in one of your Courts of Love, but we dwell in the real world. And you're not going to convince me that Eleanor, of all women, would prefer trinkets and roses and maudlin poems to a throne!"

"Jesú, men can be so dim-witted! Of course Eleanor enjoys being England's queen. But she is Harry's wife, too, and that wife has been sleeping alone for nigh on eight months now. If that is not neglect, what is? I can assure you that Raoul was never away from my bed for more than a fortnight!"

"Was that before or after he left his wife for you?" Joscelin jeered and she snatched up his cap, smacking him across the shoulders, only half in jest.

"Petra, I do not doubt that Raoul indulged your every whim. You were all of nineteen and he was nigh on fifty when he first seduced you . . . or was it the other way around?" Laughing, he ducked as she sought to pummel him again. "What else did he have to do but pamper and cosset his young bride? Whereas Harry rules the greatest empire since the days of Charlemagne. And if you think our Eleanor does not lust after that empire as much as she does Harry, then you're dafter than a Michaelmas goose!"

Petronilla cast her gaze heavenward. "Why am I talking to you about this? You know as much about women as that poor milksop Eleanor married!"

"No one on God's green earth could ever call Harry a 'milksop,' so I assume we have moved on and are now flaying the French king?"

"Of course I meant Louis," Petronilla said, and called Louis a highly uncomplimentary name that cast serious doubts upon his manhood, much to Joscelin's amusement.

"You have a very unforgiving nature, Petra. Do you judge all of us men so harshly, or just Eleanor's husbands?"

But Petronilla had lost interest in bantering with her brother. "There you are, Eleanor," she cried, hastening to intercept the woman just coming in the garden gate. "I've been looking all over for you."

"So I heard." Eleanor motioned for Joscelin to move over so she could sit down. "Harry wants me to return to Normandy straightaway."

"You do not look very happy about it," Joscelin said, wondering why women must make life so confoundedly complicated. "I thought you missed the man?"

"Of course I miss him, Jos. I'll be glad to watch English shores recede into the distance, too. But Harry's news was not good. The word out of Paris is that Louis's queen is finally pregnant again."

Petronilla and Joscelin were both startled. "Well," Petronilla said at last, "how likely is it that he'll sire a son? After three daughters, I'd say the odds are not in his favor."

Joscelin almost reminded them that women were usually held responsible for the sex of a child, thought better of it in time. "I agree with Petra," he commented instead. "With Louis's luck, it is bound to be another lass."

"I hope so," Eleanor said, surprising even herself by the depth of her bitterness. "God Above, how I hope so!"

THE FRENCH KING'S PALACE was situated on an island in the middle of the River Seine, the Ile-de-la-Cité. When his future sons-in-law, the Counts of Champagne and Blois, arrived at the Cité and sought an audience, they were escorted toward the royal gardens at the far western tip of the island. This first Tuesday in October was as mild as midsummer, and the gardens were glowing with mellow golden sunlight under a sky the color of polished sapphire. Pear trees and cypress provided deep pockets of shade, hollyhock and gillyvor flamed along the fences, and butterflies danced on the breeze like drifting autumn leaves.

It was the most tranquil of settings, a private Eden tucked away in the very heart of Paris, but the French king was deriving no solace from his island haven, pacing nervously along the walkways, heedlessly trampling the acanthus borders underfoot. He was trailed by two bishops, his brother Philippe and Maurice de Sully, the new Bishop of Paris, while his chancellor, Hugh de Champfleury, was slouched in a trellised bower, an unread book open upon his lap. Even Louis's dogs seemed affected by his anxiety, subdued and lethargic, not bothering to bark as Theobald and Henry of Blois entered the garden.

As distracted as he was, Louis still summoned up a wan smile at the sight of the young men; although they'd not yet wed his daughters, he'd already come to think of them as kinsmen. "I could not concentrate upon matters of state," he confessed. "Even during Mass, my thoughts wandered from God's Word to my wife's lying-in chamber. Her pains began last night, and the midwives say the babe ought to be delivered by sundown."

Theobald and Henry already knew this; most of Paris knew by now that the queen was in labor. They hastened to assure Louis that Constance would soon present him with a fine, healthy son, telling him what he desperately needed to hear. Louis never thought to question their sincerity and was heartened by their apparent certitude. He had to believe that all would go well, for the alternative was too terrible to contemplate. What would befall France if he could not provide a male heir? And if he could not, what did that say about God's Will? He had convinced himself that his marriage to Eleanor was cursed in the Almighty's Eyes, as proven by her failure to give him any sons. But what if Constance failed, too, in a queen's primary duty? What if the fault lay, not with his queens, but with him? The fear that God might be judging him so harshly, as a Christian, a man, and a monarch, was almost more than Louis could bear. How could the Lord have blessed Eleanor with four sons and still deny him an heir for France?

The afternoon trickled away with excruciating slowness. Twice the midwives sent word that all was progressing as it ought. Louis wandered back into the great hall, almost at once bolted outside to the gardens again. He let his brother talk him into a game of chess, but more often than not, he found himself staring blankly at the chessboard while Philippe fidgeted impatiently. As the sun began to dip toward the horizon, the River Seine turned from blue to amber, and the last of summer's warmth faded into memory for another year. But Louis seemed oblivious to the dropping temperature. He was leaning against the stone wall, gazing out at the orchards and open fields of the left bank, when he heard a throat being cleared behind him. "My liege . . ."

He was suddenly, irrationally, afraid to turn around. For a moment, his hands clenched on the wall, his palms digging into the rough stone surface. And then he pivoted to face his confessor. The priest was haggard, his gaze downcast. "My lord king," he said, very low, "God has given you a daughter."

Louis closed his eyes, feeling a sorrow so intense it was akin to physical pain. How had he sinned, that the Almighty had forsaken him like this? Four daughters. He was in his fortieth year, and two wives had failed to give him sons. Two daughters he'd gotten from Eleanor in fifteen years of marriage, and then she'd borne the Angevin one son after another. Where was God's Justice in that? Making a great effort, he said dully, "Thy Will be done." Remembering, then, to ask, "And Constance?"

The priest flinched as if he'd taken a blow. "You must be strong, my liege," he entreated. "You must remember the Almighty tests us in ways we cannot always comprehend. The queen is dead. The midwives . . . they say she began to bleed profusely when the afterbirth was expelled. They could not save her . . ."

"Constance is dead?" For a merciful moment, Louis was uncomprehending, and then he sagged against the wall as if his bones no longer had the strength to bear his weight. His confessor hovered helplessly at his side, and his brother Philippe halted several feet away, shocked speechless for once. It was the Bishop of Paris who took charge.

"Was she shriven?"

The priest flushed, shamed that he'd not thought to assure the king of that straightaway. "Oh, indeed! I cleansed her of her earthly sins and placed the Body and Blood of Our Lord upon her tongue. You need not fear for her salvation, my lord king. She died in God's Grace."

Louis said nothing, but tears had begun to spill silently down his face. When the Bishop of Paris suggested that they go to the royal chapel and pray for the queen's soul, he nodded numbly, clutching at the familiar comfort of prayer as a drowning man would grasp at anything that might keep him afloat. "Then . . . then I would see her," he mumbled, and none of them could be sure if he meant his dead queen or his newborn daughter.

Theobald and his brother watched as the other men ushered their grieving king from the gardens. They had been vastly relieved to hear that Constance had given Louis another girl, for if Louis did not beget a son, any man wed to one of his daughters might be able to assert a claim on her behalf. But the French queen's unexpected death changed the equation dramatically. As their eyes met, Theobald said softly, "Are you thinking what I am?"

"Adela?"

Theobald nodded. "Adela," he said, and they both smiled.

TORRENTS OF RAIN had turned Rouen's narrow streets into impassable quagmires, and those who lived close to the river were becoming increasingly fearful of flooding. The beleaguered citizens had begun to feel as if they were under siege and they could only hope that the storm would die away as the day did. As night fell, though, the winds intensified, rattling shutters and tearing thatch and shingles from roofs, chasing sleep from all but the boldest households.

Torches and rushlights flared in the castle, keeping the dark at bay. Entering the nursery to bid her children good night, Eleanor was puzzled to find it still brightly lit. But as soon as she crossed the threshold, she understood. What nurse would dare argue with an empress?

Maude was seated on a bench by the hearth, manipulating a puppet at her eldest grandson's urging. She looked so uncomfortable that Eleanor had to conceal a smile. Her duties as queen often severely restricted her role as mother, but when she could find time for her children, she was quite willing to play with them, to her mother-in-law's bafflement. She still remembered Maude's startled expression the day she'd come upon them in the gardens, chasing dragonflies. Games like hoodman blind and hot cockles and hunt-the-fox were alien activities to the dignified, aloof empress. Even with her own sons, she'd always maintained a certain reserve, and it was a great tribute to both Hal's charm and his persistence that he'd been able to coax Maude into this impromptu puppet show.

Eleanor wasn't surprised by her son's success, for Hal had a sunny nature, an impish smile, and a cheerful determination to get his own way at all costs. It was a pity, though, that he was the only one of Maude's grand-children to warm toward her. Even if she'd found it easier to unbend with them, the fact that she saw them so seldom made it difficult to establish any true intimacy. Both little Tilda, Maude's namesake, and Geoffrey were intimidated by this somber, austere stranger, and were sullen and shy in her presence. Three-year-old Richard did not share their unease; his utter fearlessness was a source of both alarm and pride for his parents. But he had no liking for Maude's lectures on decorum and discipline and, to judge by the mutinous pout on his face now, he and his grandmother had clashed again.

As Eleanor entered the chamber, Maude hastily put the puppet aside. The children swarmed around their mother with joyful squeals. Because they were infrequent, her visits to the nursery were always occasions of excitement. Her embraces were scented with perfume, and a perch upon her silk-clad lap was a jealously guarded privilege. Without even being aware of their knowledge, her children knew that she was beautiful and glamorous and not like other mothers. They knew that their father was someone of importance, too. He had a booming laugh, a hoarse voice, and was always surrounded by noise and confusion and fawning attention. Like a great gusting wind, he swept all before him, and his children were usually left wide-eyed and awed in his wake.

It took a while to get the children calmed down, and a while longer to convince them that bedtime was inevitable and nonnegotiable. Only Hal, in his sixth year, was given a reprieve. But he was unable to resist teas-ing Richard about his good fortune, and the younger boy kicked him in the shins, setting off such a squabble that Eleanor and Maude left the nurses to deal with it and made an unobtrusive departure.

Entering the solar, they settled themselves before the hearth with wine and wafers, and Eleanor then showed her mother-in-law the letter she'd just gotten from Bishop Laurentius, who was working with her to replace Poitiers's cathedral of St Pierre with a splendid new structure. Watching as Maude enthusiastically studied the proposed plans, Eleanor smiled to herself, remembering how sure people had been that she'd never get along with Henry's mother.

To widespread disappointment and universal astonishment, though, they had established a cordial relationship from the first. Maude the mother may have had qualms about her son's controversial bride, but Maude the empress had readily appreciated Aquitaine's worth as a stepping-stone to the English throne. It helped, too, that Eleanor had so swiftly dispelled any fears that she would be a barren queen, unable to bear sons as her enemies had often alleged. Eleanor had a theory of her own: that Maude had recognized a kindred soul, for they both were strong-willed women in a world ruled by men, loath to allow others to dictate their destinies. Nor did it hurt that they so rarely lived under the same roof. Acknowledging both the truth and the wry humor of that observation of her husband's, Eleanor laughed softly.

Maude glanced up quizzically from the bishop's letter. "I'm glad to see you are in better spirits. I detected some tension between you and Henry at supper tonight?" Her voice rose questioningly, but she would leave it to Eleanor to satisfy her curiosity or not, too proud to meddle overtly in her son's marriage.

"That must have been when I was tempted to pour my wine into his lap," Eleanor said dryly. She well knew that in any serious clash of wills, Maude would back her son utterly and unconditionally, whether he was in the right or not. But her mother-in-law could still sympathize with minor marital woes, for she'd been a wife, too, and so Eleanor felt free to voice her complaints, one woman to another.

"Ever since we got word of the French queen's death, Harry has been impossible to live with. He has been like a bear with a thorn in his paw, lashing out at anyone who gets within reach, and my patience is well nigh gone."

"That Angevin temper is his father's legacy," Maude said regretfully. "Will seems to have been spared it, but Geoffrey had his share, too. I do understand Henry's disquiet, though. It was troubling enough to learn that the French queen had gotten pregnant, having to worry that she might give Louis a son. But now . . ." Shaking her head, she said, "In some ways, this was the worst possible outcome."

"I know," Eleanor agreed morosely. "If Constance had birthed a son, we were prepared to make another marriage offer, between the lad and our daughter. But how do we stop Louis from making a disastrous marriage of his own now that he's free to wed again?"

Maude nodded, her brows puckering in anxious thought. "I suppose the most dangerous alliance would be with the House of Blois, for they bear Henry a grudge more bitter than gall. Give them half a chance and they might even try to resurrect Stephen's hollow claim to the English crown. But there are other alarming prospects, too. I would not like to see Louis look for a bride amongst the kinswomen of the Count of Toulouse—"

"Jesú forfend!" Eleanor said sharply, and took a deep swallow of wine, for the very thought left an unpleasant taste in her mouth. Before she could express herself further upon the unpalatable subject of Raymond de St Gilles, the door banged open and her husband strode into the solar, trailed by Thomas Becket.

One look at Henry's face and Eleanor half-rose from her seat. "Harry? What is wrong?"

"You will not believe the news out of Paris. Louis has found himself a bride already."

Eleanor was startled. "So soon? Who?"

"Adela, the fifteen-year-old sister of the Counts of Blois and Champagne," Henry said grimly.

Eleanor caught her breath, while Maude let hers out slowly. For a moment, neither woman spoke. Eleanor rallied first, seeking to find a few sparks of comfort midst the ashes. "Well, at least we have time to consider our options whilst Louis mourns for Constance. Mayhap by then we'll have thought of a way to thwart the marriage—"

"Not bloody likely. He plans to wed the girl straightaway."

"God in Heaven!" Maude was genuinely shocked. "His wife has been dead less than a fortnight. Where is his sense of decorum and decency?"

"Buried with Constance, it would seem," Becket said acidly; like Maude, he was deeply offended by such a blatant breach of the proprieties. "It is a sad commentary upon our times when a man of such reputed piety goes right from his wife's funeral to a young bride's bed."

"Lust is not the motivation for this marriage," Eleanor said impatiently. "I doubt that even Cleopatra could kindle Louis's ardor. No, the forces behind this union are far more sinister. Louis has always been one for doing what is proper, what is expected of him. It would never have occurred to him of his own volition to wed again with such unseemly haste. Harry and I have long suspected that he was listening more and more to the House of Blois. What more conclusive proof do we need?"

"My thoughts exactly," Henry said. "And if Theobald and his brother could coax Louis into going against his own nature like this, Christ only knows what they'll prod him into doing next. Disavowing the marriage plans of our children, God rot them!"

The scenario he suggested seemed all too plausible to the others. Seeing upon their faces confirmation of his own fears, Henry cursed again, using words he rarely uttered in his mother's hearing. "I will not let those misbegotten, treacherous whoresons cheat me out of the Vexin," he vowed. "I swear by all that's holy that I will not!"

Stalking the solar as if it were a cage, he paced back and forth while they watched. For Eleanor, there was always something mesmerizing about her husband's bursts of frenetic, creative energy. She often teased him that she could actually hear the wheels turning as his brain accelerated, but she was genuinely fascinated by his ability to cut through excess flesh to the bone. He'd halted abruptly, staring into the hearth's smoldering flames with such a glazed intensity that she knew he was mentally miles away at the French court. When he finally turned around, it was with a smile that put her in mind of cats and stolen cream.

"What have you come up with, Harry?"

"I think," he said, "that Louis is right. There is much to be said, after all, for the holy state of matrimony."

Eleanor blinked, then began to laugh. "Louis will have an apoplectic seizure," she predicted gleefully. "But can you be sure of the Templars?"

"What do you think?" he said, with such utter assurance that she laughed again, never loving him more than at that moment. Only the presence of his mother and chancellor kept her from showing him just how much, then and there.

Maude and Becket had not been as quick to comprehend as Eleanor. They spoke now in unison, in the aggrieved tones of people who feel shut out and do not like it in the least. "What are you going to do?"

Henry's smile was full of mischief, faintly flavored with malice. "I am going," he said, "to invite you to a wedding."

ON ALL SOULS' DAY, the second of November in God's Year 1160, a solemn church ceremony joined in wedlock Henry and Eleanor's eldest son and the daughter of the French king. Because of the extreme youth of the bride and groom, a papal dispensation was required. But it so happened that there were two papal legates then at the English king's court, and they graciously agreed to waive any objections to the union. Louis was not invited to the wedding. Henry explained when asked that they'd assumed Louis was too busy preparing for his own nuptials to attend.

Afterward, there was an elaborate wedding feast in the great hall of

Rouen's castle. Fresh, sweet-smelling rushes had been put down upon the floor, the walls were adorned with richly woven hangings, the trestle tables draped in white linen, set with silver saltcellars and gilded cups and flagons and even knives, for while dinner guests were usually expected to provide their own cutlery, no expense had been spared to make this a memorable meal.

Regrettably, the Church calendar had not cooperated, for All Souls' Day fell on a Wednesday that year, and Wednesday was traditionally a fast day to remind Christians of another infamous Wednesday, when Judas had accepted blood money for his promise to betray the Son of God. Denied the meat that was the fare of choice, the royal cooks labored long and hard to create a fish menu that would still satisfy the highborn guests. The meal consisted of three courses, each containing three or four dishes, and it soon became apparent that the cooks had done themselves proud, both in the quality and variety of the cuisine: baked lampreys; gingered carp; jellied pike in aspic; a spiced salmon pie baked with figs, raisins, and dates; almond rice; cucumber soup; apple and parsnip fritters; and a dish valued all the more for its rarity, sea-swine or porpoise pudding.

Each course concluded with a sugared subtlety sculpted to resemble swans or unicorns, and the servers were kept busy refilling cups with claret and hippocras and a sweet, heavy wine from Cyprus. Minstrels sang and provided music with harp and lute. The fortunate guests agreed happily amongst themselves that this was a meal to savor, one worthy of the tables of the king's chancellor.

Since the little bride was not yet three, it had been wisely decided to excuse her from the revelries, although Hal had been given a seat upon the dais. So far he was acquitting himself well, seduced into good behavior by the sheer novelty of it all and aware, too, that his mother was keeping a sharp eye upon him. The candles turning his bright hair into a crown of gold, he watched his seat-mate, Cardinal William of Pavia, and modeled his manners after the papal legate's. His proud parents beamed at him fondly, but Eleanor prudently concluded that it would be best to send him off to bed before he got tired and cranky and began to act more like a rambunctious five-year-old than a young king in the making.

Hal wasn't the only one on his best behavior. Festivities like this usually bored Henry beyond endurance, for he never liked sitting still for long; even during Mass, he was likely to start squirming on his prayer cushion and whispering to his companions if the priest's sermon was not mercifully brief. Since he had no particular interest in what he ate or drank, he could not see the purpose in lingering over a meal, which was why he was so willing to let Thomas Becket wine and dine guests on his behalf. But this was his son's wedding day, after all, and he wanted it to be a pleasant memory for Hal. And if murmurings of the feast's splendor were to echo all the way to Paris, so much the better.

Reaching for his wine cup, he took a sip, then put it aside. He preferred his wine watered-down, but since he was sharing a cup with Eleanor, he'd deferred to her taste for the products of her Gascony vineyards. The other guests were seated on cushioned benches, but those privileged few upon the dais had the luxury of oaken chairs and Henry leaned back now in his, his gaze sweeping the table.

His mother was chatting amiably with the papal legates, Becket slicing bread for Petronilla, Eleanor beckoning discreetly to Hal's nurse, the Bishop of Lisieux sharing a joke with the Archbishop of Rouen. At the far end of the table were two knights whose presence had stirred speculation and envy among the other guests. A seat upon the dais was a highly coveted honor, and there were many in the hall who felt themselves to be more deserving than Robert de Pirou and Tostes de St Omer. They were eating heartily of the dessert just set before them, a delectable concoction of cream of almonds and pears floating in heavy syrup, taking care not to get stains upon the white tunics and blood-red crosses of the Templars.

Leaning over, Eleanor laid her hand on Henry's arm. "The Templars seem to be enjoying themselves," she said softly. "I assume that they had no misgivings about yielding up the castles of the Vexin to you, then?"

"They were quite reasonable," Henry said blandly. "And why not? They were to hold the castles only until Louis's daughter wed our son. And as two papal legates can attest, that condition has now been met."

Eleanor's fingers slid along his wrist, began to caress his palm. "I think you could outwit the Devil himself on a good day," she murmured and laughed when he reminded her that the Counts of Anjou were alleged to trace their descent from the Devil's daughter.

"My father liked to tell that story," he said, grinning. "Mayhap we ought to name our next daughter after her? How would you fancy adding a Melusine to our brood, love?"

"Only if you agree to name our next son Lucifer," she parried and Henry laughed loudly enough to turn heads in their direction. Despite his chaplain's gentle chiding to thank the Almighty for his manifold blessings, he tended to take God's Favor for granted. But as he looked now into Eleanor's shining eyes, he felt a sudden surge of gratitude for all that was

his: an empire that stretched from the Scottish borders to the Mediterranean Sea, the most legendary queen since Helen of Troy, sons to found
the greatest dynasty Christendom had ever known.

Lifting Eleanor's hand to his mouth, he kissed her fingers, one by one,
and then raised his voice for silence. "I would have us drink," he said, "to
the health and happiness of my beloved son, England's next king."

WHEN LOUIS LEARNED of the wedding in Rouen, he was furious. He could not do much to punish Henry and Eleanor, but he struck
back at the Templars, expelling their Order from Paris. Theobald of Blois
then convinced him that this was not enough and they began to fortify
Theobald's castle at Chaumont-sur-Loire, casting an eye toward Henry's
lands in Touraine.

This was a mistake. Not bothering to summon the knights of Anjou,
Henry hired mercenaries instead and swooped down upon Chaumont.
Theobald had boasted that the fortress was impregnable, but Henry took
it in just three days, sending shudders of alarm reverberating as far as the
walls of Paris.

CHAPTER TEN

January 1161
Nôtre-Dame-du-Pré
Rouen, Normandy

HENRY CROSSED to the settle and kissed his mother on the cheek. The fact that she'd received him in her private chamber warned him that she had a lecture in mind; she would never berate him, a crowned king and God's anointed, before witnesses.

"Did you grant that charter to the canons of St Bartholomew, Henry?"

"I did, Mother. You know I always heed your advice."

Aware that she was being teased, Maude ignored the bait, refusing to be diverted. "I assume your men are being fed in the hall? What of your chancellor? Did he accompany you to the priory?"

"No, I sent Thomas to Caen, as I've decided to found a leper hospital there." Henry was not deceived by the casualness of her query. So Thomas was the quarry for this hunt. "Did you wish to speak with him, Mother?" he asked innocently. "He'll be back in Rouen within the fortnight."

"I have a bone to pick with your chancellor . . . as you've guessed. But I have one to pick with you, too, Henry. I have received a distressing letter from the Archbishop of Canterbury. He tells me that his illness is mortal, and it is his dearest wish that he see the two men he loves so well, you and Thomas, ere he dies. Yet he says he has been entreating you both for months to return to England, entreating you in vain."

"I would if I could," Henry said tersely, trying and failing to keep a defensive note from creeping into his voice. "You know how busy I've been, what demands are made upon my time. Not only did I have to construct three castles at Gisors, Neaupple, and Château-Neuf-sur-Epte, but I also had to lay siege to Chaumont Castle, and then fortify Amboise and Fretteville. Aside from holding a brief Christmas court at Le Mans, I've been all but sleeping in the saddle for months."

"I understand that, Henry. Yet surely you could have spared Thomas? It is his presence that Theobald truly yearns for. You are his king, but Thomas was like a son to him."

"Again, I can only repeat that I would if I could." Henry sounded irritated, but evasive, too, and Maude subjected him to a moment of intent scrutiny.

"Thomas does not want to return to England, does he?"

Henry frowned. "It is not as simple as that. Thomas harbors a deep affection for the archbishop, has fond memories of his years in Theobald's service. But he serves the Crown now . . . and serves it well, I might add. I have need of his talents, do not—"

"I do not believe," Maude said impatiently, "that you would have denied him if he'd asked you for leave to visit the archbishop on his deathbed, a good and godly man to whom he owes so much." When Henry did not respond, she shook her head in dismayed perplexity. "I should have guessed! The archbishop's letter made mention of the multitude of excuses you and Becket have been offering for his absence. The truth is that he cannot be bothered to go back."

Henry's scowl deepened. He'd long suspected that his mother had no liking for his chancellor, and she'd just confirmed it by her disdainful use of Thomas's surname; sensitive to slights, real or imagined, about his humble origins, the chancellor preferred to call himself Thomas of London.

"You are not being fair," he insisted. "Thomas does grieve for the archbishop's malady, as do I. But he has vast responsibilities, ones that go beyond overseeing the chancellory. He advises me on a host of other matters, too. I think it is greatly to his credit that he takes these duties so seriously."

Maude's sense of decorum did not permit her to snort or roll her eyes, but her skepticism showed plainly upon her face. "Does it not concern you, Henry, that your chancellor shrugs off old loyalties with such ease?"

"No," Henry said and annoyed her then by grinning. "He is not likely to find a greater patron than the king, after all!"

"I want you to promise me, Henry," she persisted, "that you will do your utmost to see that your chancellor is at the archbishop's deathbed."

He hesitated, for although he often handled the truth without care, he did not want to lie to her. "I will try," he said at last, and Maude had to be satisfied with that.

A PALE APRIL SUN dappled the ancient mulberry tree in the courtyard of the Archbishop of Canterbury's palace. Men hastened to assist the Bishop of Rochester in dismounting, showing more than the usual deference due his rank; he was also the younger brother of the dying Archbishop. As he was ushered into the great hall, he became aware of the somber atmosphere, more so than on past visits. Monks daubed with napkins at swollen, reddened eyes, and none seemed willing to meet Rochester's gaze. He glanced toward the door that led to the archbishop's private chambers at the east end of the hall. But before he could move, it swung open and John of Salisbury, the archbishop's private secretary, emerged from the stairwell. One look at his haggard, tear-streaked face and Rochester knew.

"I am sorry, my lord," John said softly. And it was then that the great bells of the cathedral began to toll, slow and stately peals that would soon be echoing across England, mourning the passing of Canterbury's archbishop.

IN MAY OF THAT YEAR, fighting broke out again in the Vexin between the kings of England and France. In September, Henry's queen gave birth to their sixth child and second daughter at Domfront Castle in Normandy; they named the baby Eleanor. In October, the warring kings met at Fréteval and made a fleeting, fragile peace.

SITUATED BY THE RIVER VARENNE, Nôtre Dame sur l'Eau was one of the oldest churches in Domfront; it was also prosperous and well maintained. Eleanor had deemed it suitable for the baptism of her daughter and namesake two months earlier. It was in honor of that auspicious occasion that Henry had chosen to hear Mass at Nôtre Dame on this cold, blustery morning in Martinmas week. Beaming at this public display of royal favor, the priest accompanied the king and his chancellor as far as the road, as did his parishioners and passersby drawn by the commotion. Henry ordered the distribution of alms, but as they rode up the hill toward the castle, he found himself being chided by his chancellor for not having been more generous.

"I am very openhanded in my alms giving," he protested, "always provide a tithe for God's poor."

"Yes, you do," Becket acknowledged. "But you should ever bear in mind how the Lord Christ admonished his disciples: 'Beware of practicing your piety before men in order to be seen by them; for then you will have no reward from your Father Who is in Heaven. Thus, when you give alms, sound no trumpet before you, as the hypocrites do in the synagogues and in the streets, that they may be praised by men. . . . But when you give alms, do not let your left hand know what your right hand is doing, so that your alms may be in secret; and your Father Who sees in secret will reward you.'"

Henry sighed, thinking that when Thomas was in one of his sententious moods, he could put the sainted Bernard of Clairvaux to shame. "This from the man who gives alms out so lavishly and publicly that he's caused at least two riots in the streets of London!"

Becket glanced over his shoulder and grinned. "Ah, but that is different. I am acting as the king's instrument, bestowing largesse lavishly so that credit might rebound to the greater glory of my sovereign!"

Henry stifled a laugh. "I am indeed fortunate to have such a selfless, benevolent servant, willing to make such sacrifices upon my behalf." By now they were riding along the High Street and he happened to notice an elderly beggar, shivering in ragged, dirty garments as he trudged toward them. "Do you see that old man? How poor he is, how scantily clad? Would it not be an act of charity to give him a thick, warm cloak?"

"It would indeed, my lord king."

Reining in his stallion, Henry smiled at the old man. "Tell me, friend, would you like a good cloak?"

The beggar blinked up at him warily, for he'd long ago learned that the humor of the highborn could be both incomprehensible and dangerous. "Yes, my lord," he mumbled, feeling it was safer to agree with whatever craziness they were up to.

Henry grinned at Becket. "There you are, a God-given opportunity. But you shall have all the credit for this act of charity." Leaning out of the saddle, he grasped the hood of the chancellor's new mantle and pulled. Becket resisted and a tug of war ensued, with both men at imminent risk of falling off their horses as they struggled over the cloak. The rest of Henry's retinue had ridden up, shouting questions, baffled by the sight of their king and his chancellor tussling like rowdy apprentices. When it became apparent that Henry was determined to prevail, Becket yielded up his mantle, although with obvious reluctance.

After calming his fractious stallion, Henry gave the mantle to the astonished beggar and then explained to the others what had occurred. Midst much laughter, several of the men offered the chancellor their own mantles. He accepted a cloak from one of his chancellory clerks, casting a regretful glance back at his lost mantle, a finely woven wool of scarlet and grey, and when Henry jokingly reminded him that "'The Lord loveth a cheerful giver,'" he laughed, too, saying that he was honored to have no less a tutor than the King of England instructing him in "'the good and right way.'"

Clutching the cloak to his chest, the beggar found himself surrounded by men who'd rarely had a kind word for him, much less a coin. Now, though, they were smiling and slapping him on the back, congratulating him on his good fortune. Several even offered to buy him a drink at the local tavern. He was sorely tempted, but as he looked at these spectators crowding around him, he saw how their eyes caressed and coveted his fine new mantle and he realized that he who'd had nothing now had cause for fear. His anxious gaze flitted from face to face, seeking a protector. His relief was vast when a priest stepped from the crowd and suggested that he give thanks to Almighty God for this blessing.

With some difficulty, the priest disengaged him from his newfound friends, steering him across the High Street toward the church precincts. "You must be heedful, Leonard, for there are those who would take advantage of your good fortune. Better that you shun those ne'er-do-wells who are always to be found in taverns and alehouses, no matter the time of day. They will be seeking to get the chancellor's cloak, by guile or force if need be. It might be better if you gave it as an offering to the church . . . safer for you, I mean. I am sure we can find another cloak for you in the collection for the poor, one that is warm but not so tempting to the greedy or godless."

Stumbling to keep pace with the priest, Leonard was only half-listening. He was still bewildered, his thoughts in a whirl, his fingers hesitantly stroking the soft scarlet wool as if he expected it to be snatched from his grasp at any moment. Halting to catch his breath, he said beseechingly, "Those great lords . . . who were they, Father? Who *were* they?"

CHAPTER ELEVEN

⚜

February 1162
Rouen, Normandy

HE EMPRESS MAUDE was very pleased that Henry had
scheduled a Great Council to be held in late February at
Rouen, for his peripatetic itinerary would have given a nomad
pause. Rarely in one place for more than a few days, he was usually to be
found on the roads of his vast realms, hearing petitioners and dispensing
royal justice and punishing recalcitrant vassals with the same zest that he
displayed in hunting for stags and wild boar. Maude cherished their infrequent reunions, and Shrove Tuesday got off to a joyful start when she
learned upon awakening that her son had reached Rouen the night before.

It had been snowing sporadically since midnight, and the priory garth
was glistening in the morning sun. Maude's spirits dimmed briefly at the
sight of her horse litter. Swinging like a hammock between the shafts, the
litter was a more comfortable way to travel than by cart, and although men
resorted to it only if they were infirm or elderly, it was an acceptable
mode of transportation for women. But to Maude, the litter was incontrovertible proof of her failing health, and she was tight-lipped as her attendants assisted her to climb inside. Was it truly more than twenty years

since she'd fled the siege of Winchester, riding astride like a man with an enemy army in pursuit?

The priory of Nôtre-Dame-du-Pré was located on the outskirts of Rouen, and the castle walls were soon in sight. In the inner bailey, servants hastily brought out a small stool for Maude's convenience. But as she straightened up, a snowball whizzed by her head, thudding into the litter's open door and splattering her mantle.

There was stifled laughter from the bystanders. Maude saw no humor in it, though, and swung around to confront the culprit, only to find herself face to face with her son. "Henry!"

Coming forward with a guilty grin, Henry gave her a quick hug. "Sorry, Mother, my aim was off."

"He was trying to hit me, and missed by a mile!" Eleanor sauntered up to greet her mother-in-law, laughing over Maude's shoulder at her husband. She was flushed with the cold, her face becomingly framed in a hood of soft ermine, snow drops melting on her skin like jeweled tears. She looked astonishingly young and very beautiful and utterly alien to Maude, who could not imagine why a queen and mother would so forget her dignity by engaging in a public snowball fight with her own husband.

"Have you both lost your senses? Surely you can find more appropriate ways to amuse yourselves," she scolded, "than this unseemly tomfoolery!"

"You're absolutely right," Henry agreed, but his grin gave him away even before he added, "Eleanor started it."

"Who dumped snow down whose neck? The truth, Maude, is that Harry could not resist the sight of that unsullied snow. He had to leave his footprints out in it, for all the world to see."

Henry laughed, then escorted Maude away from the horse litter. "Did you ever see such a splendid day, Mother? Look at the sun on the snow; it is well nigh bright enough to blind you. Let's go into the gardens. I have something I want to discuss with you both."

Maude was much more susceptible now to cold than she'd been in her youth, but she was too proud to admit it. In a sense, it was rather flattering that her son seemed oblivious to the increasing frailties of age, still seeing her as the robust, resolute woman who'd known neither fear nor forgiveness, England's uncrowned, cheated queen. The gardens were deserted, but they did have an austere beauty, the barren earth blanketed now under sparkling drifts, the bare shrubs dusted in white, holly bushes gleaming like emeralds against the snow. Escorting the women toward a bench, Henry brushed it clear, then had to blow upon his hands to warm them, for he rarely bothered with gloves.

"I want to talk to you," he said, "about finding a new Archbishop of Canterbury."

Maude refrained from pointing out that it was about time; the See of Canterbury had been vacant for the past ten months. "As I've told you," she said, "you could do no better than the Bishop of Hereford. Gilbert Foliot would be a fine choice, erudite and intelligent and ascetic, as befitting a man of God."

"I considered Foliot, but I have a better candidate."

"Surely not the Bishop of Winchester? I know he is one of England's senior churchmen, Henry, but the man could teach Judas about betrayal!"

"Do you truly think I'd so honor Stephen's brother? No, Mother, I have someone else in mind, an astute administrator who is both shrewd and subtle and utterly trustworthy."

Eleanor's smile was faintly skeptical. "Do not keep us in suspense, Harry. Who is this unlikely paragon of virtue and efficiency?"

"Thomas Becket."

Both women stared at him "Is this one of your jests, Henry?" Maude sounded uncertain, for his humor had always eluded her. But Eleanor read him better than his mother did, and she'd stiffened, her eyes riveted upon his face.

"No, it is not a jest," he said, somewhat impatiently, for this was not the response he'd expected. "I am quite serious. As my chancellor, Thomas has proven his worth more times than I could begin to count. He is clever, loyal, and occasionally crafty. Why would he not make a superior archbishop?"

"Possibly because he is not even a priest." As soon as Eleanor heard herself, she knew she'd struck the wrong note. Sarcasm would only put her husband on the defensive. But she'd been taken by surprise, and was vexed that she'd not seen this coming. For the idea did make a certain skewed sense. Harry and Becket had worked well in tandem for the past seven years. The inevitable clashes between the Church and Crown would be much easier to resolve if England's king and England's archbishop were in rare accord and of one mind—Harry's mind.

Almost as if guessing her thoughts, Henry said, "I am not seeking a puppet. Canterbury's Holy See cannot be governed by a man without stature or integrity. Thomas has both, and more innate ability and common sense than any bishop in Christendom. If it is just a matter of taking vows, that is remedied easily enough."

"I think not," Maude said gravely. As a young boy, Henry had thought she'd sounded verily like God at such moments, blessed with the divine certainty unknown to mere mortals and impossible to argue with. But that awed child was now a man in his twenty-ninth year, and Henry reacted with annoyance, not intimidation.

"Why not, Mother?"

"Thomas Becket can indeed take holy vows, as you say. Nor would I deny that he has been endowed by Our Creator with great gifts. But I do not believe he has a prelate's temperament. He is a worldly man, urbane and pleasure-loving. He has a liking for fine wines and good food, for hunting and hawking, for well-bred horses and furred mantles and silken tunics. And as Archdeacon of Canterbury, he has neglected his spiritual duties shamefully. Keep him as your chancellor, Henry, for he is well suited to that role."

"Are you saying there have never been luxury-loving prelates? Remind my mother, Eleanor, about the French king's most revered adviser. When did Abbot Suger ever deprive himself of a soft feather bed or a roasted partridge?"

"The good abbot did have a liking for his comforts," Eleanor conceded reluctantly. She was not happy with the direction the conversation had taken, for she did not share Maude's qualms about Becket's high living. Her objections to the man were more visceral and less easily articulated. She neither liked nor trusted him and begrudged his role as her husband's most trusted confidant. Taking another tack, she said, "I do not understand, Harry, why you are so willing to dispense with Becket's services. Where will you find another chancellor of his capabilities?"

"I have no intention of losing my chancellor. I shall seek a dispensation from the Pope allowing Thomas to act in both capacities. Why not? Louis's chancellor, de Champfleury, did not resign his post after being elected to the bishopric of Soissons. And the chancellor of the Holy Roman Emperor is also the Archbishop of Cologne. Once we find a reliable deputy chancellor, I see no reason why Thomas cannot serve both me and the Almighty."

Henry smiled at that, but neither woman did.

"But what if the Crown's needs and the Church's needs should diverge? What then, Harry?"

He shrugged. "I am sure accommodations can be reached. Even his enemies would not deny that Thomas is a skilled diplomat. And I have no intention of warring with the Church as Stephen so foolishly did. I will be quite content to keep papal interference to a minimum and to reform some of the worst abuses of the ecclesiastical courts. Who knows my mind in these matters better than Thomas? So who would be better qualified to carry them out?"

Eleanor was not sure how to respond, for his trust in Becket was boundless and hers was meager. "Even the most skilled jongleur can keep only so many balls aloft without dropping one. You may be asking too much of Becket."

"I agree with Eleanor," Maude said somberly. "The other examples you cited—in France and Germany—are not quite the same, Henry. The Archbishop of Canterbury is the spiritual head of the English Church. That is a great blessing and a great burden, too. I truly believe that Gilbert Foliot would be a far better choice, and I urge you to reconsider."

Henry was irritated that they both seemed unable to see as clearly as he did. "I am looking for more than an archbishop. I am seeking an ally, too, and who better for that than Thomas? If I can trust him with my son and heir, why should I not trust him with Canterbury's holy see?"

Eleanor's hands clasped in her lap, tightly enough for her rings to pinch her fingers. Henry had recently decided to place Hal in Becket's keeping, for he was just days from his seventh birthday, too old to remain with his mother. She'd agreed that it was time for their son to begin his formal education, and Becket had been the logical choice. It irked her, nonetheless, to hear Becket call Hal his "adopted son," and her earlier compliance now came back to haunt her. "If we are unhappy with Becket's tutelage of our son, we can reclaim him. But what could you do if you become dissatisfied with your new archbishop?"

An old memory surfaced for Maude, buried in the back of her brain for more than fifty years. "When I was wed to the Holy Roman Emperor, Heinrich rewarded his chancellor with the archbishopric of Reims, and the result was a grievous disappointment. Adalbert had been tireless in defending the Crown's prerogatives, but once he became an archbishop, he changed almost overnight, began to argue for radical reforms and sided with my husband's adversaries."

Eleanor gave her mother-in-law a grateful smile, but Henry was not impressed. "Obviously, Heinrich did not know Adalbert as well as he thought. But for seven years, I have been closer to Thomas than to my own brother. I have looked into his heart, seen into his soul. We have worked well together in the past and I do not doubt we can continue to do so in the future."

Conceding defeat, at least for the time being, Eleanor got slowly to her feet. "It has begun to snow again, and I think we all need to thaw out by the fire. Will you put off a final decision on this, Harry? With so much at stake, you want to be utterly sure you've made the right choice. I urge you to think upon it for a while longer."

Maude added her voice to Eleanor's, and Henry agreed that he would ponder further upon the matter. But they could take little comfort from his assurance, for they well knew that once he made up his mind, he did not often change it.

FALAISE WAS AWASH in white-gold sunlight. From the castle's solar, Henry gazed out upon a cloudless sky, as bright as the April bluebells lining the banks of the River Ante. Below in the gardens, his eldest son was romping with Eleanor's greyhounds. Becket had brought Hal to Falaise to bid farewell to his parents, and then they would depart for London, where the barons were to swear a solemn oath of fealty to the boy, acknowledging him as the future King of England. Henry watched his son's antics with a smile, and then turned back to his chancellor.

"If the weather holds, you should have a smooth Channel crossing, Thomas."

"God Willing. We'll depart for Barfleur on the morrow if that meets with your approval?"

Henry nodded. "Eleanor and I know our lad will be in good hands. Now I think it is time we talked of an English see that has been vacant too long." He was sure that what he was about to say would come as no surprise to Becket, for rumors had been circulating about his intentions for several months, fueled by his recent consultation with England's most senior bishops. "I am sending my justiciar back with you to England, Thomas. I have instructed him to advise the monks of Christ Church, Canterbury, that I would be greatly pleased if they elect you as their archbishop and greatly displeased if they do not."

Becket's smile was self-deprecating, rings glittering on his fingers as he gestured to his finely woven, fashionable tunic and buckled shoes. "And a right saintly archbishop I'd make, would I not?"

"You can switch to sackcloth and ashes if you like," Henry joked. "In fact, that might be one way to impress the monks. For whilst your election is a foregone conclusion, in all honesty, you'll not be a popular choice. When I talked to the English bishops about this, they were rather underwhelmed." Tactfully neglecting to mention that his own wife and mother were among Becket's opponents, he said, "You need to know this,

Thomas, for you will have to prove yourself to many skeptics. I can make you an archbishop. What you do with it, though, will be up to you."

Becket was no longer smiling. "And did it not trouble you, Harry, that none shared your enthusiasm for elevating me to Canterbury's Holy See? Did you never think that they could be right?"

"No, I did not. Shall I tell you why? Because I know you better than they do, plain and simple." Henry straddled a chair, grey eyes puzzled, probing. "What is the matter, Thomas? Clearly you have misgivings . . . why? And do not tell me you are overwhelmed by the high honor or such blather. You have your virtues, but modesty is not amongst them. So what makes you so wary?"

"I value our friendship, Harry. I would not want to put it at risk."

"Nor would I. But why should this jeopardize it? Yes, circumstances will change. What of it? As well as we know each other, what surprises are there likely to be?"

"I wish I shared your certainty. It is that . . . that I do not think you have foreseen the possible consequences." Becket's slight stammer was much more pronounced now, an unmistakable sign of tension. "Are you so sure that I can serve both you and the Almighty?"

Henry stared at him and then laughed shortly, amusement warring with exasperation. "I can assure you that I do not see God as a rival. That prideful I am not! If those are your qualms, you can lay them aside. The Almighty and I will not be in contention for your immortal soul."

Becket's smile was a polite flicker, and Henry's patience ran out. "Jesú, Thomas, I am offering you the archbishopric of Canterbury, the greatest plum in Christendom! I did not think I'd have to talk you into it. So you'd best tell me now if you're crazed enough to refuse."

Becket smiled more convincingly this time. "When you do put it that way . . ."

Henry studied the older man and then nodded in satisfaction. "So it is settled then."

"Yes," Becket agreed, "it is settled."

JUNE THAT YEAR in Wales was cool and wet, with sightings of the sun as scarce as dragon's teeth. The last Monday in the month dawned to skies greyer than December, and it went downhill from there. In midmorning, a rainstorm swept through the Conwy Valley, and it was still drenching Trefriw when Hywel rode in. His arrival created even more of a stir than usual, for in addition to his customary attendants and servants, he was accompanied by six kinsmen: his son, Caswallon; his foster brothers, Peryf and Brochfael; and no fewer than three of his half-brothers, the raffish Cynan and Maelgwn and the sobersided Iorwerth. Enid was in a dither, determined to entertain them in a style worthy of their rank, not drawing a calm breath until these unexpected and highborn guests were settled comfortably in the great hall with towels to dry themselves off, mead, and cushions.

"I assume you can put us all up for the night," Hywel asked, beckoning for Ranulf to join him in the window seat.

The question was a mere formality, for hospitality was a sacred duty among the Welsh. Even had Hywel led an army into Trefriw, they'd have been accommodated. "I suppose," Ranulf grumbled, "you can sleep out in the stables."

"Spoken like a true Englishman," Hywel gibed. "But where is your wife? She is the one I really came to see. Is she off visiting her sister?"

"No . . . she is in our private chambers, lying down."

Hywel's gaze had been drifting around the hall, where Peryf and Cynan had begun an arm-wrestling contest. But at that, his eyes cut sharply back toward Ranulf's face. "Is she ailing?"

Ranulf was staring into the depths of his mead cup. "She miscarried a fortnight ago, Hywel."

"Ah, Ranulf . . . I am truly sorry. I did not know she was with child again."

"We'd told none but the family. She was only in the third month . . ."

Hywel groped for words of consolation. "To lose a babe is surely one of life's greatest sorrows. But mayhap in time, she'll conceive again."

"She is thirty-nine," Ranulf said, and although the words themselves were neutral, his tone was without hope.

"So? Queen Eleanor was thirty-nine when she birthed another daughter last year, was she not?"

"Eleanor is not like other women. Childbirth seems to come as easily to her as kingdoms do."

"She might argue with you about that, Ranulf. I've heard more than one woman claim that if men were the ones bearing children, mankind would have died out with Adam."

Ranulf was suddenly very glad that Hywel was there; smiles and laughter had been absent from his household of late. "Ought I to extend my condolences for your father's marriage to the Lady Cristyn?"

Hywel heaved a dramatic sigh. "I suppose it was inevitable. But the

Lady Gwladys was scarcely in her grave ere Cristyn began planning the wedding. I half-expected her to burst into the church during the funeral service, demanding that the priest say the marriage vows first."

"Do you call her Stepmama now?" Ranulf asked innocently and then ducked, laughing, when Hywel sent a cushion whipping past his head. "So . . . how is life in the hive now that there is a new queen bee? You look hale and hearty enough, so I assume the Lady Cristyn has not been slipping hemlock into your mead?"

"No . . . but then I drink sparingly when I dine with Cristyn. In a way, I cannot blame her for wanting to protect her cubs. A pity they are such worthless whelps. God help Gwynedd if either of them ever gains my father's crown. Fortunately for Wales, I do not intend to let that happen."

"I'll drink to that." Ranulf clinked his cup playfully against Hywel's. "I surely do hope you are Gwynedd's next king. I'd hate to think I've been cultivating your friendship all these years for naught."

"You ought to have some money on the outcome, Ranulf, for few wagers are so certain of success. Peryf is offering odds of two to one in my favor. Of course if you fancy more risk for your money, he says the odds on Little Brother Rhodri are so high not even his mother would chance a wager!"

Ranulf laughed again. Owain and Cristyn's youngest son had recently turned seventeen, and by all accounts, he was proving to be a handful. "I've heard that Rhodri is becoming even more insufferable these days than Davydd, as hard as that is to believe."

"Believe it. Davydd does have a brain beneath all that bluster. But I doubt that there is much hope for Rhodri, not the way he's been strutting and swaggering about this spring. I've seen barnyard cocks show more sense. Hellfire, even I showed more sense at seventeen!"

Under Enid's sharp eye, her serving maid was offering their guests food hastily collected from the kitchen. When she reached Ranulf and Hywel now, they helped themselves to napkins and hot wafers. Sitting back in the window seat, Hywel gave his friend a curious smile. "So . . . what do you think of Canterbury's new archbishop?"

"Harry finally selected someone, did he? Who is the lucky man . . . Gilbert Foliot?"

Hywel blinked. "You have not heard? You mean I am better informed for once about English affairs than you? And here I've been assuring my father that you were worth keeping around for your superior connections to the English king's court!"

"So much for your celebrated political acumen. Now that I think upon it, I've not gotten any letters from Harry or Rainald or my sister for some weeks. Even my niece has been lax about writing and Maud is usually my most reliable source."

"Ah . . . that reminds me." Swallowing the last of his wafer, Hywel fumbled within his tunic. "I have a letter for you."

At the sight of that familiar seal, Ranulf's eyebrows rose. "Since when are you delivering my niece's mail?"

Hywel met his gaze guilelessly. "I happened to be in Chester recently, and naturally I stopped by to pay my respects to the countess."

"Naturally," Ranulf echoed dryly. "We both know you're the very soul of courtesy." Politely putting the letter away to be read later, he took a sip of mead, regarding Hywel with a sardonic smile. "So you found out about Canterbury's new archbishop from Maud?"

Hywel nodded. "You're probably one of the last to hear, for this news has been spreading faster than any brushfire. The Lady Maud says England is talking of nothing else, and once I brought word to my father's court at Aber, that was the only topic of conversation there, too."

"Why? Did Harry make so controversial a choice? Whom did he pick?"

"Thomas Becket."

Ranulf sat up straight. "You are serious? He truly chose Becket?"

Hywel nodded again, happily; he liked nothing better than being the bearer of tidings sure to startle. "The Christ Church monks elected him in late May. On June second, he took holy vows, and the next day he was consecrated as Canterbury's archbishop. From priest to archbishop in just one day; now that is what I call a spectacular promotion! He seems to think so, too, for his first official act was to decree that the day of his consecration will be a feast day from now on, in honor of the Holy Trinity."

Ranulf was silent for several moments. "I need time to think upon this," he confessed. "For once, Hywel, you were not exaggerating in the least. This will have people marveling from Rome to Rouen, and with good reason."

"That it will," Hywel agreed, thinking of his father's jubilant reaction to the news. "According to your niece, the king forced Becket upon the monks and bishops. Few think he has the makings of a good priest, much less an archbishop. But they dared not protest, for they knew your nephew had his mind set on this. Only Gilbert Foliot spoke up, with a very sour jest indeed, saying that the king had wrought a miracle, turning a soldier and worldly courtier into a holy man of God."

"Well," Ranulf said slowly, "Harry has always been one for the bold stroke, and this is nothing if not bold. I can see the logic in it, for Becket is one of the very few people whom Harry truly trusts. I can also see the risks. This will be all or nothing, either a brilliant success or an utter disaster, nothing in-between."

Hywel thought Ranulf's assessment was right on target; they differed only in which results they were hoping for. Before Hywel could respond, Ranulf was getting to his feet. Turning in the window seat, Hywel saw why; Rhiannon had just entered the hall. He stayed still for a few moments, giving Ranulf a chance to exchange a private greeting with his wife, and then joined them.

Even if Ranulf had not told him about the miscarriage, he'd have guessed that something was amiss. Rhiannon was paler than moonlight, her eyes heavy-lidded and shadow-smudged, and her smile the saddest Hywel had ever seen. "Come over here, darling," he said before she could speak. "Sit with us in the window seat."

Rhiannon had meant merely to make a brief appearance, for courtesy's sake. But Hywel would not be denied. He and Ranulf ushered her across the hall, as solicitously as if she were a queen, taking her wet mantle and finding cushions for her, offering their own cups of mead. Hywel then called for Ranulf's uncle to fetch his harp. Beaming with delight, Rhodri did.

The hall quieted as soon as the others realized Hywel was going to perform. But Hywel paid the audience no mind. Drawing a stool up, he began to strum the harp, a haunting, plaintive melody that would linger in the memory long after the music ended. "A love poem for the Lady Rhiannon," he said softly.

I love a rounded fortress, strongly built;
A lovely girl there will not let me sleep.
A bold, determined man will reach the place.
The wild wave breaks there loudly at its side.
My fair, accomplished lady's lovely home.
It rises bright and shining from the sea.
And she shines all the year upon the house.
One year in furthest Arfon, under Snowdon!
He wins no mantle who looks not at silk.
I will love no one more than I love her.
If she would grant her favor for my verse,
Then I should be beside her every night.

When the song died away, the hall erupted into applause. But for Hywel and Ranulf, the only reaction that mattered was Rhiannon's, and she was smiling through tears.

IN SEPTEMBER, Henry met with the French king at the papal court in exile of Pope Alexander III, who'd been driven out of Rome by the Holy Roman Emperor and forced to take refuge at Montpellier in France. The meeting was civil, but the wounds left by the Toulouse war were slow healing. After that, Henry moved south to the great abbey of Deols, and then joined Eleanor at Chinon Castle.

As SOON AS ELEANOR entered the great hall, she knew something unusual had happened. People were clustered together, voices raised. The first person she recognized was her husband's half-brother. Hamelin was one of Geoffrey of Anjou's bastards, acknowledged and well educated by the count until his untimely death, and then taken care of afterward by Henry. Hamelin was now in his early twenties and bore a remarkable resemblance to his other half-brother, Will. He did not have Will's equable temperament, though, was far more excitable and impulsive. Eleanor liked him, for if he was quick to fire up, he was also quick to forgive, and his joyful zest for life usually made him good company. But at the moment, his cheerful, freckled countenance was clouded, and when Eleanor drew him aside, he could barely contain his indignation.

"What has happened, Hamelin?"

"You see that Augustinian canon over there? He was sent by Thomas Becket to return the king's great seal!"

Eleanor was taken aback. "Are you saying that Becket has resigned the chancellorship?"

"Yes, my lady, he did. No letter, either, just the great seal. And when the king demanded to know why, his messenger said only that he felt scarcely equal to the cares of one great office, much less two." Hamelin's devotion to Henry was absolute, and he shook his head angrily. "Can you believe such ingratitude, Madame?"

"Yes," Eleanor said tersely. "Where is Harry now?" When Hamelin shrugged and shook his head again, she went swiftly in search of her husband. The hunt proved harder than she'd expected. Kings were rarely able to escape the constant surveillance of the curious, but no one seemed to have seen Henry. It was only by chance that she happened to glance upward, saw him standing alone on the castle battlements.

Gusting winds sent her skirts whipping about her ankles, billowing out her mantle behind her. She stayed close to the parapet wall; although she would never admit it, she had a dislike of heights. The sun was redder than blood, haloed by flaming clouds as it blazed a path toward the distant horizon. Normally such a splendid sunset would have caught Eleanor's eye, but now she never even noticed. "Harry?"

He half-turned, glancing toward her and then away. The view was breathtaking. Far below, the blue slate roofs and church spires of the town were still visible in the day's waning light, and the river shone like polished brass as it flowed west to join with the Loire. Eleanor knew, though, that her husband was blind to the valley's beauty. The hot color had yet to fade from his face, still scorching the skin above his cheekbones, and the hand resting on the merlon wall had clenched into a fist.

"Hamelin told me that Becket has resigned the chancellorship."

He nodded, almost imperceptibly.

She hesitated, for in his present raw mood, whatever she said was likely to be taken wrong. But when she touched his arm, compelling him to meet her eyes, she saw in his face as much hurt as anger, and she found herself doing something she'd never have envisioned: making excuses for Thomas Becket. "What he said may well be true, Harry. He may feel overwhelmed by the obligations and duties of his office. It must be daunting to know that all are looking to him for spiritual guidance, for he was thrust into this role, not bred for it. If men find it hard at first to move from the plains up into the mountains, mayhap he needs time to adjust to the rarefied air on the heights of Canterbury."

Henry frowned, but found her words were not so easy to dismiss. "I suppose there could be something in what you say," he conceded grudgingly. "Thomas has always had to be the best at whatever he does, satisfied by nothing less than perfection. Mayhap he truly does fear that he could not do justice to the chancellorship and the archbishopric, too."

Sliding his arm around her waist, he drew her in against him, and they watched together as the sun disappeared behind the trees. After some moments of silence, he said, "I still do not understand why Thomas did not tell me what he meant to do."

And for that question, Eleanor had no convincing answer.

CHAPTER TWELVE

May 1163
Rouen, Normandy

*M*AUDE SIGNALED to her servants to bring in the next course. Her cooks had been laboring since dawn, for she wanted this dinner to be an exceptionally fine one. Her guests were deserving of only the best, for they were family: her brother Ranulf, his wife and children, her son Will, and her niece and namesake, Maud, Countess of Chester.

The meal was an obvious success; they were eating the stuffed goose with gusto. Maude had not met Ranulf's wife before, and had never understood why he'd chosen to wed a woman without sight. She'd occasionally wondered how Rhiannon coped with the challenges of daily living, but if her behavior at the dinner table was any indication, she managed surprisingly well. Of course it helped that it was customary for two guests to share a trencher; Rhiannon's seat-mate was her husband, and he provided what assistance she needed with inconspicuous adroitness.

Watching as Rhiannon carefully laid a bone on the trencher's edge, Maude smiled approvingly. Growing to womanhood at the imperial German court, she'd learned to place a high value upon etiquette and decorum, and she decided now that her Welsh sister-in-law's manners were quite satisfactory. For certes, better than what passed for table manners in England, she thought disdainfully, remembering how often she'd seen bones thrown into the floor rushes, heard soup loudly slurped, seen meat dunked into the common saltcellar, the tablecloth used as a napkin. Maude had risked her life to reign over the English, but she had no love for the people of that island kingdom, and had not set foot on English soil since being forced into Norman exile, not even attending her beloved son's coronation. She'd mellowed some in her sunset years, but she still had not learned to forgive.

She wanted to ask about the issue weighing most heavily upon her mind: if her son's friendship with Thomas Becket had survived Becket's elevation to an archbishopric. But Will had been monopolizing the conversation since the meal began, and she hadn't the heart to interrupt; he'd always seemed so much younger than his years, in need of more coddling than his brothers.

Will was recounting their recent foray into South Wales to punish that unrepentant rebel, Rhys ap Gruffydd. "I would that all of our Welsh campaigns were so easy," he enthused. Almost at once, though, he reconsidered and glanced apologetically toward Ranulf and Rhiannon. "No offense, Uncle. I know you are friendly with Owain Gwynedd. But Rhys is a horse of another color. He deserved whatever he got, and then some."

Ranulf shrugged. "To tell you true, lad, I was glad to stay out of it. These old bones would rather sleep in my own bed, not on a rain-sodden field off in the middle of nowhere."

"You're not so old as that," Will insisted, with more courtesy than conviction, for to twenty-six, forty-four did indeed seem much closer to the grave than the cradle. Having assured himself that Ranulf was indifferent to Rhys's fate, he plunged back into his narrative with enthusiasm.

"In truth, it was more like a procession than an invasion, for we encountered little resistance. We even had Merlin on our side!" Will grinned at his mother's puzzled expression. "It seems that Merlin had prophesied of 'the coming of a freckled man of might,' whose crossing of the ford at Pencarn would set chaos loose upon their lands. Of course we did not yet know of this prophecy and the ford was an ancient one, so Harry started to cross the stream at the ford in use now. But just then trumpets sounded and spooked his stallion, who balked at crossing. To calm him, Harry rode him along the bank and crossed at the abandoned ford—just as Merlin had predicted! After word of that got about, Rhys's men lost heart and he had no choice but to surrender. How could he hope to defeat Harry and Merlin, too?"

"The fact that Rhys was badly outnumbered may have played a part in his decision," Ranulf observed dryly, and Maude seized the opportunity to divert the conversation out of Wales, toward Canterbury.

"I am glad that Henry was able to punish this Welsh rebel with a minimum of bloodshed. I can only hope that he is as successful in his dealings with his new archbishop. You sailed with Henry back to Southampton in January, Will. I understand that Thomas Becket was there to greet Henry and Eleanor. Tell me how the reunion went. Did you detect any tension?"

Will shook his head. "No . . . not that I can remember. Harry and Thomas seemed glad to see each other, joking the way they always do."

A faint frown creased Maude's brow. As much as she loved her youngest son, he was not the ideal eyewitness, blind to nuance and oblivious to undercurrents. "What of you, Ranulf? You saw Henry ere you sailed for Barfleur. What is your judgment? Think you that their friendship is still intact?"

"That is not an easy question to answer. They'd both probably insist it was, if asked. When Harry proposed that Gilbert Foliot be chosen to fill the vacant see of London, Becket agreed to his translation from the see of Hereford. And when Becket attacked the abuses of multiple benefices and demanded that the king's clerks yield them up, Harry did not object. He did insist, though, that Becket ought to practice what he preached and surrender the archdeaconry of Canterbury. I suppose you could argue that this shows they are both striving to be reasonable. But it is not an argument I could make with much conviction."

Maude leaned toward Ranulf, her gaze intent. "I've heard troubling rumors about Becket's efforts to reclaim those Church lands lost during the chaos of Stephen's reign. I am not faulting him for that, mind you. But if the stories are true, he has been arbitrary and high-handed, ordering his men-at-arms to seize disputed estates rather than seeking to regain them in court. What do you know about this?"

"The stories are true. He has revoked all leases for the Canterbury demesne. In some cases, I think he merely meant to renegotiate the terms, but many are complaining that they have been denied legal process."

"And he has rashly challenged the Earl of Hertford," Maud interjected, "laying claim to the castle and Honour of Tonbridge. Admittedly, I do not know the particulars, so I cannot judge the validity of his claim. But surely it would have been more prudent to seek recovery in the king's court? Instead, he demanded that Hertford do homage to him for Tonbridge. You can well imagine, Aunt Maude, how the earl responded to that!"

Maude could, indeed; she'd had a lifetime of dealing with prideful, thin-skinned barons. "That was foolishly done," she said disapprovingly. "What does Henry think of these doings?"

"He has been flooded with complaints and petitions coming out of Kent, and he is understandably vexed. Yet he is puzzled, too. When he granted Becket a royal writ to regain alienated Church property, he never expected Thomas to go about it in such a tactless and overbearing way. So far he is trying to give Becket the benefit of every doubt. I've been surprised by the patience he has shown, I'll admit. But then he still thinks of Thomas as his friend."

"Not for long, I'd wager." The Countess of Chester took a swallow of hippocras. "That flag of friendship may still be flying, but it is becoming more tattered by the day. Harry has been trying to convince himself that Becket just needs time to settle in, that once he feels comfortable as archbishop, all will revert back to the way it was between them. But how much longer can he cling to that hope?"

Maude was silent for a time, reflecting upon what she'd heard. "It sounds as if Becket is bound and determined to assert his independence at every opportunity. Whilst that may be understandable, it is also foolhardy and does not bode well for the future."

The silence that followed was a somber one, broken only when Rhiannon asked her husband to cut her another piece of bread. At home, she would have done it herself, but she felt self-conscious in the presence of Ranulf's formidable sister. Will had begun to fidget, for he knew from past experience that discussions about Thomas Becket might drag on endlessly, and he had news of his own to share.

"Tell me, Mama," he said quickly. "How would you like to start planning a wedding?"

"A wedding? Whose?"

"Mine," he said cheerfully. "Harry has found me a wife. I am eager for you to meet her, Mama, for she is as close to perfect as mortal woman has the right to be: fair to look upon and sweet-natured and soft-spoken and pious and—"

"An heiress, I trust?" Maude interrupted uneasily. It was obvious that her son was smitten with his future bride, and that was well and good, as long as the girl had more to recommend her than a pretty face.

"Indeed she is." Will was now grinning from ear to ear. "I am to wed Isabella de Warenne, Countess of Surrey."

"The widow of Stephen's son?"

Will nodded. "Isabella was wed as a child, was just fourteen when she was widowed nigh on four years ago. She is old enough now to be a wife and mother, and we would like to be married here in Rouen. You missed Harry's wedding, so I'd not have you miss mine." Will waited then, for her verdict. He was reasonably certain that she would approve, but he needed to hear the words; he could not imagine wedding without his mother's blessing.

The irony was not lost upon Maude that even in death, Stephen continued to shadow her path. She would have preferred that Will marry a woman with no links to the House of Blois, had never expected to share a daughter-in-law with Stephen. But it was not fair to blame the girl for a marriage made in childhood, a marriage in which she'd been given no say. And she was more than an enemy's widow; she was a great heiress in her own right, would bring the earldom of Surrey to her husband. Henry had indeed done well by his younger brother. How jealous Geoffrey would have been, she thought sadly, and then smiled at her lastborn. "I am very pleased," she said. "I am sure that Isabella will make you a good wife."

Will beamed. "So am I," he said, and when Ranulf proposed a toast to the new Earl of Surrey, he looked so joyful that Maude was able to forget, at least for a time, her qualms about Thomas Becket.

"I have long looked forward to the day of your wedding," she said, and hoped that her son would find more happiness and contentment in his marriage than she had found in either of hers.

On the first day of July in God's Year 1163, the King of Scotland and the Welsh rulers were summoned to do homage to Henry at Woodstock. As a Great Council meeting was scheduled afterward, the barons of the realm and princes of the Church were also expected to attend, and accommodations were soon filled to overflowing. By the time Ranulf arrived, he and his family had to settle for lodgings in New Woodstock, the borough Henry had founded a half-mile to the northeast.

Ranulf had fond memories of Woodstock. As a boy, he'd enjoyed visiting his father's menagerie, and he was sorry to discover that the lions and leopards and camels were long dead, for he'd wanted to show them to his children. He was particularly disappointed on Gilbert's behalf, for he knew the boy was restless and homesick, eager to return to Wales. And so when he rode over to Woodstock to let Henry know of his arrival, he took his son along, hoping there would be enough activity at the royal court to compensate for the lack of alien animals.

A small hill sloped away from the River Glyme, and upon its summit was the royal manor of Woodstock. Although it was one of Henry's favorite residences, the buildings were comfortable rather than lavish, for his main interest was in the hunting. The great hall was a spacious structure, but now there was not a foot to spare, so crowded was it with Henry's highborn guests.

Owain Gwynedd had not yet arrived, but Malcolm, the Scots king, was there, as were the lesser Welsh lords, and Rhys ap Gruffydd, who'd been held in honorable confinement since his surrender to Henry in April. Ranulf had never met Rhys and observed the Welsh firebrand with great interest. He was considerably younger than his uncle, in his early thirties, lacking Owain's commanding stature, distinguished silver-fox coloring, and regal dignity. But his dark eyes were glittering with a lively, sharp intelligence, and he still had a swagger in his step, the cocksure confidence of a man who dealt with defeat by refusing to recognize it. Ranulf doubted that Henry had heard the last of Rhys ap Gruffydd.

Ranulf knew most of the men in the hall, was kin to some of them. In addition to his brother Rainald and his cousin of Gloucester, the Earls of Leicester, Hertford, and Salisbury were in attendance upon the king, as were the Marcher lords, William Fitz Alan and Walter Clifford. The Church was also well represented. Thomas Becket was the most conspicuous of the prelates, richly garbed as always, elegant and enigmatic, a magnet for all eyes. Gilbert Foliot, newly translated from the see of Hereford to the more prestigious one of London, known for his eloquence and asceticism, but known, too, as a man who did not suffer fools gladly. Robert de Chesney, the aged Bishop of Lincoln. And by the dais, surely the most venerable and devious of England's clerics, Henry of Blois, Bishop of Winchester, Stephen's brother and erratic ally.

Maud and Will had sailed for Southampton with Ranulf and his family, but they'd gone on ahead to Woodstock while Ranulf and Rhiannon lingered for a few days in Winchester. They now greeted Ranulf and Gilbert so ebulliently that onlookers might well have assumed they'd been apart for months.

A seductive perfume alerted Ranulf to the approach of England's queen, and he turned to make an obeisance to Eleanor, pleased when his son followed his example without prompting. The queen looked lovely in a gown the color of claret; it was a shade few women could have worn well, but it suited her to perfection, as sophisticated and dramatic and distinctive as the woman herself. Ranulf marveled that she seemed to be aging with such grace and ease; had he not known she'd just marked her forty-first birthday, he'd never have guessed her to be within a decade of that age. But when he later said as much to his niece, Maud looked at him as if he'd lost his senses.

"I can assure you, Uncle, that few women age with 'grace and ease,' especially one so celebrated for her beauty. Eleanor is too shrewd not to know this is a war she cannot hope to win, but she is giving ground very grudgingly, making use of all the weapons at her disposal to keep the enemy at bay."

Gilbert seemed daunted by the noise and crowds and confusion; he didn't say anything, but he kept close by Ranulf's side, his eyes roaming the hall as if seeking an avenue of escape. Aware of the boy's edginess, Ranulf was about to suggest that they go outside to get some fresh air when Henry saw them and beckoned from the dais. His welcome was affectionate, and when Ranulf explained that he wanted to show Gilbert around the manor grounds, Henry at once voiced his approval, springing to his feet with alacrity.

"An excellent idea. Come on, let's take the lad to see the springs," he said, so enthusiastically that those around him smiled, aware that he'd have seized upon any pretext to avoid the ceremonial duties of kingship. Leaving Eleanor to preside over the hall, he headed for the closest door, accompanied by Ranulf, Gilbert, and Will. There was a time when Thomas Becket would have automatically been included in one of Henry's Grand Escapes, and Ranulf could not help remembering that as he hastened after his nephew. Looking back at the tall, stately figure of Canterbury's archbishop, he wondered if Becket was remembering, too.

Henry was in high spirits, acting like a schoolboy who'd managed to evade his lessons, and the others found his mood to be contagious; even Gilbert brightened up perceptibly. The sun had slid below the horizon, but the clouds drifting overhead were still painted in its hues, streaked with deep rose and soft purple. The sky had yet to lose its light, and the day's warmth lingered. Gilbert soon forged ahead, racing one of Henry's young wolfhounds, looking happier than Ranulf had seen him in weeks. The men followed at a more leisurely pace.

"How old is that lad of yours, Uncle?" Henry asked idly. "Nigh on twelve? I suppose he'd consider my Hal too young to bother with. A pity, for Hal has been complaining that there is 'nothing to do here,' which I take to mean he has no one to get into trouble with."

"Hal is here at Woodstock? He is still in Thomas Becket's care, is he not?"

Henry nodded. "I told Thomas to bring him along. I want the Scots king and the Welsh to do homage to Hal, too, when they do homage to me."

Ranulf glanced thoughtfully at the younger man. "I was wondering about that," he admitted. He could understand why Rhys ap Gruffydd should be required to do homage as a condition of regaining his liberty. But why summon the others? Now he had the answer: so they could swear to Hal, too. Before he could pursue this further, though, Henry asked abruptly:

"Have you spoken to Thomas yet?" When Ranulf shook his head, he looked disappointed. "I was hoping to get your impression of our lord archbishop." Although said with a smile, the words held a slightly sardonic edge. "Talk to him tonight, Ranulf. I've tried talking to him myself, and he says what is expected of him. But—"

Henry came to a sudden halt, head tilted to the side, listening intently. "Did you hear that?" They hadn't, but he paused before moving on. "Passing strange, I guess my imagination was playing me false. We're almost at the springs. I've always loved this part of the park, have long had it in mind to build a house here—"

This time there was no mistaking the sounds: raised voices, a splash, a burst of sputtered cursing. The men quickened their pace and a moment later, a woman came running through the trees. She was casting glances back over her shoulder as she ran, and didn't see the exposed root until it was too late. She stumbled, cried out sharply, and fell.

Henry reached her first, with Will and Ranulf only a step behind. She was already getting unsteadily to her feet, shrinking back at sight of the men. They could see now that she was very young, fifteen or sixteen at most. "We mean you no harm, lass," Henry said swiftly, for her torn gown and her panicked flight told a story without need of words.

Just then her pursuer came into view. He was youthful and well dressed and would have been quite handsome under other circumstances; now his face was mottled and contorted with rage. "Look what that little bitch did!" he exclaimed, gesturing toward his muddied chausses and sopping shoes.

Henry swung back toward the girl, who'd taken refuge behind him. "Did you push him into the pool?" he asked and began to laugh. "Good for you, lass!"

The girl murmured something inaudible, and the man's fury found a new target. "This is none of your concern," he warned, but his belligerence lasted only until Henry stepped from the shadows cast by the oak tree. That he'd recognized Henry was obvious, for his angry flush gave way within seconds to a sickly pallor. When he started to stammer either an apology or an explanation, Henry cut him off impatiently. He did not need to be told twice, began to back away, and then bolted.

The girl kept close to Henry's side until she was sure her assailant was gone. "Thank you, my lords," she said softly. Gilbert had arrived in time to witness the man's rout, and when the girl came forward, he drew a sibilant breath. Glancing at his son, Ranulf fought a smile, remembering the first time he'd seen girls in a new and dazzling light. Gilbert's reaction was understandable, for she was very pretty in a delicate, fragile way. Too young to wear the fashionable wimple, she'd covered her head with a veil that had been lost in her flight, and her hair now tumbled loosely about her shoulders in a splash of silver. She had wide-set eyes, the darkest blue Ranulf had ever seen, a fair, ivory-tinted complexion, and a very appealing smile; when she turned it upon Gilbert, he flushed to the tips of his ears.

"Thank you," she said again. "I did not mean to shove him into the pool, truly I did not. His foot must have slipped on one of the mossy rocks when I tried to pull away. He was sure, though, that I did it on purpose, and became so wroth . . ." She shivered visibly. "If you had not been here, I do not know what he might have done."

They were puzzled by the contradictions between her appearance and her demeanor. She wore a rather plain gown, not at all stylish, but her speech indicated education; no serving girl sounded as this one did. "What were you doing out here, lass?" Henry asked, voicing the question in all their minds.

Twilight was deepening, a soft, shimmering lavender-blue, but they could still see the blush rising in her cheeks. "My father is in attendance upon the king, and he sent for me, Godstow being just a few miles away."

"Godstow?" Henry echoed. "The nunnery . . . of course. You are being schooled there, then?"

"Yes, my lord."

"But how did you come to be with that lecherous lout?" Will asked tactlessly, and she bit her lip, looking so embarrassed that he at once regretted the question.

Notwithstanding her discomfort, she answered honestly. "I met him in the gardens. He said he was a knight in the Scots king's household and

we began to talk. He was very well spoken and courteous and when he offered to show me the springs, I saw no harm in it . . ."

"Ah, child . . ." Henry shook his head ruefully. "There is a great difference between the convent and the court."

"The fault was mine, then?"

She sounded so forlorn that Will made gallant haste to assure her that
indeed it was not, an assurance echoed by Ranulf and then Henry, who
added, "The fault lies with your father, for letting a lamb loose with so
many wolves on the prowl. He ought to be taken to task for—"

"Oh, please, no! Do not tell my father, for he'd be so angry with
me . . ." She laid a hand on Henry's arm in timid entreaty, and then
gasped. "Blessed Lady, it is you! The king!" She sank down at once in a
deep, submissive curtsy.

Henry gestured for her to rise. "Calm yourself, lass," he said soothingly. "I did not mean to cause you greater distress, will say nothing to
your father if that is your wish."

A moment ago, she'd seemed on the verge of tears. But her smile now
was radiant, so bewitching that Gilbert heaved a small sigh. "Thank you,
my lords, thank you!" The words were addressed to them all, but meant
only for Henry. "This is not the first time you came to my rescue. You
caught me when I fell out of a tree in my mother's garden at Clifford Castle. Do you . . . do you remember, my liege?" she asked, so hopefully that
Henry lied and nodded.

"Was that little lass you?" he asked, prodding his memory in vain.
"So . . . you're Walter Clifford's daughter."

"Yes, my lord king. I am Rosamund Clifford," she said, and dropped
another curtsy. She was so happy that Henry claimed to have remembered
her that she now made Gilbert utterly happy, too, by turning to him and
saying, "It was so long ago, the summer after the king's coronation. He
was putting down a Marcher lord's rebellion and stayed one night at my
father's castle. I'd climbed the old apple tree in my mother's garden and lost
my balance when I tried to get down. I was clinging desperately to one of
the branches when the king heard my cries and ran to my rescue. He
caught me just as I fell, saved me from broken bones and mayhap even a
broken neck, then dried my tears and agreed that my mishap would be
kept a secret between the two of us."

She smiled again at Henry. "So I owe you a debt twice-over, my liege,
for that little girl in the apple tree and this foolish one at the Woodstock
springs."

It occurred to Ranulf that Rosamund Clifford was looking at Henry with the same starry-eyed adoration that his son was lavishing upon her. It was dangerous for a girl to be so pretty and so innocent, too; a convent was probably the safest place for her, at least until her father found her a suitable husband.

Henry was amused and faintly flattered, his thoughts echoing Ranulf's own: that the sooner this little lamb got safely back to Godstow, the better. "The pleasure was all mine, Mistress Rosamund. But if you hope to keep your father in ignorance, we'd best see about repairing the damage done. We need someone who can be discreet, who can help the lass to stitch up the tear in her gown and find her another veil. Any ideas, Ranulf?"

"I know no one who appreciates intrigues more than Maud."

"So I've heard," Henry said, with a puckish smile that made Ranulf wonder suddenly if his nephew knew Maud had been the go-between in his long-ago liaisons with Annora Fitz Clement. It was soon agreed upon that Will would escort Rosamund Clifford to the manor and Gilbert would then go into the hall and fetch Maud, a plan that seemed to please Will and Gilbert more than Rosamund, who kept glancing back over her shoulder until she'd vanished into the gathering dusk.

Once she was gone, the two men looked at each other and laughed. "Were we ever that young?" Ranulf asked and Henry slapped him playfully on the back.

"Speak for yourself, Uncle. Need I remind you that I'm only thirty? I think I'll have a word with Clifford, though, suggest that he send the girl back to Godstow without delay. Next time she might not be so lucky." After a moment, Henry started to laugh again. "I was just thinking . . . Eleanor was about that lass's age when she wed the French king. But somehow I doubt that Eleanor was ever that vulnerable or trusting. If any man had been fool enough to force his attentions upon her, I'd wager she'd have kicked him where it would hurt the most and then laughed about it afterward!"

Ranulf grinned. "I daresay you're right." The summer darkness was flowing about them now like a river, drowning the last traces of twilight. There was no point in continuing on to the springs and they started back. "Maud was a good choice," Henry observed, "for she'll not lecture the lass. Maud, bless her, is never judgmental. Did you hear about her brother?"

"No . . . what trouble has Will gotten himself into now?" Ranulf would never understand how his brother Robert, as fine a man as ever drew breath, could have sired a son as incompetent as Will. "I saw him in the hall, so if he got himself abducted by the Welsh again, he must have paid another ransom."

"No, I'm talking of her younger brother, Roger. He is now the bishop-elect for the see of Worcester."

Ranulf was delighted, for he'd always been very fond of Roger. "A pity his parents could not have lived to see that. How proud they would have been."

"Roger is a good man, ought to make a good bishop. Even Thomas could find no objections to raise."

"You make it sound as if Thomas is deliberately being contentious. Is that what you truly think, Harry?"

"In truth, Ranulf, I do not know what I think. I'd have sworn I knew Thomas to the depths of his soul. Now . . . now I look at him and see a stranger."

By then they were almost upon the manor. It was clear that something out of the ordinary was occurring. Torches were flaring, voices raised, dogs barking. Ranulf figured it out first. "It is Owain Gwynedd," he said.

The Welsh king's entrance was so dramatic that Ranulf suspected he'd deliberately timed his arrival for nightfall. The molten-gold light of the torches flamed up into the darkening sky, casting eerie, wavering shadows, striking sparks against sword hilts and spearheads and the ruby pendant encircling the slender throat of Owain's queen. Cristyn's exotic, dark beauty had never struck Ranulf so forcefully, and he had the uneasy thought that this was a woman men would kill over, one with Delilah and Jezebel and Bathsheba. Did Hywel fully understand how dangerous it could be to underrate her?

Owain's sons had accompanied him, well armored in pride and suspicion. Davydd and Rhodri, riding stirrup to stirrup, handsome and highstrung. Cynan, looking about with unabashed curiosity, and Maelgwn, meeting Woodstock with a scowl. Iorwerth, solitary even in a crowd. Several others, whose names Ranulf knew, but whose personalities eluded him. And then Hywel, reining in at Owain's side, father and son gazing down upon their English audience, so impassive that even Ranulf, who knew them so well, could not be sure what they were thinking. With a silent, fervent hope that all would go well at Woodstock between his two kings, Ranulf stepped forward into the torch-glare to bid them welcome to his other world.

CHAPTER THIRTEEN

✦

July 1163
Woodstock, England

S ITTING ON A BENCH in the gardens, Ranulf was watching his children romp with a silver-grey puppy when he heard his name called. Rising, he moved forward to meet Thomas Becket. Two of the men with the archbishop were familiar to Ranulf, for William Fitz Stephen and Herbert of Bosham had been clerks in the royal chancellory before following Becket to Canterbury, and they exchanged amiable greetings.

"Where is the Lady Rhiannon?" Becket asked, demonstrating that his manners were no less impeccable as archbishop than they'd been as chancellor.

"She is visiting with the queen and my niece, the Lady Maud, and whilst she does, I rashly offered to keep our two hellions from wreaking havoc upon an unsuspecting Woodstock," Ranulf said with a smile.

"I see that the king has given you the puppy. He mentioned to me that he had it in mind. Apparently it is an uncommon breed?"

"Yes, a Norwegian dyrehund. The king remembered that I'd bred them years ago and thought it would please me to have one again."

"He can be very generous," Becket said, and Ranulf nodded. He was frustrated by the formality of the conversation, made necessary by the archbishop's entourage. He wanted to take Becket aside, dispense with protocol, and talk not of the king, but of Harry, the man they both knew so well. But Becket was always surrounded by others and he did not invite any opportunities. To the contrary, he maintained an emotional distance, one Ranulf had been unable to breach. Friendly but not familiar, he used courtesy and the deference due his office as a shield, effectively deflecting curiosity and intimacy, too.

Becket was talking about Roger of Gloucester's elevation to the bishopric of Worcester. He seemed to hold Roger in high esteem, which might explain his willingness to approve Roger's election. For certes, it was not to please Harry. Becket's interest in pleasing the king seemed minimal, and Ranulf yearned to know why. But that was not a question he could ask, mayhap not even one Becket could answer.

They continued making polite, meaningless small talk for a while longer and then the archbishop and his retinue moved on. Ranulf reclaimed his seat, watching until Becket was no longer in sight. What was motivating the man? Was it pride? Had his newfound independence gone to his head? Ranulf remembered his sister's foolhardy behavior when it seemed as if the crown was finally within her grasp. She'd acted arrogantly and recklessly, alienating the Londoners to such an extent that they'd rebelled and chased her out of the city. She'd lost her chances of queenship in that wild rout, and doomed England to another twelve years of civil war. Could Becket be following that same perilous path?

Or did he truly believe himself to be unworthy of the archbishopric? Did he feel the need to prove to the Church—and to himself—that he was no longer Harry's man? Did he think that to serve God, he must first sacrifice his other self, disavow the worldly chancellor who'd been the king's friend? Was he shedding his old identity the way a snake would shed its skin? Ranulf frowned, then called out an admonition to Gilbert, who had scrambled precariously up onto the garden wall. It served for naught to speculate like this. He could only hope that Becket would realize in time that neither the Church nor the Crown benefitted from confrontation and conflict.

"Ranulf? Is it really you?"

The voice was one he'd not heard in years, but he knew it at once, for it still echoed at times in his dreams. He sat, frozen in disbelief, as Annora

Fitz Clement came toward him across the grassy mead. It had been sixteen years since he'd seen her last, at Shrewsbury's fair, a memory that had yet to fade, still sharply etched and achingly vivid. She'd been clad in green, pregnant with her husband's child, glowing with contentment—until she'd seen him standing there. For at least a lifetime, they'd stared at each other, as she pleaded silently that he not betray her. He'd never forgotten that look of fear on her face; in that moment, he'd finally seen her for what she was—another man's wife.

She was garbed again in green, a moss-colored gown with tight-fitting bodice and wide skirts, the sleeves billowing out like streamers from her slender wrists. The black hair he'd loved to stroke was hidden away under a wimple of crisp white linen. She'd never been a great beauty, short and dark and so quick-tempered that he'd fondly called her "hellcat," but from the time he was sixteen, she'd been the woman he wanted, the one he had to have, at whatever cost.

She'd almost reached him and he got hurriedly to his feet, kissing her hand and then her cheek. "You always were one for taking a man by surprise," he said, with a strained smile. "It's been a long time, Annora." He winced as soon as the platitude left his mouth. It was bad enough that he suddenly felt like a tongue-tied raw lad, without sounding like one, too.

She laughed and let him seat her beside him on the bench. The conversation that followed was as proper as it was awkward: polite queries about family and health, as if there had been nothing between them but friendship. He offered his condolences for her father's death, very belatedly, for Raymond de Bernay had gone to God four years ago. She assured him that her brothers were well and related a humorous story about Ancel, the friend of his youth. Ranulf smiled and nodded and tried not to recall the day Ancel had caught them together, calling his sister a slut and Ranulf a Judas.

"I do not believe it," Annora exclaimed suddenly. "That puppy across the garden looks just like your dyrehund, just like Loth!"

"Loth was a once-in-a-lifetime sort of dog, but I have hopes for the pup . . . if only the children can stop squabbling long enough to agree upon a name for him."

"Those are your children? Gilbert and Mallt?" She made a credible attempt at the Welsh pronunciation and gave him an impish smile. "You must wonder how I know that. I met them, you see, three years ago at the Chester fair."

"Yes, I know. Rhiannon told me," he said, and saw her surprise.

"Ancel named one of his sons after Gilbert, too. What was it I called the three of you . . . the unholy trinity? I was so sorry to learn of his death . . . a riding mishap of some kind?"

He stared at her. She did not know! But then, how could she? "Gilbert died," he said, "because of me."

"Because of you? I do not understand."

"After I got your letter, telling me that you could not see me again, I set out for Shrewsbury hoping that I'd find you at the fair. When Gilbert learned that I'd gone off alone into an area under Stephen's control, he was alarmed and rode after me. He never reached Shrewsbury, though. His horse bolted and threw him, breaking his neck."

"Oh, Ranulf . . ." Reaching over, she gently touched his hand. For a time, they sat in silence, remembering and grieving and watching his children play with the dyrehund puppy. "I had to end it," she said, very softly. "I promised God that I would, if only He'd let my baby live. I could not bear to miscarry again . . ."

"I know, lass," he said sadly, "I know." But he did not want to go down that road again. "How is your daughter?" he asked hastily, and her face lit up.

"Matilda is well nigh grown, almost sixteen. She looks like me, I'm told, but she has none of my faults. She thinks ere she acts and never breaks a promise and she brightens a room just by walking into it. I wish you could know her, Ranulf." She paused. "I wish she were yours."

"Ah, Annora . . ." He hesitated, not knowing what to say, and she reached again for his hand, lacing her fingers through his.

"The Shrewsbury fair is next month," she said. "I expect to be there. Will you?"

He let his breath out slowly. "No," he said, "I will not."

Her fingers twitched, then jerked away from his. He knew how fast her temper could kindle, but she looked wounded, not angry. "I see," she said stiffly. She made no move to rise, though. "I think I have a right to know why, Ranulf."

He could give her the easy answer, that he was not free. But she'd never been one for taking the easy way, and he knew what her forthright response would be: why should his marriage vows matter more than hers? He could tell her that he loved his wife and it was the truth. He did not think she'd believe him, though. She'd never believe he could love another woman as he'd loved her. And he did not want to take that certainty from her if he could help it. "I am sorry, Annora," he said at last. "Some wounds never fully heal." He thought that sounded woefully inadequate, but at least it was not an outright lie.

She was gazing intently into his face. "Ah, Ranulf . . . I understand now." Getting to her feet, she waited until he had risen, too, and then touched her hand to his cheek in a light, lingering caress. "I shall pray for Gilbert's soul," she said, "and for your peace."

He understood then, too. Just as he'd seen her weave intricate wall hangings, she was creating a pattern out of loose threads of fact, transforming his rejection into a response she could live with. They were tragic lovers, doomed by fate and an unruly horse, kept apart by guilt and the ghost of Gilbert Fitz John. Rhiannon would remain the Welsh cousin he'd wed out of pity, a shadowy figure of no consequence, not a rival for his affections, never that. But how could he fault her for that fantasy? Had he not done the same? He'd spun out deluded daydreams about their future, justified their adultery, and given nary a thought to the impact of their affair upon her husband and stepchildren. It seemed like one of God's more ironic jokes that he could see so clearly now, years too late.

"Papa?" Mallt was sprinting toward them. "Look what I've got!" Carefully uncupping her hands, she revealed a small grasshopper. "If I put it in a jar, will it live?"

"No, love, it will soon die."

Mallt looked disappointed, but it never occurred to her to argue, for she was still at the age when a father's wisdom was absolute. Carrying her prize over to the grass, she set it free. Ranulf and Annora watched, then looked at each other in what they both knew to be a final farewell. She was smiling, but he thought he could detect a glimmer of tears behind her lashes. He stood motionless as she moved away, and then called out to his children. "Catch the puppy. I think it is time we went looking for your mother."

"HYWEL? YOU LOOK as if you've just swilled a flagon full of vinegar. What is amiss?"

"Ask your nephew," Hywel snapped, and would have turned away had Ranulf not grabbed his arm.

"I am asking you. What is wrong?"

"Why did you not warn us, Ranulf? You think my father would have given in to Cristyn's coaxing and let her come if he knew what awaited us at Woodstock? How could you let us ride into that ambush?"

"Hywel, I do not know what you are talking about. I swear by all the saints that I do not!"

"You did not know about the act of homage?"

"Yes, of course I knew about that. What of it? Harry has had the English barons swear homage to his son, so it makes sense that he would want Hal acknowledged by the Welsh, too. Surely that is not what has your hackles rising? Owain did homage to Harry at Rhuddlan Castle and the sun did not plummet from the sky. So why should it matter if he repeats the oath?"

"You truly did not know, did you? Your nephew has more in mind than a formal recognition of his heir. He means to put our kings on the same footing with his English barons, and he has begun to whittle away at our liberties and rights, imposing new demands and restrictions. He insists that we can no longer offer sanctuary to those he considers enemies of the Crown, and that is but the beginning. How long ere he attempts to introduce English laws and customs? How long ere he seeks to turn Gwynedd into an English shire?"

Ranulf was stunned by the outburst. Hywel usually diluted all of life's problems with a healthy dose of humor. He'd not known the other man was capable of a stark, searing anger like this, one that burned to the bone. He wanted to assure Hywel that the Welsh were borrowing trouble, but how honest would that assurance be? He'd told Owain that Harry had no intention to swallow Wales whole. But would he keep nibbling away until Welsh sovereignty was well nigh gone? There was a time when he could have answered that question with an emphatic "no." That was before Toulouse. His nephew's needless war against Count Raymond had been an eye-opening lesson in the cynical lore of kingship. He still did not believe that Harry meant to annex Wales outright; he was surely too shrewd to expend so much to get so little. Harry could be goaded, though, into a war of conquest. He'd warned Owain of that, could only hope that the Welsh king had taken the warning to heart.

"The English king is indeed my nephew, as you rather pointedly reminded me. But I am also Welsh, partly by blood and wholly by choice. For all that I hold English estates, my true home is at Trefriw. Your fears for Wales are mine, too, Hywel. It saddens me that I should have to assure you of that."

"Your kinship to the English king is a fact, Ranulf, not an accusation. I was not implying that you are some sort of royal spy. Only an utter idiot could suspect that you'd been dwelling amongst us for more than thirteen years, even going so far as to take a Welsh wife, all on the odd chance that should war come, you might possibly be of use to the English Crown." The corner of Hywel's mouth quirked. "So of course my brilliant half-brothers are convinced it is true!"

Ranulf took comfort in the jest, but he knew that if relations between the English and Welsh worsened, there would be others to question where his loyalties lay. "I will talk to Harry," he promised. "It may well be that you are all shying at shadows."

Hywel did not argue. His skeptical silence spoke volumes, though, and Ranulf began to realize that his nephew's actual intent might matter less than what the Welsh perceived it to be.

THE CEREMONY of homage was performed in Woodstock's great hall, in an atmosphere so charged with tension that Ranulf half-expected to hear rumblings of thunder echoing in the distance. Six years ago, the Scots king had done homage to Henry for the English earldom of Huntingdon, but the vassalage demanded of Malcolm now was more circumscribed and restrictive; he was also required to yield up his younger brother David as a hostage for his good faith. The Welsh were compelled, too, to accept a vassalage that went beyond what had been demanded of Owain at Rhuddlan Castle, a subordinate status that the Welsh found both demeaning and threatening.

If the ritual of homage to Henry and his son was an impressive demonstration of English power, the feasting that followed offered a lavish display of English hospitality. But Ranulf had no appetite for the bountiful repast, and he doubted that the Scots or Welsh did, either.

The revelries dragged on through the evening. Ranulf's edginess was only exacerbated by the presence of Annora Fitz Clement, her husband, and a stepson. Rhiannon did not yet know Annora was at Woodstock and he wanted to be the one to tell her. Feeling guiltily grateful that she could not detect Annora on her own, he kept a cautious watch upon his old love, trying to keep the two women well apart.

Hywel and Maud had eventually noticed Annora Fitz Clement, too. Hywel confined himself to a raised brow, a quizzical glance in Ranulf's direction. Maud took more direct action, pulling Ranulf aside for a hurried interrogation. Satisfied with his response, she went off to make sure that the unpredictable Annora did not take it into her head to seek Rhiannon out for an exchange of social pleasantries, and Ranulf breathed a sigh of relief, knowing he'd just gained an invaluable ally.

Not unexpectedly, he'd gotten no chance to talk privately with Henry; that would have to wait. By the time the interminable festivities had drawn to a close, he was exhausted and so thoroughly out of humor that others had begun to notice. All in all, it was a day he wanted only to forget.

Once they were back at their lodgings in New Woodstock, he sprawled on the bed, still fully dressed, watching as Rhiannon loosened her braids. She'd dismissed her attendant, a sure sign that she wanted to talk of matters not for other ears, and as she began to brush out her hair, she soon gave voice to her own anxiety.

"Do you think the Welsh are justified in their suspicions, Ranulf?"

"Well . . . I do not believe that Harry is laying secret plans to overrun Wales. He had a perfect opportunity to rid himself of Rhys ap Gruffydd this spring, chose instead to restore Rhys to power. If his intentions were as sinister as the Welsh believe, why would he have done that?"

"Then you believe the Welsh are in the wrong?"

"I would that it were so simple," he said wearily. "The problem, lass, is that the Welsh and English do not view homage in the same light. I've tried to explain to Harry that Welsh history and customs are unlike those in his other domains. In England and Normandy, the act of homage is not humbling or degrading. It is a cornerstone, the foundation upon which all else rests. A Duke of Normandy or a Count of Anjou can do homage to the French king without being diminished in his own eyes or those of his subjects. But it is different in Wales. There, it is an alien concept, imposed by the force of arms. So when Harry compels Owain and Rhys to swear public homage to him, they do not see it as part of the natural order, but rather as an act meant to humiliate, salt rubbed into their wounds. It is not surprising, therefore, that they should be so quick to suspect the worst. But Harry can no more grasp their point of view than they can comprehend his."

He sounded so dispirited that Rhiannon came over, sat beside him upon the bed. "The Almighty did you no favor by giving you such keen eyesight, my love. The man who can see both sides in a conflict earns himself thanks from neither side."

Taking the brush, he drew it through her hair. It was a beautiful color, a rich shade of chestnut; he thought it such a pity that she could never see that autumn entwining of russet and copper and sorrel. "Let's talk no more of this tonight. I've something to tell you. This morning in the gardens, I laid a ghost to rest . . . Annora Fitz Clement."

Rhiannon stopped breathing for a moment. "She is here at Woodstock?"

"It came as quite a surprise to me, too."

Not for Annora, though. She'd have known he'd be in attendance upon the king on such an occasion. Rhiannon waited until she was sure her voice would not betray her. "Was it a . . . a painful meeting, Ranulf?"

"It churned up memories long buried. But painful . . . no," he said, not altogether truthfully. "I was not sure how I'd feel upon seeing her again. It was . . . was like listening to a song I'd once loved. The words were the same, but I could no longer hear the music."

Just as on the night that he'd proposed marriage, she sat utterly still, afraid that if she moved, it would break the spell. "You have no regrets, then?"

"For Gilbert, yes, a lifetime of regrets. But for Annora . . . no. I have the life—and the woman—I want, consider myself a lucky man." When he touched her cheek then, he discovered it was wet. "Sweetheart, I am sorry. I never knew Annora caused you such unease."

"It does not matter," she said, "not anymore. Now I have something to tell you, too. I was going to wait until I was sure. But what better time than now? I think I am with child again. My flux did not come last month and we are now into the second week of July, so I am six weeks late."

Ranulf pulled her into his arms, holding her so close she could hardly breathe. "The babe was conceived in Rouen, then." He kissed her tears away before seeking her mouth, and then said what she most wanted to hear. "I shall tell Harry that we cannot accompany him on to London. Once the Woodstock council is done, we'll go home to Wales."

THE BAILEY WAS CROWDED and clamorous, for the Welsh were making ready to depart. Farewells had been said to Henry, chilled and correct, packhorses loaded, orders given. Ranulf and Hywel stood watching as horses were led out and men began to mount. Taking his stallion's reins from a groom, Hywel glanced back at Ranulf. "Ought you not to be at the council meeting?"

"They are not discussing any matters of urgency today. Harry wants to change the way the sheriff's aid is paid, hardly an issue of life or death. So I'll not be missed nor am I missing much."

"What is the sheriff's aid?"

Ranulf knew full well that Hywel cared not a whit about English taxes. He'd asked for the same reason that he'd not yet mounted his horse: to put off the moment of departure. "The sheriff's aid is a customary payment made by landowners to the sheriffs of each shire. Harry is proposing that the money be paid directly to the Exchequer in the future. That way, officials of the Crown can be kept under closer supervision, whilst limiting the opportunities for extortion."

"Dishonest sheriffs?" Hywel gave a grimace of mock horror. "What next—unchaste nuns and lecherous monks?"

Ranulf smiled. "Or tongue-tied poets? We live in an odd world indeed, Hywel. Are you sure you cannot wait and ride back to Wales with us?"

Hywel glanced across the bailey toward his father. "No . . . a good guest always knows when to go home."

Ranulf nodded, unsurprised. The Welsh had weighty matters to discuss. Upon his own return to Trefriw, he meant to visit Owain's court, do what he could to reassure the Welsh king of his nephew's good faith. And today he would try again to make Harry understand why the Welsh often seemed so skittish, so infernally stubborn. There had to be a way to bridge the gap between his two homelands, and he'd find it, by God he would.

After the Welsh had ridden out, Ranulf considered going over to the great hall where the council meeting was in session. But the prospect was not an appealing one; it seemed almost sinful to waste a summer day indoors, discussing a tedious topic like royal revenues. The choice was made for him as he drew near the gardens, for there a boisterous game of quoits was in progress. Several youths were flinging horseshoes about with reckless abandon, to the accompanying applause and jeers of a growing audience. Ranulf recognized Maud's two sons, fifteen-year-old Hugh and his younger brother, Richard, and was not surprised to see his niece midst the bystanders, cheering them on. At sight of Ranulf, she beckoned him over, and he hesitated for all of a heartbeat before yielding to temptation.

"Have the Welsh gone?" Maud asked, and then, "Good pitch, Hugh!"

"They departed a while ago. I tried to get Hywel to ride back with us, to no avail."

"What ails him, Ranulf? My impression of Hywel is that he'd be joking with the Devil on his deathbed. I've never seen him so somber as he was here at Woodstock. Why, when I told him that the Scots king was known as Malcolm the Maiden because he'd taken an ill-considered vow of chastity, Hywel merely nodded and made not a single jest! When he passed up an opportunity like that, I knew something must truly be amiss."

"The Welsh are troubled by Harry's demand for homage. They are worried that this new vassalage might well have strings attached, unseen as yet."

Maud looked amused. "Strings? With Cousin Harry, most likely enough strings to weave a spider's web."

Ranulf frowned, for he thought his niece was a shrewd judge of men. "You think, then, that Harry truly covets Rhys and Owain's domains?"

"Of course he covets, Uncle. That is what kings do, even saintly souls like Louis or our virginal young Malcolm. But I doubt that Harry is hatching any nefarious schemes to usurp Wales the way Stephen did England. To be unforgivably candid, Wales is not that great a prize. I think his true concern is to assure the succession for his son, and if that requires overawing the Welsh and the Scots, so be it. As like as not, he will—Jesú!"

Maud recoiled as an ill-aimed horseshoe thudded into the grass at her feet. "Are you so eager to be an orphan, Dickon?" she chided, and her younger son gave her an embarrassed grin. "Come on," she said, linking her arm through Ranulf's. "Apparently I am too tempting a target for my lads!"

Ranulf laughed and followed her out of the line of fire. "Quoits can be downright dangerous, especially when the players use stones instead of horseshoes. Add ale to the mix, and bystanders are likely to start dropping like ripe pears." He was about to relate an account of a near-riot that had erupted after a quoit had bounced off the hob and clouted a London alderman, when he saw a familiar figure striding toward them.

"Rainald? Is the council done already?"

"Aye, it is done," Rainald said, sounding so morose that Maud and Ranulf forgot about the game of quoits and hastened over. "Be glad you were not there, Ranulf, for it turned into a right ugly brawl. I'm half-deafened from so much shouting, am surprised you did not hear it all the way out here, for Harry can rattle shutters and raise the roof when he is in full cry."

"What stirred up such a commotion? I thought it was just the sheriff's aid that was under discussion."

"Believe it or not, that was what kindled the fire. As soon as Harry announced that he wanted the sheriff's aid to go into the Exchequer,

Thomas Becket rose up in opposition to the plan, objecting most vehemently to the proposed change."

Ranulf and Maud exchanged baffled looks. "Why? It would affect the sheriffs, not the Church."

"So Harry pointed out. But Becket insisted that the sheriff's aid was a free-will offering and was not to be changed into a royal revenue at the king's whim. Harry was taken aback and instead of setting forth his reasons for wanting the change, he lost his temper and swore by God's Eyes that the aid should be entered on the Pipe Rolls. And then Becket also lost his temper and he swore, too, by God's Eyes, vowing that he'd not pay so much as a penny from his estates or Church lands. And all the while, the rest of us were sitting there openmouthed, unable to understand how it had come about."

"Did Harry prevail?"

"No," Rainald said, with astonishment that had yet to fade. "Becket did! He cleverly shifted his ground, arguing that our ancient, revered customs must be preserved against new and potentially dangerous innovations. That carried the day with barons and bishops alike, for who amongst us is not suspicious of change? When Harry saw the way the wind was blowing, he agreed to drop the matter, at least for now."

"Why would Becket make so much ado about this? Why antagonize Harry over an issue that matters so little to the Church?"

"I'd have to be a soothsayer to answer that, Ranulf. This I can tell you, though, the bishops were asking that very question amongst themselves. For all that they rallied around Becket in public, they were as baffled by his behavior as we are. A wise man picks his quarrels with care, and Becket just squandered the king's friendship for a trifle."

"UNCLE RANULF?" Henry's brother intercepted him as he started up the steps into the great hall. "May we talk?"

"Of course, lad." Will's open, freckled face was pinched and drawn, his distress so obvious that Ranulf took his elbow and steered him away from eavesdroppers. "Were you witness to the dispute over the sheriff's aid?"

Will nodded. "I've never seen Harry so wroth, not ever. Few men would have dared to defy him like that, not to his face. I do not understand, Ranulf, how it has come to this."

"Neither do I, Will."

"Uncle . . . I had a troubling encounter with Thomas myself this morning, ere the council began. I honestly do not know if I have cause for concern or not, but I'll admit to being disquieted about it. I told Thomas, you see, that I am to wed Isabella de Warenne. And he looked at me very gravely, shook his head, and said that such a marriage would not be acceptable in God's Eyes, as Isabella is kin to me, by blood and marriage. It is true that Isabella and I are very distant cousins, and her late husband was my third cousin. But . . . but surely that is not an insurmountable impediment? Cousins get dispensations to wed all the time. Harry and Eleanor are cousins, after all, as were my parents. For certes, Thomas will be reasonable, will he not? He would not really forbid the marriage?"

Will's composure was like a thin layer of ice, barely concealing the deep reservoir of panic just below the surface. Ranulf yearned to reassure his nephew that his fears were for naught, that not even the most scrupulous clerical conscience would be so inflexible. But how could he offer Will such a surety? Who would dare to speak for Thomas Becket now?

"We'll talk to Harry about it . . . later, after his temper has cooled," he promised, and, hoping that Will's look of relief was justified, he continued on up the steps.

He was surprised to find that Henry and Becket were both still there, although at opposite ends of the hall. Like battle commanders, he thought, each one unwilling to withdraw from the field and give the advantage to his foe. Becket was talking to the elderly Bishop of Lincoln, never once glancing toward the king. But his clerks were hovering close at hand and his natural pallor was even more pronounced, his face the color of wax, his mouth ringed in white. His occasional stammer was more in evidence than usual, too. All in all, he struck Ranulf as a man with an unquiet soul, angry, agitated, and determined not to give ground. Rainald was wrong, he thought, for it was plain that Becket did not regard this as a quarrel over a trifle. Becket might be the only one who fully understood what the stakes were in this contest of wills between archbishop and king, but none could doubt that he knew they were high indeed.

The new Bishop of London was standing some distance away. Gilbert Foliot had an expressive face, and each time he gazed upon the archbishop, he gave himself away, his the queasy ambivalence of a man who'd just been proven right, at one and the same time grimly gratified and genuinely horrified. At his side was Ranulf's nephew Roger, the Bishop-elect of Worcester. Roger was the son who most physically resembled his father, Robert, compact and spare of build, with oak-brown hair and eyes, a good-humored smile, an innate reserve. Now he was speaking quietly and persuasively into Foliot's ear, like his sire, a born reconciler.

Several of the king's lords were clustered around him upon the dais. Walter Clifford and Roger de Clare, Earl of Hertford, who was smiling so smugly that Ranulf knew he'd concluded that Henry was now sure to support his claim to Tonbridge Castle. Ranulf's other nephew, Will of Gloucester, was gesturing emphatically to the Earl of Leicester, but Henry's justiciar did not seem to be paying Will much mind. From time to time, he would nod politely or absently. All the while, though, he watched the king.

So did Ranulf. If Becket was ostensibly ignoring his sovereign, Henry's gaze was following every move his archbishop made, with a falcon's unblinking intensity. His face still deeply flushed, grey eyes smoldering, he seemed to be radiating heat; Ranulf could almost believe his skin would be hot to the touch. One glance was enough to show him that Rainald was not so wrong, after all, for the friendship between Henry and Becket was indeed doomed. It was dying here and now, on this July afternoon in Woodstock's great hall.

CHAPTER FOURTEEN

September 1163
Aberffraw
Môn, North Wales

"WHAT ARE YOU DOING HERE?"

Ranulf had just dismounted in the bailey of Owain Gwynedd's island manor. He did not realize that belligerent challenge was aimed at him, not until a hand clamped down roughly upon his shoulder. Turning, he found himself face to face with Owain's youngest son.

Rhodri had inherited his father's height and topped Ranulf by several inches. His grip tightening, he repeated, "What are you doing here?"

Ranulf sought to keep his temper under rein, reminding himself that Rhodri was just eighteen and eager to prove his manhood. "I am here to see your lord father," he said, as evenly as he could. "Now would you mind taking your hand off my shoulder?"

Rhodri scowled, but after a moment, his fingers unclenched. He did not step back, though, making a provocation of his very proximity, too close for comfort. "I'll say this straight out," he said. "We want no English spies at my father's court."

Rhodri's voice carried across the bailey, quickly drawing an audience. Ranulf recognized several of the bystanders: two of Rhodri's half-brothers, Cynan and Iorwerth, and Hywel's foster brother Peryf, who nodded impassively before disappearing into the hall. Ranulf's own men shifted uneasily from foot to foot, unsure what was expected of them. His brother-in-law Celyn pushed forward resolutely to stand beside him. Celyn had been so insistent upon accompanying him to Aberffraw that Ranulf realized he'd been anticipating just such a confrontation.

Ranulf had no intention of playing Rhodri's game. "I agree with you," he said pleasantly. "There is no place at Aberffraw for English spies."

Rhodri's mouth opened, but no words emerged. Cynan burst out laughing. A few others did, too, stopping abruptly when Rhodri glared at them. Ranulf had brushed past him, and he took several hasty steps to overtake the older man. "You are not welcome here!"

Ranulf turned reluctantly. "I was not aware," he said, "that Lord Owain had abdicated in your favor. My congratulations."

Rhodri had never learned how to deflect sarcasm and his cheeks reddened. Before he could decide how to retaliate, Hywel appeared in the doorway, smiling genially.

"There you are, my lord Ranulf. Come in, my father is awaiting you."

The look Rhodri gave Hywel was both suspicious and uncertain. "Our father is expecting him? Why did no one tell me that?"

"Why, indeed?" Hywel asked, so innocently that those within hearing grinned and Ranulf felt an unwanted twinge of pity for Rhodri, so mismatched in any test of wits or will with Hywel. He could understand why Rhodri and Davydd were so consumed with jealousy, for it was like comparing a shooting star to the flickering of candles. How could they compete with a man so renowned, a man who wielded both sword and pen with daunting ease? Hywel's youthful battlefield exploits were still talked of around winter hearths, on nights when mead and memories intermingled. Ranulf knew how rare it was for a great man to sire a son of equal abilities. Too often a Robert of Gloucester produced a son like Ranulf's nephew Will, a sapling grown askew in his father's shadow. But he did not doubt that Hywel, the most celebrated of Owain Gwynedd's many sons, would also prove himself to be the most worthy.

Owain Gwynedd's greeting was cordial enough to hearten Ranulf and to disconcert Rhodri and Davydd, who distrusted Ranulf as much for his friendship with Hywel as for his kinship to the English king. This was Ranulf's first meeting with the Welsh king since Woodstock, and he was hoping for an opportunity to reassure Owain about Henry's intentions toward Wales. Owain readily granted his request for a private audience and heard him out with grave courtesy. But whether his argument was persuasive, Ranulf could not judge. Owain guarded his thoughts the way a miser hoarded coins, giving away nothing of value.

Much to Celyn's discomfort, he and Ranulf were invited to dine upon the dais. It was a signal honor, but one Celyn could have done without. Shy and soft-spoken, he had never expected to be consorting with the princes of the realm. While he tried to pay heed to what he ate and what he heard, knowing Eleri would want a full report, he took little pleasure in the experience.

Ranulf was almost as tense as Celyn, although for entirely different reasons. He was taken aback to find Rhys ap Gruffydd and Owain Cyfeiliog at Owain's hearth. It was true that Rhys was Owain's nephew and Owain Cyfeiliog was wed to Owain's daughter, Gwenllian. But they were political rivals as well as kinsmen, feuding with each other as well as with Owain. He'd not have expected to find either man dining at Owain's table, and as he watched them over the stuffed capon and venison stew, he could not help wondering what their presence here portended.

Owain Cyfeiliog was a noted poet himself, and after the meal was done, he allowed himself to be coaxed into performing his latest poem, *The Long Grey Drinking Horn*. It was a rousing success, enthusiastically received, although one line in particular resonated unpleasantly in Ranulf's imagination: *And many were the dead and dying there.* If war were to break out again between the Welsh and the English Crown, Owain Cyfeiliog's poetry might well become prophecy.

"You are doing it again," Hywel chided softly, catching Ranulf by the arm and steering him toward a window seat. "I can understand a man's wanting to borrow a horse or a knife or a winter blanket, but you are the only one I know who likes to borrow trouble. Let it lie, Ranulf. Just as babies come in God's Own Time, so, too, do wars."

"That is very comforting, Hywel," Ranulf said dryly, and Hywel thumped him playfully on the shoulder.

"You know I am right," he insisted. "No war was ever averted by fretting about it beforehand. Tell me, instead, what happened at Woodstock after we departed. Has Becket's quarrel with the Earl of Hertford been settled yet?"

"The dispute was resolved in the earl's favor. A fortnight after Woodstock, he successfully pleaded before the Common Bench at Westminster that he held Tonbridge Castle directly of the king."

Hywel grimaced. "A pity, for the earl is no friend to the Welsh. Whilst we were at Woodstock, Rhys ap Gruffydd's nephew was treacherously slain in his sleep by one of his own men. The killer escaped and took shelter with the earl, who refuses to turn him over to Rhys for justice to be done. Is there any chance you could intercede with the king on Rhys's behalf?"

Ranulf had already heard of Rhys's latest clash with the Earl of Hertford. He suspected that sooner or later Rhys would have found some reason for breaking faith with the Crown, but he had to admit that the earl had provided a particularly good excuse. He could only hope that when war inevitably flared up again between Rhys and Henry, it would be confined to Rhys's southern domains and not spill over into Gwynedd. "I doubt that it would do any good, Hywel. These days Harry has no thoughts for anything but his upcoming council with Becket at Westminster."

"What are they bickering about now?"

Ranulf sighed. "You'll be sorry you asked. Harry intends to demand that Becket cooperate with him in resolving the danger posed by criminous clerks, men in minor orders who rob and rape and plunder and then plead their clergy when apprehended. The Church insists they be tried before ecclesiastical courts, but the punishment meted out is often ludicrously light. They cannot pronounce a sentence of blood, so a murderer knows he'll not face the hangman, no matter how heinous his offense. And whilst Church courts can cast a man into prison in theory, it is rarely done in practice, owing to the expense of maintaining such prisoners."

Hywel was entertained by Ranulf's formal turn of phrase. "Feeding the poor bastards, you mean. Church law seems better crafted to find penance for sins than punishment for crime."

"Now you sound like Harry," Ranulf said with a smile. "The problem of criminous clerks has long been a thorn in his side, and he hoped to resolve it by putting Becket in Canterbury. He thought that by working together, they'd be able to come up with a solution satisfactory to the Church and Crown alike."

Hywel grinned. "But then Becket experienced that inconvenient religious conversion or whatever it was that transformed him overnight from honey-tongued courtier to crusader for Christ."

Ranulf nodded. "Becket has taken an utterly uncompromising stance, claiming that the king's courts have no jurisdiction to try a man who has taken holy orders, even if that man has committed rape and murder."

"It sounds as if you are speaking of a specific case."

"Harry and Becket have clashed over a number of cases of late. The most outrageous one concerns a clerk in Worcestershire who raped a young girl and then murdered her father. Harry wanted the man brought before his court, but Becket ordered the Bishop-elect of Worcester, my nephew Roger, to imprison the man so the royal justices could not seize him."

"That could not have been a popular decision, especially with the family and friends of the victims. Did people not protest?"

Ranulf shrugged. "Becket believes a principle is at stake and, to him, principles are obviously more important than people. This is not the first time he has intervened when a cleric ran afoul of the law. There was a clerk in London who stole a silver chalice from a church, a priest in Salisbury accused of murder, and then there was that canon of Bedford who was charged with slaying a knight."

"I heard much talk of that case whilst we were at Woodstock," Hywel observed, "more than I wanted to hear, in truth. The canon was tried in the Bishop of Lincoln's court, was he not?"

"Yes, and acquitted by compurgation, when he found twelve respected men willing to swear on his behalf that he was innocent. But that did not satisfy the slain knight's family, for compurgation is not a judgment based upon the evidence, and they appealed to the Sheriff of Bedford, Simon Fitz Peter. He agreed with them, and during an inquest at Dunstable, he tried to reopen the case. Philip de Brois, the accused canon, refused to plead and was verbally abusive to Fitz Peter, who promptly lodged an indignant complaint with the king. Harry was enraged and wanted de Brois charged with contempt of court and murder. But Becket refused to allow it, instead heard the case in his own court. He ruled that de Brois could not be retried for murder as he'd been cleared by the compurgation, and found the canon guilty of the contempt charge, depriving him of his church prebend for two years."

"Somehow I doubt that the king thought the loss of income was a sufficient punishment."

"No, he did not," Ranulf acknowledged, with a wry smile at the memory of his nephew's blazing fury. "The bishops realized that their defense of exclusive Church jurisdiction puts them in the awkward position of appearing to defend murderers and rapists, too. So Becket attempted to resolve the dilemma by inflicting harsher penalties than usual upon these particular accused. The Worcestershire clerk is still awaiting trial. But Becket ordered that the Salisbury priest charged with murder be confined for life to a monastery, and the punishment for the theft of the chalice was branding."

Hywel blinked in surprise. "Canon law does not authorize such punishment, though."

"No, it does not. In his attempt to placate the king and public opinion, Becket miscalculated. Harry was even more wroth with him after that, for he saw these acts as a usurpation of royal authority."

Hywel shook his head slowly. "You're right. I am sorry I asked."

"My lord Ranulf?"

Startled, Ranulf got hastily to his feet, then gallantly kissed Cristyn's hand while disregarding Hywel's mocking smile. Cristyn acted as if her stepson were invisible, turning all of her considerable charms upon Ranulf. She asked solicitously about Rhiannon, offered her congratulations upon learning of the pregnancy, and made him promise to let her know when the baby was born so she could send a christening gift. Ranulf was puzzled, for he'd never gotten more than grudging courtesy from her before, and when she lured him away from Hywel, he followed willingly; curiosity had always been his besetting sin.

"I was wondering . . ." Cristyn smiled at Ranulf as if they were intimate friends and he found himself appreciating how adroitly she wielded the weapons God had given her. She did not let him forget for a moment that she was a beautiful, desirable woman, but one beyond reach, for she herself would never forget that she was the wife of Owain Gwynedd. Passing strange, he thought, that she could have birthed two sons so lacking in subtlety as Rhodri and Davydd. "What were you wondering, my lady?"

"I am somewhat shy of admitting it." Her dimple deepened. "My lord husband does not like me to pay heed to gossip. But I heard an intriguing rumor from Cadwaladr's English wife. She says that the Archbishop of Canterbury has forbidden the English king's brother to wed the de Warenne heiress. Can this be true?"

"I am sorry to say that it is," Ranulf confirmed. "I had a letter from my niece, the Countess of Chester, just a fortnight ago. Will is sorely distraught, for he had his heart set upon wedding Isabella and, in truth, I think he craves the lady as much as her lands. But unless the king can persuade Lord Thomas to withdraw his objections, the marriage is not likely to be. The Archbishop of Canterbury is the spiritual head of the Church in England, and his voice echoes loudest with His Holiness, the Pope."

"Why does Becket oppose the marriage?"

"It offends the laws of consanguinity, for Will and Isabella are distant cousins, as was her late husband."

Cristyn's dark eyes shone with silent laughter. "Is that all? Owain and I are first cousins, for his mother and my father were sister and brother. But he did not let a minor matter like that deter him from taking me to wife. Poor Gwilym," she said, making use of the Welsh equivalent for William. "I suppose he'd not dare to defy the archbishop? I confess that I was not much taken with this Thomas Becket at Woodstock. Is this why the English king is so wroth with him?"

"He is greatly vexed by the archbishop's opposition to the marriage, for dispensations have been granted for those far more closely related than Will and Isabella. But this is just one more grievance amongst many."

"You know the king so well," she said admiringly, "from the skin out!"

Ranulf wasn't sure how to respond, for he still had not figured out what she wanted from him, sure only that she had more in mind than an exchange of court gossip. "Well, I am his uncle," he said finally.

"Yes, but there is a closeness between you that goes deeper than blood. I saw that as soon as I saw you together at Woodstock," she murmured and Ranulf suddenly understood her intent. She had revised her opinion of him after Woodstock, decided that he was worth cultivating on the off chance that she might be able to win him over to her side.

In light of his long-standing friendship with Hywel, Ranulf supposed he ought to be flattered that she thought it was still worth the effort. Their eyes met and he caught a glimmer—ever so briefly—of the steel beneath the silk. His gaze shifted from her face, across the hall to where Hywel was watching them, monitoring Cristyn's maternal maneuverings with sardonic amusement, and he wished that his nephew had been blessed, too, with the ability to laugh at his foes. Mayhap then this looming confrontation between Harry and Thomas Becket would not seem so ominous, so fraught with peril.

FROM THE DAIS, Henry had an unobstructed view of Westminster's great hall. The men seated upon rows of benches were princes of the Church and lords of the realm, the most powerful men in his domains. On this mild October morning, they had gathered in answer to his summons, ostensibly to heal a rift between Thomas Becket, Archbishop of Canterbury, and Roger de Pont l'Eveque, Archbishop of York. But Henry had a more ambitious agenda in mind. Now that the preliminary ceremonies were done, he held up his hand, waiting for silence.

"I would speak now of a serious matter, a grievous threat to the King's Peace." A murmur swept the hall, a rustling of leaves before the wind, and Henry rose to his feet. "I have been England's king for nigh on nine years," he said. "Do any of you know how many murders have been committed by clerics in that time? My lord archbishop?"

Thomas Becket had been given a seat of honor upon the dais. At Henry's unexpected query, he shook his head, almost imperceptibly.

"More than one hundred murders . . . committed by men of God, most of whom were never called to account for their crimes."

"We all answer to the Almighty for our sins, my liege."

Henry smiled, very thinly. "I naturally defer to you, my lord archbishop, in spiritual matters. But my concern is not with the immortal souls of these criminous clerks. Whether they be damned or saved at God's Throne does not interest me much. I seek to keep the peace in my domains and to provide justice to my subjects. And royal justice is perverted when men can rape and murder and then plead their clergy to escape the punishment they deserve."

Gilbert Foliot tried and failed to catch Becket's eye. He feared that Henry was about to bring up the case of that wretched Worcestershire cleric, an embarrassment to them all. If worse came to worst and the king demanded that they yield jurisdiction to the royal court, he hoped Becket would have the sense to temporize, offer to put the matter before the Pope. Sometimes a principle could be best defended by making a strategic retreat; the trick was to give up ground they could afford to lose.

But Henry now chose to drag another skeleton out of the Church's closet. "I daresay you all remember the scandalous case of the Archdeacon Osbert, accused of poisoning the Archbishop of York. Out of the great respect I held for Archbishop Theobald, may God assoil him, I reluctantly agreed that the man should be tried in a Church court. What was the result? A formal judgment was never reached, thwarted by the man's appeal to Rome. If Holy Church cannot provide justice to a murdered archbishop, what hope is there for victims of lesser rank? You need only ask the kinsmen of the knight slain by Philip de Brois."

Thomas Becket got hastily to his feet. "My lord king, I must protest. Philip de Brois was found innocent by the Bishop of Lincoln's court, as you well know."

"Only because he found twelve men willing to swear on his behalf. Why should a sworn oath matter more than the evidence?"

"Need I remind you," Becket said gravely, "that the act of perjury imperils a man's immortal soul? Surely few men would dare to put their salvation at risk by lying under oath."

"And surely few men would commit robbery and rape and homicide after taking holy orders," Henry shot back. "Ah, but they do, my lord archbishop . . . they do! And what befalls these renegades once they are caught? They are degraded. But do you truly think a man capable of unholy murder will care if he is stripped of his priestly privileges? You might as well seek to deflect a charging bull by scattering straw in its path!"

The bishops were shifting uneasily in their seats, for Henry seemed poised for an all-out assault upon the Church's exclusive jurisdiction. Foliot stared intently at Becket, willing the other man to tread with care; there was too much at stake for bravado. But Becket chose, instead, to fling down a challenge.

"Surely you do not have it in mind to encroach upon our courts, my liege? That issue was clearly settled in King Stephen's charter of 1136, in which it was agreed that 'Jurisdiction over clergy shall lie in the hands of the bishops.'"

Foliot winced, unable to believe Becket could have been so tactless, for Henry would be the last man alive to be swayed by precedent established during Stephen's reign, which he considered a time of "unlaw." Glancing toward Henry, he saw it was as he feared: the king's jaw muscles had clenched, his color deepening.

"I doubt that the boundaries are as well defined as you seem to think, my lord archbishop. Be that as it may, I am not proposing to deny the Church jurisdiction over its own. I am prepared to be reasonable. I seek only to punish the guilty, those criminous clerks who have already been judged in the Episcopal courts. Once these men have been found guilty and degraded, they are no longer men of God. I would have them then turned over to my courts for sentencing." Henry's voice, normally hoarse, dropped even further, coming out as a low, ominous rasp. "Surely that seems fair," he said, in what was not so much a question as a warning.

Becket shook his head slowly. "The clergy, by reason of their orders and distinctive office, have Christ alone as king. And since they are not under secular kings, but under the King of Heaven, they should be punished by their own law. Degradation is a harsh penalty, suitable for most offenses. In addition to the shame of it, it deprives a man of his livelihood. You would impose a double penalty for the same crime, and I cannot agree to that. St Jerome spoke clearly to that very issue when he said, 'God judges not twice for the same offense.'"

Henry had not expected Becket to reject his proposal out of hand, for he truly thought his reform was a moderate one. "If degradation were the 'harsh penalty' you think it is, it would be a deterrent to your wayward clerks and criminous priests. Clearly, that is not so. As for double punishment, it seems to me that a crime committed by a man who has taken holy orders is more despicable for that very reason, as it is a betrayal of God. Such men deserve no mercy. I am not willing to concede that priests and clerics are above the King's Law. But that is not at issue here. We are talking of punishing men who have been found guilty in your own courts, men who can no longer claim the protective immunity of their holy vows. Where is the injustice in that?"

For the first time, Becket glanced over at the other bishops, his gaze lingering upon their tense, pale faces. When he turned back to Henry, he said, "I, too, am prepared to be reasonable, my liege. We would be willing to agree that if a cleric was tried in our courts and degraded and then subsequently committed another offense, he should be subject to the jurisdiction of your courts."

"Would you, indeed? So you are saying that you'd not object if a former priest went on a murderous rampage and I chose to try him in my own court? How truly magnanimous of you!"

Henry's sarcasm was so savage that a number of the bishops flinched. But Becket did not back down. "I am sorry you think so little of our concession, my liege. I can only say to you what Our Lord Christ said to the Pharisees: 'Render unto Caesar the things that are Caesar's, and to God the things that are God's.'"

"Let's talk, then, of what is owed to Caesar. Would you deny that you owe allegiance and loyalty to the Crown?"

"Of course not."

"So you would be willing, then, to abide by the ancient customs of the realm?"

Becket frowned. "Just what are you asking of us, my liege?"

"You require a translation, my lord archbishop? I want to know if you are willing to swear here and now to obey the ancient customs of the realm. A simple enough question, I should think. What say you?"

"Ere I say anything, my lord king, I wish to consult with my fellow bishops."

Henry's eyes glittered. "I thought you listened only to the Almighty these days."

Becket drew a sharp breath. They stared at each other, the others in the hall forgotten, the silence fraught with suspicion and all that lay unspoken between them.

Eleanor quickened her step at the sight of her brother-in-law. "Will? Why are you not at the council?"

"We adjourned for an hour so that Becket and the other bishops could discuss Harry's demand."

He did not need to be more explicit, for Henry had confided in Eleanor his strategy: if they balked at allowing him to punish former clerks, he meant to fall back upon the ancient customs of the realm, just as his grandfather had done in a dispute with another contentious archbishop.

"I doubt that Becket will agree," she said. "He seems to think that if he yields so much as an inch to Harry, it will brand him as a heretic and apostate, unworthy to wear Canterbury's mitre."

"You think he is sincere?"

"Yes," she said thoughtfully, "I am sorry to say that I do. He'd be easier to deal with if he were not. Zealots are always more troublesome than hypocrites, Will, for they never doubt they are in the right." She almost added, "Rather like kings," but she knew Will would not appreciate such subversive humor. In that, he was very much his mother's son. She'd always been grateful that her husband had inherited Geoffrey's irony as well as his fair coloring, although it was a pity that he'd passed along the infamous Angevin obstinacy, too. Well, whatever Harry's faults, at least he was never boring, and that meant much to a woman wed for fifteen years to the French king.

Will was still talking about Becket, and she focused her attention upon him again. Alas, Will *was* boring these days, for his only topic of conversation seemed to be the wrong done him by the archbishop. She doubted that his marriage would have turned out for the best. His expectations were too unrealistic; Isabella de Warenne could not possibly have lived up to them. She was sorry, though, that he was so unhappy, for he

was a likable lad, putting her in mind of her own half-brothers, who cared
more for pleasure than politics and were blessedly free of envy or spite.

"You must not despair, Will," she said. "If Becket cannot be coaxed
or coerced into dropping his objections to your marriage, Harry will appeal to the Pope on your behalf."

"That will not help. The Pope will not want to offend his own archbishop."

"He'll not want to offend the King of England, either. As long
as Harry supports him against that puppet the Holy Roman Emperor has
set up in Rome, it is very much in Alexander's interest to keep Harry's
goodwill."

"Yes, but he can delay acting upon my request for a dispensation, neither granting it nor denying it. What better way to deal with an awkward
issue than by ignoring it?"

Eleanor thought that was an astute assessment of the workings of
the papal court, too astute and cynical for Will. "What makes you say
that, lad?"

"I asked the Bishop of Lisieux to tell me honestly what my chances
were. He said I ought not to get my hopes up, that vexatious petitions have
a way of getting conveniently lost in the papal archives."

Eleanor could not help smiling, for that sounded just like Arnulf of
Lisieux. A shrewd, worldly man in his late fifties, he was as noted for his
political acumen as for his erudition, and since his arrival from his Norman see, he'd been advising Henry how best to outmaneuver Becket. She
regretted, though, that he'd seen fit to strip Will of his optimism. Will
needed hope as much as he did air and food.

"You ought to know by now that your brother is one for getting his
own way," she chided. "If anyone can pry a dispensation from the Pope,
for certes it is Harry." The words were no sooner out of her mouth than
her husband appeared in the doorway of the great hall. She patted Will
absently on the arm, then moved to meet Henry.

"Will says Becket and the bishops are conferring in private. Could
you tell if the others seem to be siding with Becket?"

"If they do, they'll regret it," he said tersely. He didn't appear to want
to talk, not a good sign. He stalked down the steps and she had to hasten
to keep pace with him. She had never been particularly troubled by his
rages, for she came from a volatile family herself. Her father's spectacular
fits of fury had shaped her views of normal male behavior, and Louis's
mild manner had seemed neither manly nor royal to her. Her baffled and

bitter comment to her sister that "I thought I'd married a king and found I'd married a monk" could well serve as the epitaph for their marriage.

So when Henry fumed and seethed and ranted, she took his tempers in stride. She'd soon realized that there was a degree of calculation to his rages, just one more weapon in his arsenal. And she agreed with him; far better that a king be feared than loved. But his anger against Becket was different. It was stoked by pain, and she could imagine no fuel more inflammable, and therefore more dangerous.

Henry had paused on the walkway, gazing up unseeingly at the cloud-flecked sky. "I swear he takes pleasure in thwarting me at every turn. How can he be so ungrateful? All that he is, he owes to me. Yet each time I hold out an olive branch to him, he spits upon it. How long does he think he can trade on our past friendship? I will never understand how I could have misjudged him so badly—never!"

Eleanor did not fully understand it, either. How could these two men have been such close friends and yet misread each other so calamitously? Her husband had utterly failed to anticipate the archbishop Becket would become. But what of Becket? Had he learned nothing in their years together? How could he not realize what a formidable and unforgiving enemy Harry would make?

CHAPTER FIFTEEN

✦

October 1163
Westminster, England

"WELL?" HENRY'S EYES MOVED from face to face, then focused intently upon Thomas Becket. "You've had an opportunity to confer. Are you willing to swear to obey the ancient customs of the realm?"

Becket met his gaze unwaveringly. "The customs of Holy Church are fully set forth in the canons and decrees of the Fathers. It is not fitting for you, my lord king, to demand anything that goes beyond these, nor ought we to consent to any innovations. We who now stand in the place of the Fathers ought to humbly obey the old laws, not establish new ones."

"I am not asking you to do anything of the sort," Henry snapped. "I ask only that the customs which were observed in the times of my predecessors be also observed in my reign. In those days there were holier and better archbishops than you who consented to these customs, raising no controversy about them with their kings."

"Whatever was done by former kings that violated the canons and whatever practices were observed out of fear of those kings ought not to be called customs, but rather abuses. Scriptures teach us that such depraved practices ought to be abolished, not extended. You say that the holy bishops of those times kept silent and did not complain. Mayhap those were days for silence. But their example does not give us the authority to assent to anything that is done against God or our order."

Henry's breathing had quickened. "You are saying, then, that you refuse?"

"No, my liege. We have discussed your demand and we are willing to swear to honor the customs of the realm . . . saving our order."

"And what in hellfire does that mean?"

"That we refuse to acknowledge those customs which we believe to violate canon law."

"Just as I thought! This is a poisonous phrase," Henry snarled, "full of guile, and I will not accept it! You will swear without conditions and you will swear now."

"No, my liege," Becket said, "we will not."

"Does this man speak for you all?" Henry whirled around on the other bishops. "My lord bishop of London, what say you?"

Gilbert Foliot approached the dais. "I will swear to abide by the customs of the realm, my liege, but saving our order."

Henry stared at him in disbelief. "What of the rest of you?" he demanded, his gaze raking the assembled prelates. "Speak for yourselves and speak now."

One by one, they did. Stephen's brother, Henry of Blois, Bishop of Winchester, whose ambition had once been all-consuming. Roger de Pont l'Eveque, the Archbishop of York, whose animosity toward Becket stretched back as far as their youthful service in the household of Archbishop Theobald of blessed memory. Roger of Gloucester, the Bishop-elect of Worcester, Henry's own cousin. Jocelin de Bohun, Bishop of Salisbury, who'd long been out of Henry's favor. Bartholomew, Bishop of Exeter. The aged Robert de Chesney, Bishop of Lincoln. Robert de Melun, a noted theologian and Bishop-elect of Hereford. As Henry listened in growing fury, each man echoed the oath offered by Thomas Becket, adding somberly or nervously the phrase he found so odious: "Saving our order." Only Hilary, Bishop of Chichester wavered, offering instead to obey the customs in "good faith."

But to Henry, that was no concession. To the contrary, he suspected Chichester of attempting to add another qualification to the oath and cut the older man off angrily in mid-explanation. "Enough of this sophistry and equivocation! I'll put the question to you but one more time, and think carefully ere you answer. For all our sakes, think very carefully. Are you willing to swear to abide by the customs of the realm . . . or are you not?"

Becket stepped forward again. "My lord king," he said, "we have already sworn fealty to you by our life and limbs and earthly honor, saving our order, and the customs of the kingdom are included in those words, 'earthly honor.' We cannot promise more than that."

Henry swung toward his former chancellor, his one-time friend. Becket gazed back calmly. His face was impassive, but Henry thought he could detect a glint of triumph in the other man's eyes. Instead of lashing out, he somehow managed to swallow the words, as bitter as bile. Coming down the steps of the dais, he stalked up the aisle. As the bishops and his barons watched in consternation, he strode out of the hall.

E LEANOR RAISED HERSELF UP on an elbow, stifling a yawn. "I feel like I'm sharing my bed with an eel," she complained, "what with all your squirming and thrashing about. Are you never going to sleep, Harry?"

"What do you think I've been trying to do?" he asked irritably. "Sleep is not a trained dog, coming when it's called." Sitting up, he occupied himself in pounding his pillow into submission, But no matter how he molded it, it was not to his satisfaction. "It is no use," he said. "I just cannot get comfortable."

Eleanor sighed. She did not want to rehash the day's events, having spent the evening listening to her husband fulminate against Thomas Becket's treachery. She'd had no success in soothing him, and was in no mood to continue trying. If he'd listened to her when he'd first gotten that foolhardy idea to make Becket an archbishop, how much grief they could all have been spared.

She found it both frustrating and vexing that he did not pay more heed to her advice. She had been counseling him for months that he should seek to isolate Becket from the other bishops, but he'd not taken the suggestion seriously until he'd heard it from Arnulf of Lisieux. Their world was full of men who seemed to think wombs and brains were incompatible, but she did not believe he was one of them. For certes, he respected his mother's political judgment, honed as it had been on heartbreak and loss. Watching as Henry pummeled the pillow again, she remembered a remark he'd once made, that she and his mother and Becket were the only ones he truly trusted. Well, Becket was now the enemy and Maude in Normandy. Reaching over, she slid her hand up his arm.

"Becket's triumph will be fleeting. Come the morrow, he will discover that there is a price to be paid for his defiance, higher than he expected, I daresay. Now put him out of your thoughts, for there is no room for three in our bed. Lie back and relax."

"I cannot sleep, Eleanor," he said impatiently, but when he turned toward her, he saw that she was smiling, a smile filled with indulgent amusement and sultry promise.

"I am not suggesting," she said, "that we sleep."

H ENRY'S ABRUPT DEPARTURE had thrown the council into turmoil, and it had broken up in confusion and dismay. When the bishops assembled the next morning, it was evident that many of them had spent an uneasy night. Westminster's great hall was a dismal scene, empty except for servants and a few men-at-arms. To more than one prelate, the air still echoed with the king's wrathful warning: *You will swear without conditions and you will swear now.* What would be the consequences of defying him? His grandfather and great-grandfather had both had a summary way of dealing with opposition. So had his father. When Herbert of Bosham, one of Becket's clerks, chose to remind the bishops that the Counts of Anjou were said to trace their descent from the Devil's daughter, his ill-timed jest evoked no laughter.

Gilbert Foliot sat down wearily upon one of the wooden benches and was soon joined by Roger, Worcester's bishop-elect. "The king seems to be sleeping late," Roger said.

Another man so closely akin to the king would have made a proprietary reference to his "cousin," but Roger had a becoming sense of modesty, never flaunting his royal connections, and Foliot smiled approvingly. He and Thomas Becket might not agree on much, but they were united in their high esteem for their younger colleague. "I hope," he said, "that the king had a better night than I did. I was wakeful into the early hours, and when I finally did sleep, my dreams were anything but restful."

"Nor were mine," Roger admitted. "I am heartsick over this, for no good can come of it. Yet what choice had we? If we'd agreed to the king's demand, who is to say what surprises might lurk down the road, hidden in the brambles of ancient custom?"

"Just so," Foliot agreed reluctantly. What if the king used their assent to forbid them to obey a papal summons? Or if he chose to leave bishoprics vacant indefinitely, thus allowing him to appropriate the revenues?

It was not that Foliot suspected the king of acting in bad faith. But it was his experience that kings were rarely satisfied with boundaries; they were always looking to expand their influence into new spheres. And this king in particular was too adept at taking a weak claim and turning it into an indisputable one. What infuriated Foliot was his conviction that this confrontation need not have happened. There had been numerous opportunities for compromise, all lost or deliberately thrown away.

Foliot's eyes shifted, coming to rest accusingly upon the tall figure of Thomas Becket. He said nothing, though, for this was neither the time nor the place for such recriminations. If they hoped to prevail, they must present a united front to the king. He just wished he had more confidence in the man leading them into battle.

Roger was watching Becket, too, although without Foliot's animosity. Roger was easily the most riven of those caught up in this contest of wills between king and archbishop, for he was deeply fond of both Henry and Becket. He'd noticed that a few barons had begun to straggle into the hall. But there was still no sign of the king or his justiciars, and he wondered if Henry was deliberately delaying his arrival for maximum effect, playing a cat-and-mouse game meant to shred their nerves and shake their resolve.

Several of the bishops were staring toward the door, and Roger turned to see if Henry was finally arriving. At the sight of the man standing in the doorway, he frowned, for he recognized Simon Fitz Peter, the Sheriff of Bedfordshire who'd clashed so acrimoniously with the disgraced canon, Philip de Brois.

The sheriff paused and then announced in a loud, carrying voice, "I have a message for the Archbishop of Canterbury." Filled with foreboding, Roger watched as Fitz Peter moved briskly up the center aisle of the hall. If Becket shared Roger's unease, he was better at hiding it. "What message is that?" he asked coolly.

"A message from my lord king."

"He is delayed?"

Roger knew the message was more ominous than that, for it was not by mere happenchance that Henry had selected as his emissary the man mired in the middle of the controversy over Philip de Brois. He was sure that Becket knew it, too, and admired the archbishop's sangfroid even as he braced himself for trouble.

"The king is gone." The sheriff's manner was stiffly correct, but he could not keep the echoes of satisfaction from his voice. "He left Westminster at first light."

There were smothered exclamations at that, whisperings of dismay. A flicker of surprise crossed Becket's face. "He has no plans to return, then?"

"No, my lord archbishop. He said the council's business was done."

"I see. Well . . . we thank you for informing us of his departure."

It was a polite dismissal, but Fitz Peter did not move. "That was not the king's message, my lord." With a deliberately dramatic flourish, he drew two parchment scrolls from within his mantle. "As you can see, my lord, these writs bear the king's seal." He held them out to Becket. "King Henry orders you to yield up to him the castle of Berkhamsted and the Honour of Eye."

Becket had held Berkhamsted and Eye since the days of his chancellorship; he would feel the loss of their income keenly. But the public humiliation stung far worse. Reaching out, he took the writs, but made no attempt to break the seal.

"My lord archbishop . . . do you not want to read the writs?" The sheriff's courtesy was poisonous. "The second one concerns the young prince."

Becket's hand clenched on the scrolls. "What of him?"

"The king no longer wants you to assume responsibility for the education of his eldest son. You are to surrender custody of the young lord forthwith."

A BRISK NOVEMBER WIND was blowing dead leaves across the road, causing Henry's stallion to prance sideways, pawing the frozen ground. Thomas Becket was awaiting him beyond Northampton's walls, and it was Henry's doing, but he was already regretting that rash impulse. He knew his action had surprised many, including himself, but only Eleanor had dared to question him, and with her, he'd fallen back upon a half-truth: that he owed it to Will to try one last time to reconcile his own differences with Becket. She could hardly quarrel with that, and indeed he did want to salvage his brother's sinking marital hopes, if at all possible.

His motives were more ambiguous and complicated, though, than mere brotherly concern. He still could not believe that he'd so misjudged Becket. He'd never given his trust easily, even with those he loved. Very few ever got through his outer defenses. But Thomas Becket had been his closest friend. He'd enjoyed Becket's company, valued his intelligence, relied upon his discretion and steadfast loyalty. Thomas had been the perfect chancellor, shrewd and worldly and ruthless when need be. Now he was the perfect archbishop, defending the rights of Holy Church as passionately as he'd once defended the Crown and his king. Which man was the real Thomas Becket? Henry needed to know if their friendship had been a lie from the very first. Had Becket played him for Christendom's greatest fool?

And so he had summoned Becket, impulsively, before he could think better of it. The archbishop had obeyed, but brought such a large entourage that Henry's unease had flared into resentment. He'd hoped to meet a penitent, not this prideful prince of the Church, and he'd angrily sent Becket word to hold his men outside Northampton, claiming that there were not enough lodgings in the town to accommodate the royal retinue and the lord archbishop's, too. Almost at once, though, he relented, and called for his stallion.

The archbishop had turned aside into a large meadow, midst a growing crowd of curious spectators. Thomas had always been one for drawing attention to himself, Henry thought sourly, remembering his chancellor's spectacular entry into Paris five years before. Telling his men to wait, he spurred his mount forward.

Becket hastily swung up into the saddle and galloped out to meet Henry. Both men were riding spirited young stallions, though, and their high-strung destriers reacted as if this were a battlefield encounter, plunging and rearing and screaming defiance as soon as they were within striking range. Henry and Becket were skilled riders, but neither man was able to calm his combative horse. This development, as ludicrous as it was anticlimactic, would once have had them roaring with laughter. Now it roused not even a smile. After several futile attempts to divert their stallions from confrontation, they were forced to wheel their fractious mounts, ride back to their waiting escorts.

Henry's justiciar, Richard de Lucy, at once offered his own horse. One of Becket's clerks did the same. Mounting again, they rode toward each other across the barren, frost-glazed meadow, this time at a more measured pace. The wind was picking up, catching at their billowing mantles and the brims of their hats, chilling them both to the bone. Henry reined in first; how had he not realized until now just how wretchedly cold the day was?

"You wished to see me, my liege?"

Becket's words and manner were respectful—and so distant that it suddenly seemed to Henry that they were miles and worlds apart. He had rehearsed a short speech, dignified but hinting at possible concession and compromise. Those carefully crafted words were forgotten. Urging his stallion in closer, he said hoarsely:

"You were my friend. Did I not raise you from a poor and lowly station to the summit of honor and rank? Do you truly think you'd ever have become Canterbury's archbishop if not for me? How is it, then, that after so many benefits, so many proofs of my love for you, you have blotted them all from your mind? Not only are you ungrateful, Thomas, but by God, you go out of your way to oppose me in everything!"

"That is not so, my lord king. I have not forgotten your favors, which are not yours alone, for God deigned to confer them on me through you. Far be it from me to show myself ungrateful or to act contrary to your will in anything that accords with the Will of God. Your Grace knows how faithful I have been to you. You are indeed my liege lord, but He is both your Lord and mine. It would be useful neither to you nor to me if I were to neglect His Will in order to obey yours. For on His Fearful Day of Judgment, you and I will both be judged as servants of one Lord. Neither of us will be able to answer then for the other and no excuses will avail, for we will receive our due according to our acts. It is true that temporal lords must be obeyed, but not against the Almighty. As St Peter said, 'We must obey God rather than men.'"

Henry had been listening incredulously. He had bared his soul to Thomas, at last admitted to his sense of hurt and betrayal, and this pedantic, bloodless lecture was Becket's response? "I want no sermon from you!" Shame was not an emotion he'd often experienced, but he felt shame now that he could have revealed his heart's pain so nakedly. Seeking a weapon to inflict a wound as grievous as his own, he found it by recalling Becket's Achilles' heel—his pride.

"After all, are you not the son of one of my villeins?" That scornful taunt was guaranteed to penetrate Becket's shield, for in their society, few insults were more offensive than an accusation of low birth. And Becket, as Henry well knew, was sensitive about his family background; it had not been easy for the son of a London merchant to rise to the rarefied heights of power and privilege.

Just as Henry had expected, his barb drew blood. Becket's face flooded with heat. "It is true," he said, "that I am not 'sprung from royal ancestors,' if I may quote from Horace. But neither was Peter, the blessed Prince of the Apostles, upon whom Our Lord conferred the keys to the Kingdom of Heaven and the primacy over the Holy Church."

"That is true," Henry agreed. "But St Peter died for his Lord."

Becket's head came up. "I, too, will die for my Lord when the time comes."

Henry's mouth dropped open. His angry words had been a reproach, not a threat, a pointed reminder that St Peter had been loyal unto death— unlike Thomas, the faithless friend. He started to explain himself, then stopped abruptly. He stared at the other man, and it was as if he were looking at an utter stranger, someone he'd never known at all.

POPE ALEXANDER III was not pleased to find himself dragged into the conflict between the English king and Canterbury's archbishop. Alexander's position was a precarious one: stranded in French exile by the papal schism, dependent upon the goodwill of those sovereigns who'd re- fused to recognize the legitimacy of the puppet Pope, who was sheltered in Rome by the Holy Roman Emperor. When Henry dispatched Arnulf of Lisieux to the papal court at Sens, the Pope listened to his complaints and concluded that he was not proposing anything that was contrary to the teachings of the Church. Several of the English bishops had already sought to persuade Becket to compromise with the king, only to be re- buffed sharply. But Becket could not so easily dismiss those who spoke on the Pope's behalf. In December, he was visited at Harrow, his manor in Middlesex, by the highly respected Abbot of l'Aumone, the Count of Vendôme, and Robert de Melun, the Bishop-elect of Hereford.

They reminded Becket of the dangers inherent in the papal schism and urged him to take a more moderate stance in his dealings with Henry. They assured him that Henry had promised not to introduce any novel customs or make any demands that the bishops could not obey in good conscience. The Pope wanted this dispute settled amicably and would as- sume the responsibility for any harm the Church might suffer in conse- quence. Becket eventually agreed to swear to abide by the ancient customs without the qualification that Henry had found so abhorrent, and the pa- pal envoys dared to hope that this inconvenient crisis would soon be re- solved, to the mutual satisfaction of Church and Crown.

FREEZING RAIN AND SLEET had been falling since dawn and even a blazing open fire could not banish the damp, pervasive chill from the great hall. The wretched weather had not deterred Thomas Becket. Accompanied by the papal envoys, he arrived at Henry's Woodstock manor soon after dark. The hall was filled with royal retainers, barons, men-at-arms, and servants, all eager to witness this December meeting between their king and the archbishop. There was considerable sympathy for Will, who was uncommonly well liked for a king's brother, and a number of the younger knights muttered amongst themselves as Becket strode up the center aisle toward the dais.

If Becket was aware of their disapproval, he gave no indication of it, his expression somber, his gaze anchored upon Henry. He seemed composed, but Eleanor could detect signs of the toll this conflict was taking. He'd lost weight and there was a sprinkling of silver in the thick, dark hair framing his face. He was thirteen years older than her husband, less than a week away from his forty-third birthday. But he had fine bone structure, would likely age well. If she were casting for the role of archbishop, she had to concede that he looked the part, for certes. She'd known him for nigh on ten years, but he remained an enigma to her. She'd never understood men who claimed to speak for the Almighty. How could they be so sure that they had God's Ear?

As Queen of France, she'd had such a man as her greatest enemy, the much venerated Bernard, Abbot of Clairvaux. He had been dead since 1153, and if the rumors she heard were true, he might eventually be canonized as a saint. No matter what the Church did, though, she would never see Abbot Bernard as holy. Saints were supposed to be forgiving, for Scriptures said that the Lord God would forgive men their iniquity and remember their sin no more. But Abbot Bernard had not been one for forgiving his foes. He'd never doubted that he was in the right, that he was the Chosen Instrument of the Lord. She'd been scornful of that absolute certainty of his, but chilled by it, too, for who could argue with one anointed by the Almighty? She found herself hoping now that Thomas Becket did not share Bernard's fervent belief that he and he alone was doing God's Work.

Henry's greeting and Becket's obeisance were spokes on the same wheel: courteous, correct, and formal. The Abbot of l'Aumone was an eloquent speaker and he did what he could to ease the awkwardness. But this was not a social occasion, and there was no pretense otherwise. Becket had come to make amends, and Henry waited now to hear what he would say.

He did not get off to the best of starts, talking at length of the virtues and vices of past kings with an earnestness that put Eleanor in mind of a church sermon; whatever had happened to the man's sense of humor? She glanced at Henry to see if he was vexed by Becket's moralizing tone. His expression was inscrutable. Even she, who knew him so well, could not tell what he was thinking.

Becket had finally reached the crux of the matter. "Know that I shall observe the customs of your kingdom in good faith, and I shall be obedient to you in all things that are just and right."

Eleanor's head turned sharply toward Henry. It was true that Becket had dropped the qualifying phrase, "saving our order," but that still did not sound to her like an unconditional offer of obedience. Henry showed no displeasure, though, at the form of the archbishop's declaration. As his eyes met Eleanor's, a corner of his mouth curved down and a brow went up, an expression she recognized at once: one of ironic amusement. And she knew then that her husband had a surprise in store for his archbishop. Bemused and irked that he had not seen fit to confide in her beforehand, she waited to see what it was.

"All know," Henry said, "how stubborn you were in your opposition, my lord archbishop, and how careless you were of my royal dignity by contradicting me so arrantly in public. If you are now resolved to honor me as you ought, it is only fair that the retraction should be made in as public a manner as your defiance was. Therefore, I would have you convene the bishops and abbots and the other eminent ecclesiastics, and I for my part will summon my barons and lords, so that these words restoring my honor can be uttered in their presence and hearing."

Becket swung around to exchange glances with the papal envoy. Neither man had expected this, having been led to believe that Henry would be satisfied with a recantation here at Woodstock. But it was not an unreasonable demand and could not be refused without giving fresh offense. "If that is your wish," Becket said, "so be it."

Henry nodded. "We will meet in a month's time, then," he said, so nonchalantly that Eleanor alone realized what had just occurred. Becket and the papal envoy thought the dispute was done, when, in truth, it was only beginning.

H ENRY CHOSE TO SPEND his Christmas court that year at Berkhampsted, the castle he'd reclaimed from Thomas Becket.

CHAPTER SIXTEEN

✦

January 1164
Clarendon, England

T HE COUNTESS OF CHESTER reached Clarendon at dusk. She knew her son was not going to be pleased to see her, but this was his first summons to the king's council and she could not resist the temptation to watch him playing a man's role. Hugh was a good-natured boy whose greatest flaw was that he was too easily influenced, too eager to please. Maud was not a woman who'd ever harbored illusions and she knew her firstborn was ordinary, a banked fire at best. She loved him fiercely, though, intensely grateful to God that he was so unlike the unstable, savage man who'd sired him, and now that he was in attendance upon the king, she meant to see that none of the court wolves harried her lamb.

Hugh was indeed embarrassed by her maternal solicitude, but too excited by the day's high drama to make more than a perfunctory protest. "Have you seen the king yet, Mama? Did you hear what happened?"

"I spoke with Harry and Eleanor but briefly, upon my arrival. I could see that he was in a temper, though. Did he and Thomas Becket lock horns again?"

Hugh nodded solemnly. "When the council began, Cousin Harry declared that it was not enough for the archbishop and the other bishops to swear to obey the ancient customs of the realm. He said that was too vague, that there ought to be a clear understanding of what those customs were. But when he started to set them forth, Thomas Becket and the bishops balked, and he flew into a great rage. He . . . he is a daunting man to defy, Mama."

Maud thought Henry's fits of temper were mere child's play when compared to the lunatic furies of her late husband. "I am sure that is exactly what he wants men to think, Hugh. Tell me about these customs. What are they, precisely?"

Hugh looked uncomfortable. "I cannot recall each and every one," he said, so vaguely that she realized he'd been paying more heed to the fire's flames than to the fuel feeding it. "There was talk of criminous clerks again, and I think the king wants to limit papal appeals . . ."

Maud didn't bother to interrogate him further; it was obvious that she needed a more knowledgeable source than her sixteen-year-old son. And she had just the man in mind. "Where," she asked, "is your uncle Roger?"

ALL BUT THREE of the bishops had answered the king's summons to Clarendon, and no less than ten earls and numerous barons. Clarendon could not accommodate them all, and the participants had been forced to find lodgings in Old Sarum, four miles to the west, in nearby villages, even camping out in Clarendon's deer park. Becket had quartered his retinue at Old Sarum, as had many of the other bishops, but Maud's brother, the Bishop-elect of Worcester, had accepted the hospitality of the Augustinian canons at Ivychurch, a small priory just two miles from Clarendon, and it was there that she tracked him down long after darkness had fallen.

Unsullied snow shrouded the inner garth, ghostly white in the pallid moonlight. The night sky was clear of clouds, the air cold and crisp, with no hint of wind. The cloisters were quiet, providing a welcome refuge from the strife and rancor of Clarendon. Fatigue was deeply etched in the lines around Roger's mouth, the furrows in his brow. His dark eyes had lit with pleasure, though, at the sight of Maud.

Worldly and cynical as she might appear to others, to Roger she would always be the guardian angel of his childhood, the glamorous elder sister who never forgot a birthday or betrayed a confidence, now the last link to his past. He'd been faithful to his vows, had sired no bastard children like the Bishop of Salisbury, had never taken a concubine or hearth-mate. His brothers were either dead, like Hamon and Philip, living in Normandy, like Richard, or one of God's fools, like Will. Maud was all the family he had left.

Taking his arm, she let him lead her toward a bench in one of the sheltered carrels. "Is Ranulf at Clarendon?"

"No, his wife's lying-in is nigh, and he was loath to leave her. Nor is our cousin Will here, either."

That Maud already knew; Will had departed for Rouen soon after Christmas, seeking to find some solace in his mother's sympathy. "Poor Will. He deserves better than to be made a pawn in this infernal chess game Harry and Becket are playing."

Roger's frown was faintly discernible in the blanched moonlight. "I can assure you, Maud, that the archbishop's objections to Will's marriage are valid. Canon law prohibits marriage if the man and woman are related within the seventh degree, either by blood or marriage. Will and Isabella de Warenne's husband were third cousins. Moreover, the girl herself is kin to Will through William the Bastard."

"Then that makes her kin to her husband, too, does it not? So why was that marriage permitted and Will's denied? Would Christendom have been imperiled had a dispensation been granted? For pity's sake, Roger, Harry and Eleanor are distant cousins, too!"

"Yes, but the archbishop was not asked to pass judgment upon the va-lidity of their marriage," he pointed out, so reasonably that she groaned.

"You sound just like Papa," she said, "always so rational and logical!" If it was a complaint, it was also a compliment. Neither one could envi-sion a greater tribute than a comparison with the father they'd both adored. After a moment, they smiled at each other in unspoken acknowl-edgment of that family fact, and Maud said forthrightly:

"I do not want to quarrel with you. We will never see eye to eye upon the merits or the motives of your friend, Thomas Becket. But if you hold him in such esteem, I may have been too hasty in my judgment."

"I wish I could convince you of Thomas's sincerity. He seeks only to protect the Mother Church. Mayhap he has not always been as tactful as he ought—"

That was too much for Maud, who gave a derisive hoot. "Come now, Roger. The word you are groping for is *foolhardy,* not *tactless.* Bearbait-ing may well be an exciting sport for some, but it is a most dangerous one, too."

"I know," Roger said, with such stark, despairing candor that she at once regretted her levity.

"Tell me," she said, "about the council meeting today. What are these customs that Harry is demanding you all abide by?"

"He claims that those pleas concerning advowsons belong in the king's court. That no cleric may leave England without his consent. That no man holding his lands directly from the king may be excommunicated or his lands laid under interdict without the king's prior consent. That sons of villeins may not be ordained without the permission of their lords. That appeals are not to be made to the papal court without first passing through the appropriate Church courts, and then not without the king's consent. That the king should control vacant bishoprics, abbeys, and priories. That when there are evildoers whom people fear to accuse, twelve respected men of the town or vill shall be chosen to take oath that they will seek out the truth of the matter. That once criminous clerks have been taken before an ecclesiastical court, found guilty, and degraded of their clerical office, they should then be turned over to the king's court for sentencing as laymen."

It was an impressive display of memory, but no more than Maud would have expected. Her brother's keen intellect had helped, as much as his royal connections, to propel him to prominence at such a young age. "Are they, indeed, the customs of the realm in the days of the old king, Harry's grandfather?"

Roger nodded tersely. "With one or two exceptions, I would say so."

Maud reached over and squeezed his arm. "Can you not accept them, then?"

"No . . ." The look he gave her was anguished, revealing not only the conflicted state of his soul, but his bleak awareness of the high stakes involved. "In good conscience, we cannot, Maud. How can we agree to let the king circumscribe appeals to the Apostolic See? That would violate our consecration oaths. And how can we accede to the king's demand that we must secure his permission to leave the realm? That would hinder pilgrimages, at the very least. And what would I do if I were summoned to Rome by the Holy Father and the king then refused to let me go?"

"What did priests and bishops do in the old king's time?"

He was silent for some moments, gazing out upon the expanse of pristine, moonlit snow. "There must be accommodation between Church and Crown. If the king refused to unsheathe his secular sword to enforce spiritual penalties, how effective would those penalties be? The Church might, of necessity, have to tolerate certain practices that are in violation of canon law. But it is not possible to confer official sanction upon those deviant practices. So we have no choice but to refuse."

"You mean that by making this public demand, Harry has taken away your wriggling room?" It was a colloquial expression, but one that accurately summed up their dilemma, and Roger smiled in wry recognition of that. Maud understood perfectly what he meant; she was first and foremost a realist. But she understood, too, why her cousin had been driven to such measures.

"This accommodation you spoke of can work only if there is trust on both sides. And Harry no longer believes that he can trust Thomas Becket."

"I know," he admitted softly.

"What happens now?"

"When the council resumes on the morrow, we shall seek to make the king understand why we cannot accede to his demands."

"And if you cannot?"

He slowly shook his head. "Then God help us all."

THE COUNCIL was already in session the next morning when Maud slipped unobtrusively in a side door of the great hall. Her son was seated on one of the long wooden benches, next to his uncle, Rainald, Earl of Cornwall. Hugh looked ill at ease, but then, so did many of the men. The tension was almost tangible, blanketing the hall like wood-smoke. The only one who seemed unaffected by the disquieting atmosphere was Henry's young son. Hal was presiding with his father over the council; just a month shy of his ninth birthday, he was fidgeting in his seat, scraping with his thumbnail at the candle wax that splattered the wooden arm of his chair. Maud had heard that he'd become very fond of Becket during his eighteen months in the archbishop's custody, and she wondered if it was painful for him to see his father feuding so publicly and acrimoniously with Becket. At the least, she imagined it must be confusing for the boy. But his face masked his thoughts; a handsome, sturdy youngster, he looked bored and faintly sullen.

Henry was pacing like a caged lion, never taking his eyes off his archbishop. "We have gone over this again and again. I am not claiming the right to try criminous clerks in my courts. They will be judged first in an ecclesiastical court, and if found guilty, degraded of their priestly office. It is only then that they will be returned to the royal courts for sentencing. Where is the unfairness in that?"

Becket shook his head wearily. "As we've tried to make you see, my liege, that would still be a double punishment: first degradation and then whatever penalty your court might choose to mete out. That would be like . . . like bringing Christ before Pontius Pilate a second time."

Henry stared at him and then exploded. "That is arrant nonsense! There is no honesty in your arguments, my lord archbishop, nothing but prevarication and contumacy. As long as you persist in this obdurate attitude, further discussion is meaningless. I would suggest that you and your fellow bishops retire to reconsider your position. And whilst you do, bear this in mind. I have sought to convince you by logic and common sense. But if need be, I can find other means of persuasion."

Maud would not have believed that a crowded hall could have fallen so silent so fast. But in the moments that followed, there was no sound at all, no whispering or murmuring, not even the catch of indrawn breaths, only an unnatural stillness.

THE CHAMBER was heated by charcoal braziers, but they did little to chase away the cold. Roger was the youngest of all the bishops, but the stress was telling upon him, too, as their deliberations dragged on into a third day. He'd slept little that night and suspected that few of the other suffragans had either. So far this morning the arguments being made were merely a rehash of the previous day's heated discussions. They'd already exhausted all their options. Roger knew that not a man among them wanted to swear to obey these abhorrent customs, for to do so would be a de facto concession that the king and not the Pope was the true head of the English Church. But did they have the collective courage to defy him? If they held firm, would he back down? Roger felt reasonably confident that his cousin was bluffing. Harry was neither a monster nor a fool. Surely he'd not bring down the anathema of Holy Church upon his head by persecuting the greatest prelates of his realm?

But others were not as sure of that as Roger, and several of the bishops were imploring Becket to yield. The Bishops of Salisbury and Norwich, in particular, were insistent that a compromise be sought, for they were already in Henry's bad graces, and admitted quite candidly their fear that they would be the ones to suffer the most if Henry's anger were not deflected or appeased.

In truth, few among them had the stomach for this looming confrontation between Church and Crown. By Roger's reckoning, only he and Henry of Blois, the wily Bishop of Winchester, and possibly the Bishop of Hereford, backed Becket without reservation. The Archbishop of York so disliked his fellow archbishop that even his courtesy seemed grudgingly given. Gilbert Foliot had reluctantly concluded that they could not obey the customs. But he was furious with Becket for having allowed himself to be cornered like this, and his anger made him a prickly, irascible ally. Hilary of Chichester had so far taken little part in their emotional debates, which did not surprise Roger. His assessment of Chichester was of a man slippery and shallow and clever, an opportunist who'd seen the priesthood as a profession, not a vocation. The Bishops of Ely and Lincoln were elderly and ailing, poor soldiers in this war of wills. Bartholomew of Exeter and the Bishop of Coventry were good men, but not the stuff of which martyrs are made. And the Bishops of Durham, Bath, and Rochester were fortunate enough to be absent, spared this harrowing test of their own fortitude.

Roger glanced then toward the man in the center of the storm. Thomas Becket was very pale. His cheekbones were thrown into sudden prominence, and his eyes shone with feverish brightness. Roger knew, as few did, how delicate his friend's health was, and he feared that the older man might fall ill under the strain. For the full brunt of the king's wrath would come down upon those thin, squared shoulders. If they did not yield, what would their defiance cost them?

As troubling as that question was, there was one that weighed even more heavily upon Roger. What damage would be done to the Church as a result of this dangerous breach with the king? His eyes again sought out Becket. As much as he admired and liked the other man, he did not fully understand him. Although loyalty kept him silent, he agreed with Foliot that this was a battle that need not have been fought. But now that they were forced to fight it, they could not afford to lose. All they could do was to hold fast to their faith and hope that the king's rage would cool enough for him to see reason.

The tension was such that they all flinched at the sudden loud knocking. Becket gestured for one of his clerks to open the door, frowning at the sight of Roger de Clare, for the Earl of Hertford flaunted his enmity like a battle flag. "What do you wish . . . ," he began coolly, then got hastily to his feet as the earl pushed past the clerk into the chamber, with others on his heels.

"We've grown tired of waiting," Hertford declared combatively. "Do you mean to obey the king or not?"

Roger had risen, too, moving to stand at Becket's side. He recognized most of these intruders: the Earl of Salisbury; the king's bastard half-brother, Hamelin; the one-eyed John Marshal, a Wiltshire baron with the soul of a pirate; the Earl of Essex, whose father, Geoffrey de Mandeville, had died in rebellion against his king. Behind them, more men were seeking to crowd into the chamber, shoving and pushing and cursing. The bishops instinctively recoiled; only Becket, Roger, Gilbert Foliot, and the aged Bishop of Winchester stood their ground.

"We are not answerable to you," Becket said sharply. "When our deliberations are done, we will return to the hall, not before."

"What is there to deliberate? Either you are loyal to our lord king or you are not. Which is it?" Hamelin's freckled face was suffused with angry color, his eyes narrowed accusingly; he looked so much like his elder brother that the Bishop of Norwich could not suppress a gasp, shrinking back in his seat as if to escape notice. Several of the other bishops were also trying to appear as inconspicuous as possible.

But the Bishop of Winchester reached for his cane, glowering at this threatening mob with the icy aplomb of a man in whose veins flowed the blood of William the Bastard, England's conqueror. "Be gone from here," he said scathingly. "You honor neither your king nor your God by this churlish display."

"We have no intention of going anywhere," Hertford insisted, "not until you agree to obey the customs as your predecessors and betters did!"

"We have nothing to say to you." Becket sought to stare the earl down, without success. "Your intrusion into this chamber is an affront to the Almighty. Withdraw at once, lest you imperil your immortal souls!"

A few of the men had begun to squirm. But John Marshal sneered, "Better you should worry about yourself, priest! Your skin will bruise and your bones will break like any other man's. Even the Pope will bleed if cut."

"How dare you threaten the archbishop!" Roger found he was gripping his crosier as if it were a weapon, so great was his outrage. "If ever there was a man heading for Hell, it would be you, John Marshal. And the fires of Hell will be even hotter than the flames in that burning bell tower!"

Marshal scowled at this pointed reminder of the calamity that had cost him an eye. Before he could retort, though, there was a commotion to the rear. Men were reluctantly moving aside, clearing a path for the king's justiciar and the king's uncle.

The Earl of Leicester and Rainald bulled their way through the crowd, trampling on toes and jabbing their elbows into ribs. "What in hellfire are you fools up to?" Rainald's florid face was nearly crimson now. "Who told you to harry the bishops like this?"

Leicester was shaking his head in disgust. "The lot of you ought to be ashamed of yourselves, threatening men of God. Get out of here, and just hope this deplorable lapse does not reach the king's ears."

Some of the men did seem shamed by the justiciar's tongue-lashing, others merely disgruntled. But none of them resisted, and within moments all were in retreat. Leicester strode to the door, rather ostentatiously slid the bolt into place. "The king sent my lord earl of Cornwall and me to discuss this lamentable impasse—fortunately for you, my lord bishops. I regret to say that feeling is running high against you amongst the king's barons. Who's to say what those dolts might have done if we'd not arrived when we did?"

Roger swallowed a skeptical rejoinder, for he suspected this entire scene had been staged for their benefit, a not-so-subtle warning of what could befall enemies of the Crown. "Uncle," he said coldly to Rainald, while wishing suddenly that his other uncle, Ranulf, had been able to attend the Clarendon council. Mayhap Ranulf could have talked some sense into the king. It would not even occur to Rainald to try.

"What would you say to us, my lord earls?" Becket's pallor was stained by blotches of hectic color burning across his cheekbones. "Do you speak on the king's behalf?"

"Nay, my lord archbishop. I speak for myself," Leicester said, his eyes sweeping the chamber, moving slowly and searchingly from bishop to bishop. "The king wishes to know how your deliberations are progressing. But nothing has changed. He'll not give ground on this, my lords, for he has the right of it. In those lawless years under the usurper, Stephen of Blois, Crown prerogatives were lost and Church encroachments proceeded apace, if you'll forgive an old soldier for speaking bluntly. It is only natural that the king should want to recover what was lost, to restore the—"

"This serves for naught," Becket interrupted, with a rudeness that betrayed the shaken state of his nerves. "We already know the king's views on this matter. If you have nothing new to offer, I see no point in prolonging this conversation."

"How can you be so shortsighted?" Rainald glared at Becket. "My nephew is an honorable, God-fearing man, one who has the makings of a great king. But he is known to be . . . hasty in his tempers. Do not push him so far, my lords, that he takes measures he may well later regret."

Leicester nodded grimly. "I must obey the king's commands. I believe myself to be a good son of the Church, and it would not be easy to arrest an archbishop. But I would do it, my lords, if the order were given. I would have no choice."

"You do what you must," Becket said. "As will we."

After Leicester and Rainald had departed, the silence was smothering. No one seemed to have the heart for further argument. Slumped in their seats, the bishops stared off into space, each man lost in his own dark musings. Roger's head had begun to throb, and he rubbed his temples gingerly. How were they to escape this trap?

THE NEXT ONES to try their luck at breaking the bishops' resolve were the Templars—the English Grand Master Richard de Hastings and Tostes de St Omer. With a solemnity that seemed more appropriate for a wake than a council, the two urged Becket and the other prelates to reconsider, to think of the good of the Church. That argument hit home with Roger, whose greatest fear was that this acrimony would poison the well for years to come. They had spoken with the king at great length, the Templars reported, and he was willing to be reasonable. If the bishops would agree to accept the customs, that avowal would be enough to satisfy the king.

"This we faithfully promise you," the Templars' Grand Master concluded earnestly, "and may our souls be condemned to eternal damnation if henceforth the king demands of you anything contrary to your will or your order."

Becket heard them out in silence and then announced that he would go to the chapel to pray for divine guidance. The atmosphere lightened a bit after his departure. The Bishop of Winchester ordered wine and wafers to be brought in. He no longer seemed to harbor the political ambitions that had once helped to wreak such havoc upon the kingdom. Those days when he'd dreamed of the archbishopric of Canterbury for himself, the throne at Westminster for his brother, were long gone. Now in his life's winter, he still retained a healthy appreciation for the pleasures of fine wine and good food, and he ate with a relish that few of the others could match.

Roger had no appetite. When Gilbert Foliot took the seat beside him, he found for the Bishop of London a crooked smile. "Well, it has been an interesting afternoon. Shall we toss a coin to see who gets to give the king the bad news?"

Roger's flippancy didn't go over well with Foliot, who was still silently fuming at the idiocy of it all. "As soon as Becket returns, we'd best go back to the hall and get this over with whilst we can still pretend to a semblance of unity."

The Bishop of Winchester finished one wafer, reached for another. "Just be thankful," he said, "that the king's termagant mother is in Normandy. If you think Harry can be a raving lunatic, you ought to have seen the Lady Maude in one of her imperial fits of fury."

His sarcasm struck a sour note with Roger; the Lady Maude, after all, was his aunt. It was also an impolitic reminder that Winchester had been on the wrong side in the great war that had torn England asunder for nigh on two decades. He was on the verge of an equally impolitic rebuke when the door opened and Thomas Becket entered the chamber.

He had the dazed look of a man bleeding from an inner wound, so ashen that even Foliot felt a twinge of involuntary pity for his plight. Waving aside Winchester's offer of wine, he said abruptly, "If the king will have me perjure myself, so be it. I will agree to take the oath he demands, and hope to purge the sin by future penance."

Roger was too stunned to speak. He stared at the archbishop mutely, having no idea what to say. Judging from the silence, none of the others did either.

Becket's sudden capitulation was greeted by Henry's barons with surprise and jubilation. They sat upright on their benches, listening intently as the archbishop promised that he would "observe the customs of the kingdom in good faith." Even his enemies would later remark that the man looked ill, but he spoke out firmly, loudly enough to be heard throughout the hall. Henry showed no emotion, his face impassive, grey eyes guarded. Once Becket had recanted, he said:

"You have heard the archbishop's promise. All that remains is for the bishops to do the same, at his command." And that was done. It was then that Henry startled them all, barons and bishops alike, by insisting that the customs should be committed to writing so as to avoid future misunderstandings.

The law, as they knew it, was oral tradition, passed down from one generation to the next. This was an innovation, one that stirred suspicion and alarm. But Henry had the momentum and the control of events, and his opponents were too demoralized by Becket's volte-face to muster further opposition. This, too, was done as the king commanded, and the Constitutions of Clarendon were duly set down in a chirograph on January 29, the text written out three times on the same parchment and then torn so as to validate all three copies when joined together. With that, the historic and contentious Council of Clarendon drew to a close.

ROGER WAS SO TROUBLED by his friend's despairing state of mind that he concocted an excuse to accompany the archbishop upon the first leg of his journey back to Canterbury. Becket had been bitterly assailed by some of the other bishops, accused of abandoning them in the midst of battle. Even his own clerks turned upon him, and as they rode toward Winchester, his cross-bearer, a fiery-tempered Welshman called Alexander Llewelyn, dared to accuse Becket of forsaking his flock and betraying his conscience, saying boldly, "When the shepherd has fled, the sheep lie scattered before the wolf."

The archbishop offered no defense, flinching away from the words as if they were weapons. When Roger urged his mount closer so they might talk, Becket said huskily, "I have indeed betrayed my God, my friends, and myself. I do judge myself unworthy to approach as a priest Him Whose Church I have vilely bartered, and I will sit silent in grief until the 'dayspring from on high hath visited me,' so that I merit absolution by God and the Lord Pope."

Roger was taken aback by the emotional intensity of Becket's remorse. But he did not doubt the other man's sincerity and realized at once what this meant. His cousin the king may have won this battle, but the war would go on.

AN ICY FEBRUARY RAIN was drenching Winchester, turning the streets into muddy quagmires and driving people indoors, where they huddled around reeking hearths and cursed the vile winter weather. Within the castle, though, another storm raged, a battle royal between England's king and his consort.

"I cannot believe," Henry exclaimed, "that you are siding with Becket in this!"

Eleanor swore in exasperation. "Jesú! I am doing no such thing. I simply said that it might have been wiser if you'd concentrated upon a few important issues, such as the matter of the criminous clerks. You have the right of that argument and few save Becket would dispute it with you."

"I have the right of all sixteen arguments—the Constitutions of Clarendon. They are indeed the customs of the realm from my grandfather's time. I did not pluck them from the sky or invent them out of whole cloth."

'No, but you did a bit of embroidering," she insisted, with a wry humor that he did not find amusing. "Harry, I think you overreached yourself, and for certes, you'd have done better not to have demanded that written recognition—"

"Christ on the Cross, woman!" Henry was stung by her criticism, for he was very proud of the Constitutions of Clarendon and could not understand why others were so leery of change. "How can rights be properly defined if they are not set down in writing?"

"But that makes compromise so much more difficult! Why can you not see that?"

"Because I have no intention of compromising with Thomas Becket, now or ever!"

"Like it or not, you may have to, Harry. The man is still the Archbishop of Canterbury . . . and whose fault is that?"

"I have admitted I made a mistake with Becket and do not need you to throw that in my face! But even the worst mistakes can be undone and I mean to undo this one."

"I suppose it is too much to ask how you intend to bring this about? Why should you share your plans with me, after all? I am merely your queen!"

"Why should I want to tell you anything at all when this is the response I get—carping and disapproval?"

A timid knock on the bedchamber door interrupted the quarrel, although not for long; both their tempers were still at full blaze. Henry took the proffered parchment, dismissed the messenger, glared at Eleanor, and broke the seal. As Eleanor watched angrily, he moved toward the nearest light, a tall candelabra. His back was to her, but she saw him stiffen, heard his gasp, a cry broken off in midbreath.

"Harry?" When he didn't answer, she moved toward him. "Harry . . . what is it?"

He'd crumpled the parchment in his fist. "Christ have pity," he said, very low. When he looked up, his eyes were brimming with tears. "My mother has written to tell me . . ." He swallowed painfully. "My brother is dead."

"God in Heaven! Will? What happened . . . a fall from his horse?"

"No . . . he sickened. He sickened and died on Friday last. My mother says he was not ailing long. According to the doctors, he had no fight in him, just gave up . . ."

Eleanor was shocked; Will was only twenty-seven. "I am so sorry, Harry," she said, and put her arms around him. He held her so tightly that it hurt, burying his face in her hair. She could feel his breath rasping against her ear, could see the pulse throbbing in his temple. They stood in silence for a time and then he drew back. There were tear tracks upon his cheek, but his eyes were dry and hot.

"Will died of a broken heart," he said. "Even the doctors think so. In denying him the wife of his choosing, Thomas Becket brought about his death."

Eleanor did not argue with him. She reached out again, held him close, and let him grieve for his brother.

H EEDLESS OF THE CHILL, Ranulf stood in the doorway of the great hall at Trefriw, gazing across the rain-sodden bailey at the chamber he shared with Rhiannon. Faint light gleamed through the chinks in the closed shutters, the only signs of life. The wind and rain were all he heard, although he doubted that Rhiannon would do much screaming; Eleri had once confided that during her previous birthings, she'd bitten down on a towel to stifle her cries. Thinking of the proud, vulnerable woman in that lying-in chamber, laboring to bring his child into the world, Ranulf felt fear prickle along his spine. Rhiannon was almost forty-one. Women died in childbirth all too often, and the older the woman, the greater the risk. What would he do if the Almighty took her, if she traded her life for the baby's?

"For the love of God, Ranulf, shut the door!" Hywel shivered as a blast of wind invaded the hall. He and Peryf had arrived in midmorning, only to learn that Rhiannon's pains had begun before dawn. He assumed that the birthing was proceeding as it ought; Eleri's occasional updates were hurried, not alarmed. He felt confident that Rhiannon would safely deliver her babe. But then Rhiannon was not his wife.

"We've got the midwife to tend to Rhiannon. Mayhap we ought to fetch a doctor to tend to Ranulf ere the poor soul unravels like a ball of yarn." While said ostensibly to Rhodri, the words were actually aimed at Ranulf. The gibe worked; Ranulf turned reluctantly from the door, joining them at the table. He stared down at the food upon his trencher, though, as if he'd never seen stewed chicken before, and had to be prodded into swallowing a few mouthfuls.

"So . . . tell me," Hywel said with determined cheer, "what names have you chosen for the child? If it is a lad, I think *Hywel* has a fine ring to it."

That roused Ranulf from his uneasy reverie. "You ought to have put in your bid sooner. Rhiannon and I have already settled upon the names."

"Let me guess. For a daughter . . . Annora, perchance?" Hywel murmured, grinning when Ranulf threw a wadded-up napkin in his direction.

"If it is a girl, we shall name her Angharad, after my mother."

Hywel nodded approvingly. "A name I've always fancied. I've bedded two lovely Angharads." He started to joke "but not at the same time," then glanced over at Ranulf's son and thought better of it. Ranulf's daughter had been sent to stay with neighbors, but Gilbert was in his thirteenth year now, deemed old enough to remain. He was slouched at the end of the table, saying little and eating less, and Hywel decided circumspection was in order. "What if it is a son?"

"We will name him Morgan, after one of Rhiannon's brothers."

"My Morgan died young," Rhodri began somberly. As proud as he was to have the name live on in one of his grandchildren, he still felt an old sorrow at the memory of that lost son. But before he could continue, Gilbert flung his knife down, shoving away from the table.

"Why could you not have named me Morgan? Why was I the one saddled with an alien English name that no one can even pronounce?"

They were startled by the boy's outburst, Ranulf most of all. "I never knew you felt like that, lad. I named you Gilbert after my best friend—"

"An Englishman!"

"Yes, Gilbert was English. What of it? I am half-English myself, as you well know."

Gilbert was deeply flushed. No longer meeting his father's eyes, he muttered something under his breath. Ranulf could not be sure, but he thought his son said that was nothing to boast about.

"What did you say, Gilbert?"

The boy shrugged. "I am not hungry. May I be excused?"

Ranulf hesitated, then nodded, and Gilbert snatched up his mantle, bolting out into the bailey. "I had no idea that he was harboring such resentment," he confessed. "I suppose I should not be so surprised, though. Your brothers are not alone in their suspicions of me, Hywel. For all that I've lived here fourteen years, some people will always see me as the *alltud*—the alien Englishman in their midst, who may or may not be the English king's spy. Some of that suspicion must inevitably spill over onto Gilbert."

Hywel slid his mead cup across the table. "Do not make more of this than it deserves. I daresay the lad is scared and lashing out at the closest target—you. Once Rhiannon safely gives birth, it will be forgotten."

Ranulf was not convinced of that. But Rhiannon's need was paramount; Gilbert's grievances would have to wait. He drank from Hywel's cup, then sent it skidding back across the table just as they heard sudden shouting out in the bailey. For a moment, he froze, his first fear for Rhiannon.

Hywel's hearing was more acute. "A rider is coming in," he announced and within moments was proved correct. The messenger was soaked to the skin, trembling with the cold. Stumbling toward the hearth, he gratefully accepted a cup of mead, gulping it down before he drew a sealed parchment from his tunic.

"My lord," he said, dropping to his knees before Ranulf. "I bring you an urgent message from the king."

The hall quieted. Even those who did not understand French realized that something was amiss. All watched nervously as Ranulf broke the seal and read. He sat down suddenly in the closest seat, the letter slipping from his hand, fluttering into the floor rushes. "My nephew is dead."

"Which one?" Hywel asked, hoping it was the least of the lot, that fool Gloucester.

"Will . . . the king's brother." Ranulf blinked back tears. But before he could tell them any more, the door was flung open and his sister-in-law plunged into the hall.

Eleri was wet and disheveled and jubilant. "God be praised, Ranulf, you have a son!"

AFTER A VISIT with his wife and newborn son, Ranulf returned to the hall, where a celebration was in progress. Celyn soon arrived, and then their neighbors, for in Wales, word seemed to travel on the wind. Ranulf welcomed his young daughter home, assured her that her mother and baby brother were well, and generally tried to play the role expected of him, that of host and happy father. But Will's plaintive ghost lingered in the shadows and Ranulf kept catching glimpses of him from the corner of his eye; once or twice, he even thought he heard Will's voice, sounding sad and bewildered and wrenchingly young.

"When will you tell Rhiannon?" Hywel had come up quietly behind him. "I did not get a chance to say I was sorry. I know how fond you were of Will. He was good company . . ." Hywel's smile flickered briefly. ". . . for an Englishman."

"I did not want Rhiannon to know, not yet. She was fond of Will, too. I'll tell her on the morrow."

Hywel had brought over a brimming cup. "Drink this," he directed. "You look as if you need it."

"I do," Ranulf acknowledged. "When Will died in Rouen, any chance of compromise between Harry and Becket died, too. Harry is very bitter, blaming Becket for his brother's death."

"Then the accord they reached at Clarendon is not likely to last?"

"No . . . not bloody likely. Becket seems to have repented of his submission almost at once. As soon as he returned to Canterbury, he did public penance, put aside his customary fine clothes for plain, dark garb, and suspended himself from saying Mass. You can well imagine Harry's response to that."

Hywel whistled softly. "Say what you will about him, the good archbishop has quite a flair for the dramatic. So their war goes on." He hesitated then, dark eyes studying Ranulf's face. "I am loath to add to your worries. But you'll find out sooner or later, and mayhap you ought to hear it from me. Rhys ap Gruffydd has gone on the attack, overrunning Dinefar and chasing the Marcher lord Walter Clifford back across the border with his tail tucked between his legs. And we recently got word that the English king's stronghold at Carreghwfa fell to Owain Cyfeiliog at year's end."

Ranulf's breath caught. He'd known since the summer—since Woodstock—that trouble was brewing in the Marches. But he'd not expected the cauldron to boil over so soon. How long ere Owain Gwynedd cast his lot with Rhys ap Gruffydd and the lords of Powys? How long ere all of Wales took fire?

"If anyone asks after me," he said, "tell them I've gone to look in on Rhiannon."

Collecting his daughter as he left the hall, he agreed to take her along if she'd promise to be very quiet. Seeing Gilbert loitering a few feet away, he beckoned and the boy hurried over, with enough speed to give the lie to his feigned nonchalance. Leaving their guests to Rhodri and Hywel, he ushered his children out into the damp February night.

The midwife had departed, but Eleri was dozing in a chair by the hearth. She smiled at the sight of them, putting her finger to her lips and pointing toward the bed. Ranulf kissed her on the cheek and said softly, "Celyn is awaiting you in the hall. I'll stay with her now."

Mallt and Gilbert glanced at their sleeping mother, then followed Ranulf as he crossed to the cradle. Swaddled in linen strips and covered by warm woolen blankets, Morgan slept as peacefully as if he were still sheltered within his mother's womb. He was larger than either Gilbert or Mallt at birth, with a faint bruise on his temple and a fringe of tawny hair, the exact shade of Ranulf's own. The older children crowded eagerly around the cradle, but when Morgan continued to sleep on, their interest flagged and they soon slipped away. Picking up the chair, Ranulf carried it over to his wife's bed.

Rhiannon awakened about an hour later, raising up on her elbows to listen for the sound of a familiar step, a known voice. "Eleri?"

"No, love, it is me." Leaning over, he kissed her tenderly on the mouth. As quiet as they were, a sudden wail from the cradle signaled that Morgan was now awake and in need of attention. When Ranulf put the baby in Rhiannon's arms, Morgan let out a few more tentative cries, as if testing the power of his lungs, and then settled down contentedly against his mother's warmth. Rhiannon refused to engage a wet-nurse as ladies of rank usually did, unwilling to sacrifice the precious intimacy of that bond in the name of fashion. She guided Morgan's mouth to a nipple, smiling as he began to suckle noisily.

Ranulf slumped back in his chair. The chamber was lit only by firelight, the hearth flames offering just enough illumination for him to distinguish the shadowy forms of his wife and son. As he watched Rhiannon nurse their baby, it should have been a moment of tranquil joy. But his eyes were stinging, his heart thudding loudly in his ears. Trefriw was the first real home he'd ever known, and he'd been happier here than he'd have believed possible. Now a storm was gathering on the horizon: dark, foreboding clouds and a rising wind. When war came to Wales, how would he be able to keep his family safe? His earlier rebuke to Gilbert seemed to echo on the air. He was indeed half-English, half-Welsh. What if he could not be true to both halves of his soul? Could he choose without destroying the rejected self? He'd lived his entire life striving to keep faith. But what if his loyalties became irreconcilable?

CHAPTER SEVENTEEN

August 1164
Woodstock, England

S THE ARCHBISHOP of Canterbury's retinue approached the king's manor at Woodstock, villagers thronged the road to watch. William Fitz Stephen's stomach was queasy, his skin flushed and damp with perspiration. He would have liked to blame the day's sultry heat for his discomfort, yet he knew better—it was his lord's looming confrontation with the king. He cast a sidelong glance at his companion, wondering if Herbert of Bosham shared his unease. But Herbert's face was alight with anticipation. His outward appearance was so foppish and affected—tall and willowy, handsome and preening—that it was easy to forget his was the soul of a firebrand, one who thrived on controversy and scorned compromise. Fitz Stephen could only hope that Herbert's thirst for turmoil would go unslaked this day. Why would Lord Thomas seek out the king like this if he did not intend to proffer an olive branch?

They could see the manor walls now, sunlight glinting off the chain-mail of the sentries. Fitz Stephen had many pleasant memories of times spent at Woodstock, riding with Lord Thomas and the king as they hunted in these deep, still woods on hot summer afternoons like this one.

Those were bygone days, beyond recall. He glanced at his lord's taut profile and said a silent prayer that this meeting with the king would go well. It was then that guards stepped forward, blocking the gate.

The archbishop's men reined in. There was a flurry of confusion and the archbishop began to cough when he inhaled some of the dust kicked up by the milling horses. Fitz Stephen urged his mount forward. Before he could speak, Herbert demanded that the guards step aside. "Do you fools not recognize His Grace? Admit us at once!"

The guards shuffled their feet and cleared their throats, looking so uncomfortable that Fitz Stephen knew at once something was terribly wrong. They did not move away from the gate. "We have our orders," one mumbled, while the others let their raised spears speak for them.

"What orders?" Thomas Becket frowned impatiently. "The king is expecting me. I sent him word that I would be arriving in midweek."

There was a silence, and then the boldest of the guards muttered, "The king does not wish to see you, my lord archbishop. We were told not to admit you."

Color burned into Becket's face. He opened his mouth, no words emerging. For what was there to say?

AFTER BEING TURNED away from Woodstock, Becket seemed to realize just how precarious his position had become. He secretly sought to flee England, not even confiding in his own household. His first try was thwarted by contrary winds, and his second attempt failed when the sailors recognized him and balked, for fear of incurring the king's wrath.

BECKET'S NEXT RETURN to Woodstock was on a dreary August afternoon, under a weeping sky. The road was clogged in mud and the trees dripped with moisture, splattering the riders as they passed underneath. William Fitz Stephen tried not to glance over his shoulder at the smothering cloud cover, but his apprehension increased with each mile that brought them closer to Woodstock. He thought it was the true measure of his lord's despair that he'd risk another public humiliation. But he knew Thomas feared the consequences of his failed attempts to flee the country, for they were breaches of the Constitutions of Clarendon. If the king did not yet know of these transgressions, it was only a matter of time until he did. Better to face him now and offer his own defense. Fitz

Stephen understood his lord's reasoning. Yet what if the king refused again to give him an audience? What if he would not even listen to the lord archbishop's explanation? Fitz Stephen no longer harbored hopes that they'd make their peace, not after their last visit to Woodstock.

This time they were admitted by the king's guards and ushered across the bailey into the great hall. Henry was seated upon the dais, with Eleanor at his side. He greeted Becket with cool civility, his eyes as grey and opaque as the rain clouds gathering overhead. When Becket broached the subject of his abortive flight, Henry heard him out without interruption. The hall hushed then, waiting for the royal wrath to kindle. But Henry offered no rebukes, made no accusations. "Is my kingdom not big enough for the two of us," he asked, "that you must seek to flee from it?"

It was a barbed jest, yet a jest nonetheless. Relieved laughter rustled through the audience. Thomas Becket did not join in the laughter. Nor did William Fitz Stephen.

Afterward, Herbert of Bosham drew Fitz Stephen aside to comment upon how well he thought the meeting had gone. "I was sure the king would rave and rant over this breach of his accursed Constitutions. Who would have guessed that he'd take it in such good humor?"

Fitz Stephen looked around to make sure none were within hearing range. "Do you not realize what that means, Herbert? The king is done with arguing. I fear he has something else in mind for our lord archbishop."

RANULF FELT NO RELIEF when the walls of Northampton came into view, even though the sight signaled the end of a long and arduous journey. It had not occurred to him to disobey the king's summons, but never had he dreaded a council as he dreaded this one, for he knew its purpose—to declare war upon Wales. He'd known for months that this day was coming; Henry could not let Rhys ap Gruffydd's defiance go unpunished. And when an English army crossed into Wales, he knew that Owain Gwynedd would choose to fight with Rhys. What he did not yet know was what he would do.

The sky was a vibrant blue, and October was already beginning to splash its colors across the countryside. But the beauty of the season was lost upon Ranulf. Knowing the castle would be filled to overflowing, he decided to lodge his men at the Cluniac priory of St Andrew's outside the city walls, only to discover that the priory was already occupied by the

Archbishop of Canterbury. As Becket had brought with him a large entourage, including more than forty clerks and numerous household
knights and servants, there was not a bed to be found in the priory's guest
hall. Ranulf ordered his weary men back into the saddle. He had better
luck with the Augustinian canons at St James, where the harried hospitaller managed to squeeze them in, and within the hour, he was dismounting in the outer bailey of Northampton Castle.

"Ranulf!" His brother Rainald was coming down the steps of the
keep. "I was beginning to think you were not coming. The council started
yesterday."

"Wales is a long way off, Rainald. What have I missed? Nothing has
been decided yet about the Welsh campaign?"

"There has been no talk at all of Wales so far. Harry has other fish to
fry. Ere he deals with the Welsh rebels, he must deal with his rebellious
archbishop. So the first item of business was the contempt charge against
Becket."

"What contempt charge?"

"Ranulf, you truly do live at the back of beyond! When are you going to move back to civilization? Come into the hall where we can get an
ale and I'll bring you up to date on all you've been missing."

Seated in a window seat with a flagon and a plate of hot wafers driz-
zled with honey, Rainald wasted no time in launching into his narrative.
"Remember John Marshal, that lunatic who was nearly burned alive in
that bell tower ere he'd surrender to Stephen's soldiers? Well, this summer
he lodged a claim in the archbishop's court for the manor of Pagenham.
When he lost, he appealed to the king's court, as provided by the Constitutions of Clarendon. Becket then made a grave mistake. He did not appear in answer to the king's summons, sending four knights to argue that
Marshal had committed perjury in the Pagenham case. Knowing Marshal,
that is more than likely. But Becket should have come himself to the king's
court. By not doing so, he handed Harry a club to bash him with, and you
can be sure that Harry made the most of it."

"He was found guilty, then, of contempt?" Ranulf asked, and Rainald
nodded.

"That was all but inevitable since he had no defense to offer. But the
sentence passed was unusually harsh for a first offense—forfeiture of all
Becket's movable goods. The best proof that men thought it too severe
was that none were willing to pass sentence; the bishops argued that it was

for the barons to do and the barons insisted it was more fitting for a bishop to do it. Harry finally lost patience and ordered the Bishop of Winchester to do it. Becket objected at first, but was persuaded by the other prelates that he ought to accept the judgment, and all the bishops save Gilbert Foliot then offered to stand surety for any fine imposed by the court."

Ranulf was finding it difficult to concentrate upon Becket's plight when Wales was on the verge of calamity, especially since he felt that many of the archbishop's troubles were of his own making. "So the Becket case has been resolved, then. Does that mean the matter of Wales will be discussed on the morrow?"

Rainald's reply was unintelligible, for his mouth was full of wafer. Washing it down with ale, he gave Ranulf a knowing smile. "Becket might think it is over. But I'd wager Harry has a surprise or two still in store for our lord archbishop."

THE COUNCIL ASSEMBLED the next morning in the great hall. This was Ranulf's first glimpse of the archbishop, and he thought Becket was showing the strain of his war of wills with the king. He'd lost more weight, and he'd not had flesh to spare. His dark hair was feathered with more grey than Ranulf remembered, his natural pallor enhanced by the stark black of the habit he now wore, the garb of an Augustinian monk. He seemed composed, though, doubtless feeling that the worst was behind him. Henry was plainly dressed, as usual, in a green wool tunic. But he did not need silk or fur-trimmed garments to hold center stage. Like Owain Gwynedd, he projected the aura of kingship by his very presence, not by the trappings of royalty, the accoutrements of power. Ranulf needed only a few moments of close observation to conclude that Rainald's suspicions were correct—their nephew was not ready to settle for a contempt-of-court conviction.

When Geoffrey Ridel rose to speak on the king's behalf, Thomas Becket stiffened noticeably, for Ridel had been acting as chancellor since Becket's abrupt resignation of that office two years before. "There are a few other matters to be settled," Ridel said calmly. "My lord Archbishop of Canterbury owes the Crown an accounting for sums expended during his tenure as chancellor."

Becket looked perplexed. "What sums are you talking about?"

"Three hundred pounds in revenue from the Honour of Eye and the castle of Berkhamsted."

Becket turned in his seat to stare at the king. "As Your Grace well knows, I used that money to make repairs to the Tower of London."

"Not on my authorization. Did you get my consent to make these repairs? Did you even discuss them with me?"

"No . . . but . . . but that is because I saw no need." Becket's stammer had come back. "I never bothered you with minor matters like that. I took it for granted that you'd be in agreement with me."

"Well," Henry said softly, "those days are gone . . . are they not?"

They looked at each other across a distance far greater than the width of the hall. The impasse was broken by the Bishop of Winchester, who hobbled to his feet and asked for a brief recess so Becket could confer with his fellow bishops.

Ranulf had heard that Henry of Blois was no longer the conniving, ambitious opportunist who had goaded his brother Stephen into claiming the crown and thus doomed England to nineteen years of a bloody civil war. Ranulf supposed that it was possible for a man to mellow in old age, sincerely to repent the sins of his past. He just wasn't sure if the bishop was that man. His suspicions proved unfounded, though, at least on this particular occasion, for the bishops soon returned to the hall and Henry of Blois announced that the Archbishop of Canterbury was confident that he had done nothing wrong. He was willing, however, to make repayment of the three hundred pounds, for he would not have money come between him and his lord king.

Ranulf felt a surge of relief that the matter was to be settled as quickly as this. But his relief ebbed away as Geoffrey Ridel rose to speak again. "Indeed we are making progress," Ridel said smoothly. "I hope we can be equally expeditious in resolving the debts still outstanding from the king's Toulouse campaign."

Thomas Becket half rose in his seat, then sank back. "What debts?"

"Five hundred marks you borrowed from the King's Grace and an additional five hundred marks you borrowed from the Jews, for which the king stood surety."

"That money was a gift from the king, and spent in his service!"

"Have you evidence in support of that claim?" When Becket reluctantly shook his head, Ridel smiled derisively, although Henry remained impassive. After a brief deliberation, the court's decision was rendered: that the thousand marks must be repaid. By now the king's intent was plain to every man in the hall, and Becket had some difficulty in finding men willing to stand surety for the debt.

His face flushed with barely suppressed anger, Becket looked challengingly at Henry. "Is there anything more you require of me?" he asked, managing to invest those innocuous words with resounding echoes of contempt.

Henry's hand closed on the arm of his chair. When he spoke, though, his voice was quite even, chillingly dispassionate. "Just one thing more. I require from you an accounting for all the proceeds of the archbishopric of Canterbury during the period between Archbishop Theobald's death and your consecration—and an accounting for the revenues of all the vacant bishoprics and abbacies you administered during your chancellorship."

Becket blanched and there were audible gasps. This heavy-handed display of royal power was disturbing to them all.

R ANULF WAS ADMITTED into the king's private chamber as dusk was falling. Henry looked tired but satisfied, and why not? So far all had been going his way. Becket's protest that he'd been summoned only to answer contempt of court charges had fallen on deaf ears. He'd finally gained himself a brief reprieve by insisting that he must consult with his fellow bishops before responding to this latest demand, and the court had been temporarily adjourned. But Ranulf knew that the bloodletting would resume on Monday—unless he could convince his nephew to back off.

"Have you come to take supper with me, Uncle?"

"Yes, but first I would like a few moments with you—alone."

Henry hesitated slightly, then made a gesture of dismissal. As the other men obediently trooped out, he moved to the hearth, reached for the fire tongs, and began to stir the flames.

"Harry . . ." Ranulf joined the younger man at the hearth, so obviously groping for words that Henry slanted him a grimly amused look.

"Spit it out, Uncle, ere it chokes you."

"Harry, I was troubled by what occurred in the hall this afternoon."

"Not as troubled, I trust, as Becket."

"In all honesty, I think every man in that hall was troubled. You were justified to charge him with contempt, but to demand a full accounting . . . Jesú, that might well total as much as thirty thousand marks! It could take years to sort through the records, and there are bound to be discrepancies and missing receipts and errors—"

"So?"

"So it is beginning to look as if you are aiming for nothing less than the man's ruination!"

"I am," Henry said, with a bluntness that took Ranulf's breath away. "I cannot dismiss him, but I can force his resignation, and by God, I will—one way or another."

"At what cost, Harry? Have you not thought about the damage done to the Church—and the Crown—by this feud with Becket? I understand your disappointment with his performance as archbishop. For the life of me, I cannot understand why he felt the need to make you his enemy or to take such extreme, provocative positions. Yet getting rid of him might well give you more grief than ever he could. Granted that he was a mistake, but surely he is a mistake you can live with?"

"Can Will?" Henry demanded, so bitterly that Ranulf fell silent. There was no point in arguing that Becket had not brought about Will's death. That wound was still too raw.

S ATURDAY MORNING PASSED in endless and increasingly acrimonious discussion. All of the bishops had gathered in Becket's priory guest quarters and proceeded to give the archbishop advice that was distinguished only by its discord. Gilbert Foliot argued brusquely for resignation, a course of action adamantly opposed by the Bishop of Winchester, who insisted this would set an invidious precedent for future prelates and undermine canon law. Hilary of Chichester contended that compromise was clearly called for under the circumstances, and the plain-spoken Bishop of Lincoln sent shivers of alarm through the room when he blurted out that Becket's choices had narrowed to resignation or execution. "What good will the archbishopric do him if he is dead?"

The Bishop of Winchester shook off the gloom engendered by Lincoln's tactless remark, getting stiffly to his feet and demanding his cane. "It has been my experience," he said dryly, "that few problems will not go away if enough money is thrown at them. I shall go to the king and see what effect two thousand marks have upon his resolve."

Becket had been slumped in his chair, letting the arguments swirl about him. At that he raised his head sharply. "I do not have two thousand marks to give the king," he said and Winchester patted him on the shoulder.

"Ah, but I do," he said, and limped purposefully toward the door.

His departure brought a hiatus in the day's heated discussions. Some of the men went off to answer nature's call, others to find food or drink in the priory guest hall. William Fitz Stephen had been hovering inconspicuously on the sidelines. He'd been deeply shaken by the Bishop of Lincoln's terse warning, and when he saw the young Bishop of Worcester heading for the door, he swiftly followed.

He caught up with Roger out in the priory cloisters. "My lord bishop, might I have a word with you?"

"Of course, William." Roger gestured toward a bench in a nearby carrel. "What may I do for you?"

"You are the king's cousin. Surely you must know his mind. My lord, how far is he prepared to go? Think you that there is any chance the archbishop's life might be at risk?"

"No," Roger said firmly, "I do not. The king has the Devil's own temper, as he'd be the first to admit. But for all that, I cannot see him being deliberately cruel or unjust."

Fitz Stephen was heartened by the certainty in Roger of Worcester's voice and he returned to the lord archbishop's quarters with a lighter step. There he found that Hilary of Chichester was haranguing Becket on the need to resign his position, insisting that otherwise he faced imprisonment for embezzlement. Becket paid him no heed, but another of the bishops rebuked Chichester sharply, declaring that it would be shameful for the archbishop to consider his personal safety. The afternoon dragged on, one of the longest that Fitz Stephen could remember. And then the Bishop of Winchester was back, stoop-shouldered and grim-visaged.

"Well," he said, heaving himself into the closest chair, "he turned me down. If he does not want money, what then? Blood?"

Fitz Stephen knew that the bishop, a highly erudite man, was speaking metaphorically. Still, he flinched, and as he looked around, he saw that he was not the only one disquieted by those ominous words.

ON SUNDAY IT RAINED, but Monday brought flashes of sun. Henry was just finishing his breakfast when he received a message from his one-time chancellor and friend. He read it hastily, swearing under his breath, and then shouted for his uncle.

Rainald pushed reluctantly away from the table, his trencher still heaped with sausages and fried bread. "What is amiss?"

"That is what I want you to find out. Becket claims that he is too ill to attend today's session. Find Leicester and ride to the priory, see if he is truly ailing or if this is just a ruse."

Rainald looked wistfully at his breakfast, but knew better than to argue. Out in the castle bailey, he ran into Ranulf and coaxed him into accompanying them. As they rode through the town's stirring streets, they speculated amongst themselves whether Becket was feigning sickness. Rainald thought it highly likely, and the Earl of Leicester was somewhat dubious, although he did concede that he could hardly blame Becket if it were so, saying that a hunted fox would always go to earth if it could. Ranulf alone felt that Becket's purported illness was genuine, and was still submitting to his brother's good-natured raillery as they reached the priory of St Andrew.

All of their doubts were dispelled, though, with their first glimpse of Thomas Becket. He was paler than new snow, bathed in sweat, and clearly in considerable discomfort. Propped up in bed by pillows, he regarded them with dull, hollowed eyes, too preoccupied with his body's pain to worry about the king's enmity. Rainald and Leicester exchanged a martyred look of resignation, and then began their interrogation of the stricken archbishop on behalf of the king, constrained all the while to use the hushed, somber tones considered proper for the sickroom.

Ignoring the glares of the archbishop's clerks and the hostility of Master William, his physician, they extracted from Becket the information they sought: that his malady was a colic, one he'd suffered from in the past. The faint stench of vomit and Becket's occasional involuntary gasps bolstered his credibility even more than his faltering words. Rainald and Leicester were both uncomfortable in their role as inquisitors to an obviously ailing man, but Rainald knew what his nephew the king would most want to know, and girded himself to ask it.

"Think you that you'll be well enough to attend the court session on the morrow?"

There were outraged murmurs from the clerks. But the last words were to be Becket's. "I will be there," he said hoarsely, "if I have to be carried in on a litter."

THE FOLLOWING MORNING, Ranulf was standing in the bailey of Northampton Castle when the Bishop-elect of Worcester rode in. Roger handed the reins to a groom, gestured for his clerks to go on into the hall, and then headed toward Ranulf.

"How is Thomas?" Ranulf asked quietly. "Is he well enough to attend today's session?"

Roger nodded, but there was something in his face that Ranulf caught, a fleeting emotion of surprising intensity in his usually composed nephew. "What is it?" he asked. "What you tell me will go no further, Roger, if that is your concern."

"It is not that, for the king will hear soon enough." Roger's voice was low, his dark eyes troubled. "Uncle Ranulf, I fear this will end very badly. Never have I seen Harry so . . . so unreasonable. If we are to avoid utter calamity, the lord archbishop must be the one to compromise . . . and he has begun listening again to those who are urging defiance. He seems to have taken his sudden illness as . . . as a sign. When we called upon him this morning, he forbade us to take part in a judgment against him and ordered us to excommunicate any man who dared to lay hands upon him. Gilbert Foliot angrily objected, pointing out that the bishops would then be in violation of their own oaths to obey the Constitutions of Clarendon, oaths they'd given only at Thomas's command. When Gilbert threatened to appeal to the Holy Father, Thomas said he had that right, but the command still stood. He then went to say Mass . . . and he chose the Mass of the martyr St Stephen, with the Introit, 'Princes also did sit and speak against me.' He was even going to come to the castle in his Mass vestments, barefoot, carrying his cross—"

Ranulf's eyes widened. "Oh, no!"

"Fortunately he was dissuaded from that. I could not counsel him to resign, Ranulf, as some of the other bishops have done. Yet I do not want to see him openly defy the king . . ."

Neither did Ranulf. Both Henry and Becket were already teetering on the brink of an abyss; a single misstep could be disastrous. He'd come to Northampton haunted by his fear of a war with Wales, but it was becoming obvious that this feud between king and archbishop was equally dangerous. This was a storm that had been long hovering on the horizon. Yet now that it had blown up into such a threatening squall, most seemed taken by surprise, even Becket.

Other bishops had begun to arrive, and Roger and Ranulf hastened over to greet Gilbert Foliot. Still visibly angry, he made an effort to respond with courtesy, but abandoned the attempt after Thomas Becket rode into the bailey. It occurred to Ranulf that by now his nephew would have been told of Becket's defiant choice of the St Stephen's Mass; there was never a shortage of men eager to curry favor by carrying tales to a king. He decided to see if he could ease Henry's wrath before the court session began and was starting toward the great hall when a sudden outcry stopped him in his tracks.

After dismounting, Becket had taken his heavy oaken cross from his cross-bearer, Alexander Llewelyn—to the dismay of the spectators. Several of the bishops hurried over, seeking to talk the archbishop out of such a provocative act, but Becket brushed them aside. As Ranulf turned to see, so, too, did Gilbert Foliot. Ranulf was close enough to hear the bishop brand Becket as an utter fool. Striding forward, Foliot joined the others remonstrating with Becket. Alarmed, Ranulf followed.

The Bishop of Hereford had gone so far as to grasp the cross, pleading with Becket to reconsider. When Becket clung to the cross, Foliot grabbed hold of it, too, and tried to wrest it away by force, this time calling Becket a fool to his face. At that, Roger intervened upon Becket's behalf, only to be sharply rebuked by Foliot. Both Hereford and Foliot were still tugging at the cross, but Becket was younger and he prevailed. Pulling free, he recovered his balance and started toward the hall.

Hereford fell back, but Foliot hastened to keep pace. "If the king now draws his sword, you'll make a fine pair!"

"I carry the cross to protect myself and the English Church," Becket retorted, then disappeared into the hall as a new disruption broke out in the bailey. The Archbishop of York had just arrived, and he'd brought his own cross-bearer, in violation of the Pope's ban against displaying his cross outside of his own province. If Becket's dramatic gesture was throwing down the gauntlet to Henry, York's was meant to upstage Becket; the two men had a rivalry that went all the way back to their youthful days in the service of Archbishop Theobald. Gilbert Foliot looked incredulously at his posturing colleague, then threw up his hands in disgust.

"What next?" he snapped. "A bearbaiting?"

Ranulf understood exactly how he felt. This council at Northampton was rapidly spiraling out of control. And they hadn't even gotten around to discussing war with Wales yet.

HENRY HAD BEEN PERSUADED to withdraw to the upper chamber, much to Ranulf's relief. He wondered if his nephew did not trust himself to control his temper in a face-to-face confrontation now that it was clear Becket had chosen defiance over submission. The Earl of Leicester had pulled Henry aside and was quietly urging him to show forbearance. Ranulf didn't expect Henry to listen, but it was reassuring that there were a few voices of reason still to be found. Too many of the men advising the king and archbishop were arguing against compromise. Ranulf had tried again to convince his nephew to settle for the victory he'd already won—the contempt of court charge—but that was not what Henry wanted to hear. He had come to Northampton determined to force Becket's resignation and was not willing to settle for anything less. Ranulf realized he could only watch as events played themselves out. He had to keep trying, though. If he'd come upon a burning house, he'd have felt compelled to fight the flames.

Becket remained below in the great hall, still clinging to his cross, but the other bishops had joined Henry in the upper chamber. They had obviously conferred amongst themselves, designating Gilbert Foliot and Hilary of Chichester as their spokesmen. "My lord king," Foliot said, "the Archbishop of Canterbury has forbidden us to take further part in this council or to sit in judgment upon him on any secular charge. He has also commanded us to defend him with ecclesiastical censure, excommunicating any who lay hands upon him."

Henry's color alerted them to his rising anger. "That would put you all in violation of the Constitutions of Clarendon, which every one of you swore to obey and uphold. Need I remind you that Article Eleven compels the bishops to participate in all of the royal judgments that do not involve the shedding of blood?"

"We do understand that, my lord. But the archbishop's command has placed us between the hammer and the anvil. We must obey you or the archbishop—"

"You think you're being offered a choice? Think again, my lord bishop!" Henry's eyes flicked from Foliot to the other bishops; it did not escape him that none seemed willing to meet his gaze. "I suggest you go back downstairs and talk some sense into him. My patience is fast running out."

Foliot was convinced such talk would be a waste of breath. There was no point in protesting, though; that, too, would be a waste of breath. Followed by several of the bishops and a number of barons, he returned to the great hall, where Becket sat alone with two of his clerks, Herbert of Bosham and William Fitz Stephen. Before Foliot could launch his futile appeal, Bartholomew of Exeter fell to his knees before Becket. He was one of the most respected of the prelates and all fell silent, disquieted to see him in such an emotional state. Tears blurring his eyes, he reached out uncertainly toward Becket.

"Father," he entreated, "spare yourself and us, your brother bishops. The king has let it be known that he will treat all who oppose him as traitors."

Becket slowly and deliberately shook his head. "You do not understand the Will of God."

Foliot drew an exasperated breath, audible evidence of his frustration. "We tried," he said tersely, pivoting on his heel to go back abovestairs. Most of his colleagues followed, but some of the barons lingered and began to talk loudly amongst themselves, with the archbishop as their true audience. They reminisced about past clashes between kings and churchmen, reminding one another that King Henry's great-grandfather, William the Bastard, had known how to tame his clerks, arresting his own brother, the Bishop of Bayeux, and condemning an Archbishop of Canterbury to perpetual imprisonment. Rannulph de Broc, who was known to loathe Becket, chimed in with a chilling atrocity story of more recent vintage. "What about the king's father, Geoffrey, the Count of Anjou? He had the Bishop-elect of Seez gelded for his insolence!"

That was too much for Ranulf. While he had never been fond of Geoffrey of Anjou, he did know that Geoffrey had always sworn his men had exceeded their authority in the brutality of the attack upon the bishop-elect. How true that was he had no way of knowing, but he resented Rannulph de Broc's dredging up of a twenty-year-old tragedy for the express purpose of frightening Becket into surrender. Neither of the archbishop's clerks could hide their horror. Becket was better at dissembling, but Ranulf noticed his white-knuckled grip upon the cross. Did Becket truly think Harry was capable of cruelty of that sort? If so, he had misjudged Harry as badly as Harry had misjudged him.

Ranulf shoved past the loitering barons, meaning to reassure Becket and his clerks that Henry would never resort to such violence, even though he suspected that his words might sound hollow to them, coming from the king's uncle. But his other nephew had lingered, too, and Roger stepped forward now to offer Becket his own assurances, pointing out that the bishops were only to sit in judgment in those cases that involved no shedding of blood. Yet Henry was insisting that the bishops take part in the judgment. What better proof could they have that he intended no charge that involved maiming or mutilation?

Ranulf couldn't tell if Roger's reassurances had succeeded or not. The clerks were too polite to show any skepticism, and the archbishop's expression was difficult to decipher. Ranulf had an uneasy sense that Becket was listening to voices only he could hear. What had he said to Exeter? *You do not understand the Will of God.*

ABOVESTAIRS THE QUARREL still raged between Henry and his bishops. Finally even the Bishop of Winchester agreed to go down and urge Becket to resign. He had no more luck, though, than the others, and the bishops, abandoning Becket to his fate, set about making their own peace with the king. After withdrawing for a hurried consultation, they returned to the chamber with a proposition for Henry.

Once again, Gilbert Foliot was the one chosen to speak for them. "My lord king, we find ourselves caught between Scylla and Charybdis. The Archbishop of Canterbury has placed us in an impossible position. First he bade us vow to obey the Constitutions of Clarendon and now he forbids us to honor that promise. But we owe him a duty of obedience and risk excommunication if we refuse to heed his prohibition."

"Have you thought about what you risk if you do heed Becket?"

"Indeed, my lord king. Therefore, we offer a compromise. If you will excuse us from pronouncing judgment upon the archbishop, we will forthwith make an appeal to the Holy Father, accusing the archbishop of perjuring himself and forcing us to violate our own oaths. We will further promise to seek his removal."

More than a few of the bishops then held their breath. Henry did not keep them in suspense, though. After a moment to consider, he nodded. "So be it," he said, although he was unable to resist adding a sardonic aside. "I'd not want it said that I showed as little compassion for my bishops as does the Archbishop of Canterbury."

WILLIAM FITZ STEPHEN was seated at Thomas Becket's feet, Herbert of Bosham on the archbishop's other side. The tension and turmoil had given Fitz Stephen a pounding headache, and from the way a vein was throbbing in the archbishop's temple, he suspected that Lord Thomas suffered from the same malady. They were sitting in silence, for after Herbert had urged Becket to excommunicate his enemies, the marshals had warned them that no one was to speak to the archbishop. They could only wait, dreading what was being deliberated abovestairs. Fitz Stephen cast admiring glances at his lord, marveling that he could seem so composed in the face of such blatant injustice. When their eyes met, Becket smiled tiredly and Fitz Stephen found himself fighting back tears. Bowing his head, he whispered, " 'Blessed are they which are persecuted for righteousness' sake, for theirs is the kingdom of Heaven,' " only to be silenced by one of the marshals.

They were soon joined by the bishops, who'd been excused from further participation in the proceedings, and the waiting resumed. Occasionally a muffled shout of "Traitor" carried down to the hall and Fitz Stephen shuddered. His lord did not respond, though; his earlier agitation and uncertainty were gone, or well camouflaged in an almost otherworldly appearance of calm. The other bishops showed far less patience, fidgeting and murmuring amongst themselves. Herbert was glaring openly at them, making no effort to hide his disdain. Fitz Stephen was less judgmental; excepting the Archbishop of York and the Bishop of Chichester, he felt they were well intentioned. While it was a great pity they'd not shown more backbone, he could not in all fairness fault them for it. There were few men walking God's earth with the courage to defy a king, especially this king.

When they finally heard the door open and the thud of footsteps on the stairs, Fitz Stephen, Herbert, and several of the bishops jumped to their feet. Thomas Becket remained seated, though, still firmly gripping his cross. Men began to crowd into the hall and Fitz Stephen's last quavering hope was snuffed out by the sight of the triumphant grins and smirks of those barons most hostile to his lord.

There was no joy to be found in the somber expression of the Earl of Leicester. Moving with a heavy tread, as if he felt the full weight of his sixty years, he approached the archbishop. "It has fallen upon me," he said gravely, "to inform you, my lord archbishop, that you have been found guilty of treason. The sentence passed by the court is that you be—"

"I will hear no judgment, for I have appealed to His Holiness, the Pope."

Leicester was momentarily thrown off-stride by Becket's interruption. His hesitation making it clear that this was a task he was loath to perform, he started to speak again and again Becket cut him off. Leicester turned to Rainald as if for assistance. Rainald merely shook his head. At that the Bishop of Chichester intervened, but not on behalf of his beleaguered colleague.

"Your treason is manifest to all," he told Becket, with a sorrowful air that only emphasized the harshness of his words, "and you must hear the court's sentence."

"Who are you to tell me that?" Becket rose to his feet, dismissing Chichester with a scornful curl of his lip. For a moment, his eyes raked the hall and such was the power of his personality that even the most virulent of his foes fell silent. "Judgment is given after a trial," he said, speaking loudly enough so that all could hear. "I have done no pleading today. I was summoned for no suit except that of John Marshal, who did not even put in an appearance." When Leicester would have spoken, he held up his hand, halting the words in a gesture both dramatic and imperious. "I forbid you by the authority that Holy Church gives me over you to pass judgment upon me."

Leicester, looking more uncomfortable by the moment, conceded defeat and stepped back. But Rannulph de Broc was uncowed. Pushing his way forward, he said with a sneer, "What authority can a lowborn traitor exercise?"

Becket's face flooded with color. "You're one to talk! One of your family got himself hanged for a felony, which is more than ever happened to any of my kin."

De Broc sputtered, momentarily at a loss for words, and some of the other men grinned, for he had few friends, mainly allies of expedience. Becket took advantage of the pause, raising his cross and starting toward the door. He moved at a deliberate, unhurried pace, head high and shoulders squared, and as his clerks hastened to catch up with him, Fitz Stephen began to hope that they would be able to make a dignified, peaceful departure. But then Becket tripped over a bundle of faggots by the hearth and almost fell.

That small stumble was enough to embolden his foes. Rannulph de Broc lunged forward, shouting, "Perjurer!" The cry was quickly taken up by others and Becket was soon surrounded by angry, jeering men, some of them pelting him with rushes scooped up from the floor. Henry's half-brother, Hamelin, his face contorted with hatred, barred Becket's way, crying "Traitor!" in a hoarse voice that was an eerie echo of the king's.

At that, Becket's self-control snapped and he turned on Hamelin in a sudden fury. "Lackey," he raged, "bastard! If I were not a priest, you'd pay dearly for that insult!"

By now Leicester and an equally alarmed Rainald had shouldered their way through the men encircling Becket, shouting for them to get back, and as they grudgingly gave way, Becket and his clerks were able to reach the door. The dignified departure Fitz Stephen had hoped for had taken on the urgency of an escape, and when Herbert of Bosham could not find his horse, he scrambled up behind Becket onto the archbishop's stallion. But no attempts were made to stop them from leaving the castle, and there was no pursuit as they rode back to their lodgings at St Andrew's Priory. Indeed, their retreat soon turned into a triumphant procession, with the townspeople flocking out to cheer for Becket and seek his blessings.

RANULF HAD BEEN TOSSING and turning for hours. All around him, the aisles of the great hall were crowded with pallets and the blanket-clad forms of sleeping men. But for Ranulf, sleep would not come. Finally surrendering unconditionally to his insomnia, he got to his feet and padded silently through the floor rushes toward the door. Trying not to awaken the closest sleepers, he pulled the bolt back and unfastened the latch. Cracking the door, he looked out in surprise. He'd known it was raining, hearing the thrumming upon the roof shingles. Until now, though, he'd not realized how severe the storm was. Torrential rains were flooding the bailey, the wind keening like a lost soul, and lightning flared somewhere over the town, searing the black sky with blue-white sparks.

Hastily crossing himself, Ranulf shut the door, wondering how many others were lying wakeful and uneasy this night. As midnight drew nigh, it seemed as if the very heavens were warring upon Northampton. How many would see this savage storm as an ill omen, a sign of the Almighty's displeasure at the shabby way His servant had been treated in the king's court?

Since he could not go outside, he looked around for another refuge, eventually settling upon the chapel adjoining the hall, for there at least, he'd find no snoring sleepers. Groping his way forward, he creaked open the door. A lone candle still flickered upon the altar and a rushlight burned in a wall sconce, but the chapel was swirling in shadows; even the wind's wail was muffled here, the storm's fury held at bay by the thick stone walls, the lingering grace of countless heartfelt prayers for God's Mercy. Ranulf's troubled spirit eased and he drew a breath of solace. But as he moved toward the altar, a ghostly figure emerged suddenly from the shadows to intercept him.

Ranulf recoiled with a startled gasp. "Christ Jesus, Roger, I thought you were one of the Devil's own come to claim my soul!"

His nephew smiled wryly. "It would not surprise me, Uncle, to find the Devil stalking Northampton this night. But your soul is safe with me." He gestured toward several prayer cushions piled in a corner. "I have made a snug nest for myself, as you can see. I even have a flask of wine. Care to join me?"

"Why not?" Seating themselves on the cushions, resting their backs against the wall, they took turns drinking from Roger's flask. "Why are you here at the castle?" Ranulf asked, since that was a safer question than why Roger thought demons were abroad in the night. "I thought you were lodging in the town."

"And I thought you were staying with the canons?"

"I was, but I stayed so late tonight in Harry's chambers that it seemed easier just to spend the night here. You, too?"

Roger took another swig of wine, his shoulders slumping. "I went to the priory," he said, "to see how Thomas was faring. Not only have many of the knights of his household asked to be released from his service, but more than forty of his clerks have abandoned him, too. Craven louts, the lot of them," he added, with unexpected venom.

"Does it truly surprise you that men should fear the contagion of the king's disfavor as much as they do leprosy or the spotted fever?"

"No . . . ," Roger conceded. "I do not blame the knights for looking to their own interests. But it is shameful for men of God to behave like rats fleeing a sinking ship."

Ranulf agreed that it was and reached over to reclaim the flask. "So what brought you back to the castle?"

"Thomas asked me and the Bishops of Hereford and Rochester to go to the king and seek a safe-conduct for his journey back to Canterbury." Roger was quiet then for a time. "Harry said that he'd answer us on the morrow."

"And that worries you? It should not," Ranulf insisted. "He'll give a safe conduct. When Rainald and I told him of the ugly scene in the great hall and of the threats made against Becket by some of the barons, he immediately sent forth heralds to proclaim that the archbishop was not to be harmed or harassed. It is Becket's humiliation he seeks, not his blood. Do you doubt that, Roger?"

"No . . . I suppose not. It is just that . . . that this quarrel with Thomas has brought out the worst in Harry, a side of his nature I've not seen before and would that I not see again."

Ranulf could not dispute that, as much as he wanted to. He refrained from making the natural rejoinder: that the archbishopric had brought out the worst in Becket. Enough heedless words had already been said during these days at Northampton. They were sitting under the overhead rush-light, and its muted glow magnified the hollowed cheekbones and grimly set lines of Roger's mouth. Ranulf shifted sideways. "You have the look of a man with much on his mind, none of it pleasant. If talking will help, I'm willing to listen. It is the least I can do after drinking your wine."

Roger's smile flickered, briefly. For a long moment, his eyes searched Ranulf's face. He looked so much like his sire that Ranulf felt the pang of an old grief. "I loved your father, lad," he said quietly, "as I've loved few men in this life."

"I know that, Uncle. I know, too, that you could not love Harry more if he were your own son."

Ranulf set down the flask between them. "What you tell me goes no further than this chapel. You have my word upon that, Roger."

Roger let his breath out slowly. "I might be wrong," he said, "but I think that Thomas means to flee tonight."

"Understandable after what happened today. What makes you think so?"

"Whilst I was at the priory, I overheard two of his clerks talking. They were huddled in one of the carrels out in the cloisters and my approach caught them unaware. Ere they noticed me and went mute, I heard them say something about midnight and an unguarded gate in the town."

Roger seemed relieved to have unburdened himself. Almost at once, though, he reached out and caught Ranulf's arm. "Uncle, you'll say nothing of this? If Harry were to find out . . ."

"You need not fret, lad. I'll not break faith with you. Even if I had not given my word, I do not think that I'd want to deliver Becket into Harry's hands—for both their sakes."

"Amen," Roger said, and after that they drank in silence while the castle slept and the storm raged through the night.

At the height of the storm, Thomas Becket and three others slipped out of the town's unguarded north gate and spurred their horses toward Lincoln. From there, he began a slow, circuitous journey for the coast, disguised as a monk. On All Soul's Day, the second of November, he and his three companions set sail from the port of Sandwich. Manning a small boat in heavy seas, they came ashore safely in Flanders at dusk.

Henry did not actively pursue the fugitive archbishop, contenting himself with putting the ports under watch. Nor had he exploded in one of his famous fits of rage upon being told of Becket's escape. In some ways, his response was even more chilling to the archbishop's partisans. Eyes narrowing, he'd said laconically, "I have not done with him yet."

> *To his lord and friend Louis, illustrious King of the French, from Henry, King of the English and Duke of the Normans and Aquitanians, and Count of the Angevins, greetings and affection.*
>
> *Know that Thomas, who was Archbishop of Canterbury, has been publicly adjudged in my court, by full council of the barons of my realm, to be a wicked and perjured traitor to me, and under the manifest name of traitor has wickedly departed, as my messengers will more fully tell you.*
>
> *Wherefore I earnestly entreat you not to permit a man guilty of such infamous crimes and treasons, or his men, to remain in your kingdom; and let not this great enemy of mine, so it please you, have any counsel or aid from you or yours, even as I would not give any such help to your enemies in my realm or allow it to be given. Rather, if it please you, help me to take vengeance upon my great enemy for this affront, and look to my honor, as you would have me do for you if there were need of it.*
>
> *Done at Northampton.*

Henry then turned his attention to the rebellion in Wales. His council at Northampton resolved upon a summer campaign against Rhys ap Gruffydd and Owain Gwynedd, and his lords pledged to supply large numbers of infantry, more suitable than armor-clad knights for the hit-and-run warfare waged by the Welsh. Mercenaries were to be hired from Flanders and a fleet equipped at Dublin. The Marcher barons departed Northampton secure in the knowledge that there was to be a reckoning with the troublesome Welsh at long last.

AFTER THE COUNCIL at Northampton drew to an end, Henry sent a delegation across the Channel to see the French king at Compiègne and then on to the Pope, still in exile at Sens. By an irony of chance, they sailed from Dover on the very day that Thomas Becket made his escape from Sandwich. Henry's envoys were distinguished—including the Bishops of London, Worcester, Chichester, and Exeter, the Archbishop of York, and the Earl of Arundel—but their mission was a failure. Returning to England, they began the lugubrious task of finding the king and breaking the bad news to him. Perhaps because they were in no hurry to deliver disappointment, they did not overtake Henry until Christmas Eve, where he and Eleanor were keeping court at Marlborough Castle.

A LIGHT SNOWFALL powdered the castle grounds and a fire burned brightly in the hearth of the king's solar, which was festively adorned with holly, mistletoe, and evergreen boughs. But every spark of Christmas cheer had been quenched with the first halting words of Gilbert Foliot, for even his eloquence could find no way to make his news palatable: that Becket had been warmly received by both the Pope and the French king.

Henry was standing so close to the fireplace that he was in danger of being singed by its dancing flames, but he seemed oblivious of the heat. "Tell me," he said tersely. "Hold nothing back."

"We met with the French king at his castle of Compiègne, where we delivered your letter. I regret to say, my liege, that his piety has adversely affected his judgment. His natural inclination is to give any priest the benefit of every doubt, even when presented with proof of perjury and broken faith."

That was a diplomatic and discreet rendering of the French king's response, and none knew it better than Eleanor, who knew her first husband all too well. She glanced toward Henry to see if he was reading between the lines. But then the Bishop of Chichester tactlessly intervened with the truth.

"We sought to make him privy to the facts, Your Grace, but he was not wont to listen. 'Who deposed the Archbishop of Canterbury?' he asked. He said he was as much a king as the King of the English, but he did not have the power to depose the least of the clerks in his realm. Not only did he offer Becket asylum in his domains, he wrote to the Pope on Becket's behalf, urging him to receive the archbishop with kindness and pay no heed to unjust accusations against him."

Henry spat out an extremely profane oath, but whom it was meant for—Becket or the French king—none could be sure. "Go on," he said harshly. "What happened at Sens?"

As Chichester showed no inclination to relinquish center stage and Foliot was willing to let him be the bearer of bad tidings, he was the one to tell Henry the rest, the worst. "We met with the Holy Father and the cardinals, and as you bade us, my liege, we privately urged the Archbishop of Canterbury's deposition. Whilst I do not doubt that many of the cardinals would not mourn Becket's departure, the Pope insisted that he could take no action until he heard the archbishop's account of the Northampton council. Becket soon arrived, with a retinue of three hundred horsemen provided by the French king. He threw himself at the Holy Father's feet, holding out a chirograph of the Constitutions of Clarendon."

Chichester had always prided himself upon his remarkable memory and he could not resist quoting now from Becket's own words. "He said, 'Behold, Holy Father, the customs of the King of the English, opposed to the canons and decretals and even the laws of secular princes, for which we are driven to endure exile.' He then read out the clauses of the Constitutions, one by one, offering his own critical analysis of each article, and although Cardinal William of Pavia made a spirited defense of the provisions, Becket's view prevailed. He then . . ."

Chichester paused for maximum dramatic impact and Henry's eyes flashed dangerously. "What?"

"Becket was ever one for the grand gesture," Chichester said scornfully. "He knelt again, began to weep, and resigned the archbishopric of Canterbury for the good of the Church, he said, and offered his archiepiscopal ring to the Holy Father. Alas, my liege, the Holy Father was moved by his tears and returned the ring, saying 'Receive anew at our hands the cure of the episcopal office.'"

Everyone in the solar understood the significance of the Pope's act. The appeal of the other bishops for Becket's deposition would come to naught. Nor would Henry's complaints to the Holy See. Thomas Becket would remain as Archbishop of Canterbury, with the Pope's blessings—and there was nothing Henry could do about it.

There was a prolonged silence, fraught with foreboding, and then the inevitable explosion. Henry's tempers were known to them all, but even Eleanor had never seen him in such a spectacular rage as this. A sweep of his arm sent the contents of the trestle table flying off into space, books and quill pens and an open inkwell spilling into the floor rushes. With a crash that reverberated throughout the entire room, the table followed, barely missing one of Eleanor's alarmed greyhounds. The men shrank back from this violent display of royal wrath, only the king's wife and his cousin Roger standing their ground. Henry overturned a chair, then swung around upon Gilbert Foliot.

"I shall issue an order confiscating all of that whoreson's possessions down to the last farthing and the forfeiture of the archbishopric. No bishop of mine shall pay revenues to any of Becket's clerks holding prebends within their sees. Will any Church objections be raised to my writ, my lord bishop?"

Foliot swallowed. "No, my liege . . . no objections."

"Now . . . what burrow has our snake found for the winter? Is he still at the Papal Curia in Sens?"

"No, Your Grace," Foliot said swiftly, grateful that he had at least a scrap of good news to offer Henry. "The Holy Father's actions were not as one-sided as the Bishop of Chichester related. Whilst he did refuse Becket's resignation and condemned the Constitutions of Clarendon, he did not censure me or my fellow bishops as Becket expected, and he most certainly did not make him welcome at the papal court. He has sent Becket off to the Cistercian abbey at Pontigny. So you see, my liege, all is not as bleak as it might first have seemed."

His words did not have the desired effect. They did not even seem to have registered with Henry. "Pontigny," he echoed. "Good . . . let them go there then and seek shelter from him."

Foliot looked confused; nor was he the only one. "Who, my lord king?" the Earl of Arundel asked in bewilderment. "Who shall seek shelter?"

"All of Becket's household still in England, and their kin as well. They are to join him in exile, every last one of them. Let him see for himself what misery he has brought upon his own. And let the French king provide for their bread if Becket will not!"

The others were speechless, staring at him in disbelief. Oddly enough, it was the opportunist who spoke up first. Hilary of Chichester cleared his throat, then said hesitantly, "My liege, I implore you to reconsider. If you banish all of Becket's family and clerks, I fear you will be harshly judged for it by your enemies."

"Let them! You think I care?"

"My liege . . ." Gilbert Foliot had never lacked for courage—until now. "I think once your anger cools, you will not want to—"

"Who are you to tell me what I want? Becket should have thought of the consequences when he fled in the night like a thief. There is always a price to be paid for betrayal and he is about to find that out, by God!" The disapproval Henry saw reflected on their faces only fanned his fury all the higher. Gesturing toward the door, he ordered them all out. "After failing me so abysmally in Compiègne and Sens, why should I listen to you now? Go on, get out!"

They did, some hastily enough to compromise their dignity. Only Roger dared to protest further. Reaching the door, he paused, meeting his cousin's eyes without flinching. "This is wrong, Harry," he said in a low voice. "Wrong and unjust."

He did not linger; he knew better than that. As the door closed behind him, Henry swore again. But before he could react, a cushion was suddenly shoved into his hand. "Here," Eleanor said. "If you must destroy something, fling this about. It is much easier to mend a pillow than a table."

Henry was not amused. "I'm glad you're taking it in such good humor that I've just been stabbed in the back by that gutless weasel you married!"

"A pity there is no way you can blame Becket's misdeeds on me, too!"

"If you are about to remind me that you opposed Becket's elevation to the archbishopric, trust me, Eleanor—this is not the time!"

"Actually, I have a far more recent grievance. I entreated you not to send Louis that letter, warned you it would do you more harm than good, did I not? And as usual, you paid me no heed whatsoever!"

"For the love of Christ, woman, let it lie! Can you not see that I'm in no mood to deal with this now?"

"Fine," she said tartly. "Forget about Louis and the fact that you were the one to provide the dagger for that back-stabbing. Let's talk, instead, about your plan to banish those poor souls whose only offense is that they are related to Becket either by blood or service. Surely you do not mean that, Harry."

"Surely I do."

"Then this interminable feuding with Becket has well and truly addled your mind!"

"This is none of your concern! I am heartily sick of your meddling, Eleanor, will have no more of it!"

"If you bid me be silent, then of course I will," Eleanor responded, with poisonous sweetness, "for like any dutiful and devoted wife, I live only to please you." With a deep, graceful curtsy, she swept toward the door, where she paused, her hand on the latch, a quizzical smile upon her face. "About that 'weasel' I married . . . You were referring to Louis, were you not?"

He glared at her. "Damn you, Eleanor!"

"Likewise, my love," she retorted, and left him alone in the solar.

✣

ON THE DAY AFTER CHRISTMAS, Henry followed through on his threat and expelled as many as four hundred people, including Becket's sisters and nephews, his clerks and servants and their families. A steady steam of refugees made their miserable way to Pontigny and Thomas Becket was indeed distressed, as Henry had intended. But it was a Pyrrhic victory, one that left a lasting stain upon Henry's honor and his reputation.

Henry and Eleanor patched up their Christmas Eve quarrel the way they usually did, in bed, and when they departed Marlborough, she was pregnant again.

CHAPTER EIGHTEEN

✦

May 1165
Trefriw, North Wales

AR HAD COME to Wales, but the first battle was being
fought in the great hall of Rhodri's manor in the hills above
Trefriw. The summons from the English king had erupted in
their midst with devastating impact, as incendiary as Greek fire and as difficult to extinguish. For days now, the quarrel had raged and showed no
signs of abating. Rhodri had argued with Ranulf until his voice cracked.
Eleri had been reduced to angry tears more than once, and Celyn had
overcome his natural reticence to plead with surprising passion. Even the
self-absorbed Enid had roused herself to observe that it would be folly to
obey the summons, for if Ranulf fought against the Welsh, he would
alienate his family and friends and neighbors beyond forgiving.

Ranulf already knew that. He was painfully aware how high the stakes
were. If he answered the summons, he was likely to forfeit all that he held
most dear in this life. But if he did not? Disloyalty to his king was a sin of
such magnitude that it was almost beyond his comprehension. It went to
the very core of his integrity, his identity. He had supported his sister over
Stephen and never wavered in that allegiance because Maude's claim was

just and Stephen's was not, even after it cost him the woman he loved. Harry was his liege lord, his blood kin. Could he betray that bond—and live with it afterward?

An exhausted truce had finally fallen and dinner was served in a dismal silence. As it was a Friday fast day, their cook had broiled a large pike, taken from the manor's fish pond. Swimming in a pungent mustard sauce, fresh pike was a delicacy. But now much of it went untouched; only the younger children seemed to have an appetite. Rhodri was pushing his fish around on his trencher with his knife, Rhiannon intent upon feeding Morgan, Celyn crumbling a crust of the bread baked to cater to Ranulf's English tastes, and Ranulf slipping surreptitious mouthfuls of pike to Blaidd, his Norwegian dyrehund.

Eleri was the one to crack first, flinging her napkin down with an oath. "For the love of God, Ranulf, look around you! This is your home. For fifteen years, your home. How can you throw it all away like this? If you love my sister as you claim, you must—"

Rhiannon let her get no further. "Eleri, enough! I do not need you to speak for me. We've heard you out, each one of you. You've had your say. Now let it be. When Ranulf decides what he must do, we will tell you. Till then, this serves for naught."

Ranulf's throat tightened; what had he done to deserve this woman? But even as he reached for his wife's hand, their son sprang to his feet, shoving his chair back so violently that it toppled over. "I've not had my say!" Gilbert's face was flushed, his voice unsteady. "If you answer the English king's summons, you are betraying Lord Owain!"

"Ah, lad," Ranulf said softly, "if only it were that simple."

"I will be fourteen by year's end, so do not treat me like a child! At fourteen, I will be old enough to fight against our enemies—against the English! And if you fight with them, you'll be the enemy, too!"

Gilbert's voice choked and he wheeled, bolting for the door as Ranulf jumped to his feet and Rhiannon cried out his name. The boy reached the door just as it opened and he collided head-on with Hywel, whose arrival out in the bailey had gone unnoticed in all the uproar. Gilbert staggered backward and Hywel caught his arm as if to steady him, effectively blocking his flight.

"Easy, lad," he said with a smile. "The last time I saw someone move this fast, his tunic was on fire. Is dinner done then?"

Gilbert tried to wrench free and failed; over the youth's head, Hywel's eyes sought Ranulf's in a silent question. Ranulf hesitated, then slowly nodded. Better to give the lad some time to calm down. But he knew that he was deluding himself. An eternity's worth of time was not likely to bring Gilbert around to his way of thinking.

HYWEL'S ARRIVAL had defused the tension, at least temporarily. Accepting Enid's invitation to dine with them, he kept them entertained with the latest court gossip, then shared the more serious news—that the English king had returned from Normandy, doubtless upon learning of Davydd ab Owain's raid into Tegeingl. Moving with his usual lightning speed, Henry had led a quick expedition to relieve his castles at Rhudd-lan and Basingwerk, then withdrew back across the border to organize a full-scale invasion intended for that summer. When Rhodri said glumly that they already knew of the English king's plans for war, Hywel showed no surprise. His father's surveillance system rivaled, if not surpassed, those of the English and French kings and the exiled Archbishop of Canterbury, and within a day of Ranulf's royal summons, Owain had known about it.

As the evening wore on, a patchy, pale mist drifted in from the Menai Straits, slowly engulfing the river valley and eventually reaching the hill-side manor above Trefriw. One by one, the family members retired for the night, and Hywel's men bedded down in the hall. A fire burned erratically in the hearth as the last of the log was consumed. By midnight, the only ones still awake were Hywel and Ranulf.

Reaching for the flagon, Ranulf emptied it into their cups. "I think there is more mead in the buttery."

"Then I'd better fetch it, for if you stagger off in search of the but-tery, God only knows where you'll end up."

"Are you implying that I've had too much to drink, Hywel?"

"No . . . I'd say you have not had enough. If you are going to drown your troubles, you might as well do it right. The aim is to blot out all the voices."

"What voices?"

"The voice of reason, to start with. Then the voice of conscience. But we've only had two flagons . . . or was it three? Based on my experience, it will take at least four. The conscience, in particular, floats like a cork . . . devilishly difficult to drown."

Ranulf laughed, but it had a sad sound to it. "You think I'm a fool, don't you?"

"No . . ."

"That was not a very convincing denial," Ranulf complained and Hywel submerged a grin in his mead cup.

"Indeed, you are no fool. In fact, you are about as far from a fool as a man can get. Is that better?"

"But . . . ?"

"But you do have a few bad habits—one of which is that you invariably hope for the best instead of preparing for the worst. Our people have a saying, Ranulf, that you ought to take to heart: that it is dangerous to run with the hares and hunt with the hounds."

"When you say 'our people,' Hywel, that does still include me?"

Hywel set his cup down in surprise. "Of course. You're Welsh by choice as well as by blood—your besotted loyalty to the English king notwithstanding!"

Ranulf knew that the other man was joking, but it was difficult for him to find much humor in his plight. "I understand why your father and Rhys ap Gruffydd and the others have rebelled, God's Truth, I do. How could I blame them for wanting to free Wales from a foreign yoke?"

"But you also understand why Henry feels compelled to crush that rebellion."

Ranulf nodded miserably. "Yes," he admitted, "I do. As king, he has no choice." He snatched up his mead cup and drained it, too fast. "I understand too much for my own damned good." Shoving the empty cup across the table, he leaned forward, cradling his head on his arms. "But God help me, for I still do not know what I will do. . . ."

Hywel finished his own drink, then reached for a spare blanket on a nearby bench. Draping it over Ranulf's shoulders, he stood for a moment, gazing down at his sleeping friend. "God help you," he murmured, "for you do know . . ."

HYWEL DEPARTED the next day, as did Eleri and Celyn and their children. Quiet settled over the manor like a tattered, faded quilt, too worn to offer much comfort. On Sunday, Ranulf's family heard Mass at Llanrhychwyn, a small church nestled in the hills above Trefriw. Ranulf loved this whitewashed stone chapel shadowed by towering yew trees; it was here that he and Rhiannon had been wed on Shrove Tuesday fifteen years ago. As the parishioners filed out into the cool May sunlight, he caught Rhiannon's hand and led her toward a corner of the churchyard. There were tombstones there, green with moss, and the woodland scents perfumed their every breath. When he described for her a hawk gliding on the air currents high above their heads, Rhiannon smiled and then said, "You are going to answer the English king's summons."

He plucked a dandelion from a grave and crushed it into a golden dustfall. "Yes," he said, "I am. If I am with Harry, mayhap I can convince him to settle for less, a victory that does not leave Wales awash in blood."

She wondered why Harry would heed him in Wales when he had not at Northampton. But there was nothing to be gained by pointing that out. "Do what you must," she said wearily, for if there was pain, there was no surprise. She'd known from the first what he would do.

"Rhiannon . . . I am sorry. I know what I risk. Whatever the outcome of this war, it seems likely that I'll no longer be welcome in Wales."

"Hush," she said, putting her fingers up to his lips. "We can only cross one river at a time."

"I know . . . 'Sufficient unto the day is the evil thereof,'" he agreed, reaching for her hand. Although they both knew there was nothing more to be said, they lingered a while longer in the churchyard, midst the familiar sounds of spring and the enduring silence of the dead.

THE DAY HAD BEGUN with a sunburst dawn the color of molten gold, but as the afternoon advanced, dark clouds gathered along the horizon and the June warmth soon slipped away. Usually men on a hunt were boisterous and rowdy, but this hunt had been different from the first. Their quarry was a large male wolf that had been killing sheep in Herefordshire and Shropshire, so light in color it had become known as the "grey ghost." While wolves were often hunted in France *par force de chiens*—by strength of hounds—in England they were looked upon more as pests than prey, and men were commonly hired to set traps and snares when villagers complained to their liege lord of slain livestock. But as soon as Henry heard about the grey ghost's depredations, he had determined to hunt the creature down, insisting that a wolf could not be permitted to roam the countryside at will; today it was taking lambs, but on the morrow it might carry off a child.

Henry's companions knew the real reason for his sudden hunting fervor: he was growing bored and restless at Ludlow Castle, impatient to speed up the preparations for next month's invasion of Wales. The others showed little enthusiasm for tracking a wolf, an animal generally viewed with unease. But Henry was not to be denied, and a hunting party was soon galloping west into Herefordshire.

The grey ghost proved to be well named, elusive and spectral. Although the dogs had been able to pick up its scent at its latest kill, the trail soon petered out. The men finally halted in a clearing for a meal of dried beef, washed down with ale. A would-be poacher crept closer to observe them, seeing more than two dozen men sprawling in the shade, sweat-stained and muddied. He knew they must be men of rank, their dishevelment notwithstanding, for hunting with hounds was the sport of the highborn. But he'd have been stunned had he known that he was spying upon England's king, the Earls of Leicester, Cornwall, and Chester, the Bishop of Worcester, and the king's out-of-wedlock kin, Ranulf and Hamelin. Deciding to postpone his own hunting for a safer day, he made a stealthy retreat, as soundlessly as the great grey wolf itself.

Rainald announced he was going to "take a piss," shrugging off the inevitable round of ribald jokes about the dangers of stinging nettles. When he returned, he headed toward a large oak and dropped down into the grass beside his younger brother.

"I'd rather be hunting any prey but wolves," he grumbled. "There's no sport in it since they won't turn at bay the way a boar does. And if that were not enough, the wretched creature has a poisonous bite."

Ranulf swiveled around to stare at him. "Where did you hear nonsense like that?"

"It is not nonsense," Rainald insisted. "All know it to be true, most likely because they eat toads."

"Next you'll be telling me that a man who eats chickens will start to lay eggs," Ranulf scoffed, laughing in spite of himself.

Rainald grinned triumphantly. "I knew I could get a smile out of you if I tried."

"I do not have much reason for smiling these days, Rainald."

"I keep telling you this war with Wales will be over in a fortnight. The Welsh princes will submit, as they always do, and Harry will pardon them, and we'll all go home. Ere you know it, you'll be back on that Welsh mountain of yours, counting your sheep or whatever you do to pass the time."

Ranulf knew better. A sudden burst of laughing echoed across the clearing and he turned toward the sound.

"That was a most unseemly joke for a bishop to be telling," Henry declared, frowning in mock disapproval at his cousin.

"So why did you laugh at it?" Roger queried innocently, and Henry grinned.

"So I'd not hurt your feelings, of course." Getting to his feet, he sauntered across the glade toward his uncles. "Why are the two of you hiding over here? Surely you're not still brooding about the Welsh matter, Ranulf? I assure you that I want you there merely as an interpreter and peacemaker once the fighting is done. As well as you know Owain Gwynedd, you're the best man for—"

The rest of his sentence was lost in a sudden clap of thunder. The horses stirred uneasily and Rainald lumbered to his feet. "Enough is enough, Harry. We've been chasing this phantom wolf for half a day and all we have to show for it are saddle sores and sweat. I'm damned if I'll get drowned in the bargain, too. I say we go back to Ludlow."

"I've never heard of a man melting in the rain like a lump of sugar, Uncle," Henry scoffed, but the other men then added their voices to Rainald's, and he reluctantly agreed that the hunt was over. Mounting up, they headed toward the east, toward Ludlow.

But the approaching storm outran their lathered horses, and they found themselves caught in a drenching downpour while the castle was still miles away. Rain pelting their faces like liquid needles, seeping down the necks of their tunics, collecting in the brims of their hats, they were soon thoroughly miserable and arguing that they ought to find the closest shelter. Henry merely laughed at their complaints. Then the storm intensified. Half deafened by thunder, flinching each time lightning seared the black-smoke sky above their heads, the men struggled to control their skittish stallions and urged Henry to reconsider.

By now even Henry was impressed by the fury of the elements. But when his brother Hamelin suggested that they head for Avreton, where the Marcher lord Fitz Hugh had a castle, he balked. "Ludlow is only four or five miles past Avreton. We're already soaked to the skin, so we might as well press on toward—"

Lightning forked from the clouds, shooting earthward with a blinding flash. There was a bang and then the smell of burning wood as a nearby tree was riven in two. The accompanying crack of thunder filled their world with reverberating, roaring sound, and in the ensuing chaos, one of the Earl of Leicester's squires was thrown from his panicked horse.

The boy's face was pasty-white under a smear of mud and a drizzle of blood. "I am sorry, my liege," he gasped as Henry knelt by his side. "I think I've broken my arm . . ."

"You'll be all right, lad," Henry said reassuringly. Straightening up, he blotted rain from his face with a soggy sleeve. "Well, you milksops win," he said. "Avreton it is."

AVRETON PERCHED on top of a steep, rocky hill, on the Herefordshire side of the River Thames, just west of the tiny village of Boiton. A deep ditch encircled the outer bailey, a narrow causeway in the southeast side giving entry to the castle. As the men rode into a small inner bailey, a woman teetered on the steps of the great hall, flanked by servants. She was clad in an oversized mantle that enveloped her from head to toe and seemed loath to brave the storm. But from the moment that the king's identity had been shouted up to the guards upon the ramparts, events had taken on a momentum of their own. By the time they dismounted, she had overcome her reluctance and was gingerly edging around the muddiest puddles toward them.

"My liege, I . . . I am so honored," she stammered. "My lord husband is not here, for he rode to Ludlow this morn upon learning of your presence there. He . . . he will be back soon, I think. . . ."

Henry was accustomed to having this effect upon people. "Lady Fitz Hugh," he said, kissing her hand with a courtliness that would have amused Eleanor enormously. "One of our men has been hurt. We need to get him inside."

Deftly steering the flustered woman toward the hall, he supervised the move of the injured squire, while the Fitz Hugh servants hastened to lead the horses to the shelter of the stables. The rest of the hunting party and their dogs followed Henry and their fretful hostess into the hall, where confusion soon reigned. Amice Fitz Hugh was so obviously incapable of taking charge that Henry found himself giving the necessary orders: sending a rider out into the storm to fetch a doctor from Ludlow, instructing servants to heat water and stoke the fire so that they could wash up and dry their sopping clothes.

Amice, a thin, wan woman dressed in an unbecoming shade of grey, relaxed somewhat once she saw that these royal intruders were on their good behavior and she even ventured to offer a timid invitation. "If you would care to stay the night, my liege, we would be so honored . . ."

Henry stifled a smile, for she'd used the word "honored" in virtually every sentence since their arrival. "That is most generous, Lady Fitz Hugh, but we do not wish to disrupt your household any more than necessary. If you can put the lad here up for a day or two, that is more than enough. We'll be on our way as soon as the storm lets up."

Amice demurred politely, her relief obvious. Turning her attention then to the ailing squire, she showed unexpected skill in soothing the boy's fears. He became noticeably less agitated under her ministrations and even perked up enough to ask the identity of a girl just entering the hall. Amice glanced over her shoulder, then gave a shrug. "My younger sister," she said dismissively.

She was alone, though, in her indifference to her sister's entrance. Every male eye in the hall was upon the newcomer as soon as she shed her mantle, revealing a crown of curly blond tresses only partially covered by a crookedly pinned veil, and a surprisingly voluptuous body for one barely five feet. Her face was heart-shaped, her skin flawless and fair, and when she smiled, the squire momentarily forgot the pain of his broken arm. Hugh de Gernons, the young Earl of Chester, trampled on several toes in his haste to reach her side. But his gallantry was wasted, for her response was polite but preoccupied; from the moment she'd hurried into the hall, the only man she seemed to see was Henry.

Henry had noticed her, too; he always had an eye for a pretty girl. This particular pretty girl seemed vaguely familiar, though. Where had he seen her before? Ranulf was wondering the same thing. The memory was somehow connected with his son Gilbert, but it was as evasive as the wolf they'd been chasing all day. Henry's memory proved more reliable. "Woodstock," he said suddenly. "Clifford's little lass . . . of course!"

Ranulf now remembered, too. "The girl you rescued out in the gardens. I knew I'd seen her somewhere. Well . . . she has grown up for certes, has she not?"

"That she has," Henry agreed and moved to meet her. "Mistress Rosamund, this is indeed a welcome surprise. How is it that you happen to be at Avreton?"

"You remember me!" Her smile was blinding. "Amice is my sister—"

"Rosamund?" Amice was staring at the girl in disbelief. "You know the king?"

"Mistress Rosamund and I met at Woodstock two summers ago," Henry said smoothly, "and it is a pleasure to be able to renew our acquaintance."

"You are staying?" Rosamund entreated. "At least for supper?"

Amice started to shake her head, but Henry forestalled her. "Yes, we're staying. Thank you, Lady Fitz Hugh, for your generous offer of hospitality." He was speaking to Amice, but smiling at Rosamund Clifford.

ROSAMUND OFFERED to nurse Giles, the injured squire, until a doctor arrived from Ludlow, and stirred up massive envy in the younger men each time she gently bathed his face with a wet cloth or rubbed salve into his gashed forehead. Amice excused herself to change into her best gown, but Rosamund didn't bother. Utterly unself-conscious in her faded everyday blue homespun, she seemed to have a remarkable lack of vanity for a young woman of such striking appearance. Neither flustered nor flattered by all the male attention she was receiving, she conscientiously tended to Giles until supper was served, but she so rarely took her eyes off Henry that even the most smitten of her swains, the Earl of Chester, could not help but notice. Some of the men began to joke amongst themselves that the king was about to make a conquest ere he even set foot in Wales, but the bawdy humor was curiously muted. If Rosamund's bedazzlement with Henry was innocently obvious, so too was she obviously innocent, and even men who normally took a predatory attitude toward women found themselves feeling unexpectedly protective of this one.

Supper that evening was a surprisingly festive affair for men who were soon to ride off to war. Jokes flew along the length of the table, and the hunt for the grey ghost was spun out for Rosamund's benefit—greatly embellished, of course. The last course of roasted capon had just been served when Osbern Fitz Hugh arrived, accompanied by the doctor and his father-in-law, the Marcher lord Walter Clifford, who had joined the king at Ludlow several days ago. Amice Fitz Hugh had so far been sparing with wine and ale, for her husband was notorious for his frugality, not an admired trait in a man of rank. But the brash, overbearing Clifford would have none of that and immediately sent servants to raid the buttery. Wine was soon flowing freely and the only men in the hall not enjoying themselves were Fitz Hugh, who had to watch helplessly as his wine kegs were drained one by one, and Ranulf, whose thoughts kept stubbornly dwelling upon the coming bloodshed.

A harp and a lute were produced, and the members of the hunting party took tipsy turns dancing with Amice, her two ladies, and Rosamund. When Henry's brother Hamelin tripped and nearly lurched into the fire while trying to show Rosamund a new version of the carol, Henry declared that one broken arm per hunt was more than enough and put a stop to the drunken dancing. Walter Clifford then announced that his youngest daughter would sing for the king. Rosamund's reluctance was painful to the more sober amongst them, but her father was not a man to be gainsaid, certainly not by the females of his household, and she was soon obediently perched on a stool, clutching a harp. While she'd shown herself to be a graceful dancer, she'd not been blessed with a strong singing voice. Her song was hesitantly delivered, barely audible at times, and occasionally off-key. Nonetheless, she reaped a round of enthusiastic applause when she was done and only Henry's merciful intervention saved her from the cries for more.

Sitting in a window seat, an untouched cup of wine in his hand, Ranulf watched the revelries and wondered how many of these men would be dead in a month's time. The cockiness of the English notwithstanding, he was convinced that this war would be a protracted, bloody one. And whoever won, he would be the loser.

"There you are, Ranulf." Henry sprawled beside him in the window seat, showing no ill effects from a day in the saddle, and not for the first time Ranulf marveled at his nephew's almost inexhaustible store of energy. Laughing, Henry gestured with his wine cup toward Rosamund. "I could become fond of that lass. She looks as if she's made of moonlight and gossamer, but she's not all sugar. There is salt there, too. When I complimented her on her singing, she blurted out that I must be stone-deaf!"

Ranulf gave him a sideways glance. "So," he said, "when is Eleanor's babe due?"

Henry grimaced and then grinned. "Subtle, Uncle, very subtle indeed. I need no such reminders, for Eleanor is the last woman in Christendom a man could ever forget. But all wives should be as wise as she is. She knows full well that a man with an itch is going to scratch it, as she once bluntly put it."

"I was not worrying about Eleanor. I was thinking of the girl. She is an innocent, Harry, and each time you smile at her, she glows like a flower that has been starved for the sun."

"You've been living in Wales too long, Ranulf. Damn me if you're not getting downright poetic—starved for the sun?"

Ranulf shrugged. "I've had my say. I just never thought you were one for hunting a nesting quail. Where's the sport in that?"

"Not all hunts are done for sport, Uncle." But even as he mocked Ranulf, Henry's gaze wandered back toward Rosamund. As their eyes met, she smiled, then blushed, and after a moment, he sighed regretfully. "Hellfire . . . you're right, I know. A lass's maidenhead ought not to be sacrificed for a night's pleasure—even if the pleasure was to be mine. I'd not want to jeopardize her chances of making a good marriage."

"What is this talk about marriage?" Rainald demanded, weaving toward them so unsteadily that they hastily made room for him in the window seat.

"I was just taking counsel with the king's conscience," Henry said, unable to resist a good-natured jab at his uncle, whose scruples were both admirable and occasionally inconvenient.

Ranulf smiled, too, with a heartfelt hope that his nephew would listen to *the king's conscience* during the war with Wales.

From ludlow, Henry continued on to Shrewsbury, where his army was assembling. He'd hired mercenaries from Flanders, summoned vassals from Normandy, Anjou, Poitou, and Aquitaine as well as England, and had even arranged for the services of a fleet with the Danes of Dublin. By the end of July, he was ready to take the offensive, and the largest English army ever to invade Wales crossed into Powys, heading for the town known as Oswestry by the Welsh and Blancminster by the English. Owain Gwynedd and the other Welsh princes awaited their coming at Corwen in the vale of Edeyrnion.

CHAPTER NINETEEN

✦

August 1165
Powys, Wales

THE SUN DID NOT LINGER, soon plunged behind the mountain range that protected the Welsh army from the righteous wrath of the English king. For that was how Henry's men were coming to view this campaign, as a crusade against the godless and the guilty. It had not begun as such. They'd marched out of Blancminster in good order, eager to bring these Welsh rebels to heel and return back across the border, for word had soon spread among them that Wales was a cheerless, barren land with no towns for the plundering, not even taverns or alehouses where a soldier could quench his thirst and find female company.

But nothing had gone as expected. The Welsh proved to be infuriatingly elusive, phantom foes who refused to take the field against them. The roads were so narrow that the men were constantly getting slapped in the face by overhanging branches or tripping over hidden roots. When it rained, they were slogging through mud, and when it was dry, they were choking on the dust kicked up by so many marching feet. The insects were relentless, tormenting horses and men alike. During the day, they sweated in sultry, humid heat, but at night, they shivered in their bedrolls, for the temperature dropped sharply once the sun set.

A soldier's lot was never an easy one and most of the men were inured to hardship. But this was like no war they'd ever fought. At first, they'd advanced unchallenged, passing through a ghost country bereft of life. The few houses they found were deserted, empty shells hardly worth torching, for the people had fled with their livestock and all the belongings they could carry off. They'd not be able to forage for food, to live off the land as soldiers so often had to do. Wales was like an oyster shell, closed tight against them.

But it all changed once they reached the forest known to the Welsh as Ceiriog, stretching before them like a towering, tangled wall. Most had never seen woods like this, so densely grown that not even the sun could penetrate that rustling, leafy canopy above their heads. The road became a deer trail, easier to lose than follow, and those men unfortunate enough to have an unease of enclosed spaces began to feel as if they were struggling through a dark, green tunnel, with no end in sight. It was in these eerie, alien woods that first blood was drawn—English blood.

The Welsh came in the night, with flaming torches and wild yells, and, as suddenly, they were gone, leaving in their wake burning wagons and mass confusion and crumpled bodies. There had been no repetition of that abrupt midnight raid, but men went to sleep with their weapons at the ready and awoke each time a horse snorted, a twig snapped underfoot. The daily pace speeded up noticeably after stragglers began to disappear. No one ever heard or saw anything, just a tired soldier trudging along in the rear, falling farther and farther behind. Yet when his companions glanced back, he was gone. Men got cricks in their necks from looking over their shoulders and headaches from squinting into the deep shadows on both sides of the road. Fights flared up over trifles and tempers soured. But the English army continued to press on into the Ceiriog Valley, toward the looming silhouettes of the Berwyn Mountains.

NONE OBJECTED when Kort moved to the front of the line, for he was a battle-scarred veteran who'd done more fighting—for pay—in his thirty-four years than most men would ever see in a lifetime. Moreover, he was a member of that elite, a crossbowman. So awesome was the crossbow's lethal power that the Church had sought to prohibit its use, proclaiming at the Fourth Lateran Council that it must be restricted to campaigns against infidels. But the weapon's deadly force was irresistible to even the most devout of Christian battle commanders, and crossbowmen were eagerly recruited.

The twenty men in Kort's unit were Flemings, and the wild, mountainous terrain of Wales was stirring in many of them a yearning for the low-lying, fertile plains of their homeland. They liked to see the enemy coming, they muttered; here even the sunsets were sudden, more like an ambush than a natural duskfall. Kort paid their grumbling no heed, for such campfire complaints were routine, a familiar soldier's lament. Many took a contrary pride in the privations they endured. And even the worst of the malcontents were not likely to desert now, for where could they go?

Once his share of the bean pottage had been ladled into his bowl, Kort sat cross-legged under a gnarled oak and ate hungrily, using his bread as a spoon. The soup was heavily salted and the bread gritty, but he'd eaten worse. He was washing his meal down with ale when Jan joined him, lolling in the grass with the boneless abandon of youth.

Jan was never too tired to talk and as the sky darkened and night came on, he chattered on cheerfully about a multitude of topics, flitting from one to another like a dragonfly. Did Kort think the Welsh would ever be brought to bay? A poor, pitiful country it was that had no taverns. Was it true the Welsh spurned good ale for a sickly-sweet drink called mead? Had Kort ever visited the alehouse on Wolle Straete? They had a serving-maid riper than summer plums . . . what was her name? Anna . . . no, Jutka! He'd wager no Welshwoman ever born could pleasure a man like Jutka could. Rolling over onto his back, he gave Kort a companionable poke in the ribs. "What am I doing in this God-cursed hellhole when I could be back home with Jutka on my lap and a brimming ale at my elbow?"

"For the money, of course," Kort said laconically and Jan grinned.

"Speaking of money, do you want to join in our dicing tonight? Be warned, though, for I am feeling lucky."

Kort snorted "The last time you felt 'lucky,' you lost a fortnight's wages, a good dagger, and your mantle. Try to walk away tonight whilst you still have the shirt on your back."

As usual, Jan took no offense; to men of more volatile temperament, his constant equanimity could be irksome. "If you do not want to play, at least come to watch. That way you can help me carry off my winnings."

As he sauntered away, another man took his place beside Kort under the huge oak. "That one prattles on like a drunken parrot," Klaas said dourly. "Why you befriended him, I cannot for the life of me understand."

"Ah, he is not such a bad sort," Kort insisted, "just in need of seasoning," and Klaas flung him a skeptical look, for he was not usually so tolerant of the foibles of the very young. Kort could have explained that he and Jan had drunk from the same well, both of them born and bred in the beautiful city of Brugge. They'd each fished in the Rijver Rei, skated upon the iced-over canals, frequented the same taverns and browsed in the Grote Markt and mourned their dead in the great church, Onze Lieve Vrouwkert. But Kort was not a man to whom explanations came naturally, and so he merely shrugged, then watched in bemusement as Klaas shared some of his pottage with a hungry dog who'd been tagging after the soldiers.

"Why waste food on that flea-bitten cur?" he asked curiously. "Better it should fill your belly than his."

"Hers," Klaas corrected, tossing the dog the last of his bread. "I've named her Gerda, after a whore I once knew in Ieper."

Kort did not comprehend the appeal of the scrawny brown beast curled up at Klaas's feet. But as long as it wasn't his ration of food the dog was eating, he was prepared to overlook his friend's eccentricity. "I'm trying to decide who should be more insulted by your choice of names, the whore or the dog."

"Well, they're both bitches." Klaas's heart wasn't in his bantering, though. Absently stroking the dog, he glanced sharply at Kort and then away. "I wish I'd never set foot in this accursed land . . ."

Kort's jest died on his lips. "Why?"

"Did you hear that nightjar crying out last night after we made camp? A sound to make the hairs stand up on the back of a man's neck. The Welsh call it Deryn Corff . . . the Corpse Bird."

"Since when did you let yourself be spooked by a bird, even one of ill omen? Did you forget the time you brought down that raven on the wing with one well-aimed stone?"

Klaas's fingers clenched in the dog's fur, not loosening until she began to whine. "I heard it in my dream, too," he muttered. "It was a bad dream, Kort. It foretold my death."

Kort instinctively made the sign of the cross even as he scoffed, "Bah—dreams like that are as common as lice. Your nerves are on the raw and why not? I'd wager half the men in camp have had death dreams in the past fortnight."

Kort continued on in that vein and eventually seemed to have convinced Klaas. He thought he'd convinced himself, too, but he was still awake hours later, staring up at a sky afire with stars and listening for the nightjar's shrill whistle. When he finally slept, it was deep and dreamless and he awoke with a start, momentarily disoriented. The blackness of the night was retreating before the milky greyness of coming dawn and the air was cool and damp. All around him men were stirring, yawning, cursing.

The object of their wrath was Klaas's little dog. Surrounded by shouting men, she was cowering between Klaas's legs, barking frantically. Scooping her up into his arms, Klaas swore to disembowel any man who laid a hand upon her, and since he was known to be very handy with a knife, that was no idle threat. Shoving forward into their midst, Kort demanded to know the cause of this brawl.

Klaas glared at his dog's tormentors. "I got up to take a piss. But as soon as I started off into those trees over there, Gerda began to bark and she kept it up. I think she heard some Welshmen on the prowl—"

He was hooted down by the other men. When someone rudely suggested that the dog had likely been scared by a rabbit, Kort had to step between them. "Whatever caused the dog to bark, it's done and we're all up now. There's not a dog alive worth shedding blood over, so let's rouse the cooks for an early breakfast."

Hunger won out over irritation, as Kort expected it would. Klaas fell in step beside him, still insisting that his dog had warned him of unseen danger. Only half-listening, Kort found himself gazing over at a blanket-clad form beside a smoldering campfire. Recognizing that shock of bright blond hair, so fair it was almost white, he said, "I know Jan is a heavy sleeper, but even so . . . Jan? Wake up, lad!"

Unable to explain his own urgency, even to himself, he strode forward. "Jan, you hear me—God in Heaven!"

Klaas was now close enough to see, too, and sucked in his breath. Jan's eyes were open, staring up sightlessly at them. There was no horror on his face, no contorted grimace, just a look of puzzlement There was blood on his blanket. Kneeling by Jan's body, Kort pulled the blanket back and exposed the death wound: a lethal thrust to the jugular vein. Kort's fists clenched. After a moment, he said in a scratchy, harsh voice, "There are faint bruises on his cheeks. A hand was clamped over his mouth to stifle any outcry as the dagger was driven home. The whoreson knew what he was about."

Flies were already buzzing about the body and if Jan were left unprotected, they'd soon be laying their eggs in his mouth and nose. In less than a day, his flesh would be crawling with maggots. It occurred to Kort that he'd seen too many corpses, buried too many friends.

Klaas leaned over to close Jan's eyes, for there was something unnerving, even accusing, about that blind, blue-white stare, only to recoil as soon as he touched the dead man's skin. "Jesú! He's still warm!"

"I know," Kort said grimly. There was no need to say more. Jan had died as the night waned, slain by a killer bold enough to venture alone into an enemy encampment, his presence observed only by a small stray dog.

H ENRY'S WRATH was volcanic. Seething and swearing, he paced the cramped confines of his command tent, raging at the murder of his men and the treachery of the Welsh and the appalling ineptitude of his guards. No one interrupted his harangue, knowing from experience that it was safer just to let his furies burn themselves out.

"A half dozen men dead, throats slit! And no one hears or sees a bloody thing? I've a mind to hang some of the sentries. I daresay that would encourage the rest of them to stay awake on duty!"

Rainald didn't really think his nephew would carry out that threat, but he deemed it prudent, nevertheless, to deflect his anger away from the sentries and back onto a more legitimate target. "The Welsh know these woods the way one of our soldiers knows his local alehouse. They can shadow us at their ease, knowing they're well nigh invisible in that God-awful tangle of trees and brush, awaiting their chance to strike. If you ask me, it is a craven way to fight a war, a coward's way."

"It is that," Henry said tersely. "There is no honor in stabbing a man whilst he sleeps."

The other men echoed their heartfelt agreement, all but Ranulf, who was conspicuously silent. Henry's eyes narrowed. "What say you, Uncle? Surely you have some thoughts about these loathsome killings?"

Ranulf knew he should keep quiet. But he'd been keeping quiet for far too long, a mute and unwilling accomplice to this English invasion of his homeland. "If my house was broken into, my only concern would be to protect my family and my home—any way I could."

"That is a peculiar comparison, by God," Henry said incredulously. "You would equate an outlaw's crime with a king's campaign to punish disloyal vassals?"

"The Welsh do not see themselves as disloyal vassals."

"Do they not? Well, they will soon learn different, that I can promise you. For all their delusions of grandeur, they are no more than malcontented rebels on the run, afraid to face us in the field."

"If you truly believe that, you're in for a rude awakening."

"Indeed?" Henry's tone was sardonic. "So you think, then, that they might yet find enough backbone to fight us fairly?"

Ranulf's mouth twisted. "If by that, you mean in the field, one army against another, no, they will not do that. Why should they? They are winning, after all."

"The Devil they are!" Henry strode forward to glare at his uncle, as the others marveled at Ranulf's audacity. "I have enough Welsh foes skulking about in the woods, need none in my own tent!"

"I thought this was why I was here—to tell you what the Welsh are thinking. Or am I only to say what you want to hear? Like it or not, my lord king, the Welsh do think they are winning this war, and why not? Those men we are burying this morn are not Welsh, and I'd wager that the next graves dug won't be for the Welsh, either."

Henry's breath hissed between his teeth. He made an abrupt gesture of dismissal, which Ranulf was more than willing to obey. Ducking under the tent flap, he began to walk through the camp. The sky was overcast, the air uncomfortably humid; within a few steps, his tunic was damp with sweat and his hauberk felt as heavy as lead. Off to his right, a small group of men were conducting a brief funeral for one of the night's victims, soldiers standing somberly around a shallow grave. The guttural murmurs of Flemish caught Ranulf's ear as he passed and he paused for a moment, feeling a prickle of pity for any man who'd died so far from his own homeland. At least if he was struck down in this accursed war, he'd be dying on Welsh soil.

He had not expected his emotions to be so raw, his anger so close to the surface. He had thought that he could handle the pull of conflicting loyalties, as he had in the past. But this time it was different. He was betraying the Welsh by fighting with the English, betraying the English by hoping the Welsh would win, and betraying himself with each stifled breath he drew. And the end was not yet in sight.

RANULF WAS SEATED upon a fallen log, gazing out upon the forest fastness of Ceiriog, when Henry finally found him. "I've been scouring the entire damned camp for you, Uncle, began to think you'd ridden off on your own."

"I thought about it," Ranulf said tonelessly, and Henry grimaced, then sat down beside him upon the log.

"I know you do not want to be here," he said after a long silence. "If truth be told, neither do I, Ranulf. I've never hungered for Welsh conquest; what man in his senses would? Look around you," he said, gesturing toward the encroaching wall of trees and brambles. "This whole wretched country is a fortress. And we have not even gotten into the mountains yet. This campaign has not gone at all as I planned—and I do not always take it with good grace when my plans go awry."

"Do tell," Ranulf murmured, but there was a softening beneath the sarcasm, for that was as close to an apology as Henry could get and they both knew it. "So now what, Harry? Do I lie the next time you ask me how I think your war is going?"

"You know better. There are precious few people I can trust to tell me the truth, but you are one of them."

"The truth, then. I think you will be making a great mistake to continue on with this campaign. The Welsh will keep on harassing us with their contrary tactics, bleeding away your army's strength with quick raids and retreats, fading back into the woods ere you can retaliate. War by attrition, the wearing down of the enemy. In your words, it may indeed not be honorable. But it works, Harry. It works."

"I know," Henry admitted. "But I am not about to give up, Ranulf. I cannot do that, for a king who lets one rebellion go unpunished will soon see others springing up all over his domains. Think of weeds in a garden, if you will. Stop pulling them up and the garden is lost."

"What will you do, then? Just press ahead by day, keep losing men by night?"

"No," Henry said, "that would be a fool's play. The rules of this game are too heavily slanted in Owain Gwynedd's favor. So—I mean to change the rules."

F ROM THEIR VANTAGE POINT upon the heights of the Berwyn Mountains, they looked out upon the vast, green expanse of the Ceiriog Valley. They had come to see for themselves if their scouts' reports were accurate, and they stared down in silence now at the devastation being wrought below them. The woods echoed with the sounds of axes and hatchets, the cursing of men, the snorting of horses as they struggled to uproot saplings and lightning-scarred hollow trunks. Henry's bowmen fanned out in defense of the axe wielders, yelling hoarse warnings when trees began to topple. It was a slow, laborious process, but the English army was cutting a swath through the thick underbrush on each side of the road, hacking away at the trees, brambles, and scrub providing cover for Welsh bowmen or Welsh ambushers. The Ceiriog Valley would be scarred for years to come by the passage of the English army.

Hywel was not easily shocked, but this purposeful and far-reaching destruction did shock him, both by the scope of the damage done and by the arrogance of the English king. A man who thought he could impose his will even upon nature was as dangerous as he was mad. He saw his foreboding reflected upon the faces of the other Welsh princes; even his half-brother Davydd seemed daunted by what they were watching, an attack upon the very land of Wales itself.

Rhys ap Gruffydd swore, then leaned over and spat. "There is nothing worse than an enemy with imagination."

"I wonder that he did not just order the woods to part, like Moses at the Red Sea," Hywel said bleakly. To his surprise, his bitter jest seemed to amuse his father, for Owain's mouth was curving in a slight smile. Hywel's own humor rarely failed him, but to save his soul, he could not wring a single drop of amusement from their present plight. How could they hope to defeat in the field an army so much larger than theirs? "It looks as if we shall have to revise our battle plans. We were so sure they'd not get across the Berwyns, so sure . . ."

"I still am," Owain said, and they all turned in their saddles to stare at him.

"Why?" Blunt as ever, Rhys was regarding his uncle with an odd mixture of dubious hope. "Why should a mountain range halt a man willing to chop down an entire forest?"

"Have you so forgotten your Scriptures, Rhys? I suggest you think upon Proverbs."

That was less than illuminating to Rhys and Davydd. Much to Davydd's vexation, it was his brother, with a poet's love of the written word, who solved the puzzle. "'Pride goeth before destruction,'" Hywel quoted, "'and a haughty spirit before a fall.'"

"Exactly," Owain said, so approvingly that Davydd's jealousy rose in his throat like bile. "What could be more prideful than this? Only Our Lord God is omnipotent, not the King of England. That is a lesson this

Henry Fitz Empress needs to learn, and I do believe it is one he will be taught, for such prideful presumption is surely displeasing to the Almighty."

The others did not doubt that the English king was not in God's Favor, for soon after crossing into Wales, his soldiers had plundered and burned several churches. But they did not have Owain's apparent faith in divine retribution, not with the English army soon to be within striking distance of the Welsh heartland. Owain saw their skepticism and laughed softly.

"Oh, ye of little faith," he said mockingly. "You want proof of the Almighty's Intent, do you?" Wetting his forefinger, he held it up. "The wind has shifted—from the northwest to the northeast. Need I tell you what that means?"

He did not, for these were men who, of necessity, had long ago learned to read the skies and cloud patterns as a monk might study the Holy Word. That wind change signaled a coming storm.

For days, the sky had been heavy with clouds, the air muggy and uncomfortably close. Passing birds were flying much lower to the ground than usual. The last visible sunset had turned the sky a dull red. There were Englishmen as adept as the Welsh in interpreting nature's portents, and so Henry's army had fair warning that unsettled weather was on the way.

They were not men to be disheartened by a few summer showers, though. Rain was an occupational hazard of the soldier, particularly in a land as wet as Wales. As long as they no longer had to shy at shadows and fear that there was a Welsh bowman lurking behind every tree, they were willing to slog through a little mud. That seemed a fair trade for being able to sleep again at night. Morale had soared with each felled tree, each trampled bush. It was slow going, but what of it? Once they got to the Berwyns, they'd make better time, for its slopes were not as deeply wooded as the valley. Their Welsh guides would lead them across the barren heaths and bogs and over the mountain pass toward a reckoning with the Welsh army at Corwen. After that, they could go home, for few doubted that they would prevail once the two forces met on the battlefield.

There was still an hour or so of daylight remaining when the English at last reached the foothills of the Berwyn range. But the wind had picked up and the clouds to the west looked like billowing black anvils. Henry was pleased with the progress they'd made and decided to reward the men by making camp instead of pushing on till dusk. They hastily set up their tents, laid out their bedrolls, and braced themselves to ride out the breaking storm.

Soon after dark, the rains began. It was immediately apparent that this was no mere summer soaker. The winds were shrieking through the camp, collapsing tents and terrifying the horses. Men who left their shelter were drenched within moments, half drowned in the downpour. Just before midnight, hail mixed with the rain, ice pellets the size of coins pelting the ground and stinging every inch of exposed skin on the unfortunate sentries. Sleep was the first casualty of the storm and, for all, it was a wakeful, nerve-racking night.

Although his command tent had withstood the tempest, Henry had gotten no more rest than his soldiers, listening to the howling of the wind and the occasional shouts when another tent was blown down. Daylight brought no respite from the gale. If anything, it seemed to intensify, and Henry had no choice but to order them to remain in camp until the storm passed. The day was torture for so impatient a soul as Henry's. He might be drier than most of his men, but he was no less miserable, trapped in his tent as the hours dragged by and his frustration festered. The night was easier, for he finally fell into an exhausted sleep. But upon awakening, he discovered that the wind still raged and the rain continued to fall in torrents.

When Henry announced that they would break camp and head out, his audience looked at him as if he'd lost his senses. Watching as his men struggled to take down their tents and load the wagons and packhorses, he soon realized they were right. The meadow had become a quagmire and men slipped and lurched and sank to their knees in the muck. The wind hindered them as much as the mud, tearing at the tent stakes and blowing over one of the supply wagons. As sacks of flour split open and a keg rolled down the hillside, spewing out a spray of ale in its wake, Henry hastily countermanded himself, and his sodden, shivering soldiers gratefully pitched their tents again, seeking what small comfort they could find under wet blankets and dripping mantles.

For the rest of his days, Henry was to refer to the squall upon the Berwyns with the very worst of the obscenities he had at his considerable command. Never had he encountered a storm so savage, or so long-lasting. Ironically, the English would have fared better had they still been down in the Ceiriog Forest they'd been so eager to leave behind. Here upon the unsheltered moors, they were at the mercy of the elements. Fires could not be set as kindling was saturated, the ground soaked. The only food available was what could be eaten uncooked or raw, and men were soon sickening, stricken by chills, fever, and the feared bloody flux. Henry was far less superstitious than most of his contemporaries, with a skeptical streak that few besides Eleanor either understood or appreciated. But even he began to wonder if such foul weather could be dismissed as mere happenchance.

When the rain finally eased up two days later, the English army resumed its march, only to discover that the mountain road was washed away in places, the streams swollen with runoff water, and the moorlands pitted with newly formed bogs. Still, they pressed on, driven by the sheer force of Henry's implacable will. By now some of the ailing men had begun to die. They were buried with indecent haste, left to molder in an alien, hostile land, and the army straggled on. They had a new concern now—their dwindling supplies, for some of their provisions had been lost or ruined during the storm. But when they sent out a hunting party to search for game, it did not come back. Hungry and dispirited, the soldiers trudged on, cursing the Welsh aloud and Henry under their breaths.

They were higher up now and the air held a surprising chill for August. Henry had dismounted and was wrapping a blindfold around his stallion's eyes, for there was a narrow stretch of road ahead and English horses were not as accustomed to these heights as the surefooted animals the Welsh rode. The wind was still pursuing them, shrieking at night like the souls of the damned, chasing away sleep and catching their words in midsentence, so that men had to shout to make themselves heard. Now a sudden gust ripped the blindfold from Henry's hand and sent it flying. He was turning to get another strip of cloth when the screams began.

One of the Flemish sergeants lay bleeding in the road, struck by a large rock that had come plummeting from the heights above them. Before anyone could reach the injured man, other rocks began to roll down the slope, and then there was a roaring sound and part of the cliff crumbled away, a wave of mud and turf and boulders engulfing the dazed soldier and those who'd hastened to his aid. Henry clung to his plunging stallion's reins, somehow kept the petrified animal from bolting. Hitching it to the closest wagon, he ran forward. But there was nothing to be done. Their broken bodies swept along like debris in a floodtide, the men caught in the avalanche were gone.

As soon as they could find a suitable place to pitch camp, Henry ordered it done even though it was not yet dusk. He'd seen the stunned faces of his men, staring down mutely at the torn-up, flattened grass that marked the mudslide's track, and he ordered, as well, an extra ration of ale with supper. But that night he was awakened by the sound he most dreaded to hear: the drumbeat of rain upon the canvas roof of his tent.

ALL EYES were upon Henry. But no one spoke. It had already been said, the arguments made for retreat. The wretched weather. The danger of another mudslide. Men with empty bellies and loose bowels and a weakened will to fight. The specter of hunger stalking them as relentlessly as the shadowy, unseen wolves who'd learned that armies were worth trailing. Henry knew that the arguments were right, rooted in common sense and a realistic assessment of their worsening plight. But still the words stuck in his throat as he turned and finally said, "So be it. Make ready to withdraw at first light."

Every man in the tent was relieved by that grudging command, none more so than Ranulf. He sagged down on one of Henry's coffers, drawing his first easy breath in weeks. But then Henry said grimly, "We will go back to Chester and await the arrival of the fleet I hired from the Danes in Dublin. This war is not over yet."

THE ENGLISH RETREAT was disorderly and hurried, as retreats usually are. Harassed by the Welsh, Henry's army retraced its route through the Ceiriog Forest and headed back toward the border. There was some skirmishing between the more zealous of the Welsh pursuers and the English rearguard, but eventually Henry's men reached safety in Shropshire. After halting in Shrewsbury to treat the wounded and ailing, Henry collected the hostages surrendered to the Crown eight years earlier by the Welsh princes, and continued north to Chester. There he encamped his army on the Wirral Peninsula northeast of the city and settled in at Shotwick Castle to plan the next stage of his Welsh war.

HENRY'S CHAMBER in Shotwick Castle's great square keep had been transformed into a council of war. The trestle table was littered with maps of Wales—none of them very accurate, for mapmaking was not an advanced science. As the men crowded around the table, Henry gestured with a quill pen, splattering ink upon the parchment as he pointed out the proposed route his army would follow upon their return—along the coast road toward Owain Gwynedd's manor at Aber—while his fleet ravaged the fertile lands of the island called Môn by the Welsh and Anglesey by the English.

Glancing up as the door banged open, Henry flashed a smile at the sight of Ranulf. "Ah, there you are, Uncle. Come take a look at this new map—"

"Tell me it is not true, Harry! You cannot mean to take your vengeance upon the Welsh hostages?"

"Of course not," Henry said indignantly and the hurtful, heavy pressure squeezing Ranulf's ribcage began to ease.

"Thank God!"

"You, of all men, ought to know me better than that, Ranulf. That would be an unworthy act, both cruel and mean-spirited. The hostages are not scapegoats, but pledges of Welsh loyalty. It is as pledges that they must be punished, and for no other reason—"

Ranulf's mouth was suddenly so dry he could not even spit. "You cannot kill them, Harry!"

"I do not want to kill them, Uncle. They must pay the price for the treachery of Owain Gwynedd, Rhys ap Gruffydd, and the others, but I will forbear to make this a blood debt. That is why I have given the command that they are only to be blinded and maimed, not delivered to the gallows."

"'Only blinded and maimed . . .'" Ranulf's voice thickened. "Jesú, do you hear yourself? Two of the hostages are Owain Gwynedd's sons, another is Rhys ap Gruffydd's. What if you'd turned one of your sons over to the Welsh? Could you talk so calmly of a mere maiming if it were your own facing the knife?"

"If I'd given up my son as a hostage, I would have kept faith with his captors! If you must lay blame about, lay it then at Owain Gwynedd's feet! If he cared for his sons, why did he put their lives at risk?"

"What choice did he have? He loves Wales as he loves his sons!"

The other men had been listening, openmouthed, to this quarrel so unexpectedly sprung up in their midst. Their faces were as familiar to Ranulf as his own—his brother Rainald; his nephew Hamelin and cousin Hugh, the young Earl of Chester; the Earls of Leicester and Arundel—but he could find in none of them echoes of his outrage. They were staring at him without comprehension, unable to understand either his rage or his sickened sense of betrayal. Pushing his chair back, Rainald said, in the soothing tones one might use to placate a drunkard or madman:

"Ranulf, the whole point of taking hostages is that they must be sacrificed if faith is breached. Otherwise, the system makes no sense. Surely you see that? By sparing the lives of these Welsh hostages, Harry is showing considerable magnanimity and mercy, more than the Welsh deserve after such treachery—"

"There is no mercy in gouging out a prisoner's eyes or taking a knife to his manhood! It is barbaric," Ranulf charged, and blood surged up into Henry's face.

"I have been more than patient with you, Uncle. Again and again, I have made allowances for your wavering loyalties. But no more. You have sworn an oath to the English Crown—to me, your father's grandson and your lawful king. It is time you remember it!"

"Owain Gwynedd is my king, too!"

There were loud gasps at such heresy. "And a right fine king he is," Henry said scathingly. "You think I do not know about Owain Gwynedd's bloody vengeance against his own kin? He had his nephew blinded and gelded, by Christ! Where is the honor or mercy in that?"

"I care naught for Owain Gwynedd's sins. They are between him and God. I do care about your sins, Harry. For the love I bear you, do not put your soul at risk like this. Would you truly sacrifice your chance of salvation just to avenge a battlefield loss?"

"I am not after vengeance! I am doing what must be done, and it matters little if I like it not. Not only do you know nothing about the duties of kingship, you plainly know nothing about me!"

"Stephen would never have committed this cruelty!"

That was the one insult Henry could not forgive. "You dare to hold Stephen up as an example—the usurper who stole my mother's crown? Need I remind you that Stephen once hanged the entire garrison of Shrewsbury Castle, more than ninety men? Is that what you would have me do with these Welsh hostages? You tell me, Ranulf—is it to be the punishment I ordered or the gallows?"

Ranulf looked at his nephew, saying nothing. And then he turned abruptly on his heel, strode out of the chamber.

Henry stared at that closing door before swinging around to face the other men. "I have no choice in this. If I let their rebellion go unpunished, the Welsh would take my mercy for weakness. You do all see that?"

They hastened to affirm their agreement, with convincing sincerity. Somehow, though, their approval did not give Henry the balm he needed. "Why," he said, "does Ranulf not see that, too?"

Henry slept poorly that night. His anger at what he considered an unjust accusation continued to smolder. He was not introspective by nature. Rarely did he attempt to probe beneath the surface for hidden emotions, covert motivations. But he was troubled by Ranulf's challenge, that he was taking out his frustration and anger upon the Welsh hostages. Lying awake during those solitary hours before dawn, he sought to convince himself that he was not lashing out in vindictive, retaliatory rage. Not to punish the Welsh hostages would be to subvert the entire process. If men could offer up hostages with impunity, sure they'd never be harmed, what inducement had they to keep faith? Hostages were only demanded from untrustworthy allies or disaffected vassals, when honor alone was not enough to guarantee a man's loyalty. The Welsh princes had failed to live up to their part of the bargain. It was up to him now to exact a penalty for that breach. In mutilating and blinding the hostages, he would be teaching the Welsh that there were always consequences in this life, even for the highborn. Such a lesson might well deter future rebellions.

Yet his sense of disquiet lingered. As far back as he could remember, his mother's brother had been there for him—fighting in the bloody civil war to oust Stephen, offering wry advice and affection that was more paternal than avuncular. Henry's own father had died when he was eighteen, and although Ranulf and Geoffrey could not have been more different, his bond with Ranulf had helped to ease his feelings of loss. This sudden threatened rupture in their relationship disturbed him more than he wanted to admit.

He'd hoped to get word that day about the projected arrival of his fleet. It did not come. Surely they must have sailed from Dublin by now? It was September already, and as much as he wanted to quell this Welsh rising here and now, he was not so sorely crazed as to attempt a winter campaign. Welsh weather was vile enough under the best of circumstances.

After dispatching a courier with a letter to Eleanor at Angers, where she awaited the birth of another child, he found an excuse to confer with his other uncle, Rainald of Cornwall. Rainald was not usually his choice of confidants. Despite the fondness between them, Henry had never shared any secrets of his soul with Rainald, not as he had with Ranulf and Thomas Becket. Rainald was a companion for good times, a practical jokester whose bluff heartiness hid sorrows that few suspected: a mad wife, a sickly heir, and a dearly loved bastard son who would never inherit his earldom. But Rainald was the one most likely to know the state of Ranulf's mind on this morning after their quarrel.

Henry wasted no time in coming to the point. "Have you talked with Ranulf yet?"

Rainald shook his head. "I thought it best to give his temper time to cool. Now your mother and my sister, God love her, can hold a grudge until her last mortal breath, but that is not Ranulf's way. He's always been quick to flare up, no less quick to forgive. That is not to say he is not still hurting, Harry. He has a soft spot where the Welsh are concerned, for certes, but in fairness, how can we fault him for it? Not only did he have a Welsh mother, but he positively dotes upon that blind Welsh wife of his."

"I've always liked Rhiannon," Henry said, and Rainald looked at him in surprise.

"Well, I like the lass, too, Harry. But that does not change the fact that she is bat blind, now does it? What I'm trying to say is that a man with a blind wife is going to feel more pity than most for hostages about to lose their sight."

"I had not thought of that aspect of it," Henry conceded. "That does explain why he took it so personally." After a pensive silence, he gave his uncle an inquiring look. "You think I ought to talk to him?"

Rainald, who could occasionally be more subtle than others realized, concealed a smile. "I think that is a good idea," he said solemnly. "Shall I fetch him for you?"

"Yes," Henry said and, as usual, once he made up his mind, he wanted to act upon it straightaway. "Go get him, Uncle."

But Rainald was gone a surprisingly long time and when he eventually returned to Henry's chamber, his demeanor was so subdued that Henry immediately knew something was amiss. "Well? Where is he?"

Rainald hesitated. "I searched the camp over, Harry," he said at last. "But he is gone."

"Gone where?" Henry said tautly, even though he already knew the answer.

"He rode out last night after your quarrel. By now I fear he is well on his way into Wales."

CHAPTER TWENTY

September 1165
Gwynedd, Wales

*T*HE ROAD HOME was long and hard and Ranulf rode
it alone. He owed the Crown the service of four knights for
his English manors, but Henry had not claimed it of him in the
Welsh war. Spared the need to provide fighting men, he'd taken along
only two English-born squires, and he dispatched them to his closest
Cheshire manor before heading west into Wales.

A state of war still existed and so he thought it prudent to avoid the
main roads, where he'd be most likely to encounter Owain Gwynedd's
scouts and patrols. After fifteen years in Wales, he knew of the alternate
routes, the deer tracks and woodland trails and local byways. His round-
about, circuitous journey was prolonged by the continuing wet weather.
While the rains were nothing like the torrential deluge that had assailed
the English in the Berwyns, they were still substantial enough to make
travel both arduous and unpleasant. By the third day in the saddle, Ranulf
had developed a low fever and a troublesome cough.

His physical discomfort on the road was a minor matter, though, when compared to the emotional abyss awaiting him at journey's end. How could he tell Rhiannon that they must leave the only home she'd ever known, start life anew in an alien land? What of Gilbert? He was nigh on fourteen, the age of majority in Wales. Would he agree to come with them? Their entire family would be torn asunder and it was his doing. His uncle would face the eventual loss of his lands. Rhodri's sons were dead and without near male kin to inherit, his manor would go upon his death by default to his Welsh king. Eleri and Rhiannon would be separated by distance and ill will, as would their children. Mallt and Morgan would grow up never knowing their own kin, their own customs, in time even their own tongue. *Hiraeth*—the Welsh longing for one's homeland— would shadow their days in English exile.

He could not even be sure that English exile would be open to him. What if his nephew chose to declare his English manors forfeit? It was difficult for him to imagine Harry being that vindictive, that petty. But then it would have been difficult a fortnight ago to imagine that Harry would ever have given the order to maim the Welsh hostages.

When he at last reached the Conwy valley, the rain had dwindled to a light mist, its cooling touch welcome on his hot skin. He halted by the river so his stallion could drink, but he was putting off the inevitable and he knew it. Tugging on the reins, he headed for Trefriw.

His arrival was heralded by barking and, as soon as he dismounted, he was surrounded by dogs, their tails whipping about like waterwheel paddles as they welcomed him home. He was fending off his ecstatic dyrehund when his daughter came flying from the hall. With a joyful squeal, she flung herself upon him, telling him how happy she was that he had not been killed by the English.

Ranulf supposed that was something to be thankful for, and decided it definitely was a few moments later when Rhiannon appeared in the doorway of the hall. He reached her in several quick strides and found fleeting comfort in her arms. She clung so tightly that he knew she, too, dreaded what was to come.

When his uncle came limping out into the bailey, Ranulf reluctantly ended the embrace and turned to face Rhodri. His leave-taking had been angry, with Rhodri crying after him in frustrated fury that he was one of God's greatest fools. He was expecting his return to be no less resentful. But his uncle was beaming, and a bewildered Ranulf was soon enveloped in a hearty, welcoming hug.

"I knew you'd come back safe," Rhodri enthused, "I knew it."

"I wish you'd shared that certainty with me," Rhiannon murmured. "Ranulf, you feel feverish. Are you ailing?"

"I'll live," he said and slipped his arm through hers. "Let's go into the hall. There is something I must tell you all."

RANULF'S ACCOUNT of the maiming of the Welsh hostages seemed to echo in the stillness that had engulfed the hall. Rhodri's outraged oaths had soon spluttered out. Mumbling that he felt greensick of a sudden, he stumbled toward the door and Enid hurried after him. Rhiannon had listened in silence, one hand softly stroking Mallt's brown braids. Her face was shuttered and drawn; Ranulf found it difficult to guess her thoughts. When it seemed clear that he had nothing more to say, she started to rise. "You must be hungry."

"No," he said, "I could not choke down a morsel to save my soul. Rhiannon, wait. There is more. On the morrow I must ride to find Owain Gwynedd, tell him what has befallen his sons and the other hostages—"

"No! Let someone else be the bearer of that news. Not you, Ranulf, not you!"

"I must," he said, and although he spoke softly, that tone was all too familiar to her. Once he made up his mind, it was almost impossible to turn him in another direction. She did not even have a chance to try, though, for at that moment the door to the hall banged open and their son lurched across the threshold.

As clumsy in his growth spurt as a long-legged colt, Gilbert was usually self-conscious about his ungainliness, for he had always been easily embarrassed. But now he didn't even seem to notice his stumble. His face lit up, dark eyes shining. "I just heard that you'd come home!"

It had been a long time since Ranulf had heard such unguarded pleasure in his son's voice. "Yes," he said, "I am home." His last encounter with Gilbert had been even more turbulent than the one with Rhodri, and he had been braced for hostility, accusations, anything but this awkward offer of an olive branch. Getting to his feet, he started toward his son, expecting at any moment that Gilbert would back away. But the boy stood his ground, ducking his head with a shy smile as his father put an arm around his shoulders. To Ranulf, his son's sudden thawing was more than he could have hoped for, and he accepted the transformation for what it seemed to be—as close as he would ever come to a miracle in this life.

IN THE COURSE of the evening, Ranulf's cough worsened and the next morning, Rhiannon insisted that he remain in bed. When he agreed, her anxiety flared anew, for she needed no greater proof that he was indeed ailing, and she hovered by his bedside for most of the day, bringing him honey for his cough, freshly baked bread and venison soup to tempt his indifferent appetite, and the rambunctious eighteen-month-old Morgan to raise his spirits. Ranulf ate what she brought him, played games in bed with his youngest son, and took a doomed man's pleasure in the respite, knowing that his time in Wales was running out.

Just before dusk, Eleri and her children arrived in response to Rhodri's summons. When they were ushered into Ranulf's bedchamber, his sister-in-law greeted him with an elated smile and fond kisses so poorly aimed that his face was soon smeared with her lip rouge. Ranulf began to feel as if he were at a celebration where he was the only sober guest. What was going on?

What happened next was even more baffling. Their nearest neighbors, Sulien and his wife, Marared, arrived soon after Eleri, for in Wales news spread faster than summer wildfire. The last time Ranulf had run into Sulien, the older man had called him a misbegotten English Judas and spat onto the ground at his feet. Yet now that same man was approaching the bed with a jovial smile, so apparently pleased to see the Judas again that Ranulf half-expected him to announce that a fatted calf had been killed in his honor. But when he made mention of their altercation, Sulien dismissed it as a "lamentable misunderstanding," adding a wink and a nudge as if they were allies in the same conspiracy.

That night Ranulf waited until his wife joined him in bed. "Rhiannon, when I rode off to fight with the English, I was reviled and denounced by all but you. Why has that changed? Why are Eleri and Rhodri and Gilbert suddenly so forgiving? Jesú, even Sulien and Marared! This makes no sense to me."

He was not reassured by her reply. Rhiannon, usually so forthright, gave him an answer that was as evasive as it was uncomfortable. She knew more than she was telling. He did not press further, though, not yet, for there was another confession to be made. She had to be prepared for the worst. And so he told her, as gently as he could, that the least he could expect from Owain Gwynedd was banishment.

She was silent for a time. "Do you know my favorite verse of Scriptures? I learned it by heart as a girl and remember it well, even now. 'Whither thou goest, I will go; and where thou lodgest, I will lodge; thy people shall be my people, and thy God my God.'"

There was only one possible response to that. Ranulf drew her close, holding her in his arms until they both slept.

To RHIANNON'S DISMAY, Ranulf arose the next morning determined to ride out to find Owain Gwynedd. They argued as he dressed, during breakfast in the hall, and in the stables as he began to saddle his stallion. Having failed with logic and anger, Rhiannon was not too proud to resort to entreaty, not if it would keep Ranulf at Trefriw. "At least wait until you are stronger," she implored, entwining slim, stubborn fingers in the sleeve of his tunic. "What harm can a few more days do?"

"I am already on the mend," Ranulf insisted. But he undercut his own argument when he could not suppress a coughing fit, so prolonged that he sank down upon a wooden bench as he struggled to catch his breath.

"Compared to what—a man newly lain in his grave?" This sardonic query startled them both. Rhiannon swung toward the sound of that familiar voice and Ranulf's head came up sharply, his eyes blinking as he sought to focus upon the man standing in the open doorway, haloed in sunlight.

"Hywel?" Incredulously. "What are you doing here?"

Hywel stepped from the light into the shadowed gloom of the stable. "What I do best," he said, "which is saving you from yourself. What is this nonsense about riding off when you're as weak as a mewling kitten?"

"I have to find your father . . ." Ranulf was on his feet now, trying to disguise the effort it had cost.

Hywel shrugged. "Do what you must, then. But it is only fair to warn you that I'll be amongst the first to be courting your lovely widow."

Ranulf started to speak, began to cough instead. When the spasm passed, he conceded defeat. "Hywel . . . we need to talk."

"Yes, we do," Hywel agreed. "But not here."

As they headed for the door, Rhiannon stood without moving, listening to their muffled footsteps in the straw. Hywel's coming was a blessing, putting off Ranulf's reckoning with Owain Gwynedd, at least for a while longer. But his arrival also brought risk, for he was the source of the secret she'd been keeping from her husband. She waited a moment longer, drawing several deep bracing breaths, and then followed the men from the stable.

✛

R HIANNON STIRRED honey and wine in a cup, then handed it to Ranulf. Sitting on the edge of the bed, he let some of the syrupy liquid trickle down his throat, but he had yet to take his eyes from Hywel. "How is it that you're here? Why are you not still with Lord Owain at Corwen?"

"My father has returned to Aber, waiting to see what the English king does next. I am here because I know you, Ranulf, down to your very bones. Sure as hellfire and brimstone, you'd be on the road to Aber within a day of your homecoming. I thought it best to head you off."

Ranulf considered that response, which was uncommonly straightforward for Hywel, who was a master of misdirection and equivocation. "How did you know I'd returned to Trefriw? Did you have it under watch?"

"I did."

"You are a good friend, better than I deserve. Hywel . . . I have something to tell you. There is no easy way to say it. A great evil has befallen your brothers Cadwallon and Cynwrig. They and the other Welsh hostages—I do not know how many—were blinded and unmanned at Chester, upon the orders of my nephew."

Hywel thought it was very like Ranulf to stress his blood bond to Henry, assuming his share of the blame. "Twenty-two," he said softly, and repeated it when he saw that Ranulf did not understand. "Twenty-two hostages were maimed at the English king's pleasure."

"You . . . you already know?"

"My father has eyes and ears wherever there is a need for them, and that includes Chester."

"Christ, Hywel, I am sorry," Ranulf said hoarsely and Hywel twitched a shoulder.

"My father has sired so many sons that some of them are almost strangers to me. Cadwallon and Cynwrig were too young to be boon companions as I came to manhood, so I never knew them all that well. But I'd not wish such a fate upon a convicted felon, much less blood kin."

"Your father . . ." Ranulf could not find the words to ask how a man coped with the mutilation of his sons, and his voice died away.

"About as you'd expect. My father never lets anyone see him bleed, even me."

"One of Rhys ap Gruffydd's sons was amongst the twenty-two. Does he know that?"

Hywel's mouth turned down. "He knows."

Ranulf forced himself to drink more of Rhiannon's honeyed concoction; his throat was so raw that it was like swallowing sawdust and
ashes. "Your father tried to warn me that a man could not ride two horses
at once. Fool that I was, I would not listen."

"Well, you gave it as good a ride as you could," Hywel said, with a
faint smile. "Nigh on eight years ere you finally lost your balance. I doubt
if there is another horseman in Christendom who could have done as well."

"Oh, I did right well," Ranulf said, with a bitter edge that was aimed
not at Hywel but at himself. "I alienated my family, friends, neighbors,
broke faith with Lord Owain, and made it impossible for my wife and
children to live in their own land."

"And on the seventh day, you rested."

Ranulf was taken aback. "You mock me, Hywel? I can find no humor
in the wreckage I have made of our lives!"

"What wreckage? As usual, you see only the brightest white, the
darkest black, and none of the colors in-between. I am simply saying you
ought not to be overhasty in packing up and racing for the border. It is not
as if you have a band of angry neighbors baying at your heels, now is it?"

"No," Ranulf said slowly, "it is not. And that is passing strange, for the
Welsh have many virtues, but they are not a forgiving people. I would
not have blamed my uncle if he'd turned me away from his door. Instead,
he welcomed me back with open arms. So did my son and my sister-by-
marriage and even our neighbors. It occurs to me, Hywel, that you might
know why."

Hywel feigned innocence and, as always, did it quite well. But Ranulf had caught a telltale flicker, enough to confirm his suspicions. "Hywel,
what have you done? I have a right to know."

Hywel regarded him pensively. "Yes, I suppose you do," he said, "but
you'll not like it much. I put the word out that you've been our man at the
English court, spying all along on my father's behalf."

Ranulf's jaw dropped. "Tell me you're joking!"

"No, I am not. I knew that the life you'd had in Wales was over, that
not even my father's goodwill would be a strong enough shield. I understand that mulish pride of yours, knew it would compel you to obey
Henry's summons. But few others would understand. You'd be shunned,
treated as if you were an outcast, a leper—if you were lucky. More likely
you'd have been burned out by your outraged neighbors. You needed an
excuse for your inexplicable loyalty to the English king, and so I provided
you with one."

"By making me into an accursed spy, a man without honor or loyalties? Christ Jesus, Hywel, how could you do that?"

Hywel was expecting just such a reaction and shrugged. Rhiannon's response was less forbearing. "I've heard enough of honor to last me a lifetime! Where is the honor in exile, Ranulf?"

Ranulf turned to stare at her. "You knew what Hywel had done? You approved?"

"Yes, I knew, and indeed I approved! More than approved, I was grateful beyond words. My only regret was that you'd have to be told, for I knew you'd never understand. You are a good and decent man, Ranulf, but in some ways, you are as blind as I am."

Ranulf was stunned by her outburst. Their quarrels were so infrequent and so mild that he'd been lulled into believing Rhiannon was incapable of genuine rage. After the turbulence and turmoil he'd endured with the high-strung, unpredictable Annora, he'd come to cherish the tranquillity he'd found in marriage to Rhiannon. He saw now that theirs was a false peace, purchased at the cost of her conscience. Again and again she had given him her unwavering support, her understanding, her acceptance—as Annora never had. She had suppressed her own fears and misgivings, always putting his needs first, even when the price of protecting his honor might well be banishment from the homeland she so loved.

Getting swiftly to his feet, he crossed the chamber to his wife, then took her in his arms. "I am sorry, love," he whispered, "so sorry. You are in the right and I am an idiot."

Rhiannon shook her head vehemently. "No, you are not. If our sons grow to manhood with even half of your courage and integrity, they will be very fortunate and I will be well content."

Whatever she might have said next was lost as Ranulf kissed her. Hywel waited until he thought their embrace had gone on long enough and then said, "I can do without the hug, but what about an apology to me, too, Ranulf?"

Ranulf smiled at the other man over his wife's shoulder. "I guess I do owe you one," he conceded. "Actually your idea was ingenious—in a sly sort of way. I can understand how others might believe it, for you've always been glib of tongue, Hywel. But how could my uncle Rhodri imagine for a moment that I'd engage in such double-dealing? And Gilbert and Eleri—do they not know me better than that?"

"I can answer that," Rhiannon said. "They believed it because they wanted to believe it, Ranulf, because they needed to believe it. They love you enough to banish disbelief."

"Whereas you should have seen the horrified reactions of my brothers Davydd and Rhodri, who love you not." Hywel grinned, remembering. "They were looking forward to a public hanging as soon as the opportunity presented itself. When they went running to my father in hopes of a denial, they were confounded when he confirmed it instead!"

"Owain did that?" Ranulf asked in astonishment. "You must be in higher favor than I thought, Hywel!" But almost at once, his amusement faded. "I would thank you," he said seriously, "for what you tried to do on my behalf."

Hywel cocked a brow. " 'Tried to do'?" he echoed. "It seems to me that my plan was a brilliant success, if I say so myself."

"It would have been," Ranulf agreed, "if not for the maiming of the hostages."

"You think my father blames you for that?"

"His sons will never see another sunrise because of the English king . . . and I am Harry's uncle."

"You are also the one man who spoke up for the hostages. Only one voice argued against the maiming, and it was yours."

Ranulf looked searchingly at Hywel, hope suddenly soaring to the quickening beat of his heart. "Are you saying Lord Owain is willing to let me stay in his domains?"

"He said that words rarely count for more than blood, but Chester is one of those times. You may make your home in Gwynedd till the end of your days and none will challenge your right to be here, to call yourself Welsh. On that, my father has spoken."

Ranulf exhaled an uneven breath and then whirled back toward Rhiannon. She returned his embrace wholeheartedly, but her eyes prickled with tears, for she knew that the events at Chester had inflicted a grievous wound, one that would leave a deep jagged scar upon her husband's soul.

HENRY GAZED DOWN from the battlements of Chester Castle upon the ruination of his Welsh campaign. His fleet had finally arrived from Dublin, was anchored in the bend of the River Dee, and each time he looked upon that motley assemblage of ships, he felt anger stirring anew, embers from a fire that had been smoldering since their forced retreat from the Berwyns. He had contracted for galleys, but some of the ships riding at anchor were cogs. Instead of warships, he had flat-bottomed cargo vessels with which to ravage the Welsh coast . . . and not even enough of those.

"Did you ever see a more pitiful fleet in all your born days?" he demanded of the young Earl of Chester. "Shredded rigging, torn sails, lost oars—it is a bloody miracle that they did not sink like stones in Dublin's harbor. Any man setting foot on one of those wrecks had better know how to walk on water, or else have made his peace with the Almighty."

Hugh fidgeted nervously, wanting to offer reassurance or hope but checked by the reality floating below them on the river. One of the ships had been run aground into a mudbank to patch leaks, and the crew was scrambling to complete the repairs before the onset of high tide. In the shadow of another ship, a raft had been launched, and as it bobbed and pitched, several men set about recaulking the seams with a sticky mixture of tar and moss. Hugh had to admit it was a sorry spectacle meeting their eyes. Striving to shine the best light upon the debacle, he ventured to remind Henry that the ships had been mauled in a storm off the Irish coast. "But once they are mended, they may yet inflict damage amongst the Welsh."

The other men winced at that, but Henry did not erupt as they expected. This muddled youth was his favorite cousin Maud's son, after all, and so he contented himself with a barbed sarcasm. "Aye—there is always the chance that the Welsh will die laughing at their first sight of this great armada."

Hugh didn't have Henry's familiarity with other languages and he wasn't sure what an armada was, but he knew better than to ask. He was finding it a trial to be his king's host; Henry had moved to Hugh's castle at Chester to await the fleet, and now Hugh hoped that he'd decide to go back to Shotwick, where his army was encamped. Hugh had always been intimidated by his royal cousin the king, but Henry's temper was exceptionally choleric these days and it was all too easy to provoke his ire.

Henry continued to watch the beached ship, his the morbid curiosity of a man with a toothache, compelled to keep touching his tongue to the tooth to see if it still hurt. It had been two days since that tattered fleet had limped into the Dee estuary, two days since he'd realized that his hopes of continuing the Welsh war had foundered with those Irish ships. The Welsh princes had defied him and gotten away with it. He had nothing to show for all his efforts but a depleted Exchequer, a lost summer, and a trail of shallow graves.

His bleak reverie was interrupted by a shout from the gatehouse; riders were coming in. A cursory glance down into the bailey showed him that there were women among them, but he had no interest in these newcomers. He would have welcomed his cousin, the tart-tongued worldly Maud, but she was in Anjou with Eleanor, planning to remain until after the babe was born. He could think of no other female he cared to see and he resumed his gloomy surveillance of the Irish ships. But then Hugh gave a sudden whoop.

"Holy Cross, it is Mistress Rosamund!"

Turning, Henry saw that the boy was right; one of the women in the bailey below them was indeed Rosamund Clifford. Hugh was heading for the ladder, at such a pace he'd be lucky not to take a headlong fall. Henry followed more slowly and with much less enthusiasm.

The Marcher lord, Walter Clifford, was greeting his daughter Rosamund and another woman whom Henry guessed to be his wife. After making the introductions to Hugh, who'd managed to get down in one piece, Clifford ushered the women toward Henry.

"My liege, may I present my wife, the Lady Margaret?" Wherever Rosamund had gotten her uncommon beauty, it was apparently not from her mother, a pleasingly plump woman in her forties with pale-blue eyes and the complacent composure of one born to a life of privilege.

"I believe you already know my daughter." Clifford's smile was so smug that Henry's first impulse was to turn on his heel and stalk away. For the girl's sake, he resisted the urge and managed a cool civility. Rosamund was more discerning than her father and her own smile faltered. Clifford was professing surprise that his womenfolk had come to visit him, jovially asking Hugh if he could find them a bed at the castle, and Hugh, beaming, declaring nothing would give him greater pleasure, while Rosamund looked at Henry in bewilderment, not understanding. Henry excused himself, climbed back up to the battlements, and stared out over the river at his misfit Irish fleet.

SUPPER THAT EVENING was not a festive affair. Hugh's cooks did their best to provide a tempting meal, but Henry picked at the minced pork and venison pie without either interest or appetite. Hugh had gallantly invited Clifford, his wife, and daughter to join them at the high table. His attempts at flirtation proved futile, though. Subdued and silent, Rosamund kept her eyes upon her trencher, pushing food about with her knife but eating very little, occasionally casting covert glances at Henry when she thought he wasn't watching. Hugh's spirits soon flagged in the face of her obvious indifference. Clifford was growing increasingly annoyed by his daughter's diffidence, scowling at her from his end of the table. The only one who seemed to be enjoying the meal was Henry's uncle Rainald, who never let other people's discomfort affect his appetite, and he at least did justice to the varied and highly seasoned dishes prepared by Hugh's cooks.

After supper, Hugh summoned a minstrel to perform for his guests. But the entertainment was no more successful than the meal, if judged by Henry's brooding demeanor. He may have heard the minstrel's songs, but he did not appear to be listening, his private thoughts obviously far from the hall of Chester Castle. Through the open windows, the sky was turning from a twilit lavender to a rich plum color as a messenger was ushered toward the dais. Kneeling before Henry, he proffered a parchment bearing the seal of a French lord of opportunistic allegiances, Simon de Montfort, Count of Evreux. As Henry scanned the dispatch, his body language alerted those close to him that something was wrong. Stiffening in his seat, one hand clenching upon the arm of his chair, he looked up, his mouth set in a taut line and his grey eyes frosted, filled with distance. He did not share the French count's news, but rose instead, making an abrupt departure, leaving behind a hall abuzz with conjecture.

It was fully dark now, but the air still held some of the warmth of the day. The sudden stretch of fine weather had seemed like the ultimate ironic joke to Henry; where had the sun been when he'd had such need of it? One of the castle dogs trailed after him as he entered the deserted gardens, but soon veered off on the scent of unseen nocturnal prey. Henry was regretting not revealing the contents of de Montfort's letter. More precisely, he was regretting not having someone to confide in, someone who'd understand his misery without the need of words. His ambitions were dynastic, his greatest wish to see his empire ruled by his sons after his death. Eleanor understood that. So had Thomas Becket—once. And Ranulf.

He did not like the direction his thoughts had taken. Some roads were better left untraveled. He had jammed the count's letter into his belt as he left the hall. Now he pulled it out again, wishing he had a fire to thrust it into. On impulse, he drew his dagger and began methodically to slash the parchment into ribbons. He felt faintly foolish; destroying the evidence would change nothing. But he did not stop until the sheepskin was in tatters, letting the scraps fall to the ground at his feet.

"My lord . . ."

He'd not heard the light footsteps in the grass, and he spun around at the sound of a soft female voice. Rosamund Clifford stood several feet away, her face blanched in the moonlight, her small fists balled at her sides. It occurred to Henry that she looked frightened and that saddened him. It did not take much to sadden him these days. He laughed suddenly, mirthlessly. God's Bones, he was as maudlin tonight as any drunken lout deep in his cups and without the excuse of wine, for he was cold sober.

He saw that his laughter had distressed her still further, for she'd understood that there was no humor in it. She was more perceptive than he would have expected of a convent-reared virgin, the self-serving Clifford's flesh and blood. "Why are you wandering about in the gardens, Mistress Rosamund? Trying to avoid Hugh?"

Rosamund blushed; she hadn't realized that he'd noticed Hugh's attentions. "I was looking for you, my lord." She hadn't meant to blurt it out like that, had hoped he might think their meeting was accidental, unplanned. But face to face with him in the moonlight, she found herself too flustered for subtlety. She could only tell the truth, or as much of it as she dared. "I was worried about you, my lord. That letter seemed to trouble you so . . ."

"This letter I was just ripping into shreds?" Henry at once regretted the sarcasm; why take out his temper on the lass? "You might as well be the first to know. All of Paris is rejoicing; it's a wonder we cannot hear the church bells pealing across the Channel. The Almighty has finally taken pity upon the French king. On the fourth Sunday of August, his queen gave him a son."

He expected that he'd have to explain the political and dynastic significance of that birth. Rosamund did not give him the chance. "I am sorry to hear that," she said softly. "Sons-by-marriage of a king have influence for certes. But uncles of a future king will wield much more."

Henry looked at her in surprise. "So you know Louis's current queen is of the House of Blois?"

She nodded shyly. "And I know, too, that her brothers, the Counts of Champagne and Blois, are men who bear you a mortal grudge."

She could see that he was pleased she was so knowledgeable and she felt faintly guilty, as if she were flying under false colors. The truth was that he was her abiding interest, not matters of state. In the two years since their encounter in the gardens at Woodstock, she had studied him as a scholar might study holy writ, asking questions when she could, eavesdropping when she could not, learning as much as possible about Henry Fitz Empress.

She knew that he'd been crowned Duke of Normandy when he was but seventeen, that he'd become king of the English at one and twenty, that he was wed to a legendary beauty, that he could be lenient to rebels but unforgiving of betrayal, that his memory was extraordinary and he was said to have some knowledge of all the tongues spoken "from the coast of France to the River Jordan," that his energy was boundless and his curiosity all-encompassing, that his anger could scorch hotter than the flames of Hell but to the downtrodden and Christ's poor, he was unfailingly courteous, that he was unpredictable and passionate and often enigmatic even to those who knew him best, and each time she looked into his eyes, her pulse began to race and her breath quickened.

"I truly did not expect that Louis would ever be able to get himself a son, not after three wives and four daughters. He came to believe that he'd incurred the Almighty's displeasure, and I suppose I wanted to believe that, too." Henry shook his head in disgust at his own shortsightedness. "If we could foretell the future with certainty, what need would we have for prayer?"

That sounded vaguely blasphemous to Rosamund, but she decided Henry ought not to be judged by the same stringent standards that applied to other men. As King of England, he was the Almighty's anointed, after all. She was thankful for her questions and her curiosity, for the flickering improbable hope that one day their paths might cross again, as her endeavors now enabled her to comprehend the root of his discontent. He had married his eldest son to Louis's daughter in the belief that this marriage might one day make his son heir to two thrones. It had been an ambitious dream, but Henry was not one to settle for less if there was a chance he might get more. Louis had two daughters older than little Marguerite, of course, wed to the conniving Counts of Blois and Champagne, and Rosamund did not doubt they'd have made their own claims had Louis died without a son. Just as she did not doubt that Henry would have prevailed. But now it was not to be.

She struggled to find some morsel of comfort to offer him, at last said hesitantly, "Your son will still be England's king, my liege. And the lands of the French king are meager indeed when compared with the empire you rule."

Henry said nothing; she couldn't be sure if he'd even heard her. He was frowning into the shadows beyond their moonlit patch of garden, withdrawing back into himself again. Rosamund felt suddenly bereft. Desperate to slow the drift, to keep his attention for a little longer, she found the courage to ask the question that had been haunting her since their arrival that afternoon.

"My liege . . . have I offended you in some way?"

Henry was sorry she'd asked that, for there was no honest way to answer her without causing her pain. "Of course not," he said, hoping she'd be satisfied with his denial.

Rosamund bit her lip, utterly unconvinced. "Then . . . then why did you look at me like that in the bailey? You were not pleased to see me, my lord, I know you were not. Can you not tell me why?"

He was quiet for a moment, considering his options and concluding that he had none. "You are right, lass. I was displeased, but not with you. My anger was with your father."

"Because he sent for me?" she asked in a small voice, and Henry nodded unwillingly.

"Rosamund, I do not want to hurt you. None of this is your doing. You did not realize what he had in mind, using you as bait to fish for the king's favor. At Avreton Castle, he saw that I was drawn to you and he thought to take advantage of it. I should be used to it by now. But you're his daughter, by God, and he ought to care more for your welfare than his own coffers. By pushing you toward my bed, he might have gained certain advantages today, but what of your tomorrows? What sort of marriage could you make? I'm no saint, have committed my share of sins and I'm likely to commit more. But you're an innocent . . ."

Henry paused, hearing again Ranulf's voice pointing that out to him. *The king's conscience.* "I do not want to hurt you," he repeated, and this time he was not speaking of the injuries inflicted by his candor.

Rosamund was deeply flushed; even by the moon's silvered light, he could see the color burning in her cheeks. "You are wrong, my liege." Her voice was little more than a whisper. "I did realize what my father had in mind. I am indeed an innocent, as you say. But I am not a child. Of course I understood. What you do not understand is that I was willing. I wanted to come. I wanted to be with you."

The silence that followed her confession seemed endless to Rosamund; even the sounds of the night had ceased, and she could almost believe the entire world had gone still of a sudden. When she could endure it no more, she said, "You must think I'm shameless . . ."

Henry closed the distance between them, slid his fingers under her chin, and tilted her face up to his. "No," he said, "I am thinking that it would take a stronger man than me to walk away from you now."

WATCHING AS HENRY MOVED to the table and poured wine for them, Rosamund could only marvel that the King of England was acting as her cupbearer. He brought a single cup back to the window seat and they took turns drinking from it. Rosamund limited herself to several small sips, for she already felt light-headed, made tipsy by this astonishing turn of fate. All her daydreams notwithstanding, she found it hard to believe that she was actually here with Henry in his bedchamber, his fingers stroking her cheek, his every smile for her and her alone. She was touched that he was being so gentle with her, so unhurried. He'd unfastened her veil and wimple, unpinning her hair until it tumbled free down her back.

"You're very beautiful," he said, "especially with your hair loose like this. The color is remarkable, not so much spun flax as spun moonlight."

"I'm glad it pleases you," she said, and he set the wine cup down in the floor rushes at their feet, took her in his arms. He'd kissed her before, below in the gardens, but not like this. His mouth was hot, tasting of wine, and when he took her onto his lap, she felt the rising proof of how much he wanted her. She was breathless by the time he ended the kiss. He traced the curve of her mouth with his finger, his eyes shining silver in the lamplight. The loss of her maidenhead would turn her life onto a different path, a road unfamiliar and fraught with risk. She was immensely grateful that he cared about her honor, but she was not afraid. Her anxiety had vanished down in the gardens, once she realized that he did want her. She gave him a smile he would remember, one of tenderness and utter trust, and he lifted her up in his arms, carried her across the chamber to his bed.

Henry was thirty-two, had first learned about the profound pleasures of the flesh while still in his early teens. Oddly, though, he'd had little experience with virgins, for he was as pragmatic about bedsport as he was about other pursuits; his natural inclination was for the most direct route. Before his marriage to Eleanor, he'd preferred knowing, practiced bedmates and was quite willing to pay for the privilege, as that was easy and uncomplicated and avoided awkward misunderstandings. Since his marriage, he'd been faithful to his wife when he was with her, feeling free to seek sexual release elsewhere when he was not.

Rosamund Clifford was a departure from his usual pattern, and he was intent upon making sure that her first time was pleasurable for her, for she aroused more than his lust; there was something about the girl that made him want to take care of her. With Rosamund, he discovered a virtue he hadn't thought he possessed—patience—and after their lovemaking was over, he held her within the sheltering circle of his arms, fighting sleep for her sake, a sacrifice he'd hitherto made only for Eleanor.

He awoke in the morning with a feeling of drowsy contentment, and for the first time in weeks with nary a thought to spare for his failed campaign, his missing uncle, or the hapless Welsh hostages. Rosamund was curled up beside him like a kitten, blond hair spilling across the pillow and over the side of the bed; it must reach nigh on to her knees, he decided, and a stray quotation from Scriptures surfaced, that "if a woman hath long hair, it is a glory to her." When she opened her eyes and smiled up at him, he was surprised by the surge of relief he felt. He'd been confident he'd made her deflowering more pleasurable than painful, but a woman's virtue was a valuable commodity in their world and she might well have suffered morning-after regrets. He was pleased to see that it was not so, and leaned over to kiss her sweeping golden lashes, the corner of her mouth where her smile still lingered.

Afterward, they lay entwined in the sheets, reluctant to leave the private refuge of his bedchamber for the reality waiting on the other side of the door. Henry was the first to stir, smothering a yawn with the back of his hand. "People will know," he said. "Nothing that a king does escapes notice. Does that trouble you, Rosamund?"

"No, it does not, my lord." The lie came readily to her lips for she'd recognized that any liaison with Henry would have consequences that were sure to spill over into every corner of her life. Until last night she'd been known to their world as *Clifford's daughter.* Now she would become *the king's concubine.* It was a prospect she found both daunting and humiliating, but it was a price she was willing to pay for her time with Henry.

"When do you plan to leave Chester?" she asked, and was proud of herself for making the query sound so casual, as if heartbreak was not riding upon his answer.

"Probably on Friday. My Curia Regis is scheduled to meet at month's end." He thought to translate the Latin into "Royal Court" for her benefit, but she scarcely noticed, for she was counting surreptitiously upon her fingers. Four days.

"Will you have time for me tonight?" she asked, still striving for nonchalance, and was reassured when he laughed and joked about staying in bed with her for the rest of his born days. She knew better, of course, but at least she'd have until Friday. That was more than many an unhappy wife had in an entire lifetime.

Sitting up, she began to untangle her hair with her fingers, feeling an almost childish delight when Henry tossed her his own brush. He was dressing with his usual dispatch, but when he smiled at her as he pulled a tunic over his head, she was encouraged to ask if he might grant her a favor.

Henry found himself fumbling with his belt, fighting back sudden suspicion. Had he so misjudged her? Was she Clifford's accomplice, after all? He was accustomed to people wanting what a king could give, and women did their best bargaining in bed; that he well knew. But for reasons he did not fully understand, he did not want Rosamund Clifford to angle for her own advantage, to put a price upon her maidenhead. "What may I do for you?" he asked, his tone so neutral that a more worldly woman might have been warned.

Rosamund hesitated, hoping that he would not think her presumptuous. "I was wondering if . . . if when we are alone, I may call you Henry?"

Henry burst out laughing. "Well, no," he said, and when he saw she'd taken his teasing seriously, he added hastily, "Actually I prefer Harry."

She smiled, saying "Harry" with such ingenuous satisfaction that he had to return to the bed and kiss her. And when he left Chester at the week's end, he took Rosamund with him.

IN OCTOBER, Eleanor gave birth at Angers to their seventh child, a fair-haired daughter who was named Joanna.

CHAPTER TWENTY-ONE

December 1165
Angers, Anjou

IN THEIR THIRTEEN YEARS OF MARRIAGE, Henry and Eleanor had often been apart, but they always spent Christmas together. Only war had separated them and only once. But now they were separated by more than miles. Eleanor did not understand why her husband was still in England. Nor did she approve. She had acted as his regent during his disastrous invasion of Wales, and that had been no easy task, for Thomas Becket's defiance was a contagion, infecting the always contentious barons of Poitou, Anjou, and Maine. Small rebellions had been breaking out like brushfires all over Henry's vast domains, fanned by agents of the French Crown and the House of Blois. Henry was needed on the Continent, where his enemies were plotting against him, where he had an infant daughter he'd yet to see and a wife who'd been sleeping alone for the past six months. Perplexed and aggrieved by his continuing absence, Eleanor finally voiced to intimates the question that was being asked by others, too, and with increasing frequency: What was keeping the king in England?

JUST AS SHE had not allowed pregnancy and childbirth to distract her from her duties as regent, Eleanor was determined to hold a Christmas Court as spectacular as any she and Henry had hosted in the past. God's Year 1165 had not been a good one for Henry Fitz Empress—a humiliating defeat in Wales, the birth of a son to the French king, continuing discord with the exiled archbishop, Thomas Becket, echoes of rebellion on the bleak winter winds. But Eleanor had always been one for nailing her flag to the mast so it could not be struck down. She spared no expense and her guests would be marveling at the splendor of the royal revelries for months to come.

The great castle of Angers was hung with evergreen, holly, laurel, yew, and mistletoe. To enthusiastic cheers of "Wassail!" the Yule candle was lit and then the Yule log, carefully stacked so it might burn for the following twelve days. The Eve of Christmas was a fast day, but the Christmas Day feast was lavish enough to blot out all memories of Advent abstinence: a roasted boar's head, refeathered peacocks, oysters, venison, and the delicacy known as a "glazed pilgrim," a large pike which was boiled at the head, fried in the middle, and roasted at the tail. The entertainment was no less impressive than the menu: music by the finest minstrels in all of Aquitaine, dancing, a fire juggler, and then the presentation of the Play of the Three Shepherds. As bells pealed to celebrate the birth of the Christ Child, Eleanor's Christmas Day revelry came to a successful conclusion, and if her spirits had been dampened by her husband's absence, she alone knew it.

CHRISTMAS FESTIVITIES traditionally ended on Twelfth Night. The January sky was canopied by clouds, and the evidence of an earlier snowfall still glazed the ground of the castle's inner bailey. Colors of crimson and sun-gold glowed in the wavering torchlight, for most of the guests had not bothered to cover their fine clothes with mantles or cloaks. Warmed by wine and vanity, they'd trooped outdoors in good humor for the wassailing of the trees, only to discover that hippocras and the frothy cider drink called lamb's wool were poor protection against a biting wind and air so icy it hurt to breathe.

Hurriedly, the revelers crowded into the garden, twelve of them forming a circle around the largest of the fruit trees. "Hail to thee, old apple tree," they chanted hoarsely. "From every bough, give us apples enow." The rest of the rhyme was all but drowned out by the chattering of teeth and the stamping of frigid feet. Cups were hastily lifted and muffled cries of "Wassail" filled the garden. There was more to the ceremony, but the guests were already hastening back toward the great hall. Pouring the remainder of their cider onto the exposed gnarled roots of the apple tree, the twelve wassailers scrambled to catch up with their retreating audience. Soon the garden was empty of all save a lone woman who'd had the foresight to wrap herself in a mantle lined with fox fur and a youth whose arm she had linked in hers.

The young Earl of Chester was sensibly garbed, too, enveloped in a green wool mantle that billowed like a sail with each swirl of the wind. He showed neither impatience to return to the hall nor curiosity why his mother should have chosen to linger in the dark, deserted garden, and it was that very apathy that Maud found so perplexing. Hugh's abrupt arrival at Angers had taken her by surprise, for she had expected him to remain in England with their cousin the king. Whatever had possessed the lad to make a needless winter journey like this? So far he'd been as sparing with his answers as he was with his smiles, thwarting her maternal solicitude with shrugs and silence. Watching him as he brooded amongst the wassailers, as somber as if he were attending a wake, Maud had at last lost all patience.

"Are you going to tell me what is troubling you, Hugh, or must I guess?" He glanced at her sideways, with another of those vexing shrugs, and Maud's frustration spilled over into the sort of blunt speaking that her more conventional son deplored. What sort of sins would he be most likely to commit? Gambling debts? Nay, he was too cautious to enjoy wagering. "Have you gotten some girl with child?"

"No!" Hugh flushed, looking much younger at that moment than his eighteen years, and Maud almost smiled. So it was a lass, after all. Reminding herself how vulnerable first love could be, she said, not unkindly, "There is no crime in being smitten by a pretty face. Nor is there any great harm in sowing a few wild oats, provided that the girl is not already spoken for . . ." Her son's face twitched, and she said, more sharply, "Hugh, no good can come of lusting after a married woman. Even if she is only a villein, it is not wise, for—"

"Rosamund is no villein," he snapped, sounding offended. "She is well bred and gently born. Nor is she married."

"Rosamund who?" she asked, so unobtrusively that Hugh found himself mumbling her surname before he could think better of it.

Maud regarded him thoughtfully; clearly this was more serious than she'd realized. Was he enamored enough to want to marry the girl? Clifford's daughter would make most men a perfectly acceptable wife, but the Earl of Chester could aim much higher. What of the negotiations to wed him to the young daughter of the Count of Evreux? "Hugh, I hope you've done nothing rash. You've made no promises to this girl, have you?"

He shook his head mutely, and she sighed with relief. But then he added in a burst of miserable candor, "I would have, but she'll have none of me."

Maud's temper ignited. That self-serving malcontent, Clifford, dared to refuse her son? What better husband could he crave for his daughter than Hugh of Chester, cousin to the king? Forgetting for the moment her own opposition to a Clifford–Chester match, she said indignantly, "Some hawks fly high these days, need to get their wings clipped for certes!" Hugh did not seem much comforted by that, and she patted his arm consolingly. "Ah, lad, I do understand. This is the first lass you've set your heart upon, and I know it is hurtful. But—"

"No, you do not understand!" Hugh's despair was so naked that his mother fell silent, for such an emotional outburst was quite unlike him. "Hurtful, you say? You do not know the half of it! What choice did she have, a girl convent-reared and all too trusting? But I could do nothing, had to watch as he took her to his bed, with her lout of a father cheering him on!"

Maud stared at him. "What in God's Name are you talking about? Who took Rosamund Clifford into his bed?"

"Who do you think?" Hugh's mouth twisted. "The king!"

"Harry . . . and Rosamund Clifford?" She sighed again, this time sadly. Poor Hugh, no wonder he was so distraught. "Well, that is unfortunate, but it might turn out better for the girl than you think. If she was indeed a virgin, Harry will surely be generous enough to compensate for the loss of her maidenhead, and there are men who'd take a perverse pride in having a woman bedded by the king."

"You still do not understand! This is more than a grope in the dark or a quick tumble between the sheets. He is besotted with her, keeps her as close as he can. Where do you think he is now? At Woodstock—with her!"

Maud's breath hissed between her teeth. Instinctively, she glanced over her shoulder, making sure they were still alone. So that was why Harry had lingered so long in England! Jesú, but men were such fools. "Have you spoken of this to anyone else, Hugh?" When he shook his head, she reached out and gripped his arm. "See that you do not."

Hugh looked annoyed. "What do you fear, Mother, that I'd blurt it out to the queen? I have more sense than that. But my silence will matter for naught. Sooner or later, she'll hear about her husband and Rosamund."

"Yes," she agreed grimly, "she will. But it will not be from you."

M ELIORA HAD not ventured far, only to an apothecary's shop on Calpe Street, but the rain started again before she could return to the shelter of Winchester's great castle. It was a stinging, cold rain, interspersed with sleet, for although the calendar had marked the first week of March, England was still in winter's frigid grip. But Meliora was not one to be daunted by bad weather; pulling up her mantle hood, she continued on her way. Several boisterous young men came sprinting toward her, laughing and cursing as they sought to outrun the rain to the closest alehouse. A woman passing by made haste to cross the street, but Meliora didn't give the rowdy youths a second glance. Now in her fifties, she still had the bold spirit that had led her to leave her native Cornwall in search of adventure and more opportunities than any Cornish village could offer.

Twice married, twice widowed—the first marriage for fun, the second for security—she had three grown children, and a dower sufficient to keep her in a comfortable old age. But for all that her flaming red hair was now greyed, her waist thickened, and her step slowed by a touch of the joint-evil, her thirst for the unknown had not been slaked. And so when the king asked her to attend the Lady Rosamund Clifford, Meliora had accepted with alacrity.

Hearing sudden footsteps thudding behind her, she spun around, her grip tightening on the walking stick that would make a useful weapon. But the man bearing down upon her was no cutpurse, far too well dressed for that. As he drew nearer, she recognized him as the castellan's second-in-command, and readily accepted his offer to escort her back to the castle. With ostentatious gallantry, he insisted upon carrying her apothecary's sack and she relinquished it with a droll smile, knowing full well that the days were long past when young men vied for her favors. His chivalry was motivated by curiosity for certes; she'd wager the entire garrison was gossiping about the girl who'd accompanied the king to Winchester.

Meliora was not averse to gossip and answered readily enough, amused by the youth's clumsy attempts at nonchalance. She confirmed that she and her lady would be leaving for Woodstock on the morrow, weather permitting, now that the king had continued on to Southampton. No, she did not know when the king would be returning to England. Yes, she and her lady would be needing an escort, but she believed the King's Grace had arranged that with the castellan ere his departure yesterday. She was so agreeable, so affable that it was only later that he'd realize just how little she'd actually told him.

The castle's postern gate was open for there was still a trickle of sodden daylight remaining. Thanking her escort with just a trace of perceptible irony, Meliora crossed the bridge and waded through the mud, heading for the square tower in the northeast angle of the inner bailey that Henry had occupied for his brief domicile in Winchester.

Meliora knew that Henry had deliberately chosen to eschew the king's chambers and the royal bed he'd shared with Eleanor. She wondered if Rosamund did. She had a genuine liking for the king. They'd met several years ago during one of his frequent stays at Woodstock, Meliora's home for the past two decades. She enjoyed his sly humor and cavalier disregard for protocol, admired his sharp-edged intelligence, and was impressed by the generosity of the offer he'd made to her, for she knew he was not a spendthrift by nature. She'd jumped at the chance to enter his world, shrewdly sure she knew what he wanted—a shepherd to watch over his little lamb for as long as his infatuation with the girl lasted—and after four months in the king's service, she had yet to repent of her impulsive acceptance.

She huffed up the stairwell to their chamber, then shed her wet mantle, kicked off her clogs, and hurried over to thaw out by the hearth. Rosamund Clifford had been lying down, but at the sound of the opening door, she jerked the bed hangings aside. "Where did you go, Meliora? Look at you, you're soaked through." Snatching up a garment from a wall pole, she hastened toward the hearth. "Here, put this on."

Meliora snorted incredulously at the sight of what Rosamund was holding out, the new bedrobe given her by the king. Made of finely woven scarlet, the most luxurious of all woolens, it shimmered in the lamplight, a deep, rich mulberry. "Child, I'd be lucky to get my elbow into that wisp of cloth, much less my rump. And even if it fit, I'd be as skittish as a treed cat, wearing something more costly than my late husband's best cow." She sketched a cross in the air, adding a perfunctory "May God assoil him," and then grinned. "The husband, not the cow."

Rosamund grinned, too. "I was fretful about wearing this myself," she confided. "I was sure I'd spill wine in my lap or stand too close to the hearth and get smoke smudges on it, and the king would think I was shamefully careless. When I finally confessed my unease, he raised a brow in that way he has and said he was reasonably sure that ruining a robe was not a hanging offense."

Meliora was amused that Rosamund continued to observe the proprieties, always taking care to accord her lover his regal title. Henry Fitz Empress was a lucky man, she thought, for this was one royal concubine who'd never be a player in those dangerous and tempting games of chance in which no stakes were higher than the king's favor. Even after more than five months of sharing his bed, Rosamund Clifford showed no symptoms of that pernicious ailment Henry had once sardonically dubbed "Crown fever," and Meliora was worldly enough to appreciate how rare such an immunity was.

She hadn't counted upon this, upon becoming so fond of the lass. She would have preferred to keep an emotional distance, to avoid getting sucked into the whirlpools and eddies as the love affair ebbed and flowed. But it was too late; her shepherd's eye had taken on a maternal glint and she was already regretting the hurt that would inevitably befall the king's little lamb.

"Has your headache eased up any?" she asked, noting the pallor in Rosamund's cheeks, the puffiness shadowing her eyes. "You still look a mite peaked. Well, I've a remedy for that," she announced, reaching for the apothecary's sack, knowing all the while that herbs were no cure for what ailed the girl. The king had departed yesterday morning for Southampton, where he planned to take ship for Normandy, and Meliora had heard Rosamund softly weeping several times in the night, despite her efforts to muffle her sobs in the pillow. The lass would have to toughen up if she hoped to survive this perilous liaison with nothing worse than a few calluses of the heart. But for now, betony would have to do.

"My grandmother used to swear by this," she said, rooting about in the apothecary's sack, "whenever any of us was stricken with head-pain. She'd mix a spoonful of betony juice with honey, wine, and nine peppercorns, have the ailing one take it every morn and eve for nine days."

Ignoring Rosamund's half-hearted demurrals, Meliora set about preparing her potion, only to remember that she'd finished the last of the red wine during their dinner; since Henry's departure, they'd been taking their meals in the privacy of their bedchamber rather than under the curious stares of the garrison in the great hall. Rosamund protested in earnest once she realized that Meliora meant to venture out again into the storm, but the older woman laughed away her objections and pulled on her sodden mantle, then squeezed her feet back into her muddy clogs. No one ever said that a shepherd's lot was an easy one.

The rain had not slackened and it was so blustery that Meliora turned her ankle in her rush to reach the buttery. She was limping back toward the square tower, clutching the wine flagon to her chest and cursing under her breath when a shout echoed from the battlements. Men were running along the rampart walks, gesturing toward the castle's great gate with enough urgency to attract Meliora's attention. Riders were coming in, and to judge by the sudden spurt of activity, they were men of considerable importance. Meliora's curiosity, always a potent force, won out over her discomfort and she lingered to watch the arrival of these high-ranking visitors. A moment later, she was splashing through the muck of the mid-bailey, intent only upon reaching the man on a familiar, raw-boned grey stallion.

"Your Grace!" Panting, she waved to catch Henry's eye. He saw her at once, and after shooting off a barrage of instructions over his shoulder, he swung from the saddle and strode toward Meliora, who'd prudently stopped some feet away, remembering his stallion's unpredictable temper. "Is something amiss?" she cried as soon as he was within hearing range. "Why are you not at sea by now?"

Henry's shoulders twitched under his mantle in what might have been a shrug. "The weather was so foul that I decided to delay crossing the Channel until the storm passes."

Meliora could not hide her astonishment, for it was well known that he'd often sailed in seas rough enough to make the Devil himself green-sick. Henry had the grace to look somewhat sheepish as he realized how lame his excuse sounded. This time his shrug was more pronounced. "I can spare a few more days," he said, as close as he could come to admitting his reluctance to leave his young mistress. "How does she, Meliora?"

By now he'd steered her across the bailey and into the square tower. "You'd best see for yourself, my lord. You needn't wait on me, though. I'd as soon stay here till I catch my breath."

The smoking rushlight above their heads caught the gleam of his smile, the damp gold of his hair as his hood fell back. Meliora sat down on the stairs, listening to the jangle of his spurs as they struck sparks against the grooved stone steps. He was taking them two at a time, and within moments, she heard the door open, heard Rosamund cry out in wonderment: "Harry!" Meliora settled herself more comfortably against the stairwell and took a deep swallow from the flagon, unconcerned with the lack of a cup. The wine was a heavy, sweet malmsey from Crete, far superior in quality to the sour white wines of southern England that Meliora's late husband could afford. She savored the taste and smiled then in the dark, for it now seemed as if she'd have more opportunities to drink the king's fine wines than she'd first envisioned.

HENRY RETURNED with Rosamund to Woodstock, where they passed another week together. It was not until March 16 that he rode back to Southampton and sailed for Normandy. Reunited with his queen, they held their Easter court at Angers. Henry then set about punishing those lords who'd defied Eleanor's orders during his absence in England. Marching into Maine, he dealt first with the rebellious Count of Seez, William Talevas, and in a lightning-fast campaign, he forced Talevas to yield his strongholds of Alençon and La Roche Mabille. He also found time to confer with the King of France, to pressure the monks of Pontigny to expel Thomas Becket from their abbey, to summon his lords to Chinon for a council on the turmoil in Brittany, and to plan another meeting with Louis. But as spring's warmth yielded to the scorching heat of a dry, searing summer, word spilled over the castle walls of Chinon, shocking even Henry's multitude of mortal enemies. The English king was gravely ill, it was said, so ill that it was feared for his life.

THE DAY WAS HOT, the sky a brittle, cloudless blue, and the soaring, white walls of Chinon had come into view, high on a spur overlooking the River Vienne. The Countess of Vermandois recognized it with a mingled sense of relief and dread, thankful to end her dusty, uncomfortable journey but uneasy about what she would find. Sending her men to seek refreshments in the great hall, she insisted upon being taken at once to see her sister, the queen. If death had come to Chinon, better that she know it straightaway.

She was escorted across a dry, barren bailey, the earth cracked and sere. The air was cooler inside the great round keep, the Tour de Moulin, but not by much. Following a servant into the shadowed stairwell, Petronilla blinked as she emerged into the light of the solar, where windows were unshuttered, open to the sun. As she sat on a cushioned settle, she could feel perspiration trickling into the lacings of her bodice; it was so tightly fitting that it seemed molded to her skin, and she wondered why fashion must be so damnably uncomfortable. Hoping for an errant breeze, she moved to a window, but the smell from the river was too pungent and she soon retreated.

When Eleanor entered, she gave her sister a distracted embrace, then sent a servant for wine. "I never thought I'd say this, but today I almost miss those wretched, wet English fogs."

"How does Harry fare?"

"Better. His fever broke three days ago." Sitting down heavily upon the settle, Eleanor groped for a pillow to put behind her back. "It was good of you to come, Petra."

"Of course I came. Your letter made it sound as if you might be a widow at any moment!"

"If I'd listened to those fool doctors, I'd have been picking out my mourning garb." Eleanor shook her head impatiently. "I told them that unless Harry could rule in absentia, he'd never agree to die."

"You say his fever has broken?"

"Yes, on Friday, and he's begun complaining about the food and the doctors and the heat, a sure sign that he is on the mend. Although he did give us a scare yesterday. A courier arrived with word of Becket's latest outrage whilst I was lying down, and those dolts let the man in to see Harry. He started shouting like a madman, insisted upon getting out of bed, and collapsed in the floor rushes like a sack of flour since he is still as weak as a newborn."

"What has Becket done now?"

Eleanor grimaced. "On Whitsunday, he celebrated Mass at Vezelay and pronounced sentences of anathema and excommunication upon seven of Harry's lords, including his justiciar, Richard de Lucy. He also condemned the Constitutions of Clarendon and freed the English bishops from their oaths to obey them. And he even threatened to excommunicate Harry himself and lay all England under interdict."

Petronilla sighed; she was thoroughly bored by this endless squabbling between Becket and her brother-in-law. "What happens now?"

"Harry means to order the English bishops to appeal to the Pope against these censures."

A wisp of hair had escaped Eleanor's wimple and was tickling her cheek; she tucked it away and leaned back against the settle, closing her eyes. Petronilla was not surprised that she looked fatigued; she'd wager every soul in Chinon was careworn from catering to Harry's sickbed whims. "You ought to be flushed in this heat, not as white as chalk," she said critically, reaching over to feel Eleanor's forehead as the door opened and a servant entered with a flagon of wine, two cups, and a plateful of fresh-baked wafers. "Set it by me," Petronilla directed and filled the cups. The wine was a strong red Gascon and she savored every swallow. "You'd not believe the swill I was served on the road. Here, Eleanor, have one of the cheese wafers."

Eleanor shook her head, recoiling when Petronilla tried to pass her a wafer. "Just the smell of it is enough to make my gorge rise."

"Are you ailing?" Petronilla gave her sister a speculative look. "You've never been one for queasiness, except . . . Good Lord, Eleanor, has Harry gotten you with child again?"

"Well, I surely hope it is Harry's," Eleanor said tartly. She was obviously irked by her sister's disapproving tone, but Petronilla doubted that she'd welcomed this pregnancy with heartfelt joy. What woman of forty and four years would?

"I know you've enjoyed confounding those who claimed you'd ever be a barren queen, but even so . . . What are you and Harry doing, going for a baker's dozen? When is this one due?"

"In January. It happened whilst we were at Angers for Eastertide."

Petronilla scowled, thinking it a pity that Harry had not stayed longer in England. No wonder Eleanor looked so wan. If the fates had been less kind, she'd have found herself a pregnant widow, bequeathed each and every one of Harry's enemies, struggling to hold together a far-flung empire for a son who was all of eleven years. She held her tongue for once, though, and glancing at her sister's taut profile, she could only hope that this eighth pregnancy would be an easy one and, God Willing, the last.

N o s o o n e r had Henry risen from his sickbed than he was in the saddle. Conan, Duke of Upper Brittany, was viewed by the Bretons as an Angevin puppet, and a rebellion had recently flared up, ignited by a disaffected baron, Ralph de Fougères. By June 28, Henry's army was at Fougères. It was said to be impervious to assault, but it fell to Henry on July 14. He then pushed on into Brittany, where he deposed the inept Conan, betrothed his young son Geoffrey to Conan's daughter and heiress, Constance, and took possession of the duchy in his son's name.

✦

AUTUMN THAT YEAR painted the countryside in vivid shades of scarlet, saffron, and russet, and the days were clear and crisp under harvest skies. But Henry had little time to enjoy the splendors of the season. Even his passion for the hunt went unsatisfied as he passed the days in a whirlwind of councils with allies and enemies alike—the Count of Flanders; Theobald, Count of Blois; the perpetually discontented Poitevin lords; the new King of Scotland; a papal envoy; and Matthew of Boulogne, scandalously wed to King Stephen's daughter Mary, former abbess of Romsey Abbey.

By November 20, he was back at Chinon Castle, and it was here that he received his justiciar, Richard de Lucy, and his uncle Rainald, Earl of Cornwall, bearing news of yet another Welsh setback. Owain Gwynedd had taken advantage of Henry's absence from England to capture and destroy Basingwerk Castle. Under the command of the Earls of Leicester and Essex, men were dispatched to rebuild it, but they'd been forced to retreat back across the border in disarray.

CHINON'S GREAT HALL was crowded, for Henry's own retainers were augmented by the new arrivals from England and a sizable contingent of Poitevin lords, squirming under the king's watchful eye. After a time, Rainald took refuge in a window seat alcove, where he made himself as comfortable as his aching muscles would allow, occasionally intercepting a passing wine-bearer or nodding with forced joviality if he happened to spot a familiar face. The night was mild and the hearth fires well tended; Rainald was soon dozing, his chin resting on his chest, fingers loosening around the stem of a tilting wine cup. But when another hand reached over to steady the goblet, he jerked upright, blinking blearily until his tired brain processed the information that the wine thief was his nephew.

Henry was grinning. "I think you'd rally on your very deathbed if someone waved a flagon under your nose." Sitting down in the window seat, he waved aside the inevitable flock of hangers-on, indicating he wanted some semiprivacy with his uncle. As they reluctantly retreated, he handed Rainald back his wine cup. "Feeling your age, Uncle?"

Rainald's answering grin was swallowed up in a huge yawn. "Aye, lad, I am, and why not? When you reach the advanced age of fifty and six, too, you'll find that even your vast stores of energy will be well nigh empty." He was not surprised by Henry's amused disbelief. Still in his high noon at thirty-three, how could he envision a twilight waning?

"These old bones are getting too brittle for journeys like this," Rainald complained good-naturedly. "Lord knows why de Lucy was in such haste to find you, what with all our news being so bleak!" He glanced toward the center hearth, where the justiciar was chatting amiably with several bishops and the Earl of Salisbury, Henry's military commander in Aquitaine. "At least Becket's curse has gone astray," he said, pointing out the obvious: that none were obeying the Church's dictate to shun the excommunicate justiciar as one of God's castaways.

The mere mention of Thomas Becket's name was enough to sour Henry's mood. "Have you heard the latest about our archbishop in exile?" he asked, the words dripping with sarcasm. "Becket left his refuge with the Cistercians of Pontigny, is now under the protection of that fool on the French throne. Louis even dispatched a three-hundred-man escort to welcome Becket into his new roost, the abbey of St Columba, outside Sens."

"It is difficult to understand how a man of God can stir up so much of the Devil's mischief." Seeing that his commiseration had chafed rather than soothed, Rainald marveled how easy it was to misspeak if Thomas Becket was the topic of conversation, and hastily sought to change the subject. "How does Eleanor these days? Is she still at Angers?"

"No, she joined me at Rouen last month and tarried to visit with my mother for another fortnight. As loath as she is to admit it, this pregnancy has not been an easy one. She tires easily and her nerves are so often on the raw that the babe she carries must be a hellraiser, for certes!"

"And Maude? Is she still ailing?" Rainald asked, and gnawed his lower lip when his nephew gave him a terse confirmation. Maude had never lacked for enemies, but the most insidious one was proving to be her own body, nurturing a foe that stole her breath, sapped her strength, and alarmed her loved ones. Her spirit still burned with a blue-white flame— Rainald had heard how wroth she'd been when Henry captured a messenger of Becket's and put him to the knife to reveal his secrets—but few doubted that her mortal days were finite enough to count. Fumbling to cast out the shadow that had so suddenly fallen between them, Rainald brightened, remembering a choice bit of gossip he'd picked up in Wales.

"Guess who Owain Gwynedd is locking horns with nowadays? None other than Thomas Becket!"

Henry's interest was immediate. "How so?"

"Well . . . the see of Bangor has been vacant for nigh on five years now," Rainald began, and Henry was hard put to conceal his impatience, knowing his uncle could spin a tale out till the cows came home. "But of course you know that," Rainald conceded, seeing those grey eyes narrow tellingly. "Owain wanted the position filled and he rashly wrote to Becket at Pontigny, asking if, during Becket's exile, another prelate might consecrate Bangor's bishop. Obviously, he did not consult Ranulf beforehand, for he'd have warned Owain that Becket's vanity would never allow him to delegate even a scrap of authority. Becket sent a curt refusal, ordering that no election be held. But Owain is a man for getting his own way, too, and he arranged for his candidate to be elected and then sent him off to Ireland to be consecrated."

He'd hoped that Henry might be amused by this flouting of Becket's will; instead he scowled. "Ere war broke out, Owain approached me about filling the vacancy at Bangor with a man of his choosing, a monk of Bardsey. I refused, for I knew what he was about, trying to subvert English control over the diocese. So he thought to checkmate me with Becket, did he?"

"Well, it did not work," Rainald reminded him mildly, putting aside the heretical thought that his nephew was no less jealous of his own prerogatives than Becket. "He may have his man at Bangor, but the Church will not recognize him. Moreover, he has made an enemy of Becket, who is suddenly showing great interest in Owain's marriage to the Lady Cristyn, warning Owain that if the rumors of their kinship be true, she is no lawful wife and must be put aside."

Henry's eyes glittered. "I wish Owain better luck than my brother Will had," he said, and Rainald realized that he had stepped into yet another snare. If truth be told, it was impossible to talk about Thomas Becket without blundering into one quagmire after another.

He began to speak at random about any subject that came to mind—the sudden death of the Earl of Essex last month at Chester, after their rout by the Welsh; Richard de Lucy's professed intent to take the cross and go on pilgrimage to the Holy Land—knowing that there was a need to exorcise more than one ghost. It had been clumsy of him to make mention of Ranulf, sprinkling salt into an unhealed wound. He knew his nephew wanted to ask if he'd heard from Ranulf. He knew, too, that he would not ask. They were a pair, Harry and Ranulf, stubbornly keeping silent whilst their estrangement festered, each one unwilling to admit his own pain. Upon his return to England, he would write to his niece, he decided. If anyone could make peace between these two balky mules, surely it was Maud.

Richard de Lucy was approaching and Rainald welcomed him heartily; let de Lucy be the one to blunder into pitfalls for a while. Not that he would; de Lucy was the perfect royal servant, with diplomatic skills worthy of a Pope and loyalty that would put a dog to shame. When Henry informed him now that he must postpone his pilgrimage, instead journey to Rome to appeal Becket's latest excommunications, the justiciar didn't even blink, agreed so smoothly that Rainald had not a clue as to what he truly thought. Camouflaging another yawn, he watched as a courier was ushered across the hall toward them, and made ready to ask his nephew's permission to retire for the evening.

But before he could, the messenger thrust a letter from Henry's mother into his hands. Henry swiftly broke the seal, unfolded the parchment, and held it up toward the wall sconce above his head. Rainald squirmed on the seat, trying to ease his aching back. His eyelids had begun to droop again when his nephew drew a sudden, sibilant breath.

Rainald's first fear was for Maude. "Is the news bad?"

Henry shook his head. "No . . . just unexpected. My mother says that Eleanor has left Rouen and rumor has it that she took ship at Barfleur for England."

Rainald gaped, for that made no sense at all. Why would a woman brave a November Channel crossing whilst great with child? "Why would she do that? Did you not say that you were holding your Christmas court at Poitiers this year, to please her?"

Henry was frowning over the parchment again. Richard de Lucy was his usual inscrutable self, but Rainald was too puzzled for tact. "Surely Maude must be wrong. Why would Eleanor take it into her head of a sudden to go to England, now of all times?"

Henry glanced up sharply, then shrugged. "I have no idea, Uncle," he said, "none at all."

CHAPTER TWENTY-TWO

November 1166
English Channel

ETRONILLA SAT UP with a jerk, her heart racing. No night should have been as dark as this, and the cold was so damp and penetrating that it seemed to have seeped into her very bones. She was astonished that she'd fallen asleep, for although she'd been blessed with a strong stomach and rarely suffered from the seasickness that afflicted so many others, she loathed sea travel as much as any mortal could, feared it even more. Each time she set foot on a rolling, wet deck, she remembered the sinking of the White Ship. When it had struck a reef in Barfleur Harbor on a November night much like this one, more than three hundred souls had gone to God or the Devil, many of them highborn.

Their canvas tent was cramped and dank, the women huddled together for warmth. Gradually Petronilla could make out their hunched figures in the shadows. Few were sleeping and, as Petronilla sat up, one of her sister's ladies moaned and retched weakly into a bucket. A stench filled the air and Petronilla wrinkled her nose; the tent was already befouled with the acrid smell of sweat and fear and vomit, stronger even than the pungent salt–brine tang of the sea.

"Aunt Petra . . ." A slender form swaddled in blankets stirred at Petronilla's elbow and she patted the child's shoulder. "Go back to sleep, Tilda. When you awaken, we'll be in sight of Southampton." God Willing. Her niece burrowed deeper into her nest of covers and, with the resilience of the very young, soon slept again. Petronilla did not understand what had possessed her sister to allow the girl to accompany them. Granted, Tilda would be departing in the coming year for her new life in Germany as the bride of Henry the Lion, Duke of Saxony and Bavaria, and she'd pleaded poignantly with Eleanor that they not be apart till then. Petronilla still thought the girl's presence was a mistake. But her sister had ignored her arguments, and Petronilla knew from past experience that when Eleanor got the bit between her teeth, the only thing to do was to get out of the way.

A martyr on the cross of sisterly rivalry, Petronilla sighed and made herself as comfortable as she could on her pallet. Sleep would not come back, though. She was preternaturally aware of every night noise: the relentless creaking and groaning of the ship as it sank down into a trough, then fought its way to the crest of the next wave, the rhythmic slapping sound of waves against the hull, the flapping of the sail as the wind picked up, Tilda's soft snoring, an occasional moan from one or another of the seasick women, muffled curses from unseen sailors. When she could endure the tossing and turning no longer, Petronilla slid away from Tilda and rose to her feet.

As she ducked under the tent flap, the ship pitched suddenly and she staggered, would have fallen if not for the boatswain, who steadied her with a helpful hand on her elbow. The smile that accompanied his chivalry was too familiar for Petronilla's liking. He backed away when she scowled, and as she lurched across the deck, she thought she heard him chuckle. Glaring over her shoulder, she almost stumbled into the tiller, but the helmsman had observed the by-play with the boatswain and he left her to fend for herself. Keeping her balance with difficulty, she caught the gunwale for support, damning all ships and sailors to eternal hellfire.

Filling her lungs with the icy Channel air, Petronilla waited until she'd gotten her equilibrium back and then started cautiously along the deck in search of her sister. She found Eleanor standing alone near the bow. She did not turn her head as Petronilla approached, and they stood in silence for a time while Petronilla tried to think of some way to narrow the distance between them.

"That bobbing light to starboard . . . is that our other ship?" No sooner were the words out of her mouth than she winced at the fatuous nature of her query; of course that was their ship! But conversation with Eleanor these days was like venturing into perilous terrain; she seemed to make one misstep after another. "You ought not to tarry out on the deck like this, Eleanor. This cold is not good for either you or the babe."

The corner of Eleanor's mouth tightened noticeably, but she made no other response, keeping her eyes upon the surging black barrier of water that stretched toward the horizon. Conceding defeat, Petronilla retreated into a brooding silence. When she'd told Eleanor of the rumors she'd heard—the salacious, gleeful gossip about Henry and Rosamund Clifford—it had never occurred to her that her sister would act so impulsively, so unpredictably, so recklessly. But Eleanor had the right to know that her husband was lusting after Clifford's daughter. She needed to know that he'd even dared to bring Rosamund to Woodstock's royal manor. Surely she'd want to know that she was in danger of becoming a laughingstock? Watching as her sister gazed toward the night-cloaked alien shores of England, Petronilla sought to convince herself that it would all work out for the best. She'd begun to shiver, though, and it was not entirely due to the stinging winter wind.

AFTER A NIGHT in the castle at Southampton, Eleanor's party rode north to Winchester, and then on to Newbury. Theirs was a sedate, excruciatingly slow pace that soon depleted Eleanor's small store of patience, but her midwife, her sister, and even her own common sense all counseled traveling without haste. It was four days, therefore, before they finally reached Oxford.

IT SNOWED during the night, but the next day dawned clear and cold, and by midmorning, Eleanor was on the road again. Five miles lay between Oxford and Woodstock, just five miles, but it turned into one of the longest journeys of Eleanor's life. The swaying horse litter unsettled her stomach and the glare of sun on snow soon gave her a throbbing headache. Not for the first time in the past fortnight, she wondered if she'd gone stark raving mad. Why had she listened to Petra's foolish gossip? Of course Harry strayed from time to time; he was no man to live like a monk. He probably did bed Clifford's daughter, as rumor had it. After all, they'd been apart for months. But he would not flaunt a concubine before the world, and he would never have taken the wench to Woodstock, one of their favorite manors. So what was she doing on this rutted, snow-glazed road in the middle of nowhere? Why had she felt such an over-powering need to see for herself that the gossipmongers lied?

The gates of Woodstock were shut, but after a shouted command from one of Eleanor's household knights, they were hastily flung open. As the party passed into the bailey, Eleanor caught a glimpse of astonished faces avidly gawking down at her from the manor walls. She sank back against the cushions, not moving until her sister dismounted and leaned anxiously into the litter.

"Eleanor? Are you ailing? All this jolting around has not brought on your birth pangs, has it?"

"No." Eleanor held out her hand, allowing Petronilla to assist her from the litter. Lifting her chin and squaring her shoulders, she turned then toward the great hall, running the gauntlet of stares and whispers with the aloof inscrutability she'd had a lifetime to perfect. From the cor-ner of her eye, she saw the steward hurrying toward her and she released her sister's arm, moved to meet him.

She'd been coming to Woodstock for eleven years now, and Mas-ter Raymond had always been there to greet her, a tall, lanky, slightly stooped figure who put her in mind of a sober, very dignified crane. For once, his aplomb had deserted him; his face was flushed with un-even color, his mouth slack at the corners, downturned in dismay. "Madame . . . ," he stammered, dropping to one knee in the snow, "Madame . . . I . . . I . . ."

Eleanor had traveled over a hundred miles in the dead of winter, only to find there was no need to pose a single question; the answer was writ plainly in the horror on the steward's face. Master Raymond's consternation was merely confirmation, though, of what she already knew, had perhaps always known, even before she'd seen those smirking and gaping guards.

Eleanor kept her voice low, pitched for the steward's ears alone. "Where does she sleep, Master Raymond?"

He made no pretense of misunderstanding. "Oh, no, Madame! Not in your chambers, never!" Hoping fervently that she'd heard nothing of the king's plans to build a manor nearby at Everswell for Rosamund Clif-ford's private use, he hastily averted his eyes, lest she read in them the one emotion she'd never forgive—pity.

He wasn't fast enough, though, and Eleanor drew a breath as sharp as any blade. "Where is she now, Master Raymond?"

"I saw her walking toward the springs nigh on an hour ago. Shall I . . . shall I have her fetched for you, Madame?"

"No," Eleanor said tersely. "My men need to be fed and our horses cooled down. See to it, Master Raymond." When the captain of her household knights would have followed, she halted him with an abrupt gesture. She did not object, though, as her sister fell in step beside her, for it would have been foolhardy to trek alone to the springs when she was less than two months from her confinement. As it was, the walk was more taxing than she'd expected. She was soon panting, leaning reluctantly upon Petronilla's supportive arm, her skirts dragging through the snow as she silently cursed the unwieldy, weak vessel her body had become, little more than a walking womb, heavy with this burdensome pregnancy that had seemed unblest from the very beginning.

Petronilla for once was exercising discretion and they walked without speaking. The snow crunched underfoot and there came clearly to them the cawing of crows perched in trees barren of leaves, the barking of an unseen dog, and then the sound of a woman's laughter.

Eleanor saw the dog first, a wolflike, sturdy creature with a jaunty, curling tail. An uncommon breed, but one she recognized as a Norwegian dyrehund. A few years ago her husband had imported some from Oslo, nostalgic for the dyrehunds bred by his uncle Ranulf. She stopped abruptly, hearing again Henry's fond boasting about the wondrous Wolf, his cherished boyhood pet, and there was no surprise whatsoever when a female voice now echoed that very name.

"Wolf!" Still laughing, a young woman came into view. She was well dusted with snow and her veil had slipped, revealing lustrous blond braids. She had high color in her cheeks, skin as perfect as that newfallen snow, and she was young enough to take the sunlight full on, with no need for the kindness of candlelight. At the sight of Eleanor and Petronilla, she stopped in surprise, and then came toward them, smiling as she brushed at her mantle. "Wolf is friendly," she assured the women, "too much so. He just coaxed me into a romp in the snow and knocked me right off my feet!" Still seeking to tidy herself up, she shook her head ruefully. "I know I'm too old for such antics, but come the first snowfall of the winter, I find myself playing out in it like a little lass."

"How old are you?" Eleanor hardly recognized her own voice, toneless and detached, utterly without inflection.

Rosamund Clifford seemed startled by the question, but she answered readily enough, saying that she was nineteen. Younger even than Marie, Eleanor's eldest daughter by the French king.

"My lady?" A second woman was approaching, coming from the direction of the springs. She had a pleasing face, plump and good-humored, flushed now from her exertion and the cold. "Did you find that silly beast? Most likely he took off after a rabbit . . ." Her cheerful monologue trailed off as she realized they were no longer alone in the deer park. Her smile was warily polite, far more guarded than the girl's, and it was easy enough for Eleanor to guess her role: Rosamund Clifford's watchdog.

These intruders were very well dressed and Meliora dropped a quick curtsy in deference to their obvious rank. But as she straightened up, she saw Eleanor clearly for the first time. The color drained from her face, leaving her sallow and shaken. She fell to her knees in the snow, saying in a strangled voice, "My lady queen!"

Rosamund's head swiveled toward Meliora, then back to Eleanor. Hers was an easy face to read; Eleanor saw her puzzlement give way to realization and then, horror. She, too, dropped to her knees, staring up at Eleanor in mute despair, for she knew that there was nothing she could say in her own defense.

Eleanor was aware, then, of an overpowering exhaustion, unlike any fatigue she'd ever experienced. She was suddenly so weary in body and soul that she could almost believe she might sicken and die of it. There was a hollow sensation in her chest and a lump in her throat, a bitter taste in her mouth. Her gaze flickered over the girl kneeling in the snow and she could no longer remember why it had once seemed so important to seek Rosamund Clifford out, to learn the truth.

When she turned and walked away, she took them all off balance. Rosamund and Meliora stared after her in disbelief and Petronilla, no less dumbfounded, scurried to catch up to her sister.

Meliora heaved herself to her feet, but Rosamund stayed on her knees. "God in Heaven . . ." The face she raised to Meliora was streaking with tears. "She is great with child, did you see? I felt so shamed, so foul. . . . But I did not know, Meliora, truly I did not!"

"Know what, lass?"

Rosamund stifled a sob. "I did not know that she loves him. But you saw it too, did you not? That she does love him?" She gave Meliora a beseeching look, and the older woman understood what she was really asking—for reassurance that Meliora could not offer. Her silence was an answer in itself, and after a few moments, Rosamund rose, began to brush the snow from her skirt. Wiping her cheeks with the back of her hand, she managed a wan smile. "Do I look presentable enough for an audience with royalty?"

"I hope to God you do not mean what I think you do!"

"What would you have me do, Meliora? I have to face her sooner or later. And if she wants to shame me before every living soul at Woodstock . . ." Rosamund's voice faltered, and then she said, "Well, she . . . she has that right."

"Child, she is more than a jealous wife. She is a queen twice over, Duchess of Aquitaine in her own name, and you have given her no reason to feel kindly toward you. Trust me, you do not want to face her while the memory of the king's betrayal is still so raw. Better that we seek shelter in the nunnery at Godstow and send urgent word to the king—"

"No!" Rosamund shook her head so vehemently that her veil lost the last of its pins and fluttered to the ground at her feet. "I cannot do that, Meliora. I cannot burden the king with this—"

"Mary, Mother of God! You have to tell the king, and not just for your own protection. This woman is not a shunned wife to be put aside at a whim, nor is she one to suffer in silence. You truly think she will not confront the king? Better he be forewarned by you than ambushed by her!"

Rosamund opened her mouth to protest, closed it again as the logic of Meliora's argument prevailed. "You are right," she said softly. "He must know. But I will not take refuge with the nuns at Godstow. I owe the queen more than that. I owe Harry more than that."

Meliora blinked, for that was the first time she'd heard Rosamund call the king by his Christian name. "I do not understand you, child, and for certes, you do not understand Eleanor of Aquitaine!"

"I understand that she is carrying his child, that she has faced the dangers of the birthing chamber again and again to bear sons for him. And she is not young, Meliora, not any more. All my life, I've heard about her great beauty, but I saw none of it today. I saw a woman haggard and careworn, a woman grievously hurt by what I've done. I cannot change a single yesterday, cannot take back even one of those nights I spent in Harry's bed. Nor can I make amends by vowing to sin no more. I am not strong enough to turn him away. I love him," she said simply, as if that was a soul-bearing revelation, and Meliora groaned in frustrated futility, for by now she'd learned that Rosamund's deceptively docile demeanor hid a stubborn streak wider than the Thames itself.

"God help us both," she said with a grimace, and then cried out in pretended pain as she faked a stumble. Rosamund would not leave her and by feigning reluctance to put weight upon the injured ankle, she bought them both some time. Not that it would be enough. She feared that a life-time would not be enough.

When she could delay no longer, she reached for her walking stick and followed Rosamund back along the path toward the manor. A strange silence seemed to have enveloped Woodstock. The bailey was deserted; even the gate was unmanned. Rosamund came to an uncertain halt, her resolve beginning to waver. When Meliora suggested that they go to her chamber and await the queen's summons, she agreed hastily enough to re-veal her fear. But they'd taken only a few steps before they saw Master Raymond striding toward them.

Summoning up the shreds of her courage, Rosamund moved to meet him. "I . . . I await the queen's pleasure," she said, as steadily as she could.

He'd always treated her with impeccable courtesy, but she'd sensed that he did not approve of her liaison with the king. A shadow of that un-spoken disapproval showed now upon his face, confirming her suspicion that the steward was Queen Eleanor's man. "The queen," he said, "is gone."

They stared at him, so obviously stunned that he felt the need to say again, more emphatically this time, "The queen and her sister and her men . . . they are all gone."

ELEANOR PAUSED in the great hall to speak to her daughter, and Petronilla seized the opportunity to search for her sister's midwife. Bertrade was not an easy woman to miss, a statuesque, handsome widow with bold black eyes, the life-loving zest of the Gascons, and little pa-tience with fools; not surprisingly, she and Eleanor had established an im-mediate rapport and she had assisted in the births of the last two of Eleanor's children. It did not take long for Petronilla to learn that Bertrade was not in the hall, but when she turned back toward her sister, she dis-covered that Eleanor had gone, too.

With a servant in tow, she hastened across the bailey toward the queen's chambers. As she expected, she found Eleanor in the bedchamber, slumped down on a coffer as if she had not been able to muster the en-ergy to reach the bed. One glance at her sister's ashen face and she ordered the servant to find Dame Bertrade and fetch wine and food. Snatching up a laver of washing water, she knelt by Eleanor's side and began to blot the perspiration from her sister's brow.

"You look ghastly," she scolded. "When will you start paying heed to what I say? It was lunacy to return to Oxford, and well you know it, Eleanor. You've not eaten a morsel since this morn, and God's truth, but your complexion is the color of unripe cheese. It is a miracle for certes if you have not brought on early labor."

To her annoyance, Eleanor did not appear to be listening. But before she could resume her lecture, the door opened with a bang and Dame Bertrade swept in. "Madame, is there any bleeding? Have the pains begun?"

Eleanor shook her head, let Bertrade and Petronilla get her to her feet. Between them, they helped her to the bed, where she lay back onto the pillows, closing her eyes. Petronilla was terrified by her bloodless pallor, the damp, clammy feel of her skin. She knew women in childbirth could suffer both sweating and shivering fits, felt a great fear that Eleanor was wrong and her travail begun. It was much too soon, both for her and the babe. What if she delivered a stillborn child? What if she died? Childbed was all too often a woman's deathbed, too. Her gaze blurred with sudden tears and she reached out, grasping the hand of this frail stranger in her sister's bed.

"Eleanor, look what you've done to yourself! Why did you not listen to me and remain at Woodstock as I urged?"

Eleanor's lashes lifted. Her face was bone-white, the pupils of her eyes so dilated that they seemed black. "I would rather," she spat, "have given birth by the side of the road!"

Eleanor had chosen the royal manor just north of Oxford's walls over the castle within the city for her lying-in. Her decision had been dictated by convenience; the manor was more comfortable than the admittedly old-fashioned furnishings of the castle. But she was not long in regretting it, for the manor was haunted by the ghosts of happier times. It was here that nine years ago she'd given birth to her son Richard, while her husband kept anxious vigil within the castle.

As the countess of Chester dismounted, Petronilla darted out of the door of the great hall. "My lady countess, your visit pleases us greatly." The formalities observed, she embraced Maud, brushing her cheek with a perfunctory kiss as she hissed in the other woman's ear, "You must have come by way of Scotland, judging by how long you took!"

Maud looked at her in astonishment. So swiftly had she responded to the summons that she had celebrated Christmas on the road—no small sacrifice, in her opinion. She did not take Petronilla seriously enough to be genuinely vexed with her, though, and she contented herself with saying mildly, "I would have been here much sooner if only I'd known how to fly."

Petronilla did not look amused. The truth was that neither woman liked the other one very much, and Maud knew Eleanor's sister must be despairing indeed to turn to her for help. Sending her ladies and her escort into the hall, she stopped Petronilla when she would have followed. "We'll have no privacy inside. Tell me now why you are so fearful for the queen."

"Eleanor is forty-four years of age and this will be her tenth time in the birthing chamber," Petronilla said waspishly. "I should think that would be reason enough!"

"Yes, I would agree . . . if not for the fact that Woodstock is but five miles away."

Petronilla had hoped to ease into the subject. "God Above, is there anyone left in England who does not know about that Clifford slut? How did you hear?"

Maud gave a half-shrug. "There has been talk for some months."

"If you knew, why did you not tell Eleanor?"

Maud stared at her. "You were the one who told Eleanor? Christ on the Cross, Petra!"

Petronilla blushed. "She had a right to know. People had begun to snicker behind her back, and Eleanor could never abide that."

"And did it never occur to you that the timing might leave something to be desired?"

Petronilla's flush deepened. "I find your sarcasm offensive. I did not expect her to go running off to England!"

Maud bit her lip, figuratively and literally. What good did this serve? What was done was done. "Be that as it may, she did. I take it that she went to Woodstock and confronted the girl?"

Petronilla nodded. "Although I am not sure if confrontation is the right term for it. She said not a word to the little bitch, Maud, not a word! And since then, she has refused to talk about it at all." Her shoulders slumped, the anger draining away. "I have never seen Eleanor like this, never. When she is wroth, the whole world knows it. Mayhap it is because of the babe . . . I only know that I would feel much more at ease if she were screaming and ranting and vowing to geld Harry with a dull spoon. This frozen silence of hers . . . it frightens me."

It troubled Maud, too. But before she could respond, a door slammed and a young girl came flying down the steps. "Cousin Maud, I am so very glad to see you!"

"And can this be Tilda? I vow, child, you get prettier every time I see you." Enfolding the girl in an affectionate embrace, Maud saw Petronilla signaling frantically that nothing should be said in front of Tilda, and she wondered, not for the first time, how Eleanor could have been cursed with a sister so lacking in common sense. She was genuinely pleased to see the child, for she'd stood godmother to Tilda. Keeping her arm around Tilda's slender shoulders, she headed for the warmth of the great hall, leaving Petronilla to follow or not, as she chose.

THE HEARTH had burned low, providing little heat or light. Maud wasted no time summoning a servant, for it was faster to do it herself. Reaching for the fire tongs, she quickly rekindled the flames.

Eleanor watched with an oblique smile that was more ironic than amused, knowing full well that Maud would soon be prodding the embers of her marriage for signs of life, too. "So what now? How do you intend to exorcise my demons?"

Maud sighed. "Could you at least let me thaw out ere you throw down the gauntlet?"

"You'll forgive me if my manners are ragged around the edges, Maud." Adding a laconic, " Pregnancy will do that to a woman."

"So will an unfaithful husband." Eleanor's head jerked around, her eyes suddenly as green and glittering as any cat's, but Maud staved off her rebuke with an upraised hand. "I ask you to hear me out, for the love I bear you as my queen, my cousin by marriage, and my friend," she said quietly. "As you clearly guessed, I am here in answer to Petra's summons. But I would have come on my own, ready to staunch the bleeding or to . . ." She paused very deliberately. ". . . plot regicide."

Eleanor said nothing, but the corner of her mouth twitched, almost imperceptibly, and Maud took that as a good sign. "I know about Harry's dalliance with the Clifford girl. If you want to talk about it, whatever you say will go no farther than this chamber. If you do not want to talk, I'll say no more on it."

"I do not."

Maud inclined her head. "As you wish."

Eleanor did not trouble to mask her skepticism. "Since when are you so biddable?"

"I have more than my share of failings—or so I've been told," Maud said dryly. "But for all of my indiscretions, I am never indiscreet." Thinking it a pity that the same could not be said for Petronilla.

"Petra meant well," Eleanor said, and Maud acknowledged her mind-reading with a wry smile. For a time there was no sound in the chamber but the hissing and crackling of the fire. Maud studied the other woman covertly through her lashes, not liking what she found. Eleanor's skin was a waxen white, almost transparent, a pulse throbbing erratically at her temple, another at her throat, deeply etched evidence of exhaustion in the taut set of her mouth, in the furrows on her brow, and most conspicuously in the lurking shadows under her eyes, the bruises of the sleep-starved. *Ah, Harry, what have you done?*

She let Eleanor control the conversation and they talked of the latest rumors to spill out of the queen's restive homeland: that the Counts of Angoulême and La Marche were supposedly conspiring to disavow Henry and offer their allegiance to the French king. Maud was not surprised when Eleanor complained caustically about the difficulties she'd encountered as regent during Henry's extended stay in England that past year. She did not doubt that Eleanor was genuinely concerned about the spreading discontent in her domains, but her political grievances were stoked now by private pain, and Maud could think of few fuels more combustible than a sense of humiliation and betrayal.

Eleanor was fuming about a petition recently circulated at the papal court by some of the more disaffected Poitevin barons. They'd actually dared to claim that their duchess's marriage to the Angevin interloper was invalid because she and Henry were distant cousins, reminding His Holiness that these were the very grounds for dissolving her union with the French king. There was no chance that the Pope would heed their appeal, but Eleanor was infuriated by their effrontery, by the very suggestion that she was subservient to Henry's will. Maud listened and murmured sympathetic agreement where appropriate, all the while wishing that the wronged wife could speak as candidly as the aggrieved queen.

It was then that they were interrupted by Eleanor's daughter. Tilda was apologetic yet insistent, entreating her mother to help her write to her grandmother, the Empress Maude. She was being tutored in German, she explained to Maud, for that was the tongue of her husband-to-be, and it had occurred to her that the Empress might be pleased to receive a letter in the language of her long-gone youth. Maud understood what the girl was really seeking—some rare time alone with her mother—and excused herself.

This must have been a wretched Christmas for poor little Tilda. The child was probably anxious about her new life looming in Germany, and at ten, she was old enough to sense her mother's profound unhappiness, old enough, too, to understand some of the gossip she'd inevitably overheard. Maud gave her a quick hug as she headed for the door, hoping that Tilda would find more happiness at the German court than her grandmother the empress had.

As soon as she stepped out into the stairwell, she was pounced upon by Petronilla. "At last! Well? Did Eleanor talk to you about Harry and his whore?"

"No, she did not."

"Hellfire and all its furies! I was so sure she'd confide in you . . ." Giving Maud a look of unspoken yet unmistakable reproach, Petronilla slipped her arm through the other woman's. "Let's hope you have better luck later. Now we need to find a quiet place where you can tell me exactly what you said to her."

"Are you sure you do not want to hide under Eleanor's bed the next time we talk?"

Petronilla was too worried to feel resentment. "I know you think I'm meddling, but it tears at my soul to see Eleanor so stricken and to be unable to ease her heart. First she put her own life and the babe's at risk with that foolhardy journey to Woodstock, and now she shuts me out, unwilling to share her hurt. Thank God Almighty that Harry did not follow her to England! In her present state of mind, who knows what she might have said to him. At least they'll have this time apart so her rage can cool."

Maud stopped so abruptly on the stairs that she nearly lost her balance. Jesus wept, was the woman serious? Nothing could be worse for the marriage than time apart. How could Petra be so blind? But she had no chance to respond, for a door banged above them and Tilda's frightened cry froze both women in their tracks.

"Aunt Petra, hurry!"

Tilda was hovering in the doorway, staring in horror at the wet stain spreading rapidly across her mother's skirt. One glance was enough for Maud. Giving the girl a gentle push, she said with quiet, compelling urgency, "You need not fear, lass. Her waters have broken, that's all. You'd best fetch the midwife straightaway." Tilda took off and Maud moved swiftly into the chamber, pausing only long enough to close the door. Petronilla was already kneeling at her sister's side.

"Jesú, Eleanor! Why did you not tell us that your pains had begun?"

Eleanor grimaced, her eyes meeting Maud's over Petronilla's bowed head. "They had not," she said, sounding edgy and out of breath. "The waters have broken too soon."

ALTHOUGH NO ONE acknowledged it, fear was a palpable presence in the birthing chamber. Eleanor's labor had begun the evening after the premature rupture of her membranes. A day later, the contractions were coming sharp and short, agonizing but ineffective, for she should have been almost fully dilated by now and she was not.

Beset by bouts of nausea, Eleanor could not swallow the honey and wine she needed to keep her strength up; even water sometimes made her gag. By turns, she shivered violently and then broke out in a cold sweat. They felt the sharp edge of her tongue as the hours dragged by, enduring her outbursts with a stoicism that could not completely camouflage their misgivings. They were all veterans of the birthing chamber, familiar with the instinctive panic that could overwhelm a woman who knew she must either deliver her babe or die.

It was, Maud thought grimly, the ultimate trap, and a woman in hard labor did not even have the option that a snared animal did, of chewing off its own foot to make a desperate escape. The Church's position was unambiguous and immutable: if necessary, the mother must be sacrificed to spare the child. Fortunately for women, they were attended in the birthing chamber by midwives, not priests, and Maud had never known one who would not act first to save the mother.

Eleanor was vomiting again, tended by her sister with so much tenderness that Maud could almost forgive her. For one so given to posturing and frivolity, Petronilla was surprisingly capable in a crisis, showing flashes of tempered steel beneath the superficial surface gloss. Maud reminded herself that the self-indulgent Petra had endured more than her share of sorrows—the loss of an adored father, a beloved husband, and an only son, stricken with that most feared of all mortal ailments, leprosy. She was not about to lose a sister, too, not as long as she had breath in her body, and she was winning Maud's grudging admiration, both for her demeanor and her gritty determination to banish the shadow of death from the birthing chamber.

Bertrade had taken a short break, was just emerging from the corner privy chamber. Her face was blank, for she was too experienced to reveal her own anxieties or dread. Her fatigue she could not hide, however, and she seemed to have aged years in these post-Christmas hours. Untidy black hair defied its pins, revealing a smattering of grey that Maud had never noticed before, and there was such a prominent slump to her shoulders that her body was conveying her distress more eloquently than words could have done. Eleanor was caught up in another contraction, and Maud took advantage of the moment to draw Bertrade aside.

"Why is the mouth of her womb not open by now?" she asked quietly, the low, even pitch of her voice belied by the fingers digging into Bertrade's arm. "She has always delivered her babies more easily than this."

"When a woman gives birth again and again, her womb can become weak and feeble. I've also seen this happen when the waters break too soon, but I do not know why."

Maud had learned that midwives, like doctors, were usually loath to admit their lack of knowledge, and she would have given Bertrade credit for her candor if it were not Eleanor in travail. "In all the birthings I've witnessed, the waters were either clear or light reddish in color. Eleanor's were dark, a murky greenish brown. What does that mean?"

Bertrade glanced across the chamber at the woman writhing on the birthing stool, then dropped her voice so her words barely reached Maud's ear. "I am not sure, my lady. I've seen it but rarely. It can mean that the babe will be stillborn."

Maud was expecting as much. "If she cannot deliver the child, what will you do?"

Bertrade could not repress a superstitious shiver. Why tempt fate? But she was not about to rebuke the Countess of Chester, the king's cousin, and she said reluctantly, "There are herbs I can give her, dittany and hyssop and others. Or I can make a pessary with bull's gall, iris juice, and oil, and that will usually expel a dead child. God Willing, it will not come to that."

"God Willing," Maud echoed dutifully, keeping to herself her blasphemous thought that the Almighty too often seemed deaf to prayers coming from the birthing chamber. Just then Eleanor cried out, an involuntary, choked sob that sounded as if it were torn from her throat. Maud had attended three of Eleanor's birthings and never had she heard her scream like that. The Latin words came unbidden to her lips, so soft and slurred that only Bertrade heard.

"*O infans, siue viuus, aut mortuus, exi foras, quia Christus te vocat ad lucem.*"

The midwife looked at her intently. "What does that mean, Lady Maud?"

Maud swallowed with difficulty. "It is a prayer for a child whose birthing goes wrong. 'O infant, whether living or dead, come forth because Christ calls you to the light.'"

Bertrade nodded slowly. "Amen," she said succinctly, and moved in a swirl of skirts back to Eleanor's side.

E LEANOR HAD BEEN CLUTCHING an eagle-stone amulet, most valued of all the talismans said to succor women in childbed. When her grip loosened, it slipped through her fingers onto the floor. With a dismayed gasp, Petronilla dropped to her knees and scrabbled about in the matted, sodden rushes until she'd recovered it. Pressing it back into her sister's palm, she clasped Eleanor's hand around the stone and hissed in her ear, "You must not die. You must hold on, you hear me? You cannot let that little whore of Harry's win!"

Eleanor's eyes were like sunken caverns, so tightly was the skin stretched across her cheekbones. To Petronilla's horror, that familiar face had begun to resemble an alabaster death mask, and she warned hoarsely, "If you die, I swear I'll kill you!"

The other women looked at her as if they feared her wits were wandering. But that was a childhood joke between them, and Eleanor's cracked, bleeding lips twitched in acknowledgment of it. "I am not going to die, Petra . . . not today."

Petronilla's eyes blurred. "You promise?"

Eleanor nodded wordlessly, saving her strength for all that mattered now—survival. Bertrade was patting her face with a wet cloth, murmuring encouragements and reassurances that it would not be much longer and she must not lose heart. Eleanor knew that most childbed deaths occurred when the woman gave up, for there came a time when dying was easier than any of the alternatives. But she would not be one of them. She would rid her body of this alien intruder, this intimate enemy begotten by betrayal. She would not die so Harry's child might live. And that the child was also hers seemed of small matter when measured against the desolation that had claimed every corner of her soul.

He was born as midnight drew nigh, bruised and blue, a small, feeble shadow of the brothers who'd come before him. They had squalled lustily, kicking and squirming as they were cleansed of their mother's blood and mucus. He gave only a muted, querulous cry, as if to complain at his unceremonious, discordant entry into their world. The birth of a son was usually a cause for celebration. But this one was an afterthought, the fourth son, needed neither as heir nor spare.

After they'd assured themselves that he was whole and breathing, the women turned their attention to Eleanor, for she still had to expel the afterbirth, and that was often the most dangerous time of all. Bertrade had prepared a yarrow poultice and mixed a flagon of wine with boiled artemisia should Eleanor begin to hemorrhage; she also put aside a lancet and basin, in case the queen's flooding must be stopped by bleeding her. She felt blessed, indeed, when none of these remedies were needed. After swallowing salted water, Eleanor groaned and twisted upon the birthing stool and the placenta splattered into Bertrade's waiting hands. Hastily putting it aside for burial later lest it attract demons, the midwife rubbed her temples, leaving streaks of blood midst the sweat. "Well done, Madame," she said proudly. "Well done!"

The baby balked at being bathed and then swaddled, but he was in practiced hands and was soon turned over to Rohese, the waiting wet-nurse. She, too, was experienced and had no difficulty in getting him to suckle. "How black his hair is," she marveled. "Blacker than sin itself." She had nursed several of Eleanor's infants and could not help commenting upon the dramatic contrast between the other babies, sun-kissed and robust and golden, and this undersized, fretful, dark imp. None of the women responded to her chatter and she lapsed into a subdued silence, sensing tensions in the chamber that had naught to do with a difficult birth.

By the time Eleanor's chaplain was allowed entry into this female sanctorum, she had been bathed and put to bed, although the women were hovering nearby to make sure she did not sleep yet, for all knew the danger that posed to new mothers. She accepted the priest's congratulations with exhausted indifference, rousing herself to meet the minimum demands of courtesy and protocol, when all she wanted was to spiral down into a deep, dreamless sleep.

At the priest's urging, the wet-nurse produced the infant for his inspection. "A fine lad," he beamed. "If you wish, I will write to the king this very night. How pleased he will be to hear he has another son. Madame . . . the chapel is ready for the baptism. What name have you chosen for the babe?"

Eleanor did not seem to have heard his query and he cleared his throat, asked again. She regarded him in silence, and he fidgeted under the power of those slanting hazel eyes, bloodshot and swollen and utterly opaque.

It was Maud who came to his rescue. Taking the child from Rohese, she said briskly, "Since today is the saint's day of John the Evangelist, let's name him John."

The priest looked relieved to have this settled. "Does that meet with your approval, Madame?"

Eleanor nodded and Maud handed the baby back to the wet-nurse. It occurred to Rohese then that the queen had yet to ask for the infant, and she moved, smiling, toward the bed. "Would you like to hold him, Madame?"

Eleanor turned her head away without answering.

CHAPTER TWENTY-THREE

August 1167
Nôtre-Dame-du-Pré
Rouen, Normandy

AUDE TURNED AT THE SOUND of the opening door. The woman who entered was her last link to the young bride she'd once been, consort and wife to Heinrich V, Holy Roman Emperor and King of the Germans. Heinrich had been dead for more than four decades, and in just a month's time, it would be sixteen years since her unlamented second husband, Geoffrey of Anjou, had been called to account for his sins. She'd lost a crown and buried two of her three sons, and through it all, Minna had been with her, steadfast and unswerving in her devotion, loyal even by Maude's stringent standards. Age had gnarled Minna's limbs and stolen away her strength; she walked with a limp, panted for breath at the least exertion, and had asked Maude to send her heart back to Germany for burial. Maude had promised that it would be done, and quietly made the necessary arrangements, for she knew—if Minna did not—that death would find her first.

Minna was balancing a platter in an unsteady grip, scorning servants for the joy of waiting upon Maude's son herself. Maude was amused to see it heaped with sugared wafers, as if England's king was still a boy hungering after sweets. If her love for Henry was like a sword, gleaming and sharp and stark, Minna's love was as expansive and comforting as the softest of goose-down pillows. Putting her finger to her lips, she signaled for quiet.

Minna carefully set her burden upon the table, smiling fondly at the man reclining in the window seat. Henry looked younger in sleep, piercing hawk's gaze veiled by golden lashes, mouth curling up at the corners in a dream-smile. He was usually too fair to tan. But he'd passed the entire spring and summer in the saddle, and his face was evenly sun-browned, aside from an incongruous pale strip that had been shadowed by his helmet's nasal guard.

"How bone-weary he looks," Minna said softly. "Now that he has made a truce with the French king, you must insist that he stay in Rouen for at least a fortnight and take his ease, Madame."

"To get him to rest, I'd have to slip a sleeping potion into his wine."

Minna chuckled. "Even as a little lad, he was a veritable whirlwind of motion, never sitting still unless he was tied to the chair."

"I remember your threatening to do that more than once," Henry said, without opening his eyes, and Minna matched his grin with one of her own, protesting that she'd done no such thing. Maude watched in bemusement, for she'd never bantered with her sons, never fully understood Henry's humor, considering it to be—like his infamous Angevin temper—one of his father's more dubious bequests. To Maude, life was far too serious to be laughed at.

Minna had begun talking about Henry's attack in July upon the castle and town of Chaumont, where the French king had stored his arsenal. Maude shared Minna's pride in Henry's feat, for it had been a remarkable achievement. He had lured the castle garrison out to meet his frontal assault while he sent a band of Welsh mercenaries to enter the town through a channel of the River Troesne. The resulting victory had been a dramatic triumph for Henry and a great humiliation for the French king. But Maude had contented herself with a "Well done," whereas Minna was so lavish in her praise that she made Henry sound like the most brilliant battle commander since the days of Julius Caesar. After listening impatiently for several moments, Maude reclaimed control of the conversation by asking Henry if all had gone as planned at Andeley.

"Indeed it did," Henry said gravely, although his eyes were agleam with silent laughter, for he understood his mother far better than she understood him. Andeley had been evacuated of all its citizens, the town abandoned to the approaching French army. The scheme had been hatched by the Count of Flanders and Maude, who'd persuaded Henry that the French king needed a sop for the debacle at Chaumont. Henry had been skeptical, for he'd never been overly concerned himself with saving face and could not imagine gaining satisfaction from such an empty victory. But the count and Maude had accurately assessed the depths of French mortification, and once Andeley had been sacked by his army, Louis and his advisers offered a truce. Henry had been quite willing to accept, for he had rebellious barons still to be subdued in Brittany and Aquitaine. And so the war had come to a mutually satisfactory if ironic end, with the French king applying the balm of Andeley to soothe his bloodied pride and Henry getting the time he needed to put out fires in other corners of his vast empire. As for the unhappy townspeople of Andeley, they had their lives and the dubious consolation that whenever elephants fought, it was invariably the mice underfoot who were trampled first.

"You read men well, Mother," Henry said now, giving her the compliment she craved while thinking that this was a skill she'd unfortunately learned late in life. Had she not misjudged the English temperament so abysmally, she'd not have been chased out of London by her own subjects. "My truce with Louis is supposed to endure until Easter next. It will be interesting to see if it lasts that long."

Maude nodded somberly. "Where are you off to next, Henry . . . Brittany?"

"I hope not," he said with feeling, for he considered the Breton realm to be a king's quagmire. Nothing was ever resolved, troubles merely deferred. It was more than ten years since Duke Conan had overthrown his mother's husband, Eudo, Viscount of Porhoët, sworn allegiance to Henry, and been recognized in turn as Brittany's duke. Conan had proved unable to control the volatile, strong-willed Bretons, though, and Henry had grown weary of having to put down their rebellions. He'd thought he'd solved the problems posed by Brittany last summer by deposing Conan and betrothing Conan's daughter to his young son Geoffrey. But the Breton lords had rallied around Conan's one-time rival, Eudo of Porhoët, amid reports of spreading mayhem and bloodshed.

"The Bretons are as hardheaded as the Welsh," Henry complained. "But after campaigning all year in Auvergne and the Vexin, I'd like a chance to catch my breath ere I have to head back to Brittany." He also had it in mind to bring Rosamund Clifford over for a clandestine visit, as only the Lord God Himself knew when he'd be able to return to England.

He glanced away, no longer meeting Maude's gaze, for he was determined to keep her in ignorance of his plans, knowing she'd disapprove. She'd occasionally displayed a disconcerting ability to discern when he'd sinned, and he could only attribute it to some uncanny maternal instinct, as she'd always scorned gossip. She was regarding him pensively now, dark eyes too probing for his comfort. He'd been shocked to find her so frail, to see how much ground she'd lost since his last visit. His brain knew that she'd reached the advanced age of sixty-five and her health was failing; his heart still saw her as the fearless woman who'd once escaped a castle siege by walking right through the enemy lines under cover of darkness and a swirling snowstorm.

He was right to be wary, for Maude did sense that he was keeping something from her. She suspected it concerned Eleanor, who remained in England months after giving birth to John, a land for which she'd never shown much fondness. "I finally heard from Ranulf," she said at last, watching closely for his reaction.

His eyes flickered, no more than that. But Minna took the hint for what it was, a signal that Maude wanted to discuss matters of family, and found a pretext to excuse herself. As the door closed behind her, Maude slumped in her chair, allowing Henry to position a cushion behind her back. "It was not much of a letter," she said, "notable mainly for all that it left unsaid. I suppose he wanted to reassure me that he was still amongst the living. Henry . . . you've had no word from him?"

"No."

She suppressed a sigh, for she grieved over this estrangement between the two people she loved best, but her attempts at mediation had been rebuffed by both men. They would have to find their way back to each other in God's Time, not hers. "When is Eleanor coming home?" she asked instead, and saw the wine in his cup splash as his hand jerked involuntarily.

"Soon, I expect," he hedged. "She had much to do, after all, to prepare for Tilda's marriage to Henry the Lion. We want to send our lass off with a wardrobe to bedazzle even the jaded courtiers at the German court."

Maude forbore to comment that Eleanor could as easily have arranged for Tilda's departure on this side of the Channel. That there was trouble in his marriage, she did not doubt. "You've been apart for many months, Henry. Do you not miss Eleanor?"

For a fleeting moment, he looked startled. "Of course I do!" And he did, for his absent wife was more than a sultry bedmate, a shrewd confidante. She was good company, too, and he missed their bawdy banter, her irreverent humor, the unspoken understanding that had been theirs since their first meeting in the great hall of Louis's Paris palace. She was as close as he hoped to come to a kindred spirit in this world, but unfortunately she was a kindred spirit with a just grievance. He ought to have been more careful, should never have brought Rosamund to Woodstock like that. How could Eleanor not take that amiss? Who knew her pride better than he? It would be no easy task to placate her, and he could not help feeling a certain relief that she'd chosen to extend her stay in England. At least she'd had time for her temper to cool and he'd had time to acknowledge he was in the wrong about Rosamund. He ought to have been more circumspect.

Maude reached over to take a sip from his wine cup. He'd once told her that Geoffrey had claimed the best marriages were based upon detached goodwill or benign indifference. That was one of the rare occasions when Maude found herself in utter agreement with her husband. Passion was dangerous in any relationship, above all in marriage, for it was utterly unpredictable. She could only hope that her son was not about to find that out.

AUGUST HAD BEEN HOT and dry that year and the gardens at Woodstock were wilting despite the best efforts of the manor gardeners. Rosamund Clifford and her guests were playing a game out on the green, and each time one of the women rolled her heavy stone bowl toward its target, it stirred up puffs of dust and left a rut in the parched, browned grass. Whenever Rosamund's sister Lucy got a strike, she laughed and clapped her hands, attracting admiring glances from the gardeners laboring nearby. While she had none of Rosamund's ethereal beauty, Lucy was a very pretty young woman, blessed with fashionable fair coloring and more than her share of feminine curves.

The eldest sister, Amice, was neither as amply endowed as Lucy nor as radiant as Rosamund, and Meliora wondered if this was why there seemed to be so little warmth between them. Growing up in Cornwall, Meliora had squabbled and bickered with her own sisters more often than not. But for all of their jealousies and childish rivalries, they were fiercely devoted to one another, bonded by much more than blood. She sensed no such loyalties amongst the Clifford sisters and could not help recalling

Henry's acerbic opinion of Rosamund's family. Rosamund, he'd once said caustically, must surely be a foundling. After a week at Woodstock with the Cliffords, Meliora found herself in hearty agreement with her king.

Rosamund's mother, Margaret, was seated in the shade of a nearby tree, sipping a cider drink and fanning herself languidly with a napkin. Upon completing her turn at bowls, Rosamund hastened over to Margaret's side. Meliora wasn't close enough to catch her words, but she was sure Rosamund was inquiring after her mother's comfort. She had been running herself ragged since their arrival, doing all she could to make their visit a pleasant one. And her reward, Meliora thought indignantly, was to be buffeted by their unending demands and worse, to be interrogated and prodded and pestered for the smallest scrap of gossip concerning her royal lover.

But Rosamund had shown a stubborn reticence whenever Henry's name was dragged into the conversation. She willingly drew upon the resources of Woodstock to indulge her family's whims. She listened attentively to the narration of their needs, promising to bring her brother Richard to the king's notice, to seek a boon for Amice's husband, Osbern Fitz Hugh, to pass on her father's complaints about his ongoing troubles with the Welsh, to ask the king to allow her kinsmen to hunt in the royal forest of Clee. Yet when they pressed her for details of her liaison with Henry, she became tongue-tied, evasive, or shyly uncomprehending. She had yet to reveal anything but the most banal aspects of her new life as the king's concubine. She had contributed nothing to the rampant rumors of an autumn confrontation with the queen at Woodstock. And she'd breathed not a word of her impending departure for Southampton, where she would take ship to join Henry in Normandy.

Margaret Clifford got to her feet, announcing that the gardens were too hot for her liking. Her daughters at once abandoned their game of bowls and clustered around her. Meliora doubted if the queen herself had people dancing such deferential attendance upon her as Rosamund's mother did. They were heading toward the great hall when a horseman rode in through the gateway. Meliora recognized him at once, for Henry used the same trusted courier for his messages to Rosamund; ever since Eleanor's surprise visit to Woodstock, he'd become a sincere, if belated, convert to the doctrine of discretion.

Catching Rosamund's eye, Meliora jerked her head toward the rider, and then feigned a semiswoon, moaning that the sun was making her sick. None of the Clifford women appeared unduly alarmed by her distress, but she commandeered their aid by the simple expedient of stumbling and grabbing Margaret's arm in a viselike grip. Wheezing and panting and thoroughly enjoying herself, she let her reluctant volunteers assist her across the bailey, giving Rosamund the opportunity to lag behind.

She continued the charade in the great hall, gasping weakly for water, going limp, and indulging her penchant for theatrics. The stratagem worked quite well; it was some time before anyone noticed that Rosamund was missing. At Margaret's insistence, Lucy ventured out into the bailey in search of her sister, reporting a few moments later that she was nowhere in sight. Meliora gave a satisfied sigh and graciously accepted an offer of ale.

She was somewhat surprised, though, by Rosamund's failure to return to the hall. As time passed, she felt a nagging sense of unease. If Rosamund had not resumed her role as hostess and dutiful daughter, it could only mean that Henry's letter had conveyed bad news. Declaring that her sunsickness was much improved, she made an inconspicuous exit and went to find Rosamund.

Margaret had already sent a servant to Rosamund's bedchamber, to no avail, so Meliora did not bother retracing his steps. Shading her eyes from the noonday glare, she sought instead to reconstruct Rosamund's likely movements. She'd have wanted privacy to read her letter, so she'd not have lingered in the gardens. It was too hot for her to have walked down to the springs. After a moment to reflect, Meliora headed across the bailey toward the stables.

The barn was spilling over with shadows, the air still and pungent with the odors of sweat, dung, and horses. A plank had been laid across two overturned buckets and a meal set out on its rough-hewn surface— a chunk of cheese and half a loaf of bread—as if its owner had just been called away. A scrabbling in the straw and a pitiful squeak told Meliora that one of the stable cats had made a kill. Stallions nickered and snorted, and a restive dun gelding gnawed and slobbered on the corner of its manger. The country-bred Meliora made a mental note to mention to the grooms that her father had successfully treated this vice by removing the manger and feeding the horse on the floor. By now her eyes had adjusted to the gloom and as she moved forward, she glimpsed movement from the depths of an empty stall.

"Lady Rosamund?"

There was a long pause. "I'm here, Meliora." Rosamund's voice sounded as it always did, soft and slightly out of breath. But as she emerged from the stall, Meliora could see tear marks drying upon her cheeks. She clutched a sheet of crumpled parchment in one small fist; this one would not be joining the precious store of letters she kept secreted and locked in an ivory casket box under her bed.

"He is on his way into Brittany," she whispered. "He could delay no longer, for the Viscount of Léon has joined the rebellion against him."

"FIRST WASTE the land, deal after with the foe." That was a basic tenet of military strategy in God's Year 1167. The castellan of Morlaix Castle had accepted it as gospel, as did most of the men who were trained in the arts of war. But the king of the English cared little for conventional wisdom. Instead of burning crops and sacking villages, then settling into a lengthy siege of the castle by blockading all access roads and controlling the countryside, Henry Fitz Empress had once again rewritten the rules of combat, relying upon speed, surprise, and a sudden assault.

His army had appeared before the walls of Morlaix before his foes were even aware of their danger. No one knew that he'd penetrated this far into Brittany. The sleeping garrison had rolled out of their blankets before dawn to a waking nightmare, to find Henry's troops breaching the walls of the town, encountering little resistance from the startled citizenry.

The castellan had done the best he could, but his men were already spooked by Henry's abrupt, unnerving appearance in their midst, already convinced they could catch a whiff of sulphur in the air. All knew the House of Anjou could trace its descent to the Prince of Darkness himself. They knew, too, about the formidable strongholds that had fallen to Henry in the past, able to recite the names like a litany of doom. Chinon, taken from his own brother. Thouars, said to be invincible, captured in just three days. Chaumont-sur-Loire, Castillon-sur-Agen, even the great fortress at Fougères. How could Morlaix hope to hold out against one of the Devil's own?

Henry's army wasted no time in storming the castle itself, seizing the momentum as he had the town. An iron-tipped bore was soon positioned at a sharp angle of the bailey wall, the men shielded behind a wooden penthouse as they turned the handles and began to drill into the masonry. A huge battering ram was wheeled forward to smash into the portcullis guarding the gatehouse entrance, and mangonels were loaded with rocks, which were then catapulted into the castle bailey. But Henry meant to take full advantage of the chaos and confusion before the garrison could recover their equilibrium, and he ordered an all-out assault. Setting fire to sacks and brush, the attackers raced for the walls through a billowing smoke screen, braced scaling ladders, and started to scramble up onto the battlements.

Had Morlaix been expecting an assault, there would have been cauldrons ready with boiling oil and water and heated pitch to throw down upon the enemy. The castellan urgently ordered fires to be kindled, but he knew time was not neutral, that it, too, served Henry Fitz Empress now.

The castellan's pessimistic premonition was not long in proving true. The portcullis was absorbing too much punishment to hold, giving way with a shriek of tearing metal, and the ram began thrusting against the next barrier, a heavy oaken door. The bore continued to grind away at the wall, sending up clouds of dust and debris. And more and more of Henry's men had managed to heave themselves onto the ramparts, where hand-to-hand fighting had begun. But the castle's fate was not yet determined, not until flaming arrows streaked across the sky above the bailey and a fearful cry went up: "Greek fire!"

Few soldiers had actually seen this legendary incendiary in action, for its use was far more prevalent in the Holy Land. But all had heard of it, and all knew it was said to be well nigh impossible to extinguish, defying both water and sand, so combustible that it burned hotter than the fires of Hell itself. And it was known, too, that Henry's father, Geoffrey of Anjou, was the one who'd introduced it to Christian combat during the siege of Montreuil-Bellay. The castellan's hoarse, shouted denials went unheeded in the turmoil. The line of resistance wavered, then gave way. By the time the ram broke through into the bailey, Morlaix's garrison was already in retreat.

They ran for the safety of the keep, with Henry's soldiers in eager pursuit. Recognizing that he was fighting a battle already lost, the castellan gave the command to withdraw. He and the last of his soldiers barely made it, for someone panicked and fired the wooden stairs while they were still climbing. They had no choice but to plunge through the smoke and shooting flames, stumbling inside mere seconds before the door was slammed and bolted shut.

MORLAIX'S CASTELLAN was sitting on the steps of the dais, morosely surveying the great hall. So many rushlights and candles burned that smoke hovered overhead like a low-lying haze. Outside in the bailey, the sun still glowed in a brilliant blue September sky, but within the keep, the tightly shuttered windows had brought on an early dusk. Already the air seemed close and stale, and the siege had only lasted half a day. Henry had stopped his men from assaulting the keep, and the castellan understood perfectly why he'd done so: to give those trapped inside time to ponder their plight.

The castellan was doing just that. He lacked neither courage nor experience, had been caught in sieges before this. He knew what misery lay ahead—rationing their dwindling supply of food, praying that the keep's well would not go dry, never knowing when the next assault might occur, hoping in vain for rescue by their liege lord, the Viscount of Léon. Some of their men might be daft enough to believe Lord Guiomar would do battle with King Henry on their behalf. The castellan was not one of them. Guiomar had a reputation for "fearing neither God nor man" but he was as self-seeking as he was ruthless. In backing his father-by-marriage, Eudo de Porhoët, he'd assumed that he had little to fear for his western, windswept domains, confident that remote Léon would be spared the brunt of Angevin wrath. Now that the Devil was on his very doorstep, he would be rapidly reassessing his options, seeking to cut his losses whilst he still could. The castellan thought it only fair that he should do likewise.

Rising to his feet, he called out for silence. "I mean to surrender the castle." He was poised to justify his decision to the knights, if not the men-at-arms, ready to point out that Lord Guiomar had not the men to break the siege, and a garrison that held out till the bitter end forfeited any claims to mercy. But there was no need. Not a voice was raised in protest and the prevalent expression on the faces upturned to his was one of weary and profound relief.

HENRY'S HALF-BROTHER HAMELIN was jubilant. "Morlaix was said to be the strongest of that hellspawn Guiomar's castles. Wait till he hears how you took it with such ease, slicing through the walls as if they were made of butter!"

Henry was sorting through a sheaf of Guiomar's captured correspondence and merely nodded absently, intent upon unrolling another sheet. He was only half-listening to Hamelin, for he shared little of his kinsman's elation. Military victories were writ in water, as fleeting as memories, and while one might give him satisfaction or relief, it was never joy. In this case, he was pleased that Morlaix's castellan was a sensible sort and not one of those glory-drunk fools who saw combat as the ultimate test of manhood. But he was under no illusions that Morlaix's loss would come as any great revelation to Guiomar, another St Paul on the road to Damascus. Men of Guiomar's ilk shed their loyalties like a snake sheds its skin. He surprised himself then by thinking suddenly of Thomas Becket.

The great hall was a scene of bustling activity. The garrison had been confined until terms could be struck for their release, and nearby the castellan waited patiently for Henry to find the time to resume his interrogation. But there were still wounded to be tended and dead to be buried, on both sides, and the village elders to be reassured that the worst was over. Henry decided to order extra rations of drink tonight for his men, recompense for his not having turned the town over to them for their sport. The villagers could thank the castellan's common sense for their reprieve. War was a punishment for the guilty, but also a lesson for those who'd not yet strayed. A castle or town taken by storm was fair game; one that surrendered could expect kinder treatment. It was as simple as that.

Hamelin was still chattering on about the day's events, but Henry no longer even made the pretense of listening, for he'd just discovered a letter to Guiomar from his father-in-law, Eudo de Porhoët, a letter that spoke with rash candor of a possible alliance with the de Lusignans, the most disgruntled of Eleanor's Poitevin barons. Both Eudo and Guiomar would regret his careless failure to burn it, Henry thought grimly, setting the evidence aside for future use. Damn the de Lusignans! They were little better than bandits, using Lusignan Castle as a base for preying upon their neighbors and travelers. He would have to deal with their treachery next. He'd known about their plotting with the Count of Angoulême and other Poitevin rebels, but not that they'd been conniving with the Bretons, too.

His spurt of anger was short-lived. What he felt mainly was a bone-weary discontent, salted with a sprinkling of mocking self-pity. This expedition into Brittany had already cost him more than he was willing to pay. He'd hoped to be able to spend all of September in Normandy, wanting to bid his daughter Tilda farewell when she set off on her bridal journey with the German ambassadors. That would have been a good time, too, to make his peace with Eleanor. And then there was Rosamund, surely the most neglected royal concubine in Christendom. It would be winter ere he could find time for her, too late then to have her brave a Channel crossing.

Just then he caught a murmured exchange between the castellan and one of the wounded. While he did not speak Breton, finding it to be as incomprehensible a language as Welsh, he was familiar with phrases and words, one of which was *Bro-C'Hall* and another *roue*. He thrust aside Guiomar's letters and got to his feet, wanting to know what the castellan had to say about the King of France.

"My liege . . ."

Henry had not noticed the newcomer's approach. He glanced over his shoulder and the man hastened to kneel at his feet. Clad in the black of the Benedictines, his monk's habit stood out in this hall full of soldiers. As he raised his face, Henry felt a twinge of recognition. After a moment's reflection, he had a name . . . Stephen of Rouen, one of the monks of Bec, a favorite of his mother's. He started to smile, then saw the dusty, soiled condition of Stephen's habit, saw, too, the monk's reddened, sorrowful eyes.

Stephen's voice was low-pitched, hard to hear above the din of the hall. "My lord king, I am heartsick to bring you such grievous news. Your lady mother . . . she is dead."

THE NIGHT WAS MILD, starlit and still. A wind had sprung up within the last hour, cooling and damp against Henry's skin. The air had a distinctive aroma that would ever after remind him of Morlaix: brine and seaweed from the harbor vying with the lingering smell of smoke and a heavy, sweet fragrance drifting from the gardens. He had not knowingly headed for the gardens, only realized that was where his wanderings had led him when he inhaled the scent of late-summer flowers. Aside from a crater in the center of the grassy mead, where a mangonel shot had dumped a large rock, and several smashed turf seats, the gardens appeared to have sustained little damage from the brief siege. Unless the moonlight was hiding unseen horrors, just as the perfume of blossom and herbs camouflaged the odors of blood and death.

He was still in the gardens when Hamelin came in search of him. Uneasy about invading his privacy, Hamelin was making as noisy an approach as possible, wanting to give Henry advance warning. His heart was beating uncomfortably fast, his stomach churning with anxiety. What could he possibly say that would ease Harry's pain? And yet, how could he not try? If only the queen or Rainald or Ranulf were here! What a jest that he should be the one chosen by God to offer comfort when he'd likely be tripped up by his own tongue.

Henry had not turned, but a stiffening of his posture indicated he was aware of Hamelin's presence. Hamelin rubbed his palms on the sides of his tunic, thinking that he'd faced the day's siege with less apprehension. "Harry . . ." He cleared his throat, started again. "It's been so long since you left the hall and I . . . I began to worry . . ."

"I wanted to be alone." It was not until he'd spoken that Henry realized how brusque his words would sound. Hamelin did not deserve to be rebuffed like that. But he could think of no way to make amends; it was as if his brain had gone blank.

"I am sorry, Harry, so very sorry . . ."

When Hamelin's stammering had at last trailed off into silence, Henry roused himself enough for a brief smile. "I know, Hamelin."

"I grieve for her, too, Harry. She was a great lady, God's Truth, and she—" Even to Hamelin, his sentiments sounded hollow, that he should be praising the woman who'd been wronged by his very birth, the woman whose loathing for his father was legend. Yet the Empress Maude had always treated him with civility, and more important, she'd not attempted to thwart his brother's largesse.

Hamelin considered himself to have been blessed in his kinships. Geoffrey had acknowledged him from the first, generous with his affections and his bounty, and even after his untimely death, Hamelin had wanted for nothing. Henry had seen to that, taking on responsibility for Hamelin's upkeep and education and even a title, making him welcome at court, and then giving a gift of such magnitude that three years later, Hamelin was still marveling at it. For Henry had made a marriage for him with a great heiress, Isabella de Warenne, who'd brought an earldom as her marriage portion.

Hamelin was not a fool and he understood that Henry had been prompted by more than family feeling. Isabella de Warenne would have been the wife of his brother Will if not for Thomas Becket's intervention. Henry had made no secret of the fact that he blamed Becket for Will's death, and Hamelin realized that in giving Isabella to him, Henry was sending Becket an unmistakable message, nothing less than a declaration of war. But all that mattered to Hamelin was the fact that he'd been raised to undreamed-of heights for one born a lord's bastard. He did not even mind that people had begun to refer to him as Hamelin de Warenne, for his wife's name was an illustrious one. Hamelin had always known how to appreciate what was important and what was not.

On this September evening, nothing was more important to him than tending to his brother's wounds. But it was becoming painfully apparent that the kindest thing he could do for Henry was to let him be. "I'll be in the hall if you have need of me," he said and was rewarded with another one of those quick, obligatory smiles.

"I'll be in soon," Henry said. "Meanwhile, I'd like you to make sure the monk, Stephen of Rouen, is being well looked after. Then find my chaplain, tell him I want a Mass said on the morrow for my mother's soul. There's so much to be done, so many people to be told . . ."

Hamelin looked as if he'd been given a gift. "I'll take care of it all, will get a scribe and start compiling a list straightaway."

"Good lad." Henry silently willed Hamelin to go away, waiting until he did. The moon's light illuminated a pebbled path and Henry began to walk along it, his slow, measured steps echoing in the silence that had enfolded Morlaix like a shroud. It led him to the far end of the garden, where an oval pool reflected the glimmering of distant stars. It was too small to be a breeding pond. Henry supposed it could be a storage pond, and then he wondered why he should be thinking of fish stews instead of his mother, already laid to rest before the high altar in the abbey church of Bec-Hellouin.

He'd previously approved her choice of burial place, and they knew he'd not be able to halt a war in time to return for the funeral. Stephen of Rouen had described the service in great detail, assuming there would be comfort in knowing. The Mass had been conducted by the Archbishop of Rouen, well attended by princes of the Church and the monks of Bec. A laudatory epitaph would soon be inscribed on her tomb, and Stephen had dutifully copied it out for Henry. He would have to read it again, for all he could remember now were the lines:

Great by birth, greater by marriage, greatest in her offspring,
Here lies the daughter, wife, and mother of Henry.

Henry sank down on a turf seat by the water's edge, trying to decide if his father would have been amused or offended by her final revenge, expunging him from her tombstone and her history. The monk had said she'd died on the tenth, Sunday last. For the life of him, he could recall little about that day. They'd been on the road, riding hard for Morlaix. Had he given her any thought at all that Sunday? Had he admitted, for even a heartbeat, just how enfeebled and ailing she was? Christ, why could he not remember?

As he moved, his boot crunched upon the gravel and pebbles, and he reached down, scooped up a handful of the stones, small and smooth and polished. When his father had died, he'd been but eighteen. He was four and thirty now, master of the greatest empire since the days of the Caesars. Old enough for certes to accept a mother's loss. So why, then, did he feel so numbed, so utterly empty?

He must see to Minna's welfare, make sure she was looked after. So many letters to write. Rainald must be told. His cousin Maud. Ranulf. For a fleeting moment, he experienced a yearning so intense it was like a physical ache, a longing for . . . what? The company of one who understood, who needed no words. Hamelin meant well, but he'd never found it easy to share the secrets of his soul. So few people he'd confided in over the years, so few he'd truly trusted.

Closing his fist around the pebbles, he called them up, the ghosts of his past. His father. His brother Will. His uncle Ranulf. His mother. Eleanor. Thomas Becket. After a hesitation, he added Rosamund Clifford's name to the roster, for her loyalty was absolute, wholehearted. The stones clinked together like dice, and he held his hand out over the pond, loosened his grip and let them drop, one by one, into the water. He sat there for a time, watching the eddies ripple across the silvered surface of the pool until his vision blurred and his tears came.

CHAPTER TWENTY-FOUR

✦

December 1167
Winchester, England

ELEANOR COULD NOT STOP SHIVERING. Cursing the damp English winter, she moved closer to the hearth, but the flames were not hot enough to dispel her chill. It had been raining for more than a week, an icy, soaking rain that drowned all memories of sunlit springs and better days. Eleanor's small son had been affected by the gloom, too, fretting and whimpering, resisting his nurse's attempts at comfort. When Eleanor could endure John's mewling no longer, she snapped, "For the love of God, fetch Rohese. He cannot cry if he's suckling."

Eleanor's attendants eyed her warily, as they'd learned to do in the eleven months since John's birth. None complained or protested, even though one of them would have to venture out into that miserable, wet night in search of Rohese. John's fussing increased in volume, progressing from low wail to high-pitched shriek. The Countess of Chester had always been adept at soothing querulous babies, but she had no luck with John and hastily handed him over to the wet-nurse once Rohese had finally been found.

Maud then took matters into her own hands, announcing that she wanted to visit the chapel to pray for the queen's safe return to Normandy. This pious declaration earned her a startled look from Eleanor, which she blandly ignored. "Will you accompany me, my lady, so we may pray together?"

Eleanor wavered momentarily between common sense and curiosity, but the latter won. Signaling for her mantle, she rose reluctantly to her feet and was soon following the flickering glow of Maud's lantern out into the rain-drenched darkness. By the time they'd reached the chapel, her skirts were sodden, her shoes muddied, and she was convinced that curiosity must be one of the Seven Deadly Sins.

Candles flared upon the altar, and a torch in one of the wall sconces was lit, but the priest was not present. Probably warm and snug before a blazing hearth, Eleanor thought sourly, in a mood to begrudge anyone comforts she was not sharing. "The next time you get an irresistible urge to commune with the Almighty, Maud, make it a solitary quest."

"This was not one of my better ideas," Maud agreed, wringing moisture from the hem of her mantle with a grimace. "But I could think of no other place for us to be utterly alone, safe from eavesdroppers."

"There was always my bedchamber, which is not only private but reasonably dry."

"Now you're being disingenuous, Eleanor. I could not dismiss your ladies or servants. All I could do was to make you curious enough to . . ."

When she paused, Eleanor suggested, "Take your bait?"

"Well, yes," Maud admitted and then she grinned. "I will indeed pray that God gives you an easy sailing, though. Anyone who sets foot on shipboard is deserving of prayers."

"Is that also true for a wife returning to an unfaithful husband?" Eleanor asked coolly. "I'll take your prayers, Maud, but I've no need of your advice."

"No? Then why did you 'take the bait,' as you put it? I think you do want to talk about your return, and who better than me? I am good at intrigues and at keeping secrets, impossible to shock, and however dismal your marriage may seem at the moment, it is infinitely preferable to the calamity that was mine, so you need not fret that I'd respond with either smugness or pity!"

Amused in spite of herself, Eleanor leaned back against the altar, regarding the other woman challengingly. "What is there to discuss? I will be joining Harry at Rouen for his Christmas Court and you were summoned to Winchester so I could bid you farewell ere I left England."

Maud was quiet for a moment, knowing that she'd be entering a verbal quagmire, one rife with pitfalls. In their world, a husband's adultery was something to be endured or ignored. Even queens had to play by those rules. If only she could be sure that Eleanor understood that.

"How are you going to handle it, Eleanor? Do you intend to give Harry an ultimatum about the Clifford wench?"

"Of course." Eleanor's eyes glinted. "What would you have me do, compete with that insipid, ordinary child for Harry's favor?"

"No . . . but have you thought about his likely response? Even if he is already tiring of the girl, he might balk at being given a command. Men tend to get their backs up as often as their cocks. What will you do if Harry refuses?"

There was a prolonged silence. Eleanor's lashes swept down to veil her eyes, but the flickering candlelight revealed the stubborn downturn of her mouth. "I will make sure," she said, "that he greatly regrets it."

This was what Maud had feared. "I do not doubt that. I just want to be certain that none of the regrets are yours. I understand your desire to punish Harry for his betrayal, but that is such a dangerous road to start down. However justified your grievances, you cannot ever forget that a woman's power is a derivative commodity, borrowed at best—"

"Forget?" Eleanor spat. "You truly think I could forget that? After Antioch?"

As familiar as Maud was with Eleanor's combustible temper, she had never seen it take fire so fast. "Antioch?" she echoed, momentarily perplexed.

"Yes, Antioch," Eleanor shot back, and in her mouth the name of that elegant crusader kingdom became a harsh obscenity. "Do not pretend you do not know what happened in Antioch, Maud. Even holy hermits under a vow of silence heard of the great scandal caused by the King of France's wanton, wayward queen. If gossip is to be believed, I was guilty of adultery and incest and single-handedly brought the crusade to ruin."

"Yes . . . if gossip is to be believed." The stories that had trickled out of Syria were indeed salacious and shocking. It was said that Eleanor had taken her uncle Raymond, Prince of Antioch, as her lover, declared her intention to annul her marriage and remain in Antioch, and had been compelled by Louis to accompany him on to Jerusalem. Maud had not believed the rumors, though, not once she'd met Eleanor. The young French queen had been willful and reckless, but she'd never been a fool.

"The crusade was botched from the beginning," Eleanor said, with a bitterness that not even the passage of nearly twenty years had abated. "And then at Antioch, Louis balked at going to the rescue of Edessa, contending he must first carry out his vow to reach Jerusalem. I thought that was madness and so did Raymond, a military blunder that might well lose Antioch, too, to the infidels. When Louis refused to heed us, I warned him that if he did not attack Edessa as agreed upon, I would remain in Antioch and keep my vassals with me. He insisted that I must obey him and he quoted from Scriptures, that wives must submit themselves to their husbands as unto the Lord. It was then that I told him I wanted to end the marriage."

"And so his advisers convinced him that you were bedding Raymond?"

Eleanor nodded tersely. "For a time, they did," she said dismissively, making it clear that she had no interest in discussing her uncle. "They persuaded Louis that it would look unmanly for him to leave me in Antioch. And so I was awakened in the middle of the night by men sent by my husband, taken by force from my lodgings and out of the city . . . as helpless to resist as any cotter's wife, for all that I wore a crown."

"You are right," Maud conceded. "You need no lessons from me as to how the scales of power are weighted between men and women. It is just that I know you, Eleanor, I know that at heart, you are a rebel and have never been one for doing what is expected of you."

The corners of Eleanor's mouth softened, curved upward. "You need not worry, Maud. I will not do anything rash . . . not unless Harry provokes me, of course. And yes, that is a joke." She did smile, then, although without humor. "Unfortunately, so is his little blonde bauble."

PATRICK D'EVEREAUX PAUSED before entering the great hall of Argentan's castle. He moved with the careless confidence of one accustomed to attracting attention, trailing authority and honors and his long-suffering wife like the spume churned up in a ship's wake. And indeed his entrance did turn heads, for he was not only the Earl of Salisbury and Sheriff of Wiltshire; to those on this side of the Channel, his importance lay in the power he wielded as Henry's surrogate in Aquitaine.

The hall was very crowded, for attendance at the king's Christmas court was a matter of prestige as much as pleasure. A baron's absence might well give rise to rumors that he'd lost royal favor, even encourage his enemies to try to sow seeds of discord with the king. Salisbury's gaze raked the throng, noting that many of the Poitevin lords were not present even though the queen, their liege lady, was expected to arrive any day now. Their conspicuous absence did not bode well for his tenure in Aquitaine. Seeing that Henry was occupied with the Bishops of Liège and Poitiers, Salisbury decided to approach him later and instead looked about for one who would know if Eleanor's anticipated appearance was rooted in reality or gossip.

The Earl of Cornwall was the perfect choice, and Salisbury grasped his wife's elbow, heading in Rainald's direction. The two men were on friendly terms, and Rainald greeted Patrick and Ela with boisterous, wine-flavored goodwill, kissing her gallantly on the cheek and thumping Salisbury on the back heartily enough to send the earl into a coughing fit. The next few moments were awkward, for courtesy demanded that Salisbury and Ela ask after Rainald's wife, even though they both knew the frail and unstable Beatrice had not left her Cornwall estates for years. They politely pretended to believe the excuses Rainald made on his wife's behalf, but then Salisbury remembered he'd not seen Rainald since the death of the empress, and it was necessary to tender their condolences for her loss.

Rainald's Christmas ebullience was temporarily dampened by these specters of death and derangement conjured up by the Salisburys. Snatching a wine cup from a passing servant, he drank deeply. He soon brightened, declaring that his son had accompanied him to Argentan. Salisbury knew, of course, that Rainald doted upon a natural son, named Henry after the king, but as he followed the other man's pointing finger toward a youngster in his midteens, he saw that Rainald was speaking of his legitimate heir, the son born to Beatrice.

"The lad over there, standing behind the king . . . ?" Salisbury frowned then, but Ela covered for him smoothly, saying "Nicholas" so naturally that none would notice his lapse of memory. Salisbury took her adroit intercession for granted; that was what a wife was supposed to do, after all. Nicholas was richly dressed, but he lacked Rainald's vivid coloring and robust stature. The youth standing by Nicholas's side was far more impressive, tall and well favored, and Salisbury felt a flicker of family pride.

"That is my nephew talking with your Nicholas," Salisbury said, "my sister's son, Will Marshal. He was knighted a few months ago and has asked to enter into my service. He's a likely lad, a good hand with a sword, too."

Rainald made a sound that passed for polite agreement; his interest in Salisbury's kin was minimal. But then the name pricked a memory. "One of John Marshal's get?" When Salisbury nodded, Rainald turned to look at young Marshal with genuine curiosity. He was not surprised that Will needed to make his own way in the world, for John Marshal had a surfeit of sons, six in all between his two marriages, and there would be little provision made for a younger lad. But William Marshal had acquired a certain fame as a small boy, for his father had offered him up as a hostage and then dared King Stephen to hang him, boasting that he had the hammer and anvil with which to forge other sons.

Salisbury knew Rainald was thinking of that same siege of Newbury, for men invariably did upon first meeting Will. But he had no desire to discuss his brother-in-law's notoriety, Stephen's unkingly compassion, or his nephew's narrow escape, and he acted quickly to head off Rainald's reminiscences. "Is it true that the queen is expected at Argentan?"

"So I've been told. She sent the king word that she'd arrived at Rouen and would be joining him for their Christmas court, but I do not know if she's—" Rainald never finished the sentence. "Now what do you suppose that is all about?"

Straining to see for himself, Salisbury too, was puzzled, by the tableau meeting their eyes. Henry had swung around to face Nicholas and Will, interrupting his conversation with the bishops. Both youths had gone beet-red and even from across the hall, their discomfort was obvious. Rainald and Salisbury exchanged perplexed looks; had Nicholas and Will been foolish enough to offend the king?

Salisbury was inclined to let his nephew flounder to shore on his own, but Rainald's first impulse was to rush to the rescue, and he was starting forward just as Henry turned away. Their eyes met and Henry murmured something to the bishops, then headed in Rainald's direction as Ela moved off to greet a friend. Rainald restrained himself until after the exchange of courtesies, but not a moment longer. "What happened? Nicholas looked as if he'd swallowed his tongue!"

"Oh, that . . . your son was sharing some of the gossip being bruited around the court these days. I suppose he thought they were safely out of my hearing, and in truth, I only caught part of the conversation. But I heard enough to justify putting the fear of God into the lad, so I spun around and told them rumor had it that I was going deaf, too."

Rainald laughed, relieved that Henry seemed to be taking it in such good humor. He could well imagine the sort of rumor a youngster would find most interesting, the more lurid the better. There was a time when he wouldn't have been able to resist a bawdy joke, but he was developing a modicum of discretion in these, his autumn years, and he decided that his nephew would not appreciate jests about wronged wives, not with Eleanor about to descend upon Argentan like one of the Furies of ancient Greece. The classical allusion was not his own; that was not Rainald's style. He'd heard it from Arnulf de Lisieux and it had lodged in his memory, for he'd always had a healthy respect for the queen's temper, convinced that Aquitaine could match Anjou in sheer heat any day of the week.

Henry had already forgotten about Nicholas's faux pas; he had far weightier matters on his mind than a young cousin's gaffe. "Actually, I was looking for you," he confided to Rainald and Salisbury. "A messenger arrived this morn from England, bearing word that Owain Gwynedd has taken Rhuddlan Castle."

This was a significant loss for the Crown. Owain had been quick to take advantage of Henry's troubles in Brittany and Poitou, and the siege had been dragging on for more than three months. Henry was tempted to blame the castellan, but he knew the fault was his; he'd delayed too long in putting together a rescue expedition, thinking the castle could hold out safely till the spring. The Welsh prince had become overly bold, would have to be dealt with. But when? He still had to punish the de Lusignans and the rest of Eleanor's troublesome subjects. What was it his father had ofttimes said about Aquitaine? Ah, yes . . . that the barons of Poitou were as perverse as any in Christendom, likely to double-cross the Devil on a whim and then laugh all the way into Hell. They were a vexing people, his wife's Poitevins, as impulsive and unpredictable and hotheaded as his uncle Ranulf's Welshmen.

But tonight, Henry did not want to think about Ranulf or Wales. Exercising a king's prerogative to commandeer the conversation, he switched the subject from Rhuddlan to Salisbury's recent pilgrimage to the sacred Spanish shrine of St James of Compostela. But he found it difficult to corral his wayward thoughts. Each time he glanced around the hall, he encountered swiftly averted eyes, poorly concealed curiosity and speculation. Like his young cousin Nicholas, they were all wondering about his coming reunion with Eleanor, avid to know what would happen once they were alone in the royal bedchamber.

Henry would have given a great deal to know that himself. He really wasn't sure what to expect from Eleanor. Her self-exile in England for the past year was not as easy to read as it first appeared. Did it indicate the gravity of her grievance against him? Or had she deliberately stayed away to give her lacerated pride time to heal?

In the beginning, he'd been relieved by her absence, then bemused, and finally, unsettled. Her infrequent letters told him much about her days, nothing about her heart. He'd been taken aback when she did not return to Normandy after hearing of his mother's death. He'd gotten a graceful condolence letter that said all the right things, yet seemed oddly impersonal coming from a woman who'd been his wife for fifteen years and borne him eight children. Not even Tilda's departure had brought Eleanor home; she'd accompanied their daughter across the Channel, saw her off for the imperial court with the German ambassadors, then sailed back to England before Henry had heard of her brief presence on Norman soil.

Feigning interest in Salisbury's pilgrim stories, Henry acknowledged that the portents were not auspicious. Whenever he sought to convince himself that Eleanor's actions need not mean she nursed a grudge, an inner voice mocked that he was like an unwary sailor, insisting that a red morning sky did not warn of a coming storm. No, her return was sure to bring squalls and high winds. They were likely to have a God-awful quarrel; he might as well reconcile himself to that. And because she was the one wronged, he'd have to make things right between them.

But what if he could not placate her with an honest apology? What if that was not enough for her? If she demanded that he put Rosamund aside, end their liaison? Logically, that should not present a problem. He had not laid eyes upon the girl in well over a year. He could not even remember the names of his other bedmates in that year. They'd never mattered to him, and Eleanor understood that. So why then was Rosamund different? Why this reluctance to disavow her? As often as he'd been down this road, he never found the answers he sought. In truth, he did not know what he'd do if Eleanor insisted that Rosamund be forsworn. He could only hope that her price for peace would not be so high.

E LEANOR WAS wearing a gown Henry did not remember seeing before, a brocaded silk of deep gold, with a tightly fitted bodice, full, sweeping skirts, and swirling sleeves of emerald green. It reminded him vaguely of the gown she'd worn on their wedding day, stirred up memories he preferred to keep becalmed. Presiding over their evening meal in the great hall, she glittered and sparkled like the rings flashing on her fingers, looking beautiful and elegant and enigmatic. Henry silently applauded her performance; no queen ever born could play that role better than Eleanor. Nor had he expected any less from her. Even if she yearned to cut his throat with his own dagger, no one would ever guess it from her public demeanor. That would be a surprise she'd save for the privacy of their bedchamber.

And so the meal passed in outward harmony, with wine flowing as freely as the polished, courteous conversation. One advantage of having so many children and so many enemies, Henry acknowledged wryly, was that they'd never run out of something to talk about. By the time several elaborate subtleties had been wheeled into the hall, Henry and Eleanor had traded information upon their vast brood, interspersed with the latest gossip coming out of the French court, the Papal See, and Thomas Becket's self-proclaimed sanctuary at Sens.

The subtlety for the high table was a depiction of the Birth of the Christ Child, acclaimed for its artistry, but not expected to be eaten, and Henry decided he could wait no longer for the second act in this drama. Why not leave their guests to fend for themselves, he suggested, and wasn't sure whether to be gratified or aggrieved by the nonchalance with which Eleanor accepted his offer.

A NURSERY had been furnished for the three youngest of Henry and Eleanor's children: six-year-old Eleanor, two-year-old Joanna, and John, who was just days away from his first birthday. Of the older offspring, Tilda was in Germany, Hal had his own household as befitting the heir to the English throne, and Richard and Geoffrey had not yet arrived at Argentan. As Eleanor and Henry entered the chamber, John's wet-nurse leaped to her feet as if caught in some dereliction of duty. Joanna's wet nurse was made of sterner stuff and as she curtsied, she dared to put a finger to her lips, warning the parents not to awaken their daughter, who had finally and blessedly gone to sleep. Eleanor, named after her mother but called Aenor after her maternal grandmother, was permitted a later bedtime and was playing alone in a corner with a felt puppet. She seemed no less startled than the wet-nurses by this sudden intrusion into the nursery, and her greetings were subdued, even shy.

Henry was not surprised by the little girl's reticence, for she'd been apart from her mother for more than a year, and how could he be other than a stranger? How often did he see any of his children? As always, when confronted with the remote reality of royal parenthood, he felt a genuine regret, a sadness that he had developed with none of his children the sort of easy, affectionate rapport he'd enjoyed with his own father. But he no longer resolved to remedy matters, for by now he knew better. The demands of kingship were invariably going to prevail over the attractions of the nursery. Since he found his children to be more interesting as they matured, he'd assuaged any sense of loss by assuring himself that there would be time enough once they'd left babyhood behind.

Joanna was sleeping soundly, her hair a tangle of bright gold upon the pillow. But as Henry leaned over John's cradle, the boy opened his eyes. Henry had gotten only a cursory glimpse of his son upon their arrival at Argentan, for John had been asleep, well swaddled in blankets. Their other children had all been fair; John's dark hair came as a surprise, therefore, to his father. "Our first black sheep," he said softly. "He looks like you, Eleanor."

"You think so?"

"Not just his hair. He has your eyes, too." The resemblance seemed so obvious to Henry that he did not understand how Eleanor could have missed it. Yet there had been an unmistakably skeptical tone to her voice. Unless their time apart had completely skewed his instincts where she was concerned. When he'd glanced down into his son's shining hazel eyes, they'd told him nothing about the workings of that small brain, nor had he expected them to; an infant's world was an alien abode. But as Eleanor's eyes met his over the cradle, they were no more revealing than John's.

He'd almost forgotten how well she could mask her thoughts when she chose. He'd been in Paris nigh on a week, and until she'd lured him into the privacy of the rain-screened royal gardens, he'd had no idea whatsoever of her intent. Now, their eyes held, and suddenly he had no more patience for these womanly games. This was his wife and he wanted her back in his bed, in his life, wanted the ease and familiarity and erotic intimacy that he'd once taken for granted.

Her hand was resting upon their daughter's shoulder and he covered it with his own, both a caress and a claim. Lowering his voice to foil the eavesdropping wet-nurses, he murmured, "Where? Your chamber or mine?"

She regarded him unsmilingly, the candlelight giving her eyes a golden tint. "Mine," she said. "Let it be mine."

✠

WHEN HENRY WAS ADMITTED to his wife's bedchamber, she was seated on a coffer by the hearth, having her hair brushed out. The young woman wielding the brush was one of Eleanor's attendants from Aquitaine, a blithe spirit who had a penchant for practical jokes, flirtations, and games of chance. Taking the brush from her hand, Henry said with a smile, "It is early yet, Renée. Why don't you go down to the great hall and break a few hearts?"

Renée's dark eyes sought out Eleanor's in the polished reflection of her hand mirror. When Eleanor nodded, almost imperceptibly, Renée dropped a graceful curtsy and did as Henry bade, without even a trace of her usual élan. Henry would have liked to believe her uncharacteristic reserve was due to travel fatigue, but he knew better. The members of Eleanor's household were utterly and fiercely loyal to her. Glancing at Felice, his wife's favorite greyhound, he almost made a dubious jest about the dog lunging for his private parts, caught himself just in time.

Eleanor's hair flowed through his fingers like a sunless river, as dark and sensuous against his skin as a summer midnight. After he'd seen her head bared for the first time, he no longer understood why men were so taken with hair that was curly and golden. Her perfume was beguiling, an evocative, subtle fragrance that seduced with its very unfamiliarity.

"You changed your perfume?" He leaned closer, breathing in the aroma. "Abbot Bernard, God rot his sanctimonious soul, could have preached a fire and brimstone sermon after just one whiff. I think he truly believed that women were all damned as daughters of Eve, and as for you, love . . . well, he never doubted that you were the Devil's handmaiden, put upon this earth for the sole purpose of tempting men into mortal sin."

Her lip twitched at the mention of that old enemy from her past life as Queen of France. "Is that what you think I'm doing, Harry . . . tempting you into sin?"

He smiled into her hair. "Well, a man can always hope . . ." He'd liked to joke that she could kindle a flame hotter than Greek fire, predicting the day would come when there'd be nothing left of him but a pile of ashes in their marriage bed. Unfortunately, she was still able to work the same magic. His intention had been to get the worst over with as soon as possible, do whatever he must to mend the marriage, and hope she did not mean to prolong their estrangement through the Christmas festivities. But his body was balking at that battle strategy.

He had never been a man to let lust command his brain. This surge of sudden desire was distracting enough, though, for him to reconsider his tactics. She'd never been shy about speaking her mind in the past. Would she have permitted him to brush her hair like this if she was not amenable to reconciliation tonight? Sooner rather than later? Mayhap she wanted an ugly, embittering quarrel no more than he did.

Setting the brush down, he reached over and took the mirror from her hand, tossing it carelessly into the floor rushes. "You cannot possibly know," he said huskily, "how desirable you look. I came in here with my head crammed full of contrary, confusing thoughts, and all I can think now is how much I want you."

She did not resist as he drew her to her feet, but rested a hand against his chest before he could take her into his arms. Her eyes were inscrutable, intent upon his face. "You sound," she said, "as if you truly mean that."

"You need proof?" He gave a hoarse laugh, for his mouth had gone dry. "I ache with it, Eleanor, that's how much I want you . . ." And this time when he reached for her, she did not pull away.

Her golden gown was a casualty of his urgency, its lacings snapped by his impatient fingers. He had a blurred memory of rending silk on their wedding night, too, and half-expected her to tease him about that. But she said nothing, wrapping her arms around his neck as he backed her toward the bed. He recalled suddenly that he'd not bolted the door after Renée's departure, but by then, they were sinking down into the softness of the feather mattress and he was not about to stop, not even if the chamber caught fire.

Afterward, there was a reassuring familiarity about it all: the covers thrown off, their bodies glistening with sweat and tangled in the sheets, the floor littered with their discarded clothing. So often had they resolved quarrels in bed like this, more than he could even begin to count. He lay still for a time, waiting for his heart and pulse to slow their erratic racing. Mayhap that old fool Bernard was right after all and sex could indeed kill a man . . . if done right. Turning his head toward his wife, he traced the line of her cheek with a finger, not yet having enough energy to move. "Good God, woman . . ."

Her hair was half-covering her face, tousled and wild and damp with perspiration. "That is what you said on our wedding night."

She sounded out of breath, and he rolled over, kissing the soft skin of her throat. "Did I?" he said, and when he smiled, she saw that he'd echoed the same words by chance, not because he'd remembered.

Henry wasn't sure when he'd finally realized that she was not going to confront him about Rosamund Clifford. When he'd considered all her possible responses, that was the only one he'd not envisioned. At worst, he'd seen her flinging down her ultimatum like a gauntlet, demanding Rosamund's immediate and permanent banishment from his life. It was all too easy to imagine her berating him for bringing Rosamund to Woodstock, raging at him for being so careless of her pride, blistering the air with her considerable command of profanity, much of which she'd learned from him. He could even envision her so angry that she'd be tempted to heave candlesticks or books at his head; she'd confided that she'd once thrown an inkwell at Louis. Or she could have gone to the other extreme: aloof, maddeningly remote, for she could outdo his mother the empress when it came to being imperial. It had never occurred to him, though, that she might choose to deal with the problem of Rosamund Clifford so simply and effectively—by not even acknowledging there was a problem.

Henry retrieved a pillow from the floor, propped it behind his head, and slid an arm around Eleanor's shoulders, drawing her in against him. There were many reasons to be grateful that God had given him this woman, apart from the obvious ones—that she was a great heiress and a great beauty, too. She had courage and common sense, a quick wit and a passionate nature. Like him, she dreamed of empires, craved crowns for their children. But of all her virtues, the one that shone the brightest for him on this December night at Argentan was her sophistication. She was wise enough to understand that men were born to sin, and worldly enough not to let it trouble her unduly. He should have realized that Eleanor, the most celebrated queen in all of Christendom, would not be threatened by a mere slip of a girl like Rosamund Clifford.

His lashes kept flickering downward, heeding the message his body was sending his brain, that sleep would not be long denied. Stifling a yawn, he brushed a trail of soft kisses across her throat. "I have a confession, love," he said drowsily. "The only way I'll stay awake much longer is if you stick pins in me. But ere I doze off, I wanted to tell you that I've missed you this past year, am very glad that you're back where you belong . . ."

"Are you?"

He had never found it easy to talk of love, for if it was present, what was the need to mention it and if it was not, why lie? It had always seemed like a needless extravagance to lavish upon a wife, telling her what she already knew. But he sensed that this was one of those times when a woman would expect no less, and so he repeated his assurances that she'd been greatly missed, adding a slightly self-conscious "I do love you, after all" as he leaned over to kiss her for the last time that night. He supposed it would not harm him to be a little less grudging with the words, and made a hazy resolution to be more forthcoming with them in the future, his last conscious thought before he drifted off to sleep.

The chamber's candles still flickered, wavering pinpoints of light against the encroaching shadows. They'd not drawn the bed curtains and Eleanor could see flames licking the hearth log, continuing to give out a measure of heat. Her greyhound rose, paused to sniff at the clothing scattered in the floor rushes, and then padded to the bed, poking a cold nose into Eleanor's hand. She fondled the dog's silken head absently, from habit, listening to the hissing of the fire and the deep, even breathing of the man asleep beside her.

She'd given him a chance and he'd scorned it. So be it, then. Rising up on her elbow, she stared down at his face, faintly lit by firelight. He must think women are such fools. Did he truly imagine that she did not know about his continuing letters to Rosamund Clifford? Or that he'd planned to bring her over to join him in Normandy? Did he really think she'd not be able to find eyes and ears to serve her at Woodstock? Or did he just assume that she'd act the dutiful wife, expecting her to endure the shame in silence, saying nary a word of protest whilst he plucked his little English gosling?

During the months since Woodstock, her rage had slowly congealed into ice. By the time she was ready to return to his court, she believed she had come to terms with his betrayal. She had every right to object to his whoring. If she'd not cast her lot in with his, if she'd not agreed to wed, who was to say if he'd ever have become England's king? Aquitaine had been his stepping-stone to the English throne, her Aquitaine.

Over these past months, she'd deliberately dwelt upon her grievances, remembering all those times when he'd disregarded her advice, ignored her counsel, alienated her vassals with his high-handed Angevin ways. He'd not truly trusted her political judgment—this from the man who'd given the keys to the kingdom over to Thomas Becket. She'd actually wielded more influence with the dithering, hapless Louis than ever she had with Harry, and what greater irony could there be than that?

When she'd finally sailed from Southampton, she'd believed that her heart was well armored against further betrayals. She would make it clear that she'd not tolerate any more Rosamund Cliffords. She'd always been reasonable about his women, had never expected him to abstain when they were long apart. But she'd not abide his flaunting concubines at their court, in her bed for all she knew. He owed her better than that.

Nothing had gone, though, as she'd planned. The indifference she'd been cultivating with such care had cracked wide open, like a defective shield. Instead of a measured, matter-of-fact recital of her wrongs and complaints, she'd been caught up in emotions that were as raw and primitive as they were unexpected, one breaking wave after another of flood-tide fury, resentment, jealousy, and unhealed hurt. She'd given him the opportunity to make things right between them, to make her believe that Rosamund Clifford meant no more to him than any of the other harlots he'd taken to his bed. And he repaid her with a Judas kiss.

It was plain now what he wanted from her—to turn a blind eye to his straying, to accept Rosamund Clifford as his paramour, to content herself with the nursery and needlework. Did he think to set his wench up under the same roof, as her grandfather had done with the most notorious of his conquests? If so, she wasn't sure which of them was the bigger fool.

Swallowing was suddenly painful. She felt as if her throat was being squeezed in a strangler's hold, as if a heavy millstone was pressing onto her chest, forcing the air from her lungs. But she shed no tears; her eyes, narrowed on Henry's sleeping form, were dry and burning. She could still give him an ultimatum, tell him on the morrow that Rosamund Clifford must go. But what if she made such a demand and he refused? She'd not humble her pride like that, would never risk such a humiliation, not in this life or the next. Nor would she forgive.

H ENRY AWOKE to a distinct chill, soon discovered that the fire had gone out during the night. A weight lay across his feet. Blinking, he saw that his wife's greyhound had sneaked up onto the bed while they slept. Eleanor was still sleeping, her head cradled in the crook of her arm, a sweep of long hair trailing over the edge of the bed. He tried to think of a reason to get up, couldn't come up with one, and burrowed back into the warm cocoon of their covers, feeling more content than he had in months.

When he stirred again, the hearth had been tended, the dog evicted, and Eleanor's attendants were moving quietly about the chamber. Her side of the bed was empty, the bed curtains partially drawn. As he sat up, a hand slid through the opening, holding a silver cup.

"Here," his wife said, "this will fortify you to face the rest of the day."

Reaching for the cup, he took a tentative sip; it was one of her Gascony wines, well watered down as he preferred. "I always fare better whenever you're around to see to the household," he said, observing her appreciatively over the rim of the cup. She was already dressed in a gown of soft wool the color of sapphire, but she'd not yet put on her wimple and veil, and her hair was still visible, plaited and coiled at the nape of her neck. There was an agreeable intimacy about the sight, for only a husband or lover ever saw a woman with her hair unbound or uncovered. "You look very pleasing to the eye this morn," he said. "A pity, though, that you were in such a hurry to dress. We could have stayed abed a while longer . . ." He let his words trail off suggestively, and she smiled.

"Too late," she said briskly. "I've already sent for your squires." Her timing was perfect, for at that very moment, a knock sounded at the door. Renée, still looking subdued, admitted a servant bearing a tray. Eleanor took it and carried it back to Henry. "I ordered some roasted chestnuts so you could break the night's fast," she said, making herself comfortable at the end of the bed, putting the tray between them.

Henry took another swallow of wine, helped himself to some of the chestnuts. Eleanor took one, shelled it deftly, and nibbled on the nut. "I was sorry to hear about the fall of that Welsh castle," she said, and they were soon deep in a discussion of the incessant turmoil in the more troublesome regions of their domains. Her ladies continued with their tasks and when Henry's squires arrived, they knew better than to interrupt until their lord was ready to dress.

Henry had finished lambasting the Bretons and moved on to the Poitevins. Eleanor listened intently, making an occasional incisive comment about her faithless barons. They both agreed that the de Lusignans must be dealt with—and sooner rather than later.

"I think, Harry, that it is time I returned to Aquitaine," Eleanor said pensively. "My presence there might help to calm some of the unrest. Not with lawless hellspawn like the de Lusignans, of course. The Virgin Mary herself could be their liege lady and they'd still be conniving and pillaging. But there are others with wavering loyalties who could benefit from a reminder that they'd pledged their faith and their honor to me, Duke William's daughter."

Henry had been thinking along the same lines in recent months. But he'd not been able to seek her cooperation against her Poitevin rebels until they'd made their peace over his indiscretion with Rosamund Clifford. "I agree, " he said. "It has been too long since you paid a visit to Poitou. But we'd have to take measures for your safety first. Once I am sure that you'd not be at risk, we can lay our plans accordingly."

He finished the last of the chestnuts, glancing over to see if this met with her approval. It did; she was smiling.

CHAPTER TWENTY-FIVE

March 1168
Poitiers, Poitou

HE SKY WAS THE SHADE of milky pearl. The streets would soon be astir, but for now William Marshal was riding alone through a sleeping city, hearing only the rhythmic clop of his stallion's hooves and the high, mournful cries of river birds. It promised to be a splendid spring day. Will could learn to like the climate of his queen's domains, for this Wednesday morn four days before Easter was milder than many an English summer's afternoon.

Ahead lay the soaring tower of Maubergeonne, the great keep of the ancestral palace of the Dukes of Aquitaine. Will picked up the pace a bit, and was admitted into the bailey by yawning guards, for he was known on sight to the garrison. Their yawns were contagious and Will stifled one himself; sleep hadn't figured prominently among the night's activities. Nor would he have any time to steal a nap. This was the day his uncle, Earl Patrick of Salisbury, was to escort the queen to Lusignan Castle and Will would be part of the party. But he was one and twenty, young enough to consider sleep well lost in the pursuit of pleasurable sins.

The stables appeared empty. He assumed the grooms were cadging

breakfast from the cooks, for few men had the fortitude to confine themselves to the traditional two meals a day. His own hunger was waking; not
that it ever truly slept. As a squire, he'd earned the nickname of Scoff-food
for his impressive appetite. Thinking about that now, he grinned; luckily,
he was tall enough to eat his fill without fear of getting a paunch like his
uncle Salisbury.

He'd unsaddled his stallion and was turning to fetch a bucket when he
heard the voices. It sounded as if they were coming from the loft and he
cocked his head, listening. He could make out no words, but the speakers
sounded young and angry. As he emerged from the stall, hay rained down
upon his head and he glanced up in time to see a youngster teetering on
the edge of the loft. The boy made a grab for the ladder as he went over,
managing to grasp one of the rungs. He dangled there for a hazardous
moment, kicking in vain as he sought a foothold. But before he could
panic, he heard a voice say with reassuring calm, "Easy, lad. If you think
you can hold on for a few more breaths, I'll come up to get you. If not,
just let yourself drop and I'll catch you."

The boy squirmed to get a glimpse of the man below him and almost
lost his grip. "I'm letting go," he gasped and came plummeting down, feet
first, showing an admirable confidence in Will's ability to break his fall.
The impact was more forceful than Will had expected and he staggered
backward under the boy's weight before setting him safely onto the floor.
As he did, another head peered over the edge and he snapped, "Get down
here now!" not wanting to have to make two rescues that morning.

He'd gotten his breath back by the time the second youngster obeyed.
They both had reddish-gold hair dusted with straw, ruddy faces scattered
with freckles and streaked with dirt. The boy Will had caught looked to
be about twelve, but Will knew he was actually only ten and a half, the
other one a year younger. A passerby might have taken them, as scruffy as
they were, for two brawling stable lads, but Will knew better. They were
the heirs to Aquitaine and Brittany.

He regarded them disapprovingly, but they bore up well under
the scrutiny, theirs the confidence of young princes already knowing
to whom they were accountable and to whom they were not. "I do not
suppose," he drawled, "that you want to tell me what you were squabbling about."

Richard's shoulders twitched. "I do not suppose so, either."

Will would have let the matter lie if Richard hadn't come so close to
splattering himself all over the stable floor. Casting an accusatory eye upon

Geoffrey, he decided it wouldn't hurt to put the fear of God into the lad and said coolly, "Want to tell me how your brother fell? You would not have pushed him, by any chance?"

But putting the fear of God into Geoffrey was easier said than done. The boy glared right back at him. "Why should I listen to you? For all I know, you're just one of the lowborn stable grooms!"

That insult rankled a bit with Will, for he was very proud of his new knighthood. Squatting down so that his eyes were level with Geoffrey's defiant ones, he said, "Why should you listen to me? Well, I can think of two reasons, lad. As it happens, I am a knight in the Earl of Salisbury's service. And in case it has escaped your notice, I am also much bigger than you. I'd wager I'd have no trouble at all dunking you in one of the horse troughs—accidentally, of course."

He saw rage flash in Geoffrey's narrowed blue eyes; he saw a sharp glimmer of intelligence, too. The boy might be spoiled, but he was no fool. His fury at being threatened was dampened by the realization that he did not want any more attention than they'd already attracted. "I do not believe you're a knight," he said scornfully, and content that he'd gotten the last word, he stalked away.

Will shook his head, glad that he wasn't a Breton. Richard was still lingering, watching with alert interest as he returned to the stall and began to rub his stallion down. "Geoff has mush for brains," he said after a few moments. "Who ever heard of a groom wearing a sword?"

"You're welcome," Will said dryly and the boy blinked. It did not take him long to figure it out, though.

"I suppose I was lucky you were here," he said, sounding as if he were not sure whether it should be a challenge or an apology.

"I suppose you were," Will agreed amiably, and when he reached for a brush, Richard stepped forward and handed it to him.

"Why not have a groom do that?"

"A man ought to take care of what's his, or at least know how to," Will said. "Want to help?"

Richard hesitated only a heartbeat. "I guess so."

"Give me that towel over there, then," Will directed, and this time the silence was companionable. "So . . . I take it you're not going to tell on Brother Geoff? Admirable. But if it were me, I'd want to see him punished."

Richard had his father's smoky eyes, his gaze already more guarded than that of many men. "He will be," he said, and Will bit back a smile.

"I see. So you'd rather dispense justice yourself."

Richard hesitated again and then grinned. Will showed him how to inspect the stallion's feet, looking for bruises to the sole or pebbles wedged between the frog and the bar, and when he finally left the stables, he'd acquired a second shadow.

Richard scuffed his feet, kicking at an occasional rock. "Are you going to Lusignan Castle with my mother and Earl Patrick?" Will confirmed that he was, and Richard shot him a sideways glance edged with envy. "They'll not let me come," he complained. "They said it was no reason to interrupt my studies."

Will thought Richard's safety might be a consideration, too, for it was less than two months since Henry had stormed Lusignan Castle and taken it from its rebellious owners. He was not about to say so, though, sure that would only make the journey all the more irresistible to Richard. By now they'd reached the great hall, and as they climbed the shallow steps, Will reminded Richard that Lusignan was less than twelve miles distant so it would entail only an overnight stay. That did not seem to give Richard much solace, and he soon abandoned Will in favor of pursuing his own interests.

For Will, nothing mattered but breakfast, and he elbowed his way toward the tables. As soon as he was recognized, he found himself fending off jests about his nocturnal hunting expedition and speculation about his quarry. Will took the teasing in stride and helped himself to sausages and fried bread. His uncle and the queen were seated at the high table and he watched them for a while, wondering if others noticed the coolness between them.

There were no overt signs of animosity, of course; Queen Eleanor would never be that obvious. But Will knew she'd been displeased by her husband's decision not to name her as regent in his absence, instead placing her under the protection of his deputy, Salisbury. Will thought the king could hardly have done otherwise. Even though he'd quelled the January revolt with a heavy hand, some of the rebels remained on the loose. Will had heard so many stories about Henry Fitz Empress's willful queen that he was unsurprised by Eleanor's lack of feminine timidity. This was the same woman, after all, who'd coaxed the French king into taking her on crusade.

The king had departed Poitiers three days earlier for Pacy in Normandy, where he was to discuss peace terms with Louis. Will hoped he would not soon return, for he was thoroughly enjoying this time in the

queen's service and was in no hurry to see it end. One of the more ob-
servant knights had begun joking that he was smitten with the queen,
warning him that King Henry might tolerate lovesick minstrels trailing after his lady, since that was the custom of the Courts of Love so popular with
highborn women, but he'd take a much dimmer view of lovesick knights.

Will had deflected the gibes with his usual good humor, knowing it
was actually much more complicated than that. He did not approve of
Queen Eleanor. How could he, for she'd defied virtually every tenet of
those conventions meant to govern female behavior. And yet he could not
deny that she cast a potent spell.

He'd never imagined he could harbor lustful thoughts about a woman
old enough to be his mother, but he did. For all that he knew the queen's
youth was long gone, he thought she was still one of the most desirable
women he'd ever laid eyes upon. Her enemies whispered that she must
practice the Black Arts to keep the years at bay. Will suspected her continuing beauty had more to do with the fact that God had been so generous with His gifts than with a Devil's pact. Common sense told him, too,
that a queen was bound to age more gracefully than a potter's widow, for
she had the best that their world could offer.

Not that he entertained any delusions about acting upon his wayward
yearnings. He was far too practical and far too honorable. If he'd have
gone to his grave before revealing the name of Magali, his Poitiers bedmate, he was not one to fantasize about seducing his queen. But he could
admire her from a respectful distance, as he was doing this morning in
Poitiers's great hall. She was fashionably attired in a gown of forest green,
her face framed by a veil and wimple whiter than snow, laughing at something her son was saying. Will had not noticed Richard's approach until
then. The boy straightened up and backed away, displaying his courtly
manners. As he did, his gaze happened to wander toward Will, and he
grinned suddenly, almost conspiratorially. It occurred to Will that he now
had a friend in the royal household, and he grinned back at the boy.

Eleanor tilted her face toward the sky, luxuriating in the
warmth of the spring sun on her skin. The very air of Poitou had a different tang. English air was like inhaling fog. Misted mornings and drizzle
and the pungent scent of the sea—that was what she'd most remember
about the realm Harry's father had called "that godforsaken isle." The
damp winters in Paris had saturated its air in moisture, too. Amazing that

she'd survived so many years of exile without succumbing to consumption. Even the colors seemed brighter now that she was back in her own lands. She could taste nature's bounty on the wind, hear the rhythm of life in the rustling of newly budding trees.

They were only a few miles from Lusignan by now and she hesitated when Salisbury proposed that they stop for a time, as her instinct was to push ahead. But as she glanced around at her traveling companions, she changed her mind. Renée was no horsewoman and she was casting wistful looks at the whispering grass and beckoning roadside shade. Several of Salisbury's knights had the pinched pallor of men badly hungover. While neither Louis nor Henry was much of a drinker, Eleanor could not say the same for the men of her own family and this was an expression quite familiar to her. Even young Marshal was nodding sleepily in the saddle. Her resentment of Salisbury notwithstanding, she did not want to oppose his every suggestion from sheer contrariness, and she nodded her assent.

Three of the men at once sprawled in the grass, arms shielding their eyes. Renée set about unpacking a wicker basket, and soon had two young knights eager to be of assistance. Salisbury was seeking to ease a cramp in his leg, complaining jokingly to his nephew about his "elderly, aching bones." Will was nodding sympathetically, but Eleanor knew he could not begin to comprehend the ailments of age. When she'd been one and twenty, she couldn't have, either.

Jordan, her trusted clerk, was nursing a swollen ankle, but he'd insisted upon accompanying her. Now he limped toward her, proffering a flagon and cups from Renée's basket. She let him pour for them both, then found a convenient tree stump to sit upon, spreading her skirts carefully to avoid splinters. She was more restless than usual today, for she'd slept poorly the night before, troubled by fragmented, dark dreams she could not recall upon awakening.

Will Marshal was looking after the horses, leading Eleanor's mare over to graze in a patch of sweet spring grass. Eleanor watched him approvingly; he was never one to shirk duties or responsibilities. She knew full well that he was in the early stage of infatuation, but she felt sure he'd get through it without embarrassing either one of them. There was a faint satisfaction, too, in knowing this young knight did not think her charms had aged or her appeal withered. Because of his vulnerability, though, she'd taken care not to flirt with him. Her life was complicated enough without adding the hint of scandal. She stared down into the dark amber liquid in her cup, an ugly, unbidden thought surging to the surface: that Harry might like it if she gave him an excuse to pack her off to a nunnery in disgrace, for then he could bring his concubine to court, flaunt her for all the world to see.

"Madame . . ." Will had ventured closer, not sure whether he should intrude upon thoughts that did not seem very pleasant. She glanced up, blinking in the mellow sunlight as she banished her ghosts and her grievances, and then smiled.

"May I fetch you something else to drink?" he asked, gesturing toward the cup which had tilted and was spilling onto the ground at her feet.

"No, I am not thirsty. I thank you for the offer, though." Will was one of the few men in their party who was wearing his hauberk; Salisbury and most of the others had shed their chain-mail as the sun rose higher in the sky, loading them onto one of the packhorses. Studying Will now, Eleanor asked, "Are you not hot in that armor? I never did understand how men could abide hauberks in the heat of the Holy Land."

"They wore tabards over their hauberks to shield them from the worst of the sun." No sooner had Will spoken than he cursed himself for a clumsy fool. Here he was, instructing the queen about crusading warfare when she'd been there to see it for herself, which was more than he could say. He would have loved to discuss her experiences with her, to hear her firsthand account of the disastrous Second Crusade, but a queen could not be prompted or, worse, interrogated. "These are not the most comfortable garments," he admitted. "But I've gotten used to the weight by now and—"

He cut himself off so abruptly and oddly that Eleanor frowned. "Will? Is something amiss?"

"No . . . probably not." He was still staring intently toward the horizon even as he gave her a sheepish smile. "It was just that I thought I saw something in that grove of trees up ahead, like the flash of sunlight hitting a hauberk or sword . . ." He shifted to get another look, and then drew an audible breath.

"Uncle!" Whirling, he shouted to Salisbury, "Men-at-arms in those woods!"

Salisbury trusted Will's judgment enough to take the warning as gospel. Scrambling to his feet, he headed for the packhorse holding their armor. Eleanor had responded just as swiftly, and she had reason now to be thankful for Will Marshal's coolness under fire. She was reaching for her mare's reins when he shook his head.

"No, take my horse. You can ride faster astride."

She at once saw the sense in that, for sidesaddles were not meant for flight. Within seconds, he'd assisted her up onto his stallion and was running toward Renée. Jordan had kept his head, too, and was already swinging up into the saddle. All around them, men were racing to reclaim their chain-mail or to mount their startled horses, cursing as the animals shied away. But by then their foes had realized their ambush had been discovered and they were spurring their stallions out onto the road.

"Madame, go! We'll hold them here!" Salisbury paused only long enough to make sure Eleanor was heeding him before swinging back toward the plunging packhorse. Appalled that he'd let himself be taken unaware like this, as if he were a raw stripling, he was relieved to see the queen send her horse across the field at a dead run, with Jordan and Renée following behind. His nephew had caught the closest horse and leaped into the saddle, sword in hand. Their assailants were splitting into two bands, one group of horsemen peeling off in pursuit of Eleanor, the other intent upon eliminating her defenders as quickly as possible.

"After them, Will!" Salisbury roared a command that was not needed, for Will was already racing to intercept the queen's pursuers. Christ, there were so many of them! Salisbury fumbled hastily for his hauberk, but even as he struggled to pull it over his head, he ran out of time. He was bitterly aware of how badly he'd failed his queen, but he never saw the weapon that claimed his life, a hunting spear flung with deadly accuracy, burying itself in the small of his back.

Will had sent his stallion crashing into the closest of the queen's pursuers. As the man's horse foundered, Will drove his sword into that unprotected area under the armpit, then pulled the blade free in a spray of crimson. To his left, he saw a familiar figure, one of his uncle's knights, closing fast on a man astride a screaming bay stallion. Sir Roger swung a spiked mace in a lethal arc, smashing into bone and ripping away flesh. Will spurred his stallion after a knight wearing a kettle-shaped helmet without a nasal guard. Drawing alongside, he parried the other's thrust, then used his shield to club the man from the saddle; there was no time for finesse, for any of the skillful swordplay he'd learned as a squire to the Chamberlain of Normandy. He glanced over his shoulder, could not find Sir Roger in the mêlée. That distracted moment was to cost him dearly, giving one of his foes the chance to kill his horse.

As the stallion stumbled, Will kicked his spurs free of the stirrups before it went down, and hit the ground rolling. Regaining his feet, he was

almost trampled by a man on a lathered bay. He was hopelessly outnumbered by now, stranded in the midst of his enemies. Retreating toward a
thorny hedgerow that would offer some protection to his back, he blinked
sweat from his eyes, tasting his own blood on his tongue. Swords drawn,
they feinted and dodged, cursing him freely. But they kept out of range of
Will's gory sword. By the time he realized what they were up to, it was too
late. There was movement in the hedgerow behind him, a blade slashing
through the branches. Pain seared up Will's thigh. His strength draining
away in a gush of blood, he wobbled and then sank to his knees, still
clutching his sword even as they closed in.

H ER ESCORT'S HEROIC EFFORTS had given Eleanor the time
she needed to reach the woods. She checked the stallion just long enough
for Jordan and Renée to catch up to her. If they were found, it would
mean Jordan's death, for she knew he'd never stand by helplessly and let
her be taken, not even if she ordered him to yield. Renée would likely be
ransomed—eventually—but she was far too pretty to be unmolested. As
for her own fate, she knew how great a prize she'd be. The fools thought
Harry would pawn Heaven and earth to secure her release. She preferred
not to put his devotion to the test. Moreover, she could not be sure that
she'd be luckier than Renée. Men desperate enough to capture a queen
might well be careless of the conventions of warfare, the dictates of
honor. And if her suspicions were right about the identity of her assailants, they could have taught the Devil himself about sin.

There was no time to explain herself. Jordan and Renée would have
to take her on trust. As Will's stallion had outdistanced his pursuers, her
brain had been racing, too, weighing her options. Even if they could
elude these men, they were too far from Poitiers, would never make it
back. Thank the Blessed Lady Mary that these were her lands! She'd
grown up here, hunted as a girl in these woods, knew the roads and rivers
and trails as well as any poacher. Their only possible refuge was the castle
at Lusignan. But a return to the Poitiers Road would be madness, would
result in their capture straightaway.

Jordan's face was flushed with exertion; he was no longer in the prime
of youth. Renée was perching precariously on her sidesaddle and Eleanor
spared a moment to damn the fools who'd decreed that women should not
ride astride. Renée's veil and wimple were gone, ripped off by an overhanging branch, and there was a smear of blood on her cheek. Eleanor

knew, though, that the girl had courage. She'd need it; they all would. She gestured silently to her left and turned her stallion in that direction. Jordan and Renée exchanged baffled looks, but they followed after her without hesitation.

It was slow going. Like threading a needle, Eleanor thought, and she'd never been one for ladylike pastimes. A laugh welled up in the back of her throat and she quickly suppressed it, recognizing the symptoms, for this was not the first time she'd faced physical danger. Fear could breed an odd sort of excitement, an emotional rush that had something of the giddiness and caprice usually bottled in wine casks. She ducked under a jutting tree limb, but not in time; it snagged her veil. They were leaving a trail a blind man could follow, but that was the least of her worries at the moment. If her memories were false, they'd be ridden down soon enough, anyway. She resolutely refused to dwell upon that possibility, and soon thereafter her faith was rewarded by the glimpse of a familiar oak tree, splintered and seared by lightning, towering above the spring greenery like a pale, timbered tomb. This time Eleanor did not stifle her laugh. Beckoning to Jordan and Renée, she forged ahead and within moments had emerged onto a woodland path, narrow and winding, but to Eleanor as welcome a sight as the widest of the king's highways.

The wind carried to them the distant sounds of male voices, hunters tracking their quarry with too much confidence for stealth. She could understand their cockiness, their certainty that she'd soon be so mired down in the heavy brush that she'd be easily overtaken. They would stumble onto the path, too, but she knew she was less than a mile now from safety. The odds were even, and she'd never asked for more than that.

The ground was too irregular to let their horses run full out. They urged the animals forward as fast as they dared, and suddenly the woodland canopy blocking the sun was gone and they were emerging into a blaze of light. The Vonne's placid surface gleamed like a polished looking glass, and shimmering ahead in the heat was the hilltop town of Lusignan. It lay in a horseshoe curve of the river, and Eleanor felt a grudging admiration for her husband's military skills; the castle looked well nigh invincible and yet Harry had taken it in less than a week.

"Listen to me," she told her companions. "I suspect there are men in hiding, watching for our approach. I'd wager my chances of salvation that the de Lusignans are the ones on our trail. If I'm right, they'll have remembered that this forest track cuts through the woods to the castle. By now they'll have sent scouts to wait for us. They'll be out of sight, not wanting to alert the garrison. But as soon as they see us, they'll have nothing left to lose."

Jordan's beard and hair were incongruously seeded with flecks of torn foliage, but his smile never faltered. "So it's a race, is it?" he said, and Eleanor nodded. Renée was ashen. She offered a smile, too, though, or at least a game imitation of one, and Eleanor gave her an encouraging look, then assured them there was a shallow ford just ahead.

Leaving the cover of the woods, they had gone only a short distance before horsemen came bursting out of hiding, closer than Eleanor had expected. Giving Will's stallion his head, she raced for the river. He slackened speed only slightly as he splashed down the bank, and she blessed the young knight's foresight; her own mare was skittish around water. She heard a choked scream from Renée, but the girl was on her own now; they all were.

Risking a glance over her shoulder, she was sorry she had, for their pursuers were only a few yards behind. A spear struck the water to her right. If that was an attempt to intimidate her into giving up, it was a waste of good weaponry. As her stallion scrambled to shore, a flock of arrows flew over her head, but these shafts had been launched from the walls of the castle. She could see faces peering over the battlements and she opened her mouth to demand entry, but there was no need. A postern gate was opening. She asked her stallion for one final burst of speed and he surged forward, galloping through the gate into the bailey.

Reining him in, she turned in the saddle, just in time to see the gate slamming shut behind Jordan and Renée. Men were crowding around her, shouting questions, asking if she'd been attacked by bandits, if there were others in danger, any deaths. Eleanor waited until she got her breath back, and by then, someone recognized her. An incredulous cry went up: "The queen!"

Hands reached up to her and she slid from the saddle. The faces surrounding her were so alarmed, so solicitous that she thought she must look like the Wrath of God. Jordan shoved his way toward her, a supportive arm around a stumbling Renée. If she was as disheveled and wet and dirtied as they were, no wonder these men were staring at her as if doubting their own senses. "Where is your castellan?" She was still somewhat breathless but pleased by the level tones of her voice.

"Madame!" A path was clearing for him. He was one of her husband's handpicked constables. She could only hope that he was as capable as Harry thought him to be, for there was no time to lose. Stilling his questions with an upraised hand, she told him, as concisely and quickly as possible, what had happened and her belief that the de Lusignans were the ones behind the ambush. He at once put the castle on a war watch in the unlikely event that the de Lusignans should launch an attack upon Lusignan itself. He then led the rescue mission himself and that, too, won him favor with Eleanor. Only then did she let them escort her into the hall.

Renée gratefully accepted the assistance of the castellan's wife, but Eleanor declined. She had her share of vanity, as most beautiful women do, but washing her face or tending to scratches and bruises seemed of small matter, as long as the fate of her men remained unknown. It was only when she noticed that her skirt was ripped from waist to hem that she agreed to change into clothes provided by the Lady Emma. As soon as possible, she returned to the great hall, where she interrogated the garrison until she found a man who seemed reliable and dispatched him to Poitiers with a terse letter in her own hand. After that, there was nothing she could do but wait.

The two hours they were gone seemed interminable to Eleanor. Jordan and a still visibly shaken Renée had joined her vigil by now. Unfortunately, so had the Lady Emma, and in no time at all, she was rubbing Eleanor's nerves raw with her well-meaning, smothering attentions.

Eleanor understood her agitation, even her compulsive need to play the lady of the manor, offering every hospitality to England's queen, Aquitaine's duchess. But the last thing she wanted was to commiserate with Emma about "the outrage," as the castellan's wife kept calling it. Jordan finally took Emma aside and, as politely as possible, explained that the queen had faced down bandits before. She had been in a caravan attacked by the Saracens; she had thwarted several attempts at abduction by would-be suitors; her ship had even been captured by the fleet of the Emperor of Byzantium, rescued in the nick of time by the King of Sicily's galleys. Emma listened, openmouthed, to this recital. Agreeing meekly that the queen's earlier experiences were indeed more harrowing than this encounter with the de Lusignans, she promised to say no more of the unfortunate events of the day, at least not in the queen's hearing. Jordan sighed with relief, grateful that he'd averted bloodshed at least once today.

The castellan and his men returned at dusk, bearing a body wrapped in a blanket and grim word for Eleanor. They'd arrived too late to be of help, had found only the corpses of the dead and a few men too badly wounded to be worth carrying off. He was bringing the injured back by horse litter, but he held little hope for their recovery. They'd need an oxcart to retrieve the other bodies, but out of respect, he'd brought back the remains of my lord Salisbury.

Eleanor watched bleakly as the body was carried into the castle chapel. When the priest gently pulled away the blanket, she gazed down for some moments into the earl's face, and then made the sign of the cross.

"My lord Raymond?"

The castellan turned at once. "Madame?"

"The earl had a nephew with him, a young knight named William Marshal. Was he amongst the wounded?"

"No, Madame," he said quietly. "But it may be that he was amongst those taken prisoner. God grant it so."

Eleanor nodded somberly and they walked in silence from the chapel. Outside, the sky had begun to darken. This accursed Wednesday in Easter Week was at last coming to an end. But she did not yet know how many men had bought her freedom with their blood.

HENRY HAD NEVER BEEN so exhausted in all his life. Upon getting word of the attack upon Eleanor, he had immediately broken off talks with the French king and raced south. By skimping on sleep and changing horses frequently, he and his men had reached Poitiers a full day before anyone expected him. But almost from the moment of his arrival, nothing had gone right.

With an effort, he fought back a yawn. His head was throbbing, his eyes red-rimmed from the dust of the road, and he doubted that there was a single muscle in his entire body that was not aching. He wanted nothing so much as a few uninterrupted hours of sleep now that he knew Eleanor was indeed unharmed, but instead he found himself presiding over the high table in the palace's great hall, having had time only for a brief, un-satisfactory reunion with Eleanor and a quick wash-up. Even Henry's careless disregard for protocol would not permit him to miss this solemn meal of mourners. Just two hours before his arrival, Patrick d'Evereaux, Earl of Salisbury, had been laid to rest in Poitiers's church of St Hilary, far from the mausoleum in Wiltshire where his kindred were buried.

The Countess of Salisbury had been given a seat of honor on Eleanor's left. She looked wan and weary, but she'd always struck Henry as a very competent, no-nonsense kind of woman, and he expected her to cope with her husband's death as capably as she had life's other crises. For a moment, his gaze rested upon his own wife, regal in black. Wearing dark colors for mourning was essentially a Spanish custom, but once word spread that Eleanor had worn black for the Earl of Salisbury, Henry felt certain that it would become the fashion at funerals throughout Aquitaine, Normandy, and France.

Eleanor looked tired, too; the powder she'd applied with a skillful hand could not quite camouflage the shadows hovering under her eyes. But with him, she'd been infuriatingly offhand, almost dismissive of her ordeal, brushing aside his concern for her emotional well-being, acting as if her physical safety was all that mattered. He knew better than most that the mind could be wounded by violence as easily as the body; he'd seen hardened soldiers haunted by battlefield memories, and he assumed that women would be far more susceptible than men to dark thoughts and dreads. Eleanor would have none of it, though, refusing to admit her fears even to him. He'd been irritated by her bravado, reminding her that it was well and good to assume an air of public sangfroid but hardly necessary in the privacy of their bedchamber. But he'd gotten only an unfathomable look from the depths of those greenish hazel eyes, a shrug, and a murmured, "I do not know what you want me to say, Harry . . . truly."

Nor had his edgy, irascible mood been improved any by the presence of Eleanor's uncle, Raoul de Faye. The younger brother of Eleanor's late mother, Raoul was about ten years older than Eleanor, with a handsome head of silver hair, snapping dark eyes, and a cultivated air of jaded worldliness that Henry had encountered all too often in Aquitaine. There was an obvious fondness between uncle and niece, and Eleanor seemed to respect his political judgment. Henry thought that was unfortunate, for he most definitely did not. Raoul was no admirer of his, either, and the tension between the two men sputtered and flared even on so somber an occasion as this. Eleanor's constable, Saldebreuil de Sanzay, was seated at the high table, too, as well as a number of other familiar faces, all vassals of Eleanor's, including a few whose loyalties he considered suspect. Eleanor appeared to be doing exactly what he'd asked of her—mending fences with the volatile Poitevin barons, soothing ruffled feathers, healing bruised pride as only a woman could. So why was he not better pleased with her efforts?

Henry was so caught up in these brooding thoughts that he did not hear the Bishop of Poitiers's query and had to ask the cleric to repeat the question, one which only reminded him of the many reasons he had to be wroth with the meddling King of France. For all that people talked of Louis's piety as if he were almost saintly, Henry did not consider shiftiness to be a virtue.

"Yes, my lord bishop, you heard right," he said tersely. "The Count of Angoulême has sought refuge in Paris. The French king is getting into the habit of making rebels and malcontents welcome at his court." And although he was speaking ostensibly of the fugitive count, he was actually thinking of Thomas Becket, Canterbury's exiled archbishop.

The rest of the meal passed without incident, aside from an embarrassing mishap by Henry and Eleanor's son Geoffrey, who tripped and lurched into one of the trestle tables, overturning wine cups into laps and splattering gravy over the fine clothes of several unhappy guests. Geoffrey flushed to his hairline with humiliation, and Henry felt pity stir, remembering a similar accident from his own boyhood, this one involving a dropped soup tureen. Even the offspring of the highborn were taught by doing, and boys were expected to wait upon tables in the great hall as part of their lessons in courtesy and etiquette. Geoffrey had learned little this day but mortification, though, and as Henry's eyes met Eleanor's, they shared a brief moment of parental solicitude.

Leaning closer so her voice would carry to Henry's ear alone, she murmured, "I know what Scriptures say about pride going before a fall, but must it be out in the full glare of public scrutiny? At least Richard sought to cheer him up; you did notice that? Too much of the time they are squabbling like bad-tempered badgers. It is heartening to see that they can close ranks when need be."

Henry wasn't as sure of what he'd seen as Eleanor. There had been a brief exchange of words between the boys, as she said, and he supposed Richard could have been offering sympathy. But if so, Geoffrey was an utter ingrate, for he'd responded with a look of loathing. He kept his suspicions to himself, for he had nothing to go on except sour memories of his rivalry with his own brother. Remembering, too, his father's feuding with his uncle Helie, he said softly, "The House of Anjou could give Cain and Abel lessons in brotherly strife. Let's hope our lads take after your side of the family."

Reaching across the tablecloth, he clasped her hand in his. "Are you truly sure you are all right, Eleanor? This I can promise you, that Guy and Geoffrey de Lusignan will come to look upon death as their deliverance."

What was most chilling about his statement was that it was said so matter-of-factly. Eleanor did not doubt that he meant to wreak a terrible vengeance upon the de Lusignans, and the thought of their suffering did ease some of her rage and grief over the deaths of her men. She merely nodded, though, for her throat was suddenly too tight for speech. It hurt more than she could endure, this sudden glimpse of what had once been hers and was forever lost. Discussing their children and their mutual mortal enemies, she could not help remembering a time when they'd been in perfect harmony, allies as well as consorts, hungering after empires and dynasties and each other, their aspirations and ambitions as entwined as oak and ivy, impossible to separate one from the other without destroying both.

WILLIAM MARSHAL'S SLEEP was shallow and fretful, the grim realities of his captivity clawing insistently at his dreams, seeking admittance to his last refuge. When he turned over, pain lanced through his leg, jarring him to full wakefulness. He lay very still, willing the throbbing to stop. The air was musty, and with each breath, he inhaled the familiar, foul odors of straw and sweat and urine and manure. He remembered where he was now, chained in another stable in an unknown castle, with his only certainty that the morrow would bring fresh indignities, more miseries.

So far he hadn't been ill treated; the de Lusignans wanted him alive in hopes of making a profit. They were desperate for money, reduced to banditry by their failed rebellion, and had carried off all of the captured knights, save those near death. Guy and Geoffrey de Lusignan had been almost as enraged by the Earl of Salisbury's death as they were by the queen's escape. Will was a knight, too, and therefore he might be worth ransoming. Will had done his best to foster that belief, stressing his kinship to Earl Patrick at every opportunity. He did not expect his uncle's widow to barter for his freedom, though. Why should she deplete her dower on his behalf? She barely knew him. The bulk of Salisbury's estates would pass with his title to his eldest son and he was even less likely to ransom a needy young cousin. And unlike the other men seized, Will could never have afforded to ransom himself.

But there was no other way for Will to buy time. The de Lusignans had split up their men and prisoners into small groups and Will's captors could not read or write. Nor could he, and it had taken them a few days to find someone they trusted enough to write to Countess Ela. By Will's reckoning, it would take several weeks to get the countess's refusal or counteroffer. At that point, he planned to assure them that his eldest brother would pay the ransom.

Lucky for him that his father was two years dead, for Will could not see him parting with so much as an English farthing to rescue an expendable younger son. He'd made that abundantly clear at the siege of Newbury. His brother John would at least make a token offer; their mother would see to that. But John was always short of money and could not be expected to sell family lands for his sake. The game must still be played out, though, for the alternative was an unmarked woodland grave with none to mourn or pray for the salvation of his soul.

Will was by nature an optimist, and at first he'd held fast to hope. All he had to do was avoid antagonizing his guards needlessly and wait for his injury to heal. Once he was strong enough, surely he could find an opportunity to escape. But after a week in captivity, he was no longer so confident. While he'd not been abused, neither had his wound been tended. He had done the best he could, fashioning a bandage by ripping off the legs of his braies and using the cord to fasten it. He'd even been able to find a flicker of humor in his predicament, for his cordless, torn braies kept sliding down to his hips every time he stood up.

The humor had soon faded, though. His captors were understandably fearful of the English king's wrath and dared not spend more than one night under the same roof lest their presence be betrayed to Henry's spies. They put Will in mind of mice trying to avoid a stalking cat, scurrying from one burrow to another. Sometimes it was a castle of a de Lusignan ally or vassal; twice they'd had to sleep in the woods and once even in the nave of a small church.

Not surprisingly, Will's leg was not healing as it ought and with each passing day, the risk of infection grew greater. Will would far rather have died on the battlefield as his uncle had done than to die slowly and painfully from a festering wound. He had never been one to borrow trouble, feeling sure that life would invariably dole out his allotted portion. Nor had he ever been fanciful or readily spooked. But lying awake in the stable blackness, he found it alarmingly easy to imagine that Death was lurking in those gloomy shadows, no longer willing to wait.

If only they would remain here for a day or two. Every hour that he spent in the saddle lessened his chances of recovery. That night, they'd dragged him into the great hall to show the castellan their prize, giving him a sudden sense of pity for the bears chained and set upon by dogs for the amusement of spectators. As he listened to their boasting, he could feel a slow anger stirring, embers from a fire not fully banked. They had ambushed a highborn and defenseless woman, their own liege lady, had slain men not wearing armor. His uncle had been struck down from behind. Where was the honor in that?

He'd managed to contain his rage, to appear oblivious to the jeering and insults of those in the hall. He was never to know the castellan's name, but the face he would not soon forget—florid and rotund, fringed with greying hair that reminded him of a monk's tonsure, and eyebrows so thick the castellan seemed to be peering out at the world through a hedge. Will had good reason to resent the man, for he'd been the one to write the ransom letter to Countess Ela. He'd been sorry to see that the castellan had a young, comely wife, thinking that she deserved far better than she'd gotten. She was the only one in the hall who'd regarded him with a hint of sympathy, had even sent a servant over to offer him hippocras when the others were served. The wine had flowed like nectar down Will's parched, scratchy throat, but then he'd had an unsettling thought: was this to be the last wine he ever tasted?

The castellan had accorded his guests center stage long enough to let them brag of their exploits. Only then did he ruin their triumph by giving them his news. While the January rising against Henry Fitz Empress had been instigated by the de Lusignan brothers, they'd been joined by the Counts of Angoulême and La Marche, and Robert and Hugh de Silly. But Robert had ended up in one of Henry's dungeons on a diet of bread and water and, according to the castellan, he'd soon died of it. Will was surprised by Robert's rapid decline and death, for men could survive a long time on even such meager rations. He felt not a shred of pity for the dead rebel, though, and for the rest of his unpleasant evening in the hall, he consoled himself by imagining the de Lusignans in a sunless cell, sharing Robert de Silly's unhappy fate.

But if the castellan's revelation had given Will some grim comfort, it had sent his captors into a panic. Will had watched them conferring amongst themselves, failing utterly to disguise their distress, and grieved that his uncle could not have been slain fighting more worthy foes than the de Lusignans and their dregs.

A horse nickered softly nearby, as if acknowledging Will's presence in the stable. Stretching out as much as his shackles would permit, he sought to ease his aching leg in vain; no position lessened the pain. He supposed their decision on the morrow would depend upon the state of their stomachs and heads. Panic-stricken they undoubtedly were, but they were also likely to be suffering acutely from swilling down enough wine to fill the castle moat. Asking the Almighty to inflict the torments of the damned upon them all come morning, he then said a brief prayer for his dead uncle, his ill-used queen, and the other men who'd died on the Poitiers Road. After gently reminding his Savior that his own plight was in need of redressing, he finally fell into an uneasy doze.

One of his guards stumbled into the stable the next morning, wincing with each step, and Will decided his chances of spending another night here had dramatically improved. He was given water and sullenly assured that someone would remember to feed him, sooner or later. After that, he was left alone. He napped intermittently as the morning wore on and he was famished by the time another hungover captor brought him a bowl of stew and a loaf of stale bread. Not having a spoon, he ate with his fingers, concluding that it was better he not know the identity of the mystery meat coated in grease. He was using a chunk of the bread to sop up the gravy, trying not to think upon the tasty meals he'd enjoyed in Poitiers, when he heard soft footsteps in the straw outside the stall.

The girl was young, with knowing dark eyes and a tempting swing to her hips. It took Will just a moment to place her in his memory; she served the castellan's wife. She was accompanied by the same guard who'd fetched his food. The man still looked greensick, but seemed a little happier about this new duty.

"My lady said even a poor wretch of a prisoner deserves God's pity," she announced in a disapproving voice that contrasted with the flirtatious look she gave Will through sweeping lashes. "This is for you." Putting a large round loaf of bread down beside him, she sashayed out, batting those lashes at Will's captor and drawing him after her with such ease that she looked back at Will and winked.

Will sniffed the bread and sighed happily, for it was freshly baked, still warm, marked with Christ's Cross. But as he started to tear off a piece, his fingers found an oddity. Squinting in the dim light, he discovered that a section of the loaf had been removed and then replaced, like a plug corking a bottle. Extracting it, he found that the center had been hollowed out to conceal strips of flaxen cloth and a rag saturated with an unguent of some kind. The smell was faintly familiar and he thought he caught the whiff of yarrow or perhaps St John's wort. He leaned back against the wall, staring down at the bandages and ointment in his lap, and for the first time since his troubles began, his eyes misted with tears.

Never had will known a spring to pass so slowly. April seemed endless, days merging one into the other until he no longer had a clear memory of any of them. At night he was so exhausted he slept like the dead and in the morning, he'd be hustled onto a horse again, once more on the run. But the wound in his thigh no longer leaked pus or threatened to poison his body with noxious humors, and by May, he could put weight on the leg without pain.

In May, too, their hectic, panicked pace eased up, for his captors learned that Eudo de Porhoët had rebelled again in Brittany and Henry had gone west to deal with this faithless vassal once and for all. No longer fearing the dragon's breath on the backs of their necks, the men finally felt secure enough to slow their flight, and that also assisted Will's recovery. Unfortunately, they had yet to drop their guard with him; he was always bound hand and foot on horseback, chained up at night. He was content to wait, though, for a mistake to be made. What else could he do?

In mid-May, they lingered for an entire week at a castle held by a distant de Lusignan cousin. Will occupied himself by watching for their vigilance to slacken, by imagining the vengeance he wanted to wreak upon every mother's son of them, and by giving fervent thanks to the Almighty and a Poitevin lord's kindhearted wife for mercies he probably didn't deserve.

He was napping in a shaft of afternoon sun that had slanted into the stables when he was jostled by a prodding foot. Opening his eyes, he saw his captors grinning down at him and he was instantly awake, edgy and alert. There was a new face among them, vaguely familiar . . . one of Guy de Lusignan's knights, a swaggering, scarred man named Talvas who'd been in the thick of the fighting on the Poitiers Road. Will hadn't seen him since early April and he felt an instinctive prickle of unease, for he'd gotten the impression that Talvas was only too willing to dirty his hands on his lord's behalf.

Talvas was grinning, which unnerved Will even more. "I know how much you're going to miss us all, lad, but we've come to a parting of the ways."

Will got slowly to his feet. "Are you going to let me go, then?" he asked with heavy sarcasm. To his astonishment, Talvas nodded.

"Yes . . . as soon as the hostages can be exchanged."

"What hostages?" Will demanded, no longer trying to hide his perplexity.

"Since trust is in such scant supply these days, making payment of your ransom was only slightly less complicated than laying plans for a new crusade. Each side had to agree to offer hostages, who are to be released concurrently as soon as you are freed and the money paid over."

Will stared at him, incredulous, still too wary for joy. "How much was I worth?"

Talvas made a hand gesture that was, oddly, both playful and obscene. "Thirty pounds."

Will was dumbfounded. "Are you telling me that Countess Ela paid thirty pounds for my release?"

Talvas gave him a quizzical look. "You *have* been kept in the dark, haven't you, lad? The Countess of Salisbury was not the one to ransom you. It was the English queen."

THE GREAT HALL at Poitiers was packed with people, so eager to see that they were treading upon one another's shoes and trailing hems, elbows digging into ribs, necks craning to watch Sir William Marshal welcomed by the queen. Eleanor smiled as he knelt before her on the dais, then beckoned him to rise and come forward.

Will had practiced his speech dozens of times on the ride to Poitiers. Now every polished phrase flew right out of his head and he could only stammer like a green lad, thanking the queen in a rush of incoherent, intense gratitude.

Eleanor mercifully put an end to his babblings and then subjected him to a scrutiny that missed neither the gaunt hollows under his cheekbones nor the stiffness in his step. "I would have you see my physician straightaway," she decreed, in tones that would brook no refusal for she well knew how loath most men were to consult leeches. "Once he assures me that you are indeed on the mend, you may take some time to visit your family in England if you so wish. I shall expect you back by summer's end, where a position will be waiting for you in my household."

If Will had been sputtering before, he was now stricken dumb. Eleanor leaned forward in her seat, saying quietly, "Did you truly think I would forget how you offered up your life for mine? I forget neither friends nor foes, Will, and I always pay my debts."

"Madame . . . you . . . you owe me nothing! It was my honor and my duty to be of service to you," Will insisted, regaining some of his poise.

She would have to provide him with another destrier and armor. Eleanor decided to put that task in Jordan's capable hands. Will's eyes were shining suspiciously, rapt upon her face. She'd been right in her assessment of him. Royal favor was the chosen coin of their realm and this young knight was shrewd enough to appreciate his great good fortune, upright enough not to hold it too cheaply. Courage, loyalty, good sense, and a wicked way with a sword—attributes worth far more than thirty pounds.

"If you want to repay me, Will," she said, "I ask only that you be as true to my sons as you've been to me."

CHAPTER TWENTY-SIX

July 1168
Poitiers, Poitou

HE SUN WAS SCORCHING, the air so still and sweltering that Eleanor felt as if she were suffocating. The sky was blanched whiter than bone, bereft of clouds and birds. People were gesturing, mouths ajar, their words thudding after her like poorly aimed stones. But the only sound she could hear was the wild hammering of her own heart, the pulsing of fear. Ahead was a clot of men, clustered in a noisy, shifting circle. Picking up her skirts, Eleanor began to run.

The crowd broke apart as she reached them, scattering like leaves before the wind. Dropping to her knees beside her son, Eleanor eased his head onto her lap. Blood matted the brightness of his hair, freckles glowing like fever spots against the ashen pallor of his skin, and a reddish bubble of saliva dribbled from the corner of his mouth. For a heartbeat of horror, she thought he was dead and her faith turned to ashes. But then she saw the reassuring rise and fall of his chest and her fingers found a pulse in his throat.

"Richard," she said, throwing out his name as a lifeline. "Richard, open your eyes."

His lashes quivered, then soared upward, giving her a glimpse of blessed blue-grey. "Am I hurt?" he asked plaintively and she choked back a sound that was neither laugh nor sob, but akin to both.

"Not as much as you will be." An empty threat and they both knew it. When had she ever punished him for showing too much spirit, too little caution? He was struggling to sit up and she hastily bade him to lie still, wiping away some of his blood with a hanging silken sleeve.

Richard grimaced and then spat into the dust. "I bit my tongue."

"Better a bitten tongue than a broken neck," Eleanor said unsympathetically. By now her physician had arrived, flushed and panting, vastly relieved to see his royal patient was conscious and complaining. Her uncle, Raoul de Faye, had gotten there, too, and she let him assist her to her feet, her eyes narrowing as she looked over at the men who'd failed to keep her son safe.

"Whose horse was he riding?"

The question was posed in level, measured tones, but it sent a ripple of unease up numerous spines. William Marshal stepped forward, shoulders squaring as if bracing for a blow. "It was mine, Madame."

Eleanor could not hide her surprise. "You, Will? You were the one who let a ten-year-old boy ride a battle destrier?"

Will was almost as pale as his young charge. "It was my stallion," he said hoarsely, "and my fault."

"It was not!" This indignant protest came from Richard. Ignoring the doctor's futile attempts to restrain him, the youngster lurched unsteadily to his feet. "Will forbade me to ride Whirlwind! And . . . and I am nigh on eleven, Mama!"

Eleanor glanced from one to the other, seeing the truth writ plain upon their faces. "It is commendable that you do not want blame to be placed unfairly, Richard. But you need not sound so proud of your disobedience. A borrowed horse is a stolen horse if taken without consent."

"Even if taken by the heir to Aquitaine?" Richard asked, with such overdone innocence that Eleanor had to smother a smile. As young as he was, her son knew full well that many of their society's strictures would never apply to him. She was also amused—and pleased—that he'd cast his identity in terms of Aquitaine, not England. But he needed to learn a lesson and she set about teaching him one now by going unerringly for the vulnerable spot in his armor.

"Putting your own neck at risk is foolish but forgivable, Richard. After all," she said dryly, "your father and I are fortunate enough to have sons to spare. A pity Will does not have stallions to spare. If you'd crippled or lamed his destrier by your recklessness, what was he supposed to do? Walk into battle? Mayhap ride pillion behind another knight?"

Her sarcasm stung. For the first time, Richard looked genuinely contrite. Turning toward Will, he mumbled an apology that was awkward, unwilling, and heartfelt, and when Eleanor instructed him to accompany the doctor back into the castle, he did not object.

"I will be there straightaway," Eleanor assured the doctor. "Keep him in bed even if you have to bind him hand and foot." She drew Will aside, then, for a brief colloquy, praising his honor while reminding him that any guardian of Richard's needed eyes in the back of his head and a strong sense of impending disaster.

Raoul had lingered and fell in step beside her as she moved away from Will. "That was a most impressive maternal lecture," he said admiringly. "No one listening to it would ever guess that you'd committed the very same sin when you were . . . twelve, thirteen?"

Eleanor gave him a speculative, sidelong glance and then an unrepentant smile. "Twelve," she admitted. "I'd just as soon you forbore to mention that to Richard, though, Uncle. He needs inducements to mischief like a dog needs fleas."

"I am a safe repository for all of your guilty secrets," Raoul proclaimed, with mock gravity. "Even the one I stumbled onto by mere chance this past week."

"And what secret would that be?"

"That you have a spy at the French court."

"Do I, indeed?"

Raoul nodded, watching her with a complacent smile. "You are asking yourself how I could know that. The answer is very simple. Spying is a demanding profession and the price of failure can be high, indeed. So the few who excel at their craft are much in demand. Your man is one of the best. I ought to know, for I have made use of his services myself from time to time."

Eleanor shrugged, untroubled by Raoul's discovery. She had a far more extensive surveillance system than Raoul—or even Henry—realized, and her French spy was only one of many irons in the fire. "You are right," she said, "about his abilities. His last visit to the French court was particularly productive. It seems that the Countess of Boulogne is playing the spy, too, these days. She recently warned Louis that Harry met with envoys of the Holy Roman Emperor."

Raoul's dark eyes gleamed, for he liked nothing better than being privy to secrets. "And of course poor Louis panicked, sure that meant Harry is hip-deep in conspiracy with Frederick, making ready to recognize the emperor's puppet Pope." He paused deliberately. "So . . . is he?"

Eleanor's smile was cynical. "Harry likes to keep his foes off balance. I rather doubt that he is seriously entertaining the idea of accepting Frederick's lackey as Christ's Vicar, but he finds that a useful weapon to wield in his infernal feuding with the Church's newest saint."

Raoul correctly interpreted that as a sardonic reference to Thomas Becket. "That raises an intriguing question," he observed. "Is the Countess of Boulogne playing the role of a double spy here, passing on information that Harry wants the French court—and the papacy—to have?"

"That thought sounds devious enough to have been Harry's. But if so, the countess is Harry's pawn, not his accomplice. She loathes him, you see."

"Why?" Almost at once, though, a memory stirred, allowing Raoul to answer his own question. "Of course . . . she is the usurper king's daughter!"

"I suspect she has a fresher grievance than Stephen and Maude's squabble over the English crown. Or have you forgotten that Harry plucked her out of a nunnery to wed a husband he'd handpicked for her?"

As little as Raoul liked to defend Henry Fitz Empress, he could not find fault with that particular maneuver. "Well, he could hardly stand by whilst Boulogne fell into unfriendly hands, could he? Great heiresses ought not to take the veil, for it is a waste of valuable resources."

"Like having a prize broodmare and refusing to breed her?"

Raoul laughed loudly. "I see marriage has not dulled your claws any!"

"Nor my wits, Uncle."

As much as Raoul enjoyed bantering with Eleanor, he had a compelling question to put to her. "I heard a rather remarkable rumor in Paris—that your husband has a grand scheme afoot to partition his domains amongst his sons and get Louis to make a formal recognition of their rights."

"Is that so surprising?" she parried. "You know Harry has long wanted to have Hal crowned in his lifetime and doubtless would have done so years ago if not for his quarrel with Becket."

"Yes, I know about that. I know, too, that it was a highly controversial proposal, one that sent many of his most trusted advisers into a panic, for there is no precedent in English history for crowning a king's son whilst the king still lives."

Eleanor shrugged. "Harry has always seen himself as Angevin, not English, and such coronations are known in his continental domains."

"But why make provisions for the younger sons during his lifetime? Did you happen to plant that particular seed, Eleanor?"

"No . . . I merely did what I could to nurture it once it had taken root."

Raoul gazed at her in perplexity. "I understand why you would want to see Richard recognized as the heir to Aquitaine. But why would Harry want to see such a division of his empire?"

"Harry is a practical man. He knows full well how difficult it would be for Hal to control dominions that stretch from the Scots border to the Mediterranean Sea. If Richard inherits Aquitaine and Geoffrey takes Brittany, that still leaves Hal with England, Anjou, and Normandy. Moreover, he naturally wants to provide for all his sons; what father would not?"

"Why do it now, though? Does he not realize the dangers inherent in such a plan? What is to keep his enemies from playing his sons off against one another—or even against him?"

"You sound as if you assume there will be an actual transfer of power, Uncle. Knowing Harry as you do, how can you be so naïve? Harry could learn to fly easier than he could learn to delegate authority. He'll be seeking to run his sons' lives and kingdoms until he draws his last breath. And if there is a way for him to rule from the grave, you may be sure he'll try to find it."

Raoul did not enjoy being called naïve; to a lord of Aquitaine, that was the ultimate insult. Scowling at his niece, he said, "Of course I know Harry intends to keep the lads on a tight rein. I am not a fool, Eleanor. And neither is your high-handed husband. Surely it must have occurred to him that his sons will not be satisfied for long with merely the trappings of power? At fourteen, Hal might be content as a puppet king, but will he at twenty? I can only assume that Harry has some guileful stratagem in mind. What is it, though?"

"If you figure it out, be sure to let me know," Eleanor said, blandly and mendaciously. It was simple, really, so simple that others overlooked it in their haste to ascribe complicated, calculating motives to an undeniably complex man. A man who'd been scarred by his prolonged and bitter struggle for the English crown. A man who loved his sons. A man who'd move Heaven and earth, if need be, to make sure they were not denied their rightful inheritance. Stephen was sixteen years dead, but not forgotten by Henry, never by Henry.

Eleanor could see the weaknesses inherent in Henry's planning, for it was predicated upon the premise that he could control his destiny and that of those he loved, that he could mold and shape sons and wife to his will as if they were malleable clay, not flesh and blood and bone, with needs and hungers of their own. She had encouraged him in these protective, paternal instincts, knowing that she was no longer acting in his best interests. But she was not about to betray him to Raoul, to reveal that his "grand scheme" was motivated in great measure by a father's fears.

They were nearing the great hall and she quickened her step, saying, "I hope Richard has not already bolted for freedom. He could have a broken leg and we'd still need to post a guard at his door to keep him bedridden. In that, he is his father's son, for certes."

Raoul hesitated only briefly and then said boldly, "But in all the ways that truly count, he is yours, Eleanor."

She did not answer, but neither did she rebuke him, and that in itself was telling. He'd suspected for some time that she was now steering her own course, that the hand on Aquitaine's helm was no longer Henry's. She had stopped and was regarding him with a faint, feline hint of a smile, her eyes reflecting nothing but sunlight and sky, and he looked in vain for traces of his sister, a soft-spoken, gentle soul who'd lived quietly and died young, so very long ago.

HENRY AWOKE SUDDENLY, torn from a troubled dream of bloodshed and betrayal. So jarring was his return to reality that for a moment, he could not remember where he was. It was only when he saw the slender female form beside him in bed that he recognized his surroundings. This was Falaise, the house he'd leased for Rosamund, a private refuge from the brutal border wars he'd been fighting for much of the year.

Sitting up, he cocked his head, listening to the dreary sound of sleet drumming upon the roof, pelting against the shutters. The hearth had burned out and the chamber was filling with frigid air; by morning, ice would be glazing the water in the washing lavers. After a lifetime of indifference to weather woes, he was startled to find himself minding this winter's misery so much. November was always a wretched month. It was a waste of breath to curse the cold or damn the wind. But still he shivered under coverlets of fox fur and at last rolled over, seeking Rosamund's warmth.

She was drowsily accommodating, stifling a yawn and entwining her arms around his neck. She was not surprised that he was awake again. For all the gold in his coffers and the lands under his rule, sleep was the one luxury that often eluded him. She sometimes tried to visualize the workings of his brain, imagining his thoughts galloping like the fleetest greyhounds through the mazes of his mind, going too fast for respite. Even during his pursuits of pleasure—his hunting, their lovemaking—he never let the man control the king. His hunger was for empires, his dreams of dynasties. He had too much, she feared, for any mortal man to govern. A surfeit of ambitions, enemies, dominions, even sons.

She'd been quieter than usual that evening. Henry was not accustomed to giving much thought to the moods of others; that was one of the many perquisites of kingship. But Rosamund was like a wildflower on a well-traveled path, too easily trodden underfoot. For her, Henry was learning to be circumspect.

He hoped she was not still fretting over that gossip about him and Eudo de Porhoët's daughter. The Breton rebel was claiming that he'd seduced the girl during her stint as his hostage and somehow Rosamund had heard of it. When she'd gathered up the courage to ask, he'd denied it with convincing sincerity. Eleanor would have known how little that meant. He could always lie with conviction, and saw his flexibility with the truth as a venal sin, too minor to matter. Of course Eleanor would not have asked the question in the first place. She'd have understood that such slander was merely another weapon, a convenient way for the Bretons to stir up hostility against their Angevin overlord. And she'd have understood, too, that even if it were true, it meant nothing to their marriage.

Henry sighed softly, regretting that Rosamund was still such an innocent. After a moment, the humor of it struck him—that he was wishing his mistress was as worldly as his wife—and he smiled to himself in the dark. He'd lied to Rosamund before and doubtless would do so again if need be, but this time he had indeed spoken true. He'd not so much as touched the hand of de Porhoët's precious daughter. Hellfire, when would he have found the time? For the past two years, he'd all but lived in the saddle, putting down one rebellion after another, only to have his foes rise up again like that blasted serpent in Greek myth, the nine-headed Hydra.

"What are you thinking of, my love?" she asked shyly. Her skin was soft and warm, her long, loose hair flowing like a silvery stream over them both, tickling his chest. This was a favorite query of hers, and although he considered it a girlish whim, he was usually willing to indulge her. Now he pondered briefly before coming up with a suitable answer, one that was a half-truth, for his upcoming meeting with the French king was never far from his thoughts.

"I was thinking about the Epiphany council. It has taken almost a year to get this far; I'd hate to have it all fall apart at the eleventh hour."

Rosamund snuggled still closer, offering her body heat as freely as she did her heart. He'd sent for her in the spring, soon after the de Lusignans had ambushed his queen. She'd seen him seldom in these past six months, though, for he'd spent the summer in Brittany and much of the autumn warring along the Marches of Normandy. During his brief visits, he'd talked of his intent to make peace with Louis, and she knew how much it meant to him, for without the cooperation and goodwill of the French king, he could not advance his plans for his sons.

Rosamund turned her head into the crook of his shoulder. She did not fully understand why he wanted to divide his empire amongst his sons, but she took comfort in the knowledge that Eleanor backed him in this; from all she'd heard, the queen was as shrewd as any man when it came to statecraft. She cared only for his peace of mind and she'd already begun praying daily for the success of his endeavor, entreating the Almighty to look with favor upon His son, Henry Fitz Empress.

Henry was engaging in a doomsday exercise, trying to envision all that might possibly go wrong during the council. He was by nature an optimist, always expecting to win whenever he took the field. But too much was at stake for overconfidence. He wanted to be prepared for any eventuality, any ambush. God knew, he had enemies enough at the French court, pouring poison into Louis's ear every chance they got.

"If Louis wants proof of my good faith," he said caustically, "he need look no further than my agreeing to meet with that traitor, Becket."

Rosamund propped herself up on her elbow and stopped him from speaking with a lingering kiss, for she'd learned early on that talking about Thomas Becket only served to kindle his wrath and often brought on one of his infrequent, intense headaches. Henry was willing to be distracted and for a time, Becket and the French king were forgotten. Afterward, he felt a throb of tenderness toward the woman lying in his arms, wanting to give her some of the comfort she gave to him.

"Did I tell you I'll be keeping my Christmas court at Argentan this year?"

Rosamund was already dreading the coming of Christmas. Never did she feel so alone, so aware of her precarious position as his concubine as she did during days of holy celebration. "I suppose your queen will be there, too," she murmured, striving to sound casual and failing miserably.

"No . . . Eleanor plans to hold court at Poitiers. I had too much still to do in Normandy to venture down into Poitou."

Later she would wonder why the queen had not joined him, then, at Argentan. Now she felt only a surging joy. "So you'll be able to find time for me?" she asked, too delighted for coyness or coquetry.

Henry laughed. "As much time as you want," he promised, tightening his arm around her shoulders. Outside, sleet and rain continued to fall, the wind wailing through the deserted streets of Falaise. But the storm's din no longer disturbed Henry and soon after, he slept.

CHAPTER TWENTY-SEVEN

❧

January 1169
Montmirail, France

ENRY WAS HAPPY that day, happier than he'd been in a long time, convinced that the Almighty had looked with favor upon this council of kings, for even the weather was cooperating. Above his head, the sky was the glowing shade of the lapis lazuli gemstone that shimmered upon his left hand, a gift from the French monarch. The air was cold but clear, free of the hearth-smoke that hovered over the streets of Montmirail, and the open fields were revived by a dusting of powdery snow, camouflaging the drab ugliness of winter mud and withered grass. The banners of England and France fluttered in the wind, proud symbols of power and sovereignty, but nothing gave him more pleasure than the sight of his sons.

They stood as tall and straight as lances, prideful and spirited and bred for greatness. Hal, already handsome enough to attract female eyes, his the fair coloring and easy grace of his grandsire. Richard, Eleanor's favored cub, with a lion's ruddy mane and a lion's strut. Geoffrey, tawny-haired and sharp-eyed, of smaller stature than his brothers, but lacking only years, not confidence. Sons to do a man proud, the true treasure of his kingship.

They had done their homage to the French king, showing a poise that belied their youth: Hal for Normandy, Anjou, and Brittany; Richard for Aquitaine. Richard was then plight-trothed to Louis's daughter Alys, a dark-eyed lively child who giggled and squirmed her way through the solemn ceremony of betrothal. Later in the year, Geoffrey would do homage to Hal for Brittany, thus assuring his ascendancy to the Breton duchy. Watching as his sons basked in the winter sunlight and the admiration of the highborn spectators, it was easy for Henry to believe that a dream once glimmering on the far horizon was now within his grasp. His heirs would not have to fight for their inheritances. Their rights would be recognized by one and all during his own lifetime, beginning with this public Epiphany Day acknowledgment by their liege-lord, the King of France.

Raising his hand, Henry signaled and his gift was led out. Murmurs swept the crowd. The pony was small even by the standards of its breed, less than twelve hands high at the withers, its coat groomed to an ebony sheen, saddle pommel and cantle lavishly decorated with jewels. The little animal submitted composedly to the French king's delighted inspection, displaying a temperament calm enough to reassure the most anxious of fathers. They were an ancient breed, roaming the moorlands of England's West Country since time immemorial, Henry explained, ideally suited for a lad's first mount. Louis thought so, too, and beamed as all eyes focused upon the little boy who held his heart. Philippe Auguste, the son whose birth had seemed so miraculous to his father and subjects that he was called Dieu-Donné. The God-Given.

Philippe was in his fourth year, but so undersized that he looked younger. He seemed reluctant and had to be coaxed forward by his father. When Louis lifted him up onto the pony, he froze and then started to cry. Henry was taken aback, for his sons had been eager to ride as soon as they could walk. Louis's attempts to reassure the little boy were futile, his tears giving way to hiccuping sobs and then to loud wails.

Henry's sons shared his astonishment. They were soon nudging one another and grinning; fortunately he was close enough to quell their amusement with a warning glare. Louis had plucked his son from the saddle, but Philippe did not seem to realize that he was no longer astride the pony and his shrieks continued until he felt the familiar arms of his nurse. As she carried him away, an awkward silence settled over the field.

Henry took in the glowering looks of the French and knew they suspected him of masterminding this debacle. He knew, too, that his denials would count for naught; his enemies invariably ascribed diabolical motives to his every act. But it had never occurred to him that Philippe would have a fear of horses. Moving over to Louis, he did his best to act as if Philippe's terror was perfectly natural, commenting casually that the lad was just a little too young yet. Louis nodded distractedly, his eyes following the small figure of his son surrounded by attendants as he was borne from the field.

Henry glanced again at his own boys. They were perfectly at ease in such a public setting, their eyes bright with suppressed laughter, and he felt a surge of fierce joy that these young fledglings were his. He wished suddenly that Eleanor could have been here to see how their sons shone at the French court. How proud she would have been, and how disdainful of Louis's timid little whelp.

Becoming aware that someone had drawn near, Henry turned. William of Blois, the newly consecrated Bishop of Sens, was not a man whose company he enjoyed, yet another of Stephen's troublesome nephews, nursing a grudge that should have been buried with Stephen. The bishop was watching him intently, as if searching for signs of satisfaction, but Henry was not about to give him any. Smiling blandly, he said that it had been a good day, indeed, a day in which the seeds of a lasting peace were sown.

The bishop could hardly disagree and responded with an innocuous platitude of his own. But then he wiped the smile from Henry's face by saying coolly, "Let us hope that another peace will be made on the morrow, when you meet with His Grace, the Archbishop of Canterbury."

THE WEATHER on the following day mirrored Henry's unsettled mood, the sky blotched with clouds the color of snow, occasional patches of pale blue hinting at a possible reemergence of the sun. Henry and Louis were flanked by the papal legates who had arranged this meeting: Simon, Prior of Mont-Dieu, Bernard de la Coudre, Prior of Grandmont, and Engelbert, Prior of Val-St-Pierre. The legates were scanning the crowd intently, for they had a stake in this outcome, too. If they could reconcile England's king with his rebellious archbishop, they'd earn the Pope's undying gratitude. This was a quarrel that only Thomas Becket seemed inclined to pursue; everyone else simply wanted it to go away, especially now that it jeopardized hopes of another holy quest. Henry had spoken of taking the Cross, but how likely was that if his feuding with Becket continued to occupy his time and energy? It had been a long and tiresome struggle, but the papal envoys had eventually convinced the archbishop that his protracted exile served neither his own interests nor those of his Church.

Henry was not as confident as the papal legates that Becket was finally willing to compromise. They had assured him this was so, that the archbishop would make a public submission without qualification or reservation, promising him that there would be no repeat of that restrictive clause Henry had found so odious at Clarendon, "saving our order."

Henry harbored some doubts, though, for he'd bribed a man who'd been privy to their discussions with Becket, and his spy had reported to him that Becket had wanted to substitute "saving our order" with a phrase even more inflammatory: "saving the Honor of God." The legates had been able to persuade Becket that this proviso was not only unacceptable but offensive, too, implying as it did that the king cared naught for the Almighty's Honor. Henry waited now to find out if the papal mission had been as successful as they claimed.

He hoped they were right. He, too, had grown weary of the unending discord. Becket had become a distraction, a tool for his enemies to use against him, a needless bone of contention with the Church. He would never understand why the other man had betrayed him, for that was how he still saw it. And until the day he died, this was a wound that would be imperfectly healed, sore to the touch. He had no intention of repudiating the Constitutions of Clarendon and suspected that Becket's opposition to them had not weakened during his years of exile. But the Pope governed on a far greater stage than the one Thomas Becket occupied, especially now that he'd been able to return to Italy. The King of England was a more valuable ally than one aggrieved archbishop, and a peace cobbled together with strategic silences and calculated omissions was still better than no peace at all.

The Bishop of Sens had just come into view, and as the crowd parted, Henry saw Thomas Becket. This was their first meeting in more than four years and his immediate, unbidden thought was that those years had not been kind to Thomas. Becket had always been of slender build; now he was gaunt. Fair-skinned by nature, his was now the sickly pallor of the ailing. Henry suddenly believed those stories he'd heard of Becket's deprivations and denials, no longer dismissed them as self-promotion. The archbishop's eyes were hollowed, his dark hair well salted with silver, and his black beard had gone white. Only his height was as Henry had remembered. His throat tightened unexpectedly; could this be the man who'd once playfully tussled with him over a crimson cloak?

He was not the only one to be assailed by memories. For a moment at least, both of their defenses were down and he saw his own regrets reflected in the other man's face. One of Becket's clerks was tugging at his lord's sleeve, whispering urgently in his ear; Henry recognized the florid face and fashionable figure of Herbert of Bosham. Becket made no response, keeping his eyes fixed upon Henry's face. And then he was striding forward, his somber black mantle reminding Henry anew of that long-lost scarlet cloak. Dropping to his knees in the snow, Becket said huskily:

"My lord king, I place myself in God's Hands and yours, for God's Honor and your own."

Henry at once reached out, raising the archbishop to his feet, and their attentive audience released pent-up breaths, beginning to believe that this meeting at Montmirail might actually begin the healing between them. Smiling, the French king bade the archbishop welcome, and cordiality reigned. When the time came for Becket's act of submission, the sun slid from behind a cloud and all took that as a good omen.

"My lord king, so far as this dispute which lies between us is concerned, here in the presence of the King of France and the bishops and barons and the young princes, your sons, I cast myself upon your mercy and your judgment . . ." Becket paused, drawing a deep, deliberate breath before saying, very clearly and distinctly, "Saving the Honor of my God."

There were audible gasps. The French king's expression of dismay was eclipsed only by the horror on the faces of the papal legates. Henry alone felt no real surprise, just an intense sense of disappointment, and then utter rage. His temper burst forth in a blaze of profanity, scorching enough to make men marvel that the snow had not begun to melt. Moving swiftly to Becket's side, the papal legate from the priory of Grandmont began to admonish him in low, wrathful tones, soon joined by his colleagues. The archbishop bore their rebukes and recriminations in silence, watching Henry all the while. The rest of the spectators did, too, believing the peace conference was at an end.

By then, Henry had gotten his rage back under rein. Glancing around, he saw that for once public sentiment was completely on his side; even Louis was staring at Becket as if he'd grown horns. Turning toward the French king, Henry said in a voice still tight with anger:

"It should be noted that the archbishop deserted his Church of his own free will. I did not drive him into exile. He fled of his own accord in the dead of night. And now he tells you that his cause is the Church's cause and that he is suffering for the sake of righteousness. The truth is that I have always been willing, and still am willing, to allow him to rule over the Church with as much freedom as any of those saintly archbishops who came before him."

"That is not so," Becket interjected, but Henry paid him no heed.

"My lord King of France, attend me if you please. Whatever displeases him, he will declare contrary to the Honor of God and thus he will ever have the last word with me. But lest I seem in any way not to honor God, I offer this proposal. There have been before me many Kings of England, some with more, some with less authority than mine. And there have been many Archbishops of Canterbury, great and holy men. Let him yield to me what the greatest and most saintly of his predecessors conceded to the least of mine and I shall be satisfied."

Henry saw at once that he had carried the day. The words "fair" and "reasonable" could be heard, heads nodding in agreement, eyes turning expectantly toward Thomas Becket, awaiting his response. When he remained silent, the disapproving murmurs grew louder. Somewhat to Henry's surprise, the coup de grâce was delivered by the French king. Sounding more sorrowful than angry, Louis said quietly:

"My lord archbishop, the peace you desire has been offered. Why do you hesitate? Do you wish to be more than a saint?"

NEITHER THE papal legates nor the French king were able to persuade Becket to retreat from the line he'd drawn, and the Montmirail conference broke up in disarray and ill will, most of it directed against the archbishop.

AN ASCENSION DAY MASS was in progress in St Paul's Cathedral. The priest had just kissed the altar stone and was now moving toward the right side of the High Altar for the Introit. In the back of the church, a young Frenchman clutched his mantle more tightly against his chest. Although it was a warm May morning, he was cold to the bone, shivering in the shadows as he awaited his moment. His name was Meurisse Berenger and he was in London on a holy mission. He knew full well that if he were caught, he could expect no mercy, but his courage was nourished by his faith, his utter certainty that he was on the side of right, doing battle with the ungodly.

"*Kyrie eleison.*" The parishioners dutifully chanted the Greek litany, and Berenger silently mouthed the words, not having saliva enough for speech. *Lord, have mercy on us.* "*Christe eleison.*" *Christ, have mercy on us.* Even as the familiar prayer echoed in his head, he was straining to see the High Altar. The priest was extending his hands, the beautiful Latin phrases rolling musically off his tongue: "*Gloria in excelsis Deo, et in terra pax hominibus bonai voluntatis.*" Berenger closed his eyes and tried not to think of the Antichrist, England's evil king. When he opened them again, he was shocked to hear the concluding words of the Gospel. So close now to the Offertory, so close!

After kissing the altar again, the priest turned to face the worshippers. "*Dominus vobiscum.*" Berenger slid a hand under his mantle, drawing out a packet wrapped in cloth. The penitents were withdrawing, as the remainder of the Mass was only for the faithful. People had moved into the aisle, approaching the High Altar with their oblations, and Berenger joined their ranks.

The priest was smiling, murmuring words of approval. When Berenger held out his bundle, it seemed to take forever until the priest reached for it, almost as if time itself had stopped. But then the letters were in the priest's hand and Berenger grabbed the startled man's wrist, holding his arm aloft so all could see.

"Let all men know," he cried loudly, "that your bishop, Gilbert Foliot, has been excommunicated by Thomas, Archbishop of Canterbury and Apostolic Legate!"

Escaping from St Paul's in the ensuing confusion, Berenger made his way to York, where he again proclaimed the bishop's sentence of excommunication and again eluded capture. Gilbert Foliot had anticipated just such an action and had already appealed to the Pope. But he was badly shaken by the anathema and scrupulously obeyed the strictures placed upon him, not only shunning Mass but going so far as to destroy his eating utensils after every meal lest they be used by others, for no good Christian could break bread with an excommunicate.

In addition to the Bishop of London, Becket had excommunicated numerous others, including the Bishop of Salisbury; Henry's justiciar, Richard de Lucy; Geoffrey Ridel, his chancellor; the Earl of Norfolk; the Keeper of the Seal; and Rannulph de Broc. Henry was enraged. The Pope was no happier than Henry with these arbitrary excommunications and strongly urged Becket to rescind the sentences. The archbishop refused and warned that his next act would be to excommunicate the English king himself and lay all England under interdict.

T HE BENEDICTINE ABBEY of Marmoutier was one of the most celebrated in Henry's domains. For the past two years, it had been home to the Bishop of Worcester. Roger had voluntarily exiled himself from England in a brave but vain attempt to convince Henry to make peace with Thomas Becket. On this blustery, cold night in early December, Roger looked back upon a year of failures, beginning with the ill-fated conference at Montmirail and ending a fortnight ago with an equally unproductive meeting at Montmartre. Roger was by nature an optimist, but he was finding it harder and harder to hold on to hope, to believe that either his cousin the king or his friend the archbishop would ever compromise enough to reconcile their differences.

He was in good spirits, though, on this particular evening. The future looked bleak indeed, and wind-lashed sleet was thudding upon the roof, but his guest quarters were warmed by a blazing hearth, his table was laden with a surprisingly tasty Advent supper, and best of all, he had the company of a woman he loved deeply, a woman who could have coaxed laughter from Job.

Maud leaned forward, resting her chin on her laced fingers as she studied her brother with mock solemnity. "Well, you look as if you survived the bloodletting at Montmartre with all your body parts intact. So tell me . . . who disgraced himself the most, dear Cousin Harry or the saintly Becket?"

Roger shook his head with a wry smile. "Actually, they never even met face to face. The archbishop and his clerks were sequestered within the Chapel of Holy Martyrs, whilst Harry and the French king and the papal legates and bishops were gathered outside."

Maud was delighted; this was a detail she hadn't heard. "Did they really keep Harry and Becket apart? That makes sense with dogs and cats, mayhap, but with kings and archbishops?"

Roger shrugged. "I overheard one of the papal legates muttering that the Montmartre peace council would be a great success if only they did not have to invite the English king or his archbishop. He laughed then, but without much humor."

"So how was it managed? Did they send messengers running back and forth with proposals and counterproposals?" Maud asked and laughed outright when Roger nodded. "What else? Tell me more."

"I hardly think it necessary," he observed. "Did you not just come from Eleanor's court at Poitiers?"

"We know that the meeting came to naught, that Becket demanded thirty thousand marks in arrears of his confiscated estates, that Harry offered to arbitrate the matter at either the court of the French king or the University of Paris, that Becket showed his usual skittishness about arbitration and insisted he preferred a 'friendly' settlement to litigation."

She paused for breath and Roger said reprovingly, "I am trying to remember if I have ever heard you mention Thomas without sarcasm dripping from his name like icicles."

She pretended to think about it, then shook her head. "No, probably not. I do find it hard to give the noble Thomas the benefit of the doubt— damnation, I did it again, didn't I? You are right, of course. Eleanor had a full account of the meeting as fast as a courier's horse could travel from Montmartre to Poitiers. But you were there, Roger. I truly would like to hear your view of the events."

"Fair enough. It was very disheartening, Maud. The differences between the two men are so deep that I despair of ever seeing them bridged. But the papal legates were bound and determined to achieve at least the semblance of reconciliation. From what I've heard, the Pope is sorely vexed with Thomas and thinks that he is woefully shortsighted, unable to see the forest for all the trees. There is some truth in that, but they do not understand how much he cares about the liberty of Mother Church."

Maud rolled her eyes at that, thinking of the letter Eleanor had shown her, having somehow obtained a copy of the archbishop's correspondence to the Pope. Becket had complained of suffering "tribulation more severe than any which has ever been experienced since tribulation first began" and assured the pontiff that there was never "grief like unto my grief." But for once, she held her tongue, waiting for Roger to continue.

"Harry finally agreed to make restitution to Thomas 'as his ministers should advise him,' and the French king convinced Thomas that this was acceptable. Louis thought it was unseemly that a priest should bicker over money," Roger said, with a faint smile. "Alas, such a high-minded principle is one only kings can afford."

Maud nodded sympathetically, knowing that Roger had incurred huge debts in the months away from his English diocese; she would have to find a tactful way to offer a loan to tide him over. "It sounds as if they did not so much resolve their differences as agree to ignore them."

"Just so," Roger said and sighed. "Thomas agreed to drop the 'saving the Honor of God' proviso and Harry in turn agreed to forgo that counterclause he sprang upon the papal legates this summer."

Maud grinned. "I heard about that. 'Saving the dignity of my realm,' was it not? I assume he figured that one ambiguous phrase deserves another. At least Harry has not entirely lost his sense of humor about all this!"

"That is more than the rest of us can say," Roger confessed. "It pains me greatly, Maud, to see two men I cherish so hostile to each other, all the more so because they were once such fast friends."

And you're the one caught between them, she thought sadly, grist for their mills. "So they agreed to jettison those troublesome stipulations and Harry promised to restore the archbishopric estates and no one dared breathe the dreaded words 'Constitutions of Clarendon.' After coming so far, how could they then stumble over a ritual like the Kiss of Peace? Why throw away all that progress over something ceremonial?"

Roger reached for his cup, grimacing at the taste of warm ale; he had forsaken wine for Advent. "I know. It was like watching a race where the horses pulled up just before the finish. They were so close to agreement, so close. . . . But then Thomas demanded that Harry give him the Kiss of Peace and Harry refused. He said—correctly—that the Kiss of Peace was to be given only after a true bargain had been struck, and there were still serious matters unresolved between them. If he'd stopped at that, well and good. But he then went on to claim that he'd sworn a holy vow that he'd never give Becket the Kiss of Peace. Since Harry has never been one for holding oaths sacred and inviolable, that explanation was met with considerable skepticism. The legates and the Archbishop of Rouen offered to absolve him of his vow, but he declined, insisting it would look forced and false under the circumstances. He offered, though, to have his eldest son give the Kiss in his stead. Thomas balked at that, and the good ship Appeasement ran up on the rocks yet again."

"God save us from stubborn men," Maud said with a sigh. "So what happens now? Surely the Pope will continue trying to mediate between them?"

"Of course he will. However irksome he finds Thomas these days, he is still the Archbishop of Canterbury, England's greatest prelate and a prince of the Church. Nor can the Pope afford to alienate the King of England, especially since he has hopes now that Harry will take part in the coming Crusade."

"Ah, yes, our cousin the crusader," Maud said, very dryly. "I was with Eleanor when she heard about Harry's sudden fervor to see Jerusalem. She laughed so hard that she spilled a cup of good wine."

Roger did not disagree with Eleanor's cynical assessment of her husband's motives. "For all that his greatest passion is for the hunt, Harry would have made a fine fisherman, too, for he can throw out bait with the best of them. And you may be sure that the Holy Father knows that full well. But as long as there is a chance that Harry truly intends to take the Cross, it must be pursued."

"Spiders must marvel at the webs that kings weave . . . or queens," Maud added, thinking of Eleanor. "Is it true that you and Harry had a falling-out this summer? Eleanor said he was wroth enough to order your banishment."

"Eleanor doubtless knows of it as soon as a weed sprouts anywhere in Harry's domains," Roger said, smiling—although that was not entirely meant as a compliment. "I was prideful enough to think that I could make Harry see the folly of this feud. But Thomas had just excommunicated several of Harry's councilors and I knew I'd encounter them at court. So I wrote to Thomas, explaining my mission and requesting that he give me dispensation to associate with these lost souls. Regrettably, Thomas refused."

"How gracious of him!" Maud exclaimed sharply, and then, "I am sorry, but I could not help myself. If you please, continue."

"I caught up with Harry in June, ere he left for Gascony to chase down more of Eleanor's Poitevin rebels. He seemed pleased to see me; I may be one of the very few whose friendship with Thomas he is willing to overlook. He was in good spirits for a man who'd spent the spring putting out fires in Aquitaine whilst attempting to get the Pope to absolve Gilbert Foliot and the others from their sentences of excommunication. I tried to talk to him about Thomas a few times, but he was always quick to change the subject; you know how elusive Harry can be.

"Still, all was going well until we attended Mass together on the third day of my visit. When Geoffrey Ridel entered the chapel, I had no choice but to depart at once. Harry followed me, baffled by my sudden departure. I explained that I could not be in the company of an excommunicate, but that was not what he wanted to hear. One hasty word led to another and ere we knew it, Harry was ordering me from his domains. I could probably have talked him out of it, but my own temper was afire by then and I made some intemperate remark to the effect that my foot was already in the stirrup, which did not help at all."

Maud could not keep from laughing. "I'd think not. A pity that neither one of us inherited our father's calm, placid temperament instead of taking after our hotheaded mother! So what happened then?"

"I rode off in high dudgeon," Roger admitted, laughing, too. "To his credit, Harry cooled off first and sent a messenger after me, telling me to return. I refused, of course. But by the time his third summons reached me, I was done with my sulking and so I came back and we made our peace. I had no luck in convincing Harry to end his estrangement with Thomas, but for the rest of my stay, Harry saw to it that neither Geoffrey Ridel nor any of the other excommunicates came into my presence."

"What will you do if Becket goes ahead with his threat and excommunicates Harry, too? No, never mind; I do not want to know. I think we've dealt with enough sorrows and trouble for one night. Let's talk instead of more cheerful matters."

And so they did, discussing Roger's studies in canon law and theology at the nearby city of Tours, reminiscing about the marriage earlier that year of Maud's eldest son, Hugh, to the daughter of Simon de Montfort, Count of Evreux, and sharing what little news they had about their uncle Ranulf, still secluded deep in Wales. Roger told Maud, with an enthusiasm she did not share, all about Henry's ambitious plans to build a thirty-mile stretch of embankments to keep the River Loire from flooding. And she did her best to coax him into returning with her to Poitiers, lavishly praising the anticipated splendors of Eleanor's Christmas revelries.

Roger demurred, joking that there were too many temptations to be found at the royal court. After a moment, though, he frowned slightly. "I was told at Montmartre that Harry planned to celebrate Christmas with his son Geoffrey at Nantes, as a gesture of goodwill toward the Bretons. Has he changed his plans, then?"

"No, he will be holding his Christmas court in Brittany this year."

"I see. . . . But Eleanor will be at Poitiers?"

Maud nodded slowly and their eyes met in a brief moment of unspoken understanding. A pall seemed to have settled over the room, giving them both an unwelcome glimpse of the road ahead, strewn with pitfalls and snares. Maud reached for her wine, no longer having the heart to tease her brother about his Advent abstinence. "Roger . . . do you think this will end well?" she asked at last, realizing that her words could apply equally to the troubles with Thomas Becket or the unacknowledged rift widening between Harry and Eleanor.

Roger did not reply at once, crumpling his napkin as he looked into the hearth's flames. "No," he said softly. "No, I do not."

CHAPTER TWENTY-EIGHT

February 1170
Caen, Normandy

ICHARD URGED HIS MOUNT forward as they passed through the city gates of Caen, intent upon overtaking his mother. She smiled as he drew alongside, pointing out the twin towers of St Etienne's, the vast Benedictine monastery founded by Richard's ancestor, the conqueror of England known as William the Bastard. Working out the relationship in his head, Richard determined that this long-dead king was his father's great-grandfather. He remembered how he'd once delighted in making mention of William because it allowed him to swear with impunity. He was somewhat scornful of that younger self, though, for he was twelve now and such childish pleasures were beneath him.

To the east was another great abbey, this one a nunnery owing its existence to that ancient William's queen, and in-between the monasteries lay their destination: William's formidable stronghold of Château Caen. Richard glanced again at his mother as the castle's battlements loomed ahead. He knew she was not happy to be summoned back to Normandy so suddenly by his father; she and his elder brother Hal had been at Caen for much of January whilst his father punished rebels in Brittany. She'd only just arrived back at Poitiers when his father's messenger had found her. Richard was very pleased, however, by this return to Caen, for he'd coaxed her into letting him come along.

He was not particularly keen upon seeing his father, for if truth be told, the man was a stranger to him, often gone for many months at a time. Nor was he that eager to be reunited with Hal. The two and a half years between them was still an unbridgeable gap, although Richard definitely preferred his company to Geoffrey's. It was enough for him that this journey to Caen offered a respite from his studies and the novelty of unfamiliar sights.

Eleanor was well aware of her second son's excitement, but she shared little of his anticipation as they rode across the drawbridge into the bailey of Caen Castle. She expected Henry to be in a foul mood, for rumor had it that his latest envoys to the papal court, Richard Barre and the Archdeacon of Llandaff, had returned empty-handed from Benevento, having failed to undermine the Pope's obligatory support for his exiled archbishop. She assumed, therefore, that he wanted an audience for his outrage, and while that was a role she'd often played during the past eighteen years, she no longer had either the patience or the inclination to smooth her husband's ruffled feathers or gentle his untamed temper.

The castle steward was waiting to bid them welcome and informed them that the lord king was watching practice at the quintain on the open ground north of the keep. Eleanor decided to get her first meeting with Henry over with as soon as possible, and refused to let herself remember those times when she'd been eager for their reunions. Sending her ladies and their escort on into the great hall, she cantered her mare across the bailey, soon joined by Richard, who flung a challenge over his shoulder as his gelding galloped by. Eleanor laughed, urging her mare on, and they raced onto the quintain field as a team, sending up a spray of mud in their wake.

Their dramatic appearance interrupted the competition at the quintain and they found themselves the focus of all eyes. Henry came forward to help Eleanor dismount. Richard had already slid from the saddle and received a playful clout on the shoulders from his father. Henry was grinning, and demanded to know who had won. Eleanor allowed Richard to claim that honor, her eyes resting speculatively upon her husband. He seemed in suspiciously high spirits and she wondered what he was up to now, for there was nothing about him of a man bowing to inevitable defeat.

"My lady queen!" At the sound of that familiar voice, Eleanor swung around toward the quintain, handing her reins to Henry. Her eldest son was sitting upon a muddied chestnut stallion, smiling down at her. Eleanor smiled back, and Hal skillfully reined his mount in a semicircle, gracefully lowering his lance with a flourish. "Would you honor me, my lady, with a token of your favor?"

Richard smirked at Hal's studied gallantry, but his parents both laughed. Reaching under her mantle, Eleanor unfastened the silken belt knotted around her hips and tied it onto Hal's lance. Another youth was making a run at the quintain and they all turned now to watch. Although Richard was too young yet to study the arts of war, he was very familiar with the quintain and the way it worked. A post was anchored in a field and a crosspiece attached to the top by a pivot; a shield was hung from one end of this revolving arm and a sandbag from the other. Only a direct hit upon the shield would enable a rider to avoid the counterblow when the sandbag swung around, and this youngster's aim went awry. As his lance slid off the shield, he was smacked by the sandbag with enough force to knock him from the saddle. His fall was cushioned by several layers of sticky mud, but his pride was badly bruised by a wave of mocking laughter. Infuriated by the jeers and gibes of the other boys, he started to stalk off the field, had to be reminded to retrieve his horse, and that generated another burst of merciless merriment.

Richard joined in the laughter, sure that he could master this difficult skill in no time at all. His brother was taking his turn at the quintain and he found himself hoping that Hal would take a tumble, too. But when Hal hit the target with a perfectly judged blow and galloped safely past the pivoting sandbag, Richard felt a spark of surprised admiration. Hal handled a lance with such practiced ease that he rose abruptly in his younger brother's estimation, and as he made a second pass at the quintain, Richard was cheering him on.

Hal had another successful run and accepted the plaudits of his friends with a nonchalance that could not quite hide his pride in his feat. Riding back to his parents, he reaped a harvest of praise, and when Richard voiced his desire to try the quintain, too, Hal was feeling generous enough to indulge the boy.

"You'll not blame me if you end up arse-deep in mud?" he warned, and when Richard insisted that he'd not care if he broke an arm, Hal grinned and beckoned his brother to follow.

It never occurred to either Henry or Eleanor to object; they took it for granted that Richard would suffer numerous injuries while learning the use of weapons. Hastily mounting his gelding, Richard listened intently as Hal showed him how to tuck the lance under his right arm and hold it steady against his chest so that it inclined toward the left. It wasn't often that their sons displayed such a cooperative spirit, and they both took pleasure in this rare moment of brotherly harmony.

Richard was an accomplished rider for his age. He had no experience in handling a ten-foot lance, though, and in his first try, he missed the target altogether, much to the amusement of the watching youths. On his second attempt, he managed to strike the edge of the shield, and was then struck in turn by the swinging sandbag, which tumbled him down into the mud. Hal and his friends laughed so hard that they were almost in tears, but their laughter gave way to grudging approval when Richard bounded onto his feet, his mud-plastered face lit with a wide grin. "I want to try it again," he said. "I think I'm getting the hang of it!"

Henry had led Eleanor over to a nearby cart, helping her up into the seat for more comfortable viewing. She was not surprised when he chose to stand, for he'd always found it difficult to sit still for more than a few moments at a time, and against her will, she remembered their first time alone—seated together in a garden arbor on a rain-darkened Paris afternoon—remembered how she'd wondered what it would be like to feel all that energy deep inside her.

"So, tell me," she said abruptly. "What bad news did Barre and the archdeacon bring back from the papal court?"

Henry's eyes were on Richard, who'd just taken another bone-bruising fall. Wincing, he said fondly, "That lad may have no common sense, but by God, he has pluck!" Glancing over his shoulder at Eleanor, he confided, then, that the news was very bad indeed.

"It was politely phrased, but the threat was lurking just beneath the surface courtesy. Alexander will not pressure Becket to accept more reasonable terms. He will, however, absolve me from my oath to give the saintly Thomas the Kiss of Peace. Nothing like an unsolicited generosity. He is appointing yet more envoys, this time the Archbishop of Rouen and the Bishop of Nevers. And if I do not make peace with Becket within forty days, England will be placed under an interdict."

"You seem to be taking it rather well," Eleanor observed skeptically, and he gave her an amused look that confirmed all her suspicions.

"The Pope and that bastard Becket think they have found a lever to use against me. They know how important it is to me to have Hal crowned and they think they can extort concessions from me as the price for that coronation."

Eleanor could not fault his logic. "So what do you have in mind?"

Hal had just struck the shield off-center, ducking low to avoid the sandbag's counterblow, and Henry let out a raucous cheer before turning his attention again to his wife. "What makes you think I have something in mind?"

"Nigh on two decades of marriage," she riposted and earned herself an appreciative smile.

"Well . . . it occurred to me that this particular lever was more of a double-edged sword."

"I asked for an explanation, Harry, not an epigram."

Henry grinned. "Sheathe your claws, love, I'm getting to it. It is quite simple. I realized that Hal's coronation matters almost as much to Becket as it does to me . . . to us. As jealous as he is of Canterbury's prerogatives, how do you think he'd react if Hal were crowned by someone else . . . say, the Archbishop of York? It would drive him well nigh mad, and he'd be desperate to re-crown Hal, lest a dangerous precedent be set, one that el- evated the diocese of York over Canterbury."

Eleanor understood now what he meant to do. It was shrewd and bold and ruthless and might well work. She studied his face pensively, thinking that these were the very qualities she'd first found so attractive in him; thinking, too, that she must never forget what a formidable enemy he could be. "You are willing to defy the Pope on this? You know Becket has persuaded him that only Canterbury's archbishop has the right to crown a king."

Henry's smile was complacent. "Ah, but you've forgotten that I still have in my possession a letter from the Holy Father in which he gives me permission to have my heir crowned by whomever I choose."

"That letter was dated June of God's Year 1161, if my memory serves," she said sharply, irritated by how smug he sounded.

"Yes . . . but the Pope never notified me that it was revoked."

"You are taking a great risk, Harry," she said and he shrugged.

"It is what I do best, love."

She could not argue with that. "Since you sent for me, I assume I have a part to play. What would you have me do?"

"I plan to leave for England as soon as possible. Once there, I shall take the necessary steps for Hal's coronation. I want him to remain here with you to allay suspicions. But have him ready to sail as soon as you get word from me. I also want you to keep a close watch on the ports, to do whatever you must to make sure that none of Becket's banns or prohibitions reach English shores. I've already talked to Richard de Humet about this and he knows what I want done."

Eleanor did not appreciate having a watchdog, even one as competent as the Constable of Normandy. Had it escaped Harry's notice that she'd been governing Aquitaine quite capably in his absence? She had no doubts whatsoever that she could rule as well as any man. Granted, she could not take to arms and capture rebel castles as Harry so often had to do. But mayhap her Poitevin lords would not be so defiant if not for his heavy-handed Angevin ways.

She gave no voice to her grievance, though, knowing it would serve for naught. Her husband was not a man to relinquish even a scrap of power if he could help it. Passing strange that he seemed so unconcerned about elevating Hal to a kingship. Did it never occur to him that Hal might not be content as his puppet, that the lad might want authority to accompany his exalted new rank? Or did Harry just take it for granted that his will would always prevail?

But in this, they were in agreement, for she, too, wanted to see their sons made secure in their inheritances. "You need not worry, Harry," she said. "Even if Becket gets wind of what you're planning, no messenger of his will set foot on English soil, not unless the man can walk on water."

Their eldest son had switched his attention from the quintain and was making a run at the rings, braided circles of rope hung from the branches of a gaunt, winter-stripped tree. As Hal deftly hooked one of the rings onto the point of his lance, Henry and Eleanor exchanged a smile of parental pride. Echoing Henry's praise, Eleanor agreed that Hal's skill at this maneuver was indeed impressive. "During our stay at Caen, he never stopped talking about the glories of the tourney, and now I see why. He is good enough to win on his own merits, king's son or not."

Henry did not share the common enthusiasm for tournaments, thought they were a waste of time at best and an inducement to civil unrest at worst. "Do not encourage him in such foolishness, Eleanor. It is not as if he has to earn his way, like that young knight of yours, Marshal. You brought him along, did you not?"

"Will? Yes, he is in the great hall." She glanced at him curiously, for he never made casual conversation. "Why?"

"I was thinking that he would be an ideal choice to watch over Hal. From what you've told me, he has a good head on his shoulders, could rein in Hal's youthful follies whilst tutoring him well in the arts of war."

She agreed that Will would be a good choice, although she felt a prickle of resentment that Henry felt so free to appropriate one of her household knights without so much as a by-your-leave. Will Marshal would have made a fine tutor for Richard, too.

"Richard will miss Will's company," she said composedly, "for he's gotten right fond of Marshal. Speaking of Richard . . . it might be advisable to make a public acknowledgment of his right to Aquitaine now that you plan to crown Hal."

Henry had expected her to make such a suggestion and he was amused that he could read her so well. Her partiality toward their second son was obvious to all but the stone-blind. But he was willing to indulge it, for Richard would make a good duke for Aquitaine. He was fortunate indeed that his realms were vast enough to provide for all of his sons. Well . . . for Hal, Richard, and Geoffrey. There was still the little lad, John, whom he'd dubbed John Lackland in a moment of levity. But John was being well cared for at Fontevrault Abbey and he would be pledged to the Church.

"An excellent idea, Eleanor." They smiled again at each other, then cheered loudly when Richard survived his first run at the quintain, being buffeted soundly by the sandbag but remaining in the saddle.

"What of Marguerite?" Eleanor asked suddenly, thinking of her young daughter-in-law. "Do you mean to have her crowned with Hal?"

"I am not sure," he admitted. "If I do not, Louis will be grievously offended. But if I do have the lass crowned now, that will make her an accomplice in my defiance of the Pope and the saintly Becket. You know Louis far better than me, love. Which is the lesser evil?"

Eleanor frowned. "It might be easier for him to forgive a slight than a sacrilege, for that is how he will view the coronation. I think it might be better to wait and have her crowned the second time . . . once you've come to terms with Becket."

This was his thinking, too, and he was gratified to have her confirm his own instincts. Reaching up for her hand, he pressed a kiss into her palm, then turned back to watch as Hal snared another ring.

"When do you plan to sail, Harry?"

"As soon as the weather permits. Why?"

"Hal's birthday," she reminded him. "He turns fifteen on Sunday."

"Ah, yes," he said vaguely, for as finely tuned as his memory was, he had an inexplicable difficulty in remembering birthdates and the like, usually joking that it was her fault for giving him too many children to keep track of. "Well, then, of course I will not depart for Barfleur until Monday."

"Hal will be pleased," she said, wondering if that was indeed so; wondering, too, if he meant to take Rosamund Clifford with him to England.

"HOLY MOTHER OF GOD!" Henry's brother was moaning softly, curled up into a ball, knees drawn against his chest, arms clasped over his head. A foul-smelling bucket testified to Hamelin's physical distress, but the worst of his vomiting seemed to be over, probably because his heaving stomach had nothing left to disgorge. Henry leaned over and patted the younger man's shaking shoulders, all he could think to do. Like most men blessed enough to be spared the humbling miseries of mal de mer, Henry usually felt faint contempt for those afflicted with seasickness. But now he had only sympathy for Hamelin's ordeal. Henry had crossed the Channel more times than he could count, often in rough, wild weather. Yet he could not remember a storm of greater savagery than this one.

The seas had been choppy and turbulent even in Barfleur's harbor. Once they had rounded Barfleur Point out into the unprotected waters of the Channel, the full force of the squall struck Henry's fleet. In no time at all, most of the passengers on Henry's flagship were suffering the torments of the damned, retching and shivering and offering urgent prayers to Nicholas of Bari, the patron saint of sailors. Even Henry began to experience queasiness and he could count his episodes of seasickness on the fingers of one hand. He fought it back and assured his companions that the storm would soon slacken. Even if it did not, these high winds would blow their ships to England faster than any bird could fly.

He was wrong on both counts. The storm only intensified and then the wind changed direction. The hours passed and they made little progress, their ships wallowing in heavy swells, the lanterns on mastheads extinguished by torrents of stinging, icy rain. Canvas tents had been set up to shelter the highborn passengers from the weather, but they could offer little protection against a gale of this magnitude. In Henry's tent, the terrified men and women were soon bruised and sore, for even the most desperate grip was no match for the power of the elements. Each time the ship pitched, someone slammed into the gunwale or one of the coffers crammed into the tent, cries of pain muffled by the roar of the wind and the thud of waves slamming into the hull. Their prayers, too, were lost to the fury of the squall. As the night wore on, Henry was the only one aboard, including the ship's master and crew, who was not convinced that they were doomed, sure to drown in the maw of the storm.

Hamelin was mumbling again about his wife, berating himself for having let Isabella sail in one of the other ships. Now they would not even drown together, he gasped, choking back a sob.

That was too maudlin for Henry. He could understand Hamelin's fears for his wife. He had fears, too, for others in the fleet, especially his half-sister Emma and her husband. Of Geoffrey's crop of bastards, he was fondest of Hamelin and Emma, and he regretted not insisting that she sail with him. Thank Christ that Hal and Eleanor were safe in Caen and Rosamund at Falaise, awaiting his return from England. It seemed a foolish waste of regret, though, to fret about being buried with a loved one, as Hamelin was doing. If their ship went down, they'd all be food for fish; how many bodies were ever recovered from the sea?

When he could endure Hamelin's tearful remorse no longer, he said brusquely, "What's done is done, man. Better you should save your breath for prayer."

Hamelin raised his head at the sound of Henry's voice. Although the wind blotted out most of Henry's words, the impatient expression on his face communicated a message of its own, and Hamelin felt a quiver of despairing rage. Who but Harry was prideful enough to sail when the weather was so foul? Now they were all going to die because of his reckless flouting of God's Will.

Hamelin said nothing, though, for even when feeling Death's hot breath on the back of his neck, he could not blame his brother; it would be like rebuking the Almighty. But his eyes were brimming with silent reproach, and even Henry's self-confidence was not immune to the force of that mournful gaze. He'd long ago learned that a king's chess game was played with the lives of other people. Men had died to make him England's sovereign, and more would die in defense of boundaries he alone defined. It was a great and fearful power—having the right to sanctify bloodshed—and it did not bear close inspection, for otherwise it could never be invoked.

Getting abruptly to his feet, Henry stumbled as the deck rolled and maintained his footing by sheer will and some luck. "I can no longer stand the stink in here," he said, feeling the need to offer an excuse. It was true that the stench was execrable, for no one could empty the vomit-filled buckets overboard until the storm subsided. But it was also true that he was escaping the mute misery in his brother's teary, accusing eyes.

As he emerged onto the deck, he was hit in the face by the wind, sleet pelting his skin like flying needles. Sailors scrambled across the slanting deck, struggling to tighten one of the shrouds dangling loosely from the mast. The man at the windlass was spinning the spokes, cursing as his frozen fingers slipped off the wheel. Henry dodged as a burly figure skidded toward him, recognizing the ship's master only when he was close enough to touch. The man turned on Henry with a snarl, realizing just in time that this intrusive passenger was the king. He could not order Henry off the deck, but neither could he indulge in the niceties of court protocol when his ship's survival was at stake. Thrusting a wet coil of rope into Henry's hand, he tersely told the king to tie himself to one of the windlass's posts ere he was washed overboard.

Henry did as bade, taking shelter against the gunwale out of the crew's way. He was grateful that he'd chosen to sail on a cog and not a nef like the ill-fated White Ship, for nefs rode so low in the water that they'd surely have been swamped by now. He was not as confident of the ship's steering innovation, though. Instead of the customary side rudder, this cog relied upon a newfangled stern rudder, and the enthusiastic arguments of the ship's master that this was a vast improvement over the steering oar were not as persuasive now as they'd been in the safety of Barfleur's harbor.

Henry guessed that dawn must be nigh, but the skies were still black, smothered in storm clouds. As much as he strained to see, he could catch no glimpse of bobbing lantern light. Did that mean the fleet was scattered to Kingdom Come? Or merely that their lanterns had been quenched, too, by the downpour? It was eerie, not knowing what the darkness concealed, knowing only that each ship was alone in its struggle to stay afloat.

There was an alarmed yell from one of the sailors, and although Henry didn't understand the man's Breton, the fear in his voice needed no translation. He jerked around in time to see the crew members lunging toward the starboard side. A shape was looming out of the blackness. With horror, Henry realized that it was another ship.

The ship's master was screaming, "Hard on the helm!" As the helmsman jerked the tiller to the left, a sailor lurched from the bow, clutching an armful of boat hooks. When he staggered and fell, Henry was jolted out of his frozen shock, and he grabbed for the spilled boat hooks, began to toss them to the sailors clustered at the gunwale. God's Blood, what was wrong with those fools? Was their helmsman blind?

Henry sucked in his breath sharply as the other ship came into clearer focus, for he saw then that the mast was broken in half, the sail shredded. It was close enough for him to make out scurrying figures on the deck. He forgot for a moment that this other cog could be his own destruction, for he knew he was looking at a ghost ship, one manned by the living dead. Only the Almighty could save those poor souls now.

His sailors were leaning over the gunwale, desperately gripping the boat hooks that were their only defense. Henry began to fumble with his rope lifeline so that he could join them, although a boat hook seemed a frail, feeble weapon against a cog. But the distance between the two ships was not narrowing, and with a surge of overwhelming relief, he realized that his own ship was slowly, ever so slowly, responding to the helm. The crewmen were shouting in grateful acknowledgment of their reprieve, yet they fell silent as the doomed ship was swept past them, for a respectful hush was all they could offer to the drowning passengers.

Henry sagged back against the gunwale. Oddly enough, their respite had done what the storm itself could not do, and for the first time that night, he accepted that he might not survive this accursed voyage. In just two days time, he would be thirty-seven, but would he live to celebrate it? What would happen to his domains without him? And his sons? Hal was only fifteen, the other lads even younger. What would become of them if he were no longer able to protect their rights?

Henry had often faced danger, but never before had he gazed down into his open grave. As was his way, he at once set about changing the ending. God's Will be done. But not yet, Lord, not yet. He needed to live long enough to see his son crowned. Surely the Almighty could see that? Hal was still in need of his guidance, his judgment, for the lad had not yet shown the mettle of a king. He would learn, but he needed seasoning. Holding fast to the gunwale, Henry offered up the most heartfelt prayers of his life, bargaining with God for more time.

The sinking ship had disappeared into the darkness, but Henry's last glimpse of it would burn in his memory until his final breath: as the cog heeled sharply to the left, its side rudder had come completely out of the water, as useless as its tattered sail and broken mast. A sudden whimper drew Henry's attention and he glanced down to discover that his dog had crept from the tent, managed to crawl across the deck, and was huddled at his feet. Touched by such selfless loyalty, he knelt beside the dyrehund and wrapped his arms around the animal's trembling body. He considered returning to the tent, decided to remain there on the deck. Better to die under the open sky, facing his fate head-on.

Henry lost track of time, was never to know how many more hours passed before he heard one of the sailors give a joyful cry, "Land ho!" Turning his head toward the horizon, he saw a glimmer of light in the distance, and for a confused moment, he thought he was gazing upon the chalk cliffs of Dover. Surely they could not have been blown that far off course? But as the helmsman called out that he could see Culver Cliff, Henry realized that he was looking upon salvation, the steep, white bluffs of the Isle of Wight.

H ENRY CAME ashore at Portsmouth on March 3, and the remainder of his storm-battered fleet straggled into ports up and down the Channel. One of his forty ships was lost, taking more than four hundred people to their deaths, including Ranulf de Bellomont, his personal physician. But when he sent for his eldest son, Hal's voyage was uneventful. He landed safely on English soil on June 5, proceeding to London, where his father awaited him, and was crowned in Westminster Abbey by the Archbishop of York on the following Sunday.

T HE EARL OF CORNWALL was enjoying himself enormously. Rainald loved food and revelries and good company, and in his considered judgment, his grandnephew's coronation feast offered all three in plenitude. Westminster's great hall had been newly whitewashed for the occasion, fresh, fragrant rushes laid down, clean linen cloths covered the tables, and in every wall sconce, a flaming torch blazed like a smoking sun. So far the menu had exceeded all his expectations; he'd confessed to his grandnephew Hugh of Chester that he'd not thought Harry could manage an elegant meal without Eleanor's guidance.

Hugh was embarrassed by this lack of discretion, casting uneasy glances along the high table, where his cousin the king was seated. Rainald merely laughed at the young earl's attempts to shush him, insisting that Harry would take that as a compliment, not an insult. He could tell Hugh stories, indeed, about the slop that had been served at the royal table, especially when they'd been on the road all day and ended up sheltering for the night in places a self-respecting pig would shun.

Hugh went crimson and looked askance at Rainald's brimming wine cup, trying to remember how often it had been refilled. Hippocras was ordinarily saved for the end of a feast, for the red wine flavored with sugar, ginger, and cinnamon was a costly beverage. But for Hal's coronation dinner, no expense had been spared, and hippocras was being poured at the high table as if it were ale. Hugh invariably found things to worry about and he began to fear that Rainald might humiliate them both if he ended up deep in his cups.

Rainald's voice was carrying, as usual, turning heads in their direction, and Hugh swallowed his own wine too quickly, for he was nowhere near as certain as his granduncle that the king would not be offended by such talk. He never knew how to read his cousin Harry and dreaded stirring up the king's notoriously quick temper. Much to his relief now, the Bishop of London, seated on Rainald's right, adroitly introduced a more seemly topic of conversation, commenting upon the lavishness of the dishes that had so far been served.

Distracted, Rainald happily plunged into a discussion of the fine pepper sauce, the omelettes stuffed with expensive, imported figs, the venison pasties, the fresh mackerel colored green with a jellylike mint sauce, and his personal favorite, the Lombardy custard of delicious marrow, dates, raisins, and almond milk. His grandnephew's concern about his drinking was unwarranted; Rainald was feeling pleasantly mellow, but he was still reasonably sober. His exuberance was due as much to high spirits as spiced wine, for a coronation was a momentous event, one to be remembered and savored for years afterward.

Hal had been seated in the place of honor, between his father and the Archbishop of York. Already taller than Henry, adorned in a red silk tunic with a stylishly cut diagonal neckline that had stirred Hugh's envy, his fair hair gilded to gold by the flaring torchlights, Hal looked verily like a king. Rainald beamed at the youth, glad that he made such a fine impression. Not every king's heir was so promising, he thought, remembering Stephen's brutal son, Eustace. When he'd died so suddenly, choking on a mouthful of eels, Stephen alone had mourned; most men felt that the Almighty had interceded on England's behalf.

"I do not know our young king well," he confided to the bishop, "but I can understand why the crowds turned out to cheer as he rode to the abbey. He is as handsome a lad as I've ever laid eyes upon, God's Truth. I know who he gets his good looks from, too!"

Gilbert Foliot had more weighty matters on his mind than the comeliness of the king's son. It was barely two months since he'd gotten the Pope to lift Becket's sentence of excommunication, and he well knew that his participation in this day's coronation was likely to thrust him back into papal disfavor. But courtesy was a virtue and he agreed that the young king was indeed fair to look upon, adding politely that the queen had been a great beauty, after all.

Rainald chuckled, looking at the bishop indulgently. "Nay, my lord, I meant the boy's grandsire. I can find nothing of the queen in that lad. Look at his coloring, the tilt of his head, then tell me he is not the veritable image of Geoffrey of Anjou!"

Foliot had not seen the resemblance before, but now that it was pointed out to him, he marveled how he could have missed it. He had been a staunch supporter of the Empress Maude, which meant that he was no admirer of the late Count of Anjou, and he silently expressed the wish that young Hal resembled his grandfather in nothing more significant than appearance.

Rainald reached for a bread sop, dunking it in the glistening green sauce of their shared mackerel dish. "Let's hope the lad's good looks are his only legacy from Geoffrey. My sister loathed the man, and with cause, by God!"

That was tactless enough to make both Foliot and Hugh wince. No matter how cheerful Henry was this day, he'd like it not to hear his father disparaged; his affection for Count Geoffrey had been well known. Fortunately, there was a sudden bustle of activity in the hall as this course came to an end, and Rainald's comments passed unnoticed. Ewers were bringing out lavers of water scented with bay leaves and chamomile; because so much of a meal was eaten with the fingers, it was essential that guests be offered several opportunities to wash their hands. The panter was cutting new trenchers for those at the high table, as by now theirs were soaked with gravy. Not even the hungriest diners would eat their trenchers, for bread had to be coarse and stale to be firm enough to serve as a plate; as they were replaced, the crumbling, sodden trenchers were collected for God's poor.

There was a sudden stirring as Henry rose to his feet. He stopped others from rising, too, and gestured for the musicians to resume playing. As the music of harp and lute filled the hall, Henry stepped down from the dais. Exchanging brief pleasantries with the guests at his table, he paused before his kinsmen.

"There is no need to ask if you've been enjoying the dinner, Uncle," he joked, "not after all you've been eating!"

Rainald grinned and patted his paunch. "Jesú forfend that I insult Your Grace by showing indifference to this fine fare! In all candor, you've always been one for eating on the run. I trust you are not about to put an end to the festivities?"

Henry grinned back. "This is one dinner that could last into the morrow and I'd not complain. No, I have a surprise for my son."

Making his way across the hall, he waited until he saw the server approaching the door and then signaled for a trumpet fanfare to introduce the meal's pièce de résistance. Garnished with sliced apples, centered on a large silver platter, the great boar's head was an impressive culinary tribute to the young king, for it was more commonly served during Christmas revelries. The admiring murmurs gave way to cheers when Henry moved forward and took the platter himself. The sons of the nobility learned manners by waiting upon tables in great households, and a king was often served at state banquets by peers of the realm. But Henry's action was an unprecedented compliment to his son.

With all eyes upon him, Henry carried the boar's head to the high table, where he stood smiling up at his eldest son. Hal smiled, too, looking so composed and regal that Henry glowed with pride. The Archbishop of York glanced from Henry to Hal and said with the smoothness of a practiced courtier, "It is not every prince who can be served at table by a king."

Hal's blue eyes took the light, a smile still hovering at the corners of his mouth. "Yes," he said, "but it can be no condescension for the son of a count to serve the son of a king."

There was utter silence. Even those who hadn't heard Hal's retort sensed something was amiss by the shocked expressions on the faces of those at the high table. The Archbishop of York was at a rare loss for words, and Rainald nearly strangled on a mouthful of wine. Henry looked startled and then he laughed. Others echoed his laughter dutifully, but the laughter had a hollow sound. With the exception of Henry and his son, few in the hall found any humor in the young king's too-clever quip.

CHAPTER TWENTY-NINE

September 1170
Bec-Hellouin, Normandy

SOFT SHADOWS AND SILENCE. That was the boy's first impression of the interior of the abbey church. Outside, the sun was blazing across a noonday sky, but within the nave, it could have been dusk. Blinking, he stumbled over a prayer cushion and lurched into the font. The noise he'd made seemed to roil through the stillness like thunder, and he flushed, relieved when the kneeling figure of his father did not react. The marble tomb glimmered in the gloom. He wondered if it was as cold and smooth as it looked. The woman buried here was his aunt, but she was a stranger to him. He'd never even laid eyes upon her and was sure that she'd not have welcomed him into her family circle, for she had been a great lady, an empress, and he was a lord's bastard, born in sin.

"*Requiescas in pace,* Maude." Rainald rose stiffly to his feet, for physical activity without aching muscles and creaking bones was as long-gone as his youth. Peering into the dimness, he beckoned to the boy.

As they emerged into the September sunlight, Rainald collided with a man striding briskly along the cloisters walkway. "Whoa!" Recognizing the chasuble and cope of a prince of the Church, Rainald began to offer a laughing apology. "I'm not always blind as a mole, my lord, but these old eyes of mine need time to—" As his gaze rose to the bishop's face, he broke off with a cry of delighted surprise and enfolded the other man in an enthusiastic embrace. "Roger!"

Roger grinned and fended off another hug. "Nay, Uncle, my ribs will snap like twigs. For all your talk of aging eyes, your clenches could put a bear to shame."

"Only an elderly bear with the joint-evil and a potbelly! What are you doing here, Roger?"

"The same as you, Uncle . . . paying honor to Maude."

Rainald shook his head. "I can hardly believe that she's been dead three years. Will you be saying the Requiem Mass?" Getting an affirmation, he smiled, and then remembered the boy. "Come here, lad. Roger, I want you to meet Rico . . . my son. Rico, this is your cousin Roger, the Bishop of Worcester."

Rico made his father proud by kneeling and kissing the bishop's ring. Roger was impressed by the boy's good manners and he acknowledged the introductions with deliberate warmth, knowing that would please Rainald. It was a poorly kept family secret that Rainald adored this unlawfully begotten son of his and felt remorse and anxiety that he could not give Rico all that his legitimate heir, Nicholas, would one day claim. Roger had an uneasy sense that Nicholas would not long enjoy the honors of his father's earldom, for the youth had inherited his mother's frail physique and delicate health. An image of Nicholas flashed into his memory as he looked upon Rainald's other son, for the contrast between them could not have been more dramatic: Nicholas, hollow-eyed and arrow-thin, with a winter-white pallor even in midsummer, and Rico, a youngster of sturdy build and obvious energy, a handsome lad who'd likely grow into a handsome man if the fates were kind.

There was a wooden bench in one of the cloister carrels and Rainald headed toward it now, making one of his usual jokes about "old bones." Roger followed willingly and Rico dutifully. Taking pity on the boy, Roger concocted an interesting errand for him to run, and Rico was soon trotting across the grass toward the slype. Just before he disappeared into the passage, he suddenly did a handstand, for no other reason but the bliss of being ten years old and on his way to the stables on a mild September afternoon.

Both men exchanged a rueful smile, one that acknowledged the pure joys of childhood were distant memories, and thank God for it. "I thought," Roger said, "that you named the lad Henry." When Rainald confirmed that he had, the bishop looked puzzled. "Then why Rico?"

"Well, you saw him, dark as a Saracen, no? After he was born, I was joking that he looked as dusky as a Sicilian and we ought to christen him Enrico rather than Henry. The next I knew, his mother was calling him Rico and soon I was, too."

Rainald's eyes took on a fond, faraway look and Roger surprised himself by feeling a small dart of envy. He'd known when he'd taken his vows as a priest that he'd be forswearing those sinful pleasures that other men held most dear: carnal lust and good wine and bad company. He'd also be renouncing the Almighty's blessings of marriage and fatherhood. He had never repented his choice, could not even envision a life not given over to God. But there were times when he wondered about that road not taken and the sons he'd never have.

"Speaking of sons," he said, "I recently heard that Eleanor had young Richard invested as Count of Poitou this spring. I suppose that explains why she was absent from Hal's coronation."

"Well, she was also occupied with guarding the coast for Harry . . . as you ought to know, lad. She kept you from sailing from Dieppe, no?"

"So you heard about that, did you?" Roger could jest about it now, but at the time, he'd found no humor in his plight. Having learned that Henry planned to crown his son, Thomas Becket had instructed Roger to go at once to England with papal letters forbidding the coronation. At the same time, Henry had commanded Roger to return to England so that he could attend the coronation. Roger felt that he had no choice but to obey his archbishop, although painfully aware that if he thwarted Hal's coronation, his cousin the king would never forgive him. There was a certain relief, therefore, in discovering that the Bishop of Lisieux had alerted the queen about his mission for Becket and she'd given orders that no ship in any Norman port was to give him passage.

"Did you also hear about the public brawl that Harry and I had upon his return to Normandy?"

Rainald shook his head, looking so expectant that Roger had to smile; few men savored gossip as much as his uncle. "Harry was on his way to Falaise and I rode out to meet him. He at once began to berate me for not attending Hal's coronation. When I told him that the queen had forbidden me to sail, he cursed me all the more loudly for trying to lay the blame on her. By then, I was no less wroth than he, and I shouted back that he was fortunate I was not present at the coronation for I'd not have allowed it to take place. I also accused him of ingratitude, reminding him of how much my father had done to secure his crown and how little he had done for my brothers after gaining the throne."

Rainald whistled admiringly, only half in jest. He did not consider himself a timid soul, but he knew he'd not have spoken up as boldly as Roger, not to the man who was his king as well as his nephew. "Do not stop now. What happened then?"

"Our quarrel was being conducted on horseback, out on the Falaise Road, so we had a large, interested audience. Some of the knights in the king's household began to mutter amongst themselves and one man sought to curry favor with Harry by heaping abuse on me as an ingrate and traitor."

Rainald let out a short bark of laughter. "I can well imagine Harry's reaction to that!"

Roger grinned. "Yes . . . Harry damned near took the poor fool's head off! Who was this miserable wretch, that he dared to insult the Bishop of Worcester and the king's kinsman? Harry stopped in mid-harangue, as if hearing himself—fiercely defending the very man he'd been threatening but moments before—and then burst out laughing. As our eyes met, I could not help laughing, too, and no more needed to be said. We rode on into Falaise and dined together that noon. And after Harry met with the Holy Father's envoys and agreed to their terms for making peace with the archbishop, he asked me to accompany him to Fréteval, which I did."

"You were at Fréteval?" Rainald was delighted. "Word reached us in England, of course, about their accord, but an eyewitness account is more than I hoped for."

"As you doubtless know, the agreement they reached is basically the same one that they were quarreling over at Montmartre. Harry agreed to allow Thomas to return to his diocese at Canterbury and to restore the episcopal estates and to permit Thomas to re-crown Hal, along with Louis's daughter. Thomas in turn agreed to defer his claims for damages done to his lands during his exile and promised to render to Harry his love and honor and all the services which an archbishop could do for a king. Harry then promised to give Thomas the Kiss of Peace once they were in England, saying it was meaningless unless done of his own free will and not under compulsion, and Thomas accepted that."

Roger paused. "All in all, the meeting between them was surprisingly cordial and amicable, with no eleventh hour ambushes by either side. Harry had made peace with Louis on the preceding day, and he seemed quite satisfied with the results of the Fréteval council. So, too, did Thomas and his clerks. As for the papal legates, they were overjoyed."

Rainald's first impulse was to take Roger's account at face value. But Roger's narration had been curiously flat, as sparse as a skeleton, devoid of all flesh and blood and marrow.

"Then why," he asked with a sigh, "are you not better pleased by it? I should think that you, of all men, would thank God fasting for a reconciliation between Harry and Becket."

"Yes . . . if only I could believe their differences had truly been resolved. But they were not, Uncle. They were merely ignored."

"I do not follow you."

"Not a mention was made of the Constitutions of Clarendon, and that was at the heart of their antagonism. The Fréteval agreement was riddled with such dangerous omissions and equivocations. Harry agreed that Thomas had the right to discipline the bishops who'd taken part in his son's coronation, but what precisely does that mean? To Harry, that is likely to mean a slap on the wrist, a minor penalty. What if Thomas interprets those same ambiguous words much more harshly?

"Moreover, Harry will want the sentences of excommunication lifted from Geoffrey Ridel and his other men, and Thomas is already finding excuses to delay that action. And when Thomas demands an exact accounting of the moneys he claims he lost in revenues during his absence, how amenable is Harry going to be to that demand? No, Uncle, I very much fear that this was not so much a peace as a truce."

Rainald sighed again, for he wanted to believe that Fréteval had been the final destination and not just one more stop along a very rocky road. And because he'd had a lifetime's experience in exiling unpleasant thought to the peripheral regions of his brain, he managed to push Roger's qualms into a cobwebbed corner where they could be disregarded.

"Who's to say a young truce cannot mature into a full-grown peace?" he joked, and then opted for an abrupt change of subject. "Do you know why Harry is missing Maude's Requiem Mass? He had no choice about her funeral, what with his war in Brittany, but I'd have hoped that he'd make time for this."

Roger swung around on the bench to stare at him. "Jesú! You do not know, do you?"

Rainald did not like the sound of that. "Know what?" he asked warily.

"About Harry's illness. He was stricken with a tertian fever last month, and for a time, the doctors despaired of his life."

Rainald's jaw dropped. "I heard not a word of this! But I went to my estates in Cornwall after the coronation. How does he? Is he still ailing? Was it as serious as all that?"

"Yes, indeed, it was. He made out a deathbed will, confirming the partition of his domains amongst his sons, and a false report of his death even reached Paris, so grievous was his condition. I did not mean to alarm you unduly, Uncle, for he is on the mend now, although I daresay it will take another fortnight ere he recovers his strength."

Rainald didn't doubt it, for he'd had some experience of his own with the ague, and knew how debilitating those deadly chills and fever could be. "Where is he? I'll want to depart after the morrow's Mass for Maude. Is Eleanor with him?"

"He was taken ill at Domfront and he is not yet up to riding, so for once you can actually be certain of his whereabouts, at least until he is strong enough to stay in the saddle. And no, Eleanor is in Poitiers."

Rainald wondered if that Clifford chit had been there, but decided it was not a tactful query to put to a priest. "God be praised," he said, "for sparing his life. I could not envision our world without Harry. It would be like blotting out the sun." Thinking then of the coronation, he said softly, "I'd just as soon Hal's kingship remained an empty honor for some years to come."

"*Deo volente*," Roger said, no more than that, but there was something in his tone which told Rainald that in this, they were of the same mind.

Upon his recovery, Henry and Eleanor made a pilgrimage to the shrine of St Mary at Rocamadour at Quercy in her duchy of Aquitaine to give thanks. In late September, Thomas Becket joined him at Tours, arriving before the start of daily Mass, where the king would have been compelled to offer him the Kiss of Peace. One of the archbishop's most bitter enemies, Rannulph de Broc, had boasted that he would kill Becket before he had eaten one whole loaf on English soil, and the archbishop was alarmed enough to want the extra assurance of the Kiss of Peace. But Henry was alerted to Becket's early arrival, and annoyed by what he saw as the archbishop's duplicity, he instructed the priest to celebrate the Mass for the Dead, in which the ritual kiss is omitted.

O CTOBER THAT YEAR was uncommonly warm and the trees were still green and full; only an occasional flare of crimson or saffron reminded men that the autumnal season was past due. The fourteenth dawned with a summer's languor, the sky above Chaumont-sur-Loire a patchwork of bleached blue and fleecy white, the air very still, without even a hint of a breeze. Henry had just finished two days of meetings with the Count of Blois and intended to leave Chaumont on the morrow for his castle at Chinon. His plans for this humid, sultry Wednesday—to hear petitioners, hold an audience with the Archbishop of Tours, and go hunting for roe deer in the forest north of the River Loire—were disrupted by the unexpected arrival of the Archbishop of Canterbury.

Henry was not pleased, for it was beginning to seem as if his peace with Becket would unravel even before the archbishop set foot again on English shores. He'd been vexed to learn that Becket's clerks were boasting of a "glorious victory" and frustrated by the archbishop's insistence upon collecting every last farthing of the revenues that had accrued during his exile. He'd made a genuine effort to be accommodating at Fréteval and felt that Thomas Becket was already taking advantage of his generosity. And so it was with a dangerous degree of resentment that he gave orders for the archbishop to be ushered into his presence.

The last time they'd met, it had been in anger, for they'd quarreled bitterly again after Henry's refusal to give Becket the Kiss of Peace at Tours. But to Henry's surprise, the archbishop made no mention of that unpleasant altercation. Their meeting was affable, even comfortable, almost as if their friendship had never been ruptured by events that Henry still did not fully understand. An exchange of courtesies flowed easily into more familiar conversation, and Henry found himself doing something utterly unanticipated: sharing a laugh with Thomas Becket.

He'd often wondered why Becket's well of humor had gone dry as soon as the blessed pallium had been placed around his neck; God did not demand that His servants forswear laughter. They had left the stifling heat in the hall and were walking together in the gardens, trailed by attendants and several of Henry's dogs. Henry studied the other man's profile as they strolled, thinking that Thomas's face was a testament to his adversities.

Becket was more than twelve years his elder, and this coming December would be his fiftieth. To Henry, he looked at least ten years older than that, hair gone silver-grey, dark eyes circled, furrows cut deeply into

his brow. He'd been told that Thomas suffered from a painful inflamma-
tion of the jawbone and that he'd inflicted harsh penances upon himself
during his years in exile, even immersion in the drains beneath Pontigny
Abbey. Why? Why had he sought out such suffering? Why had he
spurned their friendship and embraced the Church with a zealot's fervor?

That was not a question Henry could ask. He had already done so, out
on a wind-scourged field under the walls of Northampton, nigh on seven
years ago. And it had gained him nothing but bloodied pride, no answer
that explained the mysterious transformation of this man who had once
been his most trusted friend. He took refuge, instead, in a heavy-handed
joke, one that was more revealing than he realized.

"Why can you not do what I want, Thomas? For if you would, I'd
entrust my realm and my soul to you! As Scriptures say, 'All these things
will I give thee, if thou wilt fall down and worship me.'" Remembering
then that humor had become a foreign tongue for the archbishop, however fluent the chancellor had once been, Henry added hastily, "That is a
jest, of course! I do not even demand that of my bedmates, after all."

Henry was heartened when Becket smiled, for he'd been half-expecting
a lecture on blasphemy, and as they continued along the garden path, he
laid out his plans for the archbishop's return from exile. They would meet
at Rouen after Martinmas, and he would satisfy Becket's creditors from
the Royal Exchequer. He would then either conduct the archbishop himself to England or, if that was not possible, send the Archbishop of Rouen
in his stead. As they had agreed upon at Fréteval, he would bestow the Kiss
of Peace upon his arrival back on English soil.

They faced each other on the walkway, their eyes catching and holding. "Go in Peace," Henry said. "I will follow and meet you as soon as I
can, either at Rouen or in England."

Becket nodded somberly. "My lord king, I feel in my heart that when
I leave you now, I shall never see you again in this life."

Henry was too startled for anger. "Surely you are not accusing me of
treachery?"

"God forbid, my lord."

And after that, they walked on in silence.

JOHN OF SALISBURY had already packed his coffer chest, dispatched letters of farewell to his friends in France, and paid for his passage

on a ship sailing at week's end. On the morrow he would depart for the port of Barfleur. A Channel crossing was a daunting prospect to most men, but John loved traveling. The horizons of his world were boundless, ever beckoning him onward, and he accepted the discomforts of the road as the price he must pay for admittance to exotic, foreign locales.

This trip's destination was a familiar one: England. Six years of exile, though, had sharpened his hunger for his homeland. Even if his mission for the archbishop came to naught, at least he'd be able to visit his aged mother, to breathe again the air of Old Sarum, his birthplace.

A muffled knock distracted him from his reverie and he turned toward the door with a certain wariness. By the time he'd gotten to Rouen, the archbishop's entourage had taken up most of the available lodgings and he'd been forced to seek shelter on the city's outskirts, at the priory of Nôtre-Dame-du-Pré. Since the monks were still devoted to their illustrious patroness, the late Empress Maude, John's welcome had been a frosty one; even the youngest novice knew of John's long-standing friendship with Thomas Becket.

The youth at the door was a lay servant and seemed better suited to work in the stables than in the priory guest hall, for his information was annoyingly scant. All he could tell John was that a visitor awaited him in the parlor, one of the Archbishop of Canterbury's clerks whose name had been utterly expunged from his memory during his brief dash out into the November rain. Fortunately, John had a high tolerance for the foibles of his fellow men. Picking up his mantle, he sighed, "Lead on."

His visitor was still cloaked, for the priory parlor lacked a fireplace. John knew all of the archbishop's clerks, some better than others. Hoping that this unexpected caller wasn't the tiresome Herbert of Bosham, John fumbled in his scrip until he found a coin for the servant. "You wished to speak with me?"

As soon as the other man turned around, John's polite smile faded and he began to bristle. There were few men he loathed as much as Arnulf, the wily Bishop of Lisieux, and Hugh de Nonant was Arnulf's nephew. Even though Hugh had loyally followed Thomas Becket into exile, John did not trust him, sure that any kinsman of Arnulf's was bound to be self-serving and unscrupulous.

"What are you doing here, Hugh? You think I haven't heard about your defection?"

"It is true I have left the archbishop's service, but I do not see it as a defection and I resent your describing it as such. After enduring six years of exile with him, I do not deserve to be accused of disloyalty or bad faith for departing once he made peace with the English king."

"You say that as if this peace will magically make all his problems disappear!"

"Of course I do not believe that," Hugh snapped, surprising John by his irascibility, for he'd always cultivated a languid air of jaded sophistication that John considered more appropriate in a royal courtier than a man of God. "I know full well the dangers Thomas will be facing upon his return to England," he said testily, with none of his usual studied nonchalance.

"Then why," John asked bluntly, "did you balk at accompanying him back to England?"

Hugh's mouth twisted. "Because I do not want to watch him die!"

John's breath caught. "Merciful God! What have you heard, Hugh? Have you warned Thomas? Are you sure—"

"I do not know of any conspiracy to murder the archbishop," Hugh interrupted impatiently. "That is not what I meant."

John frowned. "What, then?"

The younger man frowned, too. "I'd hoped to ease into this. But since that is no longer possible, let's have some plain speaking, then. You do not like me. Fair enough, for I do not particularly like you, either. But you are the archbishop's friend, and one of the few whose counsel can be trusted. If anyone can talk some sense into him, it would be you, and that is why I am here."

"If this is your idea of 'plain speaking,' God spare me when you're being evasive. I still have no idea what you want me to do."

"I want you to save the archbishop from himself." Hugh held up a hand to cut off John's protest. "This infernal quarrel with the king could have been avoided, and should have been, for the good of the Church. And this peace patched and stitched together by the Pope is too fragile to bear close scrutiny."

"Hellfire and damnation, Hugh, you think I do not know that?"

"I think," Hugh said grimly, "that you do not know the archbishop's nerves are as frayed as this so-called peace. Wait, John, hear me out. How often did you visit him during the last six years? Yes, you were in exile, too, but you chose to make a safe nest for yourself at Reims, not with us at Pontigny or Sens. You have not seen for yourself the toll this struggle has taken upon Thomas. For the king, Thomas is a source of anger and aggravation. Yet he also rules an empire, and I daresay long periods of time go by when he does not think of Thomas at all. For Thomas, the world has shrunk to the confines of his monastery refuge and, like any prisoner, he has been brooding incessantly about what he lost. Unlike the king, he has had no respite from his woes. He is still convinced that he has been greatly wronged, and although he yielded to the Holy Father's pressure, he will be taking his grievances back to England with him—"

"You've said enough! Thomas deserves better from you than backbiting and petty gossip. Why you thought that I, of all men, would want to hear this rubbish—"

"Listen to me, damn you! I am here because I fear for him, because his judgment is no longer to be trusted and he has surrounded himself with zealots like Herbert of Bosham and firebrands like Alexander Llewelyn, men who will spur him on instead of reining him in."

John strode to the parlor door and jerked it open. "Thomas is my friend. I'll not listen whilst you malign him."

Hugh de Nonant was deeply flushed, his lip curling with scorn. "My uncle Arnulf was right about you. I should have known better than to come here." Brushing past John, he stalked across the threshold and then turned around, so abruptly that his mantle flared out dramatically behind him. "If this ends as badly as I fear, you will not be able to say you were not warned, John of Salisbury."

John reached for the door and slammed it shut, almost in the other man's face. There was a flagon on a nearby table and he quickly crossed to it, filling a wine cup with an unsteady hand. Hugh de Nonant was the sort of worldly, devious cleric he most despised, a man who saw the Stations of the Cross as rungs on the ladder of his own advancement. Like his uncle, his piety was befouled by ambition, his intelligence corrupted by amorality. John was convinced that Arnulf never did anything without an ulterior motive, and Hugh was cut from the same shabby cloth.

Was he the king's agent, sowing seeds of dissension amongst the archbishop's clerks and councilors? Was he seeking to spread rumors about the archbishop's troubled state of mind? Thomas had enemies in plenitude: men he'd antagonized during his years as Henry's chancellor, those who mistrusted his abrupt and enigmatic conversion from king's man to king's foe, those who'd profited from his exile and feared his return to royal favor. Was Hugh de Nonant in league with some of them? It was not that difficult to believe. But there had been enough truth in what Hugh had said to leave John with a lingering sense of unease.

CHAPTER THIRTY

November 1170
Trefriw, Wales

RAIN WAS AS MUCH a part of the Welsh landscape as its
mountains and ice-blue lakes and low-lying valley mists. But
even for Wales, the weather that November had been ex-
ceedingly wet, day after day of ash-colored skies and relentless down-
pours. The rivers and streams were swollen with weeks of runoff, the
roads clogged in mud, and Ranulf's family began to curse the rain with as
much rancor as Noah. An invitation to the court of Owain Gwynedd was
a great honor, and Enid vowed that they'd attend even if they had to swim
the miles between Trefriw and Aber.

Two days before the fête, though, the inhabitants of Gwynedd were
dazzled by the sight of an almost forgotten phenomenon—the sun. And
so on a Thursday in Martinmas week, Ranulf, Rhodri, and Enid were
where they'd hoped to be, dining in the great hall of their prince's palace
in celebration of his seventieth birthday.

Rhiannon was present, too, but Ranulf knew it was a sense of duty
that had prompted her to accept the invitation. She did not enjoy being
on display, and a blind woman at a banquet was enough of a novelty to

guarantee that she'd be the object of unwanted attention. He had tried to convince her that she need not attend, knowing all the while that she would insist on accompanying him. Watching as she concentrated carefully upon the venison frumenty that had been ladled onto her trencher, it occurred to Ranulf—not for the first time—that there was a manifest measure of gallantry in his wife's brand of quiet courage.

Taking a swallow of mead, he resumed his role as her eyes, continuing his description of the hall and guests. "Cristyn looks bedazzling, as usual, in a gown the color of plums. And Owain . . . well, the only word for him would be 'regal.' He most definitely does not look like a man who has reached his biblical three-score years and ten. Three of his sons are seated at the high table: Hywel, of course, and Cristyn's fox cubs. Neither Davydd nor Rhodri seems very pleased to see me; if looks could kill, I'd have breathed my last ere the servers brought in the roast goose."

They'd been speaking softly in French, for discretion's sake. Rhiannon wiped her mouth with her napkin, then murmured, "*Ni wyr y gog ond ungainc,*" and Ranulf grinned, for that was an old Welsh proverb: *The cuckoo knows but one tune.* Hywel had once said of his half-brothers that they'd ever been ones for fleeing the smoke so they could fall into the fire, and as he intercepted their sullen, baleful glares, Ranulf found himself in full agreement with his friend; Davydd and Rhodri had so far shown no sign whatsoever that they were capable of learning from past mistakes. The most successful rulers—like Owain or Harry—knew when to hold fast and when to give ground. The ones who did not were likely to end their days like Stephen, dying alone and unmourned.

But Ranulf did not want to harbor any regrets today, and made a conscious effort to banish these ghosts, casting both his doleful dead cousin and his estranged nephew out of his thoughts. Mead helped, he soon discovered, and as his eyes met Hywel's across the hall, he raised his cup in a playful salute.

"Who else is here?" Rhiannon resumed, and Ranulf took another look at their fellow guests.

"Owain's brother, Cadwaladr. He's been given a seat at the high table as a courtesy, but no one seems to be paying him much mind. Passing strange that he was once considered a threat to Owain's rule, so completely has Owain brought him to heel. Also on the dais is Owain's son-in-law, Gruffydd Maelor of Powys, and Owain's daughter Angharad. And at Owain's right is Rhys ap Gruffydd."

Ranulf was impressed by Rhys's presence at Aber, for his own lands lay many miles to the south. Rhys had come with a large entourage, as much to reflect his own prestige and power as to honor his ally and uncle, but his wife, Gwenllian, had remained behind in Deheubarth; Rhys was not known for being uxorious.

"Several of Owain's other sons are here, too, although not at the high table. Cynan seems to be enjoying himself; that one could find sport at a wake. And Iorwerth, who always looks as if he is attending a funeral, Lord love him. There are clergy present, as well; I recognize the Archdeacon of Bangor and I overheard someone say that the Cistercian monk with Rhys is the abbot of Strata Florida, that abbey in Dyfed."

Rhiannon found that as interesting as Ranulf did. "So the Welsh Church is not recognizing Owain's excommunication?"

"It would seem not." Ranulf was not surprised by the recalcitrance of the Welsh clergy, not if the views of his neighbors in Trefriw were any gauge of public opinion. When the Archbishop of Canterbury had excommunicated Owain for his refusal to end his marriage to Cristyn, most of Owain's subjects reacted with outrage, sure that Becket was punishing Owain for their conflict over the bishopric of Bangor. Ranulf had his suspicions, too, although he usually tried to give Becket the benefit of every doubt. But the timing did seem odd to him, that as soon as Owain had defied Becket by having his candidate consecrated as Bishop of Bangor in Ireland, his marriage to his cousin was suddenly a matter of grave concern to the Church.

Cristyn had never been popular with her husband's people, for her position was by its very nature an ambiguous one. She was scorned by some as a concubine who'd usurped the place of Owain's lawful wife, and to these judgmental souls, she had not been redeemed by her subsequent marriage. To others, she was seen as guileful and sly, willing to do whatever was necessary to disinherit Hywel and ensure that her sons would succeed Owain as rulers of Gwynedd. But the animosity of Thomas Becket had done what she herself could not, transforming her into a more sympathetic figure to many of the Welsh.

Once the meal was done, the trestle tables were cleared away and the entertainment began. Owain's *pencerdd* came forward as the hall quieted. Poets were accorded great respect in Wales and he had an attentive, enthusiastic audience for his songs, the first celebrating the glory of God and the second a paean in praise of his lord. After his performance, it was the turn of Owain's *bardd teulu,* the chief minstrel of the court, and as the sky darkened over the Menai Straits, the prince's palace at Aber resounded with music and mirth.

Servers were circulating throughout the hall with mead and wine, and Hywel's foster brother Peryf amused Hywel and Ranulf by appropriating a large flagon for himself. "You need not fear," he assured them, "for I might be persuaded to share."

"Assuming there is so much as a drop left," Hywel scoffed. "I've seen you in action, Peryf, remember?"

They had withdrawn to a window seat alcove. Seeing that Rhiannon had concluded her conversation with Owain's daughter Angharad, Ranulf hastened over to bring her into their charmed circle, where they had an unobstructed view of the dancing and the intermingling of the other guests. Once she was settled onto the cushioned seat and Hywel's flirting had run its course, Ranulf asked the question that was foremost on his mind.

"Are you still planning a voyage to Ireland, Hywel?"

"Must you say it in the same tones you'd use to inquire after my trip to Purgatory? I know the Irish Sea is aboil at this time of year. But I have no choice, for there are matters about my lady mother's estate that demand my presence. And now I will impress you and the lovely Lady Rhiannon with my abilities as a soothsayer, for I can predict your next question. The answer is yes. I mean to take your lad with me."

Ranulf and Rhiannon had the same parental response, a discordant mixture of pride and concern. They were gratified that since joining Hywel's household, their son was rising so fast in Hywel's favor. Yet they worried about his making a winter journey to Ireland, although they would do their best not to embarrass Gilbert by giving voice to their qualms.

"Speaking of the devil," Hywel said, and they saw that their firstborn was heading in their direction. Seeing Gilbert away from home and hearth, Ranulf invariably felt a prick of surprise that his son could be nineteen now, a man grown. Gilbert was smiling, but his parents knew him well enough to pick up on the subtle signs, indications of unease.

Once the pleasantries were over, Gilbert hesitated. "Has Lord Hywel told you that I will be accompanying him to Ireland?" Getting a confirmation, he paused again and then, as was his wont, plunged in headfirst. "There is something I need to tell you ere I go and I might not get another chance. I have decided to change my name. I've never felt comfortable with Gilbert, as you know. I am of an age now to choose a name more to my liking, a Welsh name. I wish to call myself Bleddyn."

Ranulf felt as if he'd just taken a blow to the midsection. He stared at his son, stunned that Gilbert could offer such a mortal insult in this public setting. Did he truly think it was merely a matter of names? That Gilbert Fitz Ranulf could become Bleddyn ap Ranulf as easily as that? Gilbert was rejecting half of his heritage, the Norman blood running in his veins, and at that moment, it seemed to Ranulf that his son was rejecting him, too.

Before he could respond, he felt Rhiannon's hand on his arm, gently but firmly pulling him back from the brink. He covered her hand with his own, giving it a grateful squeeze. "This is not the time," he said, as evenly as he could manage. "I think it would be best if we continue this discussion later."

His son agreed all too readily and made his escape within moments thereafter, leaving Ranulf, Rhiannon, Hywel, and Peryf behind in a cloud of dust. There was a long silence and then Ranulf slowly shook his head. "Whatever possessed him to raise this now?"

"Has it been that long since you were young?" Hywel gibed. "This was an ambush, man! Your lad picked his time and place with care. I'll wager that you'll need a pack of lymer hounds to track him down ere we sail for Ireland." He laughed, but stopped when Ranulf did not. "There's less to this than meets the eye, Ranulf. Take a moment and think it through. The name he chose . . . Bleddyn. You think he picked it at random?"

"Does it matter?"

"I think so. You told me once that yours is an old Norse name, dating back to when they invaded Normandy. 'Shield of the wolf,' right? Well, what does Bleddyn mean in Welsh? You ought to know, for you named one of your dyrehunds Blaidd!"

"Wolf," Ranulf said softly. "Bleddyn means 'young wolf,'" and Hywel gave him the indulgent smile of one tutoring a slow student. At that moment, Hywel saw that his father was beckoning to him from the dais, and after kissing Rhiannon with his usual flourish, he took his leave. It was soon clear that Owain had invited him to perform and the hall quieted in anticipation.

Hywel took a seat, accepted a harp. "I would sing," he said, "of the battle of Tal Moelfre."

Those words were enough to roll back time for Ranulf, and the torchlit hall gave way to a summer's day in God's Year 1157, to the tangled, dense greenwood of the Cennadlog Forest, riding with Harry into a

Welsh ambush. While they were escaping by a hair's-breadth, Hywel had been routing the English at Tal Moelfre on the isle of Môn, and he'd afterward composed a poem to commemorate the battle. Ranulf had heard it many times, and while he appreciated the imagery in such lines as "When ruby-red flame flared high as Heaven, home offered no refuge," he'd teased Hywel unmercifully over the hyperbole of the boastful last verse, in which Hywel bragged of sinking "three hundred ships of the king's own navy." If Harry had ever had three hundred warships, he'd pointed out, all of Wales would be an English shire by now. Hywel's response was always the same: a laugh, a shrug, and a claim that poets could not be held to the same exacting standards as mere mortals.

Others in the audience assumed with Ranulf that Hywel would be performing his own composition. There were murmurs of surprise, therefore, when he began, for the words were not his. The song was one of praise to Owain, but the poet was not present. Gwalchmai ap Meilyr had been Owain's chief bard for many years. They'd had a falling out, though, and Gwalchmai was no longer in favor. So Hywel's choice was a startling one, and Ranulf noticed how both Davydd and Rhodri pushed their way through to the dais, jockeying for position like eager spectators at a public hanging.

Hywel seemed oblivious to the tension in the hall. But then he happened to catch Ranulf's eye and winked. Ranulf knew him as well as one man can ever know another and he knew then that Hywel had selected the disgraced Gwalchmai's song to honor a fine poet. There was little that Hywel took truly seriously, but his love of poetry was the lodestar of his life, greater even than his love of women. Ranulf felt sure that Hywel had been motivated by mischief, too. He'd rarely been able to resist poking his stick into a hornet's nest.

Hywel had a rich, mellow voice and he infused Gwalchmai's words with a passion that was contagious. By the time he lauded Owain as "The Dragon of Môn," his father's stern mouth had relaxed into an amused, fond smile. No one watching could doubt the depths of Owain's pride in his firstborn, and when Hywel was done, the hall erupted into applause.

Ranulf was laughing and cheering, too, when Peryf nudged him and hissed gleefully, "The she-wolf looks like to choke on her own bile!" And he turned in time to see Cristyn's court mask slip, to see her handsome face harden into stone, dark eyes narrowed to slits of pure, primal rage as she gazed upon her husband's best-loved son.

NORTH WALES had another week of dry weather, and then the rains returned. At night, the temperature dropped and a thin glaze of ice skimmed the surface of ponds. The last of the swallows disappeared and badgers dug winter dens and trees were silhouetted bare and sparse against the November sky.

The last Wednesday in November was wretched in all aspects. Rain poured down incessantly and a cold, piercing wind drove even the hardiest travelers from the roads. At Trefriw, none ventured outside willingly, and in the stables, cats played deadly feline games with shelter-seeking mice. Ranulf awoke with a dull headache and a disheartened realization that worse was to come: dwindling hours of daylight and smoky hearths and storms and meal after meal of salted herring and the daily deprivations of Advent and Lent and months to go before the reviving clemency of spring.

By midafternoon, the household was in turmoil, most of it due to the antics of Ranulf and Rhiannon's six-year-old son. Morgan did not mean to wreak havoc, but he was bored and restless and trapped indoors, and the result was chaos. He spilled Ranulf's inkwell, snapped a string on Rhodri's harp, lost a knife Rhodri was using to carve wooden spoons, took Rhiannon's best boar-bristle brush to groom his father's dyrehund, and knocked over a barrel of wood ash that the women intended using to make into soap. After this last mishap, Ranulf grabbed the boy and, snatching up their mantles, hustled him out into the rain.

"Better you should risk drowning out here, lad, than certain death inside," he chided, and Morgan did his best to look as if he was being punished, although he had no objections whatsoever to getting wet and muddy. He was trying to coax Ranulf into wading across the bailey toward the dovecote when shouts erupted from the direction of the gatehouse.

To Morgan's delight and Ranulf's astonishment, a lone rider was being admitted. Swathed in a soaked mantle, plastered with mud, the man staggered as soon as he slid from the saddle, and Ranulf, remembering his manners, came forward hastily to bid this miserable traveler welcome.

"Good God, you're half-frozen! Come inside and thaw out."

Their guest did not argue, and as soon as a groom hurried out to take his horse, he stumbled after them toward the hall. Ranulf still did not recognize him, able to discern only that he was of middle height and stocky. He could hear the chattering of the man's teeth, could see the reddened chilblains on his hands, and wondered what urgent mission had put him out onto the roads on such a foul day.

Their arrival in the hall created a flurry of confusion and noise. Silencing the barking dogs with difficulty, Ranulf led the man toward the hearth as Rhodri limped over with a cup of hot, mulled cider and Enid sent a servant for blankets and towels. Gulping down the cider in three swallows, the man began to struggle with his mantle, emerging from its dripping folds like a rumpled butterfly from a soggy cocoon. To Ranulf's surprise, the face revealed when the hood fell back was a familiar one.

"Peryf? What are you doing so far from home?"

Peryf started to speak, began to cough instead. Signaling for more cider, he drank as if he could not get enough. He was standing so close to the open hearth that steam rose off his sodden clothes. "So tired . . . ," he panted, ". . . left Aber at dawn . . ."

Ranulf's sudden chill had nothing to do with the winter weather. "Peryf, what is wrong?"

"Lord Owain . . . he is dead."

There was a muffled cry from one of the women, a choked oath from Rhodri. Ranulf had to swallow before he could speak, for his mouth had gone dry. "How? What happened?"

"Monday morn . . . he . . . he complained of a pain in his arm, said he felt queasy of a sudden." Peryf's voice was still hoarse, but steadier now. When Ranulf shoved a stool toward him, he sank down upon it gratefully. "Then he fell over. Everyone panicked, people rushing about, bumping into one another, Cristyn shrieking like a madwoman, dogs underfoot, children crying. Lord Owain was the only one who kept calm. . . . Lying there in the floor rushes, his head cradled in his wife's lap, he told us to fetch a doctor and . . . and a priest."

Rhodri hastily crossed himself and Enid began to sob; so did her maid and their cook. "Was there time for him to be shriven?" This voice was Rhiannon's and Ranulf reached out, drew her to his side, thinking that she always went straight to the heart of the matter. Their relief was enormous when Peryf nodded vigorously.

"Aye, there was. He lived long enough to confess his sins and to be given extreme unction . . . and to name Hywel as his heir."

The full import of Owain's death hit Ranulf then. "Hywel . . . he's gone?"

"Aye," Peryf echoed, looking at Ranulf with swollen, fear-filled eyes. "Hywel sailed for Ireland ten days ago."

THE DAY was surprisingly mild for late November, and England's young king was taking full advantage of the weather's clemency to practice in the tiltyard of Winchester Castle. Rainald cheered loudly each time Hal made a successful pass at the target, but even allowing for his avuncular partiality, Hal's performance was deserving of applause. Astride a spirited white stallion, Hal was displaying both skilled horsemanship and a deft control of his lance, and he'd soon drawn an admiring audience. He would make a fine king one day, for certes, blessed with good looks, good health, and winning ways. If his judgment was still unduly influenced by impulse and whim, Rainald preferred to believe that these were flaws which would be remedied with maturity.

Reining in his stallion, Hal accepted a flask from one of his friends. As his eyes met Rainald's, he grinned. "What do you think of Favel, Uncle? This is only the third time I've ridden him and already he anticipates my every command."

"You've got a good eye for horseflesh," Rainald agreed amiably. "Listen, lad, there is someone here who'd like a word with you. See that anxious soul in the brown mantle?"

The man pointed out by Rainald was small of stature and modestly garbed, and Hal's gaze flicked over him and then away, without interest. "I was about to make another run at the quintain."

"It will take only a few moments," Rainald insisted, raising his hand in a beckoning gesture. "You met him earlier today, at your public audience in the great hall." Seeing no recollection on Hal's face, he added helpfully, "John of Salisbury." Hal still looked blank. "He's a noted scholar, a good friend to Thomas Becket, who has sent him on ahead to make sure the Fréteval accords are being implemented."

By then John of Salisbury was within hearing range and Rainald could offer no more prompting. He knew Hal was not pleased, but the youth dismounted as John approached, and that, too, Rainald had known he would do. He was more good-natured than his younger brothers, rarely showed flashes of his family's infamous Angevin temper, and was usually willing to be accommodating if it didn't inconvenience him greatly.

John bestowed a grateful glance upon Rainald before making a deep obeisance to the young king. Hal had greeted him with affable courtesy during their initial meeting, reminiscing about his years in Archbishop Thomas's household, but he'd been flanked at all times by the chief lords of his court, men so hostile to the archbishop that their very presence hobbled John's tongue. This chance to speak more candidly with the youth was God-sent.

"Lord Thomas will be returning to England within the week. When we last spoke in Rouen, he expressed his desire to see Your Grace as soon after his arrival as can be arranged. May I write and assure him that you, too, are eager for this reunion, my lord?"

"Of course I would be gladdened to see the archbishop again," Hal said politely. "But you need to consult with my lord father's chancellor about such matters." If Hal appreciated the irony of fortune's wheel—that the chancellorship which had once been Becket's was now held by Geoffrey Ridel, one of his bitterest adversaries—it was not evident upon his face. "He will be better able to tell you when the archbishop can be made welcome."

"Thank you, my lord," John said hesitantly. At fifteen, Hal was already as tall as many men grown, towering over the diminutive scholar. His smile was easy, his manners polished, his hair sun-burnished, his eyes the color of the sky.

There was so much that John had planned to say. He'd meant to stress the dangers that awaited the archbishop upon his arrival to England, to speak of the archbishop's many enemies, men of wealth and power who feared being dispossessed of the estates and honors they'd been enjoying during his long exile. He'd hoped to gain the young king's assurances that he would not heed these enemies, nor listen to the malicious gossip they'd be murmuring in his ear. With King Henry still in Normandy, his son's attitude was of the utmost importance, both to the archbishop and his foes.

"My lord king!" Geoffrey Ridel was striding hastily toward them, poorly concealing his alarm that his young charge should have slipped his tether. Giving John an irate look that spilled over onto Rainald, too, he was breathless by the time he reached them, intent upon ending this impromptu audience straightaway.

He need not have worried, for John had already realized that his mission was doomed to failure. The archbishop had been sure that Hal would be on his side. But John was an astute judge of men and he'd seen only one emotion in the depths of those sapphire-blue eyes: indifference.

CHAPTER THIRTY-ONE

November 1170
Wissant, France

THOMAS BECKET WAS WALKING along the beach, gazing out across the sun-sparkled waters of the Channel. It was a cold day but clear, and the chalk cliffs of Dover could be seen glimmering in the far distance. Now that they were so close to ending their exile, some of his clerks were eager to return to their homeland and they'd been complaining among themselves about the delay in sailing. Although they were trailing behind the archbishop, the wind carried the words of one grumbler to Becket's ears. Looking back over his shoulder, he queried, "What was that you said, Gunter?"

Gunter of Winchester smiled self-consciously, but his years of exile with the archbishop entitled him to speak candidly. "I said, my lord, that I was feeling like Moses, who saw the promised land and could not enter."

Becket's smile came and went so fast that some of the clerks missed it. "You ought not to be in such a hurry, Gunter. Before forty days are up, you will wish yourself anywhere but in England."

This was not the first time that he'd made such ambivalent statements about their homecoming, and his companions exchanged worried glances. Becket had resumed walking and they hastened to catch up, Herbert of Bosham jockeying for position beside their lord, to the amusement of the others. When Becket stopped without warning, Herbert nearly ploughed into him, but the archbishop didn't appear to notice, his attention drawn to a man striding purposefully across the sand toward them.

The newcomer was elegantly attired in a fur-trimmed woolen mantle and leather ankle boots, carrying in one hand a knitted pair of cuffed silk gloves. He looked like a royal courtier; in fact, he was a highly placed churchman, the Dean of Boulogne. He was also a fellow Englishman, and there was genuine pleasure in Becket's cry of recognition.

"What are you doing here, Milo? Ah, I know . . . you heard we are about to sail and you're hoping for a free ride with us to visit your kinfolk."

Milo acknowledged the jest with a polite, perfunctory smile. "If I might have a word alone with you, my lord archbishop . . . ?"

Becket acquiesced and, as the clerks watched intently, the two men walked together for a time along the shore, heads down, their mantles catching the wind and swirling out behind them. When they moved apart, Becket smiled and clapped Milo on the shoulder, then beckoned to his companions. "We are going back to our lodgings, where the Dean of Boulogne has graciously agreed to dine with us."

The offer of hospitality was made with deliberate wryness, acknowledging the reduced circumstances of an archbishop in exile, and Becket's clerks smiled dutifully. But they kept casting uneasy glances toward the dean, and when the opportunity presented itself, two of them dropped back to walk beside him.

Milo knew them both: Gunter was one of the archbishop's most devoted clerks and, Master William had long plied his medical skills in the highest circles of the English Church, first as physician to Theobald, Archbishop of Canterbury, and then to his successor, Thomas Becket. It was easy for the dean to guess what they wanted to ask and he saw no reason not to tell them.

"I was sent at the behest of the Count of Boulogne," he said quietly. "He wanted to warn the archbishop that his enemies are awaiting him at Dover, with evil intent in mind."

They showed no surprise, for this was only one of several warnings that Becket had received in recent weeks. Neither man bothered to ask

Milo what the archbishop had replied, for they already knew that. He'd been saying to anyone who'd listen that nothing would stop him from returning to England, that if he died en route to Canterbury, they must promise to see to his burial in Christ Church Cathedral.

"We must convince Lord Thomas to put in at any port but Dover, then," Gunter declared and veered off to suggest that to one of the most persuasive of Becket's clerks, Alexander Llewelyn, his Welsh cross-bearer.

Master William remained at Milo's side. His shoulders hunched against the wind, hands jammed into the side slits of his cloak, he was scuffing his feet in the sand, trampling shells underfoot as if they were the enemy. "You do not look," Milo observed, "like a man eagerly anticipating a return to his homeland, Will."

"I fear what awaits us," the physician said with despairing honesty. "If Lord Thomas's enemies are already plotting against him, what will they do once they hear of the excommunications?"

"What excommunications?" Milo asked sharply, and Master William looked about furtively, then deliberately slowed his pace so that they lagged behind the others.

"I might as well tell you, for all will know soon enough. The English king has acted with his usual guile, and upon learning of his bad faith, Lord Thomas fell into a great rage and . . . and did something I fear we may all regret."

The Dean of Boulogne came to an abrupt halt. "God in Heaven, do not tell me he has excommunicated the king!"

Master William shook his head dolefully. "No . . . but this morning he sent a trusted servant to Dover with papal letters of censure for the Archbishop of York and the Bishops of London and Salisbury."

"Why would he do that? Has he lost his mind?"

"You must not be so quick to judge him," Master William said defensively. "You do not yet know what the king did to provoke him. Despite his talk about peaceful cooperation, the king decided to fill the six vacant bishoprics ere Lord Thomas could be restored to power in England. York, London, and Salisbury had gathered at Dover, making ready to escort electors overseas to vote for the king's nominees. But Lord Thomas learned of their duplicity ere they could sail for Normandy and acted to thwart them."

Milo swore a most unclerical oath, stalked to the water's edge and back again, mentally heaping curses in equal measure upon the heads of

England's king and archbishop. They were a matched pair, he thought angrily, prideful and obstinate and racing headlong into disaster. The worst of it, though, was the damage that had been done to the Holy Church by their infernal feuding. And, just as so many had long feared, there was no end in sight.

> *Henry, King of England, to his son, Henry the king, greetings. Know that Thomas, Archbishop of Canterbury, has made peace with me according to my will. I therefore command that he and all his men shall have peace. You are to see to it that the archbishop and all his men who left England for his sake shall have all their possessions as they had them three months before the archbishop departed from England. And you will cause to come before you the more important knights of the Honor of Saltwood, and by their oath, you will cause recognition to be made of what is held there in fee from the archbishopric of Canterbury . . . Witnessed by Rotrou, Archbishop of Rouen, at Chinon.*

Earlier that day, the Archbishop of Canterbury had been welcomed joyfully into Southwark. He'd been escorted to his lodgings at the Bishop of Winchester's manor by the canons of St Mary, followed by local priests and their parishioners. Hours later, church bells still pealed on both sides of the river, and the bankside crowds had yet to disperse, slowing William Fitz Stephen's progress so that an early December dusk was already descending by the time he was allowed to pass through the great gate of Winchester Palace.

Fitz Stephen's nerves were on edge, for he was not sure of his reception. He'd seen the archbishop only once in the past six years, a brief meeting at Fleury-sur-Loire. At the time, Thomas Becket had not indicated that he bore Fitz Stephen any grudge for failing to follow him into exile. But Fitz Stephen knew that others in the archbishop's entourage were not as forgiving, and he feared that their rancor might have poisoned his lord's good will.

He was not long in discovering that his qualms were well founded. He saw several familiar faces, but none greeted him, averting their eyes as if he were a moral leper, one infected with some dreadful malady of the soul. And no sooner had he entered the great hall when a known figure stepped into his path, barring his way.

"Master Fitz Stephen, as I live and breathe! Passing strange, your turning up here. I was reading Scriptures a few nights ago, Leviticus 26:36, if memory serves, and suddenly it was as if you were right there in the chamber with me."

Fitz Stephen was not the biblical scholar that Herbert of Bosham was; the other man even had knowledge of Hebrew, a rarity in the most learned circles. But Fitz Stephen, subdeacon and lawyer, was well versed enough in the Scriptures to appreciate the insult. *The sound of a driven leaf shall put them to flight, and they shall flee as one flees from the sword, and they shall fall when none pursues.*

His first instinct was to strike back with scriptural weapons of his own; Matthew was certainly apt, with its admonition to *judge not, that ye be not judged.* But that would be an exercise in futility, exactly what Herbert wanted him to do. Instead, he smiled blandly. "It is always good to be remembered."

Herbert's dark eyes glowed like embers. "You are not welcome here!"

"That is not for you to say."

"You abandoned our lord in his hour of jeopardy and embraced his persecutor!"

"I made my peace with our lord king, as the archbishop himself did at Fréteval!"

"A false peace, just as you are a false friend!"

"Could you say that more loudly, Master Herbert? I doubt that they could hear you across the river in London."

At the intrusion of this new voice, both Herbert and Fitz Stephen swung toward the sound. Herbert scowled, for Becket's Welsh cross-bearer was the only one of the archbishop's clerks who could match him in rhetorical flourishes, boldness of speech, and pure lung power. While he acknowledged Alexander Llewelyn's unwavering loyalty to their lord, a trait he found to be conspicuously rare amongst the Welsh, he was invariably perplexed by the other man's drolleries and insouciance. He assumed now that this was a jest of some sort, although the humor of it escaped him, as humor always did.

"If you choose to consort with apostates, Master Llewelyn," he said loftily, "that is your right. I, however, do not." And he made a dignified departure, marred only by the hostile glare he flung over his shoulder at Fitz Stephen as he strode off.

"Why is it," Alexander wondered, "that I always feel the urge to applaud after one of Herbert's speeches?"

Fitz Stephen grinned, for that had been a standing joke between them, that Herbert of Bosham secretly yearned, not for a bishopric as most clerks did, but for the starring role in a troupe of players. His pleasure was sharp at this proof that their friendship had survived the vicissitudes of the past six years. "You do not blame me, then, for making peace with the king?"

"You did what you had to do," Alexander said, accepting life's inequities and anomalies with the fatalism of the true Celt. "My family is safely out of the king's reach in Wales, but yours was in . . . Gloucestershire, was it not? Who could blame you for not wanting to see them banished from England? How are your sisters? And that brother of yours? They are well?"

"Yes, thank God Almighty, they are. Ralph has entered the king's service, in fact." Fitz Stephen hesitated, but his were the instincts of a lawyer; better to scout out the terrain first. "Sander . . . does the lord archbishop feel as you do? Or as Herbert does?"

Alexander gestured toward a window recess. "Let's talk over there." Once they were seated, he took his time in answering. Fitz Stephen was a patient man, though, content to wait.

"I remember something that the Bishop of Worcester said to me last year. He said that any friend of the archbishop's was an enemy of the king's, with one exception . . . himself. And he was right. The king is fond enough of Lord Roger to overlook his dual loyalties. I think that also holds true for you and Lord Thomas. We both know that he and the king share the same creed: 'He that is not with me is against me.' But I can truthfully tell you that I have not heard Lord Thomas speak against you, not once in all those years of our exile. He does not doubt your fidelity, Will," the Welshman said seriously, and then laughed. "Much to Master Herbert's dismay!"

"God grant it so," Fitz Stephen said softly. "I rejoiced to hear of the archbishop's accord with the king, Sander, for I'd given up hope that it would ever come to pass. Herbert called it a 'false peace.' Is there truth in that?"

Alexander's amusement vanished as if it had never been. "I fear so," he said at last. "We've been back in England less than a fortnight, and little has gone as it ought. There is continuing strife with the de Brocs. They still hold Saltwood Castle and they've shown no willingness to surrender their grip on the diocese as the king ordered. They even went so far as to collect the Christmas rents in advance from the archbishop's tenants! And they have been harassing our lord in ways both petty and great. The king sent wine as a gift to the archbishop and they seized the ship and cargo, throwing the crew into gaol at Pevensey. They have stolen Lord Thomas's hunting dogs, poached his game, felled his trees. And I am sorry to say that the young king has so far done nothing to rein in their malice. That is why we are at Southwark, Will. Lord Thomas means to go to the young king's court at Winchester and assure him that there is no truth in the rumors the de Brocs are spreading, that he intends to overturn Hal's coronation."

"The de Brocs are evil men," Fitz Stephen said grimly, "verily spawn of Satan. Did you know that Robert de Broc is an apostate Cistercian monk? It is only to be expected that they are stirring up as much trouble as they can. I thought the king was supposed to return to England with Lord Thomas. Why did that not come to pass?"

Alexander grimaced. "When we got to Rouen, the king was not there. He sent a message from Loches in Touraine, claiming that he'd had to hasten to Auvergne to fend off an attack by the French king and telling Lord Thomas to go on to England with the escort he'd provided. You care to guess who the escort was, Will?" When Fitz Stephen shook his head in puzzlement, he said, after a dramatic pause: "The Dean of Salisbury, John of Oxford."

Fitz Stephen's response was all that Alexander hoped for. He gaped at the Welshman in disbelief. "But Lord Thomas loathes John of Oxford! He even excommunicated him once! Whatever possessed the king to make such a choice? Was it meant as a deliberate insult?"

"That was Lord Thomas's suspicion, too," Alexander admitted. "He was quite indignant at having such a man foisted upon him. And that was not all. The king had promised our lord that he'd give him five hundred marks when they met at Rouen and take care of the debts he'd incurred in exile. But there was no money and our creditors had trailed after us all the way to Rouen. The Archbishop of Rouen was so embarrassed that he offered Lord Thomas three hundred pounds out of his own funds."

"Hellfire and damnation," Fitz Stephen muttered. There was much that he admired about his king, but he deplored Henry's bad faith. He was not so naïve as to believe that all promises were hallowed. Men of intelligence and goodwill understood which ones could safely be broken and which ones must be honored. Alas, the king did not.

"It does not sound like an auspicious beginning," he said, and Alexander gave a short laugh.

"You do not know the half of it, my friend. Whilst we were waiting to take ship at Wissant, the Count of Boulogne warned Lord Thomas that the de Brocs and the Sheriff of Kent were planning to arrest him upon his arrival at Dover. As a precaution, we landed instead at Sandwich, but word soon got out and the de Brocs, the sheriff, and one of the king's justiciars, Reginald de Warenne, came galloping up from Dover with a force of armed men."

"Jesú! What happened?"

"Well . . . we wronged the king by doubting his motives in sending John of Oxford with us. John proved to be a godsend. He stopped them in their tracks, for all the world like a broody hen protecting her chicks!" A reminiscent grin crossed his face. "He would not even allow them into the archbishop's presence until they'd disarmed. He insisted upon accompanying us all the way to Canterbury to make sure there would be no further trouble. Lord Thomas was impressed enough to write to His Holiness the Pope and commend his good services, and I never thought I'd live long enough to hear him speak well of John of Oxford!"

Fitz Stephen was not easily roused to anger, but he felt a deep, slow-burning rage beginning to kindle, directed at the archbishop's enemies, wolves harrying one of God's own. Because it was in his nature to look for flowers among weeds, he sought to reassure Alexander by saying resolutely, "Once men find out that the archbishop has been restored to the king's full favor, these provocations will cease."

"It is rather more complicated than that." The Welshman lowered his voice to the confidential tones of one privy to secrets of consequence, and then revealed that Thomas Becket had dispatched letters of censure for the Archbishop of York and the Bishops of London and Salisbury.

Fitz Stephen was stunned. "Are you saying that the archbishop excommunicated them on the eve of his return to England?"

Alexander's smile was beatific. "Indeed he did, and I'd have been willing to beg my bread by the roadside for the chance to witness their Judgment Day at Dover!"

Fitz Stephen did not share his friend's satisfaction. "I know the depths of his anger toward them, justified anger. But . . . but why would he strike out at them now of all times, just after making peace with the king?"

"He'd not intended to do so. Remember that I said this was 'complicated'? When Lord Thomas first heard of the illegal coronation of the king's son, he was told that Henry had perverted the coronation oath, demanding that his son swear to observe the ancient customs of the realm as set forth in the Constitutions of Clarendon. He wrote to His Holiness the Pope of this, with understandable outrage, for that would indeed have been salting the wound."

"I agree. But the traditional oath was sworn, with no mention made of those accursed Constitutions!"

Alexander smiled ruefully. "I know. We soon learned that the first report was in error. But in the press of events this summer, getting ready to meet the king at Fréteval, Lord Thomas forgot to advise the Pope of this mistaken claim. In October, the papal letters reached him at Rouen, suspending the Archbishop of York and five other bishops and ordering that the Bishops of London and Salisbury relapse into the excommunication that had so recently been lifted. Lord Thomas at once wrote to the Holy Father, asking for another set of letters in which no mention was made of the customs of the realm or the perverted coronation oath, giving him the choice of suspending or excommunicating the offending bishops at his own discretion."

Fitz Stephen was frowning. "Then how did this come about? He could not receive new letters of censure until after Christmas, at the earliest. So he must have made use of the first letters, the ones based on faulty information. Why, Sander? Why would he do that?"

"Because he learned that the three of them were going to advise and aid the king in his plan to fill the six English bishoprics that are still vacant."

The pieces were coming together for Fitz Stephen, in a pattern as ominous as it was familiar. The king had acted with his customary arrogance, and the archbishop had reacted with fury as calamitous as it was understandable. "Clearly, word of these excommunications has not become public knowledge, for I'd heard nothing of them. Does the king know yet, Sander? You realize that he will take Lord Thomas's actions as a declaration of war?"

"I do not know if the king has heard yet. If not, he soon will, for all that the bishops would prefer to keep this quiet in hopes of pressuring Lord Thomas to relent. That was the chief demand made upon him by the Sheriff of Kent and the others when they confronted him at Sandwich. As for the king's rage, I do not doubt that it will be spectacular. But the archbishop has more than one arrow in his quiver. When he made peace with the king at Fréteval, the king agreed to let him discipline those bishops who'd taken part in the coronation."

Alexander delivered this last revelation with the complacent pride of a court jongleur who'd just demonstrated an impressive sleight-of-hand trick. Fitz Stephen did not respond as expected, though. "He consented to further excommunications?" he said, sounding so skeptical that Alexander's smile faded.

"Well, no, not exactly . . . not in those words. But he did concede that the archbishop could exact punishment upon them for defying the Pope."

Fitz Stephen shook his head slowly. "And you truly think that is one and the same? Even if I did not know the king, I could tell you that he'd never equate a vague, ambiguous term like 'discipline' with the most lethal of the Church's weapons. Knowing him as I do, I can say with certainty that there was no agreement, for there was no meeting of the minds upon this."

Alexander shrank back in feigned horror. "Saints preserve us, you're sounding like a lawyer again! Be that as it may, Will, it is done and the archbishop is not likely to undo it. He told the sheriff and that whoreson de Broc when they threatened him at Sandwich that the sentences were passed by the Pope and so only His Holiness could absolve the bishops."

To Fitz Stephen's legally trained mind, such an argument was a sophistry, for the archbishop had set the censures in motion by seeking them from the Pope. There was nothing to be gained, though, by saying so. He found it very easy to understand his lord archbishop's fury and frustration, his need to strike out at his foes. But if only he'd stayed his hand! If only he'd waited until the storm provoked by his return had passed. Fitz Stephen suppressed a shiver, for he feared that Lord Thomas had given to his enemies a sharp sword indeed.

There was a sudden stir at the end of the hall. Fitz Stephen jumped to his feet, nervously smoothing the crumpled folds of his mantle as Thomas Becket appeared in the doorway of the Bishop of Winchester's private chamber. He was flanked by Waleran, Prior of St Mary's of Southwark, and Richard, Prior of St Martin's, a respected cleric from Dover. Fitz Stephen tried to take heart from their presence—physical proof that his lord did not stand alone—and reminded himself that not all of the bishops would side with the king. For certes, the Bishops of Winchester and Worcester and Exeter would hold fast for the archbishop, he concluded, and tried to shut out the insidious inner voice whispering that Winchester and Exeter were elderly and ailing and Lord Roger far away in Tours.

Trailing after Alexander, Fitz Stephen threaded his way through the crush toward his lord. Once there, he stopped as if rooted in place, eyes stinging with tears, for the archbishop's face was etched with the evidence of his travails; he looked haggard, even frail, all too intimate with pain of the body and soul. Like one consumed by a flame from within, Fitz Stephen thought sorrowfully, and cried out hoarsely, "My lord!"

"William!" As Fitz Stephen knelt, Becket gestured for him to rise. His smile was warming, blotting out the years of separation as if they'd never been. "I am gladdened by the sight of you," he said. "Have you come to welcome me home?"

"Yes, my lord, and to serve you . . . if you'll have me."

"There is always room in my heart for a faithful friend." Fitz Stephen was still on his knees and Becket reached out, offering his hand. "It is well that you are here," he said. "'You also shall bear witness, because you have been with me from the beginning.'"

Becket sent the Prior of St Martin's to the young king at Winchester, preparing the way for his own arrival. The prior returned to Southwark with unwelcome news for the archbishop: he'd been received very coolly and soon dismissed, being told that a reply would be dispatched by a royal messenger. The court of the young king was hostile territory, he recounted. Geoffrey Ridel, King Henry's chancellor, was utterly opposed to allowing the archbishop to meet with the young king, and in that, he seemed to have many allies. Only the lad's greatuncle, the Earl of Cornwall, had spoken out in favor of the proposed visit.

The prior's pessimistic report was soon borne out. A delegation of high-ranking lords rode in from Winchester. The young king, the archbishop was told, did not wish to see him. He was to return to Canterbury straightaway and remain there upon pain of incurring the royal wrath.

Becket was very troubled by his failure to see the young king; Hal had once been educated in the archbishop's household and he was quite fond of the boy. He'd known that there were many in England who resented his return, men who'd profited by his exile, others who bore him grudges for past disputes. But he'd not realized how well entrenched they were at Hal's court. Not a man to accept defeat easily, he decided to send Prior Richard back to try again. And since the Earl of Cornwall seemed most amenable of the young king's advisers to reason, he sent a trusted confidant to the earl, his personal physician, Master William.

RAINALD HAD ACCEPTED the hospitality of the Augustinian canons at Breamore, not far from Fordingbridge where the young king was then residing. He was so alarmed by the arrival of one of the archbishop's men that Master William was easily infected by his own panic. Dismissed by the earl, William wearily set out for Canterbury, bearing a message that seemed heavier with each passing mile. He reached the archbishop's palace at dusk on Saturday, the nineteenth of December, and was ushered into Becket's bedchamber to deliver his bad news.

The archbishop was attended only by one of his oldest advisers and friends, the noted scholar and cleric, John of Salisbury. They were seated by the hearth, his lord's chair just scant inches from the flames, for his extreme susceptibility to the cold made winters an ongoing ordeal. He smiled at the sight of William and beckoned him forward.

"Come sit with us, William, and warm yourself. John, you remember my physician. He is the one who treated me when my jaw became inflamed at Pontigny. William has just returned from a covert visit to the Earl of Cornwall and, to judge by his demeanor, his mission was not a success. Do not try to sweeten the brew, William. If it is as bitter a draught as I fear, it is best to drink it fast."

Master William gratefully settled onto a stool, stretching his feet toward the fire. "You are right, my lord. I bring troublesome tidings."

John of Salisbury stiffened his spine, like a man bracing for bad news. But Becket's face remained impassive. "Go on," he said. "Tell us all."

"Earl Rainald was not pleased to see me, my lord. He was blunt-spoken and said that you had created a great disturbance in the kingdom and that unless God intervenes, you will bring us to eternal shame. He went so far as to say that we should all end up in Hell because of you. Later, when we spoke in private, he told me in confidence that your enemies are plotting against you. I asked him if the young king gave credence to their charges and he shrugged, saying that he was but fifteen and not much interested in political matters. There is a real fear amongst his advisers that you mean to undermine royal authority. Some believe that you will seek to overturn the coronation, and there is much talk about your evil intent, talk that you are riding with a large army."

"A large army?" John echoed indignantly. "We took five knights as an escort back to Canterbury—five!" Becket remained silent and, after a moment, William resumed.

"Earl Rainald said that there was much sympathy at court for the bishops; men were irate that you acted so unfairly and vengefully, especially in the season of Advent. He said that he was not necessarily voicing his own views, merely telling me what others were saying."

He paused uncertainly until Becket nodded, signaling him to continue.

"The next day the young king sent over from Fordingbridge a gift of venison for the earl, and by mischance, the bearer recognized me, crying out loudly, 'That is Master William, one of the archbishop's household!' He was assured that I was the earl's doctor, but the earl was greatly disturbed by this incident, not wanting others to believe he was your ally. He insisted that I leave at once, telling me to get as far away as I could. And . . . and he bade me warn you, my lord, to look after yourself. He said that you are not the only one in danger, that so are John of Salisbury and Alexander of Wales, and if they are found by your enemies, they will be put to the sword."

John gasped, his eyes flooding with tears, but Thomas Becket regarded William calmly. Stretching his neck, he tapped it lightly with the palm of his hand, saying, "Here, here is where they will find me."

ON CHRISTMAS MORNING, Becket preached a sermon to the townspeople of Canterbury, assembled before him in the cathedral nave, based upon the text *Peace on earth to men of goodwill*. He then excommunicated again those men who had transgressed God's Laws: Rannulph and Robert de Broc; Henry's chancellor, Geoffrey Ridel; and his keeper of the seal, Nigel de Sackville; and he published the papal censures against the Archbishop of York, the Bishop of London, and the Bishop of Salisbury.

"Christ Jesus curse them all!" he proclaimed, and flung the lighted candles to the ground where they flickered and guttered out.

CHAPTER THIRTY-TWO

December 1170
Canterbury, England

ILLIAM FITZ STEPHEN was seated at a table in the great hall, drafting a letter to the Archbishop of Sens. Once it was done, he would take it to the archbishop and if it met with his approval, it would then be turned over to a scribe who would make a final copy. Fitz Stephen was a gifted Latinist, far better than Becket, and it pleased him greatly to put his skills at the service of his lord. He was so intent upon his task that he did not look up until his name was called close at hand.

Edward Grim was standing by the table with two full cups. "I thought you might like a cider."

Fitz Stephen was agreeable to a work break, and after carefully putting aside his parchment, quill pen, inkhorn, and pumice stone, he made room at the table for his new friend. Edward Grim had been at Canterbury only a few days. Like many visitors to the archbishop, he was a supplicant, bearing a letter of recommendation from Arnulf, Bishop of Lisieux. A testimonial by Arnulf was suspect in some quarters, given his reputation for slyness and his closeness to the king, and Grim had been treated with coolness by several of the archbishop's clerks. But Becket had received him cordially, and Fitz Stephen thought that he had a good chance of getting the archbishop's help. He'd been given the benefice of Saltwood Church by the Abbot of Bec, only to be forcibly ejected by the de Brocs, and by aiding him to regain his office, Becket would accomplish two benefits: righting a wrong while injuring his foes. When Grim asked now about his prospects, Fitz Stephen was able to offer him honest encouragement.

"Your grievance is one that needs redressing and I think Lord Thomas will decide to uphold your claim to the benefice at Saltwood. But I would not want to make less of the difficulties you'll be facing. The de Brocs are likely to maintain their greedy grasp upon Kent until the king himself comes over to evict them."

Grim nodded morosely, and the same thought was in both their minds: the latest offense by Robert de Broc, the apostate monk. On Christmas Eve, he'd stopped a servant of the archbishop's delivering supplies to the priory kitchens, and cut off the tail of the man's packmare. Fitz Stephen did not doubt that he'd then gone back to Saltwood Castle to brag of his deed, for that sort of alehouse humor was sure to win favor among the riffraff followers of his uncle, Rannulph de Broc. These were men who deserved the utmost contempt, but they were dangerous, too, and one forgot that at his peril.

He said as much to Grim, who nodded again in bleak agreement and then asked him about the tension he'd observed between the archbishop and Odo, the Christ Church prior.

"The last prior died during Lord Thomas's exile and the monks chose Odo to succeed him. But my lord does not recognize his election and plans to replace him with his own choice."

"Ah . . . I see." Edward Grim tactfully asked no more questions, thinking that this conflict between Lord Thomas and Prior Odo explained much. He'd been baffled by the obvious undercurrents at the priory, by the silent, smoldering resentment that existed between the archbishop and some of his own monks.

"Will?" Alexander Llewelyn was coming toward them, and after one look at the Welshman's somber expression, Grim rose and politely excused himself. Straddling the bench vacated by the young priest, Alexander gestured toward Fitz Stephen's half-finished letter. "Is that the one I'm to take?"

Fitz Stephen nodded and then glanced across the hall, where Herbert of Bosham was standing by the open hearth. His eyes glassy, his face feverishly flushed, he looked so wretched that Fitz Stephen felt a twinge of pity. Alexander was hiding his distress better than Herbert, but Fitz Stephen knew him well enough to discern his inner turmoil. By now all in the religious community knew that Lord Thomas was sending Herbert and Alexander to consult with the French king and the Archbishop of Sens, and all knew, too, that both men were obeying with extreme reluctance, loath to leave their lord in the midst of his enemies.

Trying to offer some comfort, Fitz Stephen observed that Alexander could be thankful, at least, that he'd not been the one chosen to visit the papal court, for he'd be able to return from France within a fortnight if luck and good winds were with him. Alexander did not seem much heartened by that. Absentmindedly helping himself to Fitz Stephen's cider, he stared down into the cup as if it were a wishing well. "Listen," he said after a long, brooding silence, "I want you to stay close to Lord Thomas whilst I am gone. I fear he is making a grave mistake to send Herbert and me and the others away. I have a bad feeling about all this, Will . . ."

Fitz Stephen would normally have joked about his friend's Welsh second-sight. Instead, he said earnestly, "You must not let your fears run loose, Sander. Keep them tightly reined in, for your own sake. None would dare harm an archbishop, not even the Devil's leavings like the de Brocs."

Alexander's mouth twitched down. "We both know better than that. But I am worrying about more than those Saltwood vipers. It is Lord Thomas's state of mind that gives me concern, too. After the Christmas Mass, he spoke to me of the martyred archbishop, St Alphege, and said there would soon be another."

Fitz Stephen blinked, and then said hastily, "He had just condemned men to eternal damnation. Is it so surprising that his mood would be low at that moment?"

Alexander muttered something which Fitz Stephen assumed to be a Welsh oath. "Lord Thomas's anger does not drain him. If anything, it sustains him. But even if you were right, that does not explain what I overheard him say to the Bishop of Paris when he came to bid the French king farewell."

Fitz Stephen did not want to ask, suddenly sure that he did not want to know. He said nothing, watching uneasily as Alexander set the cup down too forcefully, splattering cider onto his sleeve, the table, and even the sheets of blank parchment.

"You know that the French king advised him not to leave France

without obtaining the Kiss of Peace from King Henry. The Bishop of
Paris was of the same mind and sought to convince him to wait until his
safety was assured." Alexander's eyes were shining with unshed tears. "Lord
Thomas . . . he told the bishop that he was returning to England to die."

H ENRY HELD his Christmas court that year at his hunting lodge
of Bures, near Bayeux in Normandy. Any hopes he and his family had of
enjoying the holiday were dashed a few days before Christmas by the arrival of a courier bearing the news of the censure of the Archbishop of
York and the Bishops of London and Salisbury.

E LEANOR WAS SURVEYING the great hall at Bures with poorly
concealed dissatisfaction, wondering if she'd go stark raving mad before
she was able to return to Poitiers. Never had a Christmas court been so
bleak, so boring, so utterly endless. Nothing had gone right so far. The accommodations were cramped and modest and not at all to her liking. She
had been assured that the lodge at Bures was quite acceptable. She should
have known better than to believe Harry. When he was hunting, he'd be
perfectly happy to shelter in a cotter's hut.

There was not even room enough for the royal family and their attendants and servants, much less adequate space for Henry's barons and
bishops and the inevitable petitioners trailing after the king in hopes of
gaining an audience. Eleanor's children had been quick to take advantage
of the chaos. Richard and Geoffrey were soon disappearing from dawn till
dark, up to mischief she'd prefer not to know about. Nine-year-old
Aenor, betrothed that year to the twelve-year-old King Alfonso of Castile,
was no trouble at all, though, so docile and well behaved that Eleanor
could only marvel this placid child could have come from her own womb.
Joanna was the daughter most like her mother; as Eleanor watched now,
she was running about the hall like a small, lively whirlwind, playing
a game of hunt-the-fox with the little brother she rarely saw, four-year-
old John.

Eleanor had been surprised by Henry's wish to bring John from
Fontevrault Abbey for their Christmas court. When he'd mentioned that
all of their children would be with them except for Hal in England and
Tilda in Germany, she'd not even thought of John, destined for the

Church. But here he was—dark, slight, silent—so different from the other sons she'd borne that it was difficult to remember he was hers.

She supposed she ought to collect Joanna and John before they did something to vex her husband. It would not take much, God knows. Ever since he'd learned of Becket's Advent excommunications, his temper had been like a smoldering torch, ready to flare up at the slightest breath of wind. Before she could act upon that decision, she saw her uncle making his way toward her. Raoul's presence at the Christmas court had surprised many, for the mutual animosity between him and Henry was well known. But he had done the king a great service in negotiating Aenor's marriage to the young king of Castile. Only Eleanor knew that he'd acted at her behest.

"Well?" he asked. "Has the king decided where he goes from Bures? Any truth to the talk that it might be St Valery?"

Although they were speaking in their native Provençal to thwart eavesdroppers, Raoul was taking the added precaution of employing code. Eleanor smiled thinly, acknowledging his joke: that her husband would be heading for the port from which William the Bastard launched his invasion of England.

"Not likely," she said. "He has already dispatched a protest to the Pope and, for now, plans nothing else. Although the papal letter had to be sealed in a fireproof lead casket, lest the royal courier leave a trail of flames from Bures to Frascati."

Raoul grinned, thinking that her jest was not far off the mark. He was in sympathy with the Angevin, for once, could not blame him for reacting with volcanic temper to Becket's latest outrage. "I think the king would do well to send a doctor to the good archbishop," he said, "for he must be suffering from a brain fever. How else explain his behavior?"

He needed to display no discretion in speaking of the archbishop, for Becket was being damned in all quarters at Bures; men eager to curry favor with the king were outdoing themselves in the virulence of their abuse. That was not a game that Eleanor cared to play, though, and she shrugged, thinking that Harry had brought so much of this upon himself by his stubborn refusal to take her advice. She'd warned him that he was making a great mistake in entrusting Becket with such power, but Jesú forfend that he pay heed to a woman . . . or anyone else, for that matter.

Just then there was a commotion outside, sudden shouts penetrating the normal noise level of the hall. Eleanor turned toward the sound with jaded curiosity, wondering what fresh trouble was about to be dumped at their door.

GEOFFREY RIDEL and Richard of Ilchester had no compunctions about speaking their minds even as excommunicates. Lent eloquence by their anger, they had taken turns accusing the Archbishop of Canterbury of sins running the gamut from bad faith to outright treachery. But Gilbert Foliot and Jocelin of Salisbury were far more scrupulous about adhering to their proscribed status as spiritual exiles.

"My lord king," the Archbishop of York asserted, "I was suspended from my sacred calling, but I may still defend myself and my brothers in Christ." He gestured toward the two bishops, standing mute and miserable behind him. His dramatic declaration was needless, for everyone in the hall knew that an excommunicate was not only denied the holy sacraments, prayers, and burial in consecrated ground; he was also deprived of the right to participate in the common blessings of the Christian community.

York drew a deliberate breath, making sure all eyes were upon him. "My liege, Thomas Becket has done us a great wrong. Nor does he mean to confine his vengeance to us. It is his intent to excommunicate all who consented to the coronation of the young king, your son."

"Does he, indeed?" Henry's scowl put Eleanor in mind of lowering storm clouds. "If all who were involved in my son's coronation are to be excommunicated, I am not likely to escape, either."

"That would be an evil way to repay you for the many kindnesses you've done him over the years. He owes all to you. How could a man of his humble pedigree ever aspire to the most exalted office of the English Church? But he seems to know nothing of gratitude. He even dared to claim that you'd agreed at Fréteval that he could cast my brethren out into eternal darkness!"

"He did what?" Henry said, in so ominous a tone that those closest to him began to back away. "He said that he had to discipline them for defying the Pope. Nary a word was said about excommunication!"

"Alas, my liege, Becket's veracity is only one of our concerns. I have grave doubts, too, about his motives. Many believe that he has it in mind to overturn the young king's coronation."

"No." Henry was shaking his head impatiently. "I gave him the right to re-crown my son. There is no need to annul the coronation."

"I am sure you are right, my lord. It may be that these suspicions are unwarranted. But you cannot blame men for taking alarm, not after Becket has been riding about your realm with a large armed force—"

"An armed force?" Henry echoed incredulously. "This is the first I've heard of that!"

"Indeed, my lord. He took a large escort on his procession to and from London. Moreover, he disobeyed your son's order to return straight-away to Canterbury and remain there. Instead he went from Southwark to Harrow to meet with the Abbot of St Albans. Once more he shows his contempt for royal authority—"

Again there was an interruption. This time it came from the Bishop of Salisbury, who was stricken by a fit of coughing. Jocelin de Bohun was elderly, not in robust health, and many in the hall began to mutter indignantly. A man darted forward from the crowd and assisted the bishop toward a seat. As he turned around, Eleanor recognized Reginald Fitz Jocelin, the bishop's son.

Reginald was his father's archdeacon and had once been in the Archbishop of Canterbury's service. Salisbury's friends had long insisted that Becket's animosity toward him was the result of his son's defection to the king's service in 1164. The situation was further complicated by Reginald's claim that he'd been born before his father's ordination as a priest, a claim Becket hotly disputed. It occurred to Eleanor now that in the race to make enemies, her husband and his archbishop were heading for the finish line neck and neck.

Salisbury allowed Reginald to seat him on the nearest bench, but when his son attempted to help him drink from a wine cup, he shrank back, vehemently shaking his head lest that be interpreted as sharing a meal, a transgression which could taint Reginald with his own pollution.

Reginald's face was streaking with tears, but his voice was harsh with rage. "Look, my lords," he cried, "look how they have ill-used my father! What has he done to deserve such cruel treatment? We all know why he has been persecuted by Thomas Becket—because of me! The archbishop seeks vengeance for my loyalty to the king."

The Archbishop of York reclaimed center stage now by saying, loudly and combatively, "Nor is that likely to change. This man Becket has naught in his heart but hatred. It spews from his lips like venom, sparing neither the righteous nor the just. His own words convict him. He has called the Bishop of London and myself 'priests of Baal and sons of false prophets.' He slandered Reginald Fitz Jocelin as 'that bastard son of a priest, born of a harlot' and he invariably refers to Archdeacon Geoffrey as 'that archdevil.' When he learned that the Bishop of London had been absolved of his unjust excommunication at Easter, he even reviled the bishop as 'Satan.' Again and again, he has resorted to the rhetoric of the gutter, the vulgarisms of infamy!"

That was too much for Eleanor's uncle. Raoul nearly strangled trying to stifle a laugh, amazed that the bombastic York could make such a charge without even a trace of irony. He nudged Eleanor playfully, but she ignored him, unamused by what was occurring. This was too dangerous a discussion to conduct in a public forum, where collective outrage could easily ignite a veritable firestorm. She signaled to one of her children's attendants, who swiftly gathered up Joanna and John and led them from the hall. She saw no indication, though, that her husband was going to do the prudent thing and hear the rest of this incendiary report in private. Doubting that he'd have listened to her cautionary words, she remained silent, a witness both intent and oddly detached.

"The Archbishop of York speaks true, my liege," Geoffrey Ridel exclaimed. "We earnestly beseeched Thomas Becket to absolve the bishops, reminding him that these excommunications were contrary to the peace made at Fréteval. He knows nothing of good faith, nothing of gratitude. I, too, have heard that he has been raising an army, and I cannot help wondering what use he means to make of it."

Henry could not believe that a fire he'd thought finally quenched was flaring again. Savagely damning Becket to the hottest abode in Hell, he retained just enough control to keep from saying it aloud. Swinging back toward York, he demanded to know what they would advise him to do. Salisbury and Gilbert Foliot were looking more disturbed by the moment, but York seemed quite calm, almost complacent.

"We think you ought to take counsel from your barons and knights, my lord king," he said sententiously. "It is not our place to say what should be done."

Richard of Ilchester had brought a stool out for Gilbert Foliot, insisting that he seat himself. Foliot resisted at first, but he was in his sixth decade and soon capitulated. He was so flushed that he looked feverish, so obviously shaken that he aroused considerable sympathy in the hall. Richard gestured angrily toward the older man. "Here is yet another victim of Becket's vengeful scheming. Bishop Gilbert has devoted his entire life to Holy Church, first as Abbot of Gloucester Abbey, then as Bishop of Hereford and now London. None have ever questioned his faith or besmirched his integrity—none but Becket! He even dared to accuse Bishop

Gilbert of the vilest sort of treachery. His very words to Bishop Gilbert were: 'Your aim has been all along to effect the downfall of the Church and ourself.' Notice how he equates the Mother Church with his own selfish interests!"

Engelram de Bohun stepped forward to add his voice to the fracas. As the Bishop of Salisbury's uncle, he felt that he had more right than most to vent his spleen against his nephew's enemy. Like the others, he made a point of calling the archbishop "Becket," spitting it out as if it were a curse. Eleanor understood why quite well. It went beyond denying him his rank as a prince of the Church. By making use of the surname Becket himself shunned, his foes were emphasizing the archbishop's greatest vulnerability: his shame at being the son of a mere merchant.

As a descendant of Charlemagne, the proud daughter of a prideful and ancient House, Eleanor agreed, of course, that bloodlines were of profound significance. But she found herself feeling a growing sense of exasperation with all concerned. She had learned through painful lessons that words must be weighed with care and that actions had consequences. Looking back upon the rash, headstrong girl she'd once been, she winced at the naïveté and foolhardiness of that younger, indiscreet self. How was it that Harry and Becket had learned nothing from their own mistakes?

Others were joining now in the chorus. The young Earl of Leicester admitted that his late father, the justiciar, had been too solicitous of the archbishop, but vowed that he himself would never associate with an enemy of the king. Men dredged up memories of Becket's past offenses and dwelt upon them at considerable length. Reginald Fitz Jocelin accused the archbishop of every sin but lust, and several even cast doubt upon that exemption. Mention was often made of the archbishop's "English army." Arnulf, the Bishop of Lisieux, lamented the archbishop's obstinate, willful nature, and the Archbishop of Rouen and the Bishop of Évreux expressed anger that the Holy Father had been misled by the archbishop in the matter of the young king's coronation oath. Geoffrey Ridel and Richard of Ilchester bitterly blamed Becket for their own excommunications. The only men in the hall who did not speak against Becket were the two that he'd silenced by anathema, the Bishops of London and Salisbury.

As his court denounced and damned Becket, Henry paced before the open hearth, his anger rising with every insult, every stride. When was this going to end? Was he never to be free of Becket's malice? How many times must he play the fool and put his trust in this faithless friend and disloyal subject?

Engelram de Bohun had worked himself up into a frenzy and was bellowing that the only way to deal with a traitor was to find a rope and a gallows. A Breton lord, William Malvoisin, was recounting a rambling story of his return from the Holy Land, saying that in Rome he'd been told of a Pope who'd been slain for his "insufferable insolence." That brought down the wrath of several bishops upon him. While they castigated Malvoisin, the Archbishop of York drew closer to his king and said softly, as if sorrowing over his message:

"I fear, my lord king, that whilst Becket is alive, you will never have a peaceful kingdom."

"I know!" Henry snapped. "Christ smite him, I know! No matter what I do, he betrays me at every turn. He owes all to me, but repays me with treachery and deceit." Stalking so close to the hearth that he kicked one of the fire tongs, sending up a shower of sparks, he glared at the barons and knights milling about the hall. "What miserable drones and traitors I have nourished and promoted in my household, who let their lord be mocked so shamefully by a lowborn clerk!"

E LEANOR WAS already in bed, her long hair braided into a night plait. Her ladies, Renée and Ella, were asleep on pallets piled high with blankets, for there was no fireplace in the bedchamber. When Henry and his squires finally came in, Eleanor was still awake, for she wanted to learn the outcome of his council. He had belatedly retreated from the turmoil in the great hall, gathering the most trusted of his barons and bishops and crowding into a small antechamber where they could determine in privacy how best to deal with the crisis. Once again Eleanor had found herself relegated to the outer perimeters of power, and she did not like it at all.

She lay still, listening as Henry's squires assisted him in undressing and then bedded down themselves. There was a pale flicker from a solitary candle as the bed hangings were parted and the mattress shifted under Henry's weight. As soon as he drew the hangings back, they were cocooned in darkness. Eleanor waited for several moments before saying, "Well?"

Henry started and then sank back against the pillow. "Good God, were you trying to make my heart stop beating? I thought you were asleep."

"What did you decide to do about Becket?"

"I am going to give him an ultimatum. Either he absolves the bishops from their lawless excommunications or he shall be arrested."

"That is likely to go well."

"What do you expect me to do, Eleanor? Let him defy me with impunity?"

"Are you actually asking for my opinion, Harry?"

"What ails you, woman? I have troubles enough with that whoreson Becket, need none from you!"

It was a strange sort of quarrel, one conducted in utter darkness and the illusory intimacy of the marriage bed. After an aggrieved silence, Henry said testily, "On the morrow I am sending Richard de Humet to England to let Hal's advisers know of my will. At the same time, the Earl of Essex and Saer de Quincy are to guard the ports in case Becket seeks to flee to France again."

"Do you truly think he would?"

He exhaled an exasperated breath. "If I could penetrate the maze of that man's brain, do you think we'd ever have come to this? I know not what he is likely to do. Nor do I care."

That was such an obvious untruth that Eleanor chose to let the matter drop. She asked no more questions and their argument waned, a fire damped down but not entirely extinguished. They lay side by side in a suffocating stillness charged with foreboding, and it was nearly dawn before either slept.

THE LAST Tuesday in December, the morrow of Holy Innocents, was chill and grey. The sky was mottled with clouds, and a high wind was tearing the last of the leaves from an aged mulberry tree in the outer courtyard of the Archbishop of Canterbury's palace. William Fitz Stephen was hurrying along the south range of the cloisters, shivering in the wintry morning air, when he saw a figure slumped upon a bench in one of the carrels. Recognizing the cellarer, he swerved in that direction, for this was not a day to be enjoying the outdoors.

"Richard? Is something wrong?"

The cellarer looked up, his face as ashen as the sky, and Fitz Stephen sat down hastily beside him on the bench. "What has happened?"

"A cousin of mine is wed to a retainer of the Lord of Knaresborough, Hugh de Morville. He sought me out last night in Canterbury to warn me that the archbishop is in grave peril."

This was even worse than Fitz Stephen had expected. "What did he tell you?"

"Hugh de Morville and three other lords and their knights landed at Winchelsea yesterday and rode straight for Saltwood Castle. They told the de Brocs that they'd come from the king's Christmas court, that he had sent them to arrest the archbishop. But Martin—my cousin's husband— said that he'd begun to doubt this was true. He overheard them talking amongst themselves and was no longer sure they were doing the king's bidding. His misgivings finally became so strong that he slipped away from Saltwood and came to alert me to the danger."

"You've gone to the archbishop with this?"

"Of course I did! He heard me out and seemed to believe me. Yet he has done nothing to protect himself, Master Fitz Stephen, nothing! There is no use in seeking aid from the Sheriff of Kent, for he is an avowed foe of the archbishop and hand in glove with the de Brocs. We could still rally the townspeople, summon the knights who owe fealty to the archbishop, send urgently to the young king's court. But Lord Thomas will not even bar the gates to the priory!"

Fitz stephen was sitting at a table in the great hall, staring vacantly off into space. It was his inactivity, so unusual in one of the most industrious of the archbishop's clerks, that attracted the attention of Edward Grim. Although they were only recently acquainted, the two men shared much in common: an excellent education, a reluctance to demonize their foes, spiritual piety entwined with secular ambition, and an abiding faith in the rightness of the archbishop's cause. There was concern as well as curiosity, therefore, in Grim's quiet query.

"Will? I do not mean to intrude, but you seem sorely troubled. May I help?"

Fitz Stephen looked up dully, then gestured for Grim to join him. No sooner had the young priest seated himself than the words came pouring out, each one more alarming than the last. By the time he'd finished, Grim was staring at him, aghast.

"You talked to the archbishop about this?"

Fitz Stephen nodded. "So did John of Salisbury and Robert of Merton, his confessor. He heard us out, but paid us no heed. We are not exaggerating his danger, Ned. Either these men are plotting to murder him in the hopes of gaining royal favor or they are acting at the king's command. Whichever is true, the outcome is likely to be the same, for I do not think Lord Thomas will allow himself to be arrested."

Neither did Grim; even in his brief stay at Canterbury, he'd observed how mindful Lord Thomas was of his archiepiscopal dignity. "These men you named . . . is much known of them? Are they as ungodly and foul as the de Brocs?"

"If so, we are all doomed. Three of the four are not only known to Lord Thomas, they were his vassals whilst he was chancellor. Hugh de Morville remained for a time in his service after he became archbishop. His family is a respected one; his father was a Constable of Scotland. William de Tracy is well connected, too; his grandfather was a baseborn son of the old king, the first Henry, and he holds the barony of Bradnich. Reginald Fitz Urse's father was Lord of Bulwick in Northamptonshire and he has lands in Somerset and Montgomery. Lord Thomas was the very one who secured for him his position at court. It defies belief, Ned, that any man of Christian faith could so reward good with evil. The fourth man is younger than the others, one Richard le Bret. I think he once served in the household of the Lord William, the king's late brother, but I am not altogether certain of that. Richard the cellarer says that his cousin's husband told him that they had enough men-at-arms with them to require two ships for the Channel crossing." He paused to swallow, his mouth as parched as his hopes, and then added tonelessly, "And Saltwood Castle is just twelve miles away . . ."

Grim had always prided himself upon his logical thinking. He struggled now to remain calm, to subject this information to a dispassionate analysis. "So they are not lowborn rabble, but men of property, of substance. Are they of sufficient rank, though, to be dispatched to arrest the archbishop?"

Fitz Stephen pondered that for several moments. "I would think not," he said doubtfully. "King Henry has a fearsome temper, one that has gotten worse over the years. I have witnessed several of these outbursts myself, and to hear him ranting and raving in the throes of a royal rage is to understand why men say the Angevins are of the Devil's stock. I was told that he threw a truly terrible fit at Chinon four years ago, upon hearing that Lord Thomas had excommunicated his justiciar, Richard de Lucy, as well as Richard of Ilchester and John of Oxford. It may be that his temper caught fire at Bures, too, and these lords took him at his word—"

He broke off in midsentence, half-rising from the bench as John of Salisbury hastened toward them, his expression so stricken that they knew the news he bore was bad.

"They are here," he panted. "They've just ridden into St Augustine's!"

"The priory?" Grim was dumbfounded. "Why? Surely they could not expect aid from that quarter!"

Fitz Stephen and John looked at him in surprise, then remembered that his appointment to the benefice of Saltwood was a patronage plum and he'd probably spent little time in the parish before being ejected by the de Brocs.

"Lucifer himself could rely upon a welcome at St Augustine's," John said caustically. "Their prior, Clarembald, is a disgrace to the clergy and Church. He is a worldly sinner who was rewarded with an abbacy for his service to the king, a man who cares only for his carnal pleasures, feuding with his own monks, and siring so many bastards that he's known as the stud of St Augustine's."

Fitz Stephen was already well acquainted with the scandalous history of Abbot Clarembald. "Let that be, John. Tell us what is happening at the priory. Does Lord Thomas know of this?"

"Yes, he knows."

"And . . . ?" Fitz Stephen prodded impatiently. "What did he say?"

"I told him that his enemies had arrived at St Augustine's and were having dinner with Clarembald, and he . . . he said that we should make ready to dine, too."

AFTER DINING on pheasant, Becket withdrew to his private quarters at the east end of the great hall. Once all of the monks, clerks, knights, and lay members of the household had finished their meal, it was the turn of the kitchen staff and servers to eat. By now word had spread of the arrival of the armed men at St Augustine's Priory. William Fitz Neal, Becket's steward, had been considering his precarious position as liegeman to both the archbishop and the king. Leaving his own dinner untouched, he followed Becket to his bedchamber and asked his permission to depart, saying candidly that "You are in such disfavor with the king and all his men that I dare not stay with you any longer, my lord."

Becket's clerks bristled, but he accepted the defection with surprising composure, telling his steward, "Of course you have my leave to go, William." Fitz Neal ignored the accusing looks thrown his way and returned to the hall. It was now almost 4 P.M. and winter's early twilight was already beginning to chase away the daylight.

While Fitz Neal was planning to abandon the archbishop's sinking ship, a large contingent of knights and men-at-arms had left St Augustine's and were entering the city through its Northgate. Leaving their men at a house close by the palace gateway, Hugh de Morville, Reginald Fitz Urse, William de Tracy, and Richard le Bret rode into the palace courtyard. Dismounting by the mulberry tree, they removed their swords and scabbards, then entered the great hall. Declining Fitz Neal's polite offer of refreshments, they demanded to see the archbishop.

Thomas Becket was sitting upon his bed, conversing with one of the monks. Others of his household were seated or kneeling in the floor rushes. Fitz Neal announced the four knights, who strode into the bedchamber and sat on the floor, too. Fitz Stephen, frozen by the door, almost forgot to breathe. For what seemed forever to him, the archbishop ignored the knights and they said nothing. Finally the impasse was broken by Becket, who acknowledged their presence coolly, only to get a response so terse as to be deliberately discourteous, a growled "God help you" from Fitz Urse. Becket flushed and another silence ensued.

After exchanging glances with his companions, Fitz Urse assumed the role of spokesman and declared that they carried a message from the king. Did the archbishop want it said in private or public? To Fitz Stephen's horror, his lord said that was for them to say, and Fitz Urse responded with a succinct "Alone, then." As his clerks and monks started to leave the chamber, Becket suddenly changed his mind and recalled them. Still seated on the bed, he said to the knights:

"Now, my lords, you may say what you will."

"We have been sent to escort you to the young king at Winchester, where you are to swear fealty to him and make satisfaction for the offenses you have committed against the Crown."

"It was my dearest wish to meet with the young king at Winchester. I was prevented from doing so by his advisers, who ordered me to return to Canterbury. I will gladly swear fealty to him. But I have committed no offenses against the Crown and I will not go to Winchester to be put on trial."

Fitz Urse seemed taken aback by the archbishop's defiance. By now all of the knights were on their feet. "The lord king commands you to absolve the bishops, both from damnation and the bond of silence!"

"I have not excommunicated the bishops. It was the Lord Pope, whose power comes from God. And if His Holiness has seen fit to vindicate me and my Church against grave injury, I am not sorry for it."

Fitz Urse's jaw jutted out. "The excommunications were still your doing, so you will absolve them!"

"Indeed, I will not. Only the Lord Pope can do that. Moreover, this was done with the king's consent."

Fitz Urse whirled toward his companions. "Have you ever heard such deceit? He accuses the king of betraying his closest friends! This is beyond endurance."

John of Salisbury mustered up the courage to intercede at this point, realizing that there was a great and gaping chasm between what the archbishop and the king believed to have been agreed upon at Fréteval. "My lord archbishop, this serves for naught. You ought to speak privately about this with your council."

Fitz Urse, who so far had maintained a respectful distance, now took several steps toward Becket. "From whom do you hold your See?"

"The spiritualities from God and my lord the Pope. The temporalities from my lord the king."

"You do not admit that you owe all to the king?"

"No, I do not. We must render unto the king what is the king's, and to God what is God's. I will spare no one who violates the laws of Christ's Church."

"You dare to threaten us? You mean to excommunicate us all?"

When Fitz Urse strode closer still to the bed, the archbishop rose to his full height, towering over the knight. "I do not believe that you come from the king," he said and at that, the other men burst into loud, angry speech. For several moments, there was chaos, all speaking at once. They cursed the archbishop for breaking the peace and seeking to uncrown the young king and foment rebellion and even to make himself king. No less wrathful himself, Becket denied those charges with passion and leveled accusations of his own, reminding them that they'd once sworn fealty to him on bended knee. This enraged them all the more, and to the frightened witnesses, it seemed as if violence would erupt then and there, in the archbishop's own bedchamber.

"You threaten me in vain." Becket's voice was hoarse, his dark eyes blazing. "If all the swords of England were hanging over my head, you could not turn me from God's Justice and my obedience to the Lord Pope. You will find me ready to meet you eye to eye in the Lord's battle. Once I ran away like a frightened priest. Never will I desert my Church again. If I am allowed to perform the duties of the priesthood in peace, I shall be glad. If not, then God's Will be done."

As more members of the archbishop's household were drawn by the commotion, the knights seemed to take silent counsel, communicating by meaningful looks. Fitz Urse turned toward their audience, saying roughly, "We warn you all in the king's name to abandon this man!" Stunned, the monks and clerks remained motionless, and he amended his order. "Guard him so that he does not flee!"

They turned, then, began to push their way toward the door. Becket strode after them, crying out, "I am quite easy to guard, for I shall not run away. You will find me here!"

Fitz Urse swung around, his hand groping for his belt, the instinctive gesture of a man accustomed to the weight of a sword at his hip. "Thomas, in the name of the king, I repudiate your fealty!" The other knights also repeated this most solemn oath of renunciation and a chill swept through the chamber. Even Becket appeared shocked.

Shouting "To arms!" the knights shoved through the doorway, seizing Becket's steward as they exited. As they pushed him ahead of them, he looked back over his shoulder at the archbishop. "My lord, you see what they are doing to me?"

"I see," Becket replied. "They have the force and the power of darkness." There were loud gasps, for those clerks and monks familiar with Scriptures at once recognized that as a paraphrase of the words spoken by the Lord Jesus Christ as He was arrested in the Garden of Gethsemane.

As the knights clattered down the stairs to the great hall, Becket returned to his chamber and sat down upon his bed. At first, there was a deathly stillness and, then, uproar. Most of the monks and clerks began to voice their opinions. Some dismissed the knights' threats as drink-sodden posturing, for it was evident that Fitz Urse and his companions had drunk their fill at Abbot Clarembald's table; they'd also appeared to be utterly fatigued, not surprising in light of their nonstop journey from Bures to Canterbury. Others insisted that they'd not dare to commit violence at Christmastide. Those who knew better moved to the windows on the north side of the chamber and fumbled to unlatch the shutters so they could monitor the moves of the men outside.

"My lord, it really is quite amazing that you never will take any notice of our advice." John of Salisbury sounded fretful and reproachful and, above all, fearful. "You always say and do what seems right to yourself alone. Was there any need for a great and good man like yourself to provoke those wicked men still more by following them to the door? Would it not have been better to have given a softer answer to men who are plotting to do you all the harm they can?"

Becket regarded his clerk and friend calmly. "We all must die, John.

We should not swerve from justice for fear of death. I am more ready to meet death for God and His Church than they are to inflict it on me."

"We are all sinners and not yet ready for death. I can see no one here who wants to die needlessly, apart from you."

Some of the clerks were offended that John should dare to speak so disrespectfully to the archbishop. Becket merely said, "May the Lord's Will be done."

John would have argued further had Fitz Stephen not put a restraining hand upon his arm. As their eyes met, they shared a moment of frustrated, haunted understanding, the awareness that as clay was in the potter's hands, so were they all in God's Hands, and they could not save Thomas Becket unless he chose to save himself.

Just then there was a sharp cry from Edward Grim, standing watch at one of the windows. With a young man's keen eyesight, he'd seen in the fading light what the older sentinels had not, the activity under the ancient mulberry tree. "They are arming themselves!" Hanging so far out the window that he was in danger of falling, he soon reported, "Men are pouring into the outer court! They've seized the gatehouse and . . . Jesus wept! My lord, your steward has joined them! He is helping to guard the gate!"

Through the open windows, they could hear now the shouting, the Norman battle cry of "King's men, king's men!" Other sounds were coming from the west, the laments of townspeople gathered outside the priory walls, crying out their fear that the archbishop and his monks were "sheep for the slaughter." The noise was intensifying, curses and heavy pounding filling the air. Within the archbishop's bedchamber, some of the monks and clerks fled while they still could, realizing what that new clamor meant: that quick-witted servants had barred the door to the hall and the knights were attempting to force their way back in.

"My lord, we must get to the church!" Becket's confessor was tugging at his sleeve and others at once added their pleas to his, entreating the archbishop to flee whilst there was still time. Becket refused, insisting that he would not budge a foot from this chamber, for here he would await God's Will. The hammering suddenly stopped and Fitz Stephen darted toward the windows in the south wall, where he soon confirmed his worst fears.

"Robert de Broc has led them around the side of the hall. They are going to try to enter by the external stairway!"

Someone said that the stairway was being repaired and was not accessible, but Fitz Stephen had to puncture that faint hope. "The workmen left their ladder and tools there and de Broc is climbing up! Once he gets into the hall, he'll take them right here!"

The monks renewed their pleading, imploring the archbishop to seek safety in the cathedral, and again he refused, scorning them for their cowardice. It was Edward Grim who finally offered a reason for leaving that Becket could not reject out of hand. "Vespers is nigh, my lord. Would you keep the Lord and your flock waiting?"

When Becket hesitated, the other men took physical action, seizing his arms and compelling him toward a long-unused door that led down to a private passageway to the cloisters. The door had to be forced, but they could hear now the splintering sound of wood and knew that Robert de Broc had broken into the hall. Shoving the archbishop into the stairwell, they fled into the corridor, fear making them fleet. But then they discovered that the door to the cloisters was barred. Some of the monks began to panic, crying out that they were trapped. When the bolt was suddenly lifted on the other side of the door, only the narrow, cramped space kept them from dropping to their knees in wonder at this miracle of God. A moment later, the door swung open, revealing the Almighty's instrument to be none other than Richard, the cellarer.

Spilling out into the cloisters, the archbishop's clerks and monks continued to push him toward the door leading into the northwest transept of the cathedral. He eventually stopped struggling once he realized he could not prevail against them and sought to preserve his dignity, insisting that his cross-bearer proceed ahead of them with his archiepiscopal cross. Nor would he permit the cellarer to bar the door to the cloisters.

When they reached the church, vespers for the monks was already in progress, but the service was halted in confusion. As some of them came down the steps leading up to the choir, Becket ordered them to "Go back and finish divine office." Monks and clerks continued to crowd into the church, and a cry soon went up that there were armed men in the cloisters. Several men ran to close the door and slide its heavy iron bar into place.

"No!" Becket's voice carried loudly and clearly across the cathedral, halting the men in the act. To their utter dismay, he commanded them to reopen the door. "Christ's Church is not a fortress. Let anyone enter who wishes."

They dared not disobey and he returned to the door, shoved it open, and pulled in a few stragglers seeking refuge in God's House. He then turned and walked without haste toward the choir. He was mounting the steps when Fitz Urse and the other knights burst into the cathedral.

Darkness had fallen and the church was lit only by a few oil lamps up in the choir and candles at the High Altar. The knights peered uncertainly into the murky, swirling shadows, their task made no easier by the fact that Becket and the Benedictine monks were clad in black. Advancing warily into the transept, one of them shouted, "Where is Thomas Becket, traitor to the king and realm?"

Their demand was met with silence. Fitz Urse swore and then called out, "Where is the archbishop?"

Becket turned and slowly started down the steps. "Here I am, no traitor to the king, but a priest of God. What do you want of me?"

Some of the monks had already faded away into the blackness of the nave. Now Becket's clerks abandoned him, too, even John of Salisbury and Henry of Auxerre, the cross-bearer substituting for the absent Alexander Llewelyn. They hid behind altars, fled down to the safety of the crypt, up the stairs to the Chapel of St Blaise. Only Robert of Merton, his confessor, Fitz Stephen, two monks, and Edward Grim stood their ground behind him on the choir steps.

The knights were a terrifying sight, having shed their mantles to reveal chain-mail underneath, naked swords in one hand, the stolen workmen's axes in the other. Neither of the de Brocs were with them, although Robert de Broc's renegade clerk, Hugh de Horsea, was. As they fanned out, approaching Becket from the left and right sides of the massive central column, one of the two remaining monks lost his nerve and bolted for the stairs. Hugh de Morville took up position between the nave and the choir, sword leveled menacingly at a few citizens who'd arrived early for the second Vespers service. Becket continued down the steps, moving at a measured pace, and then halted by the pillar between the Lady Chapel and the Chapel of St Benedict.

Without warning, Fitz Urse raised his sword and used its point to flick Becket's tonsure cap from his head. There were muffled cries from the monks cowering in the shadows, but Becket did not even flinch.

"Absolve the bishops!"

"I have already said what I will and will not do."

"If you do not, you are a dead man!"

"I am ready to die for God and the Church. But in the Name of the Almighty, I forbid you to harm any of my own."

"Come with us, then!" When Becket refused, Fitz Urse dropped the axe and grabbed for his mantle.

Becket jerked free and shoved the other man, sending him reeling back. "Let me go, you pimp!"

Fitz Urse snarled and lunged forward, seizing Becket again. The other men moved in, too, and attempted to drag him from the church. Bounding down the choir steps, Edward Grim joined the fray, throwing his arms around the archbishop to keep them from moving him from the pillar. He was resisting so fiercely that, with Grim's help, he was able to shake them off.

Fitz Stephen was still standing on the steps, unable either to flee or to go to the archbishop's defense, unable to move. The scene had lost all reality for him. He heard Grim shouting that the men must be mad, heard William de Tracy calling the archbishop a traitor. And then he saw a shivering glimmer of light as an altar candle reflected off Fitz Urse's upraised sword.

Grim flung up his arm to shield Becket and the blade came down upon them both, slicing off some of the archbishop's scalp and all but severing Grim's arm at the elbow. Both men began to bleed profusely. Fitz Stephen made a shaky sign of the cross, closing his eyes as de Tracy struck. The confessor standing beside him would later tell him he'd said, " 'The waters that were in the river were turned to blood.' " But he had no recollection of his own words. He remembered only what Thomas Becket said as he fell to his knees. "Into Thy Hands, O Lord, I commend my spirit."

Fitz Urse and de Tracy stood over the fallen archbishop, swords dripping blood. Hugh de Morville was still holding back the people in the nave. Richard le Bret rushed forward to deliver the death blow, almost slipping in Becket's blood, and brought his sword down with such force that it split the archbishop's skull and broke in two upon the pavement. "Take that for the love of my lord William, the king's brother!"

Grim was trying to crawl toward the altar. The knights were staring down at Becket's body as if stunned by their own deed. It was suddenly quiet, with no sound but the rasping of labored, ragged breathing. Becket's killers raised their swords again, threatening any who would dare to stop their escape, and then plunged toward the door. But Robert de

Broc's subdeacon turned back. Setting his foot on the archbishop's neck, he thrust the point of his sword into the gaping wound and scattered Becket's brains over the floor.

"Let's go," he said. "He'll not rise again."

ROBERT DE BROC had remained in the archbishop's private chambers to watch over Becket's treasure chests, and after the killing, his men looted the palace. They took all the papal letters and documents they found, in the hope that they'd prove treasonous. But they also took Becket's silver plate, his gold chalice, costly vestment cloths, jewels, and silver coins. Loading their plunder upon horses from the archbishop's own stables, they rode out of Canterbury, leaving behind a scene of utter devastation.

Men began to emerge from their hiding places in the cathedral. Few dared to approach the archbishop's body, keeping their eyes averted as if that would somehow allow them to deny that murder had been done in God's House. Fitz Stephen and Robert of Merton, Becket's confessor, shook off their paralysis and rushed over to the crumpled form of Edward Grim. To their great relief, he was still alive, still conscious. They were soon joined by Master William, who set about halting the bleeding. It was not long before other victims staggered into the church, for the servants caught in the hall had been brutally beaten by de Broc's men.

The silence was absolute, eerie. People wandered about aimlessly, faces blank and dazed. Fitz Stephen still knelt by Grim's side, cradling his head as Master William improvised a bandage. John of Salisbury had crept out from the altar where he'd taken shelter. He sagged down upon the choir steps, and Fitz Stephen and he looked at each other across the wounded priest. Although neither spoke, Fitz Stephen knew what they both were thinking. The only one who'd tried to protect Lord Thomas was a stranger, a man who'd known him but a few days.

By now most of the monks had thronged into the nave and choir. Prior Odo had surfaced from the crypt and, striding over to them, began to ask abrupt questions about Edward Grim's prospects for recovery. Fitz Stephen felt rage welling up. Odo was so eager to assert his authority that he could not even wait for the archbishop's body to cool. Doubtless he felt Lord Thomas's death had been his own deliverance, his fears of removal seeping away with the archbishop's lifeblood.

Fitz Stephen been focusing all his attention upon Edward Grim, awed and shamed by the priest's courage and not yet ready to accept what he'd just witnessed—an archbishop butchered in his own church. But Odo's presumption had jarred the protective cobwebs from his brain, and his numbness began to ebb, giving way to an emotion as crippling and fierce as the most physical pain.

He was becoming aware of a low droning of disapproval. The archbishop's relationship with the monks of Christ Church had often been a fractious one and not all had welcomed his return from exile. To some, he had remained the worldly, high-living chancellor who'd been forced upon them, never truly one of them, and a violent death, while deplorable, did not change every mind. There were monks now expressing that skepticism, implying that Becket had been an accomplice in his own demise. Several spoke of the archbishop's willfulness, his antipathy to compromise. Mention was made of his prideful manner, his vainglory, his inability to forgive wrongs. Someone muttered: "He wanted to be a king, to be more than a king. Let him be a king now."

Fitz Stephen, a man of the most equable temperament, found himself fighting back the urge to spill yet more blood in the defiled cathedral. Then he noticed Osbern, the archbishop's longtime chamberlain. His face was bruised and swollen, several teeth knocked out by pummeling fists, for he had been the one who'd barred the door to the great hall. Kneeling by Becket's body, he tore off a sleeve of his shirt and using it as a bandage, he wound it carefully around the archbishop's shattered skull. There was such tenderness in that simple, futile gesture that Fitz Stephen's throat closed up and his eyes burned with hot, bitter tears.

Townspeople had ventured into the cathedral and were gathering around the body, weeping and wailing, crouching to kiss Becket's hands and feet, ripping off pieces of their clothing to dip in the puddles of coagulating blood. Prior Odo and several of the monks hurried over to disperse them, eventually managing to clear the church of all but the members of the religious community.

Slowly, haltingly, men began to function again, to deal with the immediate aftermath of the murder. Edward Grim and the other injured were ushered out to be tended at the infirmary. Fetching a bier, some of the monks lifted the corpse and carried it up into the choir and onto the High Altar. Benches were dragged into the transept and positioned to keep anyone else from stepping in the spillage of blood and brains.

It was then that Robert of Merton chose to reveal the archbishop's secret. Lifting Becket's black mantle and bloodied surplice and lambskin pelisse, he uncovered the monk's habit beneath. The priory monks were deeply moved by this evidence of his camouflaged solidarity, evidence that he'd been one of them after all. But the confessor had one more surprise to disclose. Pulling up the habit, he showed them that Becket was wearing a hair shirt, even a pair of hair braies. The drawers were so tight that the seams had gouged a furrow from knees to hip and the skin was abraded and chaffed from continual contact with the rough, coarse cloth. The hair shirt had been split so that Becket could bare his flesh to daily flagellations and his back was scarred with the marks of past scourging. That very day, the confessor told them proudly, he had endured three such penitential whippings. As the awestruck, stunned monks crowded in closer, they saw that the braies were infested with vermin, swarming with lice and fleas, some of which had even burrowed into his groin.

Pandemonium resulted. Men wept at this painful proof of sanctity. Monks expecting to find the archbishop garbed in silken braies and furs of fox or vair were overwhelmed by this discovery of his daily torment. Sobbing, they kissed his hands and feet, proclaiming him "Saint Thomas, martyr unto God." A few thought to return to the transept where they carefully scooped up as much of the blood as they could, some of it undoubtedly Edward Grim's. The broken blade of Richard le Bret's sword was recovered and put aside with the archbishop's bloodied clothing, to be cherished as holy relics, and many no longer mourned, rejoicing instead that their lord had died for God and Holy Church, martyr to the True Faith.

The following day, Becket's body was hastily buried in the cathedral crypt after the monks were threatened by Robert de Broc, who vowed that he would drag the corpse behind his horse to the nearest cesspit. The church had been polluted by the shedding of blood so there could be no funeral Mass. The archbishop was dressed in his hair shirt and the vestments he'd worn at his investiture eight years before. He was not washed, as he had already been washed in his own blood. The first miracle occurred three days later, when a woman stricken with palsy was reported to have been cured after drinking water sprinkled with a few drops of Becket's blood.

CHAPTER THIRTY-THREE

January 1171
Argentan, Normandy

*T*HE ARCHBISHOP OF ROUEN had been summoned to the king's solar for further discussions about the looming confrontation with the Archbishop of Canterbury, but he was still lingering in the great hall, not at all eager to jump back into that particular fire. Henry's combustible temper had even more fuel to feed upon; yesterday he'd learned of Becket's Christmas Day excommunications. The archbishop had long harbored a secret apprehension that this clash between two such stubborn, strong-willed men could not possibly end well, although he'd struggled to ignore his doubts and do whatever he could to make their peace a permanent one. But the peace had not even lasted through Christmastide, and he was grimly certain that far worse was to come.

Getting reluctantly to his feet, he was adjusting his surplice when his attention was drawn by a new arrival to the hall. Waiting for the Bishop of Lisieux to join him, he said wryly, "You're just in time, Arnulf, to enter the Valley of Death with me."

Getting no response, he subjected Arnulf to a closer scrutiny and felt a sudden chill, for the bishop was the color of curdled milk. What news could have so unnerved a man as worldly and urbane as Arnulf of Lisieux?

THEY HUDDLED in the stairway by the solar door, Arnulf and Rotrou of Rouen and a travel-stained, disheveled young courier too fatigued for fear. Arnulf at last reached for the latch, mouthing the cry of the crusaders, *"Deus vult,"* in an attempt at sardonic bravado that rang hollow even to his own ears.

The solar was crowded, well lit by flaring torches. Henry was standing in the center of the chamber, listening to several men at once. When the door opened and the two prelates entered, he greeted them with a scowl and sarcasm. "How kind of you to belatedly honor us with your presence, my lords."

Arnulf, as skilled as any diplomat in the arts of discretion and circumspection, could not believe that he had volunteered for such a thankless task as this. Balking at the very edge of the cliff, he decided to throw the hapless messenger into the void and beckoned the young man forward. "My liege, this is Lucas, whose lord is Hugh de Gundeville. He has come from Canterbury with grievous news for you."

Lucas stumbled and sank to his knees before Henry. "My lord king, the Archbishop of Canterbury is dead."

"What?" Henry stared at the man as if the words had no meaning. The blank look on his face was one Arnulf had seen before, a moment of desperate denial before the Apocalypse.

"The young king sent my lord Hugh to Canterbury. We got there on Wednesday morn, after the murder was done."

Lucas paused, waiting politely for his lord's response. When there was none, he made the sign of the cross, saying softly, "The archbishop was slain Tuesday eve at Vespers." Remembering, then, the letter he'd almost forgotten in his exhaustion, he held it out.

Henry took the letter, but he made no attempt to read it. His fingers tightened around the parchment roll, as if of their own volition. He looked at the horror-struck faces of the men encircling him, saying nothing. And before any of them could speak, he'd turned away and was gone, the door closing quietly behind him.

WHEN HENRY'S SON, the young king, was told of the archbishop's murder, he exclaimed aloud, "Alas! But God, I give Thee thanks that this was done without my knowledge and that none of my people were involved."

THEY WERE WAITING in a private chamber in Eleanor's palace at Poitiers. They had gathered to consult with their duchess about the latest crisis threatening to engulf the Angevin empire. They'd just begun, though, when Eleanor was called away. She'd not been gone long, but the delay was eroding their patience. They were experienced enough to know that she'd not have interrupted the council for a routine message.

When she finally returned, it was to a sudden silence. Her face was expressionless, and to these men who knew her so well, the appearance of her inscrutable court mask was as sure a sign of a coming storm as northeast winds and a haloed moon. She paused for a long moment in the doorway and then strode into the chamber, head high and eyes guarded and opaque. The men were watching her, so only Raoul noticed as her son slipped inconspicuously in behind her and took up position in the shadows. He was not about to give the boy away though, believing that if Richard was old enough to sneak in, he was old enough to hear.

"I've just received word from Argentan," Eleanor said without preamble. "Thomas Becket was murdered in Canterbury Cathedral on the morrow after Holy Innocents' Day."

Even the most irreverent of her lords could not suppress a shiver, for there were few crimes more sacrilegious than the killing of an archbishop in his own church. Once the initial shock passed, not all were displeased by the news. No one had yet asked the fateful question, but in a sense, it was not even necessary. Whether Becket had died at the English king's connivance or not, the blame would still be laid at Henry's throne.

"The killers were four English knights, some of whom may be known to you," Eleanor said dispassionately, "Hugh de Morville, William de Tracy, Reginald Fitz Urse, and Richard le Bret. The de Brocs were involved, too, although they apparently took no role in the actual slaying. They claimed that they were doing the king's bidding. That is not true."

They already knew that was so, for she'd reported that her husband's decision at Bures had been to demand that Becket absolve the English bishops or face arrest. A few speculated whether an assassination order might have been given without her knowledge, but none were foolhardy enough to suggest that. It was left to her trusted confidant and seneschal, Saldebreuil de Sanzay, to give voice to the other truth, the obvious truth.

"I do not doubt that, Madame," he said. "But it may not matter. Lord Henry's enemies will care only that a weapon of incomparable sharpness has been delivered into their hands."

"I know," she acknowledged, and for a fleeting moment, she allowed her frustration and dismay to show. "What monumental, unforgivable folly . . ."

It was then that Richard emerged from hiding. Eleanor stiffened at the sight of her son, but she did not send him away; it was too late for that. Richard had experienced a growth spurt that autumn and it was a minor surprise to realize that his eyes were level with her own, that it was like looking into her husband's eyes, clear and sea-grey and impenetrable.

"Will men blame my father for this killing?"

Eleanor was not going to lie to him, not to Richard. "Yes," she said, "I fear that they will," and he nodded, apparently satisfied by her candor. What he thought about Becket's murder, she did not know, would not know unless he chose to tell her.

Raoul dared then to pose the question that many of them were wondering. It had not escaped him that she'd been ambiguous about the source of her information. He suspected that if she'd heard of the murder from Henry himself, she would have said so, which meant that the rumors of marital strife were becoming more and more credible. Nothing could please him more, but he took care to keep his voice perfectly neutral as he asked, "My lady . . . will you go to the king at Argentan?"

Eleanor was not fooled by the detachment of his query; she well knew the depths of enmity between her husband and uncle. She regarded Raoul pensively, trying to decide if she should answer honestly, answer at all. "Yes," she said, very evenly, ". . . if he sends for me."

"My lamb, you must cease your weeping. You'll sicken upon your tears if you do not."

Rosamund paid no heed to Meliora's commiseration, continuing to sob into a sodden pillow. Meliora sat down heavily beside her, reaching out a hand to stroke the tousled fair hair. She had tried to keep the news of the archbishop's murder from Rosamund, but the story was spreading faster than wildfire, on everyone's lips, the topic of all conversation in the streets of Falaise. She did not doubt that this heinous crime would rock Christendom to its very foundations.

"Men are saying he did this, that he gave the command . . ." Rosamund sobbed again, then hiccuped. Her beautiful blue eyes were swollen to slits, puffy and sore. She knew Meliora was right, that she was making herself sick. But she could not control her tears, her grief, or her fear. "He would never have done that, Meliora, never!"

"I know, lamb, I know," Meliora said soothingly, while hoping that Rosamund's faith in her royal lover would not be shaken, or worse, betrayed.

"If only he would send for me, Meliora . . ." Rosamund shifted so that her head was in the other woman's lap, taking faint comfort in these maternal attentions, an unknown luxury in the Clifford family. "If only I could go to him! He is heartsick about the archbishop's death, I know he is. And I can do nothing to help, nothing . . ."

FROM A LETTER of Louis, King of the French, to Pope Alexander: "Let the sword of St Peter be unsheathed to avenge the martyr of Canterbury . . ."

From a letter of William, Archbishop of Sens, to Pope Alexander: "Avenge, O Lord, the blood of thy servant and martyr, the Archbishop of Canterbury, who has been slain, nay, crucified, for the liberties of the Church . . ."

From a letter of Theobald, Count of Blois, to Pope Alexander: "Those dogs of the court . . . showed themselves true servants of the king, and guiltily shed innocent blood. . . . May then, Holy Father, the Almighty aid and counsel you. . . . May He both instill into you a wish for vengeance and the power of obtaining it, so that the Church, put to confusion by the magnitude of this unheard-of crime, may have reason to rejoice . . ."

From another letter of William, Archbishop of Sens, to Pope Alexander: "And indeed, I believe that the outcry of the world must have filled the ears of Your Holinesss, how that this, not King of the English, but enemy rather of the English and of the whole body of Christ, has lately committed wickedness against the holy one. . . . For this crime is one that by far deserves the first place among all the crimes of the wicked that are read or related; as all the wickedness of Nero, the perfidiousness of Julian, and even the sacrilegious treachery of Judas does it exceed . . ."

THE BISHOP of Worcester was taken at once to the king's solar, where he was greeted by a trinity of churchmen: Rotrou of Rouen, Arnulf of Lisieux, and Giles of Évreux. His mantle was wet with melting snow and sleet, for Argentan was in the grip of an icy January storm. They hovered around him, fatherly and concerned, offering to find dry, warm garments, to provide food, mulled wine. Roger brushed off their suggestions with terse courtesy; he did not want their solicitude.

"I do not know why I am here," he said, and Rotrou began to describe the king's anguish. Arnulf cut him off, understanding what Roger was really saying.

"It is possible," he said, "to mourn for the archbishop without forsaking your cousin the king."

"Is it?" Roger asked bleakly and Arnulf shrugged.

"You are here, are you not?"

"Yes," Roger admitted, "I am . . ." Pulling off his mantle, he flung it across a chair. "Tell me why you think I can help."

"If you cannot," Arnulf said bluntly, "I fear for the life of the king."

Roger's left eyebrow shot up in a skeptical arch that was uncannily like Henry's. "Is his grief as great as that? Or his guilt?"

Arnulf shrugged again. "I suspect they are horns on the same goat. I can tell you, though, that his sorrow is very real. He has been secluded in his bedchamber for more than three days now, refusing to admit anyone, refusing to eat, to accept any comfort at all."

"The queen is not here?"

Rotrou shook his head. "Would that she were, but she and the king parted after Christmas, he riding north and she returning to Poitou."

They were watching him hopefully, expectantly. Roger stalked to the hearth, held his hands out toward its warmth. "Ask him," he said, "if he'll see me."

THE CHAMBER was dark, shutters latched, candles and lamps quenched. It was cold, too, for the hearth fire had gone out, only a few feeble embers still aglow. Roger was blind, unable to see anything but blackness. "Harry?" There was no reply and he waited until his eyes adjusted to the lack of light, until he could discern a motionless figure in a window seat. He hesitated and then carefully crossed the room and sat down beside Henry.

"Jesú!" Cold air was seeping through the shutters, the window seat under siege by icy drafts. "Are you not half-frozen by now?"

"No."

Roger was encouraged that he'd gotten an answer, any answer. Sure that he could outwait his cousin, he said nothing, let the silence settle around them. He could hear Henry's breathing, shallow and uneven, could hear the other man shifting position on the seat. When Henry finally spoke, his voice was as constricted as his breath.

"As God is my witness," he said, "those men did not murder him at my bidding."

"I know," Roger said, thankful that he need not lie about that.

There was another prolonged silence. "Do you think that Thomas knew that?"

"Yes, he did," Roger said, with such certainty that Henry came abruptly to his feet.

"If I wanted to be fed pap, there are more than enough men eager to serve it up to me. That question was not easy to ask. I agreed to see you because I thought you'd be the one man who'd give me an honest answer!"

Roger rose, too, unable to endure the window seat chill any longer. "You want more from me than honesty, Harry. You want absolution."

Henry started to make an angry denial, stopped himself. "What if I do?"

"I cannot give it to you," Roger said and again it was quiet.

"I know," Henry said at last, so softly that Roger barely heard him.

"But I can give you this much. I can tell you for certes that Thomas knew his killers were not there at your behest. He said so, you see. When they first confronted him in his bedchamber, he told them that he did not believe they came from the king." Thrusting into the pouch at his belt, he drew out a letter. "This was written by William Fitz Stephen within hours of the murder. Read it for yourself if you doubt me."

Henry reached out, but his fingers just brushed the parchment. Roger turned away, dropping the letter onto a nearby table, and strode toward the hearth. Picking up fire tongs, he began to prod the embers back to life. "I am going to light a candle now," he said and when Henry did not protest, he did so, cupping the flame once it had kindled and holding it aloft.

Henry flinched away from the light at first, but then he raised his head and met Roger's gaze full on. "Do I look like a man with blood on my hands?"

"You look," Roger said, "like a man who has not slept or eaten for days." Setting the candle down, he started toward the door. "If I order milk of almonds, will you drink it?" Taking Henry's silence as assent, he opened the door just wide enough to issue instructions. Neither man spoke until a timid knock announced a servant's arrival. Thwarting the curiosity of those hovering out in the stairwell, Roger did not admit the man, taking the tray himself and closing the door upon the waiting world.

Henry accepted the cup with indifference, but with Roger's eyes upon him, he took a swallow, then another. His gaze shifted several times from his cousin's face to Fitz Stephen's letter. He was not ready to read it, though, and began to pace, retreating back into the shadows beyond the candle's solitary glimmer.

"It does not matter that I never wanted this. I will be blamed for it."

It was not posed as a question, but Roger heard the echoes of one nonetheless. "Yes," he said, "you will."

Henry halted his pacing. "Do you blame me?"

"Yes," Roger said implacably and Henry drew a sharp breath.

"You said you believed me! You said you knew I did not order his death!"

"I do believe that. But if you are not guilty, neither are you innocent. Your hot, heedless words set the killing in motion."

"I did not want him murdered!"

"But he was murdered, and by men who killed in your name."

Henry shook his head vehemently. "It was not my doing, Roger! I spoke out in anger, no more than that. You know my temper, quick to kindle and quick to cool. I admit that my words were ill chosen, but this was not the first time that I'd flared up over one of Becket's affronts. I cursed him out soundly and publicly at Chinon after learning that he'd excommunicated my justiciar, and I daresay my language was intemperate, even threatening. But no one acted upon my words!"

"Well," Roger said, "this time they did," and that, Henry could not deny.

CHAPTER THIRTY-FOUR

†

January 1171
Trefriw, North Wales

PERYF AP CEDIFOR looked haggard and tense, like a man in dire need of sleep, one who'd forgotten how to laugh. Arriving at mealtime, he'd politely accepted the invitation to dine with them, but he'd yet to swallow a mouthful. His brothers Caradog and Brochfael, had eaten very little, too, and since Cedifor's sons were as known for their prodigious appetites as for their powerful, wrestlers' physiques, their indifferent eating did not pass unnoticed. Enid fretted and apologized for the "poor fare," Rhodri kept urging them to try various dishes, and Ranulf's own appetite dwindled each time he glanced at Peryf's transparently troubled face.

Once the meal had finally ended and the servants had cleared the table, Ranulf chose to confront his demons head-on, waiting only until Morgan and Mallt were shepherded out of the hall. "I know you sent word to Hywel of his father's death. But can you be sure your messenger reached him?"

"No," Peryf admitted, "I cannot. Tathan is a good man, one I'd trust with my soul's last breath. But soon after he sailed, the weather turned foul. For all I know, his ship was one of the hundreds that have foundered in that accursed Irish Sea. Even if he landed safely, he could still have come to grief ere he found Hywel. I was told that there was a man so eager to catch the ship that he was rowed out to board whilst it was making ready to leave the harbor. I could not help wondering if that unforeseen passenger had an urgent reason of his own—an ungodly one—for wanting to take Tathan's ship."

Rhodri looked perplexed, but Ranulf understood at once. He was taken aback, though, for Peryf's fears were much darker than his. "You truly think they would try to murder your messenger?"

"What better way to keep Hywel from learning of his father's death? To keep him in Ireland until it's too late?"

Rhodri always kept his crutch within easy reach. As he pushed his chair back now, it clattered to the floor and he never even noticed. "What are you saying, Peryf? Who are *they?*"

"Cristyn and her brood. Who else?"

Peryf's candor hushed the hall. Ranulf leaned across the table, clamping his hand upon the other man's arm. "Have you any proof of these suspicions?"

"I do not need proof. I know in the marrow of my bones that Cristyn would scruple at nothing to gain power for her sons."

Ranulf had often heard Hywel joke about his foster brother's "doom and gloom disposition," but he could not dismiss Peryf's fears as easily as Hywel would have done. The natural optimism of his youth had been tempered by life's ongoing lessons, his equivocal status as one who was both a king's son and a bastard, and the sobering realization that the race was not always to the swift, nor the battle to the strong.

"What would you have me do, Peryf?"

Peryf's smile was rueful. "Am I as easily read as that? I have indeed come to ask for your help, Ranulf." Holding up his hand before Ranulf could respond. "Wait! Do not be so quick to agree, for it is no small favor I seek. Would you be willing to sail for Ireland and find Hywel?"

Ranulf's acceptance would once have come as quickly and unthinkingly as his next breath. But it was not enough to understand that his wife deserved a say in their family's future, not unless he also acted upon it. A winter voyage to Ireland was often a widow-maker. He looked over at Rhiannon, and with the intuition honed by two decades of marital intimacy, she sensed his eyes upon her, heard his unspoken question.

"Yes," she said unhesitatingly, and Ranulf thanked the Almighty for giving him this remarkable woman.

"I owe Hywel more than I could ever begin to calculate and he is as dear to me as my brothers in blood. I will right gladly go to Ireland to fetch him home."

Ranulf's first thought had been to take ship at Chester, for it was far larger than any of the Welsh ports and attracted numerous ships engaged in the Irish trade. But Peryf was as methodical and far-sighted as he was pessimistic, and he'd sent scouts to keep watch over Môn's harbors and cove-notched coastline. He was able to tell Ranulf, therefore, that there was a cog at Aber Menai, doing rigging repairs. And so Ranulf and the sons of Cedifor took the Llan-faes ferry across the Menai Straits and then headed west.

Aber Menai was the island's most ancient port, a natural crossing for Welsh princes on their way to the royal manor of Aberffraw, and according to Peryf, both Davydd and Rhodri were reported to have been at Aberffraw for the past fortnight. Ranulf was rapidly developing respect for Peryf's surveillance system, and it occurred to him that Hywel could do far worse than to make Peryf his seneschal. For himself, he sought no such honors. His soul would always be riven in twain, torn between his love for Wales and his loyalty to the English Crown.

After a cold, clear night strewn with stars, the day was born with an ice-edged caul. Snow from a midweek storm still clung in spots, and Ranulf's breath was frosted in cloudlets of wispy white. The island climate was usually milder than the more mountainous heights of Gwynedd and this spell of frigid weather had surprised the sailors, slowing their repairs. But the ship's master had assured Ranulf that they'd be ready to sail by the morrow and Ranulf could only take the man at his word.

Picking up shells, Ranulf sought to skip them across the water's roiling surface, without much success. The cog was anchored out in the harbor, its single mast and furled sails silhouetted against the horizon like a tree stripped of leaves. Several children were playing at the water's edge, chasing a spotted dog. The small cluster of houses looked out of place, as if dropped there by accident, naked and vulnerable to wind and the treacherous tides of Yr Afon Fenai. The church was tolling a mournful "passing bell" to seek prayers for the soul of one hovering near death. All in all, it was as bleak a scene as Ranulf could envision, an accurate mirror of his own mood.

He suspected that his edginess was due to the looming sea voyage. Despite the many times that he'd braved Channel crossings, he had never ventured out into the ocean itself, and he'd have been quite content to go to his grave with that particular challenge unmet. Now that he was committed to the endeavor, though, he was impatient to start, finding this time ashore to be as unpleasant in its own way as the time aboard was certain to be.

"Ranulf!" Turning at the sound of his name, he saw Caradog ap Cedifor ambling toward him. Caradog was the youngest of Cedifor's many sons, with more than twenty years stretching between him and Peryf, and in consequence, he was the least-known to Ranulf of Hywel's foster brothers. Like Peryf, he was of medium height, stocky and well muscled, with wind-blown hair the color of wet sand and eyes bright with the intrepid spirit of the young. He would be accompanying Ranulf to that distant isle known to the Welsh as Iwerddon, and he actually seemed delighted at the chance to risk drowning in the frigid waters of the Irish Sea.

"Peryf intends to row out to the ship and see if he can coax or coerce the master into sailing tonight. You want to come along?"

"Why not?" Ranulf followed Caradog up the beach, shivering as they headed into the wind. Knowing that Caradog's father had Irish kindred, he asked the younger man if he'd ever been to Ireland, getting a toss of Caradog's sandy head in reply.

"Nay, I have not. But Peryf crossed the Irish Sea when he went along with Hywel to visit Hywel's lady mother." Caradog's smile soon became an impish grin. "Hywel says if ever there was a man born to spend all his days a hundred miles inland, it is Peryf. He fed the fish from Môn to Dublin and back again, and for a good year afterward, he'd get greensick at the mere mention of ships or the sea. That is why he dared not offer to come with you to find Hywel. Even rowing out into the harbor will likely cost him dear."

"I'd wondered about that," Ranulf confided. "I've been wondering, too, why Peryf turned to me. Since you'd already offered to go to Ireland on your own, why the need for me?"

Caradog's laugh was carried off by the wind. "You ought to be able to guess the reason for that! Hywel says you were the old king's youngest son."

"Yes, I was . . ." Ranulf was puzzled and then amused. "Peryf still sees you as his little brother, does he?"

"Of course, and he secretly fears that I'd either drink myself into oblivion or become so besotted with the Dublin whores that I'd forget altogether about Hywel!"

Caradog laughed again, with such infectious humor that Ranulf laughed, too, glad that at least he'd have good company on this perilous journey. It was then that they heard the shout, saw Peryf running up the beach toward them.

PERYF WAS PANTING and his first gasped-out words were not all that intelligible to Ranulf. "One of your men just arrived with news of a ship seeking entry into the harbor at Cemlyn. That I understand, Peryf. But why do you think it is Hywel?"

"Because . . . because Cemlyn is not a port for trading. If a ship were bringing over goods from Ireland, it would most likely head for Llan-faes or Pwllheli. Why would it put in at Cemlyn? There's no town there, and the nearest royal manor is at Cemais. Hywel must have paid them to let him ashore. Nothing else makes sense."

Ranulf was still not convinced. "Suppose it was just coming in for repairs?"

Peryf's messenger spoke up then. "It did not drop anchor, my lord Ranulf. The winds were contrary and it was unable to enter the harbor. After several failed attempts, it sailed off to the east, hugging the coast. If they had an urgent need for repairs, surely they'd have kept on trying? I followed for a time and it seemed to me that they were seeking another harbor on the sheltered side of the island. As I told Lord Peryf, I truly think their intent was to put passengers ashore."

"Nothing else makes sense," Peryf repeated. "I think we should ride for the east coast. There are several coves and harbors suitable for landing. Dulas, for one. But the best harbor by far is at Traeth Coch. I am certain that Hywel means to land there."

"And what if you're wrong and the cog sails ere we can get back to Aber Menai?"

Peryf shrugged. "We'll make it worth his while to wait."

The other man's sudden, uncharacteristic extravagance proved—if it still needed proving—just how worried he truly was. Ranulf conceded the argument with a joke about getting Hywel to pay for the additional expenses, and hoped that he was not motivated by a desire to put off his sea voyage for another day.

THE ISLE known as Anglesey to the English and Môn to the Welsh had once been called Ynys Dywell, the Dark Island, so heavily wooded was it in bygone times. But by God's Year 1171, much of its deep, primal forest had been cleared away, for the low-lying, fertile land was ideally suited to farming, and Môn had long functioned as Gwynedd's granary. With neither mountains nor wealds to hinder their progress and less than fifteen miles to cover, the men expected to reach Traeth Coch before dark. Skirting the edges of the vast river marshes of Cors Ddyga, they soon had the sun at their backs. The morning's chill had been overtaken by an afternoon warming, giving rise to patches of the fog so common to an island climate. By the time they were in sight of the church at Pentraeth, which overlooked the bay, dusk was beginning to cast lengthening shadows and the day's light was slowly ebbing. The waters of Traeth Coch had darkened from sapphire to a twilight indigo and a ship was anchored in the cove.

As they drew nearer, the sails unfurled and took the wind, a sudden burst of brightness against the hazy sky, and then the ship was in flight, gracefully cresting the waves of the bay as it headed for open water. They began to yell, spurring their horses forward. But then they saw the men standing at the water's edge, saw the one taller by a head than the others, hair the color of the sun, legacy of the silver fox, and their shouting changed timbre, soaring skyward with great relief and even greater joy.

THE REUNION was noisy, jubilant, and somewhat chaotic, for two of Peryf's brothers had accompanied Hywel to Ireland and now had to be welcomed home, too, as did Hywel's son Caswallon, and Ranulf's son, the newly named Bleddyn. For a time, voices merged, laughter rang out, and they were able to forget that death had brought them together, the death of a well-loved father and a formidable prince.

Tathan was the man of the hour, lavishly praised for accomplishing his challenging mission with dispatch and aplomb. He had located Hywel within two days of his arrival in Dublin, bearing his heavyhearted message of Owain's death. Hywel had at once made plans to return to Wales straightaway, but the Irish weather was even more erratic than in Wales and winter gales had stranded him for weeks, unable to find any ship's master foolhardy enough to venture out into the cauldron of the Irish Sea.

"Is it true," Hywel demanded, "that you were really going off in search of me?" When Ranulf nodded, he burst out laughing. "Once or twice in your cups, you pledged to go to Hell for me if need be, but nary a word was ever said about Ireland!"

"Rhiannon made me do it," Ranulf said, and Hywel laughed all the harder. Caradog joined in with mock indignation, wanting to know why he was not being commended for his willingness to accompany Ranulf, and his brothers roared when Hywel pointed out that he was crazed enough to think a sea voyage to Ireland in the dead of winter was an opportunity for adventure.

Hywel wanted to know all that had happened during his absence, more amused than alarmed by Peryf's dour suspicions about Davydd and Rhodri. "I know folklore holds that an apple never falls far from the tree, but Cristyn's Dead Sea Fruit landed halfway between Limbo and Purgatory."

That sally sparked much merriment among Hywel's audience, and Ranulf thought, not for the first time, that Hywel could transform words into weapons with the ease of an alchemist. He shared what little he knew of happenings in England, then, that Thomas Becket had landed on English shores on the first of December, after excommunicating the bishops on the very eve of his departure. Hywel did not seem surprised by this, commenting dryly that Becket would do well to heed an ancient Welsh proverb; a wise man ought not to let his tongue cut his own throat.

Hywel also had news to impart, briefly relating the current turmoil in Ireland, where Dermot, the King of Leincester, had allied himself with one of the most powerful of Henry's Marcher barons, Richard de Clare, Lord of Pembroke, in an attempt to stave off his Irish adversaries. "Dermot offered de Clare his daughter and the promise of his realm upon his death. I daresay the English king would like to see a Norman kingdom in Ireland about as much as he'd enjoy watching Becket consecrated as the next Pope. So I think it safe to say that the next time he gets to hungering for lands not his, he'll be looking toward Ireland, not Wales."

Among Hywel's talents was one particularly valuable to a prince: the ability to inspire confidence and hope in his followers. Now that he was back on Welsh soil, safely back in their midst, the morrow was once more full of promise. They well knew that the loss of Owain could have dealt a death blow to Gwynedd if he'd not had a son worthy to succeed him, if he'd not had Hywel.

The day was done, which meant that the night must be passed on

Môn, for no man in his senses would attempt an evening crossing of the
Menai Straits. In his urgency to return to Wales, Hywel had taken the first
ship from Ireland whose master was willing to make a January voyage, one
that had been too small to transport horses. Now, after some discussion, it
was decided to head for Llan-faes, where Owain had a manor and stables.
Amid much good-natured bickering and jesting, some of Peryf's men offered their mounts for the use of the new arrivals, and horses were found
for Caswallon, Bleddyn, and Peryf's brothers Iddon and Aerddur. The rest
of Hywel's men agreed to wait at the Pentraeth church until additional
horses could be dispatched from Llan-faes, and by the time it was all
sorted out, dusk had staked its claim to the island and sea fog was swirling
in to hide the horizon.

Hywel had brought back an Irish keepsake, a young wolfhound as big
as a pony, and it loped easily beside his stallion as they rode toward Llan-
faes. He'd named it Cúchoigríche, he explained, which meant "hound of
the border," laughing at Ranulf's futile attempts to get his tongue around
the unfamiliar Irish. He'd said little of his father so far, asking only for assurances that Owain had been buried in consecrated ground despite dying
excommunicate. Ranulf knew him well enough not to push, though. Hywel's grieving had been done in private, for he did not find it easy to offer up glimpses of his inner soul, not even to so close a friend as Ranulf.
Instead, he entertained Ranulf and Peryf and the others with a rollicking
account of Bleddyn's romantic conquests, claiming that the lad had broken numerous female hearts in Dublin during his short stay. Bleddyn
flushed and denied all, but Ranulf could see that his son was secretly
pleased by the attention and he made careful note of the names Hywel
was bandying about—Áine and Mór and Sorcha—to tease him in the days
to come.

Llan-faes was just five miles from Pentraeth, and Ranulf was thankful
for it, as his back had begun to protest so many hours in the saddle. Slack-
ening the reins, he let his stallion ease its pace, not wanting Hywel to notice his discomfort, knowing he'd be tormented mercilessly if he did.
Dropping back inconspicuously, he was soon riding in the rear, where he
occupied himself by trying to think of a suitable gift for his niece; Maud's
birthday was coming up after Candlemas. He had no warning, would
never know what caused his stallion's misstep, but he could tell at once
that something was wrong. Dismounting by the side of the road, he examined the animal in the dimming light and quickly discovered the injury,
a back tendon hot and tender to the touch.

Ranulf swore softly and with considerable feeling. Only his stallion's obvious distress kept him from losing his temper entirely. After briefly contemplating his options, none of which appealed, he took the reins and started to lead the horse slowly back toward Pentraeth. It was not long before he heard hoofbeats behind him. Turning toward the sound, he let his hand drop to his sword hilt from force of habit, and then smiled at the sight of his son.

"Papa?" Reining in beside him, Bleddyn gazed over at the limping stallion. "Roland's gone lame? What foul luck!"

Ranulf was inutterably touched that Bleddyn should have observed his disappearance and come back to check up on him. He said nothing, of course, not wanting to embarrass them both, and so they spent several moments discussing Roland's injury. "He seems to have strained a sinew. It could be much worse, but he cannot be ridden like this. I'll have to walk him back to Pentraeth, soak the leg in water, and make a bran poultice. Most likely I'll have to leave him overnight with the priest, damn the luck."

"I'll keep you company," Bleddyn said and would have dismounted if Ranulf had not shaken his head.

"No, Bleddyn, I'd rather you catch up with Hywel and tell him of my mishap. Tell him, too, that if he laughs, I might remember the time he was flirting with two sisters at Nefyn and Smoke shadow-jumped, tossing him head over heels into a briar patch." Bleddyn said nothing, but there was such an odd look on his face that Ranulf added, "Is something amiss?"

"Nothing at all. It is just . . . that you'd not called me *Bleddyn* before." Bleddyn smiled then, a smile so like Rhiannon's that Ranulf could only marvel how he'd missed the resemblance.

As Bleddyn disappeared into the mist, Ranulf began trudging again toward Pentraeth, stopping frequently to rest and comfort his horse. He was tired and hungry, but happier than he'd been in months, relieved to be spared that harrowing journey to Ireland, grateful that he'd heeded Hywel's advice and accepted his son's name change. He found himself wondering suddenly if Harry and his sons were traveling a road as rough hewn as the one he'd been riding with Gilbert-Bleddyn for so long. Why were daughters so much easier to rear? Mallt had given him nary a worry over the years. Whereas Morgan was already a hellion at six; God forbid what he'd be like at sixteen!

The sounds were muffled by the fog, but far too familiar for Ranulf to mistake; he'd fought in enough battles to recognize the din in his sleep. He stood still for a heartbeat, listening to the metallic clash of swords, the cries of men and horses, and then hastily looped Roland's reins over the nearest bush before he began to run.

"Gilbert!" He wasn't even aware that he was shouting his son's name. "Gilbert!" The fog was inconstant, drifting over the land like sea smoke. One moment he'd break free of it, only to plunge into another cloud. The air was mild and damp, and he felt as if he were trying to breathe underwater. The fog distorted sounds and he could no longer trust his senses, could not judge distance. He fell once, was up even before his bruised body could register the impact. And then suddenly he was there, emerging from the mist onto a scene of carnage.

The fighting was over, the battlefield strewn with crumpled bodies, dropped weapons, and several downed horses. Unlike most battles, there had been no looting and the attacking force was already gone, in their hasty retreat leaving behind riderless stallions and bloodied or broken swords. Ranulf came to a halt, stunned, unwilling to believe what he was seeing. Drawing his sword in a reflex action, he peered blindly into the night, but could find no foes, none but the wounded, the dead, and the dying.

"Papa!"

Ranulf spun around as Bleddyn came stumbling out of the fog. He looked dazed and blood was flowing from a gash on his forehead, but he was alive, he was breathing, and Ranulf dropped his sword, lunged forward to embrace his son. Bleddyn was trembling, and for a long, shuddering moment, he said nothing, just held tight.

"I came upon this . . . ," he said, his voice so constricted and choked that Ranulf would never have recognized it. "Dead . . . all dead . . . the men who'd attacked them were fleeing . . . I never even saw who they were . . . I set after them, not thinking, just . . . I wanted to kill, to make them pay . . . and then my horse swerved to avoid trampling a body and I went right over his head . . . God, Papa, Jesus God . . . what happened?"

"Hush, lad, hush. It's over, it's all over." Steering the shocked youth toward the closest shelter, a lanky sapling, he got Bleddyn to sit upon the ground. Fumbling for his dagger, he slashed a strip from his mantle and urged his son to hold it to his bleeding head. "Stay there, lad. Do not move. I'll be back, I swear I will."

He thought then to retrieve his sword, shoving it into his scabbard. But he was at a loss as to what to do next. Everywhere he looked, there was need. *Hywel . . . where was Hywel?* Moving like someone in a trance, he knelt beside the closest body, saw that the man was beyond help, and went on to the next victim. This one, too, was dead, and somewhere in the back of his brain, he recognized Iddon, one of Peryf's brothers. He could hear moaning now, cries of pain. The rank smells of death—blood, urine, and spilled entrails—were strong enough to make him queasy. *Hywel . . . Jesú, where was he?*

He found Peryf next, so limp and still that he was amazed to be able to detect a pulse. Peryf had been the only one wearing a hauberk, mocked by his brothers for his excessive caution, but Ranulf suspected now that the chain-mail had saved his life for he could find no wounds on Peryf's body, just an ugly, swelling bruise above his eye.

"Mary, Mother of God!"

Ranulf whirled toward this new voice, saw one of the men who'd been left behind at Pentraeth standing several yards away. The rest were coming into view now, too, moving instinctively toward Ranulf, all talking at once, some swearing, others saying that they'd heard the clamor, one man just whispering "Merciful Jesus" over and over, as if he knew no other words.

The priest was there, too, having followed them as they raced past his church, fearing the worst and finding it. After a horrified pause, he began to move among the bodies, seeking to do what he could, stirring the others to action, too.

Peryf was groaning, his eyelids fluttering. Coming back to consciousness, he came back, too, to immediate recall, and started to struggle upright, had to be restrained by Ranulf and Tathan. "Davydd," he gasped. "It was Davydd and Rhodri . . . Christ, it happened so fast, Ranulf! They were upon us ere we knew it and we were so outnumbered—Hywel! Where is Hywel? Find him, Ranulf, find him!"

"I will," Ranulf promised. "Just lie still, Peryf. I'll be back." Beckoning Tathan aside, he said softly, "Stay with him. Whatever . . . whatever happens, he's already lost a brother. Iddon is dead."

Tathan blanched. "God help him, for so is Brochfael."

They looked at each other, neither knowing what to say. And then Ranulf turned away to hunt for Hywel.

The fog hid the worst of the bloodshed. So did the utter blackness of a January night. With no stars, no lanterns, they stumbled around in the dark, going from body to body, seeking to find the living midst the dead. Ranulf had not seen so many casualties since Lincoln, that long-ago battle of his youth, which ended with the capture of a king. Would Hywel be as lucky as Stephen? That was a question with no answer, a question to raise the hairs on the back of his neck and start icy sweat oozing down his ribs.

He almost fell over Caradog, twisted aside just in time. Kneeling, he touched the young man's face. His skin was still warm, but the eyes staring up at Ranulf were sightless, empty. Ranulf reached out and gently closed them, trying not to think of all that Caradog would never see now. Coming slowly to his feet, he continued to search the field for Hywel.

He heard someone shout that Caswallon was alive, and that emboldened him to call out for Hywel. His cry was quickly taken up, for men were no more equal in death than they were in life, and Hywel's blood was worth more to Wales than any spilled by the other victims of this island ambush. Ranulf began to shout for Hywel again, shouting until he was hoarse, hearing only echoes on the wind. But then he saw the dog.

The wolfhound was crouched by a low hedge of hawthorn, shivering with fear. It whimpered as Ranulf approached, shrinking back as he held out his hand. With a leaden step, he drew closer. He moved around the hawthorn and there he found Hywel.

He lay motionless on the ground, a bloodied spear protruding from his side. Crying out for help, Ranulf dropped to his knees beside him. There was a moment of wild hope when he saw Hywel's chest rise and fall. Hywel's breathing was shallow and labored, his heart not yet ready to stop beating, and when Ranulf gripped his hand, the fingers closed weakly over his. But blood was trickling from the corner of his mouth and his dark eyes were losing the light. He did not look afraid or even in pain, just surprised. He struggled for enough breath to speak as time ran out, and his face blurred for Ranulf in a haze of hot tears. When he blinked them back, Hywel was gone and the hand in his was inert, unresponsive.

Men were cursing and crying. From a great distance, Ranulf heard a wail of anguish, and he wondered numbly if Peryf knew that at least three of his brothers had died with Hywel. The priest was beside him now, giving the last rites to the man who so many saw as Wales's best hope, giving them all the only comfort he could, the salvation of Hywel's immortal soul. Ranulf did not move, no longer hearing the babel of voices. He looked up at the fog-shrouded sky, down at Hywel's body, and then he wept, for himself and for Hywel, for Peryf and his brothers, for all the good men who had met sudden death in the vale of Pentraeth, but above all, for Wales.

CHAPTER THIRTY-FIVE

March 1171
Poitiers, Poitou

OW MANY DAYS until Maundy Thursday?"

Raoul de Faye's question seemed idly put, innocuous. Maud knew better. It was a sly thrust at her cousin the English king, for it was customary for the Pope to issue excommunications and interdicts upon that day, the Thursday before Easter.

"I have not been keeping count," she lied coolly, as if she had not been grudging every day's dawning for the past month. Henry's envoys had departed for the papal court weeks ago, racing the calendar to arrive before Maundy Thursday. Thomas Becket's cross-bearer, Alexander Llewelyn, was known to be on the road to Italy, too, bearing letters from the French king and outraged French bishops. If he reached the Pope before Henry's emissaries, a Maundy Thursday thunderbolt was almost a certainty.

"It is less than a fortnight," Raoul supplied helpfully. "I wonder how far the Angevin's minions have gotten by now. For all we know, they are snowbound somewhere in the Alps, using his papal petitions for firewood."

"You sound as if you hope that to be true," Maud observed, and he gave her what he thought was a candid, disarming grin, allowing that he'd not be heartbroken if Henry's agents were lost until the spring thaw.

Maud studied him with speculative, critical eyes. Raoul had been verbally sparring with her since her arrival in Eleanor's capital the preceding week. At first she'd dismissed his sniping as an echo of Petronilla's antagonism, but she was reassessing that assumption. Petronilla was jealous of her intimacy with Eleanor, and obviously so was Raoul. But Petronilla's resentment was personal and his was political. He wanted no rivals for Eleanor's ear, no trusted confidants to offer advice that was not his. Not for the first time in her life, Maud marveled that men could be such fools. As if Eleanor would ever be any man's pawn, be he husband or uncle.

Raoul's smug satisfaction grated upon her nerves. They were jackals, she thought scornfully, nipping at Harry's heels, hoping against hope that the lion was cornered at last. She had a weapon of her own—knowledge that Raoul did not possess—and she used it now to retaliate.

"It grieves me," she said gravely, "that you find such joy in wishing misfortune upon the king's ambassadors. One of them is my beloved brother, the Bishop of Worcester." Although addressed ostensibly to Raoul, her retort was actually aimed at their audience, and it achieved the desired result. Her sorrowful dignity stirred chivalric urges in the listening men and their disapproval discomfited Raoul. In the indolent, pleasure-seeking society of Aquitaine, bad manners were often judged more harshly than sins.

MAUD HAD NOT LINGERED in the great hall after her victory; she had no interest in exchanging poisoned pleasantries with Raoul or Petronilla. Her confident pose was just that: a pose. She was deeply concerned for her cousin, fearing that Henry would be branded as an enemy of God by the enraged Pope. She worried, too, about Roger, for a winter crossing of the Alps was fraught with peril. And in the past few days, she'd become aware that Eleanor was troubled by more than her husband's jeopardy.

She discovered the queen's secret later that night, purely by chance. She'd gone into the chapel upon discovering that it was unoccupied, for solitude was rarely found midst the clamor and commotion of a royal court. After saying prayers for the souls of her parents and dead brothers, for friends long gone and the husband who was surely burning in Hell these seventeen years past, she then prayed for the salvation of a Welsh prince whose laughter was stilled, his music silenced.

She was about to depart when she heard footsteps out in the stairwell leading up to Eleanor's private chamber. One of the queen's men was escorting a woman muffled from head to foot in a dark, enveloping mantle, an odd choice of apparel on a mild spring eve. Maud's curiosity was piqued by the clandestine behavior of the couple; had one of Eleanor's ladies dared to tryst with a lover in her mistress's own bed? As they passed the chapel door, whispering furtively, she acted on impulse and stepped out to confront them.

Recoiling sharply, the woman grasped the hood of her cloak, drawing back into its folds like a turtle into its shell. The man reacted with equal dispatch, hurrying her by Maud before any words could be exchanged. Maud stood utterly still in the stairwell, staring after them. A cry rose in her throat, a name that never left her lips. For just the span of an indrawn breath, she'd looked upon the other woman's face, no more than that, but time enough for recognition. This mysterious, shrouded figure being spirited from the queen's chamber with such secrecy was Bertrade, her midwife.

ELEANOR HAD unbraided her hair and was brushing it out, a nightly ritual that should have been soothing in its very familiarity. Not tonight; her thoughts continued to careen about: unwelcome, illogical, and unexpected. Picking up a mirror, she examined her metallic reflection with critical eyes, seeing a tired, pale woman gazing back at her, an aging stranger.

The sudden pounding startled her and she frowned toward the door, vexed by this proof of the edgy state of her nerves. Before she could respond, it was pushed open and her cousin by marriage burst into the chamber. But this was a Maud she'd not seen before, white-faced and tense, so obviously agitated that Eleanor felt a surge of alarm.

"Maud? What is wrong? It is not Richard—"

"No," Maud said hastily, "nothing like that. The last I saw of him, Richard was in the hall, playing chess with one of your household knights too new to know better."

Eleanor smiled faintly. "Richard turns every game into a life or death struggle. And when he loses, he demands an immediate rematch. But if nothing is amiss, why did you come running in here as if the palace was afire?"

Maud hestitated, for this was one of the rare times when she'd reacted on instinct, not thinking out beforehand what she would do. The sight of Bertrade had propelled her up the stairs, for the memory of Eleanor's last birthing was still harrowing even after the passage of more than four years. Not knowing what to say, she could only fall back upon the truth. "Eleanor . . . I saw her leaving."

"Saw whom?"

"Bertrade. It was not her fault; she was being very circumspect." Eleanor's face was a graven mask, utterly unrevealing, but Maud forged ahead, nonetheless. "I know I am intruding and I know that trespassers risk being—"

"Maud, I am not with child."

"If it is still early enough, there are herbs like artemisia and pennyroyal or savin—"

"You are not listening to me. I am not pregnant."

This time Maud believed her. "But you thought you were." Reading Eleanor's silence as assent, she crossed the room and took the brush from the other woman's hand. Eleanor didn't object and for a time it was quiet. Maud concentrated upon brushing the queen's hair until it gleamed like a long, dark rope.

"You have beautiful hair," she said. "Did you ever wish that it was a fashionable flaxen shade?"

"No," Eleanor said, and then, "I've had to start dyeing it."

"To hide the grey? Me, too."

"I thought I was . . . pregnant, I mean. I've not had a flux since December. But Bertrade says no, that I've reached that time in life when a woman's menses cease. She says it usually happens by age fifty." Eleanor's shoulders lifted in a slight shrug. "I'm forty-eight."

Maud kept silent, continuing to brush Eleanor's hair.

"It makes no sense. I was horrified to think I was pregnant again, Maud. I've been drinking wine mixed with the juice of willow leaves so I'd not conceive. I should be so relieved . . ."

"I understand," Maud said softly. "Any woman would."

"But no man." Eleanor rose suddenly, moved to the table, and poured wine into two gilded cups. Handing one to Maud, she said, "I took your advice, after all."

"Which advice was that?"

"A long time ago, it was, more than eleven years. I was wroth with Harry for failing to win Toulouse, and Petra was adding fuel to the fire. You told me—not in so many words—that I was being foolish and short-sighted. It took a while, but I came to see that you were right."

Maud glanced quickly toward Eleanor, their eyes catching and holding. She remembered. She had warned Eleanor that she must either accept Harry as he is or learn to love him less.

POPE ALEXANDER was so appalled by the news of Thomas Becket's murder that he refused to meet with Englishmen for more than a week. But Henry's envoys were still able to persuade him not to issue a sentence of excommunication, taking oaths that the English king would abide by any papal judgment. The Pope contented himself with pronouncing a general sentence of excommunication against the murderers of the archbishop and all who had given them counsel, countenance, aid. Nor did he lay England under interdict, although he subsequently confirmed the interdict laid by the Archbishop of Sens upon Henry's continental domains. He also confirmed the sentences of excommunication and suspension imposed by Thomas Becket upon the Bishops of London and Salisbury and the Archbishop of York, prohibited Henry from entering any church for the time being, and announced that he would be sending papal legates to Normandy to meet with the English king and judge whether he was "truly humbled."

GERALD DE BARRI always felt his heart swell upon his first sight of St David's. Hidden away in a secluded hollow by the River Alun, the cathedral burst into view like a flower in sudden bloom, resplendent even in a chilly Welsh downpour. The original church had been built in the sixth century by the patron saint of Wales. The present cathedral was a lodestone for the faithful, attracting pilgrims from the far-flung corners of Christendom. For Gerald, it was much more; his uncle was the Bishop of St David's.

Urging his mount forward, Gerald vowed to make sure the poor beast got a rubdown and a bran mash, rich fare for a hired horse. He knew, though, that he'd pushed the animal mercilessly. The ride from Pembroke was less than twenty miles, but the day was wet, the September weather foul, and he'd set a punishing pace, so eager was he to reach Menevia while the English king was still there.

After finding a trustworthy groom to take care of his horse, he took time for a quick wash-up before seeking his uncle and the king; both vanity and practicality dictated that he not appear before them in muddied disarray. He then plunged out into the rain again, hurrying toward the church. He arrived just as the Mass had ended and slipped inconspicuously in the south door, mingling with the canons and English lords as he awaited his chance.

It came sooner than he expected. The king had halted in the nave, surrounded by his entourage and well-wishers and royal watchers. Murmuring an excuse to his highborn guest, the bishop hastened toward the door. Gerald darted forward to intercept him just as he stepped out onto the porch.

"Uncle David!"

The bishop blinked "Gerald! What are you doing here, lad?" Not waiting for his nephew's response, he enfolded the young man in an affectionate embrace. "Why did you not write that you were coming home? Ah, but you'll never guess who is inside the cathedral!"

"I already know! I heard as soon as my ship dropped anchor at The Cross. He's staying at Pembroke Castle whilst awaiting favorable winds for Ireland. People in the town were talking of nothing else. I had planned to head for Manorbier first, but when I heard the king was at Menevia . . . well, I thought if we met, he'd be likely to remember me in the future." Gerald acknowledged his aspirations with a forthright grin; in his family, pride was not one of the Seven Deadly Sins. "Has a king ever visited St David's ere this? When you heard he was at Pembroke, did you dare hope he'd come here?"

"I hoped he would not," Bishop David confided softly, and when Gerald stared at him in surprise, he glanced around surreptitiously to be sure they were not overheard. "It is a great honor, of course. But it is also a great burden, for we have not the resources of an English cathedral. We do not have enough in our larders and pantries to feed so many and I am loath to shame us by providing a meager meal for the king. Moreover, the longer he stays, the more dire our straits. A three-day visit could eat up our entire winter supplies."

Gerald was very fond of his uncle; David was paying for a first-rate education at the University of Paris. But he deplored his kinsman's shortsighted approach to life. Were he the Bishop of St David's, he'd gladly have put the canons on starvation rations if that earned him the favor of a king—even a king in disgrace.

"Where does he stand with the Church these days, Uncle? In Paris, rumor had it that the Holy Father was still deliberating his fate. Is there any chance that you are entertaining an excommunicate?"

Bishop David shuddered. "Jesú forfend!" Even though they were alone on the porch, he lowered his voice still further, continuing in a throaty whisper. "I assume you know that the Bishops of Worcester and Evreux and Lisieux were able to persuade the Pope not to issue an excommunication on Maundy Thursday. His Holiness then appointed a commission to investigate the king's complicity in the murder of the martyred Thomas. But they have reached no conclusions. In fact, I believe they are still en route to Normandy. So at least I need not fear that I have invited Ishmael into God's House!"

Pope Alexander had also forbidden the English king to enter a church until his guilt or innocence could be determined, but Gerald kindly forbore to remind his uncle of that. For all he knew, the Holy Father had lifted this proscription; he had, after all, absolved the Bishops of London and Salisbury of their excommunication. Gerald was a student of history and he knew that kings were rarely cast out into darkness, for most Popes were astute practitioners of political power. Only outright defiance could guarantee a papal thunderbolt, and the English king was too shrewd to fall into that trap.

" 'Ishmael'? Discussing Scriptures, my lord bishop?" This new voice was low-pitched and ironically amused, the voice of a man who never had to raise it to be heard. Gerald guessed the identity of the speaker even before he swung around to face the king of the English.

Bishop David flushed and began to fling words about as if they were lifelines, hoping that one of them might be his rescue, distracting Henry from what he may have overheard. He made the introductions with over-hearty enthusiasm, and as his nephew knelt before the king, he babbled on nervously about Gerald's accomplishments, the fine career ahead of him in the Church once his studies were done.

Gerald was not easily embarrassed, scorned false modesty, and usually enjoyed hearing his virtues lauded. But not under these circumstances, and he earnestly entreated his uncle to desist, insisting that the King's Grace could not be interested in the doings of an "obscure scholar."

"Not obscure for long, I'd wager," Henry observed, for he knew Gerald's family and there was not a one of them born without a craving for fame and fortune. Gerald de Barri was the grandson of a celebrated Marcher lord and a Welsh princess, a woman so lovely that men had called her the Helen of Wales. The Lady Nest gave Henry an incongruous link with the young clerk, for Gerald's beautiful grandmother had become the mistress of his own grandfather, the lascivious old king, Henry I.

Henry could think of any number of bawdy jokes to make about this dubious connection, but he regretfully refrained, for he was supposed to be on his best behavior. Reminding himself of that, he ignored the tempting subject of the Lady Nest, instead offered some courtesies about the cathedral, the saint's shrine, and the bishop's hospitality.

Bishop David gulped and then did what he must, declaring that the King's Grace and his entourage were welcome at St David's for as long as it might please them, seeking to disguise his discomfort with lavish compliments and much talk about the "honor" of this royal visit.

Henry knew better. "That is most kind of you, my lord bishop. We will, of course, be pleased to dine with you. But I regret that we cannot accept your generous invitation to stay at Menevia, for I must return to Pembroke this eve."

Bishop David's relief was so transparent that Henry had to hold back a smile. His uncle Ranulf had often joked that a royal visitation was about as welcome as a biblical plague of locusts, stripping bare every cupboard and blade of grass in their path. Had the bishop looked upon life with more humor, Henry might have jested about his plight. As it was, he contented himself with the knowledge that his pilgrimage to St David's had gone so well. Facing a fearsome sea voyage to Ireland, it behooved a man of faith to court the goodwill of one of the most celebrated of Christendom's saints. And if word of his visit—and his offerings of brocaded silk and silver coins—got back to the Holy See, so much the better. He well knew that his papal currency had dwindled down to a handful of farthings, not enough to buy delay, much less absolution.

"I NEED HAVE NO FEARS of Purgatory when I die, for I am expiating all of my sins on the road to Pembroke," Rainald moaned, no longer bothering to clutch his mantle close against the gusting rain; he was already drenched, wetter than any fish.

"Somehow, Uncle, I doubt that your sins can be as easily shriven as all that."

Rainald turned in the saddle to glower at his companion. It wasn't Roger's joking that offended him. He was vexed that his nephew could sound so cheerful under such drear circumstances: riding along a muddy mountain path in a pouring rain as night came on, all because his other nephew was a lunatic. Who but a lunatic would drag them out into a storm when they could be snugly abed back at the bishop's palace?

Roger knew exactly what he was thinking, for Rainald had been complaining nonstop. "We're almost there," he said encouragingly. "Surely you can endure a few more miles?" Getting another groan in reply, he kicked his stallion lightly in the ribs and overtook his cousin, riding just ahead.

Henry slanted a smile over his shoulder. "Is Uncle Rainald hurling more curses at my head?"

"Be thankful he does not practice the Black Arts or you'd have been struck down miles ago." Roger grinned, for he was still young enough to share Henry's indifference to the weather. "I think you are to be commended, Harry, for sparing the bishop's larders and his pride. It was plain to see that he could not afford the openhanded hospitality that we'd find in Normandy or England. As it was, some of our men had to eat standing up even though you'd deliberately limited your escort to three hundred. If we'd stayed overnight, St David's might never have recovered from the honor!"

The rain was coming down too heavily for Henry to see his cousin's face, but Roger's voice held a levity that he hadn't heard for almost a year. Roger had defended him before the French court, and then made the dangerous winter journey across the Alps to argue his case to the Pope. He'd accompanied Henry back to England in August, ending his self-imposed exile, yet Henry knew that Roger held him responsible for Thomas Becket's death. Roger did not confuse the legal concepts of "innocent" and "not guilty," nor would he pretend otherwise. But Henry had noticed a thawing in recent weeks.

It had begun at Wolvesey Palace, when he and Roger paid a visit to Henry of Blois. The aged Bishop of Winchester was blind and feeble. He had not minced his words, though, bluntly telling the king that once he'd unleashed the hounds of Hell, he could not claim he was blameless for the destruction they did. Very few people had ever dared to speak to Henry with such uncompromising candor. Winchester had known he was dying and that may have unbridled his tongue. Henry had known he was dying, too, and so he'd accepted a judgment he thought to be unfair and biased; how likely was he to receive impartial justice from Stephen's brother? He'd tried to view his silence as penance, for even at his most defiant, he could not deny that his reckless words had set in motion the bloody killing at Canterbury. But on this rain-sodden Michaelmas night, he saw the first flickering of light after months of darkness, the realization that his friendship with his cousin Roger might one day emerge from the shadow cast by Thomas Becket's murder.

ALTHOUGH HE'D NOT have admitted it, even Henry was relieved when they finally rode into the bailey of Pembroke Castle. Warming himself before the hearth in his bedchamber, he waved his squires aside when they would have helped him to undress. "Later, lads. For now, just fetch me some red wine."

The youths exchanged startled looks, for that was a rare request. Eager to please him, they made a hasty departure for the buttery, already starting to squabble over which wine to select, Gascon or Rhenish, even though they knew Henry would want whatever they chose watered down.

As soon as they were gone, Henry sat down on a coffer, stretching his muddied boots toward the fire. He'd been detained at Pembroke for a fortnight, his will thwarted by westerly winds, and the delay was shredding his patience raw although his stay had been quite productive so far. In addition to his pilgrimage to St David's, he'd made peace with the most powerful of the Welsh rulers, Rhys ap Gruffydd, accepted the submission of the erring Earl of Pembroke, and even enjoyed several successful hunts, the rain notwithstanding. But he was eager to be on his way and he knew these contrary winds could continue to blow for weeks to come.

He'd just taken his boots off when a knock sounded. "Enter," he said, not bothering to turn around. But it was not his returning squires. Glancing over his shoulder, he was surprised to see both Rainald and Roger beaming at him. "Why are you two not abed?"

"We've brought you a visitor."

"At this hour? What would you have done if I'd been asleep?"

Rainald dismissed the objection with an airy wave of his hand. "We'd have had to awaken you, of course." He and Roger exchanged grins, looking more like gleeful coconspirators than earl and bishop, stalwarts of the king's council.

Puzzled and faintly irked by their complacent smiles and baffling behavior, Henry got to his feet as they stepped aside, revealing the man standing behind them in the doorway. And then a smile of his own slowly spread across his face.

"What are you waiting for, Uncle?" he said. "Come on in."

After a barely perceptible hesitation, Ranulf did.

Henry's squires had fallen asleep on their pallets. So had Rainald, who was sprawled, snoring, in the window seat. Roger held out longer, but at last he, too, was nodding drowsily and stifling yawns. "I'm going to bed now and leaving word that I'm not to be awakened until Friday." Ignoring Henry and Ranulf's gibes of "milksop" and "weakling," he headed for the door.

They'd been conversing easily, interrupting each other freely, lapsing back into the bantering familiarity of a lifetime, almost as if the past six years' estrangement had never been. They had discussed Henry's plans for Ireland, where he meant to foil the ambitions of his Marcher lords, put a halt to the ongoing strife, and aid the Irish bishops in their attempt to bring Irish Church practices into conformity with Roman law. They had talked of Henry's family, scattered throughout the Angevin empire like feathers on the wind: Eleanor in Poitiers with Richard and Joanna and Aenor, Hal in Normandy, Geoffrey in Brittany, Tilda in Germany, and John with the nuns at Fontevrault Abbey. And they had spoken of the smoldering tinderbox that was Wales.

North Wales had fragmented in the aftermath of Hywel's death at Pentraeth. Gwynedd had been divided up amongst Owain's surviving sons, with the lion's share going to Davydd and Rhodri, Môn to Maelgwn, Nanconwy to Iorwerth, and the commotes in the west to Cynan. Few doubted, though, that this partitioned peace was doomed, kindling for yet another Welsh war of succession.

In the south, it was different. Rhys ap Gruffydd had none to challenge his supremacy, none but the might of the English Crown, and he had made a coldly calculated decision to ally himself to that alien power. He'd come to Henry near the Welsh border, offering hostages, horses, oxen, and fealty. Ranulf understood why he'd done so, and thought that Owain might have understood, too. But he did wonder if any mention had been made of the hostage son who had suffered for Rhys's broken faith, the son now known as Maredudd Ddall, Maredudd the Blind.

When Roger shuffled sleepily off to bed, Henry had been telling Ranulf that he'd waived payment of most of Rhys's proffered tribute, rec-

ognized Rhys's right to lands claimed by the Marcher Houses of Clare and
Clifford, and returned to him another son long held hostage at the English
court. But now that he and Ranulf were alone for the first time, their
conversation's flow began to ebb, soon slowing to a trickle.

They studied each other silently in the fire's erratic glow, listening to
the crackle of flames, the raspy sounds of Rainald's snoring, the rhythm
of rain upon the roof. Henry sipped his wine, oblivious to what he was
tasting. "I grieved for you when I learned of Hywel ab Owain's death," he
said softly. "He was a brave man, a gifted poet, and good company."

Ranulf inclined his head. "Yes . . . he was."

"I was concerned on your behalf, too, Uncle, for I very much
doubted that Davydd ab Owain would let you dwell unmolested in domains now his."

"He did not."

Henry waited a moment and then prodded, "Well?"

"I thought it best to depart Trefriw lest I drag my uncle Rhodri down
with me. My elder son joined the service of Hywel's brother Cynan, and
Rhiannon and our younger children are dwelling now at my manor in
Shropshire . . ."

Color had crept into Ranulf's face, spreading upward from throat to
forehead, and Henry set his cup down in surprise once he noticed the
older man's discomfort. Ranulf was quiet again and Henry shifted impatiently, but this time he did not prompt, waiting for Ranulf to continue
on his own.

Ranulf was still deeply flushed. "I realize you might well think that
this is why I am here, Harry, to mend fences now that I've returned to England. But that is not so. I came not to regain royal favor—"

Henry had been staring at him incredulously and now burst out
laughing. "Jesus God, Ranulf! In all my life, I've never known a man so
uncalculating, so lacking in avarice. Did you truly think I'd doubt your
motives? After you turned down an earldom?"

Ranulf joined in his laughter, somewhat sheepishly. "You will admit
it was an awkward coincidence, though, that I should seek you out once
I am back on English soil. I could hardly blame you for harboring some
suspicions."

"And I usually breathe in suspicions as I breathe in air," Henry conceded. "But not with you, Uncle." He hoped that Ranulf understood his
assertion for what it was, the rarest of compliments. Death had claimed

his confidants one by one—his parents, his brother Will—leaving only Rosamund and Eleanor and his sons, who were still green, untried lads. "Whether it be the doings of the Almighty or your 'awkward coincidence,' Ranulf, I am not likely to question it, just to be glad of it."

Ranulf's smile was still the smile of his youth, curiously untouched by time. "I'm glad, too," he said. "I've missed you, lad."

Henry's answering smile never reached his eyes. "I ought to leave well enough alone," he said, "but I'd not mislead you by my silence. I deeply regret our falling-out over the Welsh hostages. I am sorry that there are men who dwell in darkness because of my command. But in all honesty, if I had to do it over again . . . most likely I would, Ranulf."

"I know." Ranulf had spent much of his life watching those he loved wrestle with the seductive, lethal lure of kingship. It had proved the ruination of his cousin Stephen, a good man who had not made a good king. For his sister Maude, it had been an unrequited love affair, a passion she could neither capture nor renounce. For Hywel, it had been an illusion, a golden glow ever shimmering along the horizon. He believed that his nephew had come the closest to mastery of it, but at what cost?

Henry rose and padded barefoot across the chamber to pour more wine for Ranulf, spilling only a splash into his own cup. He detoured to snatch a blanket from his bed and drape it over Rainald's shoulders before returning to the hearth. "The drawbridge is down, the parapets unmanned. You may not get another chance to catch me with my defenses in such disarray. Are there any questions you would put to me?"

Ranulf smiled and shook his head, and Henry's brows shot upward. "Not even about Thomas Becket?"

"No."

Henry studied Ranulf's face intently, and then exhaled a breath soft as a sigh, for he saw that his uncle was utterly sincere, free of all doubts or misgivings about the manner in which Becket met his death. "A pity the Pope does not share your certainty," he said, with a flippancy that did not deceive Ranulf in the least.

"I know that the Pope has dispatched two cardinal legates to investigate the killing, and I know, too, that both men are said to be strongly predisposed in Becket's favor," he said and Henry grimaced his agreement.

"I think we can safely assume that there will be some finding of fault."

"Is that why you are going to Ireland, then, to delay the reckoning with the Church?"

Henry feigned indignation. "Such cynicism ill becomes you, Uncle. Would you have me sit on my hands whilst my Marcher lords carve out Irish kingdoms for themselves?"

"But Roger told me that the Earl of Pembroke hastened from Ireland to meet you at Newnham and made an abject submission to assuage your wrath," Ranulf pointed out, and Henry shrugged.

"Yes, he came to his senses right quickly. By that time, though, I already had an army assembled. If you go to the trouble of saddling a horse, you're going to want to ride it."

Ranulf was amused by his nephew's ability to avoid giving a direct answer. "If lamprey is not your favorite dish, it ought to be, for your slipperiness could put any eel to shame. I know you can give me reasons beyond counting why you must go to Ireland, beginning with that Papal Bull you were granted some years ago to bring Ireland under subjugation to Rome. Nor do I doubt that you want to teach your Marcher lords that if they try to fly too high, you'll clip their wings. But I still say that if the Irish isle was not even more remote than Wales, you'd not be so keen to spend the winter there."

Henry yielded, then, with a grin. "I see these past six years have not robbed you of any of your stubbornness. If you must hear me say it, so be it. The longer I can stave off the Church's verdict, the less likely it will be an excommunication or interdict and the more likely they'll offer terms I can live with."

Ranulf raised his cup in a fond, sardonic salute. "Now that I think of it, there is a question I want to ask you. Rumors about the Canterbury killers have taken root in every alehouse, every marketplace, and are sprouting faster than the hardiest weeds. I've been told that they have gone on Crusade to make amends, that you've dispatched men to hunt them down without mercy, that in the months since the killing, they've all begun to sicken, stricken by unknown maladies that have no cure. What is the truth of it, Harry?"

"The last I heard, they had gone to ground at Hugh de Morville's castle at Knaresborough in Yorkshire, where I daresay they are hoping to ride out the storm."

"But you have not moved against them?"

"No," Henry said, frowning into the depths of his wine cup. "They thought they were doing my bidding, Ranulf. Even though they wounded me almost as grievously as they did Thomas, they were arrows launched from my bow, men who were acting upon my own angry, imprudent words. I admit that I have been known to dissemble at times, for that is an essential aspect of statecraft. But I am not a hypocrite."

"No," Ranulf agreed, although not as wholeheartedly as Henry would have liked. It was not that Ranulf disbelieved him. But life had taught him that men learned to justify themselves almost as soon as they learned to talk, and he suspected that kings had more need than most to vindicate their acts. "What do you think will happen to them, Harry?"

Henry shrugged again. "If they are wise, they'll confess their sins, repent, and throw themselves upon the mercy of the Church. Of course the only penalties they'd face are spiritual. The ultimate absurdity of this, Ranulf, is that their crime is one the Church would deny me the right to punish. Thomas insisted unto his final breath that only the Church could judge the offenses of men in holy orders and any crimes committed against them."

"I do not imagine Thomas would appreciate the irony of that," Ranulf said dryly. "From what I've heard, he cast off humor when he put on the sacred pallium."

"For certes, he did when he donned that wretched hair shirt," Henry agreed, sounding more perplexed than sarcastic. He'd been shaken by the revelation of Becket's secret mortification, and months later, he still could not reconcile that man with the one he'd known—or thought he'd known. He waved Ranulf off when his uncle would have refilled his cup, for wine was not the key to the enigma that was Thomas Becket.

"I thought he was the hypocrite," he admitted. "In that, I was wrong. No man would wear a filthy, lice-ridden garment next to his private parts if he did not believe utterly in the sanctity of his cause. The chafing alone must have driven him half-mad!" He smiled then, without much humor. "How could I have so misjudged him, Ranulf?"

Ranulf did not answer at once, for he understood the honor inherent in the question; he was likely the only man to whom his nephew could pose that query. "I think," he said slowly, "that Hywel saw him with the clearest eye. He said once that Thomas reminded him of a chameleon, changing his color to reflect his surroundings."

Henry raised his head, considering that. "Well," he said, "if Hywel is right, the fault is still mine, then, for insisting he take the archbishopric. If I'd kept him as my chancellor, we both might have fared better."

"I'd heard that the Pope has agreed to absolve the Bishops of London and Salisbury. But what of the Archbishop of York? Does his suspension still hold?"

"For now it does. I expect, though, that he'll eventually get it lifted."

"And the de Brocs? What of them?"

That was a question Henry preferred not to answer. He didn't doubt that they had been implicated in Becket's murder, but he still had need of their services in Kent. He sought to divert Ranulf's attention by changing the subject. "I do not suppose you've heard about the latest misfortune to befall Gilbert Foliot? He took ill this past August, was burning with fever until they began to despair of his life. The Bishop of Salisbury had come to give him comfort, and he kept urging Gilbert to let him pray to Thomas for deliverance. Gilbert finally agreed, his fever soon broke, and within a few days, he was well on the road to recovery."

Ranulf grinned. "Was his misfortune that he was so gravely ill . . . or that he may have owed his recovery to Thomas Becket?"

"Both, I suspect," Henry said and laughed. "Poor Gilbert. He is truly torn between his dislike of the man and his awe of the martyr!"

It was quiet for a time after that, but it was a companionable quiet, bred of intimacy and affection. Henry absentmindedly scratched the ears of one of his wolfhounds and Ranulf smothered a yawn.

"I think I shall have to be off to bed," he said. "These old bones of mine need more rest than yours."

Henry glanced up, then nodded. "Ranulf . . . do you think Thomas Becket was a saint?"

"I do not know, Harry."

"There is much talk of miracles at his tomb and the like. But surely that is not proof? There are fools aplenty who are credulous enough to believe any nonsense that reaches their ears."

"I've heard of these miracles," Ranulf acknowledged, "and in truth, I do not know what to make of them. To us, Thomas was a mortal man, one like any other, with his share of flaws and follies. It is difficult to envision him a saint."

"Well nigh impossible," Henry commented trenchantly. "Did I ever tell you what he was reported to have said about the expulsion of his kinfolk and servants? When he was told that some of them were on their way to join him at Pontigny, he replied that as long as their souls were saved, he cared not if they were flayed to the bone. How saintly does that sound?"

"Well . . . not very. But I suppose it could be argued that saints care only for the spiritual and not the corporeal."

"Do you believe that?" Henry demanded and Ranulf shook his head, smiling.

"No, not really. I cannot answer your question, Harry, doubt that any-one can. I do know, though, that saints are not judged like ordinary men. That is, after all, what makes them saints."

Henry drained the last of his wine, then looked up at Ranulf, his ex-pression an odd one, at once skeptical and regretful. "Saint or not," he conceded, "Thomas got the last word for certes."

H EAVY RAINS and westerly winds continued to keep Henry at Pembroke. Another week went by. Roger departed, returning to Nor-mandy to await the arrival of the papal legates. Rhys ap Gruffydd arrived and Henry agreed to an elaborate banquet, as much to banish boredom as to honor Rhys.

Seated at the high table with Henry, Rhys, Rainald, the Earls of Pem-broke and Hertford, and the Bishop of St David's, Ranulf drank the wine offered and ate the venison and fresh pike and pheasant, but he was not really enjoying himself. He missed Rhiannon, missed his children, missed Hywel and the life he'd lost at Trefriw. He was glad that he and his nephew had made peace; their breach was a wound that had never fully healed. Yet even his pleasure was diluted these days and left an aftertaste.

When the meal was done and the trestle tables cleared away for the entertainment, Henry signaled for silence. "Did you know, Uncle, that Hywel's foster brother has written a tribute to him?"

Ranulf shook his head, glancing from Henry to Rhys, back to Henry again. The Welsh prince's bard had come forward, claiming the center of attention and waiting until his audience quieted. "This elegy is not mine, although I wish it were. The poet is Peryf ap Cedifor, and he writes of what he saw, what he felt, what he lost at Pentraeth. Peryf agreed that I could sing his words, share his grief, and it is my great honor to present *The Killing of Hywel.*

While we were seven men alive, not three sevens
Challenged or routed us;
Now, alas, dauntless in battle,
Of that seven, three are left.

Ranulf balled his fists at his sides, grateful that Peryf was not the one performing his lament. Four brothers he'd lost at Pentraeth, and Hywel, brother in all but blood. He was no longer listening to the bard's words, his eyes misting with tears. But then the tone changed, from mournful to embittered.

Because of the treachery brewed, unchristian Briton,
By Cristyn and her sons,
Let there be left alive in Môn
Not one of her blotched kindred!
Despite what good comes from holding land,
World is a treacherous dwelling:
Woe, to you, cruel Davydd,
To stab tall Hywel, hawk of war!

Only Ranulf, Rhys, and his men understood the elegy, as it had been recited in Welsh. But the hall had fallen silent, for there were haunting echoes of heartbreak in the pulsing plaint of the harp. Henry moved toward Ranulf, his eyes marking the tear tracks upon his uncle's face. "I thought it would please you to honor Hywel. Was I wrong?"

"No . . . I'm glad you did. It would have pleased Hywel, too." Ranulf mustered up a shadowy smile. "He always did have a liking for center stage."

As Henry turned away in response to a query from the Earl of Pembroke, Ranulf took the opportunity to withdraw. He'd lost enough loved ones to know that even the greatest pain would eventually dull its edges. His grieving for Hywel no longer pressed against his chest like the heaviest of stones, no longer tore at his lungs with each constricted breath. If not fully tamed yet, the hurt was becoming accustomed to being handled; almost broken to the saddle, he thought, with a flicker of black humor that Hywel would have approved. It was the regret that he found hardest to live with. He sometimes pictured a wheel in his brain, spinning over and over in remorseless rhythm to those most tragic and futile of words: *if only, what if.*

It was then that he overheard it, a casual comment made by Rhys to one of his retainers. Peryf's lament drew its strength from his sorrow, not his style, Rhys observed, adding that his poetry could not hold a candle to Hywel's.

Noticing for the first time that Ranulf was within hearing range, the Welsh lord gave a half-humorous, half-embarrassed grimace. "You caught me out," he conceded. "I did not mean to slight Peryf's talent. It is just that I think Hywel was a better poet, one who'll be remembered far longer than Peryf."

"No offense taken," Ranulf said. "I doubt that even Peryf would argue with your assessment. Hywel's poetry will live on even after his memory fades." And when he realized how much truth there was in that prediction, he found it gave him considerable solace. Hywel had made words soar higher than hawks, his songs celebrating his love of life, women, and Wales. That might be a legacy more lasting than even a kingship.

HENRY'S FLEET had assembled at The Cross, just downstream of the castle at the mouth of the River Pembroke. It was an impressive sight, for he'd required four hundred ships to transport thirty-five hundred men, five hundred knights, horses, and provisions. On this Saturday in mid-October, the waiting was finally over. With favorable winds at last, anchors were raised, shrouds tightened, sails unfurled, and the fleet got underway.

Ranulf and Rainald had bade Henry farewell, then mounted their horses to ride along the north shore so they could watch the ships enter the estuary. The sun was sinking in the west and the sky was a dusky copper, obscuring the horizon in a golden haze. The first stars had not yet appeared, but the absence of clouds promised a clear, moonlit night. The tranquillity of the scene was illusory, though, for sixty miles of open sea had to be navigated before the ships saw land again.

Waving frantically at the fleet's flagship, Rainald shouted, "Go with God, Harry!" Much to his delight, a man in the bow waved back. "You think that is him?" He squinted, uncertain but hopeful. "By the Rood, it is! He's got the lass with him, Ranulf. See her blue mantle?"

Ranulf swung around in the saddle. "'The lass,'" he echoed. "You mean . . . Rosamund Clifford?"

"Well, with all due respect to Eleanor, I'd hardly refer to her as a lass, now, would I? Yes, I mean the little Clifford. You did not know he was taking her along?" When Ranulf shook his head, Rainald grinned, pleased to be the bearer of scandalous tidings. "Mind you, he does try to be discreet. He did not even sail with her on the same ship for Portsmouth. And he kept her hidden away at Pembroke, too. But he told me that she has a fear of the sea—sensible lass—so I suppose he thought it would be easier for her if they traveled together to Ireland. That is a longer voyage than a Channel crossing, after all."

Ranulf said nothing and they sat their horses in silence as the ships were piloted from the river mouth into the estuary. The sunset was flaming out and in that fleeting, ephemeral interval between day and night, it seemed as if the world was afire, as if time itself was suspended until the last dying rays were submerged in the crimsoning waters of the sea. And then the moment was over, the spectacle ended, and darkness began to descend. Ranulf continued to watch, though, as long as the sails were still in sight.

AUTHOR'S NOTE

I always look forward to doing my Author's Note, as it is a way for me to speak directly to my readers. It also gives me an opportunity to invite readers backstage, so to speak, and acquaint them with some of the behind-the-scenes choices and tactics that go into a novel's creation. In this case, I'd like to begin with an explanation. *Time and Chance* was originally supposed to be published several years ago, and I know the long delay has perplexed many of my readers. My own favorite query was a very succinct e-mail in which a reader asked simply, "Did Eleanor get lost in Aquitaine?" The truth is much more mundane; I was unlucky enough to be sidelined with an eighteen-month siege of mononucleosis. College students can shake it off in a few months, but it flattens aging baby boomers like a runaway steamroller, and not even Henry and Eleanor could make any headway until it ran its course.

In writing *Chance,* I took an occasional small liberty with known facts, a common sin for writers of historical fiction. In the ambush scene in Chapter Three, I gave Ranulf credit for another man's heroics; he was not the one who snatched up the fallen royal banner and forestalled a rout.

This is as good a time as any to acknowledge that Ranulf is a rarity in one of my historical novels, a character who owes his existence solely to my imagination. As I explained to readers in *When Christ and His Saints Slept,* since King Henry I had at least twenty known illegitimate children, I figured one more couldn't possibly hurt.

I took another liberty in sending Hywel to Toulouse with Ranulf and Henry, although not a large one; one of the chroniclers did report that a Welsh prince accompanied the king on his Toulouse campaign. The "cloak scene" that I dramatize in Chapter Ten is perhaps the best-known anecdote about Henry and Thomas Becket, related by a very reliable source, William Fitz Stephen. With apologies to Fitz Stephen, plot considerations forced me to move this incident from London to Normandy. And I embellished Henry's meeting with King Louis at Montmirail in 1169. As far as we know, Henry did not present Louis's young son Philippe with a pony. Philippe's aversion to horses is well known, however, and so I did not see this scene as such a stretch. One final confession. In my *Saints* Afterword, I admitted that I'd failed to find a death date for Eleanor's sister, Petronilla. I am very glad I red-flagged this there, as I later discovered a reference to her death in 1151! But because I'd allowed my fictional Petronilla to live on in *Saints* beyond her real-life counterpart's demise, I saw no harm in extending her lifespan into *Chance*.

As many readers are familiar with the Salic Law barring women from the French line of succession, I think I should mention that it did not become operative in France until the fourteenth century. So a daughter of Louis VII could have inherited the French throne had he been unable to sire a son. Owain Gwynedd was the last Welsh ruler to call himself a king. I could not resist borrowing from Richard Coeur de Leon's famous exchange with the French king, when Philippe boasted that he would take Chateau-Gaillard if its walls were made of iron, and Richard riposted that he'd hold it if its walls were made of butter; I give a similar statement to Henry's half-brother Hamelin.

In view of all the controversy John managed to provoke during his lifetime and afterward, it is not surprising that even his birth date should be a source of dispute. Some readers of my novel *Here Be Dragons* might remember that John was born in 1167, a year later than his birth in *Chance*. According to Ralph of Diceto, Dean of St Paul's Cathedral, John was born on Christmas Eve in 1166. The Abbott of Mont Saint-Michel in Normandy, Robert of Torigni, gave John's birth date as 1167 and this is the one most commonly reported. It is, however, in error. Henry and

Eleanor were in different countries during the time when John would have had to be conceived, if John were, indeed, born in December 1167, and not even Eleanor's most virulent enemies cast doubts upon John's paternity. To complicate matters, I've come to doubt the accepted birthday for John as Christmas Eve. He was named after John the Evangelist and since the Apostle's saint's day was December 27, I think it is more likely that John was born on that date.

So many myths and legends have sprung up around Eleanor during her own lifetime and in the centuries following her death. That she presided at Poitiers over Courts of Love is one such legend, no longer given serious credence by most historians. Did she confront Rosamund Clifford at Woodstock? We know that she suddenly left Normandy and made a hazardous winter crossing of the Channel while in the late stages of pregnancy. We know that upon her arrival at Southampton, she traveled on to Oxford. We know that Oxford is but five miles from Woodstock, where Henry was keeping Rosamund Clifford. And we know that Eleanor then remained in England, a land she little loved, for over a year, not rejoining Henry in Normandy until December 1167. I leave it to my readers to draw their own conclusions.

As always when writing of the Plantagenets, I must reassure readers that even the most improbable events actually occurred. The bitter quarrel between Henry II and Thomas Becket is possibly the best documented episode of the Middle Ages. We have no fewer than five eyewitness accounts of the archbishop's murder in Canterbury Cathedral, and more than a dozen biographies written by Becket's contemporaries, including letters and testimony by three of the men who knew him best: John of Salisbury, William Fitz Stephen, and Herbert of Bosham. So in many of the key confrontations between Henry and Thomas Becket—at Woodstock, Westminster, Clarendon, Northampton, Montmirail, Canterbury—I had the rare privilege of letting my characters speak for themselves.

SKP
August 2001

ACKNOWLEDGMENTS

I could never have completed *Time and Chance* without the help and support and encouragement of the following people: My family and friends, particularly Earle Kotila and Valerie LaMont. My agents, Molly Friedrich and Mic Cheetham. My editors at Penguin, Tom Weldson and Harriet Evans. Above all, my editor for twenty remarkable years, Marian Wood.